Planet of the Orange-red Sun

Series Volume 13

Eagles's Seed and Origins

Planet of the Orange-red Sun Series

Volume 13
Eagle's Seed and Origins

by Vic Broquard

For Morgan and L. Ron Hubbard

Table of Contents

Part I Point of Origin

Chapter 1 Footholds
Chapter 2 Getting Acquainted
Chapter 3 The Linguists
Chapter 4 The First Archaeologists
Chapter 5 Uncovering Clues
Chapter 6 Captured
Chapter 7 Your Hand in Marriage
Chapter 8 The Telepath
Chapter 9 Above the Law
Chapter 10 Changes Come
Chapter 11 Countermoves
Chapter 12 Implementation
Chapter 13 Revenge
Chapter 14 Help
Chapter 15 Recovery
Chapter 16 Reconstruction
Chapter 17 Terrorists

Part II Contagion Spreads

Chapter 18 Switched
Chapter 19 Toughening It Out
Chapter 20 Recovery
Chapter 21 Of Electronics and Resurrection
Chapter 22 The Rise of Electronics
Chapter 23 Hell Comes to the Federation of Planets
Chapter 24 Unraveling Threads

Chapter 25 The Great Escape
Chapter 26 Perversions and Hidden Standards
Chapter 27 Revolution and Pirates
Chapter 28 Recovery and Stabilization

Part I Point of Origin

Chapter 1 Footholds

14:30:00. June 2, 1381. Reich Spaceport, Hoffdorf, Cass-C. Three very powerful men within the Federation of Planets met in secret. Cass-C was one of the hub worlds of the Federation. Their method of identifying the planets of a sun was to append a letter after the star's name, with 'A' being the closest planet to the sun. Hoffdorf was Cass-C's United Capital City. On the edge of the sprawling city lay the gigantic Reich Spaceport, so large that it was able to service five battleships at the same time, though only one was in orbit above the world at the moment, the Tamerlane, the flagship of Admiral Jason Tremors of Scappa-F, another hub world. He was forty-five with short brown hair and eyes. Of the trio who met this day, he was the most conservative. He was also Scappa-F's representative to the ruling body known as the Admiralty Round Table.

Joining him at this top-secret meeting was Ambassador Riley Jones, a forty year old black man from Rigel-F. He was their most influential ambassador, cutting a trim figure. His black moustache gave him a distinguished look or so he considered. It was he who had called for this hasty meeting, though the last person to join them would have called for the meeting had he not. That was Werner Kettlebohn, Commander of the Hub ID, the Intelligence Division of the hub section of the galaxy on the Federation side. He was from Cass-C. The blonde haired, blue-eyed man was highly suspicious of nearly everything, as befitting one of the top leaders of the many Intelligence Divisions.

Upon entering, he said not a word, but began a thorough scanning of the room, looking for spying devices. Finding none, he silently activated his own small voice and signal scramblers, placing them at strategic points around the room. Satisfied, the small stature man then spoke. His native language was German, and his English accent was rather terrible, but he didn't want to trust the Ear Translators that were commonly used within the Federation of Planets. These were small devices placed in one ear, which roughly translated the various languages spoken in its vicinity into the one selected by its wearer.

He knew Ambassador Riley spoke Bantu, while Admiral Jason spoke Swedish. In his rather broken English, he barked antagonistically, "Okay. All secure. I won't have our conversation overheard by any means. We've two key situations to handle here. Ambassador Riley, you go first." Actually, Commander Werner was following the long-standing protocols among the ruling elements of the Federation. The entire Federation of Planets was ruled by a group known only as The Seven, considered a mystical number from antiquity. Its members were supposed to have once been Admirals themselves, but were known only by their number: One, Two, and so on through Seven. Their number also indicated their importance within The Seven. Many believed that One controlled everything, but perhaps that was just a rumor.

Below The Seven were two branches: the Admiralty Round Table and the Intelligence Divisions. For the most part, everyone saw the Admiralty Round Table as the "rulers" of the Federation. Each member world was allowed to send one of its admirals to sit at the Round Table. Quite why it was "round" no one knew for sure, but most believed it symbolized that no one admiral was "above" or more "important" than the others. Currently, two thousand six admirals met to conduct Federation business. Admiral Jason was Scappa-F's representative to this important group. Scattered around the Federation spiral arm were ten Intelligence Divisions, each controlled by a Commander, who had the authority to do any and all types of spying and subterfuge. Each division also had a top-secret SF Unit, a Special Forces group, which carried out all manner of covert operations within its area of operations.

The Ambassador Pool represented the political arm of each member world, which elected one ambassador to represent them. The Ambassador Pool had little actual authority, but carried their recommendations to the full Admiralty Round Table. Thus, they were theoretically subordinate to the Round Table. However, if the situation warranted it, an ambassador was also permitted to address

The Seven directly, though few ever did so, for that meant bypassing the Admiralty Round Table and accepting the repercussions of that action.

Ambassador Riley spoke in English as well. As an ambassador, he prided himself in his ability to speak twenty-two languages. "Ah, thank you, Commander Werner. I do hope these security measures are not needed. We have an interesting development. I have received word from Emperor Bino Sanguro, the ruler of the Ataro Empire of the Twelve Sacred Planets of the Wasps. As you know, it was his people who gave us ample warning about the supernova explosion. He wishes to establish friendly relations with the Federation of Planets. It is his belief that perhaps people from the Federation of Planets settled his worlds and those of the defunct Imperium. He's requesting we allow one of their transport ships to visit various Federation worlds seeking such knowledge. He assures me there will be no military personnel on this ship, merely women who are historians and a couple of gypsies who are astronomers. As you know, Emperor Bino now controls the strongest group of planets in the old Imperium spiral arm. I told him I would see if such permission could be obtained."

He ended by saying, "I strongly believe we should allow this initial contact, though perhaps we should carefully monitor them."

Admiral Jason spoke up, "You say they're bringing only women and a couple of gypsies? I can't see any harm in that. We've always had the meddling gypsies around. While I suppose women could be trained as spies, from what I've heard of this Ataro Empire, they don't use women that way. I agree. We should allow them passage, but watch them of course. Ideally, I would like to see one of our people actually traveling with them. That way, they could be properly guided among the Federation worlds and could also keep a very close eye on them."

Commander Werner grinned, hearing that last phrase, an obvious deference to the ID. "Yah, that would be prudent, admiral. I concur. While I can't believe tracing origins is the real purpose of this trip into our space, we also cannot dismiss it out of hand, since they did give us fair warning of the supernova. If ve are agreed on this, I vill send the proposal directly to The Seven and get their authorization today." Both other men nodded and he continued.

"Now then, for the second reason for this meeting. I've been contacted indirectly by certain members from the ex-Imperium hub world of Hernion-3. They wish to join the Federation of Planets. I also know the other hub worlds have formed up three other alliances, in the west, north, and south hub zones. Of course, the east zone is where the massive genocide attacks have been occurring with alarming frequency. Gentlemen, a golden opportunity has fallen into our laps. If we can bring this heavily populated world into the Federation, we'll have our first foothold into the old Imperium!" Werner exclaimed animatedly.

"Sehr gut!" Ambassador Riley replied in Werner's language, adding a bit more clout to his expression or so he hoped. One can never be too accommodating to commanders of Intelligence Divisions.

"Ah, this is excellent news, Commander Werner, most excellent. Our enemies now join us. They nearly lost the war, you know. While they negotiated a truce, we really did defeat the Imperium, causing its total collapse. To the victor go the spoils. It's about time we got our reparations," Admiral Jason declared. It was still a sore point with him, that the Federation had yielded to the truce just when they were about to defeat the Imperium. At least, that was his opinion of history, which he studied in his youth. "However, can we trust them?"

Commander Werner smiled wickedly, "Of course. We'll apply all the normal rules and regulations that we do to any other world in our spiral arm that wishes to join the Federation. I assure you that we'll have appropriate spies among them in short order. Our initial contact is a General Amil of the Battleship Royale out of Hernion-3. Gentlemen, with your approval, I'll also send this request on up to The Seven. We should hear back from them shortly. Today may well mark the beginning of the integration of all the Imperium into our mighty Federation of Planets!"

Ambassador Riley spoke up, "Oh do be sure to mention

to The Seven that it was we three who first proposed these actions. Let the fame fall upon those who have earned it, I always say."

Commander Werner detested Riley's constant propitiative attitude and countered antagonistically, "Yes, but if this backfires, it'll be on our heads. The sword cuts both ways, ambassador, both ways. Okay. I'll send the two messages and contact you as soon as I hear back, and we can go from there. If they agree, much will have to be done in short order."

"Indeed it will, Commander Werner. Much," Ambassador Riley added. His covert smile told all, namely that he would be playing a key role in the establishment of Hernion-3 into the Federation, gaining more fame for himself. After all, fame was everything, vastly more important than mere money. History remembers the famous, but not the rich. That was his guiding principle.

By evening, the three men were once more meeting in secret, summoned by Commander Werner. His smile announced his achievement. "Gentlemen. Both proposals have been approved! You are going to have your fame, ambassador. The Seven have requested that you two meet with this General Amil and work out the details of the Joining. I will, of course, send along one of my men to observe and gather data. I've been charged with planting an 'observer' and guide onboard this transport ship of the emperor's. No need for you to worry about them. They're my responsibility. Yours is this proposed Joining. My man will contact you shortly. I'll leave you to make your plans. History may well be in the making, gentlemen." Both nodded, and Commander Werner rose and left the two, who began discussing how best to proceed. He had his own situation to handle.

Handle. He needed to get one of his people onboard this ship called the Eagle's Seed. On the surface, the person would serve as their guide among the many Federation worlds. Beneath that, the person would be ensuring that no sensitive information was gathered by these people, and they would also be spying on them to see what their real objective might be. No one was remotely interested in ancient history. Distant past was utterly irrelevant in the present as far as Commander

Werner was concerned. He doubted very much this was their true objective. No, he'd bet anything these women were on some form of clandestine spying mission.

Women. That was his problem. Few women held any real power in Federation worlds. Men did. True, some backward worlds still had queens, princesses, and even aristocracies. A very few did sport women presidents and other leaders, but those were rare. One even had a female admiral, but she was merely a junior admiral at the Round Table, seldom listened to as far as his reports indicated. Commander Werner's problem was just who could he insert in this ship filled with women? He rejected placing a man there. Sexual relations could well jeopardize the spy mission. It would have to be a woman.

He spent an hour searching the hub Intelligence Division personnel records, looking for a suitable candidate. At last, he zeroed in on Molly Maud Porsche, a twenty-five year old, single woman of mixed ancestry. Her mother spoke English and was from Nova-C, while her father was Hermann Porsche, a famous industrialist on Cass-C. His enterprises build the powerful engines that were in use in all the Federation battleship class space fleet. She, on the other hand, had no interest in his business and was something of a rogue, having joined his Intelligence Division at nineteen. Her records indicated she longed to become an active field agent. "Well, Miss Porsche, you're going to get your wish." He sent off a secure email, requesting her presence in his office at nine tomorrow morning.

Molly Maud Porsche reread the secure email three times, not believing her fondest wish had somehow magically come true. She was about to get her first Field Agent assignment! Long ago, she knew the Federation was an Old Boy's Club, men only. They held most all positions of power. Her highly influential father would not even consider leaving his company to her or any of her younger, now married sisters. Women had to fight to gain any kind of power or respect. That she knew well. Something of a rogue, she decided the Intelligence Division was where she wanted to make her mark. Why them? Certainly, women would have to be used in the spying business. Her hope was to prove she was as good as any man out in the field. Molly Maud was a driven woman thus far in her young life.

She did treasure her "mixed" family, which is why she went by both her names, the one her mother gave her and the one her father did, Molly Maud. She was quite blonde with sky blue eyes and an angular face, one that people never forgot. Yes, Molly Maud was quite an attractive young woman. Backed by all the money anyone could want — that was her father's statement to his daughters, she owned only the finest in apparel and accessories. She dressed and looked the role of a wealthy industrialist's daughter. Her wavy blonde tresses fell to the small of her back, and she always wore just the right amount of makeup, bringing her features. Long ago, she decided she wasn't above sleeping her way to the top. Thus far, however, she had not had to use her sexuality to get what she desired, though she was prepared to do so if the opportunity arose.

Just now, she was glad she hadn't had to play that card. Field Agent. She had been promoted and was about to receive her first assignment at nine tomorrow! Dress like a professional woman, she thought, and began laying out just what she would wear to this meeting with the Commander of the ID no less, the most important man in the whole division and here in the hub for that matter, save perhaps The Seven, if they really were located here in the hub section. No one knew that for sure, let alone their identities.

Molly Maud laid out three outfits, trying to decide which would make the best impression on the Commander. She knew from many office rumors that he loved to see nylon-covered legs and taller heels on women. Hence, she discarded one outfit and studied the other two. Grey was too subdued. Satisfied, she kept the black skirt and white silk blouse with a black blazer out, storing the others back into her large, walk-in closet filled to overflowing with outfits and shoes. She then picked out a pair of black patent pumps, opting for the pair with a tiny, five inch spiked heel. Satisfied, she showered and washed her hair. Time seemed to move so slowly, she thought.

Molly Maud rose early and fixed a healthy breakfast, as

she always did, having been taught by her mother that a good breakfast starts the day right. Today, she needed everything to go absolutely right! She did the dishes and sat down to prepare her appearance. She put on her pointed bra, the one that accentuated her small breasts. Every woman in the Federation always wore a bra. Quite why, no one knew for sure. To be seen without one was scandalous. She donned her white garter belt and slipped on her finest black seamed nylons. After slipping on her silk slip, she brushed out her blonde hair and did her makeup. Satisfied that she looked perfect, she then dressed in her professional outfit, donning her heels when she was finished. That done, she rose and walked to her full-length mirror to examine her appearance. Something was lacking. After some thought, she donned a red scarf around the collar of her blouse. Satisfied, she checked on the time. Finally, she rose and headed off to her private shuttle, arriving ten minutes early at the ID Building in downtown Hoffdorf. She clipped her ID card to her jacket and strode into the main entrance, her heels clicking on the granite floor.

"Morning Miss Porsche," the guard at the welcome desk called out. "You are looking extra fine today."

"Thanks. Big meeting," she relied, flashing him a grin.

"Knock'em dead, Miss Porsche," the guard replied jovially. That, she intended to do.

"Ah, Miss Molly Maud Porsche," Commander Werner barked, as she entered his office on the ninety-fifth floor, the top-most office. She tried not to look at the spectacular view from the windows that covered all four walls of his office suite. He sat behind an unassuming desk, but had positioned her chair such that he could easily see her legs and heels. This, she noticed at once and took her seat, making sure her legs were crossed and giving him a proper view of them. Anything to make sure she received this promotion and became a real Field Agent!

"Congratulations. I've promoted you to a Field Agent. I've got an immediate assignment for you," he began, eyeing her legs and then moving upwards. For a moment, Molly Maud wished that perhaps she had done her one-inch nails. There was one tiny chip in their red polish. Perhaps, he wouldn't notice, she thought.

"Thank you. It's my life's dream to be a Field Agent. I'll do my very best to live up to the standards you've set for all agents," she replied demurely, rocking one leg a little and noticing that he was noticing it.

"Indeed. I'm sure that you will. This assignment is a very delicate one, possibly fraught with danger, but it must have a woman's touch. Emperor Bino Sanguro, the ruler of the Ataro Empire of the Twelve Sacred Planets of the Wasps, is sending a deep space transport here into Federation space. Their stated objective is to visit many of our worlds in search of the original planet from which the galaxy was populated. Obviously, this is a ruse. No one could be interested in such. It is a total waste of time and effort. Who cares where humanity rose? No one. It has nothing to do with the price of bacon on Hoffdorf. No, they must have some other secret mission, probably spying out our worlds, though I've no idea what they are looking for. Perhaps military secrets? Who knows?"

He went on a little belligerently, "Anyway, The Seven have given their permission for this ship, the Eagle's Seed, to travel around Federation space, visiting our various worlds. Further, I've learned quite a lot about this particular ship and crew. They've been on a very lengthy mission, exploring the worlds in the northern galactic halo! They've made some significant contacts. Plus, they were also testing two new engines, one of which the emperor has agreed to share with the Federation, in return for allowing them to research their origins. So, Molly Maud, this crew has invaluable information, which we desperately need to know. What worlds? What technology? What alliances? You know — all the usual intelligence data. Somehow, someway, I need you to pry this out of them."

"You'll be joining them shortly as the Federation representative, escort them to the worlds they wish to see, and be their 'tour guide.' That's your cover story. Just make damned sure they see nothing that they should not see. Show them around and all that, but make darn sure you find out all you can about their previous trip into the halo."

He slipped a thick, sealed folder over to her, covered in

red tape marked "Top Security," forcing her to have to put her legs down and lean over to reach it, giving him an even better view of her legs. She noted this, though, and inwardly smiled.

"This is everything we know about the Eagle's Seed and its crew. I'm told they're coming here with a skeletal crew — ten women and one man. However, as you'll see when you review that folder, they are all hermaphrodites. Yes, the freaks," he added, seeing her startled reaction to that announcement. He added with a barely detectable sneer, "I'm sure you can handle that detail superbly."

"I want progress reports over a secure channel when possible without raising suspicions. You'll be rendezvousing with the Eagle's Seed at our Space Station #109 just at the edge of our hub space section at nine in three days. Allowing for travel time, your transport will leave in two days. Here's the docking bay. Good luck, good hunting, Field Agent Molly Maud Porsche." He declared with some finality, indicating the meeting was finished. She thanked him, rose, and left, carrying the precious folder with her.

As she took the elevator down to her own floor, the fifth, she tried to keep her emotions in check. She wanted to yell, to cheer, and to punch her fists into the air. Instead, she took several deep breaths. She was calm by the time she reached her desk in its private cubicle. She sat down, opened the folder, and began studying its contents. There were somewhat fuzzy images of their Captain Nia Elain Compton-Jereni and other crew members. By the time she'd finished reviewing what was known about her and this crew, Molly Maud was quite impressed and in more ways than one. Here were women who held true power. This emperor had seen fit to entrust her with a critically important and vital mission, wholly unlike the Federation.

She envied these women but soon began rereading the proposed purpose of the extended visit of Federation worlds. They wanted to trace ancient history of many worlds and that meant actually landing on them. This then dictated the clothing she would need to bring along. Important women always dressed appropriately. Hence, she began mentally going through her wardrobe picking out various outfits to bring with her. Halfway through, she wondered if these aliens would have appropriate apparel with them. She made a mental note to check on this as a first action. If they didn't, she'd have to make a stop and purchase them proper apparel to wear planet-side. That evening when she finished packing, she had five shipping crates filled. That done, she spent the rest of her time again studying the folder, learning as much about these people as she could, bearing in mind much of the data could well be erroneous. That much she knew well from her clerking duties here at the Intelligence Division. At last, the day of departure arrived, and she eagerly headed to the spaceport, ready to begin her great adventure as a real Field Agent.

General Amil had little choice but to seek an alliance with the Federation of Planets. His president had given him strict orders. The position of Hernion-3 was precarious at best. With the breakup of the Imperium, already most of the other hub worlds had formed up their own alliances, leaving the eastern portion of the hub to fend for itself. True, many of their highly populated worlds had been destroyed in the genocide attacks. Still, those that remained were no match for the other three alliances. Worse, General Amil didn't trust the Ataro Empire, not since he learned that one of their worlds, Aquila Prime, had been behind the recent genocide attacks. While he'd eliminated that threat, he still feared retaliation. Did other of these Ataro Empire worlds also possess this awful biological weapon? If so, Hernion-3 could be wiped out in a flash. They needed protection, and the only way that they could get it seemed to be to join the nearby Federation of Planets, once their sworn enemy, but now possibly their saviors.

His request had been honored and a meeting set. Now would come the hard bargaining. What would Hernion-3 have to give up to get the protection they needed? He knew he was to meet Admiral Jason Tremors and Ambassador Riley Jones. He dressed in his parade uniform. Looking as impressive as possible, he headed off to welcome the arrival of the Federation Battleship Tamerlane and his two guests, hoping the price of admission would not be prohibitive.

The introductions went well, and soon Ambassador Riley began outlining the benefits of becoming a member of the Federation of Planets. While General Amil didn't need the sales pitch, he listened politely. "So the first steps are the application fee, non-refundable, and the world study report. If as you say, we find there are about ninety-three billion on Hernion-3, then the yearly tithe is what we just discussed. The only two problems I can foresee is the monetary systems and the fuel used by your warships. The Federation uses the Gold Dollar Standard in much the same way as your Imperium credit, if I understand you properly. You see, each of our dollars is backed by an equivalent in gold bullion. So as long as you have gold enough to back your credits, I'm sure some arrangement can be made. We do this sort of thing all the time when new worlds join up."

Admiral Jason took over. "Indeed, the only real problem is that your ships use a totally different fuel than ours. At least, we both use similar hyperdrive coordinate systems, so navigation shouldn't be a significant problem. Usually, for those worlds, which do not have any proper battleships that are up to Federation standards, we request that they pay one of the member worlds to build them one or two. I believe I can make a case here that we, the Federation, ought to have your propulsion battleships operate here in what used to be Imperium space. That would alleviate Hernion-3 from having to purchase some. Of course, one of your battleships would need to have one of our fleet crew manning it, at least for a few years until you and we get familiar with each other's equipment and tactics."

General Amil breathed a sigh of relief, but tried not to show it. "I can foresee no problems with any of these requirements. I can take the paperwork to our President, and we can get the ball rolling, as they say."

"Excellent, excellent, General Amil," Ambassador Riley poured it on a bit heavy. "As soon as we get the documentation signed, we'll need you to appoint or elect your new ambassador and your admiral. Admiral Jason and I will then be spending a good deal of time with them grooving them in on the various procedures and formal protocols. Once the payments are completed and approved by The Seven, we'll then escort the two to the Admiralty Round Table and the Ambassador Circle, and formally introduce them, allowing Hernion-3 to take its place in the Federation of Planets. Congratulations, General Amil. It is indeed an honor to welcome you to our Federation. I do so hope that other nearby worlds will follow your lead."

On July 1, 1389, Hernion-3 became the first ex-Imperium world to join the Federation of Planets. General Amil was promoted or rather his title was changed, and he became Admiral Amil and their representative in the ruling body, the Admiralty Round Table. By the end of the year, all the other eastern hub worlds had also joined the Federation of Planets, seeking a way to protect themselves from the other three hub alliances of planets. For the first time in almost a half-century, these worlds of the eastern hub finally felt safe from attacks. Now, an attack on them was an attack on the mighty Federation of Planets, the strongest force in the galaxy, as far as anyone knew.

Chapter 2 Getting Acquainted

June 10, 1381. Space Station #109 was close to the imaginary line that marked the old Imperium-Federation border in the central hub of our galaxy. Anya opened up a comm channel on the frequency we had been given. Lacking any knowledge of the language spoken here, I used Imperium Standard as a starter. "Eagle's Seed on approach as requested. I need docking orders, please. Over."

We all had our ULATs turned on, but when a voice replied, Marisol, Martina, and I recognized it at once as a derivative of a common one found within the Imperium — er, I mean the ex-Imperium. I'm still having a hard time remembering the Imperium is history. I switched to speaking in our derivative language and sensed relief from the voice at the other end. Docking was quite different from what I was used to handling, but hey, the docking process is pretty much the same action everywhere. In five minutes, the Eagle's Seed was parked inside a huge bay, large enough to handle a heavy cruiser. We could see another ten transports beside us being serviced. Swarms of men were busily working, but many took time out to stare at my ship, which admittedly looked very different from theirs.

Following our instructions, Danika and I opened the bay doors and stepped out onto the metal ramp. Dizzying. That would be an excellent description. We stood on this narrow ramp protruding out into empty space. Far below us were more bays, just as there were above us and to our left and right. This giant station could well house a hundred or more ships at one time. I rather picked up a flash of history from this place. At one time, the station was jammed with ships loaded with troops for an invasion of the Imperium! I blinked and that image was gone, replaced with that of a young woman waving towards me, while she walked out from a door at the far end of the ramp, one that must lead into the heart of the station.

Danika and I saw an attractive woman, dressed much

like a professional woman, to use Martina's description. I was attracted to her long, wavy blonde hair that fell to the small of her back. She wore a grey skirt, white blouse, and grey business jacket. From a distance, her legs appeared dark, but as she drew closer, I could see she was wearing black nylons and black pumps with three-inch heels. Her lips were rather full and quite red, matching her inch long nails. Her eyes were an incredible shade of blue, nicely accentuated with eye shadow.

She in turn saw two raven-haired young women about her own age. My hair was thick and wavy, falling equally as long as hers. I wore a simple, comfortable pants suit and tennis shoes. Danika wore her favorite supple leather pants suit with padded leather moccasins. She had her traditional bangs trimmed to fall just above her eyebrows, just the way she had worn it when we first met years ago on Metcalf-4. It seemed a lifetime ago now. However, we all had the usual melon-sized breasts found on Ashford-5 and of course tiny waists, a residual effect from the genetic bio agent modification. So I wasn't surprise to see her eyes focusing on our extreme "shapes."

"Hello. I am Molly Maud Porsche. You must be Captain Nia Elain Compton-Jereni?" she said politely. Her voice was a very mellow alto, quite pleasing to hear.

"Yes. Pleased to meet you. This is my mate and navigator, Danika Jereni-Compton. Welcome to the Eagle's Seed. We're very pleased to have an official guide on this trip. Honestly, we know almost nothing about the worlds of your Federation, though our gypsies have traveled a bit around some of your beautiful gaseous nebulae. Please, come onboard and meet everyone else. Pardon our outfits. We didn't anticipate we ought to dress up."

"This ship is so unusual looking. It belongs to you?" she asked, as we walked up the bay ramp into the cargo hold area where everyone else had gathered, Jen included. I noticed she was wagging her tail.

"Yes, inherited it from my parents. Here's everyone. I'm afraid we're down to a skeletal crew on this trip," I replied. "This is Martina Wells and her mate Tesla Niko-Wells. She's our electronics technician. This is Anya Pavel-Bellweather, our comm expert, but her husband isn't with us on this trip. This is Jovanna Darvin-Gervasi-Jones and her twin sister Jana Darvin-Childa. Their husbands aren't with us either. Both of them are our ancient historians and mean cooks. You're going to eat well on this trip. This is Marisol Gervasi-Hammil and her mate Beth Hamil. Marisol is our linguist, though I'm pretty good with languages too. Beth is our zoologist and botanist, and this is her border collie Jen. Finally, our two gypsies, Anwyn and Dylan Braith, our astronomers. The other astronomers aren't with us this time. As I said, we've got a skeletal crew. Gang, this is our guide and host, Miss Molly Maud Porsche." Everyone shook hands, welcoming her onboard.

"Well, I can see I'm a bit overdressed for now," Molly Maud teased. "I do hope you have some nice outfits to wear when we get planet-side."

"Yes, but we would appreciate your guidance on what to wear and when, since we know almost nothing about Federation protocol," I replied. "Come on; let's show you around the ship. I see the men are bringing your crates now. We actually have quite a lot of room on this trip. Last time, we were a bit crowded, what with twenty-two of us, some forty-seven of our children, and twenty-three robots. Of course, we had four additional modules attached, giving us more room." I chatted, as we gave her a quick tour and gave her a pick of the available cabins. She chose the one that Alexandra and Zarita had used, the one closest to the front of the ship and nearest the comm center.

Once we all helped her get her crates stowed, we headed to the meeting room, which seemed positively empty this trip compared to the packed room before. Jana provided some hot tea, and we got down to business. I had to, in order to get us going from this space station.

"Okay. Here's what we are trying to do," I began. "We have several clues that the original settlers of our spiral arm probably came from your spiral arm. I'll let Marisol explain one of these clues."

Marisol tossed her shoulder length brown hair back and

began, "You see, for a long time, we linguists have studied the many languages spoken throughout the Imperium, rather ex-Imperium. While there are hundreds of them, there are thousands of worlds in our arm. Thus, many languages are nearly identical, but naturally with local variations. True, there have been just a few worlds on which their language is totally unique, but only ten such worlds. Statistically, this suggests that most all our worlds were settled by overlapping groups, perhaps no more than a few hundred different ones. Further, many of these languages are quite similar to each other, forming close-knit families."

She continued, "Through our minimal contacts with people from the Federation of Planets, we know these same hundred plus languages are also spoken on their worlds or yours rather, with some variations naturally. Hence, this suggests to us that our ancestors came from some of your worlds, one or more. Jana, take it from here, please."

Jana grinned. "Okay. On our original world, Metcalf-4 out on the rim, where my sister and I, along with Danika, Tesla, and Anya were born and met Nia Elain, we discovered two spaceships crash landed there, but in different centuries. Those original survivors gave rise to our two groups, the Sud and the Rus. Likewise, on Ashford-5, they've discovered traces of the original settlers, who also probably crash landed and somehow survived, giving rise to the three distinct cultural groups there. Jovanna," she waved to her sister, who turned on her projection system and continued.

"You see here the different colored dots. They represent the earliest known people on various Imperium worlds, at least as far as we have been able to trace. Here's Ashford-5 way out here. The blue dot indicates their settlers came within the last millennia. Over here in the central hub, you see a lot of yellow dots. These represent worlds that can trace their ancestors back almost ten millennia. However, none of the Imperium worlds has a population that goes back more than about ten millennia. So we believe that initially, our spiral arm was settled by people from your arm around ten millennia ago. Later on, some settled in the mid-arm regions, and more recently, some have reached the rim worlds. Beth, care to elaborate the final point?"

Beth grinned, "You bet. You see, on nearly every Imperium world, there are some local flora and fauna that are unique to that world. However, nearly every one has cows, chickens, pigs, horses, and sheep. Further, they are all domesticated and quite similar. In fact, you would have a hard time telling the difference between samples from our worlds. Likewise, there is absolutely no trace of a 'primitive' man on our worlds. This is further evidence that all our worlds were settled by relatively common ancestors who brought along their domesticated animals."

I wrapped it up. "So the purpose of our exploration trip is to visit many of your worlds, checking out the languages spoken there, the domesticated animals, and trace their ancient history in a similar manner as we've done for our worlds. We are hoping to find out where human life began, what world spread out into the galaxy."

Molly Maud looked a bit perplexed. "But why? So what if you find one world from which we all came? That's totally ancient history at the very best. I don't understand why you want to know this."

Marisol answered before I could. "For one thing, we may find your people and ours are related. It's in everyone's best interest that we learn to respect and value the others. If we find this common ground between the people of our arm and yours, then that might go a long way towards unifying us as a group. For another thing, we all believe strongly in through knowledge comes the only true power. I know, some believe might makes power or that money does. But not in the final analysis. It's knowledge that sets you free and makes you more able. If nothing else, think of this as a philosophical exploration. Perhaps, others could understand us better if we put it that way. We are simply a curious lot."

Molly Maud was still confused. "But you are not like the rest of us. Aren't you all hermaphrodites? That makes you entirely different from me, from us, from the rest of us."

I fielded this one. "We all were like you and the rest of humanity. However, we've had the misfortune to have been the targets of a terrible genetic biological agent that drastically modified our genes. Heck, I've been so attacked several times now. Thank heavens that there are some very brilliant geneticists on Ashford-5 who have found cures for some of the genetic modifications!"

"Oh. So that's why you and Danika are together and Martina and Tesla are a couple?" Molly Maud asked, still confused a little.

I laughed. "Heavens no, Molly Maud. We are together because we love each other. Same with Martina and Tesla. We marry for love. It is merely fortuitous that we are able to have children now, but that's not why we are together. Don't your people marry for love?" I decided to turn it around a bit.

"Well sometimes, I suppose. I know quite a few who marry for other reasons, you know, to be rich, to have a higher social status, to become more powerful. Wait, you all have arms. I thought that bio agent thing caused you to lose them," she countered.

"Yes, it does," I validated her statement. I launched into a lengthy description of just what all it actually did to our bodies. "So you see, our hair, lips, feet, arms, and bosoms have been cured or rather put back to where they ought to be. Our waists are still tiny, and we've all got working dual organs, much to the men's dismay."

"But your breasts are mammoth," she protested. Compared to hers, ours were.

"That's got to do with something in the air on Ashford-5. Any woman living on our world for more than half a year has hers grow to these sizes. Even if you use a medical machine to reduce them again, they grow right back."

"Oh, I think I see. But wait. You got attacked while you were out exploring the halo? How could you even survive? Without arms, I mean? And how could you even walk?" she asked many questions that rather popped into her mind all at once.

"We have robot assistants. Alexandra and Zoe were thoughtful enough to get some to the ship while we were in that four day coma."

"Oh. So the robots did all the work," she replied.

"No, we told the robots what to do. They simply

followed our orders and directions. Believe me, it wasn't fun, but we're survivors and carried out our mission in spite of the barriers thrown our way," I answered.

I decided I ought to also level a bit more with her. "One other thing that you should know. Everyone except Martina and the Braiths are telepaths. Don't worry. We aren't reading your thoughts. We consider doing that without your permission to be mental rape. None of us would ever do that." Note: Martina never wanted anyone to know she was a telepath now, a gift from Rafe and Rafaela. We honored her request.

Her face flushed. She blurted out, "So you really are spies!"

"Oh don't be silly. No, we aren't spies. Never have been. Never will be," I countered. "Look, we needed our skills on that mission in the halo." I found myself outlining much of what we had done, focusing on the Achtnag and Ceri who only communicated via telepathy. "So without our skills, we would never have been able to communicate with them and establish a working relationship with them."

"I guess I can accept that, but why isn't there a man in charge of this ship? I would have thought there wouldn't have been any women sent on the trip into the halo. I know our people would never send a woman on such an exploration trip," Molly Maud asked, growing more curious by the minute.

"Why should they send only men? That's stupid. No, I chose my crew very carefully, picking the best qualified personnel, regardless of sex. Though I also admit that I also chose mostly married couples, since the duration was so incredibly long. That worked out well."

"How very strange. You must be the exception — I mean as far as women go. Surely, men control everything on your worlds. Men hold all the positions of real power and authority, right?" Molly Maud asked with a wry grin. I sensed she felt she was making a point of some kind. I could have touched her mind lightly and seen what she was driving at, but I didn't.

"Heck no. Within the Imperium, er ex-Imperium, men and women are more or less equals. The best qualified are the ones chosen. However, I'll be the first also to admit that this is not always the case. Some men still insist women are inferior and all that. But on most of our worlds, men and women are more or less equal. Martina, I'm going to pick on you, if you don't mind." She grinned and nodded, telepathically sending me her approval.

"Over a century ago, Martina here was the top leader of the Imperium ID."

Martina corrected me, "Hub Sector 1 Intelligence Division Minister, Nia Elain. I haven't been that for many, many years now. I stepped down after I got genetically modified and helpless during a terrorist attack shortly after our war with the Federation. So don't worry, Molly Maud, I've nothing whatsoever to do with them any longer. In fact, that organization doesn't even exist anymore."

"You were the top leader? Incredible! Are there other women in positions of such power?" Molly Maud asked rather enthusiastically.

"Of course. The governor of Ashford-5 is a woman, quite competent too," I replied.

"Incredible. Kind of hard to believe though," she admitted.

"Hold on," Martina interrupted. "Are you suggesting that within the Federation women are not equals of men? That we will find no women in positions of power? Are women considered second class citizens?"

"Er, well, yes. I mean there are a very few worlds that have a queen or princess, but those are very few. Usually the king has the real power. We women are considered sexual objects for the most part. Women are supposed to look pretty and attractive for men. I worked very hard to get this position here on your ship." I sensed she was withholding something key from us, but didn't probe. Undoubtedly, she was under orders to spy on us. I certainly didn't care. We had nothing to hide.

She went on, "That's why I asked if you had dresses. If we land on some of our worlds, you simply have to look at least like I do. Otherwise, you won't get anywhere with those in charge of whatever you are wanting to see or visit. Don't you wear bras?" she asked.

Martina replied, "Sorry. We've not heard that word before. What's a bra?"

Molly Maud flushed and fumbled for an explanation. She finally undid her blouse to show us. Okay, a picture is worth a thousand words. I laughed. "Those things don't exist anywhere within any Imperium world. Sorry. We don't have such garments."

"Oh my! Well, if you don't wear them on our worlds, you will be taken for low life prostitutes. Only such women don't wear them. Don't worry. Part of my job as your host is to make sure you have what is needed. Of course, dress customs vary from world to world, so we'll have to be a bit cautious and make sure we have or acquire what we'll need, but we can do that as we go along," Molly Maud replied, somewhat relieved.

She then asked, "Dylan is the only man onboard. So you don't have any security guards at all? What do you do if trouble comes? There are an awful lot of unscrupulous men around and some might try to take this ship from you."

Danika laughed heartily. "I'd like to see them try! You are looking at one very deadly bunch of people."

"Oh, we do have d-guns around here somewhere," Martina suggested. "Ought we dig them out and wear them when we go planet-side?"

"Huh? Well, as visitors, you won't be allowed to carry d-guns, but I'll carry mine for protection. I suppose we can hire some security men to guard us," Molly Maud suggested, biting her lip slightly.

Danika roared. I replied, "We won't need security guards. Trust us, Molly Maud. We can handle things."

Dylan and Anwyn laughed. He added, "Hey, you can protect us, me and Anwyn. We'll need protecting, not those women."

We were getting dangerously close to revealing our *mentales* gifts. I hastily spoke up, "I've had a lot of martial arts training and have killed men with my feet. Danika here is quite the fighter. We should be all right, just clue us in when we get to worlds where we need to be careful, okay?"

"Yes, of course," she replied, though I sensed she was

still considering hiring some private security men. "One thing is for sure, we will need to make some apparel purchases."

"Oh yes, money. We have a lot of Imperium credits, but we don't have any of your funds, nor do we know how your financial institutions work," I pointed out, moving the conversation away from our gifts.

"Well, that's an easy one. We can use the usual methods that we use when a new world joins the Federation. We base the exchange on gold bullion. You figure out how much a pound of gold is worth in your currency and arrange to purchase that amount of gold. Then, I do the same with the Federation dollar. You give me the gold, and I deposit it in a new Federation dollar account. The bank will then give you a card that allows you to make purchases and deposits on any Federation world. It's all automated you see. So this is the first thing that we ought to do."

Okay, we actually do have a pound of gold onboard. It's worth about thirty-two thousand credits. Can we open up an account with that little? I can then somehow arrange for more gold to be purchased and transferred to say this station here, if they can then make the deposit for us," I replied.

"Oh! So you know about this already and came prepared?" Molly Maud asked.

"Well, no. We have it as a universal means of exchange. We found that platinum was in high demand in the halo worlds and used it for local currency," I replied.

She giggled. "Okay. A pound is worth thirty thousand Federation dollars. We can get it setup from the station here, at least I hope so."

"Good. So do you think that another ten pounds of gold will be enough funds to bring along?" I asked.

"Oh for heaven's sake yes! More than enough, I should think. That'll give you close to three hundred thousand dollars to spend. Your emperor must be financing your trip very well indeed," she replied somewhat animated.

"No, it's from my account. I suppose that the emperor will reimburse me later if I ask him. We've all got more funds than we could ever spend," I explained.

"Wow! Incredible. Okay, then grab your gold; let's go to

the admin office and see about getting this arranged," Molly Maud suggested. An hour later, I had a new account, but also any of my crew could also tap into the account as well. Plus, I arranged for another ten pounds to be sent here and added to it.

With that taken care of, we again met only this time in the galley where Jana served up supper. "So what or where do you want to go first?" Molly Maud asked.

"We probably need to talk to an archaeologist who knows a good deal about ancient history on many worlds," I replied. "Secondarily, we ought to talk to a linguist, who is familiar with your many worlds and their languages."

"Oh dear, I really don't know anything about those. I never went to the University. That's where those kinds of people are," she replied, frowning at her own lack of knowledge.

Martina volunteered, "In our worlds, we have such data online in educational databases that can be accessed from many different places. Surely, the Federation has something similar where we could use a computer to browse through what's been published about such things."

"Let me do some checking on that. Probably, we ought to go to my home world first, Cass-C. Hoffdorf has a University. That's my hometown. I should be able to arrange something. We do have libraries. Maybe that will help. Say, what are those little boxes you have on those belts around your waists?"

I explained the ULATs to her, and she giggled, removing her earpiece, showing us their counterpart. Hers was much smaller and had to be programmed for a specific set of languages that she expected to need, subject to a maximum of three different ones. That settled, we got the coordinates for Cass-C and entered them into our nav system. I was greatly relieved to discover that the Federation's hyperspace coordinates were complimentary to ours, unlike those worlds in the halo. While I backed us out of the docking bay, everyone else gathered by the view ports to watch the action. True, I took my time, went very slowly, and then rotated the ship so they could get a good outside view of the busy station. Then, I made the jump into hyperspace, and Danika announced we would be arriving there around nine the next morning.

After that, everyone retired for the night, though I sensed Molly Maud was making some secure calls on her small comm device, piggy backing on our much larger comm center. I wasn't worried about that. I figured she had to report to her boss about our activities. I know if the situation were reversed, we'd be doing the same thing. So far, there weren't any secrets being revealed. We really had nothing to hide, except for our *mentales* gifts.

"Oh dear," Molly Maud exclaimed, looking at how we were dressed. We'd had an early breakfast and then following her dress suggestions; we'd gotten dolled up preparatory to landing at Hoffdorf, Cass-C. We wore our satin, pencil style gowns, hose and lower heels. "Don't you have any higher heels? Don't you wear makeup? The dresses will be passable, as long as we get you into some bras. We can visit a nail salon and get your nails done up properly, so that won't be a problem." She wore a red chiffon dress with a flair beginning at her waist expanding outward perhaps eighteen inches and ending just above her knees. Her knees on down exposed her black nylons, extremely risqué as far as we were concerned. She also wore matching pumps with six-inch heels that ended in tiny metal spikes.

I ducked back into our bedroom and returned wearing the usual six-inch oxfords so popular on Ashford-5. Remembering to take tiny steps, I rejoined Molly Maud and asked, "These more like it?"

She breathed a sigh of relief. "Well, yes they are. Much better. You don't have any shorter dresses do you? It's important for us to show a lot of nylon covered leg along with our heels. The men expect this from the best women, you see."

I laughed, "Hardly. That's considered really, really risqué on our world. And no, we don't wear makeup, though there are some worlds where the women do." Martina smiled. Descartes-3 women did, but usually minimalist makeup.

"Remember to flirt with men. After all, women are supposed to be sex objects," Molly Maud pointed out.

"But we're not sex objects," Martina protested. "How

utterly archaic."

"No, more like barbaric and primitive!" Marisol spoke up. "It would appear the Federation of Planets is far more backwards than the Imperium ever was."

"When on Proxima Prime, do as they do," Beth reminded her mate.

"Yes," Martina sighed. "She has a point there. We are visitors, and we do want to make a good impression and not violate their expected customs here. That's not going to get us the information we need, gang. Put on your highest heels and let's get going." The others grumbled a little. After all, we had only recently gotten our feet back and loved being able to walk normally in comfortable flats.

Satisfied we were as presentable as possible, Danika and I headed back to our positions and prepared for landing at their spaceport. Ten minutes later, the Eagle's Seed touched down on the first planet in the Federation. Martina opened the bay doors, and we all headed there, ready to explore this new world.

I began to think all spaceports were pretty much similar. My first breath inhaled traces of fuel fumes, oil, and metal. The temperature was warm and rather balmy, with a light breeze. Comfortable. In the distance, we saw a concrete building, probably the control center or administration tower. A man dressed in a brown suit with a yellow spotted tie stood waiting for us, along with six men armed with d-guns, probably his security guards. I picked up surface thoughts and realized he was Molly Maud's boss. All seven men leered at us, as we teetered clumsily down the ramp in our tall heels. Their eyes were torn between our legs and our very large bosoms. I blocked their thoughts, which were most disconcerting. Once everyone was out of the ship, I entered some codes, and the bay doors shut and locked securely.

Molly Maud did the introductions, "This is Commander Werner Kettlebohn, head of the Hub Intelligence Division." She introduced me first, but he interrupted her before she could introduce the rest of my crew. I sensed that he considered them of little importance.

"Ah Captain Nia Elain. Pleased to meet you. Molly

Maud, we really do have to get them to a beauty salon before we can allow them to visit our libraries. No offence, but I'm afraid you all do look like prostitutes, what with no bras and such. You should reveal far more of your gorgeous legs too. Molly Maud will take care of this at once. Then, I would like to speak to you privately, Captain Nia Elain, if I may. You really don't have any men with you do you?"

I sensed Dylan's ire rising, but he wisely didn't say anything. I knew he was very much embarrassed by his appearance. I replied, "We are on an educational mission, and I didn't think we would need any security men. I look forward to meeting with you shortly." Honestly, I had no such notion. He was radiating lecherousness, and I was the target of his intentions.

"This way. We can take a shuttle bus," Molly Maud hastily took charge. I purposely sat close to Dylan, as we climbed into the bus, which ran on the ground. How quaint. It had rubber tires, and soon I saw they had concrete paths or roads all over the place.

As we zipped along into the city proper, I whispered to Dylan. "Perhaps, you might consider dressing like us. Far less questions that way."

"Maybe I should have stayed on the ship. This is humiliating, Nia Elain."

"I know, but the alternative is worse. They've never seen hermaphrodites before. Pretend you are putting one over on all them."

He grinned. "Hey, I like that idea. Okay, I'll do it. Say, I don't trust these people. Be careful with that Werner fellow. He gives me the creeps."

"I expect we're going to see a whole lot of things we aren't used to seeing on this trip," I replied. Little did I know then how much of an understatement that was.

An hour later, Danika complained, "I really don't like all this goop on my face. This dress is way too short." We had entered The Haufbrau Boutique, and been "fixed up" by Molly Maud and the friendly women who ran the establishment. It had to be upscale though. Every other woman here was probably wealthy, judging by the cost of the apparel. She added, "This bra thing is worse than wearing that metal stay corset!" I wasn't any too comfortable myself.

Ada, the saleswoman who waited on us continued to preach, "Lovely ladies such as yourselves simply must look as attractive as possible. Just do as Molly Maud suggests. She knows what she's doing. After all, you do want men to pay attention to you, don't you?" None of us answered that one.

We strutted out of the Haufbrau Boutique looking like many other women of Hoffdorf. We had our nails done. They added some extensions so that they were an inch long and painted them to match our choice of lipstick. We wore various dresses quite similar to Molly Maud's and the bras. I do have to say they did have a hard time fitting us, both with bras and with dresses. Molly Maud explained we needed H cups while she only needed a B cup, whatever that really meant.

As we pranced along out on the street heading towards a bus stop, I got a good look at the citizens of Hoffdorf, as they went about their business. The men wore dark suits and ties, quite formal I thought. The women either looked like us, teetering on their high heels, or wore a "professional" woman's outfit, much like Molly Maud did when she met us. However, man after man leered and gawked at us, just as they did nearly every other woman on the street. Some even whistled, embarrassing us slightly. Molly Maud merely took it in stride.

She held the bus for me when we arrived at her office building. "I'll take you up to see Werner. The rest of you wait here. It shouldn't be long, and then we can go to the library as you planned," she explained.

"Morning Miss Porsche," the lone security guard called out as we entered and walked up to his desk.

"Morning. I need a visitor's pass for Nia Elain. Werner is expecting us."

"Yes, he has already alerted me," he replied, handing her the pass, which she clipped onto my dress shoulder strap. Even the guard covertly watched our every wiggle, as we teetered to the elevator.

Once on the elevator and alone, I asked, "Doesn't it bother you? I mean all the leering stares and such?"

She flushed, "Well, yes. But I can't do anything about it,

so why worry. Here we are. I'll take you in, but I'm sure he won't want me present when he talks to you."

A few minutes later, I was sitting across from his desk far enough out from it so he had a good view of my overly exposed legs. While I felt a bit uncomfortable, I suppressed those feelings. "Well," Werner began, "this is more like it. I say, you are very attractive now."

"Thank you. So what did you want to see me about?" I asked, pushing him back on track.

"I've heard from some hub worlds of yours that on your last mission, you were testing a new form of hyperdrive engine. Is that true?" Werner asked with a hint of disbelief in his voice.

"Yes. Hans developed it, and we tested it thoroughly. It works well. Why?"

"I see. And it is a big improvement over current engines?" Werner asked pointedly.

"Yes."

"Can you elaborate, captain?" he insisted.

Okay, I wanted him to squirm and actually ask me for more information. If he was going to get his jollies off looking at my legs, then I was going to exact my revenge, if only a little. "I could sir."

"Would you?" he sounded a bit exasperated with me.

"Sure. Its top speed is five times faster than current drives using half of the fuel at top speed. At cruising speeds, it uses about fifth of normal fuel consumption. Once we installed it in the Eagle's Seed, we've never taken it out. Works perfectly. Great savings on fuel and faster travel times."

I could see him drooling and not over my legs this time. "Any chance we could get access to that technology? We would pay you handsomely, captain."

I laughed. "Sorry, but I don't need money. Got millions that I don't know what to spend it all on." I noticed that he cringed a little, and I suspected I'd just dashed his hope of paying me for the technology. I went on, "Your best bet is to contact our Emperor Bino Sanguro of the Ataro Empire. He is in charge of marketing it. I know he's already giving out Alexandra's new hydrogen propulsion system, which revolutionizes sub-light cruising, at least here in the disk. He is easy to work with, at least I think so." I gave him the calling frequency, which he dutifully jotted down and dismissed me, though he watched my teetering and wiggling as I walked out of his office. I couldn't help but think: Dirty old man! But then, so were all the men we'd seen here in Hoffdorf.

I met Molly Maud just outside his office, where she'd been waiting for me. She looked relieved when I appeared. At first, I thought that was because she had been standing on these tall heels for so long, but I quickly sensed an entirely other reason. She was worried for my safety! Still, I didn't probe her mind, though I was curious. We soon rejoined the others in the bus and headed off to their library.

The Hoffdorf Public Library was a huge, stately, old building, made from red bricks and in the shape of a large box with ornate columns at the entrance. We entered, following behind Molly Maud. I expected to see and smell books, but I saw none. Instead, I saw dozens of small rooms, each filled with monitors, and I realized everything was probably electronic, computerized. That was a relief, but short-lived.

The librarian we met was dressed as a "professional" woman. As we went up to her, she said, "Is it true? You are the captain of the expedition ship from the Imperium?"

"Yes, that's me. My crew, at least part of them who came on this trip," I replied.

"Incredible! So few women ever get such opportunities here. What's it like? I mean to be in charge of a whole exploration ship? No one to give you orders and all that," she gushed, more or less ignoring Molly Maud.

"We always pick the most qualified person for the job at hand. Gender usually doesn't play any role, but of course, there are always a few men around who don't accept women in power positions. Personally, I like being in charge, but you have to have the knowledge and training first. I grew up in the ship, and by eighteen, I could run most everything in the ship."

"Incredible. Knowledge. That's the answer then, but our universities don't take too many women, only those with exceptional IQs."

"Well, you have a library here. You can learn from here

just as well," I suggested. "That's why we're here, to learn about the Federation worlds and languages," I suggested. "In our world, knowledge is the true power."

"Incredible. Funny, we never thought about learning from here. I'm going to spread the word! Oh, Molly Maud, you're in Room #12. We've reserved it for you and your guests." She pointed in the right direction.

As we walked down the carpeted hall, Molly Maud explained, "I arranged for us to have a private room so we can talk and discuss things. People are talking, you know, about you. We've never had an exploration ship come here with only women onboard, much less a woman as the ship's captain."

The room had four separate systems; we paired up, and sat down to make use of their system. Molly Maud hatted us up on how it worked. However, as our first screen appeared, we realized the fatal flaw in our plans. While it is one thing to be able mostly to speak a foreign language, it is quite another thing to be able to read it. The screens looked foreign to us all!

"Oops!" Marisol exclaimed. "Duh. Sorry, Molly Maud. We can't read your language. We're a bunch of idiots. We should have thought of this."

She laughed. "Well, I thought you must be geniuses or something. Okay. I can read it for you, just tell me what to enter or click on, all right?"

This was frustrating, until Marisol had a bright idea. "Say, can this machine show the pages in a different language?"

"Oh sure. Lots of them. Which one?" Molly Maud replied hopefully. She wasn't enjoying this either.

Marisol tried speaking in her native Midlands Dialect. "Oh, yes, I recognize that one. It's English or something similar. Okay, give me a minute. Sorry, I can't read this one though." She'd brought up a translation page. All of us chorused, "Unbelievable!" rather startling Molly Maud.

Marisol explained, "We can read this more or less. It's like our own Midlands language. How very interesting!"

"What? I don't get it. Midlands? No, this is English. It's spoken on a number of Federation worlds, along with other big ones, like French, Italian, Spanish, Chinese, and of course my own German," Molly Maud explained.

On a hunch, I found a link that switched it to Spanish. "More amazing by the minute! Look at this, Marisol. Here's their Spanish, which is our Westerlings language! More or less anyway."

"I don't understand," Molly Maud broke in. "How can you read these?"

Jana answered her. "It's why we are here really, Molly Maud. We suspected our Imperium languages are very similar or akin to some spoken here in the Federation of Planets. Now, it seems we are right. Why is this important? Because we believe our ancestors came from some Federation worlds, settling our many worlds in the distant past. Now, if it will translate into Imperium Standard — nope, doesn't do that," she added.

"I think I am really beginning to understand why you are here. This is important, isn't it?" Molly Maud replied.

"Yes indeed. We may have common ancestor ties to some of your worlds. Perhaps when that becomes known, it may help create stronger bonds between our peoples," Jovanna added.

I got everyone back on track. "Okay, let's start making a list of people and planets we should be visiting. Linguists and archaeologists."

A half hour later, I came across a most unusual topic: Forbidden Planets. I clicked on it and got a list of worlds. "Molly Maud, what is this? Forbidden planets? I don't understand."

"Oh! You don't want to go to any of those. They are forbidden," Molly Maud said the obvious. From our curious faces, she took the hint and elaborated. "You see, there are some worlds we've encountered where it's not safe to land. Most all do not have space travel or very limited travel at best. They are forbidden because some are totally decadent worlds, filled with drug addicts or constant fighting between factions or filled with psychotics who have launched nuclear attacks on others on that world turning it into a radioactive mess. Some are so awful that the Federation has refused them admittance into our league until they clean up their act. Some are run totally by mobsters, criminals. Then, there are a few worlds that are really, really primitive, like in the stone age or something. Forbidden worlds for very good reasons."

"Wow. Okay. Looks like quite a few of them. We certainly don't want to visit any of them," I replied mostly to calm Molly Maud down. She'd gotten rather agitated and worried we might be considering one of these to visit.

We narrowed our search down to two linguists and four archaeologists who seemed promising. Miss Gabrielle Duparte of Bernard-D and Miss Marilyn Tonby of Capella-D were the linguists. Both were highly renowned with ratings actually higher than men had. Okay, I admit just now we were a bit biased against men of the Federation. The archaeologists consisted of Mrs. Elena del Gotto of Centari-C-C, Mrs. Glynis Dolyn of Spica-C, Dr. Lujan Ho of Mira-C, and Mrs. Bianca and Donatella Bellini of Vegan-C. Molly Maud carefully wrote down the list and their contact information.

"All right. I'll have to spend a few days getting in touch with these women and setup our visits. Plus, I'll need to get us the proper apparel to wear while on those worlds. You see men mostly all dress similarly, you know, suits and ties. However, Federation regulations require visiting women to dress appropriately. What we are now wearing will work for some of these, but not all. You know, women of each world often have their own customs, apparel, and looks. As visitors, we must be presentable or the men in charge will not allow us to leave the ship when we land. In the meantime, you can have a tour of Hoffdorf. Anyway, it's time for supper. I know this nice restaurant. Dinner is on me tonight," Molly Maud offered.

Again in the restaurant, we were not over-dressed, if anything possibly under-dressed. However, the waitress and manager spent some time chatting with us. They'd not seen aliens before. Further, they drilled us about the roles of women in the Imperium. We spent four hours at dinner. Then, Molly Maud put us up in a fancy hotel for the next few days, while she worked on making the arrangements. Our very nice rooms did have computers in them, and quickly we began browsing for sights to see while we waited.

Commander Werner barked at his three Field Agents. "You couldn't even crack a simple security code? You don't deserve to be in the ID! Incompetent idiots. Get out of my sight!" The three men left his office hurriedly. "Damn. Now. I'll have to make that call to their stupid, ignorant, armless freak of an emperor!" His walls didn't respond to his outburst, though.

Martina found something called the Women's Chamber Orchestra, which was holding a concert the next night. When we told Molly Maud about it, she went ahead and got us tickets. Around fifty women attended plus us. The group of a dozen women played stringed instruments. I must admit we loved their sound and music. Afterwards, they asked to meet us, and we suspected Molly Maud had alerted them to us. Again, this led to a four-hour chat, well into the night. Once more, they were particularly interested in the role of women in the Imperium, which we explained in detail. Here, as professional musicians, these women had risen to about as high a position as was possible for them. Male musicians commanded concert halls filled with patrons. The women were equally gifted musicians, but were often considered totally second-rate. I left them with the notion of forming up a tour of some Imperium worlds, playing for packed concert halls.

A footnote: they did just that. About two years from now, we caught them at a sold-out concert on Winno-3. Their leader sent me a note at the end of their tour thanking me and telling me they had made so much money that they were now all quite wealthy women. Fascinating. More important, they barely escaped what followed later on.

When we finally returned to the Eagle's Seed, I ordered a complete systems check. Anya reviewed the video surveillance log. "Gang, they tried to break into the ship. Look at this," she pointed out antagonistically. She was right. Four times, groups of men attempted to crack the entry pad code, but failed miserably. Someone definitely wanted access to our ship, but I didn't really know why, unless it was for our new hyperdrive. I vowed to take some extra security precautions in the future.

We saw the fuzzy video images of the attempted break-ins, including Molly Maud. "Back in a few minutes. I need to do one more thing before we depart," she explained.

"That's okay, we need to recheck our security measures too," I declared a bit testily. I admit I was miffed and not just a little.

From the women's restroom at the spaceport, Molly Maud opened a secure line to Commander Werner. "Ah Field Agent Porsche. Something to report?" She heard the slick voice of her boss. She was furious.

"Your men tried to break into their ship! That's what! They made a video of the attempted break-ins. While it's a bit fuzzy, I recognized three of our Field Agents. What are you trying to do? Sabotage their visit? What am I? A decoy to lead them away from their ship so that you can steal it?" Until now, Molly Maud would never have considered raising her voice to a man, let alone her boss and the Commander of the Intelligence Division, one of the most powerful men in this zone of the Federation. However, she felt used, dirty, and betrayed.

Holding his hand over the microphone, Commander Werner cursed softly. These simpleton women were sharper than he'd estimated. "A misunderstanding. It won't happen again."

Having calmed down slightly, Molly Maud realized she'd just raised her voice to her boss and hastily backed down. "Well, all right then. They're all quite upset over the attempted break-in, but they don't know who the men were, and as far as I can tell, they are not going to report it."

Commander Werner breathed a sigh of relief. His Field Agent was calming down. It wouldn't do to have a woman all emotional on him. That's why he never considered using women in the field before — too emotional. At least that was his opinion of women. He picked up on something she mentioned. "Good. They aren't reporting it, and we won't try that again, so no harm has been done. Are they about ready to depart?" He changed the topic, and she went along with it, saying so and ended her call.

Yet, Molly Maud was still angry. She hopped in her own

shuttle and headed across town to the corporate headquarters of Porsche Industries. Field Agent Molly Maud marched into the building, past their security guards who recognized her and didn't interfere, and on into her father's plush office. Hermann Porsche was in his mid-fifties, slightly overweight, but dressed in a three thousand dollar grey suit. He was smoking a cigar and studying some papers, when she marched into his office. He looked up to see the fuming face of his lone, unmarried daughter.

"Come on in, Field Agent Porsche," he welcomed her rather jovially, teasing her about her supposed promotion, which he knew she received only because of the circumstances surrounding this assignment.

"How dare you!" she barked at him. "You are compromising my first mission and betraying me!" He couldn't help noticing that she was flushed and highly emotional. Well that was why women could never be trusted with real power, he mused.

"What are you talking about?" he countered, allowing his own anger to rise slightly.

"You know damned well. Your men tried to break into the Eagle's Seed. Three times! Bet you didn't know they had a video system hooked up to the ship. Captured your men trying to bust the security code on the shuttle bay doors. Three times!" she slammed her accusative words at his face. Never before had she been this confrontational with her powerful father, but this time he had gone too far.

Damn! Those women are sharper than I've given them credit for, he thought. He needed the specifications for their new engine. If his competitors got their hands on it first, his vast enterprises would suffer greatly, perhaps even go out of business. Greasing hands was just part of doing business, and Commander Werner had come through, tipping him off to this revolutionary new hyperdrive technology. That the bumbling Commander had failed to gain entry had given old Porsche a chuckle, but then his own men had failed three times now.

"Business, daughter. Can't expect you to understand business." He thought for the thousandth time, why did I have to have four damned daughters and not one single son?

"Business? Stealing from our visitors from the Imperium? They've already said that you could negotiate with their emperor for the hyperdrive engine. Isn't that good enough for you? You do this again, and I'll have no choice but to report you to the Intelligence Division. Then see what happens!" she replied angrier than she could ever recall being.

"They haven't reported it, have they?" he asked the only thing that meant anything to him.

"Not this time. I swear, if you do it again, I'll insist they report it and send along the damming video as well! How could you? This is my first assignment. I'm a real Field Agent now," she attempted to harpoon him, anything to get under his skin.

The pudgy industrialist heard what mattered. No report. He picked up on her last line, which raised his ire. "Get real, woman! Field Agent? Hah. Women cannot be *real* Field Agents and you know that. You are simply a temporary figurehead. It wouldn't be prudent or wise to send a man along with the all-woman crew. Commander Werner had no choice but to send along a woman representative and one close to their ages. Once this little trip of theirs is finished, you'll be back on filing duty where you damn well belong. Now get out of my office," he barked.

Her cheeks flaming, her ire fuming, she felt her world collapsing in around her. Her father was right. Commander Werner had chosen her for just those reasons. She wasn't a real Field Agent and never would be. Men were all powerful, and women were mere sexual objects, pretty distractions for men. Her emotions swelled, but she had the strength to turn on her tall heels, and march out of his office without betraying her wildly swinging emotions. Molly Maud headed for the first available women's restroom. Alone in a stall, her emotions surfaced. Tears streamed down her cheers, messing up her makeup.

I don't want to be a pretty bauble. I want to be a Field Agent. I want to amount to something. God damn all men, everywhere! Pull it together, Molly Maud. He can't win. You won't let him. Get it together. She dabbed her eyes, took a deep breath, and left the stall, stopping to redo her makeup before departing from the headquarters building. A short while later, she rejoined the others on the Eagle's Seed, but didn't say anything about her experiences.

Chapter 3 The Linguists

Our first stop was Bernard-D, the fourth world around a relatively dim star in the middle of their spiral arm. This world had unified centuries ago, establishing French as their predominate language, superseding all others. As we approached this new world, Molly Maud used her laptop computer to show us the acceptable fashions for women on Bernard-D. I groaned. Enormous ball gowns.

"Hey, they were once very popular on Ashford-5," Marisol pointed out. "At one time, all the noblewomen wore them, compliments of Elegant Fashions Inc. I tried one on once, what a royal pain. I'm glad they're now out of fashion, though sooner or later what was old will once again be new."

"How do we even get into these things?" Beth complained.

"I had a whole lot of help when I was on Krazdorf, Narsten Cluster. I should have paid more attention," I moaned.

Molly Maud merely chuckled. "We have to be presentable or the men in charge won't let us off the ship. Come on; it can't be that bad, can it?" Hours later, she changed her opinion. Combined with the requisite tall heels, getting around was more than a little challenging. Only this time, I didn't have any servants to assist me. We were on our own.

My gown's hoop was at least twelve feet across, sky blue. However, I must say we looked quite good in them. Dylan was finally enjoying himself, masquerading as a woman. His comment was simply, "Well, now they won't be staring at our legs and up our short dresses." We chuckled and struggled to get to the bay doors without falling down.

As we stepped out and avoided falling down the bay ramp, several men in the usual dark suits met us. It was here we first learned Molly Maud Porsche was officially a Field Agent of the Hub Intelligence Division. The customs man looked us over and said questioningly, "Field Agent Molly Maud Porsche?" She flushed slightly and stepped forward to sign the official documents requesting permission for us to visit this world. She signed them, and we followed the men inside their administration building, where we were photographed and given temporary ID cards marked "Alien Visitors." At least, we passed their dress code inspection. No one said anything about our gowns.

That done, I returned to the Eagle's Seed, closed the bay doors, and entered the secure locking codes. This time, Anya had rigged a signal system. If someone tried to tamper with the keypad, a sensor would activate, sending an alarm to a small pocket receiver she had stuffed in one of her dress's hidden pouches. That was one of the main benefits of these enormous gowns. They had a dozen sneaky pockets in them where we could store smaller items. Molly Maud had her d-gun in one of hers. At least, we didn't have to wear all that makeup, though she continued to do so.

The weather was cool. Someone said it was early fall. Again, they had rubber wheeled transport vehicles, a bus it was called. However, the doors were very wide accommodating our giant hoop skirts. The seats were also wide, though only one of us could sit on a given bench seat. As we were driven through the city of Marseille, their architecture literally demanded our attention. We had never seen anything so ornate as their buildings! Usually stone was the primary construction material, but what a job they had done. Each building tried to outdo all the others on the block. I swear they had ornaments on top of ornaments in an over-the-top, grandiose manner. In many ways, it reminded me of the fantastic cathedral back in Exchange City, Saint Shane's Basilica, with its giant columns and vaulted ceilings.

The entrance doors were extremely wide, which I figured were designed to allow us women with our billowing gowns to enter easily. We spotted a good deal of people on the sidewalks. At once, I could see we were not "overdressed." Every woman we could see wore similar ball gowns, but more often than not, a well-suited man had her arm, though some were going about their business unescorted. Try as I might, I couldn't see any woman who wasn't wearing one of these billowing dresses. However, they varied considerably in color, design, and ornamentations. No two were entirely alike, at least seen in passing from a distance.

We arrived at what on many worlds would be considered a mansion or royal estate, a huge, ornate building of brown stone construction, three stories tall with a low stone fence around its neatly trimmed lawn. We could see a paved walk strolling through a small formal garden. Two men wearing suits were doing some gardening. I thought they were very over-dressed for such things, though. The bus stopped before 42 Rue d'Amor, home of Miss Gabrielle Duparte, the linguist.

As we walked up the cobblestone path to the portico entrance with its enormous doors, a doorman stepped out, holding the doors open. A man in a well-made black suit stepped out. He was in his fifties. Speaking in French, he said, "Ah, Miss Molly Maud?"

"We," she replied, stepping forward, offering him her hand, which he took, leaned over, and placed a brief kiss on it, before releasing it.

"I am Monsieur Ansel Duparte. I believe you have come to discuss linguistics with my daughter, Miss Gabrielle?"

"We. That we are," Molly Maud replied politely. "May I introduce our guests from the Imperium world of Ashford-5?"

"Mais naturellement, madame," he replied. Hastily, Molly Maud introduced each of us. He insisted on kissing each of our hands, bowing to each of us in turn. Very formal. Pleasant even. "This way," he led us inside his home. Okay the grandeur on the inside surpassed that on the outside, if such can be even envisioned! Art works were jammed into specially made niches, hung prominently on walls, or even hung suspended from the tall, ten-foot ceilings. Even those were highly decorated, with either painted frescoes or elaborate and intricate carvings. I later learned they were plaster castings, a very big industry on Bernard-D.

He led us into a giant sitting room, where a young woman our own age was sitting, though she rose as we entered. Her giant gown was five shades of pink, the darkest being closer to the floor. She had wavy brown hair, full and shoulder length. "Bon jour," she said pleasantly, with a hint of real excitement in her voice. "I'm so very pleased to meet you." Once more Molly Maud did the introductions, though her French was not all that good.

Monsieur Ansel said, "I take it you women are going to discuss linguistics, no?"

"We," Molly Maud replied. "That's why we've come to see Miss Gabrielle."

"In that case, Gabrielle, I give you permission to discuss your language things. I bid you all good day." He turned and left the room, closing the door behind him.

"You must forgive my father. He wanted to make sure that was all you wished to discuss with me," she replied, sitting back down on a very soft, but wide chair. Apparently, she knew our numbers, and there was a chair for each of us. I was amazed at how wide they were, accommodating our giant skirts rather well.

"We've chosen to talk to you about linguistics, because as far as we can tell, you are one of the foremost experts in your field," I began.

"True, but I can't publish anything until my father approves of it. He doesn't know much of anything about linguistics. I think it rather bores him, but still, I have to have his permission, as do all women scholars. This is, after all, a man's world, and we women are wholly secondary. Yet, in linguistics, I have found my true calling. Your accent, though, is atrocious, Captain Nia Elain."

I laughed and got right to the point. "You see, within the Imperium worlds, there are only a hundred or so spoken languages, really only a few dominant ones. Further, we are finding they are very closely related to languages here in the Federation." I began outlining our theory, though Marisol added far more details.

Miss Gabrielle produced what she called her Overview Listing, on which she listed all the known languages spoken within the Federation of Planets. An asterisk beside one indicated spoken only, not written. Further, she had them arranged in predominance order. There were thousands on her list, but the vast majority was quite isolated ones, found only in smaller, remote areas of some worlds. On a separate list, she had them arranged into families of related languages. "Some of these are mere dialects or variations of the major languages," she explained.

She went on, "There aren't that many of what I call major languages in use, though each has many variations, which is what one would expect. When two planets speak say French, one can expect to find local variations, naturally. The major ones include French, of course, Spanish, Italian, Russian, English, German, Chinese, and Slavic. These are what I call the Big Eight."

Marisol and I indulged ourselves and traded sentences in these eight with Gabrielle, who was delighted with this, pointing out slight pronunciation differences and word meanings. Okay, I admit the others were pretty bored with the whole thing, especially as the hours passed by so darn quickly. Before long, Monsieur Ansel interrupted us, asking us to stay for supper, which we accepted.

Their dining room was fit for royalty, but we soon learned that most homes were similarly done. He had two servants who prepared and served the meal. "My wife died two years ago, so I had little choice but to hire Claude and his wife Dione to assist us. My older children are, of course, married and on their own. I'm left with dear Gabrielle here, who has so far refused all offers of marriage, though I cannot see why. She has gone overboard on her linguistics studies, but then we do so indulge our women here on Bernard-D. So what is it like on this Ashford-5 world from which you come? And how is it that your men are not with you? Surely, they would not allow you women to venture so far from home on your own. It is so unseemly," he asked.

Over a delicious meal, we chatted a good deal about our world and theirs. We learned he was a famous architect, designing mostly these elegant homes. Half of their population worked in construction and the arts in some manner. With so many fabulous buildings, I could see why that was. I also asked if their women always wore these giant gowns. "But of course!" Monsieur Ansel replied. "We would not think of having any woman be disgraced. It's the worst possible disgrace for a woman ever to be seen not wearing one of their fabulous gowns. There is even a dress subsidy for those most unfortunate women who cannot afford to purchase them. We want all our women to look their very best, and we take great pains to make every building on Bernard-D totally accessible for their wide skirts. Every woman is a princess to be cared for and prized."

I wanted to laugh at that bit of insanity. All women were not princesses nor were they alike, not even remotely, just as no two men were identical. Yet, these people were equating every woman with each other, all identical. I found it rather suppressive that Gabrielle, an obvious linguistic expert, had to get her father's permission to even publish anything! However, both were utterly appalled to learn within the Imperium women were often just as independent and powerful as men were, more or less.

Monsieur Ansel was very much bothered by this revelation, but then he came to grips with it. "Well, that then explains why you women are here on your own without the governance and protection of your men. Still, such simply is never done here. Oh no, not ever."

Miss Gabrielle, on the other hand, was quite fascinated and eager to know more about the freedoms that our women had within the Imperium. After Monsieur Ansel excused himself and left, that was all she wanted to talk about. "We don't dare say such things when father is around or any man for that matter. Please, tell me more." We did until the hour grew late.

She explained, "We don't have enough rooms for everyone to stay here with us."

I suggested that everyone but Marisol and I return to the ship, while we two would stay the night, continuing our discussion tomorrow. That met with total agreement. I didn't need my gifts to sense the relief from the others who were not into linguistics. Jana and Jovanna, however, did want to stay as well, and Miss Gabrielle said they could share one of her sister's rooms.

While we five continued to chat far into the night, Anya sent me a telepathic message. *We're almost back to the ship. The alarm went off again. Someone is trying to break into the ship. My system is working, but I'm going to build us a robot for more protection. Maybe we can surprise them and catch them in the act. Don't worry, Molly Maud has her d-gun out. More later.*

Later that night, Anya reported back. Her new system worked well. When someone tried to enter the combination and did so three times incorrectly, her new system turned on a bunch of exterior lights. Hence, the video had very good images this time. The sudden lights also scared the robbers off. I could only grin at the resourcefulness of Anya and Tesla, who had helped her assemble the new system.

The next day, we delved into theories of linguistic spread, aided by the data gathered by Jana and Jovanna. We spent the day in deep discussions, entirely fascinated with the data Miss Gabrielle had, as she was with ours. When Gabrielle learned we had a huge database of all our spoken languages, she pleaded with us to have access to them. "We can learn so very much from comparing your versions to ours. We can study how the language was modified as it spread throughout the galaxy!"

She went on, "I know of another linguist who has prepared something similar on all our languages, Miss Marilyn Tonby on Capella-D. She and I have been helping each other with our studies. While we've never met, she and I have to get our father's permission even to email each other. But she's been developing a similar database, I think. You've just got to talk to her."

I laughed. "Gabrielle, like minds think alike. We already have her on our list to visit. She's next, in fact."

Gabrielle's eyes lit up. "Oh! That's wonderful. I would love to meet her, and I know she would love to meet me. We've sent hundreds of emails to each other, but our fathers won't allow us to actually visit with a live connection."

"Sure, you can come along, but won't you need to get your father's permission?" I countered. I figured he wouldn't dream of letting her go off-world with us. We then got back on track.

That night over supper, she popped the question to her father. "Father, Captain Nia Elain is next going to visit Miss

Marilyn Tonby on Capella-D, you know, the linguist I have been working with these past six years. Captain Nia Elain has a complete database of all their spoken languages — learning disks actually. If I could go with them, I could get a chance to study this vast amount of Imperium world languages in great detail. Then, I could publish them, and the whole Federation would benefit greatly from that."

"You want to go to Capella-D? On your own? Unthinkable, Gabrielle, you know that. Women just don't do such things," he replied.

"But I wouldn't be alone. I'd be with Captain Nia Elain and all her crew. Please, this is so very important. Think of the benefits to the whole Federation, father," she pleaded.

The arguments flew back and forth for ten minutes. Only once did he ask me if it was even acceptable for her to come along. She added, "Besides father, Miss Molly Maud is an official Field Agent for the Hub Intelligence Division, so it's got to be a safe trip." At last, he said that he would consider the matter.

We spent two more days pouring over her limited distribution data. She kept saying that Marilyn had far more data on this aspect than she did. However, we could see a possible similarity with the overall current distribution of languages within the Imperium. The historical time line was missing though, but Gabrielle insisted that Marilyn could fill in those gaps. At supper that second night, her father relented.

"I've talked with the President's Office. They agree a good database of the spoken languages of the ex-Imperium worlds would be valuable. They talked with Hub ID about this too. So I'll go along with their suggestion to allow you to travel with Captain Nia Elain and Field Agent Molly Maud this one time. However, I want you to go to the Formal Dance tomorrow night. I know Gerald wants to propose to you. I've given him my permission. If I let you go on this extravagant trip, then I want something in return. When you get back, I want your promise to marry one of the men who've proposed to you. I don't even care which one. It's unseemly that at twenty-five you are still unmarried, Gabrielle. I won't have any more of your incessant delays. Agreed?"

She sighed and agreed, but asked us to come along to their formal dance. When we were alone, she said, "This is terrific! I get to come with you."

"Yes, but that's awful. You have to marry when you get back. What kind of a deal is that?" I replied, annoyed. I know. It wasn't any of my business. Still.

Gabrielle sighed. "I know. But that's what women have to endure. We can't do anything on our own. None of the men who have asked for my hand is even remotely interested in linguistics. Several have told me outright that all that will have to stop when I marry them. Of course, I refused them, politely mind you. Still, what choice do I have? I can't do anything about it, not really. It's the way things are and always have been for us women."

"That's a load of crap," I spouted off. "I do what I want to do. All my crew does. Just because it has always been done that way doesn't make it have to be that way or make it right. We marry for love. Our spouses support us, as we support them. You are a brilliant linguist and should keep on with it."

"But father has all the money. If he disowns me, I'd have nothing and no place to even live," she explained. I could sense the pit of sadness in her voice though.

"Well, let's focus on the here and now, shall we? Make the very most of this special time," I countered.

"True, I must. Say, you've been wearing the same dress for days."

I laughed. "I know. It's the only one I have."

"Come on; let's see if some of my skirts would fit."

What she called a limo came by right after supper the following night to take our large group to the Formal Dance. None of us had any idea of their dance steps, but Gabrielle said it wouldn't matter. Of necessity, they were very simple. "In these heels, we can hardly do much at all. Mostly, it is just a grandeur show." She showed us how to do the simple box-like steps.

The L'Arch, where the Formal Dance was held, was more like the inside of the cathedral of Saint Shane's Basilica! The vaulted ceiling dwarfed us. The male musicians played from a gallery high overhead. Something like five hundred younger couples attended. The music was interesting, slow and majestic, fitting for us women in our giant skirts and tall heels.

However, what surprised me was the rather obvious fact that somehow a large number of young men knew we were from the Imperium! Almost the second that our group walked into the spacious, granite-floored space, various young men came up to us, bowing, kissing our hands, and asking for this dance. I heard all manner of comments, such as "A young woman should never be out without her escort." "You don't look like an alien." "How very strange your men didn't bring you on this trip." Of course, we had all sorts of other offers, including one overly enthusiastic young man who wanted to marry me. He looked crestfallen when I told him that I was already married and had six children back home. That calmed his hormones down considerably.

Nevertheless, we did enjoy the dance and the near constant attention of the young men. Poor Gabrielle. This Gerald fellow was not the most handsome lad and clearly wanted to dominate her. I even overheard him tell her that when she got back from this trip, she could forget about all this silly linguistic nonsense. While we rather enjoyed ourselves, Gabrielle didn't and left very sober indeed.

"Well, we should pack your things tomorrow and head for the Capella-D planet as soon as we can," I said in the limo on our way back to her home.

That brought her spirits up. "Oh yes! I wonder how many of my dresses I ought to bring with me?"

Molly Maud laughed. "Oh just a couple. I've researched women's fashions on the worlds they plan to visit. None of them has these giant skirts. Heels, yes, but not these types of gowns. Don't worry; we'll be able to purchase appropriate clothing when we get there. I'm making all the arrangements. No cost to you, Gabrielle. It's coming from my ID expense account. Might as well stick it to those men anyway." That brought chuckles all around.

After packing and sending one crate off to the spaceport, we said our farewells. Yes, I thanked our host Monsieur Ansel Duparte for everything. He puffed up some, grinning broadly at the compliments. However, he spoke to his daughter just as she was leaving, "Remember your promise, Gabrielle. No more of this linguistic nonsense when you get back. And marry someone."

All the poor woman could do was mutter, "Yes father." He just had to dampen her spirits on the day we were leaving. Gr. However, by the time that the Eagle's Seed appeared, Gabrielle was quite enthusiastic once more. She was about to have the time of her life!

Once onboard the ship and after a tour and getting her settled, Molly Maud quickly produced a satin pencil style gown for her to wear. "Look, moving about on this ship in those billowing skirts is nearly impossible. Besides, dresses like this are what they wear on Capella-D." I was pleased our usual dresses would be in fashion. While I couldn't wait to get out of this ball gown, I decided to follow Molly Maud's suggestion and wear our usual dress-up pencil style gowns instead of our usual everyday pants and blouses. It would make both women far more comfortable.

Once Danika had clearance for us to depart, I took the controls and gently lifted us off Bernard-D, and shortly after that, jumped into hyperspace. Purposely, I set a reasonable speed, deciding to give us more time to reflect and discuss our next moves. Danika then announced to everyone, "We'll be arriving there in forty-three hours."

As we met in the galley for a snack, Molly Maud spoke up. "Okay. Fashions for Capella-D are different. We can wear these dresses, but we'll need to continue wearing our six-inch heels and nylons. However, they do have one most unusual custom. They keep their nails six inches long. I've no idea why, but that's their custom. I've researched this a bit and found they provide nail extensions for visiting women. I've taken the liberty to acquire them for us. They were delivered to me while we were on Bernard-D. I think we should apply them now and try to get used to having such enormously long nails before we get there." Groans echoed.

Jana pointed out, "Well, our Imperium senator's wives used to always have to have six inch long nails, while the female senators used to have to have them twelve inches long.

That was the custom for centuries. I guess if they could manage, we can too. Does anyone know how to apply them?" No one did, but thanks to Molly Maud's foresight, she had good instructions.

Hours later over supper, I complained, "This is for the birds! I can't pick up anything, and I keep poking myself in my eyes." Everyone roared. In a way, they were relieved, having similar difficulties adapting. Molly Maud was right; we did need time to get used to them.

During the two days of travel time, Gabrielle and Molly Maud spent much of it gabbing with my crew about the roles of women in our part of the galaxy. Jana and Jovanna were delighted to go on at length about such. Our guests were eager listeners.

Capella-D was a very bright world. Used to the dim orange-red sun of Ashford-5, Capella-D was positively brilliant, almost painfully so. I rather wished we had a supply of sunglasses, the type worn at high altitudes to block the sun's harsh rays where the atmosphere was so thin. This time as we teetered down the slope of the bay ramp, we were met by Miss Marilyn Tonby herself, along with several official representatives, whose names and positions I've forgotten. Blinking from the harsh light, I did see she too had similarly long talons painted a dark red matching her lipstick. She was about our age with curly blonde hair. She spoke English or Midlands dialect, which pleased my crew, though Molly Maud had to rely upon her ear wig for translations. Once we passed through customs and had our temporary ID cards, Marilyn led us to a waiting minibus, which she had rented.

Finally, alone with her at last, we could speak freely. "I'm so glad you could all come, especially you, Gabrielle. I've been dying to meet you for ages and ages. There are so few of us really competent female linguists, you know."

"Me too. It's going to cost me dearly, but I just had to make this trip!"

"I'm so glad you could," she repeated herself. "We are having fabulous luck, you know. Mom and dad are off on a month's vacation to the southern paradises, so we have the whole place to ourselves. My brothers and sisters are all married and have their own places. So I was able to have you all come without having to put up a nasty fight with my dad. He probably would have vetoed your coming to visit. He thinks my linguistic studies are for the bananas, and keeps ordering me to hurry up and get married. I told him no way. That's why they decided to take a long vacation, thinking I'd be bored out of my mind home alone. Ha. I've been catching up on a lot of work, since I don't have to beg him to even send an email to another linguist." She chatted gaily on while driving us along the busy streets of her city, West Hampton, about five miles from the spaceport.

"How come everyone here has such long nails?" Molly Maud asked what most concerned her. She had tried to operate her d-gun and failed miserably. I'd seen her and hoped such wouldn't be needed.

Marilyn laughed, "Cause they are super sexy. Men love them, and so do women," she chatted on showing us the sights of her city before we arrived at her home. I found this city most unassuming and rather familiar. The residential buildings were wooden, but the downtown had the usual steel and concrete skyscrapers. Her home was a modest structure with four bedrooms. We could squeeze in here nicely. It had a homey atmosphere, nothing gaudy or ornate. Everything had a purpose here, and I felt instantly at home. I think the others did too.

Quickly, we launched into a heavy linguistic discussion. Most of my crew decided to take a stroll around the block, which wasn't so easy in these tall heels. I quickly discovered Marilyn had assembled a large set of linguistic sample files of most all languages. Further, her interests lay in the spread of a given language through time across many worlds. She gaily showed us her dozens and dozens of charts, each one outlining the historical spread of a language. She even had spreads of language families as well. Of course, when she heard that we had a complete language database for all major Imperium languages, she wanted to trade with us, just as Gabrielle suggested.

We spent days pouring over her time lines of distributions, correlating them with ours. It became clear that their major languages had spread out from somewhere within the middle of their spiral arm, first towards the hub. Based on her time lines, we could see that their settlements of the hub worlds preceded the settlement of our hub worlds by about a millennia. Jana and Jovanna now had a good working hypothesis that exploratory ships from the Federation hub worlds had been the ones to discover and settle our own hub worlds. The dates of first settlement here were between eleven and thirteen millennia, whereas those of our hub worlds dated from around ten millennia ago.

Then, we discovered a secondary out-thrust beginning around eight millennia ago, heading from their mid-arm regions towards our own mid-arm worlds. Marilyn theorized that they began traveling across the arm regions instead of going the long way around, in to their hub, over to our side of the hub, and back out down our arm. However, that migration was short lived for unknown reasons.

There was a third pattern, a more recent one, in which expansion had moved out towards the rim of their arm, beginning some six millennia ago. What we found fascinating was they crossed over into the outer rim of our arm beginning no earlier than two millennia ago, but more likely only one millennia in the past. As far as Marilyn's data suggested, that spread was still going on, though the recent war with the Imperium had more or less ended that expansion.

Marilyn pointed out the obvious, "Look, all humans are really related, coming from the same original people, just spreading out over some dozen millennia." When she heard we were really going to visit some of the key worlds looking for archaeological evidence of the point of origin of humans, she gushed, "Please, can I come along? I want to know this too. It fits my research. I just have to see this through too. Besides, my father isn't here to tell me no! I'll never ever get such a chance ever again! I just know it. Eventually, he's going to force me to marry, and then all this will be over. Please, I can pay my way somehow. I'll do whatever you tell me to do."

Hearing Marilyn saying this, Gabrielle chimed in, "Hey, me too. I want to come along as well. We are the two best linguists in the Federation, well among us women. Please, you just have to let us come. You know dad's going to force me to marry when I get back and leave all my linguistic studies behind me forever. Please, you just have to let us come."

How could I refuse them? I couldn't. "Okay. You both can come along. We just won't tell your fathers about it until we get back. After all, it'll take quite some time to organize and swap our two large language databases, right?"

"Sure, sure a *very* long time," Marilyn caught on to my pronouncement. We all laughed. Besides, I knew it was going to take the wizardry of Tesla and Anya to make the two totally different systems somehow communicate with each other. All the data was in completely different electronic formats, naturally.

Just then, Anya sent me another telepathic message. *Hey, someone is trying to break into our ship again. Tesla and my new system is working. We should have some good images when we get back.* She and the others were out exploring the city. After that, I ordered them to go back to the ship and keep it safe. Now, I was getting worried. Someone must be following us and still trying to gain entrance to our ship. If they stole it, we'd be stranded here. I decided from now on, someone ought to remain behind to guard the Eagle's Seed. However, I didn't mention this to the three Federation women.

On our sixth day here in West Hampton, a news crew pulled up outside and demanded an interview with us aliens from the Imperium. At least they sent along a female reporter accompanied by four males. I decided to give the woman the exclusive interview, much to the dismay of the men. Still, we were news, and they had no real choice but to consent.

"This is Mary Ann Trestle here live with the aliens from the old Imperium," the blonde woman began as their video systems rolled. "As you can see, they are proper women, just like us, nails, heels, and all. I'm speaking with their leader, Captain Nia Elain Compton-Jereni. Would you like to tell the viewing audience what brings you so far from your home world? Why there are no men with you? Some say you're outcasts. How do you answer those charges?"

Finally, she let me answer. "We're here investigating the

origin of the human species. We know the Imperium worlds were all originally settled by colonists and explorers from your Federation of Planets. We've been gathering sufficient proof of that, particularly since combining our data with that of your linguists. There are no men with us on this trip for a very good reason. Within the Imperium or rather ex-Imperium worlds, women are normally on an equal status with men. Hence, we always pick the most qualified personnel for any given mission or post. I've done just that. We are no more outcasts than you are, Mary Ann."

"Equal status?" Mary Ann noticed my innuendo. I couldn't have played her any better had I been using my gifts.

"That's right. I'm appalled with the lot of women here in the Federation. My goodness. Your men are ignoring the most knowledgeable linguists that we've discovered, Miss Marilyn Tonby here and the visiting Miss Gabrielle Duparte of Bernard-D. When we finish our joint work, the Federation should have a workable database of all languages spoken in the Imperium and vice versa, something unheralded within both our domains. If people cannot communicate easily with each other, difficulties often arise."

"Appalled? Surely, you don't mean that. After all, you and your crew look just like any one of us women here on Capella-D," Mary Ann refused to let this go.

"Yes, we've been told we wouldn't be allowed to land and visit here unless we dressed and appeared appropriately. When we were on Bernard-D, we had to wear their giant ball gown skirts. Here, we have our nails done in your manner. We don't wish to appear like some kind of alien freaks among you. After all, we're all human beings and women in this case. It's just we have cultural differences between us. We have a saying that is quite dated now, but when on Proxima Prime, dress as they do. If we dressed totally different than you do, that alone would begin to erect barriers of differences between us, making real communication and cooperation between us rather difficult to impossible."

"But just what appalls you?" she continued to probe.

"Well you asked for it. The simple fact that women here seem to be considered second-class citizens, pretty wallflowers, sexual objects, things, and have no positions of real power and authority. While within the ex-Imperium worlds there are some men who think similarly, the vast majority do not. Each person is regarded based on what they know and can do, not their gender. Let me be more specific."

"On our last mission involving many things including exploration of the northern halo worlds, we also tested out two new engines. One, the hydrogen propulsion system, is revolutionizing sub-light travel. A woman, Mrs. Alexandra Khristos-Laag, invented it. Her new system worked to perfection, and as I understand it, already the design has been shared with some of your Federation worlds. The other, an improved hyperdrive, was invented by a man, Hans Valen."

Mary Ann pointed out, "But surely this Alexandra was highly educated."

"Of course. However, here as I understand it, women are seldom allowed into your Universities, a men-only rule or some such silliness. From one woman to another, it's education and knowledge, which are truly important. If nothing else, use your public libraries. Half of my crew has never been to our equivalent of your University, our Academy. Yet, they took it upon themselves to learn at least that much on their own and have proven that they are qualified for their positions. Look, I've never been to a University or Academy, and yet, I'm the most qualified person to head up the exploration of the halo worlds and now this minor trip to your Federation. True, I also have a goodly number of Academy trained women with me as well. Pick the best qualified person is my motto and that of most knowledgeable people in positions of authority."

"What a radically novel notion you have. Anyway, there are many reports that you and your crew are outcasts or I believe the word being tossed about is freaks. How do you answer that? It's obvious that you are massively endowed." Mary Ann didn't want to let that detail go.

"As you may know, during the recent war with the Imperium, some of our idiots thought the way to win the war was to drop genetic biological agents on your key worlds. In secret and answering to no one, they developed this horrific genetic agent. It's just awful. Victims fall into a coma for days, while the bio agent mutates their bodies via an accelerated gene alteration. Yes, they all become hermaphrodites. Men and women end up with dual, fully functional sexual organs. But that's the least of the mess. They lose their arms. Their lips become slit, and they must wear giant lip plates. Their hair develops pain neurons, grows down to their ankles, and cannot be cut without intense pain. And their feet become malformed, forcing them to walk only on their toes. Breasts become much larger than heads. Naturally, without total assistance, the victims quickly die from either dehydration or starvation. It's nothing but genocide."

"Some idiots on some Imperium worlds did believe this was a weapon and used it on their enemy worlds, committing mass genocide. Worlds with hundreds of billions of people on it were infected and only a few could be saved. It's not a weapon; it's cold murder of innocent men, women, and children. So yes, many of us have suffered some of these terrorist attacks. Thank we have some very brilliant women geneticists and men too back on our world of Ashford-5. They alone have been able to work out a cure for most of these genetic mutations, all save the hermaphrodite one. We hope in time they will be able to cure that one too."

I went on, "As far as our large bosoms now, it is natural for women who live on Ashford-5 to be so well endowed. Makes breast feeding lots easier, more milk."

Mary Ann just wouldn't let this one go. "So you do admit that you and some of your crew are these freaks, these hermaphrodites?"

"Yes, some of us were victims of these terrorist attacks. Personally, I've been a victim more than once, but I have also been cured three times now."

"And you are married to another woman?" Mary Ann said with some disgust in her voice.

"Most everyone in the Imperium marries for love, for both admiration and respect. Okay, I'll grant you that some don't, choosing to marry for money or position. But most of us follow our hearts. I think that makes for a far healthier marriage, in my humble opinion."

Mary Ann just had to comment, "Well, not everyone has the luxury of marrying for love. Now then, formal records seem to indicate that you and some of your crew are telepaths, Class V it says, whatever that classification may mean. Care to comment on that?"

"No. I'm sure that there are telepaths within your Federation of Planets as well. We're just people too."

"So you read minds. Some say your real purpose is to use your skills to spy on Federation secrets. Care to comment on that one?" Mary Ann asked quite pointedly.

Damn, they sure did know a lot about us. Well, no use in hiding those details. If we had been secretive and then had such things discovered, it would be hard to convince them we weren't spies. I replied, "Sorry, we're not spies. We have no governmental connections. Besides, to my knowledge, we're not going anywhere near anything that could be considered 'secure.' We also have a Hub Intelligence Division Field Agent escorting and traveling with us everywhere we go, Miss Molly Maud Porsche. She carries a d-gun and knows how to use it. So I'm sure if we turn out to be spies, she'll simply blast us. I don't know about you, but I sure don't want to go up against a d-gun." That brought a brief smile to Mary Ann's face.

"Well, that's all the time that we have. This is Mary Ann Trestle signing off for now." She then said, "Cut." The crew began to pack up their gear. The male reporters hastily took off, leaving her still standing before me. After she got rid of her microphone, she moved a little closer to me.

"So are you really serious about women holding positions of power and influence on Imperium worlds? Not just the occasional queen or princess. That they really do hire the most competent person, regardless of gender? Women are treated as equals and not sex objects?" Mary Ann whispered to me.

"Yes, of course. Although I'll be the first to admit that occasionally you'll run across some men who don't, but mostly those are the exceptions. I really am appalled at how women are treated here. I'm hardly the sex object thing."

"Well, you are rather attractive," she said with a coy grin. "But do you really have one of those, well you know, a man's thing too?"

I decided against embarrassing her and said simply, "Yes."

"Curious. Well, I was really impressed with the equality point. Take myself for example. They sent out five of us reporters, four males. They all wanted to do the interview and were not going to let me near you. Then, they had a change of heart and let me do it, mostly because they thought that a woman could get more out of you."

"I already guessed that was what was going on."

"I mean I've worked darn hard to be a fair and accurate reporter, to get those whom I'm interviewing to say what they mean. But I get so few interviews. The men hardly ever let me do my work. Really, there are so very few opportunities for women besides mundane chores. I refused to be a silly receptionist, getting coffee for the men and all that. I hope they air that whole interview. You really called it as it is, as far as I'm concerned. If they don't, I'm going pirate on them and get it aired anyway I can. Women deserve to hear it. Thanks for being so honest with me. I hope I didn't embarrass you too badly."

I smiled. "No. You did well. Keep up the good work, Mary Ann. I best get back to our linguistic work." We shook hands, and I watched her walk away, her heels clicking on the pavement.

Once back inside, the others wanted to chat some about the interview, and I let them vent their feelings before getting everyone back on track. After a bit more review, we decided we were ready to take the exploration to the next level and visit some of the archaeologists on our list. Both Gabrielle and Marilyn were coming with us to work on getting our language database converted over into some form that they could use. After helping Marilyn pack a bag, we headed to the spaceport and my ship.

Naturally, we spent a bit of time giving Marilyn a tour and setting her up in the cabin next to Gabrielle. Once settled in, those two, Tesla, and Anya began working together on the linguistic databases. Getting the proper electronic conversions worked out would be the hardest part. Data transfer would take a lot of time, but would be mostly automatic, once they had the proper methods established. Meanwhile, Molly Maud and I reviewed the list and decided to visit Mrs. Glynis Dolyn of Spica-C first. She had apparently uncovered some curious hominid skeletons. Also, Molly Maud pointed out that our current dresses and tall heels would suffice there. That decided, Danika entered the coordinates, while I got clearance to depart. A half hour later, we entered hyperspace once more, bound for Spica-C. Arrival was three days off, giving our linguists time to work out the database conversions, with Marisol lending them a hand with it.

Six hours later, Tesla sent, *Nia Elain. Troubles. I've just done a thorough check of all systems and found something. We've got an electronic bug on the outside of our ship. Meet me in the comm center.*

Damn. I moved as quickly as my heels allowed, which wasn't fast. I found her and Anya there, hovering over a small display. "Hi. On that monitor, you can see it's signal, the repeating beeps. Anya and I are now triangulating its location. Probably something stuck to our metal hull."

"Well done, both of you. Once we locate it, what are our options to remove it?" I asked, thinking along those lines myself.

"Can't do it while in hyperspace. We'll have to drop out. Of course, once we do, someone would have to suit up and take a spacewalk. The problem with that is whoever planted this will likely drop out alongside of us. With a spacewalker outside, we would be sitting ducks for a boarding party. Clever of them. They know we wouldn't risk leaving one of us outside," Tesla explained, theorizing a worst-case scenario.

"Right. We have to remove it while in hyperspace," I countered. "Find it. I think I have an idea, but I will need its precise location down to a millimeter. Also a way to find that spot from the inside. Anya, open up an intercom line. I best alert everyone. This could get dangerous."

A minute later, I finished explaining the situation. "So I think I have a way to get rid of it, but it can be dangerous. More, once we locate it. Hang in there everyone." Anya switched it off as I nodded to her.

"Got it. Zeroing in on it now. Going to be hard to get it that precisely," Tesla commented, just as everyone else joined us in the comm center.

"Looks like it may be accessible from inside. I'm going to change into work clothes. Darn these long nails anyway," I grumbled and made my way to my quarters. After a good deal of fumbling, I got changed into my pants and flats. Considering how difficult it was for Molly Maud to get these nail extensions on us, I decided to try to work with them. I headed rapidly for the small workshop and found what I needed. A laser drill, a can of Helium, and the Insta-metal repair kit. That latter was one of the more useful items carried on all spaceships. There's no telling when a ship can accidentally run into a piece of space junk, usually tiny particles traveling at high velocity. Shields usually deflect them, but occasionally one can strike the hull, puncturing it with a tiny hole. Enter Insta-metal. Point and squirt. Instant metal bond, stronger than the metal skin.

With my arms full, I headed back to the comm center. "Boss, I have it down to the millimeter. I'll bring my secondary monitor with me, and Anya will monitor both until I've got the precise location on the inside. So what's the plan?"

Molly Maud looked a little pale, but the other two women looked on fascinated by our seeming calmness and competence. I explained, "A little physics is going to come to our rescue. I'm going to drill a microscopic hole through the inner hull, through the insulation, and through the outer hull just beneath the tracking device. Don't worry; this tiny hole is only a few atoms across. Then, I'm going to make use of the peculiar property of liquid Helium-II. When it is almost at absolute zero, the temperature of our outer hull right now, it becomes almost completely frictionless. It can even crawl up the sides of a container. My theory is that when I release the Helium gas, it will liquefy when it reaches the hull. The peculiar property will cause the liquid Helium to seep under the connection that the tracking device has on our hull, releasing it. With luck, it will simply float off into hyperspace. Once done, I'll repair the tiny hole with the Insta-metal."

"Will it work?" Marisol asked slightly worried.

"Hope so. If not, then Plan B is to make a larger hole and push the device off of us with some kind of probe and seal the hole," I replied.

"How do you know about all these things?" asked Gabrielle, very much impressed with us.

"Lots of self-study. You can know all these things too, if you spend lots of time at your library studying up. Come on; you're welcome to watch. There's not any real danger, I hope." I tried to sound fearless, but any spacer will tell you deliberately punching a hole in your hull is just asking for trouble.

It took us nearly a half hour to pinpoint the precise location on the inner hull just behind the center of the tracking device. With the others watching me from a distance, I fumbled around with the drill, silently cursing the long nails. We held our breaths as the drill activated. I don't know why we all did that, but we did. Perhaps it was fear of something about to happen. It didn't take the drill long to penetrate the inner hull and the outer hull as well. I turned it off, and we all took a breath and then laughed. "See, the air isn't escaping," I commented, sensing this was what everyone was scared of happening.

Next, I formed up a seal and slowly released the Helium. Now we could only wait. The reaction on the outer hull could not be seen. Instead, Tesla brought a laptop in and displayed a science lab video showing this peculiar property of liquid Helium-II. It did amaze everyone to see the peculiar stuff flowing up the sides of the container and out as though by magic. Meanwhile, Anya continued to monitor the tracker from the comm center. I never heard such welcome words over the intercom. "It's working. The tracker is moving. Yes, it's moving away from us. Give it a bit longer so I can be sure it won't just come back." Five minutes later, she cheerily reported, "Okay. It's three feet from our hull. Seal the hole."

Everyone watched me as I fumbled with the Insta-metal can. Soon a bright metal patch appeared and the hole was sealed. "Back to the comm center. Let's be sure the device is staying away from us," I ordered. Many heels clicked on the metal floor, and I found myself having to take abnormally small steps, but they were going as fast as they dared.

"Yep, you did it, boss. It's now ten feet from us," Anya reported.

"Well done everyone. I'm going to go to the pilot's seat and give us a tad bit of acceleration and see if we can leave it far behind us," I explained. A few minutes later, Anya reported she lost contact with it completely. Everyone let out a loud cheer, and I smiled, joining them.

"Impressive!" Marisol praised me.

"Indeed. Incredible," Molly Maud added.

For the benefit of our three passengers, I said, "Teamwork. Knowledge is the true power, ladies. Not money. Not force. Knowledge. There is so much to know that one person can't know it all. Besides, we all aren't interested in the same things. That would be mega-boring. Tesla knows her electronics far better than I do. Anya here can make a whole comm center from spare parts. Danika can navigate in the dark, I swear." Several chuckled. "Now, I hope Jana and Jovanna have supper ready. I'm hungry, and no, ladies, I can't cook, but I can boil water for tea, I think." More laughs followed.

More importantly, when we finally dropped out of hyperspace, Tesla and Marisol had worked out the database conversion process going both ways. Further, they got the two computers working together, namely Marilyn's and ours. Marisol proudly announced, "The linguistic database transfer has begun! Of course, it'll take days to complete. But once it's done, ladies," she spoke to Gabrielle and Marilyn, "you two will possess something of immense value to the Federation. Heck, you could sell it to them for a fortune."

I realized what she was doing. Clever lady. She had just planted an idea in their minds, one that could well allow them to remain independent women. I wondered how it would finally play out weeks from now.

Meanwhile, Molly Maud consulted her Intel on Spica-C and reached another conclusion. "Everyone, I think that we can simply dress like professional women on this world. Perhaps, we don't even need to dress up even that much, but I would like to play it safe. A professional appearance can't hurt us. We could shorten our nails if we wish."

"But I don't want to cut mine," protested Marilyn. "I'd feel really naked or something without them."

Out of deference to her, we all silently agreed to keep our nail extensions on for now. We could always remove them later if needed. We were not planning to go on any archaeological digs; rather we intended to discuss their findings.

Molly Maud added, "We'll need to use our ear wigs. They speak a version of Welsh on this world. I don't speak that language."

"Neither do I," added Marilyn. We all echoed her. My group adjusted our ULATs to Welsh, while the three guests did the same with their ear wigs.

Chapter 4 The First Archaeologists

I began my approach to Spica-C, while everyone else watched the view from our several view ports. We certainly got an eye-full this time! Spica turned out to be a binary star. The main sun was a giant B type star, extremely luminous and bright. Its companion was a much smaller star, rotating about it fairly closely. The planet in question lay some distance from the orbiting pair of stars. Anwyn pointed out, "If Ashford-5 was the same distance from Ashford as this planet is from the twin suns, then you probably couldn't even see Ashford without a telescope." That was worth pondering. Even so, as the planet drew steadily larger, I realized we were going to be landing on a very brilliantly illuminated world. Again, I wished for mountain sunglasses.

This time, Beth produced them! She found a box of them in storage and handed each of us a pair. "You're going to need them. I think their suns are going to be extremely bright." She was right. Later, we thanked her for finding the glasses for us!

As we slowly descended, I thought here was another world that needs Jan's supernova prediction program and hoped that it didn't go off while we were here! It seems that every time I come across a giant or supergiant star, I begin to worry. Silly me. This spaceport seemed a little rundown to me. Still, it had the expected security men and control building. Unlike the Imperium, here in the Federation, each world had their own notions of what a spaceport should look like. This one looked more like some heavily fortified defensive structure. Blockish in shape, I thought it appeared rather ugly, but functional. A man dressed in a dark brown corduroy suite walked up to our bay door, accompanied by the uniformed men with their d-guns.

This time, we stepped down to meet them dressed as professional women, three inch black heels, black skirt that covered our knees, white blouses, and black blazers. ULATs and ear wigs were definitely needed. Their language was very difficult to grasp but for an entirely different reason, one which took us all by surprise. Their teeth.

All their front teeth looked like they had been filed down to points. Each incisor was shaped like a 'V,' pointed at the tip and sharp. Later, I notice all their other teeth behind their canines were normal though. Still, we were taken aback when we first saw them. Our dark sunglasses partially hid our surprise as we talked with this man. Marisol pointed out the impact this had on their speech. "All of their labial-dental sounds are allowing lots of extra air through the V gaps, adding that ssss sound to everything." When pronouncing a word, which had a 'th' in it, the sounds that came out were more like 'ssthssss.' Well, I now had one more question to ask this archaeologist.

The man led us into the bunker building, where I paid the small landing fee. After stating our business on this world, he gave us our temporary ID cards. He was kind enough to give us directions on how to find the woman in question. While he didn't know her name, a government official had given him her address. Molly Maud's people had previously gotten clearance for our meeting, and the permission had filtered down to this man. Unfortunately, she lived in a rural area on the other side of the world.

In order to get there, we would have to take their commercial transportation, something called an airplane and then a bus. That said, we headed back to the Eagle's Seed to work out our next step. Making matters more uncomfortable, the air positively stank! Oil, tar, and some type of chemical stench filled the air. This was the worst spaceport air I'd ever encountered. However, we would soon learn that here the air was fresher than at most other areas. Exhaust pollution was rampant across their entire world. Moreover, it was hot, far too hot for comfort. At least, that bunker had been air-conditioned. By the time that we got back onboard, our blouses were soaked, and I decided we'd abandon our blazers.

Considering the difficulties in reaching our archaeologist, only a few of us would make the long trip. I took Jana, Molly Maud, and Marisol. Gabrielle and Marilyn decided not to make the trip. Both were having a hard time breathing this foul air and were quite uncomfortable. Once we four left the ship, Danika closed the bay door and turned the air filtration system on full. Soon, they had clean, cool air to breathe once more. Not us, however.

A shuttle car drove us two miles across the steaming tarmac to their associated commercial airfield. Here we saw giant airplanes landing and taking off, belching out voluminous quantities of exhaust fumes, causing us to gag slightly. This was a miserable world to live on, I decided. Inside the public building, with Molly Maud's assistance, I bought us four tickets on the next flight. At least inside it was cool, though the air still stank.

An hour later, we joined a hundred others filing onto the airplane. While we were not overly dressed, we were certainly "dressed up" and received many stares, though we stared back at their teeth mostly. It was freaky seeing all those V-shaped teeth. I figured that they must have one heck of a bite, like some vicious wild animal. The ride was long and tiresome, not to mention bumpy and full of undo accelerations. We sat next to an older woman who insisted on chatting with us.

"You must be foreigners. Your teeth, you see. Well, we do need visitors. Do you have global warming where you come from? We do here. They say it is only going to get hotter every year, but then that's to be expected what with all this pollution that no one can seem to get under control. Speaking of control, did you see that newscast a while back where that hub star exploded? Well, it was all over the news here. Some say that Spica-A is going to blow up one day. Well, it hasn't done that yet, but they say that some fellow can predict when it will. No one's done that here yet, though I don't know if the government would actually tell us if they knew. Might cause panic, you see. I suppose it will only get hotter here when it does blow up. So where are you pretty things from?"

Molly Maud kindly answered for us. "Hoffdorf on Cass-C out in the hub. Yes, that supernova over in Imperium space did wipe out two of the Federation worlds, but they gave us a warning in time for most of the people there to evacuate to nearby worlds. The explosion was quite spectacular. I believe our scientists are studying it now, and the Imperium man has given his theory of prediction to our leaders. I expect someone will soon be working out when Spica is going to blow. Probably there will be time to get everyone evacuated. It's so hot here now."

"Ah, that is good news then. Yes, it gets hotter every year. Pollution. They say that's the cause, but I don't know about such things. I came to the spaceport here to see my daughter off. She's on her way to Taurus-C as an ambassador. She's a good girl, studied hard. You know, they have to, especially us women. But then, they needed a woman representative, and she was chosen. Quite an honor. She claims she's only the third female ambassador of ours this century. Don't know about that, but if she says so, it must be so."

So the hours passed. From her chatter, we did learn quite a lot about this world. When a child reached adulthood, their front teeth were filed down to the sharp 'V' shapes. This had been done as far back as they had any written record. No one knew why, only that everyone had their teeth filed, but they sure had good bites. The old woman speculated that at one time, they were used to rip meat apart.

Once we got off the airplane, we found a bus to take us the rest of the way. Molly Maud was a pro at arranging transportation, and we praised her for her skills, pleasing her a good deal. The bus dropped us off at a rural gravel road. There was a metal box on a post, which displayed the address prominently so we knew we had the right location, but we had to walk about a quarter mile up the gravel road to an old wooden farmhouse, quaint and picturesque. By the time we arrived, all four of us were rather soaked and irritable. This was anything but fun, and I hoped she had air conditioning inside. Molly Maud knocked on the front door.

Shortly, a woman in her early thirties appeared at the door, wearing an apron over her cotton dress. Her brown hair was tied up in a bun. "Come on in. You must be the alien visitors. I was told to expect you. I've baked some muffins and have lemonade chilling in the fridge. Don't mind all the kid's toys. They are out back in the swimming hole cooling off."

We were formally introduced to Mrs. Glynis Dolyn, ex-archaeologist. After we cooled down some, devouring several muffins and two glasses of the ice-cold lemonade, we explained why we had come to see her.

"I'm so sorry. You see, shortly after I made that discovery, I had to get married, and my husband flatly refused to allow me to continue my archaeology work. He insisted I be mother and housekeeper here on the farm. My initial findings indicated I'd uncovered fossil remains that might be pre-humans, but just as I was getting married, I was able definitely to prove they were a local race of monkeys that died out millennia ago. However, he wouldn't even allow me to publish that or even to retract my initial wrong suggestion. I'm so sorry you made this long trip for nothing. But we women just can't do anything about such things. Men control everything. I have three young sons and two daughters, all healthy, thank heavens. So I guess I can't complain," she admitted.

Well, this cleared up one point that we had on the origins. Had the remains been those of pre-humans, then the spatial distribution would have been askew. In spite of everything, this was good news to us, and I pointed this out to her, sparking or rekindling her love of antiquities. As we talked more, she became more and more alive. We'd sparked the goals she'd originally had as a young teen.

"Say," she volunteered, "I saw that interview you did with that reporter, what's her name, oh, Mary Ann. Are you really hermaphrodites? Can you really impregnate yourselves?"

I laughed, "Yes. Danika and I have six daughters of our own now. We can't have boys, obviously. So just between us, there's a benefit to this awful genetic bio weapon. She and I can have our own children."

"Well here in the Federation, I don't think that's such a good benefit, having daughters I mean, but no one can do anything about it, not really. We're stuck in being men's slaves or toys. Always have been as far as history goes. You are really lucky to be living in the Imperium," she replied.

"As long as women believe they can do nothing about it, then they can't," I pointed out. Okay, I was growing tired of their self-defeating attitudes.

"Point taken. You are right. We make up half the population. If we went on strike, we'd shut nearly everything down. Look, the men have really turned our whole world into a disaster zone. Pollution is taking its toll. The average lifetimes have shortened some ten years and that's just in the last decade. You know, if we women don't do something soon, we won't be here much longer. I can see that clearly. Now if I can only get other women to see it too."

"Perhaps they can," I suggested, reminded of that older woman and her lengthy chat on the airplane. I told Glynis about her. "I bet you could easily drum up support."

Molly Maud checked her watch, and said there was still time to catch the bus on its return trip to the airport. Hence, we said our goodbyes to Glynis and wished her the best of luck. She also took down our frequency so that she could get a hold of us later on. Once more, we headed out into the late afternoon heat, melting by the time we got on the bus. Thank goodness, it was air conditioned too.

I admit we were too lax on our security. What happened next is as much my fault as theirs. While we were cooling off, three rough looking men with d-guns got onboard and came back to where we were sitting near the rear of the bus, which could hold about fifty people, though only we four and three others were present when they boarded. The men came back to our seats and had their guns drawn before we realized that they were after us.

"Aliens. Don't make a move or we'll shoot you," one barked softly.

Looking up, I was startled to see a gun pointed at my head. "What do you want?" I asked trying to be polite and trying to size up the situation. The driver was intent on the road ahead. The other three passengers were up front, no help there.

"You are going to get off at the next stop with us. Boss wants you alive, but he didn't say that you needed all your pieces," he replied antagonistically.

"I am a Hub ID Field Agent. Do you know what you are getting involved in?" Molly Maud countered bravely. I sensed she felt guilty about having let her guard down. She was playing the only card remaining to her, her position.

"Yeh lady. We know. We won't hesitate to drill you. Boss doesn't want you, just them alien bitches. So shut up," he barked.

I'll take the one in front of me. Jana, you get the one in the green shirt. Marisol, you get the brown shirt. Count to three and do it, I sent and counted to three as I focused. Three psi-crystals around our necks glowed with a pale blue light. All three men slumped to the ground, dropping their d-guns in the process. I'll admit I over did it a bit and turned my man's mind into mush. Blood seeped from his nose, ears, and eyes. Molly Maud looked shocked and startled by their sudden collapse. The bus driver called out, "What's going on back there?" He'd seen the men falling down in the rearview mirror.

I called out via my ULAT box, "Heat's got to them. We'll get them seated. They'll cool off soon enough." That satisfied the driver who didn't pay us any more attention. After a bit of a struggle, we got the three men into some seats in front of us.

Only then did Molly Maud whisper nervously, "What just happened? Why did they collapse? That one is bleeding."

"Confiscate their d-guns, Molly Maud," I ordered, "just in case they wake up before we get to the airport." She did as asked, fumbling a bit with her long nails while trying to pick them up. She stowed them in her purse.

"But what happened to them? One minute they were kidnaping us, and the next, they just collapsed," she whispered. I could see that she was trembling a little. So I sent her calming thoughts.

"We sort of put them to sleep for a while," I replied, non-specifically.

"I can see that, but how? That one is bleeding," she countered.

"It's too hard to explain, but we sort of knocked them out mentally," I replied. "You know — telepaths?" I tried to assign it to mere telepathy, hoping she would buy that explanation and not press the issue further. I wanted to focus on what these men were trying to do and why? "We should search them for clues," I suggested.

That did the trick. Molly Maud replied, "Yes, we should. I'm shirking my duties. Yes, let's search them. Darn these nails anyway." Trying to go through their pockets was quite a challenge, but we found nothing. "Here comes the next stop. I'm going to have my d-gun at the ready in case more come onboard. Do you want to use their guns?"

"No, I'm allergic to them," I teased her. "I'm sure you can protect us if more come. We were just taken by surprise that's all." She smiled and readied her gun, watching the front of the bus. Marisol and Jana kept watch on either side of the bus.

"There are more men and some kind of vehicle," Jana whispered. "They are looking at us."

I decided to be coy. I waved and smiled at the men who quickly looked away. The bus pulled back on the road, leaving them behind. "Could you tell what they were thinking, what they wanted from us?" Molly Maud asked.

"Well, no. Probing another's mind without their consent is like mental rape. We almost never do that. The situation is under control. If it wasn't, then we might do that," I explained.

"Oh, I see. Well, I sure would have — if I had telepathy, I mean, probe their minds," Molly Maud said determinedly. "Beasts. Why did they want to kidnap us? They were obviously planning to drive us away in that truck. It didn't have any markings on it either. Suspicious. Well, I'll certainly report this to my boss!"

The long drive passed without further incident, though the men remained unconscious and were still so when we got off. As I passed the driver, I said, "Those men are sleeping until they get to where they are going. Guess they were tired." He nodded appreciatively, flashing his V-shaped teeth, which I still found spooky. We headed on into the airport, where Molly Maud had gone on ahead to purchase our tickets for the return flight. A bit later, we sat in the waiting area, watching other airplanes landing and taking off. Finally, our flight was announced, and we rose to get into line to walk down the corridor and into the plane.

Just then, I spotted three more ruff looking men

coming our way. I could see bulges in their pants where they had concealed d-guns. *Three behind us. Take them out quietly,* I sent. Again, our crystals glowed briefly, and the three men dropped to the floor, causing a bit of a disturbance while we and the other passengers glanced back but headed on and into the plane. After finding our seats, we kept a look out to see if the men got onboard. They didn't. We'd knocked them out fairly well. At least this time, I didn't kill one of them.

The long flight was boring, cramped, and generally uncomfortable. We were all starving by the time we arrived at the spaceport. Besides that, it was full dark. Cautiously, we made our way across the tarmac towards the Eagle's Seed. I messaged Tesla, and she turned on the bay lights. Now, I felt more comfortable. If they wanted to try it again, they'd have to do it under our lights. I did sense the minds of others not far away in the darkness, but I think they thought better of risking an attack in the bright lights of our ship. We got onboard as fast as we could and shut it behind us.

"Keep the lights on, Tesla. I think there are some unsavory men outside," I ordered.

"Supper's waiting," Jovanna called out.

"I'm taking off first. We've been attacked twice now," I replied, heading for the pilot's seat up front.

As I sat down, Danika explained, "We were too. Tesla drove them off with her new invention. She somehow electrically charged the hull and shot great sparks into the men. Harmless. Just made their hair stand up on end and made their bodies jerk about. She thinks that'll deter them from trying anything else. Where to, boss?"

I chuckled. "Just into hyperspace for now. We'll figure that out over supper. This one was a total bust." I got my clearance to depart and a half hour later, we were cruising at the slowest possible speed in hyperspace. Danika and I headed back to the galley to join the others for supper. Already Marisol, Jana, and Molly Maud had told the others about our adventures, and Tesla, hers.

"Should have seen them jump when my Tesla Coil arced into their bodies. Harmless, but it sure shook them up," Tesla explained.

Jovanna said, "Well, it wasn't a total bust. We can scratch the possible anomaly of Spica-C off our lists. That's something. So where now?"

"How about Mira-C?" Jana suggested.

Dylan looked it up on his laptop. "Boy, you sure do pick the weird planets. Mira is a binary star. The main one is a red giant, but it has a white dwarf companion star very close to it. That smaller star is gaining mass from the red giant. There is a plume of gas flowing from it to the white dwarf. About every ten thousand years, there is another giant pulse. Plus there are smaller periodic increases in brightness."

"Is it dangerous there?" Jana asked.

Molly Maud also brought up the star on her laptop. "It's a desert type of world, pretty arid. Most of the energy output of the pulses is in the infrared, which means it get hotter at those times. They seem to have their bases covered. Something called an IR Burst Warning. When those are issued, people stay indoors. Looks like another major burst isn't due for at least another millennia, so we only have to worry about the IR Bursts. So why are we going here? Surely humankind didn't evolve here," she suggested.

Jovanna answered her. "No, it didn't. However, Mrs. Lijuan Ho wrote a key article about skeletons recovered in an abandoned museum on a deserted world. These skeletal remains are definitely linked to our human anatomy, though they are nearly two million years old, if the dates she provided are accurate. We need to talk with her and find out more about these and from where they originated. Good clues, you see. Shouldn't take very long to find out what she knows. So what's their dress code like? Can we get rid of these long nails?"

"But they are so sexy," Marilyn protested. I suspected that she wouldn't cut hers even if we did.

"Well, the women wear golden colored neck bands that immobilize their necks. I once saw an ambassador's wife in Hoffdorf. She couldn't turn her head and had to turn her body to look to the side. I hope we don't have to wear them. Dress-wise, we are okay again with the professional woman look, unless we want to go out in the field. Then, they wear light cotton dresses, which look like they would be substantially cooler, and sandals too. I do hope that we aren't going out into the field on this one," Molly Maud answered.

"Not if we can help it. Her address seems to be inside a city called Ho Min," I replied, looking over Dylan's shoulder at the map that he brought up. We were getting better at dealing with Federation databases that were available on the right frequencies.

That decided, Molly Maud make the arrangements for us, after Danika plotted our course. We were due to arrive there in three days, timing our arrival with early morning at their spaceport. That done, we decided to get rid of the clumsy long nails, though as I expected, Marilyn kept hers.

As we dropped out of hyperspace, the binary star was so spectacular that Anwyn and Dylan began making a video recording of it as we made our approach to Mira-C, a world far from the two close stars. It had to be, considering the intense red luminosity from the red giant. The mass bridge from the giant to the white dwarf was clearly visible and quite fascinating to see. Then, the inhabited world appeared, a brown and blue world. At least they had oceans, which meant that the world wasn't completely a desert. I followed the landing instructions, but needed the ULAT to understand them. The people here spoke a Chinese dialect I didn't know, and I rather wished the Cho family were with me. They probably could understand them or so I mused.

We landed at their spaceport. Stepping off, it was hot and dry, but the air was relatively clean with the usual oil and metal odors found at so many spaceports. A party of six armed men in uniforms accompanied a man wearing a thin linen, white suit approached us, waving his arms in greetings. Well, this is friendly enough, I thought.

Once more, Molly Maud introduced us, and I was surprised she could speak their language, as could Gabrielle, Marilyn, and Marisol. For once, I was glad to have the linguists along. It made things simpler. We were definitely welcome. After paying the nominal landing fee and being photographed, we were presented with our temporary ID cards. The white suited man was Commander Bo Lin Huan, and he then dropped the bombshell on us.

"If you wish to travel beyond our spaceport, you must be fitted with our customary neck rings that all women wear. We have just such a facility here on the base where you may obtain them, as do all female visitors to our world and at no cost to you, a courtesy extended by our government." His voice was all sweetness and polite, but I sensed that inwardly he was laughing at us.

"You have an unusual custom. Why do all of your women wear them?" I asked just as politely.

"They are called the Jinwei, the Golden Dragon, the mother of us all. Women are considered the mother of our people. It is worn with high honor. Many women even have a Golden Dragon tattoo on their backs, but you are not required to obtain such a tattoo, only the Jinwei," he explained, growing rather bored with the conversation. I sensed he'd given this speech a thousand times.

I told him that some of us would get them. We headed back to the ship to discuss just who would go with me to visit Mrs. Lijuan Ho. Naturally, Molly Maud insisted on coming. Marisol, Marilyn, Gabrielle, and Jovanna wanted to come with us. The others decided to remain and monitor for any of the IR Burst Warnings. That decided, we six headed back to their main control center, where Commander Bo Lin Huan was waiting for us, giving the appearance of being quite patient with us.

"Ah, six of you to receive the high honor of the Jinwei is it?" Commander Bo asked.

"Yes. Will it hurt?" I asked.

He grinned, "Oh no, no. It doesn't hurt at all. This way, honored women," he replied, leading us down a long hallway. A sign protruded from above a doorway. It showed a golden dragon, and we entered this small room. "Six to receive their Jinwei," he said to the older man who sat beside a strange looking machine. The man was incredibly bored, but he brightened up when we entered. "I will leave you in his capable hands." Commander Bo bowed respectfully and left.

"Please lie down on the couch and place your head on the head rest," he said. I decided to go first and did as he asked. He carefully pulled my long hair back and out of the way, as well as the top of my blouse. From prior experience, we chose not to wear our blazers, not in this heat. With my neck fully exposed, he closed the machine around my entire neck, forcing my chin up somewhat.

He explained, "Each neck has its own height. The machine will fit you with a perfect fitting Jinwei." I heard a hissing sound and felt small, cold metal encircling my lower neck. Then another hiss and I felt it again slightly higher up my neck. Six more times it hissed, but on the last one, I felt strong downward pressure on my upper shoulder and my chin. The process was finished, and he opened the machine while the others stared at me. My neck was encircled by eight golden rings, but they were held tightly against each other, pressing hard on my shoulders and my upper head. As I tried to get up, the first thing I noticed was that my head was immobile. I couldn't turn it even a half inch! The rings held my neck as though it was in some kind of vice grip. I got up and began to deal with being so constrained. I had to turn my body now and not my head, awkward in the extreme. Worse, I had to bend to look downward. I felt a sudden pang of deep sympathy for what the women of Mira-C had to endure all their lives.

One by one, the others were given their Jinwei. "Well, this is horribly confining," Molly Maud confessed. I can't see to draw my d-gun! I'll have to do it by feel." I noticed she said this in English, hoping the old man didn't understand her. He gave no sign that he did.

"Well this is different," Marisol commented, as we six walked back down the hall, turning our bodies slightly to see to each side. "Awkward at the very best. I wonder how the women here deal with this? I'm going to ask Mrs. Lijuan Ho about it."

"I can't bend over to see my purse. Getting my bank card out is going to be difficult," Molly Maud added. We agreed to help each other with things and walked up to the information desk to see about getting transportation to our archaeologist's home. Again, we were able to obtain an inexpensive bus ride. We had to bend at our waists to see the steps as we boarded the bus. I knew we had some adapting to do and fast. Our necks were effectively in a rigid brace. It was annoying to have to turn on your butt just to look out of the window!

"It's only for a few hours," Jovanna tried to make light of our situation. An hour later, we had seen many, many women on the streets wearing their Jinwei. As much as we could, we watched them to see how they managed, as we drove by through heavy city traffic. Indeed, from the little we could see, they were adept at twisting and bending. Then, the bus pulled up at a stop, our destination, well nearly. We were at the right street. Molly Maud tried to get her notebook out of her purse and failed miserably. I bent over and retrieved it.

"Thanks. This is crazy. Okay, we're looking for number 1543. It's on that side. All the odd numbers are there," she pointed out. We six then headed on down the street, occasionally pivoting to our left to see a house number. The homes were mostly brown sandstone, but palm trees lined the street. Multicolored birds darted about, and we heard a few dogs barking. The lawns were pretty dried out, but their bushes looked rather foreign to us. I knew that Beth would have loved to stop and examine them. We walked on for another two blocks before we found the right house, an unimposing brownstone home. Six professional looking women walked up to the front door and knocked.

Shortly a woman in her thirties opened the door. "Mrs. Lijuan Ho?" Molly Maud inquired politely.

"Why yes. You must be the alien guests that called. Please, come inside out of the heat," she said. She wore a thin cotton dress, had long black hair braided into a single strand that touched her rear, and of course the golden Jinwei. "I've been expecting you. I've prepared our traditional tea. Please this way. I am so honored by your presence," she explained, leading us into her home and living room. There, we sat down on two couches which had low tables before them. Elegant china teacups on saucers sat on them waiting for us. She squatted down and picked up the teapot, done in gold leaf ornamentation. Bending over, she poured each of us a cup and then herself, before sitting down. Unused to our constraining neck rings, we watched to see how she managed to sip her tea and then emulated her. Meanwhile, Molly Maud introduced each of us to her. She politely bowed to each of us by bending slightly at her waist.

The tea tasted a little funny to me, but then I was on a strange world. I sipped more, and then I felt slightly dizzy. I tried to say something, but my words were slurred. Then blackness came. At the last moment, I realized that I'd been drugged!

Six men then came out from a back room, handed the woman a stack of bills, and she rose and left the house. She didn't notice another man following behind her in another vehicle. As she approached the street corner, the vehicle sped up, intercepted her. A side door opened and another man physically jerked her into the vehicle. Her body was found months later decomposing out in the desert south of the city.

Meanwhile, another vehicle pulled up, and the six men carried each of us out and into the vehicle, which they called a van. We were whisked away, far out of the city and into the desert. Time passed.

I finally roused only to find myself bound to a chair. My arms ached. They were pulled tightly behind me and tied together and to the back of the chair. My feet were similarly tied tightly to the legs of the chair. The neck rings prevented me from looking down at my bindings or to either side. All I could do was move my eyes. Off to my left, I saw some of my companions, but off to my right, I saw a woman around our age. She too had her arms bound behind her and to the back of her chair. Her legs were secured to each leg of the chair as well. However, I could see she had taken a severe beating. Her shoulders were black and blue, as was that part of her chin that I could see. What was probably dried blood had congealed below her mouth. Her hair was still braided and quite long. She was conscious, her eyes straining to see my companions and me.

Seeing me rousing, she whispered, "Are you the aliens who came to see me?"

"Mrs. Lijuan Ho?" I whispered back, convinced that the woman we had met was an imposter.

"Yes. Are you hurt? What happened to you?" she whispered.

"We went to your house, but an imposter was there; she drugged us with some tea, and here we are, wherever here is. Nia Elain Compton-Jereni," I answered. "What's going on? Are you all right?"

"What's happening?" I heard Molly Maud whispering as she came to. One by one, the others roused, but fortunately, none screamed.

Lijuan whispered, "I thought they were after me because I'm leading the revolt. We all heard your interview, Captain Nia Elain. Some of us are trying to do something about it. They came, took me last night, and beat me some, but they later gave me a drink of water. Why have they taken you?" she asked, resigned to her fate.

"Don't know. Sh. Someone's coming," I whispered.

Two men entered and walked up to me. One spoke crude English but with an obvious Chinese accent. You are the captain?" he addressed me.

"Yes, why have you taken us prisoners?" I replied.

His hand slapped me across my face. My head didn't move, making it sting far harder than normal. I felt a trickle of blood. He'd slit my lower lip a little. "Answer only my questions. Do not speak otherwise or I'll beat you senseless. Understand woman?" I said so.

"Now then, we want your ship, the combination that'll open the bay doors. If you give it to us, then we'll not harm the rest of your crew and will bring them safely here to you. If not, we'll let you sit in that chair until you are willing to give us the combination, though we'll probably beat you severely from time to time, just like we've beaten that bitch there, Lijuan. So tell us the combination," he spat at me.

"If you hit me again, you are a dead man," I spat back, hitting him with a bit of bloodstained spittle. He pulled back his arm to smack me another time. My crystal glowed and I focused. I admit it. I was fighting mad, and I didn't withhold anything. He dropped dead before me. Marisol cried out, but Jovanna acted, dropping the second man as he moved towards the first.

She whispered, "Should I kill him?"

"Best that way," I replied. "I wonder how many more of

them there are?"

"There were six at one time," Lijuan whispered. "What happened to him? Is he really dead?"

"Sorry, I got pissed. No one slaps me like that. Yes, he's dead. So is the other one now," I whispered back. *Good going, Jovanna.*

Right. I've had enough brutality back on Metcalf-4 to last me a lifetime. Now what?

"We wait until more men come and then kill them too," I whispered.

"But how can they be dead? We're helpless, tied up. We can't do anything," Molly Maud whispered back. "Is it like that man on the bus?"

"Yes, sorry, but he pissed me off. No one has the right to beat helpless women. Not in my book," I replied, thinking hard.

Marisol whispered, "I contacted the others on the ship and told them what happened. They are having their own problems. Men are trying to break in by force, but they are holding them off."

"Damn. We have got to get out of here," I stated the obvious.

"But I can't move anything," Marilyn whispered. I thought she and Gabrielle were holding up well, all things considered. "What is this code that they want?"

"The combination that will let them steal my ship and kill my crew. No way are they getting that out of us," I answered.

"I suppose we could get a commercial transport back home if they let us go," Gabrielle theorized.

"They won't let us live. We're out in the desert," Lijuan whispered back. "Listen, I think I hear more coming." We shut up and played dumb as two more men walked in. They looked stunned to see their two dead companions lying on the stone floor in front of me, mostly.

"What the hell is going on?" one said, running up to the fallen men and turning them over, while feeling for a pulse.

"Heart attack?" I suggested. "Heat stroke?"

He looked up at me accusatively, "What did you do to

them?" he barked.

"I can't move a muscle. Get real," I retorted. That stopped him. He looked each of us over briefly, verifying we were still tightly bound.

"Carry them out. I'll question her," he ordered. His companion began dragging one of the bodies out of the room. "Okay, woman, we need the combination to your ship. Give it to us, and we'll let you and your crew on the ship live. Refuse and you'll get beaten until you do give it to us."

"Touch me and you'll be as dead as those are," I replied. "Untie us now, and we won't kill you."

He reached back to wallop me a good one. I certainly didn't want to get hit that hard. With my rigid neck, he'd probably break my facial bones or jaw. Again, I acted, but Jovanna was only a fraction of a second behind me. Both men simply dropped onto the floor, their brains had become liquefied, a trick we'd learned a long time ago from Zarita.

I whispered, "Four down, two to go." We waited in silence for some time. Finally, another two men entered with drawn d-guns.

"What the hell is going on here?" one yelled, looking around the room as though he expected to see others here. While they were looking about and distracted, I acted. The problem with d-guns being held in hands is that they have a tendency to go off. One fired and took out a chunk of the roof. The other one fired as Jovanna brought him down. Unfortunately for her, the beam shot slightly upwards underneath her chair and between her legs, hitting her bound arms.

Jovanna cried out, "I'm hit! Pain! I think I lost my left hand. I'm. . ." She fainted.

I yelled, "Can anyone see her? Is she dying?" I was frantic with worry and extremely angry. This was the last straw. I struggled mightily, but couldn't move my arms or legs.

"She's passed out. Can't tell more," Marisol's frightened voice hit me hard.

"Okay everyone. Think. Knowledge is power. We need a bright idea and fast!" I called aloud.

Her voice shaking, Marilyn said, "If we had a knife,

maybe we could cut the ropes."

"Good idea. Does anyone see a knife on these men? I can't move enough to see them," I called out.

Marisol had recovered her shock. "Boss, if we lift them up, then we can search them. Surely one has a knife on them."

That meant that she was willing to display our true *mentales* gifts. Well, we had done that already, though rather mysteriously. Up to this point, our three companions had not seen us really "do" anything, just bodies falling over dead. They had no idea their brains were now liquid mush.

"Okay. You lift. I'll search. Probably on their legs or in their pockets," I replied. "Gang, you are not seeing this." My voice had a definite teasing sound to it.

The four watched in complete disbelief as one of the dead men rose into the air, upside down. His pant legs seemed to be being pulled down my unseen hands. I found what I needed on the third man. He had a large knife strapped to his right lower leg. I unfastened it and they watched the knife float over to us.

"Well, now I can't see a damned thing. No way to cut us free, Marisol. Ideas?" I asked.

"If we could bust up the chairs," Marilyn suggested, "but I don't know how. I can't move."

I lunged forward a bit and the back legs of the chair came off the ground a little. Lijuan said, "I think you are doing it a little bit." She was doing her best to encourage me. I decided that while I might not be able to break the chair, if I was on the floor, I might be able to see the back of one chair. If so, I could levitate the knife and free one of us. I didn't want to break my neck, so I focused and sort of levitated myself as I tipped over and fell. I wasn't in a position to see very well, so I tweaked my position with a little telekinesis power. Then came the hard work, getting the knife to work only by levitation. One slip, well, I didn't want to think about that.

I decided to gamble on freeing Gabrielle first. Why? It would raise her morale if she could at least free the rest of us. Besides, I could now see her best. It took me a half hour but I did cut her arms free. However, she had a bit of difficulty leaning over well enough to untie her legs. I silently curse these darn neck rings again. Still, my goal was achieved. Gabrielle sprung free and stood up looking for the knife.

"I'll cut you all free right away. Gosh, it's hard not being able to bend my neck so I can see. I hope I don't cut you," she gushed. The pride she displayed when she had cut us free was impressive. Next, while Marisol and I tended to the still unconscious Jovanna, the others discussed what to do.

I planted a thought in Molly Maud's mind. She spoke up, "We should blow their heads with a d-gun. That ought to hide whatever you did to them and make a more believable story." She went ahead, did just that, and then clumsily gathered up the other d-guns, giving one to Lijuan to use. "I'm going with her to see just where we are," she announced with some pride herself.

Meanwhile, Marisol and I focused and did what little healing we could on what remained of Jovanna's left lower arm. The d-gun had taken it off at her wrist. A little higher and it would have hit her in her abdomen and probably killed her rather painfully. At least, we got some pinkish skin covering the wound. Once we got her back to the ship, we could use the medical machine on her and truly heal it.

The others returned and Lijuan reported, "We are out in the desert. I'm not sure where. It's an abandoned warehouse facility of some kind. There is a van we can use to get away from here."

Molly Maud added, "I put in a call to Commander Werner and told him about our abduction and the wounding of Jovanna. I was furious with him, so I think he might actually do something about it, but who knows. He's a man after all."

"We need to get Jovanna back to our ship, but we need water and food," I spoke up.

"I know a safe place. We'll be all right if that van has a Nav system in it. I'll go check and see if there's any water around here. Come on ladies; let's search this place," Lijuan suggested. Meanwhile, Marisol and I worked together to levitate and push Jovanna's body out to the van. By the time that we had her lying comfortably on the back seat, the others joined us.

Marilyn proudly handed out bottles of water to everyone. Let me tell you, water never tasted so good! After that, we climbed in and Lijuan punched in some coordinates, and the Nav system began to give her directions. "We've got about an hour's drive. Keep watch for the enemy," she suggested.

It was dark when we arrived at the outskirts of the city. Lijuan took us to another abandoned building. "This is where archaeologists often store their finds while they clean, catalogue, and study them. Right now, there's no digs so the place is deserted. We have beds and a little food stored here. Come on; let's get her inside."

An hour later, we were finally full and Jovanna had awakened as well. The intense pain was gone, but her stump was exceptionally tender and would be until I could get her back to the ship and our medical machine. I figured now was the time for our chat. It would give Jovanna something to think about besides her missing hand.

"We came to see you about the pre-human skeletal remains that you wrote about," I began our lengthy explanation. Marisol and our two linguists added their linguistic evidence, while Jovanna bravely explained the rest of it to the archaeologist.

"Well, I was forced to retire when I got married. My husband flatly refused to allow me to continue my work. I had to stay home and care for our two boys. He has them now. He ran off to his parents when I took up the Free Women's mantle. You see, after I heard that interview of yours, I realized what all I had given up. Besides, life is a bitch with these damned Jinwei that we women are forced to wear. They put them on us when we are twelve. They are sealed on and cannot easily be removed. However, several times in a woman's lifetime they do have to be replaced. Our shoulder bones get pushed down so much that our necks are no longer held securely in place. So they put more and larger rings on us."

"But why?" Jovanna asked.

"It's traditional, Jovanna. It goes back to the dawn of our written history, but it's worse than you think. After a woman has worn the Jinwei for around ten years, her neck muscles have atrophied so much that she cannot live without the Jinwei holding her neck motionless. When they have to remove them to replace them with larger rings, they have to be exceedingly careful. Some women have choked to death or accidently broken their necks and died. So as much as I'm now fighting for the freedom of all women on Mira-C, I'll always have to wear the Jinwei. I've worn it now for fifteen years. I had them enlarged once and nearly choked to death when they took the old ones off me. Scary."

"So I got into big trouble when I started this Free Women's movement a few weeks ago. But we're starting to make inroads, I hope. As soon as I can, I'm going to make a pirate broadcast telling everyone how the government thugs kidnaped me and beat me. I won't mention you people though. It'll fuel even more anger and drive more women to join the rebellion. I'm planning a general strike in a month. If enough of us women refuse to do our work, I do think we can shut the whole world down. That ought to get the attention of the men, but we'll see."

"Now then, about your questions," Lijuan continued getting back onto what we needed to know, "those skeleton remains were finally dated at two million three hundred thousand years old. They came from a world called Earth. However, that world is not listed in any Federation database. So I gave up trying to find where it was. The remains were brought to that museum as a show and tell exhibit, as near as I can decipher the ancient writings."

"Your data is most intriguing. I agree with your findings, based on linguistic spread. The point of origin must be in this spiral arm somewhere between the midpoint and about the three-quarters outward point. And you are right, there are additional pre-human skeletal remains on both Vegan-C and Centauri-C-C. Vegan-C is much closer though. Two archaeologists there, what were their names, oh, Bianca and Donatella something or others. I've forgotten. I did read a dissertation they wrote on their remains, but again that was years ago now. I've not been able to do anything at all in archaeology since I was married six years ago. I did try several times, but my husband discovered it and beat me silly twice. When your neck doesn't move, even a slap is quite nasty. So I gave up. I couldn't do anything about it. Well, that's changed now, especially after they kidnaped you and me too. I'll shut this damned world down until women get the rights and respect we deserve. And I know just how to do it too. We archaeologists know quite a bit about how societies and civilizations work. They won't know what hit them when I get through with them," she swore.

I noticed Molly Maud, Gabriella, and Marilyn were paying very close attention to her. When we turned in for the night, those three stayed up and chatted privately with Lijuan, who proceeded to give them advice that they could use on their own worlds. I began to wonder just what influence I was bringing to the Federation!

The next morning after we ate leftovers, Lijuan made a call and hired a man, whom she trusted, to take us straight to the spaceport. We said our farewells and promised to stay in touch with her. The polite man did just as he was asked. He drove us to the spaceport and got us as close to our ship as regulations allowed. We would have to walk from the parking lot across the tarmac to our ship, about a mile. We thanked him and began our long walk, keeping a sharp eye out for troubles.

When we drew closer to our ship, we saw a number of men still fighting a fire on the tarmac some distance from our ship. The asphalt that covered this section of the tarmac was still smoldering. Once we got closer, Commander Bo stepped out of his building and came directly at us. We couldn't avoid him.

"Ah, there you are. I'm sorry there has been such troubles near your ship, which is unharmed, I assure you. It seems some men with jet fuel somehow caught fire, and the intense heat even caught the asphalt on fire as well. If you will go around the men, you can reach your ship. I assure you that your ship suffered no damage." He sounded completely propitiative and sincere in that he believed that was what had happened. I already knew better, thanks to the telepathic reports from my crew. They had dropped walls of fire on the men who were trying to cut their way into the ship with a blowtorch during the night.

We did as suggested and quickly entered the Eagle's Seed. Jovanna cleverly kept her stump hidden from his view, but as we entered, her sister rushed her aside, insisting she go straight to the medical machine. I brought up the rear and closed the bay doors behind me, sealing this world off from us. I got quick status reports from everyone while I was also heading to the medical machine in our small med center. While we didn't have our Doctor Leann with us, Martina and I were both very competent med technicians. I found her already there, helping Jovanna get into the machine.

"Well Nia Elain, how do we want to proceed with her? My recommendation is to prepare the stump for a prosthetic hand. Unfortunately, we don't have them onboard, but she'll be ready for one the second we get back," Martina proposed.

Jovanna joked, "Maybe I'll just take another dose of that bio agent, get modified, and then get the geneticists to regrow everything again." We all laughed. It wasn't a half-bad idea though. A half hour later, Jovanna now had a perfectly conical stump that was barely an inch across at her wrist, where the prosthetic hand would be attached via suction. As she looked it over, she commented, "Well, I was lucky. I'm right handed." We all laughed.

I then asked, "Okay, can you all take a look at these damned neck rings and see how to get them off of us? There must be a way to do it. Lijuan said that they sometimes have to have theirs replaced."

Now, everyone hovered over us, had us lie down, roll over, and so on, while they carefully examined our rings. I commented, "I sure don't want to go back out there to the building. I don't trust them at all. So I hope you can figure out how to remove them."

Molly Maud teased, "Well, we do have perfect posture now." Several chuckled. I regretted not having brought along at least one engineer, but then I didn't have the heart to pull them away from their work on the alien flying saucers. After a half hour of study, no one had the slightest idea how they could come off.

Molly Maud then had a bright idea. She used her laptop, though somewhat awkwardly, to research these neck rings, bringing up web sites that discussed them, but she had to have Marilyn translate for her. She couldn't read their Chinese language. She called out, "The rings are brass. That's why they are shiny and golden. Ah, they are cold-forged around your neck. Here we go. It says that the rings begin as brass bars of the correct length based on the neck's circumference. They are about a quarter of an inch thick at the middle of the ring but at the top and bottom edges, they are slightly thinner on the outside surface, so when bent into shape, they look like rings. Then under intense hydraulic pressure, the machine bends them into a ring, cold forging the joint. Now how do you get rid of them? Hang on," she called out.

I waited patiently and then somewhat impatiently. Some fifteen minutes later, she said, "Okay I found it. They are removed by the same machine, which first subjects the cold-forged joint to enough pressure to snap the joint, and then hydraulic pressure is used to bend them back sufficiently so they can be slipped off the neck. After that, they are once more subjected to hydraulic pressure and re-formed back into their original bar shape, ready to be reused again. Captain, it doesn't sound too hopeful that we can get them off you, not easily. It doesn't say how much force is actually needed anywhere," Marilyn admitted. "Now what?"

"Well," I said, "we have two choices. One, we can live with them and continue with the mission. We only have two more archaeologists to check out and then have our engineers remove them somehow when we get back. Or two, we can take a gamble that Commander Bo isn't in cahoots with the kidnapers and see if his people can remove them."

Molly Maud volunteered, "Do we get a vote or something? I mean I'm really afraid that Commander Bo was in on it all. I don't trust him. He could just force you to give up your ship or something. The rings are not life threatening, just a darn nuisance and inconvenience."

"She's got a point," Gabrielle spoke up. "What if he's in on the plot too? We could all be maimed or worse."

Marilyn added, "Can you guys use your telepathy thing to find out if he is with the kidnapers? That way we could make the best decision."

I grinned. "Okay, okay. I can take a hint. Give us a little time, and we'll see if we can get a definitive answer on Commander Bo."

"Let me try," Marisol suggested. She was perhaps the best at such things so I agreed. She focused and her psi-crystal began glowing with a pale blue light. The three now wanted to know what that was, so I whispered a lengthy explanation that they magnified our powers.

"How long will it take?" whispered Molly Maud, growing very curious.

"No way to tell. It could be right away if he is thinking about it. If he isn't, then it takes time subtly to suggest that he think about past events. We could simply pry it out of him, but then he would know someone had been probing his mind and be very antagonistic towards us, maybe even preventing our departure with force," I replied.

"Sounds complicated," Marilyn whispered. I grinned and nodded. We waited.

I also knew that Marisol would have preferred to wait until late at night when he was asleep. Then, she could literally probe his mind. Whatever she touched upon would seem only like a dream to him, and he would not be aware that she was searching through his memories. However, I didn't feel we dared wait that long. After all, it wasn't even noon yet. A whole lot could happen between now and midnight.

A half hour later, the glow died and Marisol roused. "Well, this is interesting. He isn't directly involved yet, but he is about to. He's received orders from someone above him to take us prisoners when we return to have the rings removed. When we arrived, he was under orders not to mention to us that we didn't need the rings on our bodies if we swore we would only be among their people less than a day. Had we known that, we could have avoided this whole mess. Now, he is supposed to hold us and notify his boss. He's also supposed to direct the tower not to give us clearance to depart. We've gotten ourselves into a very sticky mess."

"Well, that settles it. We'll have to endure the darn neck rings until later on. We need to get off this world somehow," I replied. "Everyone, get to your posts. Guests, best get into your quarters; the ride might be a bit bumpy." Danika and I headed for our positions up front.

"So what's the plan?" she asked, as I sat clumsily in my seat and took the controls.

"Anya, please record the conversation I'm about to have with the control tower." She acknowledged me. "We're going to pretend to ask for take-off clearance. Of course, we now know they won't give it. However, it's customary to fire up the engines before making that call. That'll give us an edge. The second you hear clearance to take off is denied, hit the cloaking button. I'll take off anyway. We'll make the jump to hyperspace immediately. Enter some coordinates just a little ways from here."

Danika grinned. "Dear, you are really devious and clever. Okay, coordinates entered and all set. Fire up the engines. This ought to be cool! The idiots!"

I fired up the engines. Once the preliminary checkouts were done, I called the control tower. "This is the Eagle's Seed requesting permission for take-off. Over."

"This is the Control Tower. At this time, permission to take off is denied. I repeat. Do not take off at this time. Acknowledge. Over."

"Take off? Okay. Goodbye," I replied politely as though I'd not heard him correctly. Already Danika had activated our cloaking device. The ship was invisible, but one could still hear the engines whine, as I lifted her off the ground. A hundred feet above ground, Danika punched in the hyperdrive, and we vanished from normal space. Even if there had been a valid reason for not taking off just then, such as another ship on a landing vector, at such a low altitude, we would have avoided any chance of a collision. Now in hyperspace, we were once more un-trackable, unless another bug had been planted on the ship's exterior.

I spoke over the intercom. "Tesla, complete systems check. Find out if there is another tracking bug on our hull. Everyone else, you can relax. We are in hyperspace and safely out of their reach. Jana, how about some lunch? I'm starving. We need to figure out where we go next."

Over a light lunch, we decided to follow Lijuan's suggestion and visit Vegan-C next, since it was closer. Danika entered the coordinates, and I adjusted the speed some so we would make planet-fall around nine the next morning. True, I was using a bit more fuel than I might have liked, but we had plenty in reserve.

Meanwhile, Molly Maud filed a complete report with her boss and then brought up all the information she could on Vegan-C. "Well, you sure do pick the stranger worlds, Nia Elain. This one is also a hot and dry world, but weird. It seems that on this world, men have harems of wives. They wear belly-dancing clothing. My god, we'll be almost nude! Oh, they even chain their women. Look at these pictures. It says that beginning at age ten, young girls have their legs chained so that they can only take tiny steps. Once they marry, their arms are chained to a neck collar, severely limiting their arm motions. I guess they don't want their many wives to run away or something. Looking for visitor requirements now."

After a long pause, she added, "Visiting women are required to have their legs bound. If they are also married, they are required to wear the neck collar and have their arms bound to it as well. Apparently, that is a safety precaution to prevent their men from attempting to seduce visiting wives. Oh, I can see why. Ladies, look at this image. Now that's a hunk if I ever saw one!"

Everyone gathered around to have a look. Indeed, the man was about the handsomest fellow I'd ever seen. Almost perfection. Our guests were literally drooling over his good looks. "They speak Italian, so that should not be a problem. It says this is a very romantic and passionate world," Molly Maud added. "Oh, it also says visiting women: beware. Well, I certainly can see why!"

"Scenery is lovely too," Beth broke in.

"Honey, you are looking at the wrong things!" Molly Maud teased her.

"Cool your hormones, ladies. We don't need any romantic affairs complicating matters," I teased everyone.

Several roared with laughter.

"Yes, but we can admire from a distance," Gabrielle spoke up. "Look, there is an online sample of their men. Everyone is a real hunk! No wonder they end up with harems!"

"That doesn't mean they are any good in the bed," Marilyn pointed out. Several laughed again.

I decided we ought to pick our visiting party beforehand. Jana was unwilling to leave her sister alone on the ship, understandably. I didn't dare take Danika with me. If something happened to me, she was as good a pilot as I was and would be needed here. After yesterday's experiences, Gabrielle and Marilyn decided not to go planet-side in spite of the promise of romantic, handsome men. Molly Maud had to come since she was officially our host. Marisol agreed to venture forth one more time. I limited the ground party to just the three of us, just to be safe.

Later at supper, Molly Maud announced, "Now, I know what's going on with these planets that you've chosen to visit, Nia Elain. Each one is, well weird, in some way. Decadent might be a better choice of phrasing. I spent the afternoon doing some checking on other worlds. I've found an interesting correlation that explains a lot, even the planets on the Forbidden List."

"Do go on," I encouraged her. She'd done some of her own research, and I wanted to validate her for it.

"Well, there is a sharp correlation between the age of a world's civilization and its decadence level. It's not really scientific, but I sort of assigned a decadence level between one and ten to the worlds, with a ten being those worlds on the Forbidden List. No one wants to visit a drug den. Anyway, based on the limited data I can find for how old any given civilization on these worlds is, I have found something quite interesting. You are visiting worlds whose civilization can be traced back between fifteen and twenty millennia, and they have a high decadence level. Worlds whose civilizations are around ten millennia old have a moderate decadence level, while those which only go back five millennia or less have a low level. Isn't that interesting?"

Tesla jumped on her findings, "How keenly interesting,

Molly Maud. As civilizations age, so they decline in values. Wow. Make a copy of your lists for me. Well done indeed. When we get back to our space, I'm going to work out similar lists for our Imperium worlds. How have you classified the decadence levels?" The two began to discuss this in great depth, and the rest of us let them have at it. Tesla was keenly interested in forms of government as well as political science.

Gabrielle said to me, "So you are visiting the older worlds and that's why her decadence level is so high? So Bernard-D is decadent?"

"No, Bernard is in the middle zone. Honestly, wearing your giant gowns is a far cry from these dismal neck rings or the chains we're about to encounter on Vegan-C. Both your civilization and that of Capella-D are nowhere near as old as these we're now visiting. We're looking for the oldest fossil remains of pre-human type creatures and those happen to be on these decadent worlds," I explained.

Chapter 5 Uncovering Clues

Around nine the next morning, I began my approach to Vegan, a rather hot main sequence star, according to Dylan. "Nothing unusual about this star," he declared. That was a relief. It was just a hot world not in danger of natural disasters for once. As we drew close to the third planet out from the sun, once more we saw pale blue and light brown, laced with green patches. It was rather picturesque sliding down towards the planet, particularly as you get closer. Only a mile above their capital city of Po, we began to see the architectural marvels that helped form the identity of this twenty millennia old civilization. Marble columns supporting concrete roofs over the open-sided structures — my first thought upon seeing the nature of so many such buildings was "so much for privacy."

Oh's and ah's echoed throughout the ship, as the others caught glimpses of these fabulous buildings. We even spotted an open-aired theater or coliseum perhaps not too far from the spaceport. No skyscrapers. No steel and concrete monsters, just these incredible works of art, the open-aired structures. A bit lower and their many formal gardens were quite distinguishable. It was summer or so we presumed from the thousands of colored flowers in the height of bloom. You name a color and hue, and we could find such a flower. I knew that Beth, Jana, and Jovanna would dearly love to explore this world! A botanist's dream planet — that was Vegan-C.

Yet amid such wonders of nature, men had twisted the very nature of women, binding them as one might their dog. I wondered if it was true, what Molly Maud had discovered, that all civilizations, given enough millennia, would fall into utter decadence, dying a slow death. I swore to myself if I heard the phrase, "I can't do anything about it," just one more time, I was going to scream! Did time always ravage the sense of ethics and morals of a people? I wondered if that was going to be my next big project to research.

"Eagle's Seed, you are cleared to land at Slot 166. Acknowledge. Over." The sweet sounding voice of the tower controller brought me back to the present, though I couldn't help wonder what his body must look like. Was he as handsome as his voice?

"Acknowledged. Slot 166. Over." I replied in Italian, or the Easterlings dialect.

The voice added, "Once you are down, please contact Generalissimo Bernardo Bertolini on frequency 1123 regarding your visit. Over and out." I knew that Anya had already written the frequency down and was preparing a connection even as I finished landing our ship. I do have a feather touch with this ship. Touchdowns could only just barely be felt. Perhaps, I was also levitating it a bit, though my psi-crystal didn't glow, and I doubt I could lift anything as heavy as this ship.

"Another perfect landing, love," Danika commented, as she and I rose and headed for the comm center. "Hope this is a fast trip," she added. I did too. I hated the constriction of my neck, making everything miserable, but Jovanna had it worse. She'd lost her left hand. I cursed myself for having somehow allowed that to happen.

Anya called out, "Placing the call to Generalissimo Bernardo Bertolini now, boss."

I sat down before the video camera as the connection was made. "Calling Generalissimo Bernardo Bertolini per instructions. This is Captain Nia Elain Compton-Jereni of the Eagle's Seed. Over."

We saw a handsome man with short black hair and moustache wearing a uniform filled with medals looking into his video camera. He was probably fifty. "Ah, welcome to Vegan-C, captain. Generalissimo Bernardo here. I have your visitation request here, filed by Field Agent Molly Maud Porsche. May I ask, is she any relation to the famous industrialist Hermann Porsche?"

I smiled. "His daughter."

He smiled back. "Excellent. It is a very great honor to welcome her to our world. Now then, about your request to visit two of the wives of Carlo Bellini. There is a problem. It seems that the two wives, Bianca and Donatella, have mysteriously vanished several days ago. The police have been investigating their disappearance, but as yet, we have no leads.

I'm so sorry they are not available for your visit. Perhaps, someone else may fulfill your needs? If so, you only have to ask. Meanwhile, I have the full list of your crew at hand along with their marital status, compliments of Field Agent Molly Maud. I will await your word on which of your personnel wish to visit our world, and I'll personally see that they are properly bound as per our customs. Also, I'd be delighted to make suggestions on the sights to see here in Po or if you wish to travel to other areas, I can put you in touch with the very best people who will guarantee you the very best that we have to offer. Just let me know. Over and out."

"Sorry. I didn't know about their customs when I forwarded the list of everyone when I made the advance arrangements," Molly Maud hastily spoke up, very apologetically.

"No harm. You were doing your job. No, what's bothering me is the missing women," I replied. "Everyone, conference time. Bring your laptops too."

We tried to get access to the local news, but found nothing of interest. "Look, perhaps you can just visit the museum where the skeletons are kept. Maybe you can find additional information on them there?" suggested Molly Maud.

"True. That's probably the best route, Nia Elain. We know from our research none of the male archaeologists have published anything about the pre-human remains. So maybe there is something useful with the exhibit," Jovanna suggested. Jana agreed with her sister. "It ought to be a very quick trip. Out and back in no time," she added.

"I wonder if those two women are in trouble because of us," I ventured, vocalizing what was still bothering me. "Look, they kidnaped Lijuan because we were supposed to meet her. Now, we get here and find our two contacts have suddenly gone missing. Coincidence? I think not. I just feel we're responsible for what has happened to those two women."

"Dear, I see your point," Danika defended me. "It's got to have something to do with us — their disappearance I mean. But what I don't understand is the why? We've told them to contact Emperor Bino about the hyperdrive. I'm sure he'd make the technology available in some way. So why try to steal our ship? Even if they did, they would have to reverse engineer the modifications that Hans made. Why go to all this trouble? Isn't kidnaping and theft against the law in the Federation?"

Molly Maud replied, "Yes, of course. They are illegal. It has to be the ship that they want. After all, positively no one is remotely interested in what you are researching, the planet of origin of our ancient civilizations."

"She has a point," Jana volunteered. "Our research is purely academic. I can't see any real practical applications of knowing our planet of origin, save for a better understanding of history, ancient history at that. It has to be the ship they are after. Molly Maud, doesn't the Federation have deep space exploration ships?"

"Why yes. Yes of course. I can bring some models up on my computer if you want to see what they look like," she answered. "But is there anything else about your ship that is unusual, besides your new hyperdrive that is?"

After a brief pause, Tesla said, "Nope. No criticism of you Nia Elain, but there's nothing unique about the Eagle's Seed. It is similar to hundreds of other exploration ships. The hyperdrive of Hans is the only part that is different."

"So why risk an international incident by kidnaping us and stealing the ship?" I asked pointedly. "That could only create severe repercussions between the ex-Imperium and the Federation, a violation of the peace accords."

"Perhaps you've said it," Tesla offered, "ex-Imperium. Maybe the Federation now believes there is no Imperium and thus no repercussions?"

Molly Maud sighed, "Well, she has a point there. Still, theft is illegal, Imperium or no Imperium."

"Let's get back to the main issue," I suggested. "I'm worried the two women are missing because of us. If so, I owe it to those women to find them and rescue them."

"She has a point," Molly Maud backed me up. "If my setting up these arrangements has in anyway caused their disappearance, then I'm as guilty as anyone. It's my obligation to locate and rescue them or to bring the culprits to justice if they've been murdered."

"Okay. Here's the plan. We three will go planet-side as planned, paying a visit to the museum and seeing the pre-human remains firsthand. Meanwhile, the rest of you monitor this world's communications, and see if you can find any word on the missing women. Surely, a local newscast would have carried the story. The only thing I'm still considering is if we should pay a visit to their husband and offer our apologies for what happened to his wives? It would be common courtesy, but it could also be risky for us as well."

Molly Maud again backed me up and had a suggestion. "She's right. If they were abducted or harmed because of us, then it is only polite for us to offer him a sincere apology. Since that could well be risky, it is also acceptable to send him an official letter of apology. Still, a personal apology is far better, but do we dare risk that?"

I made a decision. "Yes, we risk that. I won't lower my sense of ethics, of honor, just because others are being unethical or that this whole world is bonkers. If we are responsible, as I believe we are, I won't feel right until I apologize to this Carlo Bellini personally. Whether or not I think having multiple wives is proper, having them kidnaped just because we wanted to speak with them about their archaeology studies deserves a face to face apology on my part. You with me, Molly Maud?"

"Yes. It could be dangerous, but I feel I owe it to him somehow. We could pay him a quick visit, then hit the museum, and be back by suppertime or sooner," she suggested. Marisol also agreed and that became our plan.

Since we were going to have to change our clothes and wear native outfits, we decided to dress as simply as possible. While I was struggling to change into a simple cotton day dress made difficult by my immobile neck, Tesla joined Danika and me. She explained, "We've been through being chained before." This was an obvious reference to the Slavers and that awful period when we first met. "So I've taken the liberty of making you a safety valve. Here, let me put this hair fastener in your hair."

"But that's a cutter," Danika recognized the disguised cutting tool we had used to free everyone on Metcalf-4. "Oh you clever dear!" She grinned broadly.

"Thanks! Well done. I do feel better about this already," I praised her inventiveness.

Wearing flats and casual, plain dresses, we three walked down the bay ramp onto the tarmac of their spaceport. I could not help noticing our ship was parked well away from the main areas currently in use. I didn't like the feeling that gave me, but it was perhaps understandable. If we were staying a while, they didn't want our ship hogging primary landing spots. Besides, we were aliens to them, another justification to keep us separated from their usual ships.

It was a long walk to the control tower and administration building. Here was one of the very few buildings that we'd seen from the air that wasn't open on its sides. Still, it was made of marble with a concrete sloped roof with quite ornate columns decorating its outer facade. We could see numbers of ships being serviced from other areas closer to the tower. Those, of course, looked alien to us just as our ship must appear to these people.

As we drew closer to the building, Generalissimo Bernardo came out to greet us personally. Even though he was an older man, he still looked highly attractive. I sensed even Molly Maud was a bit smitten with him and his perfectly done, black moustache and most polite manners. "Welcome, welcome Miss Molly Maud Porsche. It is a great honor to meet you at last. I am so very glad that you've chosen to pay a visit to our special Vegan-C world." He bent low and gently kissed her hand.

Suave. That's the thought that popped into my head. "I see that you three prefer the customs of Mira-C. And this must be Captain Nia Elain Compton-Jereni." Again, he bowed and kissed my hand. "Welcome to our magnificent world, captain. Is this your wife?"

"No," I chuckled. "She is our linguist, Mrs. Marisol Gervasi-Hammil." He repeated his greeting to her and kissed her hand as well.

"Please, this way. I'll have my Welcome Crew get you properly attired in no time. While they are doing that, are there some arrangements that I can make for you?"

"Well, as a matter of fact, Generalissimo Bernardo, there is. We would like to pay a brief call on Mr. Carlo Bellini to offer him our sincere apologies for what has happened to two of his wives. We feel we are somehow responsible for their disappearance. After that, we wish to visit the museum, the one that has the pre-human skeletal remains on display. We'll be returning here after seeing those remains. Short trip, I'm afraid," I replied.

"Excellent, excellent, my ladies. You may count upon me. I'll have a driver prepared and ready to take you there. I have both addresses, and I'll see the driver has them in his GPS system. A to B, as I always say, is the best route to take. Don't you agree, captain?" he said smoothly.

"Of course, A to B. We should be back before suppertime," I replied.

He then added, "Of course, you are most welcome to stay longer. There are so many delightful sights to see in Po. That is, if you have the time. So many come here for a relaxing vacation and pampering. We have mineral spas, hot springs, massage parlors, and of course, so many formal gardens that one could spend a year here and not stroll through all them."

I grinned. "We'll see how it goes today, Generalissimo Bernardo." We had been strolling along beside him, and as we reached the main doors, he gallantly opened them for us. We then headed to the right, down a long hallway. I noticed the change in atmospheric odors at once. Outside, the heady fragrance of a multitude of flowers was mingled with that of tar, oil, and machinery. Inside, the air had no fragrance at all. Filtered air, pure. The difference was striking.

He led us into a room where two women were sitting on sofas browsing through some magazines and a handsome young man was reading an electronic book on his small reader. All three looked up as we entered. The man hastily put his book down and stood erect, a soldier I suspected. Generalissimo Bernardo said, "Three to be prepared. Miss Molly Maud Porsche isn't married. See that they are very well attired as our most honored guests. Ladies, I will go now and make the arrangements for you. I assure you that you are in the most competent hands with Donato here. His wives Mona and Natale will give you proper instructions and great care. Until later then," he bowed and left us.

We could not help noticing his two wives were about our ages. Natale had wavy, long brown hair, while Mona's hair was slightly curlier and black. Both women wore leg chains, preventing their feet from moving more than a foot from each other. They had a golden neckband with a loop in front. The long chain that connected each wrist went through the loop, allowing only one hand to be extended while the other was raised up to their faces or both hands lowered only partially, barely reaching below their bust lines. Even more shocking were their clothes or should I say lack thereof! Their tops covered only their breast areas with the thinnest gauze of a fabric. Their nipples and breasts were clearly visible. They wore panties which at least did obscure their privates, but over that, they wore the shortest skirt imaginable made from the same nearly transparent gauze material as their tops! Both top and bottom were very loose fitting. Well, such an outfit would be quite cool in the heat of this world. They also wore leather sandals on their feet.

"Signore, I'm truly honored to be the one to bind such beautiful women as yourselves," Donato said smoothly. Even his voice sounded handsome, if voices could be so said. "If you will accompany my wives, they will assist you in changing into far more comfortable clothing of our humble world. And please do pick your favorite colors. We wish you only the best time here on Vegan-C."

Accompanied by rattling chains, we followed the two young women, noticing carefully how they even managed to walk. It wasn't easy. The chains prevented them from placing one foot more than just ahead of their other foot, sort of a shuffling gait, extremely slow at that and accompanied by the constant jingling of their golden chains.

Once in a private dressing room, Natale took charge. Moving up close to us so they had the use of both hands, they proceeded to help us undress completely. Natale exclaimed, "Oh Nia, Marisol, your breasts are just to die for! So big! So utterly perfect! You are making us jealous. All men of Vegan-C are going to be after you two! Are they natural?"

"Yes, all women on our world have whoppers like ours," I replied honestly. "We all rather wish they were smaller, like yours."

The two women gasped. Natale exclaimed, "Oh no. Don't say such a thing! Any one of us would die to have such perfect breasts!" It took them a while to get us undressed completely. They had to work together, since their arm chains prevented more than one hand to be extended at a time. Of course, they also gasped when they discovered Marisol and my extra privates. Both women giggled, and I briefly had to explain our modified bodies.

They both thought this was fabulous and not freakish at all. "So you can satisfy any woman. How utterly fantastic!" Mona gushed. "You would be the center of any harem! Loved by all the wives as well as the husband," she explained.

I chose a red colored outfit, if there was even enough material in them to display the red. Okay, I admit I thought these were beyond risqué! I felt nearly naked and so did my companions. Marisol chose a dark blue, hoping it would help hide her breasts. It didn't, of course. Molly Maud went with brown for the same reason and was just as disappointed as Marisol was. After fastening the soft sandals on our feet, they bid us follow them and we soon rejoined Donato.

He began by fastening metal leg collars three inches tall around each leg. The collars were covered in a very plush fleece lining and felt quite soft around our legs, resting just above our ankles. They fit snugly and he locked them into place, hitting them once with a spot welder. That ensured they could not be taken off, at least not easily. With the collars secure, he then brought out a foot long golden chain, bronze probably and fastened it into the single loop of the collar. Once more, he touched his spot welder to the two links around the loops and that was that. The leg chains simply could not be removed without un-welding them.

He then tried various sized metal collars until he found some large enough to go over our neck rings. Again, the collars were fleece lined, but in our case, this detail was wholly unimportant. After spot welding it shut, he moved the single loop to the front and proceeded to fit each of our wrists with a similar fleece lined metal bracelet, two inches wide. Again, they were spot welded shut. He then measured our reach and fastened the arm chain to each wrist loop, passing it through the neck loop before spot welding the two links.

"There, all finished," he spoke suavely. "If you will permit me, I must say that you three are the very finest looking women I have ever had the pleasure of meeting and handling. Queens could not look more attractive than either of you. No, you put them to shame. All men on Vegan-C would just die to wed either one of you. Of course, you do not need to wed to enjoy our company and services. After all, there are no finer, no handsomer men in the galaxy than we Vegan-C men, but you already know that." He lowered his voice and winked at us, "If you want to have a good time right now, my wives and I would be extremely honored to take you into our private chambers for some elegant, delightful pleasures."

I felt Molly Maud's strong urge to burst out with a big "Yes!" "I'm sorry, Donato, we are on a tight schedule. We have to visit two places yet this morning, if possible. Perhaps, we can partake when we return from our most urgent business?"

"Oh that would be fabulous, signore. We three will count the hours until your return!" he exclaimed. After that, we three rose and tried to walk. Shuffle would be a better description. We kept stumbling, taking too large a step and nearly tripping ourselves.

"This is awful!" Molly Maud whispered, afraid of being overheard.

Just then and right on cue, Generalissimo Bernardo appeared, coming around a corner to meet us. "Oh my, oh my! I never imagined how gorgeous you three women actually look. Stunning beyond imaginations. If I didn't have my duties here at the spaceport, I would treasure being your driver for this day! In fact, if you are back by supper, I and my wives would be most honored if you three beautiful ladies would join us for supper. You are the prettiest women to ever set foot on Vegan-C!"

"Why thank you," Molly Maud gushed, quite taken by his unexpected compliments. She played into his hands.

"Thank you, Generalissimo Bernardo. Let's see how our

day progresses. If we are back in time, we would surely like to dine with you," I replied politely. I didn't dare refuse him, not just yet. Best to have an ally, even if it was likely all fake.

"Absolutely perfect! If you will follow me, I will take you to your personal driver for the day. No expense. It is on me. You must allow me this trifle indulgence, Miss Molly Maud, Captain Nia Elain." I did notice he slowed way down and was obviously quite used to walking at the only speed we could manage, pathetically slowly. He did notice our bumbling efforts and added, "Please. Slow down. There is no rush. Women on our world never, ever have the slightest need to rush. Walk slowly, smell the fragrances of millions of flowers. Appreciate the beauty of the day, which pales in comparison to your beauty," he said most suavely.

We slowed down and found it a bit easier going, but we were annoyed at the constant jingling of our chains on the floor, announcing our coming miles ahead of us. Okay, that's an exaggeration, but I didn't like to proclaim my presence so loudly. Any remote attempt at stealth was entirely gone, and I hoped we never needed either speed or stealth on this trip. I was also very thankful for the cutter holding my hair back.

Our driver was a handsome young man, barely twenty-one at most. His youthful face was incredibly well formed. I began to wonder if all men on this world looked this good. Then, I realized the men so far believed they were God's gift to women! No wonder they felt they should have many wives. The reverse was true. The men were incredibly handsome to we women, incredibly so. Molly Maud was almost fawning over our driver, Alfredo Zonatelli.

His voice was very mellow and sweet, almost as sweet as the fragrances in the air just outside the building. "Incredible luck. I've never seen such beautiful women as you three. When I got the call from our Generalissimo, I figured I'd have a very boring day driving some matrons around our lovely Po, but no! I find I'm escorting three goddesses! Signora, Alfredo is most humbly yours for the whole day. In any way I can be of service to such goddesses as you are, you only have to ask." He flashed us a big smile, totally disarming Molly Maud!

I took the bait though, and asked, "So tell me, Alfredo, are all men on this world as handsome as you are?"

He looked terribly affronted. "Oh no, signora, no. Alfredo, he is not so handsome. I'm afraid I'm rather ugly by Vegan-C standards. That's why I'm a mere driver."

Molly Maud gushed, "Oh no you are not ugly, Alfredo. You are an incredibly handsome young man. You must have many young women fawning over you. I know I sure would."

He flushed slightly. "You compliment me, Miss Molly Maud, but I do not have women coming after me. I'm only just barely able to get a date occasionally, though I do try. You'll see; I'll do my best to show you the very best of times. Allow me to assist you into the car," he said.

She'd tried to step into the car, but found her leg chains preventing that and stood there at the door rather baffled. He put his strong hands around her waist, just below her bosom. He lifted her up and sat her inside. One by one, he did the same for us. "You see, this is how we men are to assist you women. None can get into a car without assistance, at least not elegantly." I ended up sitting beside him in the front seat, much to Molly Maud's dismay. She had hoped to sit beside him, and I couldn't help but pick up that surface thought.

Alfredo looked at me, and I told him to take us to the home of Carlo Bellini. "Oh, the wealthy industrialist! Indeed, he is a famous young man who runs Bellini Industries. They make fancy automobiles, the very best ones. Yes, I have the coordinates. You see, this car has a GPS Nav system that shows us the route to take. As we drive, would you like me to point out the more famous sights? Some of these you just have to see, that is, if you have a few more days to spend here," he chatted away.

"Are all homes open-aired on all sides?" I asked. Once more, we began to see their unusual buildings, more like an ornate concrete roof supported by carved marble columns.

"But of course, it is far too hot all year round. We make use of the air currents. At night, we lower side curtains to permit some privacy. Besides, there are so many flowers, flowering bushes, and trees that we would never wish to block them out. We are, as you say, one with nature, except in that awful spaceport building. I just hate going in there. The air is just putrid, stale. Gone is the fragrance of life. I try not to go in there unless I absolutely have to. Didn't you notice how bad it was in there?"

"Yes we did." I replied, still observing the homes. You could see right through the entire home. It looked positively strange to see all of the household items totally visible because there were no inside or outside walls. It was like looking at a three-dimensional, full color x-ray! Strange beyond belief. I wondered what the nighttime curtains were like. This place sure was not big on personal privacy. As the morning progressed, the temperature rose rapidly. Alfredo soon removed his white cotton shirt, revealing his very well formed chest. Poor Molly Maud was nearly beside herself trying to get a look at him.

Outside, we saw that most men had now removed their shirts as well. I began to see why everyone wore the thinnest possible garments. The heat was rather high, but dry. In our gauze that passed for dresses, we were in fact comfortable. He did point out the sights, including formal garden after formal garden, figuring we women were more interested in them than other buildings. Molly Maud didn't care. She just wanted him to talk more.

It took a half hour to reach the home of Carlo Bellini. Again, it was a huge home. Dozens of marble columns rose skyward, supporting the ornate, sloping roof. Yet, without any walls, everything was clearly visible, as the car stopped before the main entrance. We could see a man wearing shorts and sandals, putting down a paper, and rising to meet us. Further back, we saw two other women apparently in the kitchen, preparing jasmine tea as we would soon learn.

Alfredo assisted us to exit the car. Slowly, we shuffled up to the front entrance, though one could really enter from any side, but you would have to step up two feet to the main floor on several other sides. Here at the front, there were very low steps, which we women could just barely manage. "Ah, you must be the aliens who wished to see me," Carlo Bellini spoke up as he approached the main entrance from the inside. There were no doors, per se. Strange.

He was in his forties and sported a black moustache. His chest rippled with well-toned muscles. His biceps were perfectly formed, but I could see there was a difference between him and Alfredo. He was considered extremely handsome, while Alfredo was merely handsome. On any other world, these men would be top models at the very least. That was Molly Maud's thoughts anyway.

"Yes, I'm Captain Nia Elain Compton-Jereni. My linguist, Marisol Gervasi-Hammil. Field Agent Molly Maud Porsche," I did the introductions. Like the generalissimo, Carlo bent and kissed each of our hands, ignoring the clanking of our chains as we extended one hand.

"Ah yes. Most welcome. Generalissimo Bernardo called me to tell me that you wished to stop by. I'm now most pleased that I delayed going to work today. Never have I met such beautiful women. Please, please come on in. I've had my other wives prepare some tea for you. Such an honor to have the daughter of the famous Hermann Porsche visiting my humble abode. Please, this way." He led us into the living room, where we sat on plush sofas.

His two other wives shuffled in, carrying trays, one with a china teapot and the other with cups. "This is Milana and Mimi, my older wives." He introduced us to the pair.

Each had shoulder length brown, wavy hair, nicely done with a purple flower protruding above their right temples. I noticed a private garden out back. The women could have been top models on any other world. They were absolutely stunning. I felt my male appendage rising on its own and flushed slightly, wiggling a bit on the sofa, hoping it wasn't too visible. I couldn't even bend my neck to see if it was.

I hastily did what I came here for. "I'm truly sorry your two other wives have gone missing, Carlo. I cannot help but feel that somehow, someway we are responsible for their disappearance. If we had not tried to meet with them about their archaeological work, perhaps they would still be here. Have you heard anything about their disappearance? Have the authorities any clues about what happened to them?"

"Yes, we were all quite surprised to hear you wanted to meet with them. I made them give such silly things up when we married. Women belong in the home, like the gorgeous flowers that they are, not out digging up old bones or playing around with them. The dead are dead. Life is within us all, and we should cherish and nurture that life, that incredible beauty that is a woman." He poured it on a little too thick for my taste. "But no, the authorities have yet to uncover any clues. They have just vanished without a trace. They were on their way to the grocery store but never made it there. No one has seen them. It is a big mystery. They are such beauties, that I suspect someone has stolen them away from me. That is sometimes done, you know, stealing wives."

"How awful," I admitted.

"Indeed. If they do not turn up soon, I'll have to court more women and find two replacements, won't I, dears?" he looked lovingly at Mona and Milana, who smiled and nodded affirmatively. Just then we heard a ringing sound. "Oh, excuse me. That's the phone. Perhaps, someone has discovered something." He rose and headed to another room, leaving us with his two wives.

"So tell me, why do you believe that he needs two more wives?" I asked Milana.

She giggled. "Because we women need each other's help with things. Chains." She rattled hers a little. "We four always work together. With Bianca and Donatella gone, it is very hard for us to do our duties and care for Carlo. He is simply gorgeous, is he not? Kind, loving."

"And a top provider," Mona interrupted. "Being married to a wealthy, very important, and handsome man is everything any woman could dream of having!"

I changed the topic. "We are new to your world and customs. Why is it all women here are bound in these chains? We can just barely walk, and with our arms chained, everything is terribly difficult to do."

Both women giggled. Milana replied, "It has always been this way. Our world is ancient, and women have always been bound here, just as all men hardly ever wear shirts. Of course, Donatella or Bianca could recite other reasons. They used to pour over ancient writings. Bianca once told me that even three millennia ago, women were bound just as we are today."

"But isn't this just awful? So hard to do anything?" I asked.

Milana explained, "That's why each man has three or four wives. We always help each other. That is the way it is. It could not be otherwise. Come; would you like to see our private gardens? We are most proud of it, and spend as much time taking care of it as we can. Carlo often complains we love the garden more than we do him."

Mona giggled. "He might be right. We have two hundred three different types of flowers and bushes in ours. It's beautiful and the smells, divine. Come; you simply must see it," she insisted. We rose and shuffled along behind the two women, watching how they moved. Seductively. They wiggled their butts, and I again found my private growing hard, embarrassing me further. I glanced at Marisol who also had a slight flush on her face. These women were just too darn attractive!

As we walked along the stepping stone path, Marisol asked if they had any children. They each had two, but they were all at school right now, along with Donatella and Bianca's. That was ominous. No woman would abandon her children! I was convinced they had been abducted, probably to keep us from meeting with them. But this made no sense at all. We wanted to talk about ancient bones, nothing more.

There was nothing more to be learned here, and Carlo said that he really did need to get to work. Hence, we said our farewells. Carlo hinted we were welcome to return anytime and further that he would love to court us. "After all, I'm in need of some new wives," he added.

As we shuffled slowly to the car and Alfredo, Molly Maud whispered to me, "Can I sit up front this time? He's really quite a hunk, isn't he?" I let her have my seat, pleasing her. As we drove on to the museum, she never once took her eyes off Alfredo! I began to wonder if some of the fragrances in the air were aphrodisiacs! If so, that would explain much, including my embarrassing wet spot on my red panties and Marisol's too.

A half hour later, we arrived at the museum. Here was

one of the few buildings that had walls, ostensibly to protect the fragile nature of its contents. As we entered, a male guide in his late twenties came up to assist us. He too wore no shirt, but had shorts and sandals on. Once more, Molly Maud was completely smitten by the handsome man. "We came to see the pre-human skeletal remains, sir," I explained.

"Of course, signora. This way," he led us through the maze of halls and display rooms. Molly Maud clung to his arm, rubbing her hand up and down his rippling muscles, while her other arm sort of dangled before her face.

The exhibit was a simple one, with the bones laid out appropriately to where they must have once belonged on the creature. Only about half of the bones were present. Nearby was an artist's sketch of what he probably looked like, a small, three-foot tall human-like person, covered in fur. Not much to see, really. I looked around for a plaque or something that might tell us more. I found a brochure and attempted to decipher it. While I could speak the Easterlings dialect somewhat, I couldn't read it. However, Marisol could.

"Say, this was written many years ago by Bianca Bellini. Ah, here's what we are looking for. It says this pre-human was a gift from a wealthy patron who had moved to Centauri-C-C, donated to Vegan-C some four millennia ago. Apparently, it was Bianca and Donatella who dug up the ancient records and found this information. There is no mention where it came from before then. So we are right. Centauri-C is perhaps the closest world to the world of human origin. I wonder where they got it?"

"We are going to have to go there next, that's for sure," I replied. "Say, it's lunchtime. I wonder if Alfredo knows of a good place to eat?"

A half hour later, we entered The Olive Grove, one of the finer restaurants in Po. Again, it was all open-aired. A huge gardens lay just behind the dining area and we saw many women and a few men strolling through them, presumably after dining. Molly Maud invited Alfredo to dine with us. He protested slightly, but her intense persuasion won out. She clung to his arm, as we entered and were seated. She sat beside him and across from us. If anything, the odors here were even more intense. The smells of delicious food mingled with the heady aroma coming from the gardens just behind us, brought to us on a very light breeze, just enough to be felt.

The atmosphere of The Olive Grove was simply superb as was their food. None of us bothered with the tab that Molly Maud covered. While we really didn't know what was what on the menu, I had something that tasted remarkably like a Cornish hen that I once had back on Descartes-3. While eating was awkward at best for us, somehow that seemed of no important to us, whatsoever. No, this place, these smells, the gorgeous hunks of men who were also here dining either alone or with other women — these were what demanded our intention, our support.

We had just finished the main meal, when Carlos Bellini spotted us at our table. Funny, we had somehow missed seeing this fabulous looking man come into The Olive Grove. Apparently, he too had finished eating his lunch, and he came over to our table, his bare chest displaying his magnificent form. "We meet again, most beautiful signora. Had I known that you would be dining here, I would have made arrangements to join you."

"Oh please do sit, Carlo. We are about to have our tea," Molly Maud gushed.

"I see that there are only four places. Alfredo, would you mind waiting outside in the car for these ladies?" Carlo said. He handed him something, but I couldn't see what it was. Later, I learned it was a large denomination bill, probably more than he earned driving us around all day! A waitress brought our tea, which we sipped, and stared at this really handsome man, though we were unaware that we were leering at him.

"You should take a stroll through their fabulous formal gardens, that is, if you are not in a rush," Carlo suggested. "I've the afternoon off. It would be my greatest pleasure to accompany you three through these gardens." He rose and offered Molly Maud his arm, which she took without the slightest hesitation. He then offered his other arm to me. I found myself also taking it, but also I fumbled around with my other arm trying to take hold of Marisol's arm. Of course, the chain prevented it, but she found a way to slip her right arm up into my raised left arm. That bit of confusion passed, Carlo led us out the back and onto the cobblestone path that wandered among hundreds of different species of blooming flowers and bushes.

The aromas were even headier this close to them. We inhaled deeply, as we shuffled slowly along, our chains clanking along behind us. We could hear the chains of other women moving along other paths, but the growth was tall and hid them and us from view. Before long, we turned and now the diner itself wasn't visible. Cradled here and there were white marble statues. Carlo explained them to us; they represented historical figures. We weren't really paying attention to what he was saying though. No, we just wanted him to continue speaking to us in his soft, sensuous voice. We just wanted to continue to rub our hands along his well-muscled arms and stroll, stroll aimlessly through this surreal garden.

We had been walking for some time, when Carlo leaned over and gave Molly Maud a passionate, but gentle kiss on her lips. She responded, stopping and trying to put her arms around him, to hold him tightly, but her chains interfered, frustrating her. I too wanted a kiss, and I rather pushed my way between them. He leaned and gave me an equally passionate kiss as well. Then, I too struggled annoyingly with my chains, unable to get my arms and hands to work properly. They seemed to have to go in opposite directions somehow. Marisol scooted in between us, leaned up to partake of his thick, sensuous lips, and wasn't disappointed either.

We were in some isolated location within this wonderful garden. Ahead of us, we saw soft, green grass, large enough for us all to lie down and bask in the beauty of the warm sun, flowers, and each other. Driven mad with lust, I pulled Carlo down, and he complied. We three women were all over him, though he was enjoying himself as well. His hands felt electrified, as he gently massaged our mammoth breasts. I think I was moaning, but certainly wanted more, more. Now, I understood why the women here wore such skimpy clothing, so easy to get out of the way of one's pleasure when the need arose. That Marisol's male organ was stiff along with my own was more than obvious to everyone, but Carlos seemed not to care in the slightest. Heavenly.

Wham! Out of nowhere, a woman slugged Carlo in the head with a chuck of wood. Another woman joined her. The first one spoke gently to us. "Please come with us now!" Her voice was filled with an urgent sensuousness I'd never felt before. I felt totally compelled to obey her. She was beautiful too, a gorgeous model, I thought, even my own age. She wore pink, while her companion, equally beautiful, wore a light purple. Chained as we were, getting ourselves upright was terribly awkward, and I felt delighted that one of these rare beauties deigned to assist me to rise. The other helped Molly Maud and Marisol get up as well.

She slipped her thin, smooth arm around mine. I wanted to caress it, and was able to slide my fingers up and down her arm. Meanwhile, Marisol saw what I was doing and reciprocated, running her hand up and down the woman's left arm. Molly Maud was doing much the same with the other woman. Now, we were somehow walking, shuffling along the path, our chains clanking lightly. I really did want to stop and make passionate love to these two beauties. I think I must have said so. "Later, when we get to a safe place," she whispered to me, filling me with lust and hope.

Somehow, we ended up near the street and a parked car. Before we could protest, the two helped us inside. "Please be patient. It won't be long now. Won't a soft bed feel good beneath you?" the woman with the lovely brown hair said to me. Was she the one that I wanted to bed? I couldn't remember. The other woman had very light brown hair with bangs over her forehead, reminding me of Danika, my sweet love. Where was she now? No matter. This woman would do, fulfilling my every desire. Now, we were moving, traveling through the streets. Why? Oh, to find that soft bed.

"Here we are at last," my bangs-headed woman said softly to me. "Inside, we have soft beds. Won't that be perfect?"

"Oh yes, yes, I can hardly wait," I exclaimed.

"I can't wait! I'm so wet," added Molly Maud, wiggling

around on her seat.

The car stopped, and they helped us out and into the building. I didn't really notice that it was some kind of warehouse with real walls. Soon, we entered a dimly lit bedroom with two very large beds beckoning to us. This must be heaven, I thought, trying to pull the bangs-headed woman up close to me.

"Let's cut those chains first. Don't they interfere with you?" she said ever so sweetly. I didn't ever want her to stop talking! I only vaguely recall hearing the chain links snapping. They had some giant cutters. I didn't really know that they had removed our wrist and ankle cuffs as well as the ring around our neck rings. I only recall her saying, "Now, let me help you lie down." I felt the gentle touch of her lips upon mine, felt her hair gently touching me as she came down upon me. My passions exploded. I believe we ended up in a five-way embrace, before I was totally exhausted and fell into a deep sleep.

I awoke, smelling freshly brewed coffee. Struggling to sit up, I was lying naked on one of the beds with Molly Maud and Marisol on either side of me, likewise naked. What had happened to us? I flushed, realizing that we'd probably had sex with all them. I focused and sensed my body fully. Yep, we had. Quickly, I adjusted my own body, having it reject the fertilized egg. Marisol must have gotten to me. One by one, I did the same to the others, and then got up to my feet to meet these strange two women. Only then did I realize fully that they'd removed all of our bindings, except the fused neck rings of course. They were naked too but fixing breakfast in the adjoining room, though I could catch glimpses of them moving about.

One saw me and said, "Wake up sleep heads. Coffee is ready. I'm Bianca Bellini, by the way. She's Donatella Bellini. You must be Captain Nia Elain, we think. She's Molly Maud. At least we're certain of her. She's from Hoffdorf. We've seen her image on the Net."

"I'm sorry. I don't know what came over us. We're not like this normally. We wanted to meet you, but were told that you had vanished. Oh, that coffee smells really good. May I?" I said walking into their makeshift kitchen.

"Yes, help yourself. You need it after last night. We got to you just in time," Bianca said. "Ah, the others are rising. Come on ladies. Coffee is waiting for you." I took a moment to focus and make sure they would not also become pregnant because of our licentious behavior. Then, I sipped the brew. My god, coffee never tasted so good. Something was definitely out of kilter with my body. Normally, I much prefer tea.

"I'm sorry. I don't know what came over me. Did we all. . ." Molly Maud said, her voice failing to complete her obvious question.

Bianca laughed. "Yes, we all did. I must admit that was something else. We've never seen hermaphrodites before, but after last night, we want more! You two were fantastic, better than any male, that's for sure. I guess you have a woman's touch not a man's." I flushed. So did Marisol.

"I'm sorry we lost all control. We're very happily married," I rapidly apologized.

"Not to worry. It wasn't your fault. It was the Purple Droga," Bianca said.

"Huh?" I replied rather stupidly.

"The Purple Droga. It's a beautiful flower, but it has a super aphrodisiac property. It grows in nearly everyone's gardens. It causes men and women to lose all control, craving sexual intercourse with anyone and everyone. Foreigners are particularly prone to its effect. You three were so zonked out yesterday that we had no choice but to let you satisfy yourselves, though we both admit it was simply incredible for us as well," Bianca teased.

Donatella added, "We believe the Purple Droga is one reason nearly every male has a harem, and why we women insist on being in a harem."

"And probably why we women insist on the ancient custom of binding," Bianca added. "We got to you just in the nick of time yesterday afternoon. Another few minutes, and you would have lost it completely, begging Carlo to marry you and join his harem, just as we did years ago. Had you done that, there would be no turning back. It's like an addictive drug. You would have spent your days pining for the evening's pleasures."

"She's right. Another half hour and you would have sold yourselves to Carlo, and he would have greatly desired you as well," Donatella added. "We brought you here to this old archaeology warehouse where the air is filtered, removing the Purple Droga spores. As long as you are inside here, you won't be affected again. Go outside and those urges will return once more."

"What happened to our bindings?" Molly Maud asked, realizing that she was free from them.

"We cut them off of you when we got you here. You see, when we heard that you wanted to meet with us to discuss our archaeological findings — that jogged something in us. When we married Carlo, we were under the influence of the Purple Droga. After that, it didn't take much persuasion from him to have us abandon our work and live for the hour when he came home to us and our beds," Bianca explained.

Donatella continued. "We realized what had happened to us and sort of came out of our stupor. Plus, we then saw that interview you did with that reporter, and it clicked with us. Everyone on this world is running on one big can't do anything about it, whatever 'it' may be. We realized what would happen to you if you did come here, but we had no way to get a hold of you. Plus, Carlo was furious with us for abandoning his bed at night. So we snuck off one day. Found the cutters and freed ourselves too," she added.

Bianca explained, "Since then, we've been on a crusade to destroy all the Purple Drago plants that we can find. Already it's beginning to have some effect. In that small section of Po where we've killed those plants, the harem women are waking up and trying to find ways of abandoning their marriages. The men are likewise dismayed that they have so many wives, and are willingly letting some walk away. Of course, there are miles to go, but we are doing something about it! That's what matters."

"Incredible. Yes, you are absolutely right. You are doing something about it," I validated them. "In time, big changes can come about as a result."

"We're counting on that," Donatella replied. "So what

did you want to talk to us about? That old early pre-human skeleton?"

Over breakfast, we chatted and fully explained our mission, discoveries, and theories. They agreed with much of our results thus far. Bianca said, "Yes, you really should visit Centauri-C. That's where that skeleton came from. Now, whether it came from that world originally, we can't say. Such records, if they ever existed, are long lost."

Chapter 6 Captured

After breakfast was finished and we had our very lengthy chat with the two women, I tried to contact Danika to let her know that we were okay and to try to explain what had happened. I was shocked with her reply!

Late afternoon, Anya complained, "Well, I've hacked into bunches of their comm channels, got all sorts of really boring news, but not one word on the missing two women. Rats. You would think someone would be reporting such things."

"Perhaps those women are not really important enough to be on the news," suggested Marilyn.

"Hardly. No police reports either. I don't think Carlo has even bothered notifying them about his missing wives, though he must have told the generalissimo about it," Anya complained. They chatted about it and dropped this line of research.

Meanwhile, Jana had not given up on helping her sister and the two linguists, who were having a terrible time with their immobile necks. She recalled how I had used the drill to cut a hole in the hull just a few atoms wide. Plus, she was well aware of just how the cutter tools worked, thanks to her terrible experiences back on Metcalf-4, when we first met. There, the thief Kisha had used my cutter to cut safely through the metal bands fastened to her legs. She put two and two together. Later, she explained her reasoning to me. "Look, if this drill is so very precise, I ought to be able to make a controlled cut in the ring without touching her skin beneath it, since we know that the ring is a quarter of an inch thick. If I make a number of successive passes with the drill, I ought to be able to take an appreciable slice out of the ring, separating it. Using that gap, I might be able to fit a screwdriver blade in it and bend the brass outwards a bit. With a larger gap, I might be able to then have a way to bend it even straighter, and get it wide enough to slip out from around her neck."

That's precisely what she did. Being extremely careful,

she made over a dozen vertical cuts on one of the ring's bands, until she could see the gap. She used a tiny bladed screwdriver to bend the gap open a bit larger and inserted successively bigger screwdrivers until at last she had a quarter inch gap in it. From here, she was able to get several other tools into the opening. With Tesla helping her by pulling opposite of her pull, the two bent the ring more and more open, until at last the gap was large enough to slip off her neck. Suddenly, she could move her head some, gaining a good deal more freedom. Embolden by this, she set to work on removing one ring from Marilyn and Gabrielle. The others pitched in and soon those two could also move their heads without having to turn their whole bodies. That was quite a relief.

Having proven this would work, everyone worked in pairs on each of the three. By bedtime, they had all of their debilitating rings removed and celebrated. Their spirits were considerably dampened a moment later. Why? They tried telepathically to contact Marisol and me to tell us the good news.

"Something is very wrong. I can't reach her!" Jana exclaimed. Quickly, the other telepaths tried to reach us and failed too. Now, they really began to worry, none more so than my mate, Danika, who continued to try to reach me until nearly midnight when she finally fell asleep.

Around one in the morning, Beth's border collie Jen began barking loudly, rousing Beth and everyone else. "Quiet Jen! What's the matter with you?" Beth complained sleepily. "Quiet, you'll wake everyone." The dog continued to bark. Beth had no choice but to get out of bed to try to calm the barking dog down. "My god! We're moving!" She sensed motion and cried out a warning, "Everyone! Wake up! Something's very wrong. We're moving!"

A sleepy-eyed crew was suddenly totally alert! Dressing partially in a hurry, everyone dashed to various posts throughout the ship, trying to ascertain what was happening. Danika rushed barefoot to the pilot's seat. Her fear was that somehow a control got bumped, and the ship had somehow lifted off the ground. A glance at the controls told her the engines were not turned on, but the altimeter read a thousand feet about the tarmac! She screamed loudly, "We are being pulled up into the air — a thousand feet up so far!"

Tesla yelled back, "Tractor beam! Someone's got a tractor beam on us!"

"What the hell is going on?" Danika yelled.

"Someone's snatching our ship," Martina yelled up to her, "and with us in it."

"Okay, firing up the engines. We'll break free," Danika yelled, doing just that. Martina raced to join her up front, while the others began analyzing sensor data. Anya turned on a live exterior video feed and could see that they were slowly rising from the spaceport below.

By the time that Danika had the sub-light engine revved up, Martina was in the co-pilot or navigator's seat, ready to assist her. "Breaking free now," Danika cried out, applying full power to the engines. The ship twisted and vibrated fiercely, jarring everyone.

"Turn it off before you rip the ship apart!" Martina yelled. Danika had no choice but to kill the power fast. "The only ship with that kind of powerful tractor beam is a battleship. Good God! What have we run into this time?"

"A freaking battleship? Damn, they sure want this ship bad!" Danika cried. "I'm not going to surrender this ship! Come on; how do we break free?"

"We can't Danika. The tractor beam of a battleship exceeds the amount of force our ship can generate. If you try it, you'll simply rip the engines out of the hull, killing us all. There has to be another way. We have to use our minds on this one," Martina yelled.

Anya called out, "Hey, someone's calling us. I think you got their attention, Danika. You want me to answer it or do you?"

"Coming. I'll take it. I'm second in command," she replied, running back down the hall to the comm center. "Captain Danika Jereni-Compton here. What the hell are you doing to our ship? I demand you release us immediately!" She didn't bother saying "over."

"Admiral Berthold Brecht here. We are confiscating your ship. You are almost onboard my battleship. Once we have you locked down on the flight deck, you'll evacuate your ship, turning it over to us. We'll return you to Vegan-C where you can join your captain and other crew members. Sit tight and don't try those engines again, you'll rupture your ship. Over and out." He spoke English but with a German accent.

Martina called out, "Okay, everyone, gather around. We need to talk this out." Hastily, everyone ran up to her as she arrived in the comm center, midship. "Okay. No way are we going to give up this ship without a fight. I assume we can take what he says as factual, namely that we are being tractored into the docking bay of a battleship of the Federation. That being said, he is right, we can't fight the tractor beam. Once we are inside, they can close the bay's outer doors and turn off the tractor beam. However, unless we had a large gun or torpedo, we can't smash through those bay doors. Even if we did, they'd just put their tractor beam back on us. So we need some other ideas about how to handle the situation."

Danika spoke up, "Our gifts. They don't know about our *mentales* gifts. Nia's got Zarita's giant crystal in our room. I say let's liquefy the brains of anyone who approaches our ship!"

"I'm all for that!" Tesla agreed with her, as did Anya.

"We can drop walls of fire around the bay area, cause massive destruction," suggested Jana, who loved fires.

Martina asked, "Who's got the strongest telekinetic force among us?" Normally, that might have been me, but I wasn't there.

"Maybe I do," Anya suggested. "Nia's stronger than me."

"Okay, join with the giant crystal and see if you can generate enough force to rip those bay doors open so we can slip out," Martina suggested.

"Hey, we can cloak. That will only add to their confusion," Tesla suggested.

"Good. I'll monitor the comm center while Anya is trying to rip the bay doors apart. Everyone, let's get ourselves ready. I think we're in for one hell of a fight!" Martina declared emphatically.

Danika raced to our cabin, found Zarita's giant crystal,

and brought it out for Anya to use, or for any of the rest of my crew who could join with it. Anya focused and began to try to adapt to its unique resonance, attuned to Zarita's personal frequency. She soon realized that was going to take some time for her to do.

Now, my crew waited. They could do nothing until the Eagle's Seed was brought into the bay, and the tractor beam turned off. While Anya was tied up struggling to master Zarita's frequency, Tesla stepped in to keep an eye on the external video feed, announcing periodic reports. The admiral was taking it slow and easy, preferring to gain altitude before actually docking our ship in its bay. Giant battleships do not maneuver well at a thousand feet above the ground. One tiny goof and the ship crashes. Po was a large city and the collateral damage would be huge. He had to gain sufficient altitude before bringing the exploration ship into his bay, where he knew my crew would be highly resistant.

It was around seven the next morning before the battleship was three miles above Po and had finally tractored the Eagle's Seed into its docking bay. At that point, they closed the outer blast shields and turned off the tractor beam, shining many bright lights onto my ship. A number of well-armed soldiers came running down the corrugated metal walkways, heading towards the Eagle's Seed.

"Now," Tesla called out. Suddenly, soldiers simply collapsed dead on the walkways. Others were lifted up and tossed off the ramps, falling helplessly hundreds of feet to their deaths. In one minute, some twenty soldiers were dead, and the walkways empty. Round One went to the *mentales* gifted.

Martina appointed herself our battle commander, having had the most experience of any of my crew dealing with tough situations such as this one was. "Okay, that was just a feeler. My guess is that they will bring out some big guns, trying to blow a hole in the side of the ship so they can rush us with sheer numbers of men. Danika, put all power on the shields and prepare to cloak us on my command. Beth, you, Gabrielle, and Marilyn keep your eyes peeled on the entrances to this bay. A whole lot more men should soon come charging at us."

Tesla spoke up, "I have an idea, Martina. I can sense their power lines."

"Good. We can use that. Marilyn, Gabrielle, do you know what powers the Federation battleships?" Martina asked.

Gabrielle said, "I think I once heard they have a number of nuclear power plants that provide unlimited power, but I'm not totally certain."

"Hey, I can work with that," Tesla suggested. "Don't disturb me unless you need more fire power." She focused and began following the electrical current back down the cables that carried it to the bay.

My crew waited patiently for nearly a half hour before Marilyn called out, "I think they are coming again." Martina glanced over at the monitor displaying our hull camera's video stream.

"Okay, get ready. They are bringing in what looks like some small cannons. Don't let them get a chance to fire them. Danika, cloak now," she barked and focused herself.

Outside, over a hundred soldiers in full battle armor stormed into the bay. Some wheeled in their small assault guns, ready to blast holes in the hull in the forward sections. Their general figured the engines were in the rear, and the controls were obviously up front in the nose. The ship winked out, no longer visible parked in the berth. Obviously, the ship was still there, but could not be seen. Walls of fire dropped down on the men, but this time they were more protected. However, they weren't ready to be lifted up and dropped like some child's toy, falling hundreds of feet down the huge bay. Some hit other decks and were sent spinning wildly on down. Loud crashes announced the end of their lives. Their battle armor didn't protect them from taking a three hundred foot fall onto solid, unyielding steel.

The fires had another side effect beyond adding to the confusion. This time several power cables began burning, shorting out, and showering voluminous sparks everywhere. Several unlucky soldiers were electrocuted in the process. Lights flickered and some went out, while others dimmed. One cannon was able to fire several salvos into the side of the ship. The shields held, deflecting the shots, which went on to take out some bulkheads, ripping open an inner wall, exposing more of the great battleship's interior.

Another lull quickly followed, after the last of the hundred men and cannon went over the side of the ramps. "Well, you handled that one. I don't know how you are doing it, but it's simply fantastic," exclaimed Marilyn.

"We're not out of the woods yet. We're like a fish caught in a net. We're still fighting, but we're doomed unless we can escape the net," Martina pointed out. "Danika, fire up the engines and nudge us out say a hundred feet. Point us towards the bay doors and raise us up another hundred feet. With luck, they'll not be able to locate us easily. Now, ideas on how to get those bay doors open?"

Just then, Admiral Berthold Brecht appeared on a monitor. His face was twisted and red; anger seethed through his entire body. He yelled, "How dare you murder my soldiers! This is your last warning. Surrender now, and we will let you live. If you do not, then your lives are forfeit, and we'll take the ship anyway!"

"Hey look!" Gabrielle pointed to another monitor. Martina saw commandos sliding down a dozen ropes from far overhead. Each one carried a contact mine. She instantly knew their plan. They would land on the hull, plant their mines, and descend to safety. The mines would detonate, ripping gaping holes in the hull, giving soldiers the breech they needed.

"Well, we've confused them for a bit," she called out, watching their flailing arms, searching for the ship which wasn't where it had been parked by the tractor beam. One by one, Jana and Jovanna used their gifts to severe the commandos' ropes. Martina watched the men suddenly accelerating swiftly downward. Several explosions followed, but the video cameras couldn't pick up what happened that far away.

The disembodied voice of Tesla spoke softly, "Reactor One is going off line." A tremendous explosion somewhere distant from the bay could barely be heard. However, half of the lights that were still functional suddenly went out, leaving the bay very dimly illuminated. That was both good and bad, harder for them to see my ship, though it was currently cloaked, but harder for my crew to see what their next move might be.

Martina whispered, "Nice job, Tesla." She opened up a line to the battleship, using the same frequency the admiral was using. "Admiral Berthold Brecht. This is the last warning from the Eagle's Seed. Open the bay doors and let us go now. If you do not, your ship will be destroyed." She switched off the frequency, meaning her sudden termination was like a slap in his face.

"Will they do it? Let us go?" whispered Marilyn.

"Hardly. But two can play this psychological head game," Martina replied. "Stay alert for their next assault."

Another distant explosion could barely be felt within the Eagle's Seed. Tesla had taken out another nuclear power plant. She didn't know it, but that one had provided guidance power. While the big ship still had all its massive engines, the ship could not be guided on any given course, let alone plot such.

Danika, what is going on? I sent just after breakfast.

We are fighting a massive battle. No time to chat. A battleship put a tractor beam on us last night, pulling us into their shuttle bay. We've been fighting off wave after wave of attacks. They are trying to take the ship. Martina's in charge. Gotta go. You okay? Oops. Talk later, Danika sent me, but abruptly ending the connection. Her attention was needed on the present situation.

This time, Martina could see some massive, armored assault vehicles, usually used to crawl along on the ground, destroying points of resistance. Long barrels pointed out into the bay as they rolled along the strongest points of the metal walkways used to service the docked ships. "Good god. How do we stop these beasts?" she whispered.

Tesla came to the rescue. She focused again and pervaded the enormous steel I-beams that formed the reenforcing structure below the metal platforms over which the heavy vehicles were slowly moving towards the bay where the Eagle's Seed had been parked. While it was no longer there, these beasts could fire their shells around the bay and eventually hit the shields of the ship. Martina knew there was a limit on just how much force the ship's shields could withstand, probably not what they were going to be hit with.

Tesla began molecularly altering the composition of the steel I-beams. It didn't take much. A hideous creaking sound carried well in the space of the bay. As Martina and the others watched, the floor carrying the first of these massive assault vehicles bent and twisted. Like butter on a hot piece of toast, the assault vehicle slipped sideways off of the platform and plunged into the dark depths of the bay. The resounding crash and explosion when it hit shook the whole battleship, and the air concussion jarred the Eagle's Seed, sending everyone who was standing onto the floor.

Anya was sitting at her post, fully in rapport with Zarita's giant crystal. It had taken some concentration on her part to match frequencies or wavelengths of Zarita, but she'd done it. Now, she felt the raw power of the crystal flowing through her, one with her. She focused on the bay doors, giant monsters of metal. Pretending she had a giant's hands, she latched onto them and began prying them apart. As far as Martina could tell, these doors just twisted and ripped off their runners, falling down into the dark space below, eventually landing on the growing pile of debris on the floor of the bay. Anya ripped enough away that the Eagle's Seed could slip through.

Danika needed no encouragement. As soon as she estimated the gaping fissure was large enough for the ship, she nudged the controls and began moving slowly towards the newly formed exit. Anya continued to rip more and more sections of the doors off, enlarging the opening. She didn't stop until she'd ripped them all off! Now, the entire bay was open to space! Worse, it could not be sealed off. Repairs would not easily be made!

Tesla continued following the electrical flow of energy through the miles of wiring. Of all my crew, she had an uncanny affinity for all things electrical. After this event, I knew why. Tesla knew that Anya would probably be able to open up the doors so Danika could drive the ship out of the bay. But she also knew the battleship had simply massive guns, and they would be firing like mad at them when they flew out of the bay. While the shields could protect them from normal encounters, she doubted they could long prevent these giant cannons of the battleship from penetrating the Eagle's Seed. At last, she sensed what she was looking for, the enormous power cables that led to the deck guns. Martina saw a faint smile purse her lips. As the Eagle's Seed's nose began to protrude from the bay, another massive explosion shook the battleship.

Tesla broke out of her reverie. "Well, they won't be able to fire their giant deck guns at us. I took out their power plant. They have three nuclear power plant meltdowns to handle now. Never mess with Tesla. Oh, good going Anya. You ripped them all off," she praised her dear friend, as she saw the gaping hole and stars ahead.

Taking no chances at all, as soon as the ship cleared the bay, Danika executed a wild, random series of rolls, feints, and repositions, designed to elude anything sent their way. After pulling clear, she jumped into hyperspace. Moving over to her usual seat, she punched in another set of coordinates, moved back to my seat and executed the maneuver, dropping back out of hyperspace three miles south of the spaceport at Po. Still cloaked, the ship was invisible and safe.

After touching my mind, which was a turmoil of frantic worry by now, Danika sent me, *Okay love. We're free of the battleship and hovering over Po. What's up? Where do we pick you up?*

We are at the edge of the city in an old warehouse with walls. Hang on. I'll get specific directions from Bianca. After a few minutes, I gave her more specific ones. On most Imperium worlds, Danika's next move would not have been possible. She brought the ship down to a few thousand feet above the ground and began circumnavigating the outer edges of Po, looking for our building. We couldn't see them, and there were a fair number of these particular walled buildings around the perimeter of Po. City planners refused to mar the beauty of the heart of the city with walled buildings. Therefore, most all storage facilities lay around its outer edge. So much for city growth, I thought. Hence, with Bianca's help, I made a big X on the ground just outside, using bed sheets.

Finally, I heard the most welcome words in my mind. *We see your X. Stand back, going to land nearby.* However, as we five stood there waiting the ship, we could smell the Purple Droga in the air. "How long do we have?" I asked Bianca, fearing another round of drug-induced orgy.

"Hours. If you leave soon, you should be all right. We wear masks when we go out now. Give us a few years, and Po will finally wake up from its drugged stupor," Donatella explained. We had already exchanged frequencies, so once they had access to comm equipment, they could get in touch with us. While we were waiting, we said our farewells. I didn't want to gamble on being drugged again. Neither did Molly Maud and Marisol, though Molly Maud was awfully silent and quite embarrassed over what she'd done last night.

Soon we heard the engines, but saw nothing. Then, Molly Maud spotted sand and dust swirling around, and pointed to that spot. Shortly after that, we saw the bay ramp appearing out of nowhere and Martina's smiling face. She waved to us, and we waved back. "Bye and thanks for everything. Good luck on your rescue operations," I said to the two women, who grinned. We three dashed for the ramp, running up it into the ship. Martina shut the door after us, sealing us inside. At once, Danika accelerated upwards and within a minute dropped us into hyperspace, where we would be totally safe, though Tesla once more did a thorough check. She found no bugs and joined us to hear our exchange of tales. Admittedly, theirs was far more exciting to hear than ours was.

Molly Maud was aghast at what had happened to the ship. "Come on. I've recorded the whole thing," Anya offered.

"You did? Fantastic! I'd love to see it. This is wholly criminal. I want those responsible to stand trial and be punished!" she declared with more anger than I'd seen her produce before. A while later, she shrieked. I went to see what was the matter.

"I know that man. He's a close friend of dad's. Admiral Berthold Brecht. This cannot be tolerated! I've got to make a call to my boss and tell him about this treasonous act!" Molly

Maud declared very antagonistically. She marched off to her quarters to do just that.

I decided we'd spend three days traveling to Centauri-C-C. Why? I wanted Jana to get these infernal neck rings off us and to give us all time to recover and check out all of the ship's systems for possible damage or compromise. Also, I wanted a full analysis of our next destination. I'd had more than enough of these clandestine actions against us.

Chapter 7 Your Hand in Marriage

Dylan and Anwyn began our education on our final destination star. "Originally, it had the name Alpha Centauri. Not sure where that comes from," he explained, throwing up an image of the triple star system that he'd found while searching the Federation databases. Thanks to Anya and her special programming, we were able to review many of their databases. The two yellow main sequence stars are a close binary system, with one slightly larger and whiter than the other, which has a slight orange tinge to its yellow color."

Anwyn added, "The third one, which has the planet we're heading for orbiting it, is much smaller and far dimmer. If it were not for the brighter close double stars, this planet would be far dimmer than Ashford-5 and redder. So daytime on Centauri-C-C is going to be really strange. When the red sun comes up, it's really dim, but when the pair rises, they provide far more light, though they are far more distant. Plus, the orbital swings of the planet are a bit wild too, yielding some strange, at least to us, phenomenon. Some winters are really summers and some summers end up being winters. Very confusing. I think we'll be arriving in a summer that really ought to be a winter. They call it La Estacion Opuesta. I find their calendars most confusing indeed."

"Okay I can handle summer. What's their women's dress code like?" I asked.

Molly Maud spoke up, "They are modern. A professional woman would be appropriate, but with our taller heels. Oh, and very vibrant colors. We'd call them clashing colors. Here's a professional woman's image." She showed us a photo on her laptop. The woman wore a bright red blouse with a canary yellow skirt that fell to just below her knees. That contrasted with her quite black hose, but her heels were red, matching her top. She wore a bright green blazer, and had very black hair, curly and draped down just over her shoulders. Her face was darkish with rather angular features. Her eyes were black. She also wore a matching green belt.

"Well, we certainly don't have wild combinations like that," I commented.

"Maybe we can make do," Jana suggested. "We can wear one of our colorful satin gowns. Then, put a contrasting skirt on over it, plus a blazer. If we trade around among us, surely we can make up some outfits that are sort of similar."

For the next few hours, we women were preoccupied with trying on each other's clothes, trying to come up with a combination that was "wild" from our point of view. Since this world seemed safe, compared to what we had encountered, the landing party would consist of our three guests, Marisol, Jana, Jovanna, and me. Jovanna insisted on coming in spite of her missing left hand. Further, I found that Marilyn and Gabrielle were more determined than ever to make a difference. Their contributions in the battleship fight had somehow hardened them to the realities of the universe. Since this was to be our last stop, they wanted to see the sights, before we returned them to their own worlds. I couldn't refuse them either. Hence, we had to "invent" seven wild professional woman's outfits. At least tall heels were not a problem.

During the three days before we were to arrive, Molly Maud chatted directly with Elena del Gotto. She wanted to make darn sure the woman wasn't kidnaped or harmed. No surprises this time became Molly Maud's mantra. "She's the wife of the mayor of their city. Alcalde Ruperto del Gotto runs Cordoban. She has a five year old son, Salvador, and a three year old daughter, Adelina. She says Alcalde Ruperto will be giving us the ceremonial key to the city. So with us in the limelight, the bad men won't dare try anything this time. We'll be too visible in the public eye." I certainly hoped that her analysis was correct.

This time, everything sounded quite normal. Honestly, we needed some normal interactions. However, that was not to be. The day before our arrival, Molly Maud came up with more startling discoveries and hastily called up Elena again. When she ended her call, she explained to us.

"Well, this one is really strange. All married women have their non-dominant hand cut off! Mano Cortada it's called! How brutal, but Elena says that this Mano Cortada tradition goes back as far as their written records go. She says that they give their hand in marriage to their spouse, literally! She gave up archaeology work after she got married."

Jovanna teased us, "Well, I will fit in perfectly." We all gave a tense laugh.

Molly Maud continued. "So I talked with Elena about this. We get a break. Visiting married women are not asked to have their hand cut off. Rather, they have a special binding that they do, one that is easily removed. When on Centauri-C-C, do as the Centauri-C-C do."

"Well then perhaps this won't be so bad," I admitted.

"Right, we don't need our non-dominant hand too much, not with our *mentales* gifts. Our three guests are not married and should be a-okay," Marisol suggested as upbeat as she could manage. "Just clumsy. I would suggest that we keep the visit as short as possible."

Weird. That would be a total understatement of what this world looked like, as I began our descent to Centauri-C-C. The bright binary stars dominated our view, dwarfing the dim red star around which the planet revolved in its wild orbit. I didn't need my astronomers to tell me that their seasons would be rather wild ones indeed. Soon, the planet became more visible. We could see a number of other ships on a descent pattern as well as some taking off. This world was a busy one in this sector of space.

Cordoban was not their capital city, but still had a population of several million people. Hence, I soon got ordered onto a different trajectory, and we left the swarm of descending ships behind us, joining only a few that were also heading to Cordoban. As we drew closer to the ground, we could see their buildings. In the heart of the city, glass and steel skyscrapers rose, but not higher than a dozen floors. We would later learn that was a safety factor, since earthquakes were somewhat common, particularly during certain times in the planet's peculiar orbit. However, most of the buildings were built of stone. Red, brown, grey, and black predominated, good, sturdy structures, but usually only one story tall. Roofs were uniformly red tile and added more contrasting color.

As we approached touchdown at the spaceport on the

edge of the sprawling city, we could see formal gardens and plenty of green lawns, along with grey roads filled with more of the rubber-tired vehicles we'd encountered here in the Federation of Planets. Anya also spotted several fountains, which Jana decided we should visit and take some pictures of them for her. Shortly, I sat the Eagle's Seed down on Pad 42, as directed. We were not all that far from their Admin Tower, where we would need to check in, pay our landing fee, and go through customs.

As quickly as we could, we seven got dressed up in our strikingly wild colored "professional woman's" makeshift outfits. Again, we had to wear our six-inch heels, but I was more worried we would be far too hot with all these layers that resulted in our looking as close to Molly Maud's example of dress that we could get without purchasing clothing here. Since we weren't planning to spend much time here, I vetoed that idea. All set at last, we seven teetered our way down the bay ramp, arms moving about to help us keep our balance.

The air had a fresh smell to it, though as always it was mingled with oil and metallic odors so often found at spaceports. "Well, hopefully there isn't Purple Droga here," Molly Maud commented, adding a sigh to the end of her words. She added, "Honestly, those men were incredibly handsome."

We saw others moving out from the building and others heading towards it, as well as some baggage carts transporting crates of various sizes. It was still a busy place. Since their spoken language was Spanish, which was a variation of our Westerlings dialect, we felt confident we could handle the language barrier here. Indeed, we quickly discovered we could more or less read their written language as well. Signs directed us to the customs entry point.

There, we met a polite man, who accepted our landing fee, and verified our names and marital status. He then explained, "Well, your dress is, shall I say, quite strange indeed."

"We were trying to look like your professional women," Molly Maud defended us. "It's the best that we can do."

He chuckled. "Well, that's better than most visiting

women. However, we have a Dress Machine here, and we can whip our proper dresses, which will be vastly more appropriate for your stay and for a very slight charge. Of course, the married women will need to have their non-dominate hand bound up for the duration of your visit."

"We were expecting that. I do believe we ought to take advantage of your offer on the proper dresses," Molly Maud replied.

He smiled. "Of course. Looking your best goes a long way towards acceptance by ordinary Centaurians. If you will follow me, we'll have you fixed up in no time. I can have your old garments sent back to your ship saving you the time, if you like."

"Please do. That would be most kind," she replied.

"Also, I believe that you will prefer our style shoes. They will have a most difficult time trying to tie those shoes." He was referring to our Ashford-5 oxfords. "Here, our married women prefer simple ones that they can take off and put on most easily."

We entered a room. At once, our noses were assaulted with the odor of fabric material and leather. A middle-aged woman stepped out of a back room. Her appearance was much like the image that Molly Maud had shown us on the ship. Her color scheme was quite striking, but I noticed that she was missing her left hand, indicating that she was married. "Ah, my charming wife, Abella. These visiting women wish to obtain proper professional outfits. Here's the list of their names, dear, and which ones are married. I'll leave you in her competent hand. Also, I'll let the Acalde's wife know you are about ready to meet her. Abella will let me know when she has you dressed properly, and I'll return and take you to her. On behalf of Cordoban, we welcome you to our lovely city."

Hastily, we undressed, though retaining our undergarments. Abella handed us a large bag, and we stuffed everything in it. One by one, she had us stand inside a strange looking machine. "It uses suction to obtain proper measurements of your bodies. Once done, all we have to do is pick your color scheme," she explained. I went first. It did feel a bit strange, almost a tickling sensation, but the process took less than a minute. I stepped out and over to the menu display.

"What color blouse would you like?" Abella asked. We conferred a bit, and we went along with her color suggestions based a lot on the color of our hair. I ended up with a bright red blouse, a bright blue skirt, and a green blazer. The belt was canary yellow. My six-inch pumps were made from real leather, very high quality, and bright red to match my blouse. Once the colors were entered, the machine made a high-pitched noise, and three minutes later, my new outfit appeared. Meanwhile, Abella handled Molly Maud.

I got dressed in my new outfit, and by the time that I was satisfied, Molly Maud was also dressed. In fact, the total time spent here was less than a half hour. Incredible. Here was a machine I would have loved to purchase! Next, we had to endure the binding part. This turned out not to be as bad as I was anticipating. She had me ball up my left hand into a fist. I then stuck it into another small machine. It wrapped it with an elastic type bandage. When I pulled it out a minute later, it looked more like I'd severely injured my hand. The clips that held it in place could easily be removed. However, I certainly didn't have the use of my left hand, not remotely.

While she was handling the others, I stole a good look at her stump. Her hand had been removed at the wrist and her lower arm bones there at the wrist joint had not been altered in any way, unlike Jovanna's, which was now quite conical and ready to be fitted with a prosthetic hand once we got back. I also noticed Abella used her left arm constantly, mostly in support of what she was doing. Her motions with it seemed wholly natural to her. I filed that observation for later, because her husband arrived, ready to escort us to meet our host, Mrs. Elena del Gotto. "I say, you do look quite stunning now. This way, the Acalde's wife is expecting you."

"Say, can someone one purchase a machine like that one that makes these clothes?" I asked him, as we walked slowly down the long hall, our heels clicking nearly in unison.

"Senorita, I'll check and let you know upon your return," he replied cordially.

He led us to a private area, where we spotted Elena waiting for us. She rose from a soft chair as we approached.

She too wore a professional woman's outfit, rather similar in color to mine. Her hair was black and wavy, falling to just below her shoulders. I guessed she was in her mid-twenties, but she was quite attractive and had charming eyes that were fully alert. Her heels were bright red and as tall as ours. Her left hand was missing and her wrist looked rather like Abella's. No attempt had been made to fit it for a prosthetic hand. In fact, it looked as if they simply had cut off her hand at her wrist. Barbaric I still thought!

"Welcome to Cordoban. I'm so very pleased to welcome you to our world. It's not often that we have such visitors. In fact, we've never had anyone from the Imperium here. I'm Elena del Gotto. Oh, I see at least one of you has given her hand in marriage," she looked at Jovanna.

Jovanna giggled, "Not really. Lost it in a battle recently." I hastily did the introductions.

Elena then explained, "You will be staying at my home. We have extra rooms for visiting guests. My husband is our city's Alcalde or mayor. Normally, I do the cooking for our family, but I have hired another cook. I need an extra hand with so many of you. Alcalde Ruperto will join us for supper. I know he is dying meet you too. This way, I've a limo waiting to take us to our place."

We chatted briefly during the limo trip, but mostly Elena pointed out the sights. I was surprised she did her pointing with her left stump. We quickly saw that these married women did not feel the slightest bit embarrassed about not having one hand. They used that arm just as readily as they did their other one, only they used it to apply pressure, to hold, or to secure something. These women were quite comfortable with making whatever use they could with their handless arm, as though this was completely normal. Well, for them, it was, as we quickly discovered.

Their home was a spacious red stone building with a white picket fence around a green lawn. Out back, she had a small flower garden, her pride and joy. Inside her home, we saw nothing really fancy, exotic, or expensive for that matter. She and her husband were quite practical people. We did meet her two children, who ran out to see her and meet us, but quickly they scampered off to play outside in the warm sunshine.

With the kids off, she led us into her study. "As you know, I used to be an archaeologist before I met Ruperto and got married. I know our Mano Cortada custom or tradition must seem entirely strange to you, especially those of you from the Imperium, or rather is it the ex-Imperium now? I've heard rumors it has fallen."

"Yes, it's been disbanded. Indeed, we do find it quite strange, brutal from our point of view," I replied.

She laughed. "I assumed so. That's why I wanted to show you my wedding ceremony to Ruperto. I want you to have a better appreciation for our ways and a better understanding of us. After all, I do believe that understanding is the fundamental building block for all relationships, especially with aliens from the Imperium. For so many years, everyone thought your people were the Devil Incarnate, to be annihilated utterly. Now, we are at peace with you, and here you are in my home. So indulge me a little on this."

"Please, we would love to see your wedding, Elena," I replied enthusiastically. This might well answer our many questions.

She played a computer recording for us, and we watched it on a large monitor. I realized at once that this was her comm center. "I was nineteen when I got married." We watched, as she appeared wearing a flowing white wedding gown, and walked down an aisle accompanied by some delightful music that was quite upbeat, not solemn or foreboding. She looked incredibly happy, as she walked up to Ruperto and the Wedding Official, who performs these ceremonies. Ruperto took her left hand in his, as the two met and stood before the official.

We listened to the two exchanging their marriage vows, not so different from those found on many other worlds, at least I thought so. Near the end, the official opened a white box-like machine resting on a pedestal just between them that I'd not paid any attention to before. Ruperto then gently placed her left hand into the box and the official closed it over her hand. It covered most of her lower arm as well. The official then said, "Ruperto, please take the hand of your future bride in yours." He reached around to the front of the machine that was facing away from us.

The official then spoke directly to Elena. "Elena, is this your non-dominate hand?"

"It is," she replied softly, but a bit nervously. What bride isn't nervous on her wedding day? But I would have thought that she'd be terrified, even panicking.

He then said, "Elena, do you wish to give your hand in holy marriage to Ruperto del Gotto, knowing that what is given out of your love for Ruperto can never be taken back?"

Nervously, Elena replied, "I do."

"Ruperto, will you accept the offered hand of Elena, given to you freely and out of her deep abiding love for you, knowing that this bond between you cannot ever be broken or undone, from this day forward?"

Just as nervously, he replied, "I do."

"So be it. Since the dawn of time, this precious gift of her hand in marriage seals their bonds through sickness and health, through good times and bad, until death parts your ways. The precious gift of Elena symbolizes her undying faithfulness to Ruperto. His acceptance of her hand in marriage fills him with the never-ending responsibility to care for her, to cherish her, to remain faithful to her until death parts their ways. Ruperto, your acceptance of her hand in marriage is final and cannot be undone. Should you become unfaithful to Elena, you will be marked as a pariah and wholly shunned by all society. It is done. You may take her hand now, Ruperto, and place it upon the Holy Altar of Lord God who has borne witness to your vows."

I noticed he was now exceptionally nervous. His right hand was shaking a little as he withdrew it from the box. I almost gasped as I saw her left hand in his! At least it wasn't bloody. Still shaking, he placed it upon a white cloth on the altar before him. The official lifted the lid of the box and Elena removed her left arm, which was missing its hand. There was no wound. It was fully healed. What a terrible use of a medical machine, I thought!

Ruperto put his right arm around her left handless arm

and the pair turned to face their friends. The official now said, I give you Ruperto and Elena del Gotto." Cheers arouse; the happy couple walked gracefully down the aisle, and the video ended.

"Sorry, I didn't want you to see the reception part. I was foolish and didn't practice beforehand. I was very awkward and clumsy at the reception. I was supposed to bind my hand like yours for months beforehand so I could get accustomed to being without it. I didn't and paid dearly for that with embarrassment at our reception. You see, it is a thing to be treasured. I felt no pain, nothing at all. When he opened the machine, my arm was completely healed, although for some time after that I kept having ghost feelings from my non-existent hand and fingers."

"So you see this is not a brutal thing, but something to be treasured. Honestly, if Ruperto ever betrays me, the pariah would ruin him completely. He would be a marked man. No woman would ever go near him, and most married men would shun him completely. He would be a total outcast."

I spoke up, "But isn't it hard to do many things without that hand?"

"We get by fairly well. Ruperto is always here to help me if I can't handle something. In time, I use it for everything that it can be used for. No sense in favoring it," she replied. "Certainly, it's nothing to be ashamed of or embarrassed by, not anywhere on our world, though I understand the loss of a hand is treated quite differently on other worlds."

"But what happens if Ruperto dies unexpectedly soon?" I asked.

"Well, we certainly can't give up our good hand," she laughed, as though this was funny. She explained, "That does sometimes happen. In that case, I would go to the hospital, and they would shape my lower arm much as Jovanna has hers. They would give me an artificial hand. Mind you, they don't actually work or anything like that. But when I remarry, ceremonially, I would give that artificial hand to my new husband in a similar ceremony. In that case, it is a more symbolic gift. I'm really surprised that on other worlds the brides don't live up to this pledge, giving their hand in marriage. They also have that saying. I traced it when I was studying archaeology in school. Nearly every world has that saying, giving my hand in marriage or asking for your hand in marriage. Yet, none of them *actually* does it. Perhaps, that is why the divorce rates are staggeringly high on so many Federation worlds. They aren't actually giving their hand in marriage, so the only bond is their word. And we all know how easily words can be manipulated."

She then said, "I hope this helps you understand our people better."

"It certainly does," Jovanna replied. "But aren't there things that you can't do without your other hand? I can't tie my own shoes anymore."

Elena laughed. "Of course there are. That's a big one and why we professional women always wear these pumps. All married women wear shoes they can handle easily. The other really big hassle is getting dressed and putting on our black nylons. When I have no help to dress, I always allow an hour to get the job done. My advice to you, Jovanna, is to allow extra time. Always try to use your left arm to help. I never favor my left arm in the slightest. Now then, I would like to ask you many personal questions as well, but I'll wait until supper because I know Ruperto would love to hear your replies too. He will be incredibly honored to have you dine with us. In the meantime, I know you are here to see me about other matters. Perhaps, we should pursue them now?"

"Okay. That sounds fine with me," I replied. Without further preamble, I began outlining what we knew about the origins of humankind. Marisol, Jana, and Jovanna did most all of the talking, though. We spent a good hour discussing this in depth.

Elena was an excellent listener and added observations of her own. She was also highly encouraging. "Honestly, this is fantastic work, extremely valuable. It offers a sort of bond between the people of the Imperium and the people of the Federation. You simply must publish your findings in depth both in your worlds and ours."

Marilyn and Gabrielle promised they would do so here in the Federation, and Jana and Jovanna promised to do so within the Imperium. After that, our focus became the pre-human remains she had researched as a beginning archaeologist. She did explain she'd given up her professional career shortly after getting married, because she became pregnant with Salvador. Once the children were grown, she planned to restart her career. At least she hoped so.

"My research into the most ancient records we have gave only a tantalizing clue to their origin world. They suggest an archaeologist named Enrique Mundo brought several sets of remains from his excavations on a world called Earth. However, I could not find any planet with such a name anywhere among the known worlds of the Federation. One other thing, from the sketchy documents, this Earth must not have been too far from here. He mentions a short travel time, but then who knows what that may have meant some eighteen millennia ago. Technology is always changing," she explained.

Of course, this rather dampened our hopes of finding this world of origin. I knew that further research and a combing of stars for planets in this zone of space would be required. Additionally, after what we'd been through, I doubted that we could get such permission just now.

Elena commented, "It is so utterly incredible that you are able to speak our Spanish as well as you do. And yet it is called Westerlings dialect on your world. Fascinating. You say perhaps a deep space exploration ship may have crash landed on your world centuries ago. I wonder if there are any records of lost ships? I'll make some inquiries and let you know. Fascinating."

"What's fascinating, dear?" a male voice broke in on our conversation. We looked around and saw Ruperto walking into her study. He came up to her, and she raised her handless left hand. He bent over and kissed its end gently, before turning to face us.

"Our esteemed guests," she explained and began the introductions. "Alcalde Ruperto, this is Captain Nia Elain Compton-Jereni. Did I get that said right?" she asked. I nodded, and he took my left hand and planted a kiss on it just above the elastic bandage.

When she introduced Jovanna, Ruperto exclaimed, "Ah

a true wife this one is! My compliments." He kissed the tip of her stump as he had done with his wife. "Your husband must be a very honored man for your greatest of gifts." Jovanna didn't have the heart to tell him she'd just recently lost her hand.

Over supper, Elena and Ruperto plied us with questions, beginning with our large breasts. After I explained some, Elena said, "How interesting. All women on your world. Anthropologically, this is significant. Perhaps it is genetic too?" Marisol told her that it wasn't genetic and that we had some of the best geneticists in the Imperium on our world.

A bit later, Ruperto commented, "You know, we did see that interview you had with that reporter, Mary Ann somebody. Of course, someone translated what was being said in a scrolling banner below the images. Speaking for Elena and myself, I have to say we were somewhat startled and surprised to hear some of what you were saying about women. Is it really true that on Imperium worlds women are often in positions of great power? Here for example, the position of alcalde is one of the most influential and powerful ones in Cordoban."

"Absolutely true. If Cordoban was on some of our worlds, we might be addressing Alcalde Elena," I answered. "Mind you, there are other places where men attempt to keep women from positions of power, but those are in the minority."

"But I wouldn't want to be the alcalde. I have enough trouble handling the home and children, what with my single hand," Elena countered. "I don't know I could physically do the work he does. Besides, I have no interest in doing the work that men do, no more than men are interested in doing the work we women do. I just can't see Ruperto here doing my needlepoint or sewing. I certainly don't want to be the Jefe de Policia here in Cordoban. What would I do with the criminals? Hit them over their heads with my stump? No, dabbling in archaeology is probably as far afield as I would ever like to go. Don't get me wrong, I admire you, Captain Nia Elain, for being the captain of your ship. It's just that I have no such interests."

"That's perfectly fine, Elena. As I said to that reporter, people regardless of their gender ought to be able to do what it is that they are interested in doing, as long as they are competent in it. We've found on the worlds we've visited here in the Federation, men are simply not allowing women to pursue their own interests. Gabrielle and Marilyn can testify to that."

Jovanna spoke up, asking quite pointedly, "But don't you think losing your hand when you marry is limiting the roles or positions that a women could potentially have within Cordoban?" I knew she in particular felt that this practice was horrid.

"I can answer that one, Jovanna," Ruperto spoke before Elena could. "I see your point, but you must see ours. Here on our world, we have the lowest divorce rate of any world within the Federation of Planets. In fact, it is a factor of a hundred below the second lowest world. Our women are glad to give up the potential for a few occupations, which they might not seriously be interested in holding, for the total security of their marriages. For years now, our Federation ambassadors have been trying to convince other worlds to follow our marriage practice. You see, so many other worlds are so decadent, what with all the drugs, promiscuity, and crime. You have heard, I presume, of the Forbidden List of worlds?"

"Yes we have. I've shown it to them," Molly Maud volunteered. "I'm not so sure I would want to give up my hand when I marry. After all, what if the man turns out not to be truly compatible with me or I, him?"

"You must choose wisely," Elena answered, "and not rush into a marriage."

After this point, our chat became more mundane, what was life like on our world, did we have seasons, what did women usually wear, what did our homes look like, and so on. As the hour grew late, Elena remembered and asked, "Dear, are the listing of deep space exploration ships that were lost and never heard from again in the library? Tomorrow, I've promised Nia Elain I would try to find them, since it may well be possible that their world was settled by some of our explorers. Wouldn't that be something?"

"Yes, I believe so. Ask the librarian. She ought to be able to put her hand on those records. Indeed, that would be something," he replied. "One final question, you all are telepaths, right?"

"Yes, but not Molly Maud, Gabrielle, and Marilyn," I answered.

He grinned sheepishly. "Well, I wondered how weird it would be to hold a conversation with telepaths. Now that I've done it, I could not even tell that you are. You are just like normal people."

I laughed, "Of course, we are just like normal people. We never pry into another's mind unless they ask us to. We consider doing that to be mental rape, and it just isn't done."

"I see. How very interesting. Well, it is getting late. I do hope you'll stay with us a few more days. I can arrange for a tour of our city. I'd like to present you with the Key to Cordoban. I know, it's symbolic, but it is an honor."

"Sure. We'll stick around a while yet. We want to see what your library holds tomorrow," I replied. "It's that we only have this one outfit."

Ruperto quickly replied, "Elena, take them to Pablo's tomorrow and see that they each get another three outfits. On Cordoban, ladies. It's the least that we can do to honor you." We thanked him.

Later, as we turned in making use of three of their guest rooms, I began to think perhaps this time we would have some fun and no serious problems. Certainly, the next day proved so. An hour at their library produced a hard copy of all their lost expeditions with dates and theoretical destination locations. There were too many to make any definitive adjudication quickly. Jana and Jovanna needed time to study them and Ashford-5's own records. Later, we entered Pablo's Dresses. I won't bore you with eight women on a shopping spree. I'll just say it was closer to suppertime before we arrived back at Elena's home, loaded with bags, seven very happy shoppers.

Chapter 8 The Telepath

Severino Tono was quite a wealthy man. Some hinted he was the wealthiest man in Cordoban, perhaps on all Centauri-C-C. He was fifty-two, somewhat overweight, but continued to say that one day he would go on a diet, though he never followed through with that. He had built his fortune with his vast Tono's Import-Export Company. His ships traveled throughout the entire Federation, including worlds that were on the Forbidden List. Three months ago, he'd been cheated, and he was still fuming over that. "No one cheats Severino Tono!" he'd screamed at his office walls. Ordinarily, if someone wanted to sell him something whose price exceeded a million gold backed dollars, he insisted on seeing the product firsthand.

This special transaction had cost him ten million, and he had been cheated, that much he knew. A contact on the hub world of Cass-C had put him in touch with a very special seller. Telepaths are exceedingly rare. The seller had one for sale, and Severino had jumped at the opportunity, against all his better judgment. The deal was simple. Deliver the money and return with the telepath. It would have to be sight unseen, since Cass-C was half the galaxy from Centauri-C-C. For days, he dreamed of how much more wealth he could amass with a telepath working for him, overseeing all his more significant business deals. It had been his own greed that had overridden his own safety precautions. He'd sent the funds, and his company ship had returned three months ago with the telepath, one Zuzana Ruzickovana, age twenty-six.

He had no doubt that she was a telepath, of that he was certain. However, after even a couple of days with her, he knew that he'd been cheated big time. She was an emotional basket case and wholly dependent upon others for everything. She'd been severely abused by her former owners. There had been six, if she were to be believed. When she arrived, she had no hands, no eyes, and plenty of bruises about her face, torso, and legs. He managed to get some of her story out of her. Her first owner had to force her to work for him by blinding her. That didn't work out well, and she was sold to another man. This one cut off her left hand at the wrist in an attempt to get her to perform for him. A later owner in utter frustration cut off her remaining hand, hoping that would get through to her and make her cooperate with him. She was such an emotional wreck by this time, that she made so many mistakes that he too sold her. Her last owner had taken to beating her silly, but that only made things worse, and he'd cleverly sold her to Severino, sight unseen, recouping his losses and then some.

Hence, after just a couple of days with Zuzana, Severino realized he'd been swindled out of ten million, and he was furious. At least, he didn't take it out on the poor woman. Instead, he felt sorry for her and had his own wife look after her for the time being. Daily, he sat in his office and fumed, trying to figure out how to get revenge and even. Thus, when the call came from Commander Werner of the Hub Intelligence Division, he was all ears.

"I'll do it, but the telepaths are mine," he bargained. He was amazed the Commander agreed to his stipulation. He then said, "What about your Field Agent?"

Commander Werner replied, "She's just a woman. Do what you like or send her back. Best not to harm too badly the two linguists. That could cause us difficulties." Just what those difficulties would be, Severino didn't know or care. This commander only wanted the ship intact. In his mind, this sounded too good to be true.

Having just been cheated out of ten million, Severino did his own checking, dropping by the Alcalde's office to check up on the aliens, who were due to arrive sometime in the next week. There, he was able to verify there were quite a number of telepaths onboard. Satisfied Commander Werner was telling the truth about these aliens from the Imperium, Severino set about making his plans, assigning one of his thugs to keep an eye on the spaceport and another one to watch the Alcalde's home, since they were supposed to be paying them a visit.

At last, his men reported they had arrived. Unfortunately, they were nearly always in the company of the Alcalde's wife, complicating matters. "Okay, Zuzana, I need you to do one more thing for me. After that, I'll see that you are set free and taken care of. Will you stop your crying and do this for me. It's a simple thing."

"Who will take care of me?" she whimpered.

"I'll find a very nice woman and a nice house. That's the least I can do for you. All right?" He sensed her in his mind, and quickly he imagined a pretty house with a kindly old woman to look after her needs.

"All right then. Just this once," Zuzana whimpered. "Just don't hit me."

"Have I ever hit you?" he replied, his ire rising. He'd done many things in his life, but he'd never hit a woman physically.

"I can't tell. I can't see anything."

"Well, I haven't. Now get to work. The alcalde's wife, Elena. I need to know where she plans on taking her visitors tomorrow," he repeated his request.

After several minutes, Zuzana whispered, "To the Natural History Museum to see the pre-human. You promised me."

"I know. It'll take me a few days to arrange things. Be patient a little longer." He headed out to go to his office. He had plans to arrange and only one night to make his preparations.

The third day of our visit, we spent quite some time sorting out our new dresses, deciding what to wear today. Elena had promised to take us to see this pre-human skeleton, and she could get us access to the ancient records that had accompanied the remains when they were brought here to Centauri-C-C. We also realized Elena was right. She did need a whole lot more time to get herself dressed and ready to go. While she donned a simple robe to help fix breakfast for her family and us, she then had to get dressed up in her professional woman's outfit. As the Alcalde's wife, she had to look good when she was out in the public's eyes. Still, what with our lengthy decisions on what to wear, we timed it about right.

"The museum is not too far. Is it okay if we walk there?"

Elena asked.

I dreaded walking a long way in these six-inch heels, but agreed. If she could do it, so could we. We left around ten that morning, strolling along the streets of her city. She pointed out several interesting places we should visit, if we had the time. The day was warm and the air, fresh, though filled with traces of oil and machinery, pleasant enough. Around eleven, we strolled slowly into the museum, where she had worked as a teenager, when she was studying archaeology. Unerringly, Elena led us through the many corridors to the exhibit.

"It does look like the similar one on Vegan-C," Molly Maud stated, "but then I'm not an expert on old bones."

Elena chuckled. "Come. I'll take you down to the records department."

Just as we turned to leave the room, someone tossed a gas grenade into the room. Billowing smoke rapidly flooded the room. While I tried to hold my breath and head for an exit, I moved too slowly in these heels and had to gasp for air. One inhale was all that it took. I felt dizzy and darkness swept over me. I didn't even know I'd collapsed onto the floor along with everyone else. None of us saw several men enter wearing masks and pushing garbage bins. We didn't feel them lifting each of us up and depositing us into the bins. Nor did we sense being rolled out of the museum, hoisted into a truck, and driven away. All I saw was the blackness of unconsciousness.

Then, I began hearing a whimpering woman's voice. "Hello. Is anyone there? Please. Is anyone there? I hear breathing so you must be. I need help. Please, is anyone there?" She continued to whimper more or less the same thing. Groggy, I opened my eyes and blinked several times, trying to clear the haze from my eyes. I felt bindings again and blinked all the harder. At last, I could see and heard others rousing, mingled with the incessant whimpering from the other woman.

At last, my vision cleared and I gasped noticeably. We were in some warehouse, empty except for nine chairs arranged in a semi-circle so we could see each other. I saw the source of the whimpering voice, a woman around our age. A rope was wrapped around her waist, holding her securely to her chair. Her legs were also tied together. What caused my initial gasp was the fact that she had no hands. Then, I also saw her eyes were gone. She was also blind.

I glanced at my own body's situation and gasped again. My left hand was gone. The wrapping was lying in a pile with many others off to one side, but my hand wasn't in sight. A rope held my waist to the chair, while another rope bound my feet tightly together at the ankles. My arms were tied together at my elbows and lying in my lap so I could get a good view of my new stump. Gasps came from all around me. One quick glance and I saw we were all in a similar position. Further, everyone in my group had their left hand removed! (Well, Jovanna had already lost hers.)

Hearing our gasping sounds, the door opened, and a man in a grey suit walked in. He had a triumphant look on his face. Molly Maud screamed, and Marilyn and Gabrielle lost it and joined her briefly, causing the whimpering woman to call out even more loudly than before.

The man yelled, "Ladies, shut up!" His bark did the trick. Silence.

Elena cried out next, "Severino? Severino Tono? Is that you? Help us. Someone kidnaped us."

Severino laughed, "That would be me, Elena. Now shut up. I have important business to handle. Okay you telepaths. You now belong to me. As long as you obey me and work for me, you'll be well treated. If you resist, I'll remove your other hand. If you still don't work properly for me, I'll remove your eyes, like Zuzana over there. Got it?"

"Yes," I said quietly. Since Elena knew this man, any number of theories raced through my fuzzy mind. I needed more data and time to recover from the knockout drug.

"Good. Now, I understand there are more of your telepaths on your ship. I want you to contact them and have them open the ship's door and go to Elena's home, where my men will be waiting for them. They'll then come join you. One big happy family."

Elena barked, "My kids are there! Don't you dare harm them!"

150

"I said shut up, Elena. You keep quiet, and the kids will be okay."

"Why should they leave the ship's door open? That's against protocols," I spoke up, fishing for more information. I know, I could have just kill this thug right now, but perhaps, I could find out who was really behind all this. At the very least, now that Molly Maud had been mutilated, she deserved to know, if I could find out. I could use my skills to force it out of him, but it would be better for her to hear it herself. More believable.

"Cause they want the ship. I want you telepaths. He screwed me out of ten million gold dollars for that pathetic wimp over there, the blind one. She's a basket case, but still a telepath, pretty useless right now though. You cooperate with me, and you'll get rich and live fine lives."

"We're cooperating, but who wants our ship? Don't you? We're aliens you know. Our ship doesn't use the same fuel Federation ships use. I don't think there is anywhere around here to refuel," I rattled on, playing dumb on him.

Severino laughed. "No harm telling you. Commander Werner Kettlebohn of the Hub Intelligence Division. He wants the ship and so does her father, the famous industrialist Hermann Porsche. Those two have been fighting over it ever since you entered Federation space. Looks like old Werner beat your father to it. Both of them are utter fools. The real prize is you telepaths. Do you realize each one of you telepaths is worth at least ten million dollars, maybe more if you act nice and cooperate? When you put your skills to work, the sky's the limit on how much cash you can make, more than enough to keep you women in the finest clothes and heels money can buy. Cooperate and you'll be extremely wealthy women."

I heard Molly Maud's sharp inhale when he mentioned her boss and her father. So I decided to pump him a wee bit more. "Sir, what about Molly Maud? She's a Field Agent. Then there are these two linguists and the Alcalde's wife, Elena here. What about them? They aren't telepaths."

Severino laughed again. Werner said I can dispose of Molly Maud, but I have to keep the two linguists alive and healthy. We don't want an international incident with their worlds. He'll probably return them to their home worlds. As far as Elena is concerned, as long as she behaves, she'll live a little longer, at least until we have the rest of your crew rounded up at her place. She behaves and her kids will live. After that, she can join Molly Maud. We'll arrange a little accident." Again, I heard sharp inhales from both women.

As far as I was concerned, I had heard all I wanted to know. I turned to look at Molly Maud. Her face was stark white, shocked beyond words. Not only had her boss turned on her but had been using her all along. Even worse, her own father was in on it. That she was about to be killed probably also had something to do with her shock. Time to act.

Anya, have you gotten all this recorded, I sent to her, more than pleased. After our last narrow escape, she and Tesla had worked up this spy technology apparatus. I had a small video camera disguised as a hairpin.

Got it. Video is good, but the audio is spot on. We were unable to track you in time to prevent them from cutting off your hand. Sorry about that. You doing okay?

Yes, I'm taking him out now. Contact you shortly. I focused and used my telekinesis powers to yank his d-gun out of his hand, tossing it across the warehouse. Then, I levitated him up to the ceiling. "I'll hold him up. Marisol, you keep alert for anyone else coming to his aid. The rest of you, see if you can get us untied somehow. Oh, Molly Maud, Anya has made a complete recording of all this, video and audio. It ought to be enough to convict all three men."

"What? What? Anya? How? Yes, if I had that recording, I could bring them to justice," Molly Maud stammered, not totally believing me.

"Spy camera in my hair. Tesla and Anya worked it up after that mess on Vegan-C. They recorded everything. Please, get us untied somehow."

"Jana's on it, boss. Don't distract her. She had a cutter concealed in her bra. These uncomfortable things do have their uses. Give her time to levitate it out. Kind of a tight fit," Jovanna said softly, trying not to distract her sister.

"Someone's coming," Marisol whispered. We all sat still, but the moment that the doors opened and two thugs stuck their heads in to confer with their boss, Marisol and Jovanna struck, sending a powerful blast of energy into their minds. The result was semi-liquid brain matter, much like one would get by placing it in a microwave for a couple of minutes. Both men dropped to the floor very dead. "I'm back on watch duty," she whispered.

"What — what happened to those two men?" Elena whispered.

"Dead," I whispered back. "Don't worry; we'll get to your children soon. I'm sure they'll be all right. Trust us." She took a deep breath, but there was a heavy grief catch in it. Elena was really scared for her two children.

Jovanna whispered, "Okay, I'm free. I've the cutter now. Have you all free soon." Using her good hand, she began cutting Jana's bindings and then moved on down the line of us. She cut the blind woman free last.

As soon as Elena was free, I asked her, "Elena, is there any way you can contact Ruperto and get the police here to arrest Severino?"

"Yes, if I can find my purse. I've got my phone in it."

"Okay. Start hunting around. It's probably around here somewhere," I said hopefully. She rose but was still a little wobbly. She began walking around the spacious warehouse.

"Oh god!" she exclaimed.

"What?" Marisol called out.

"Just found your hands. Awful. Sorry."

"That's okay. Keep looking," Marisol said, so that I could keep focusing on holding Severino high in the air. I had half a notion just to drop him and be done with it, but I sensed that Elena wanted justice.

"Found it. Calling him now." We heard her part of their frantic exchange. A bit later, we heard sirens, and I began lowering the still fighting Severino, who had no idea what was happening to him. Not long after that a very worried Ruperto came rushing into the warehouse along with a dozen uniformed men, their local security men or police as they called them.

"Oh dear god!" Ruperto exclaimed, as he saw our missing left hands and us. He turned to stare at his onetime friend, Severino. "How could you?"

"They are telepaths, you fool, worth a giant fortune! Let me go, and we can work something out."

"Take him away and lock him up. Throw away the key while you are at it!" Ruperto yelled at the police, who smiled and obliged. "Elena, I sent a dozen more to our house. The kids are fine. Arrested the six men there. They didn't want to put up a fight." He hugged Elena and then kissed her stump, honoring her sacrifice as he had done every day since they were married.

He turned to me, "I'm so terribly sorry! This should never have happened."

"Hey, we got the goods on those behind it. Let's get out of here," I replied.

Whimpering sounds reminded me of the other woman, Zuzana. "Sorry Zuzana. We forgot about you. You are coming with us. We'll take good care of you," I called out to the poor woman.

"I have her, boss," Jovanna said, walking over to her and helping her up. "It will be all right. I've still got one hand, so I can help you some. Put your arm around me. Right, just feel for me. Good. I'm wearing tall heels so let's go slow. I'll guide you, Zuzana. You are one brave woman," Jovanna chatted encouragingly to the terrified woman.

An hour later, escorted home by many policemen, we followed a still worried Elena and Ruperto into their home. Their two children came running up, nearly knocking Elena over. It's hard keeping your balance on such tall heels. She finally broke down, sobbing for joy. Just then, their temporary cook came walking into the room. "What's all the excitement about? Lunch is ready. Police were here and arrested six men, who said they were waiting for you to return. Oh my, what happened to your guests?" she exclaimed, suddenly seeing all of our missing left hands.

Normalcy is just what the doctor ordered. We all sat down for lunch. Elena explained everything that had happened, more or less. She didn't have any reasonable explanations for some of the things that she had seen, preferring to call them magic tricks that worked. We allowed her to do all of the talking, knowing from Basic Therapy that this was good for her. Since she wasn't actually harmed, her trauma was mostly fright and the knockout drug.

When the long lunch was finished, Ruperto left to go to the police station to make sure Severino was properly handled. Elena put the kids down for their afternoon nap and then came to us. "Look, I know this is awful for you. The least I can do is to share all of the tricks I have learned with this," she raised her handless left arm up. Dressing is a real chore with only one hand to do it. Even going to the bathroom poses problems. Come on; let me do this for you."

Considering the mess we were in, I thought this would be a very good idea. We spent the afternoon watching how Elena did something and then trying to emulate her. "Always use your left arm. It's nothing to be ashamed of or embarrassed by. Use it. It makes a great holder-in-placer. Getting our nylons on is the hardest of all to do. Here's how I do it." Unfortunately, Marilyn and her six-inch nails on her right hand simply couldn't do it by herself, not without ripping them.

"I don't want to cut them," she wailed, "then I'll look like a freak or something."

"There, there, Marilyn, don't give up. We just have to work out another way for you to do it," Elena bravely said. It was a very long afternoon as we seven tried to come to grips with our missing hands.

During this time, Zuzana was sleeping. Over lunch, we noticed she was malnourished along with being an emotional wreck and physically abused. Jovanna fed her well and then got her into a bed. The poor woman slept all afternoon, but awoke at suppertime and needed help once more. She was also filthy and her hair matted. When supper was done, Elena volunteered to give her a good scrubbing, while we rummaged through our new clothes to find some that would fit her. We used some from Molly Maud, Gabrielle, and Marilyn. Our busts were way too large for the woman.

Jovanna soon headed off to assist Elena in giving Zuzana a good bath. Secondarily, she wanted to see what physical damage Zuzana's body currently had and to heal what she could. *I sense you. You feel good to me*, Zuzana sent.

I know. I'm checking your body for injuries and will try to help heal them. You are among friendly, good telepaths now, Zuzana. You'll never be mistreated ever again. I swear to you. She did sense Zuzana's relief. Elena was surprised to see so many of the ugly bruises disappearing while she was bathing the woman. It took the pair of them nearly two hours to get Zuzana truly cleaned up and her hair thoroughly washed. She had no idea when it was last washed or brushed out.

As they were drying her off, I joined them and added my own touches to help heal her bruises. She did have a cracked rib, but Jovanna had already handled that detail. By the time we had her hair dried, all traces of her bruises were gone, much to the surprise of Elena. While Elena began gently brushing out her hair, Jovanna and I practiced what we'd learned during our afternoon session with Elena, dressing her with the borrowed clothes.

"We're dressing you up in a professional woman's dress. Is that okay with you?" I explained.

"Sure. I once liked nice dresses," Zuzana admitted. I described each item and its color, as Jovanna and I struggled some to get them on her.

"Use your stumps more. Don't be shy about them," Elena kept on coaching us. "They won't bite or hurt. Yes, use them to hold it steady. Make them work for you."

"It's hard," Jovanna admitted.

"Well yes, I recall it was at first, but you just keep at it. Never back off from using it every way you can," Elena advised. "My Zuzana, you have really long, lovely blonde hair. It hasn't been cut in ages has it?"

"I can't remember when it was last cut. Long time," Zuzana admitted. "I can't tell time any more. I can't do anything anymore." I knew she was sitting in the middle of a huge amount of grief, but now wasn't the time to handle it.

"I've got very long hair myself. I just love it long. Yours is so pretty, Zuzana. Now that Elena's got it brushed out so nicely, can you feel it down your legs? It'll fall to the back of your knees. You really are a very pretty young woman, Zuzana.

Never let anyone tell you different."

She flashed us the first smile ever. However, now that we had her dressed, we had a shoe problem. The only ones we had were the six-inch pumps. Elena's feet were much smaller than Zuzana's. "Well, the only problem we have, Zuzana is the heels. All that we have right now that will fit you are the same ones we are wearing. They have six-inch heels. Very sexy, but hard to walk in."

"I can try if someone helps me. I once saw heels such as these must be. Do they match my dress?" Zuzana asked.

"Absolutely. There, now you do look like the rest of us, a professional woman, Zuzana," I said.

"Really? I feel good. Thank you all. My body isn't aching anymore either."

"Come on. Let's get you up and walking around so you can get used to the heels. Take small steps," I advised.

I've never been around a blind person before so all this was new to me as well as Jovanna. Zuzana ignored the difficulty she was having dealing with the heels. She simply felt like a woman again, something she hadn't felt for many years. We led her out into the living room where everyone else was listening to the newscast reporting our kidnaping, mutilations, and the arrest of the culprit. Considering Severino was one of the wealthiest men in Cordoban, this was news.

"Wow! Look at Zuzana! She looks positively stunning!" Jana called out. Her sister alerted her, and she poured out the praise we felt Zuzana needed to hear.

"Really?" Zuzana whispered.

"Really. You are a knockout. Love your long blonde hair. Elena has worked a miracle on it. You look just like us now, a real professional woman, Zuzana," Jana exclaimed.

Now, Zuzana really did break into a broad smile. She ran her arms up and down her body, feeling for her hair. Finding it, she smiled even more. We helped her sit down. "So where are you from?" I asked what we needed to know.

The smile vanished. "I — I don't know. I was on a farm. I was only thirteen. Then the men came and took me away during the night. That's all I know."

"That's okay, Zuzana. So you don't know your planet. At

least you know your name."

"Zuzana Ruzickovana."

"Linguists, little help here," I asked.

"It could be Slavic or Russian," Marilyn spoke up. "Zuzana, I'm going to say a couple sentences in each. Let me know if you recognize any of the words. Don't use telepathy to understand them. We are trying to figure out your native language. Obviously, you can speak Spanish but with a thick accent. Okay?"

"Sure."

The linguists rattled off quite a few with many variations. Her native language turned out to be Slavic, amazingly similar to that found on Metcalf-4! We were making some headway.

"Even if you can find where I come from, I can't go back there. Bad men will just come and take me away again," Zuzana whimpered.

As far as I was concerned, that was it. She didn't want to go home, wherever that may be. "Okay, Zuzana. We'll take you with us to our world, where there a lot of us telepaths around. How's that sound?"

She brightened up again. "Very good. Please, take me with you. You are kind. I want to look like a professional woman too." Now, I understood her better. She was stolen away while she was just a child and horribly mistreated. She still had the mind of a child. She needed all the Basic Therapy we could give her. For that matter, all of us now did, particularly our three hosts. I knew right then I simply could not take the three back to their home worlds without getting them their Basic Therapy somehow, someway.

"Well, we had all best head to bed. It's getting late," I suggested.

"True. Zuzana, you can sleep with me and my sister," Jovanna insisted. "Come on; up you go." Both had to help her get up. Zuzana was wholly unused to the extreme heel height. Slowly, the three headed off to their guest bedroom, while the rest of us followed.

"I can hear my heels and yours too. They must be really sexy, but it's hard to walk in them. Is it so for you?" Zuzana asked, innocently.

"Yes, we have to watch our steps too. We're watching them for you. After all, you have to look as a professional woman too," Jana replied. Zuzana grinned broadly. Jana could not help think about her own robbed youth. The Slavers had ruined her life completely, until I and my friends arrived at the Slaver's town. We had salvaged her and given her back her life. Now, she and her sister fully intended to pay it back with Zuzana.

We had to stay in Cordoban for several more days, assisting their legal personnel with the highest profile criminal case ever brought in their city. Ruperto was both apologetic and sympathetic towards us. "Nothing like this has ever occurred in Cordoban. I'm so sorry. Whatever can we do to make this up to you and your people? And to think he was my friend for so many years. I had no idea." After a while, I grew tired of this and just wanted their legal proceedings to wrap up.

What I thought more interesting, no one said a word about the two dead thugs in the warehouse. Instead, the focus was on Severino Tono and what he'd done. While I expected he would be charged and convicted of kidnaping us and mutilating our hands, surprisingly those became completely minor charges. Everyone focused on his abuse of their Mano Cortada marriage tradition! This was the serious crime for which he was convicted on the third day. At least their justice system moved swiftly. We watched in disbelief as he was ordered to pay each of us a million gold dollars, which he hastily arranged, a total of six million. Since Molly Maud, Gabrielle, and Marilyn already had Federation accounts, the sum was directly deposited in theirs. I accepted the funds for Jana, Marisol, and me, since those two didn't have an account here. That done, Severino was then officially declared an outcast to be shunned by everyone under penalty of arrest. The man walked out of their Justice Office a free man!

"Well, that's that. Justice is served," Ruperto declared, as we all walked out together. "See, Centauri-C-C justice is swift and effective.

Jana was fuming. "You mean that's all the punishment

that he gets? We have to live like this," she waved her left arm around, "and he just pays a fine?"

"No, he's shunned. No one will do business with him again. He cannot even purchase groceries. He will have to leave Centauri-C-C somehow, probably on some foreign transport ship, since none of ours will take him. He is ruined here. Perhaps, he can start a new life on some other world," Ruperto explained.

This did nothing to defuse Jana's ire. I sensed the same anger from the others too. They had a strange sense of justice from our point of view. Fortunately, Jana kept her cool and said nothing more. Back at the del Gotto home, we packed our things and said our farewells, promising to stay in touch. Elena had our comm center frequency and could call us any time. Ruperto arranged for a fancy bus to take us all back to the spaceport, and we were only too glad to walk up that ramp, though Jana and Jovanna had some difficulty assisting Zuzana up the ramp.

Martina took charge of us once we were onboard. "To the medical lab, all of you. Danika will lift us off of this perverted world!"

"Why? We're fine, sort of," Marilyn asked. We headed there anyway as Martina explained that she wanted to use our medical machine to prepare everyone's stumps for a prosthesis. "But those mechanical hands are pretty much useless," she protested a little.

"We are going to get you all Imperium prosthesis. They work electronically, picking up your nerve signals as though it was your real hand," she explained, breaking down her protest and allowing a tiny ray of hope to sprout. Still, Martina could sense the overwhelming sense of loss and grief she was bravely suppressing. Like me, Martina knew that somehow we needed to give these women Basic Therapy and soon. Zuzana was another matter. Blind, prostheses would not help since she would have no feeling in the artificial hands, but Martina went ahead and did her two stumps as well, if only to make the woman feel like she was now one of us.

I felt the ship liftoff and relaxed, letting Martina handle things while I pondered the best action to take next. Molly

Maud interrupted me though. "I need to contact my people and file charges against dad and Commander Werner. This has to be done right away before they try anything else." I had my doubts after seeing Centauri-C-C justice.

Jana wasn't through with Severino though. While waiting her turn at the medical machine, she focused and swept her attention back over the world that we'd left, locating Severino. No one saw a sly grin appear on her face when she found him. She took control of his body and walked it to the warehouse where the Mano Cortada machine was still being kept. The shocked and frightened man was unable to control his own body. Worse, as he saw his body moving of its own accord up to the machine, he tried to scream for help, but Jana tightened his vocal cords so only a guttural noise came out. The panic-stricken man saw his own left hand being inserted into the machine and the lid closed. Again and again, he tried to regain control of his body, to open that lid, to save his hand, all to no avail. The lid opened, and he pulled out his left stump. Then, his right hand went into the machine. He fought against it with every bit of his will power, but Jana's will was steel. His right arm came out missing its hand as well. Only then did she let go of the man who had maimed her and us. A hideous scream filled the space of that warehouse, but no one heard it. Later, Jana told us she had obtained real justice for us, bringing a sense of relief to our three guests.

Chapter 9 Above the Law

"Yes, I want to bring all manner of formal charges against my father, Hermann Porsche, and against my boss, Commander Werner Kettlebohn. They have been trying to steal the Eagle's Seed and kidnap the telepath crew. I have proof. I'm sending along video files that show dad's men trying to break into the ship and Commander Werner's men doing the same thing. Plus, I have the video confession of the man they hired. He kidnaped us, cut off our left hands, all to force the telepaths to work for him, while Commander Werner's men were to steal the then empty Eagle's Seed. This is high treason at least," Field Agent Molly Maud explained politely, but somehow managing to hold her seething anger at bay. She was talking to the Prosecutor General of Cass-C, the highest legal official on her world.

"These are very serious charges you are making, Field Agent Porsche. I do hope you have this proof," the man barked.

"Sending the many files now," she replied. "Watch them and see for yourself. A little digging into their financial records will also prove how much they paid their thugs to carry out these actions."

"Very good, Field Agent Porsche. Files are coming through now. I'll review them and get back to you. Over and out."

Molly Maud sat back and rubbed her conical stump, imagining her fingers were still there. She fought back some tears. *Not now. Not until this is all done, and I get them,* she stoically thought, suppressing her seething emotions, but barely.

Meanwhile, I also called Emperor Bino and told him what had happened. We also discussed the Planet of Origin situation and all of the correlated results we'd found. He replied, "I'm now totally convinced our ancestors came from worlds within the Federation of Planets. They are in a sense our relatives. Yet, I am bothered by the overall decadence of these far older civilizations. Still, they currently possess the strongest military force in the galaxy, what with the dissolution of the Imperium. What are your plans now? Going to look for the actual planet among the Forbidden List? Over."

"We are going to see how Agent Molly Maud's charges play out. Then, we do need to get them Basic Therapy. After all, they were harmed while in our service. Over."

"I agree. We can see how their justice works. It should be an interesting commentary on the Federation, knowledge, which we must have. Thus far, I have not made a decision on their request to have the designs for Hans' modified hyperdrive system. Keep me posted. Over and out."

Judicious of him, I thought. Although perhaps his not giving up those plans had forced Commander Werner and Hermann to take the more extreme measures that they did to acquire this new technology. Still, that was only justification.

I tried to relax and get more used to life without my left hand. In spite of Elena's coaching, everything was just damned difficult. You don't realize how much you need both hands until you miss one of them. While she had a point — that we should not be embarrassed about it and use it in the most optimum ways we could, it didn't solve the awful awkwardness that accompanied so much of what I did. Yet, that was really what it was awkwardness, a far, far cry from being handless like poor Zuzana was or like being armless from the genetic bio agent. It was more annoying to me than anything else was.

The next day, Field Agent Molly Maud received her answer from the Prosecutor General. He called her and set up a four-way conference call. I joined her to help back her up. The screen divided into three side-by-side windows. The Prosecutor General faced her from one window. Her father faced her from another window, while her boss Commander Werner faced her from the third window. I didn't like how this was proceeding at all!

"Field Agent Molly Maud, I have very, very carefully reviewed the video testimony you sent me yesterday. Indeed, it is most compelling, quite damning. I then sent it to Hermann and Werner and asked them about the veracity of these charges," the Prosecutor General explained, choosing his words carefully. "Commander Werner and Hermann would like to state their views for the official record. Commander Werner, go ahead."

Our eyes shifted to the next window. "Field Agent Molly Maud. I'm sorry about the loss of your hand. That said, the rest of your accusations against me are fundamentally correct. Obtaining either the plans for the new hyperdrive or a ship with it installed is absolutely critical for the survival of the entire Federation of Planets. Imagine the horrific disadvantage we would be in should the Imperium forces, which have this new hyperdrive, decide once again to wage war against us. We would be nearly defenseless. With this kind of speed, they could sweep into anywhere within the Federation, strike a killing blow, and be gone long before our ships could arrive to counter them. Our Federation could very easily be brought to its knees. So yes, I'm doing everything possible to get this new technology for the Federation."

He went on, "And yes, I have been working with Hermann Porsche as well, since his companies would be manufacturing these new drives. He wants this technology as much as I do. It is regrettable you've lost your hand in the line of duty, but you knew the risks involved in being a Field Agent. Be thankful you are still alive. Hermann," he nodded and ended.

Hermann cleared his throat, clearly disgusted with his renegade daughter. "Commander Werner is correct. I, we, the Federation simply must have this new hyperdrive. The why is as plain as the nose on your face. Anyone can see why we must have it. Further, since my industries manufactures all the hyperdrive engines in use in all Federation war ships, think of the damage that could be done to my industries if some other company obtained the new engine. We'd have complete chaos and incompatibilities in the very engines of the spaceships upon which the entire security of the Federation rests. I have no choice but to do everything in my power to obtain this new hyperdrive engine. The loss of your hand is on your shoulders. I told you repeatedly to get married, but no, you had to go and join the Intelligence Division. Now, you've paid the price. Prosecutor General," he wrapped up.

The Prosecutor General then spoke again. "So you see, Agent Molly Maud, these men are not denying any of your charges."

"Then have them arrested and put on trial for what they did," Molly Maud cried out vehemently. Her voice was acid cold, as she glared at her father and then her boss.

The Prosecutor General smiled coyly. "I'm sorry, Agent Molly Maud, but legally there has been no crime committed here by either party."

"What?" she screamed at the top of her lungs, before I could send her calming emotional waves.

"That's right. Do you not agree Captain Nia Elain and her crew are aliens to the Federation?" the Prosecutor General asked calmly, ignoring her fiery outburst.

"Well yes. They are Imperium citizens from Ashford-5, Ataro Empire," she replied.

"There you have it. There is no law anywhere in the Federation that prohibits any and all kinds of actions against aliens to our worlds. Kidnaping aliens isn't a crime. Even mutilating them isn't or killing them. Certainly stealing their advanced technology isn't a crime, technology, which we vitally need for our own survival, militarily and commercially. Think how devastating it would be to our interplanetary commerce if suddenly Imperium traders began moving our cargo at speeds five times faster than our ships can go. I'm sorry, but while the evidence is most damning, none of it is against any of our laws, with the sole exception of the mutilations of the two linguists. I have Hermann's and Werner's sworn statements made under oath that they did not in any way order this Severino Tono fellow to do what he did to these women. I checked with Centauri-C-C and found this man has already been tried and convicted of that crime. That case is closed."

Molly Maud looked positively crushed. All she could say softly was, "So they are above the law."

The Prosecutor General replied, "There is no law concerning the aliens for them to be above. I must dismiss all the charges that you have brought against both men. Case closed. Over and out." His window closed.

"You are hereby fired, ex-Field Agent Molly Maud Porsche," Commander Werner declared without the slightest emotion. His window closed.

"Don't bother coming home," Hermann grumbled and his window closed, leaving a blank screen facing Molly Maud, who just stared at it in utter silence. I wisely said nothing, giving her time to come to grips with what just happened. After a couple silent minutes, Molly Maud slumped in her chair and tears came uncontrollably. Once more, I just let her be. Sometimes, crying is the best medicine. I sent Danika a message. *Dear, set course for Ashford-5 at top speed. Don't announce it yet.*

Amid her sobs, she said repeatedly, "Above the law. I can't believe it. They are above the law. They got away with it." I let her cry for nearly a half hour. At last, she rubbed her eyes on her blouse and looked up at me.

"You did well, Molly Maud. I understand. Come on. We're heading to Ashford-5 for a brief stop. We have this thing called Basic Therapy. It is simply amazing stuff, removing all the trauma a person has suffered. Plus, we all have to get some really good prosthetic hands. Between you and me, I don't think this conflict is over yet. You may have just lost the first round, but there are more rounds to come, and we're on your side." That cheered her up some.

I then announced over the intercom, "Everyone, we are officially heading for Ashford-5 for a break. Some of us need hands and Basic Therapy. We'll regroup for a time. Be there in about five hours. Can't wait to see my kids."

"Five hours?" Molly Maud asked, trying to grasp everything. "I thought Ashford-5 was on the outer rim of your arm."

"It is. We are now making use of our new top speed. Uses maximum fuel. We're going nearly three-quarters across the whole darn galaxy. Impressive speed," I answered.

"That's — that's unreal," she exclaimed. "I had no idea it could go this fast."

"We didn't have any need for speed before. Now we do. I'm not taking what's been done to us and you three lying down. We regroup and figure this one out. Come on; we've just got time to grab some lunch."

"I can't feel anything with it, though," Molly Maud commented, as she made the fingers wiggle on her new, top of the line prosthetic hand. We'd landed and the two queens took us at once to the Imperial Castle. They were prepared to handle our needs immediately. Thus, Molly Maud, Gabrielle, Marilyn, Jana, Jovanna, Marisol, and I found ourselves whisked to the med lab, where were checked up and now fitted with the very latest in artificial hands. I wiggled my fingers too.

"It's amazing, they do sort of seem to do what I want the fingers to do," she said while continuing to move her fingers. "It's so strange. I can't actually feel anything with them. I can see what she means; we have to be careful with them to avoid knocking things over."

"Let's see if we can pick up some silverware with them," I suggested.

"Weird. I can't feel the fork," Gabrielle commented. "This is hard. Oh, there I got it. No, I dropped it. Well, maybe this will somehow sort of work," she said softly. I sighed. No getting around the fact that life was going to be more problematical for the seven of us.

Zuzana insisted on not being parted from Jana and Jovanna, and she sat quietly listening to our conversation about our new hands. I knew she wanted hands too, but they would be useless to her since her prime sense was now touch. I think she also realized this. More importantly, she was still recovering. Her overly thin body was craving food now, and we were feeding her frequently, trying to get some meat back on her frame. She would need that before she could get the intense therapy that I knew she desperately needed.

With our new hands working properly, we were then assigned a therapy giver and headed into our private sessions. Meanwhile, our many doctors and geneticists worked on Zuzana, overriding her wishes to sit beside Jana or Jovanna while they got their therapy sessions. The first thing they decided to do was to put her whole body into the machine. When they took her out of it an hour later, her body had been fully healed and restored. She looked a thousand times better and commented, "Somehow, I do feel lots better. I think I have more energy."

"Yes, you certainly do," Doctor Leann replied.

"Do I still look like a professional woman? I must. Jana and Jovanna do, and I must look like them," she said innocently.

"Of course you do. Now, let's get some food in you and into your first Basic Therapy session too, just like Jana and Jovanna are getting." That brought a smile to her face.

Jana, Jovanna, Marisol, and I spent about a week in rehab, working with our new hands, getting therapy sessions, and thoroughly enjoying our families and children, who were more than eager to see us. Zorina and Nadia just had to see and touch my stump and play with my new hand. Then, our kids wanted to hear all about our great adventure. Danika laughed and began telling them about it. For me, this was one terrific pleasure week. How I missed our children.

What pleased me the most was that Rafe herself handled Zuzana's therapy. "Nothing but the very best for her!" was Jana's comment to me when we found out Rafe was running Zuzana's sessions. I also knew it was going to take weeks for her to recover fully from the extensive brutalities she'd suffered.

After about two weeks, Marilyn, Gabrielle, and Molly Maud finished their Basic Therapy. I had three very much alive young women on my hands now. It was time to discuss the next step for these three. We held a chat between them, Emperor Bino, our two queens, and myself.

"Look, Marilyn and I want to publish this definitive linguistic database within the Federation," Gabrielle pointed out. "It's really needed the more contact we have with your worlds."

Via the comm center, Emperor Bino said, "I believe that is a most excellent project. I will back you financially. When you get back to your worlds, whatever equipment and support you need, I'll find a way to supply it." Both women were extremely pleased and ready to head back and get started on it. He added, "Once you have it done, I expect that you'll both become rather wealthy." They giggled.

"Now then, the more difficult matter," I broke in. "We need to help Molly Maud out."

Emperor Bino interrupted me. "Yes, we most definitely do, Captain Nia Elain. I know just how to do it. Molly Maud, you no longer want revenge do you?"

She tossed her hair back a little and laughed. "No, not revenge. But things simply must change and for the better."

"Agreed. I can think of no better way to counter them than for you to flourish, to prosper far beyond anything they could ever imagine. What would you say if I gave you and your new company the sole rights to the new hyperdrive in the Federation? All that your company would have to do really is a small retrofit. I'm told by my engineers that it's not that big a deal."

Molly Maud's eyes opened wide. "Sir, I'd have every spaceship in the Federation knocking at my door to get it. Oh! I see what you mean. My company would effectively compete with dad's. It might even cost him an enormous amount of business. Hurt him where it matters, his damned bank account. Show him women are not second-class people. This would be fantastic. Count me in. I've now got some startup money from the Severino settlement."

"Indeed you do. It'll take more than that to get you firmly established. I do hope you can handle an explosive growth business," he teased her. "I will, of course, assist you financially as well. I've been studying the legal laws of the Federation of Planets in some detail. I believe if you file the proper legal papers, you'll be untouchable."

The discussions continued for nearly an hour, ironing out the many details. After that, we prepared to depart once more. Emperor Bino insisted we stay close to Molly Maud until her company was fully established, providing "protection" as only we could provide. However, before we departed, Jana and Jovanna had to let Zuzana know about this.

Fortunately, Zuzana's sessions were going very well, and she felt far more comfortable in her new surroundings. Plus, the doctors and geneticists had devised a plan that might truly help the woman. When I accompanied Jana and Jovanna to meet with Zuzana, I was quite surprised to hear what that plan actually was.

Doctor Leann explained it in simple terms. I wasn't ready for the heavy genetics side of it. "As she now is physically, she can't have much of a life. So with her permission, we are going to expose her to that genetic bio agent."

"What?" I exclaimed a little shocked.

"Once she's been modified, we're going to subject her to the same massive cures that we did for you. At the very least, she'll have her arms and hands back. The geneticists are also hoping the process will also restore her damaged eyes," Leann explained.

I relaxed. "Well, becoming an hermaphrodite is a small price to pay to have your hands and eyes back. Honestly, if it works, she truly will have her life back."

"Yes, that's the idea. She's agreed to it, but just between us, I don't think she really has a clue about it. Her education is marginal at best. If she comes through with eyesight, we can then get her on a crash course of learning," Doctor Leann added.

Now, I did feel very relieved. Zuzana would be well taken care of while we were gone. I had hoped to be spending a long time with our daughters, but I still owed Molly Maud. Besides, I really did want to help do something about the plight of women within the Federation of Planets.

Chapter 10 Changes Come

Late August 1381, the Eagle's Seed took off once more, but made a short stop on Winno-3 to pick up six engineers and a large amount of supplies that Molly Maud would need to get started on the retrofits. After departing Winno-3, once more I used top speed, dropping off Marilyn on Capella-D six hours later and then Gabrielle on Benard-D not long after that.

We went more slowly to Cass-C, timing it so we would arrive just after nine, when the legal offices opened for business. We dressed for our roles on this world, the professional woman. Wearing similar grey skirts, white silk blouses, a matching grey blazer, and of course black pumps with their requisite tall, spiked heels, Molly Maud, Martina, and I walked into the Legal and Professional Building shortly after nine. She carried her precious briefcase with the signed legal forms Emperor Bino had provided and authorized. Our heels clicking in unison, we three marched into the building with polished granite floors. Glass and steel formed the superstructure of this impressive building.

She stopped at the information desk and got directions, then led us to the elevators. On the tenth floor, we entered the Legal Patent Office. "I'm here to officially register my patent," Molly Maud said to the receptionist, who looked a bit startled, but buzzed the lawyer.

"Highly unusual, women don't file patents, not often anyway. If you'll step this way," he said cordially, though taking a very good look at our legs and heels.

After we sat down at his immaculate table, Molly Maud fumbled a bit to get the briefcase open and the documents out. While her new hand was working, the lack of sensation in it still caused us problems. She didn't even try to hide the fact that she'd lost her left hand. The lawyer did notice it right away and realized who she must be. "So you are here on behalf of your father, I presume," he said, figuring this now made sense. Hermann had merely sent her to file the patent.

"No, I'm here on my own behalf. Here are the proper

forms all notarized and signed by all parties," Molly Maud replied. She insisted on watching him actually file them. We were taking no chances the lawyer might pull some skullduggery on us. At first, he did try, but I kept him honest with a bit of "persuasion."

"But you realize this will put you in direct opposition to Hermann Porsche Industries," he cautioned her.

"Of course it does, the old fool. We women are not stupid or second-class citizens. I aim to turn this into a giant business. I'll keep you as my corporate lawyer, as long as you truly work for me and not against me. Your fee," she slid a bank draft over to him with her artificial hand, just to make the point more poignant.

Next, we headed to a realtor, marching into his office as a determined trio. "We need to purchase a warehouse and office complex at the spaceport," Molly Maud explained to the realtor, who couldn't take his eyes off our legs.

"And this is for what company?" he asked. "I assume that you are his secretaries."

"No, it is my new company. Sorry. I don't have any secretaries just yet," Molly Maud began enjoying herself, making these men uncomfortable. None was used to dealing with actual female customers. It took two days to find just the right location and the right size space. She paid cash for it, which also took the realtor by surprise. He was anticipating her having to take out a loan and then having the loan rejected because she was a woman.

A day later, a small ad appeared all over Cass-C. "Wanted. Competent women for worthwhile careers in the hyperdrive industry. Full training will be provided. Men need not apply." Below that was her contact information at the new office. That same day, a large sign was installed: Molly Maud Porsche Hyperdrives.

Now we waited. I wasn't sure the ad would bring us any candidates. She was prepared to run another ad asking for male workers, but that was a last resort. Late that first afternoon, two young women walked in, rather hesitantly. "Is this the right place? Hyperdrives?" one asked. Molly Maud smiled and took over, hiring her first two trainees.

A week later, she had twenty-four women on her staff, and all were being trained by the engineers from Winno-3. For starters, she purchased an old transport ship and this was used to demonstrate the installation procedures. At the end of the week, she handed out the two dozen paychecks. One woman who had been a receptionist exclaimed, "Miss Porsche. This must be in error. The check is more than I made in two months as a receptionist!"

"Oh no. It is correct, dear. Of course, once you are trained and installing the new hyperdrives, why the amount will be substantially higher," Molly Maud replied, enjoying watching the faces of the women. She was paying industry standard wages for male workers.

The following week, word had spread like wildfire. She added fifty more women and another fifty the following week. More importantly, when the six engineers certified the original two dozen women, she then placed another ad. "Molly Maud Porsche Hyperdrives is now accepting transport ships to be retrofitted with the new superhigh speed hyperdrive engines from the Imperium. Guaranteed five-fold increase in speed with a lower rate of fuel consumption." Her contact information then followed.

"Now we wait. This should be interesting," Molly Maud teased me.

A day later, her new receptionist, Elke, came walking into her office, her tall heels clicking on the concrete floor. She too was dressed as a professional woman. "A man is here about the ad for hyperdrives. Should I send him in?" Molly Maud nodded and a tall man in his fifties, dressed in a brown suit walked in.

"I'm here about the hyperdrives. I'd like to speak to the owner, miss," he said politely, while eyeing her legs and heels, before rolling his eyes over to mine.

"I am the owner. Miss Molly Maud Porsche. Please have a seat, mister. . ."

"Wilhelm Gunther. Are these the fancy drives that the Imperium has that we've heard rumors about?" he asked politely.

"Yes, of course they are. Straight from the Imperium

manufacturers. I'm the sole licensee and installer of these new engines. I hold the patent on them. From personal experience, they live up to their speed specifications. I traveled about three-quarters of the way across the galaxy in mere hours. However, at this time, I'm only accepting transport ships to be retrofitted. No war ships. How can I be of service, Mr. Gunther?"

"I can't believe a woman is running this, but I need those engines. Okay, I'll bring one ship in and have it done. Then, I assure you I'll fully test it," he replied accusatively.

"I would be terribly disappointed if you did not fully test it, Mr. Gunther," she replied calmly.

"Well, if it works and lives up to all this hype, I'll want the rest of my fleet converted."

"And how many transports are we talking about?" she inquired. "I want to make sure I have enough engines on hand, as well as technicians to install them."

"Fifty-three," he answered, and Molly Maud smiled.

The next day, he brought a deep space transport by and her two dozen technicians poured over it, working together. By the time he'd written the check for the work, they had it ready to go. Molly Maud cautioned him, "Each engine has a unique power up code sequence that it goes through, assigned by my company. This engine is licensed to this particular ship. It cannot be copied or installed in another ship. Why? When a new one is powered up, it checks itself against my database. If it isn't in it, the engine does not operate. Safety precautions. I won't be ripped off, but my work is guaranteed, Mr. Gunther. Your ship is ready now."

He was shocked that it was done so soon. As he left, he admonished her, "I aim to check this out thoroughly."

She countered, "You darn well better, Mr. Gunther!" He gave her a queer look.

Two days later, he returned to work out a schedule to get all fifty-three ships converted as soon as possible. Even better, two more men dropped by to get one ship done and tested. Within a week of placing the ad, she finally had to begin a short waiting list, while she added even more employees.

Two weeks after that first install, she had a dozen companies lined up. Each wanted their entire fleet converted. Further, she had suddenly become big news and reporters hounded her for an exclusive interview, which she gladly gave, putting in her own ad for more women who wanted a rewarding career. She allowed them to interview some of her workers, who only sung her praises. "We're being paid a man's wages and doing a man's work!" one enthusiastic worker exclaimed on camera.

The female reporter teased her, "Maybe I should quite the reporter business and come to work here." She meant it as a jest. The worker showed the reporter her latest pay stub. Off camera, the reporter gasped. After her crew packed up and left, she hesitantly walked into see Molly Maud, who hired her to help make promotional materials for her company. The woman's pay just quadrupled overnight. And so the rapid expansion began.

The third week began with quite an unexpected turn. As we settled in at our desks, Hermann Porsche himself walked in, bypassing Elfe, who was too slow in her tall heels to stop him from barging in. "Well hello father. What could possibly bring you into my company's office?" she said with a wry smile.

"You know damned well why I'm here, daughter," he barked.

"Sorry, but you did tell me never to come home again. I'm obeying you, father," she replied coolly.

"You know you've gotten every merchant company on Cass-C lined up to get these new hyperdrive engines, don't you?"

"I'm not sure I have every merchant company yet, but I expect I soon will have. Already word has reached our nearest neighboring worlds. I'm anticipating their business fairly soon."

"Don't you see you are bankrupting me? You are sinking Porsche industries."

"I believe you have done that to yourself father, when you repeatedly attempted to steal Captain Nia Elain's prototype ship. All you had to do was chat with Emperor Bino of the Ataro Empire, and you could have had them legally. I did, and I'm now the patent holder. You know the law on that one. If you even try to copy the engines, I'll sue you for every last penny your company has, father."

"Daughter," his voice changed completely, "can't we come to some kind of agreement here?"

"What did you have in mind, father? Have me sign over my company to you and go quietly away somewhere?"

"I — I think I've badly misjudged you, Molly Maud, badly. What you've done — it's what I would have expected a son of mine to pull off, making him worthy of inheriting Porsche Industries," Hermann admitted humbly.

I sent her, *He's sincere, not faking it.*

"Well father, I'm not your son, but your daughter. I hope you now realize I'm not a second class citizen, that I've a good mind and feel for business, and that I'm quite competent at it."

"Yes, yes. I admit it. You most definitely are. Please, can we not somehow reconcile our differences somehow, someway?"

Molly Maud thought for a moment before replying. "Father, are you still planning to leave Porsche Industries to Uncle Wolfgang?"

His face flushed, and I knew Hermann Porsche was thinking faster than he ever had in his life. He knew she had just given him perhaps his only possible way to reconcile with her and to save his own companies. *Damn, she is acutely smart! Better than any son I could hope for.* He sighed and took the only step possible that could ever lead to reconciliation with her. "No. I believe I must change that. You have earned the right to inherit Porsche Industries, Molly Maud."

She thought for a second and replied. "Dad, I simply cannot trust you just now, not after what you did to me, to us. Bring me the official papers that so stipulates my inheritance, and we'll talk, after I have my lawyers go over them with a fine-tooth comb. If you are really serious about this, then perhaps we can reconcile after all. I really don't want to be your enemy, dad. Really I don't."

Two days after that, we marched into the lawyer's office once more, bringing the papers for him to go over. After giving them a very careful study and making some calls to verify several aspects, he said, "Well now, this is most unusual. No, it is a first. These papers are an ironclad agreement that you, Molly Maud, a woman, will inherit Porsche industries when your father steps down. Congratulations are in order." He rose and actually shook her good hand firmly, as he would if she had been Hermann's son.

After that, she and I were invited for supper at her parent's home. "Does it hurt much?" he asked, referring to her stump. "Can I see it?" She gladly removed her prosthetic hand, and both parents carefully examined her arm and the hand. Hermann commented, "This Imperium workmanship is utterly remarkable. Such technology in a hand." The ice was finally broken between them. Soon, the two were discussing how best to handle all the millions of retrofit orders that were sure to be coming soon. Literally, every transport in the Federation of Planets needed to be upgraded to this new hyperdrive. Plus, there were all the military ships to consider.

What I found truly interesting was that less than a month later, Hermann Porsche decided to retire and enjoy his remaining years. I stood with Molly Maud as Hermann officially handed over the reins of one of the largest Federation of Planets industries to his daughter, much to the dismay of his Board of Directors. In her first speech to the Board, she outlined her plans for the companies and added, "You can expect we'll be hiring many more women in the technical areas, not just as secretaries and receptionists. If you can't handle this, I'll accept your resignation." Several hostile men did resign, but more than half stayed on. My guess was they wanted to see what would happen down the road.

I stuck around until late November, making darn sure all went well. I was the Emperor's eyes and ears, though I knew he had others too. For obvious reasons, he wanted to make sure that things were going well before allowing military vessels to obtain the new hyperdrives. By now, I was convinced changes had indeed come to Cass-C. Hundreds of women were now enjoying good paying jobs, earning respect for themselves in the process. In fact, here it seemed to be steam rolling along.

As I now look back and reflect on the whole initial journey into Federation space, I can see the overall level of decadence of their major societies and their long standing treatment of women had reached a critical level. Using one of their expressions I picked up on Cass-C, the situation was like a giant powder key which only needed a tiny spark to ignite and explode. I believe my Eagle's Seed crew and I were indeed that spark.

I kept in touch these past three months with others whom we'd met and with the general news from many Federation worlds. We were learning all we could about Federation worlds. Jovanna, Jana, and Tesla were cataloging and organizing this on a daily basis, sending weekly summaries back to the emperor.

My interview with Mary Ann Trestle on Capella-D had gone viral, to use another Federation term I picked up. That interview had been translated into many languages and re-broadcasted many times. If I was the spark, that interview was the gunpowder. Daily, we heard about a new women's revolt. The first one occurred on Capella-D, where for one week most all women simply refused to do any work, bringing the entire world to its knees. The government had no choice but to hastily pass new laws, giving women far more rights and opportunities.

November saw the coordinated release of the Galactic Linguistic Database, published by Misses Gabrielle Duparte and Marilyn Tonby. Almost overnight, their massive compilation combined with learning disks became a best seller. Every world had to get multiple copies, to say nothing of the many universities and libraries. Those two became extremely wealthy almost overnight. Their success fueled the women's revolution on their worlds as well.

On Mira-C with their neck rings, the women's shutdowns resulted in a new law that made beating a woman a high crime, punishable with ten years in prison. Bianca and Donatella were equally effective. By November, they'd destroyed so many of the Purple Droga plants that the whole city began to have withdrawal symptoms, coming out of their centuries old drugged state. That forced a completely new appraisal of their society as well. As the first of December on our calendar rolled around, I counted no less than sixty of the major Federation worlds on which women were rebelling and gaining more rights than they ever had in millennia, if ever. I admit I was mostly ignorant of their history.

Thus, my December report to the emperor was filled with a genuine hope for the future of the women of the Federation.

Chapter 11 Countermoves

"Look, Hermann, something has to be done about these women," Commander Werner complained bitterly. It was November 1381. He'd located the new retirement home of Hermann and paid him a call.

"Well, my Molly Maud is more than my equal, Commander Werner. She out-played me. Now, if only she was my son, I could be truly content. I'm retired now. I just want to enjoy the fruits of my long years of work."

Commander Werner realized he'd get nowhere with his old acquaintance. He had to look elsewhere. He said his goodbye and left, pondering his next move. Things were definitely getting totally out of hand, and not just on Cass-C, but on far, far too many heavily populated worlds. Something had to be done or these infernal women would soon be taking over everything. Further, everyone was now talking about this women's right phenomenon, spreading like a wildfire in all directions. He regretted not just outright ordering the total destruction of the Eagle's Seed ship when it first came to Cass-C.

Only two major institutions still were holding out, the Admiralty Round Table and the Ambassador Circle. Well also The Seven, whoever they were. On his return trip to Hoffdorf, he received a secure call from Number Seven! The Intelligence Divisions hierarchically reported to The Seven, but it was rare for one of them to directly contact him. "Secure channel confirmed, Number Seven. Over."

A disguised voice spoke, "Commander Werner, we have a very serious problem with the women's uprisings. Over."

"Aye, that's for damned sure! It's like an unstoppable wildfire. Over." He wanted to add, "And soon they will take your place," but thought better of that. He was Number Seven after all.

"Indeed. Something must be done about it. The Seven have decided we must act, but we have also decided directly attacking these women rebels will only fuel the blaze and destruction. While it would be an easy thing to do to just assassinate their leaders, that is a guaranteed route to failure. So we've decided what's needed is some kind of damper. Something that will rapidly slow the movement down and likely put out this fire, which threatens to destroy the Federation. Over."

"I agree. I could have just had Molly Maud killed, but then that would only fuel the fires. A damper, you say? I like that idea. What did you have in mind? Over."

"This mess with the aliens on Centauri-C-C has come to our attention. We would like you to meet in private with Ambassador Ricardo Santiago of Centauri-C-C and listen to what he has to say. Think about it and then get back to me on this frequency. Over."

"That old kook? Okay. Will do. We sure do need a damper of some kind. Over."

"Yes, that old kook. He's been making a larger than normal stink at the Ambassador Circle since that alien mess on Centauri-C-C. Over and out."

He punched in the alternate coordinates, heading for the Ambassador Circle building instead of his office. What could this kook possibly say that would be a damper on these women running rampantly out of control, he wondered. Ambassador Ricardo was about the last person he wanted to talk to, but Number Seven had given him a direct order, and he dutifully followed it, arriving there shortly.

The Ambassador Circle was just that, an enormously large, single story building circular in shape so that inside, the entire assemblage of ambassadors could sit at tables arranged in a circle. No one was "above" the other; all were equals here. Next to this imposing building was a skyscraper that housed the quarters and offices of the many ambassadors. He parked his shuttle and entered the tall building, stopping at the information desk where a woman manned it. He cringed, but she wore a professional woman's dress. He gave her that much credit. "Ambassador Ricardo Santiago please."

"Floor ten. Suite 6," she replied politely. Glancing at her legs and heels, he smiled and headed to the elevator. Women should be seen, not heard. Why can't they be happy just being admired, looked at, and screwed? A few minutes later, he entered the office of Ambassador Ricardo. A receptionist looked up at him. She too wore the requisite professional woman's outfit, and he dutifully noticed her nylons and heels. That she didn't have a left hand he also noticed.

"Commander Werner to see Ambassador Ricardo," he said politely, taking a seat from where he could get a very good view of her legs and heels.

Shortly, the middle-aged man came out of his office, "Commander Werner. So good to see you again. It's been far too long. Come in, please." Werner rose, took one last look at her legs and followed him into the office, sitting down across from the ambassador. "To what do I owe this visit? How may I help you?"

"Well, I'm not sure. It's this nasty business on Centauri-C-C with the aliens," he began, unsure how to proceed.

"Ah yes. The total violation of our most sacred ceremony the Mano Cortada. Indeed, that has been a total disgrace almost beyond bearing."

"Please, tell me more about this Mano Cortada ceremony," Commander Werner improvised. He had no idea what Number Seven wanted him to hear. This was good enough, he thought.

Ambassador Ricardo began highly enthused, "I know our Mano Cortada tradition must seem entirely strange to you. First, let me show you one of our wedding ceremonies, taken at random." He played a short video for Commander Werner, noticing the man didn't just get up and leave as so many others did. Perhaps, he thought, this man will actually listen to me.

Werner watched as the young bride wearing a flowing white wedding gown walked down an aisle accompanied by appropriate music. It was upbeat, not the solemn music that attended his own wedding. The woman looked incredibly happy as she walked up to the man. "That's the Wedding Official who performs these ceremonies," Ambassador Ricardo whispered. The groom took the bride's left hand in his as the two met and stood before the official. He listened to the usual type of marriage vows, not so different from those he and his wife had said.

Near the end, the official opened a white box-like machine resting on a pedestal just between them. The groom gently placed the bride's left hand into the box and the official closed it over her hand, covering most of her lower arm as well. The official then said, "Please take the hand of your future bride in yours." Werner saw the groom reach around to the front of the machine that was facing away from him. The official then spoke directly to the bride. "Is this your non-dominate hand?"

"It is," the bride to be replied softly, but a bit nervously.

He then said, "Do you wish to give your hand in holy marriage, knowing that what is given out of your love for him can never be taken back?"

Nervously, the bride to be replied, "I do."

Turning to the groom, he said, "Will you accept the offered hand, given to you freely and out of her deep abiding love for you, knowing that this bond between you cannot ever be broken or undone, from this day forward?"

Just as nervously, the groom replied, "I do."

"So be it. Since the dawn of time, this precious gift of her hand in marriage seals their bonds through sickness and health, through good times and bad, until death parts your ways. The precious gift of the bride symbolizes her undying faithfulness to her husband. His acceptance of her hand in marriage fills him with the never ending responsibility to care for her, to cherish her, to remain faithful to her until death parts their ways. Your acceptance of her hand in marriage is final and cannot be undone. Should you become unfaithful to her, you will be marked as a pariah and wholly shunned by all society. It is done. You may take her hand now and place it upon the Holy Altar of Lord God who has borne witness to your vows."

Werner noticed that the groom was now exceptionally nervous. His right hand as shaking visibly as he withdrew the dismembered hand from the box. Werner didn't flinch. He'd seen far worse things. The groom placed it upon a white cloth on the altar before him. The official lifted the lid of the box and the bride removed her left arm, which was missing its hand. There was no wound. It was fully healed. The groom put his right arm around her left handless arm and the pair turned to face their friends. The official now said, "I give you. . ." The video ended, preserving the privacy of the couple.

With the video over and Werner still here, he said, "You see, it is a thing to be treasured. The bride feels no pain. This is not a brutal thing, but something to be treasured. Honestly, if the husband ever betrays the bride, the pariah would ruin him completely. He would be a marked man. No woman would ever go near him and most married men would shun him completely. He would be a total outcast from all society. I would also point out that as far as the brides are concerned, their missing hand is never, ever anything to be ashamed of or embarrassed by, not anywhere on our world."

Werner was still listening. Emboldened, the ambassador added, "Now, if the husband should die prematurely, the widow is given a prosthetic hand so she'll have a hand to give to another man, should she remarry. What we Centauri-C-C people don't understand is why no one else follows the very words that they recite. On every world, the brides pledge to give their hand in marriage and the man accepts her hand, and yet they do not do so."

"Our holy ceremony has tremendous benefits for society, Commander Werner. The divorce rate on our world is nearly nil. The divorce rate here on Cass-C was seventy-two percent last year, according to your government's figures. We believe it's this high because the women here aren't actually giving their hand in marriage. The only bond is their word, and you and I both know just how easily words can be manipulated."

Commander Werner finally said something. "Yes I know just what you are saying. I suspect you've had a hard time selling this to other worlds."

His face fell. "Yes of course. I keep trying. The Federation would be so much better if no one got divorced, if all men treasured their wives. Surely, you can see that. Families should stay together, grow old together."

"Indeed. I don't want to give you any false hopes, but I will take what you've told me quite seriously. May I return and discuss this with you in more detail at a later date?"

"Oh please do so!" exclaimed Ambassador Ricardo, exuberantly. Finally, someone in authority actually listened to him!

An hour later in his secure office, safe from all manner of scrying and electronic monitoring, Commander Werner placed a secure call to Number Seven. "Werner here. I talked with Ambassador Ricardo. He went on and on about their Mano Cortada wedding ceremony."

Number Seven replied, "Indeed. Would this be a damper do you suppose?"

Like an electric jolt, suddenly Werner grasped the situation and just why Number Seven has sent him to the kooky ambassador. "Brilliant! I see it now. Yes, yes, it most certainly would act as a damper! But how the hell can we sell such a thing? Women would surely protest violently against it."

Number Seven suggested, "Approach it as a solution to the dismal divorce rate, a critical problem that must be solved. Plus, as an added incentive, also give women more legal rights. I suggest you take this approach when you visit with Admiral Fritz Gerhardt. I can tell you he controls a secret block of admirals, all of whom are very much concerned over this wildfire of the women. They are looking for a solution. Give them one. Over and out."

Commander Werner smiled. Number Seven is always a step ahead of me, he mused. He checked the admiral's schedule online. He was free just after supper. He placed a secure call to the man's office and left a message with his receptionist that he wanted to visit with him at seven tonight. Now, he sat back and began to frame his arguments, knowing they would have to be quite persuasive. A little later, he had a callback from the receptionist. The admiral wanted to meet at the Officer's Club at seven. Even better, he thought, a more relaxed and private setting.

At seven, he entered the exclusive club catering only to the many admirals who stayed here on Cass-C and met weekdays at the Admiralty Round Table. He flashed his badge, which allowed him to enter. There were no women allowed, even if they were their world's admiral representative. He looked around the plush entrance room filled with the best chairs and fully carpeted in a dark red, thick fabric. He saw Admiral Fritz waving towards him, and he walked briskly over to the man. He said, "Welcome Commander. Will this do or should we be more private?"

"Private."

"This way," the admiral said, casting him a very quick, stern look. They entered a small side room with just two chairs in it. They sat facing each other. "What's on your mind?"

"The situation with the women on many worlds is getting completely out of hand. Something needs to be done to tone it down, to dampen it, if possible."

"And you have an idea?" the admiral inquired, suddenly paying full attention to the head of the hub spy network.

"I believe so. Are you familiar with the Centauri-C-C marriage custom of Mano Cortada performed at their wedding ceremonies?" Commander Werner asked, hoping that he didn't need to elaborate further.

"Ah yes. Nasty bit of business you had there on that world. You handled it nicely though. Too bad for everyone you failed to obtain the hyperdrive then. Now, it's costing us some, though not too much."

"Indeed," Commander Werner replied and moved on hastily. He hated to have his failings pointed out to him. "Suppose the Round Table passed a law that said all married women must have the Mano Cortada done immediately and that all future weddings incorporate the ceremony. The angle to use is our dismal divorce rate. Theirs is almost nil, according to the latest figures, while ours is over seventy percent. Approach it as a family thing. Think of all the children who get psychologically messed up by the divorces and strangers becoming their fathers."

"You think that is sellable?" he asked.

"Might be, especially if it was also accompanied by severe laws for unfaithful husbands and laws granting women more legal rights, whatever those might be. Stress saving the family unit and it ought to sell. However, from an enforcement perspective, we'd need the legal right to use force to bring about compliance. I should also think it needs to be done rapidly across all major Federation worlds. Otherwise, we might see an exodus of people, particularly women. What do you think?"

"It has distinct possibilities. Surely, Commander Werner, you didn't think all this up on your own."

His face flushed. "No sir. Been chatting with Number Seven about it. He's behind it. We have to do something and fast before this movement gets so far out of control that the whole Federation crumbles."

"Ah, then it is as I suspected. This has gotten the attention of The Seven. Indeed, Number Seven is behind it you say. Interesting. I have quite a few influential Admirals I'll need to consult. Let me get back to you next week. Keep up the good work, Commander Werner. That will be all."

He knew he was being dismissed, but he'd said what he needed to say. Plus, the admiral hadn't rejected his idea out of hand. Werner left feeling a bit more upbeat. Perhaps, something could be done about it before it was too late.

Admiral Fritz immediately sent word to his close group, asking them to join him. When they arrived, he quickly outlined what Werner had told him, with particular emphasis on the fact the Number Seven was behind this move. "We don't dare bring this up on our own at the Round Table. It would be best if we were seen reacting to public outrage and public demand that something be done," Admiral Fritz explained.

"And how do you suppose that can happen?" one asked.

"We use the press. Call in some favors. Make this divorce rate, this disintegration of the family unit, seem like the greatest threat to the Federation ever. Interview young boys highly disturbed by their parent's divorce. If we play this right, we can have the public demanding we do something about it."

Another said, "Have to be coordinated across fifty worlds — simultaneous implementation. Have to be universal. No exceptions for anyone's wife. Black and white."

Another added, "True. Needs severe punishments for those who refuse or those who become unfaithful. We've got to cover all the bases on this one or someone will begin to poke holes in it or see the real reason before we can get it fully accomplished."

"We'll need thousands of those machines. In addition, we can use our soldiers, sending them house to house. We'll need a list of all married women and their addresses. Moreover, this has to be seen as a religious ceremony. There aren't enough priests around. It can't go slowly. It must be done rapidly and efficiently, with a strong emphasis on its profoundly religious aspect. Hence, it must be kept secret until we're ready for its implementation," Admiral Fritz added.

The first one spoke up, "Plus, we'll need the fifty main worlds to tightly coordinate this, even going so far as doing it at the same time. Tricky. But our soldiers are really bored right now."

Another added his suggestion. "We can prepare a 'Holy Script' and train and dress one of our soldiers up as a priest and have him officiate. Use the Fabrication Machines to make as many of these devices as we'll need. Once the mass job is finished, donate them to everyone who is legally permitted to marry a couple."

"Say," one who had been silent finally said, "what do we do about the unusual matings. You know, the lesbian couples and the gay couples? Shouldn't they participate too? If so, do both lesbians lose their hand and does one of the gay lose theirs?"

"Fair is fair," the first one replied. "Have them make their choice as to which one is being the role of wife and take hers or his." Several chuckled. "Or take them both off."

Fritz added, "We'll need to call in all of the favors we can from the many minor admirals. With their support, we can pass it through the Round Table fairly easily and quickly. However, we are going to need to keep this as top secret until it can be physically executed."

Everyone was in agreement. Fritz then began working out the myriad details, confident that soon the problem of the unruly women would be stamped out once and for all. This threat to the Federation just had to be ended soon.

For my own part, I did notice that during December the

newscasts seemed to be playing up the really high divorce rate and its severe repercussions on the family. It seemed obvious to me the basis of society and humankind was the basic family unit, so I took this raising of public awareness of the problem a positive thing. In hindsight, I ought to have known better, but at the time with everything working out so well, I only saw this as another positive step forward. Lowering the divorce rate would be a very good thing for a society to do. Save the family became a battle cry as late December rolled around.

Admiral Fritz Gerhardt began meeting daily with his secret group of other major world's admirals, orchestrating their plot, and assigning some tasks to his fellow admirals. He formed up a complete checklist of actions to be taken. Mid-December, he presented his group with a card. "Admirals, here is the script that our 'priests' will be using. Look it over now and make suggestions for changes, if any." The admirals read the following:

The Holy Marriage Confirmation Ceremony
Priest:
> Arrange the machine in the center of the room.
> Place the white cloth over the box just in front of the machine.
> Make sure the upbeat music is playing softly.
> Have the couple stand before the machine and you face them.

Say to them both:
> We are here today to conduct the Holy Marriage Confirmation Ceremony, the
> Mano Cortada.

Say to husband:
> Husband, please take your wife's non-dominate hand in yours.

Ask the woman:
> Is this your non-dominate hand?

Priest:
> She must answer. If it is not, find out which it is and put that one in the machine.

To husband say:

>Place her hand on the resting place of the Holy Confirmation Machine.

Priest:

>When he has done so, verify hand is properly positioned.
>Close the machine and press Start.
>Make sure Red light is now on.

Say to her:

>You are giving him your hand in holy marriage, knowing full well that what is given out of your love for him can never be taken back.

Say to him:

>You are accepting her offered hand, given to you out of her deep abiding love for you, knowing that this bond between you cannot ever be broken or undone from this day forward.

Say to them both:

>Since the dawn of time, this precious gift of her hand in marriage doth seal your bonds through sickness and health, through good times and bad, until death doth part your ways. The precious gift of the bride symbolizes her undying faithfulness to you, her husband.

Say to him:

>You sir, by your acceptance of her hand in marriage commits you with the never ending responsibility to care for her, to cherish her, to remain faithful to her until death doth part your ways. This acceptance of her hand in marriage is final and cannot be undone.
>
>Note this well, sir, should you become unfaithful to her, you will be marked as a social demon, and you will be wholly shunned by our entire society and prosecuted by law.

Priest:

>Make sure Green light is on. If not, stall until it is on.

Say to them both:

>It is done.

Say to him:

>Take her hand, which you are still holding, and place it upon

the Holy Altar of Lord God who has borne witness to your vows.

Priest:

Indicate with your hand the white cloth over the box.

When he has done so, fold the cloth over the hand.

Say to them both:

Your shared gift of her hand this day is a symbol unto God of the undying, eternal love that you share for each other. She has felt no pain or discomfort.

Think not of this as a brutal thing, but rather as something to be treasured for all of your lives.

Say to her:

Your missing hand is never, ever anything to be ashamed of or embarrassed by — not anywhere on our world. On the contrary, it is the visible symbol of your love for your husband and your family. Always show your handless arm with the greatest of pride! In your daily life, make use of that arm in any way that you can.

Say to them both:

May God bless you both, filling your lives with richness and happiness.

Priest:

Firmly shake each one's hand.

Turn off music.

Pack up machine.

Take wrapped hand, box, music, and machine with you as you leave.

Report the name of the couple just handled to Program Administration.

When the admirals finished, they had nothing but praise for the script. One commented, "If this is followed by all of our soldiers-turned-priests, this can't fail! Ingenious indeed. Well done, Fritz!" Others echoed his sentiments.

In total secret, soldiers were formed up into teams of three men. One was appointed to act as the priest. One served as the record keeper, tracking which homes they were to visit each day. Both were also to carry their d-guns and handle any protests or refusals to allow the ceremony to proceed. One was given training in administering a sedative to any unwilling woman, who might protest and refuse to go along with it. Essentially, he was to come up from behind her while his buddy was distracting her and insert the syringe into her neck. She would be tractable within a minute, and the ceremony would then proceed as planned. Ditto if the husband was a problem.

For a week, the three men were drilled and drilled on their roles until they could do them in their sleep, rapidly and efficiently. Each city had five hundred such trio teams ready to go when the time came. Further, it was estimated they could handle three couples per hour, twenty-four per day, one hundred forty-four per week. This tallied to an expected nearly seventy-two thousand couples handled per week. Depending upon how it went, the admirals were prepared to field an additional thousand trio teams, if necessary.

Admiral Fritz had not gotten to his top position on Cass-C merely by superior military skill. Rather, he considered himself to be something of a political scientist as well, wise in the arts of manipulating people. In point of fact, that is precisely how he got himself appointed the Admiral for Cass-C some fifteen years ago. It wasn't enough just to force this on the married population of the cities. No, the backlash, the protests, the outcries might be too great thereby endangering the whole plan.

Admiral Fritz knew the art of making a population or person actually *desire* something. First, you *force* it on them by any means possible, including insisting they simply must have it or else. Next, you *inhibit* them from having it by any means possible, denying it to them. After that, he knew from experience that they would then actually begin to *desire* it or want it or demand to have it. In this case, he had to be careful and not reveal precisely what was going to occur. He told his fellow conspirators to follow the newscasts, but to say nothing. "Let me be the sole spokesman. I'll have them begging us for the solution before the new year comes." They agreed, and he began to put his plan into operation.

After the newscasts had carried all manner of terrible reports on the high divorce rate and its ramifications, he held a news conference, but insisted it be broadcast on all major worlds of the Federation. By creating an air of mystery, he got the civilian news networks to agree, and he then held it. Surrounded by a wall of microphones and dressed in his parade uniform of office, Admiral Fritz stood before a crowd of his own soldiers, dressed as civilians.

"As you know, we on the Admiralty Round Table are charged with making the laws of our mighty Federation of Planets. Normally, our focus is on mundane things, such as taxes. However, we too are married, and we cannot ignore the social decay of our worlds. Unless you've been in space this past year, totally out of touch, you are well aware of our terrible divorce rate. It is high on almost all major worlds. I must compliment your news reporters for focusing in on this enormous problem that we face today. And it is truly an enormous problem. One does not need to be a genius to know the family unit is the basis of society. Without a thriving, wholesome home life, being raised by both parents, our children are and have suffered horribly. Our own future generations are being threatened by us adults."

He allowed his "audience" a moment to give him a loud round of applause, before continuing. "We of the Admiralty Round Table cannot sit idly by and let our very society decay any further, crumbling into dust. I've been meeting with many of my peers and together, we have come up with a very simple, practical solution. This solution is extremely inexpensive. No new taxes will have to be raised. It can be done in a relatively short amount of time. But more importantly the solution is guaranteed to nearly wipe out divorce rates!"

Again, he allowed the applause and cheering to die down. "The plan has been thoroughly tested and is virtually guaranteed to work. I call it the Save the Family Plan. Of course, if the Admiralty Round Table passed this plan, it will apply to all married couples, even to non-traditional unions. We'll be strictly enforcing this plan broadly. No exceptions allowed. It's everyone participating or no plan. If we have to, we'll use the armed forces to force unwilling couples to abide by the Save the Family Plan. We can't have even one exception made."

"I know there will always be some couples who will protest and refuse to cooperate. Again, for the Save the Family Plan to work, it must have one hundred percent participation by all married couples and unions. Hence, right now, we are working out just how we can enforce this plan on those who might refuse to go along with it. Thank you for your time."

A reporter shouted, "Admiral Fritz, tell us some of the details of the plan? How does it work? Why will some refuse?"

He worked the reporters like a knife spreading butter on one's morning toast. "Since the plan has not yet been finalized and passed by the Round Table, it would be premature for me to release such details. Surely, you can understand that. As you also know, no matter what law the Round Table passes, there are always those who protest against it. And that is the critical detail that we have yet to iron out, namely how to force the unwilling to participate. The plan simply will not work if we allow even one exception, one couple to opt out of the plan."

"Admiral Fritz," shouted another reporter, "will the plan actually lower the divorce rate? Will it keep families healthy? After all, couples are divorcing for valid reasons are they not?"

"Yes, the plan will nearly eradicate the divorce rate. I ask you to look at it from the child's point of view. He sees mommy and daddy arguing, perhaps even fighting. All he wants is peace and stability, but he is powerless to stop them. Sometimes, children even believe they are the reason mommy and daddy are fighting. Everyone knows just how difficult it is for children from broken homes to make it. So I ask you, shouldn't those who are heading for a divorce do what is truly best for their children, our future generation?"

Someone shouted, "What about widows and widower? Are they in the plan?"

"Of course not. While we realize untimely deaths do occur and that there are many single parents out there, they will only become part of the Save the Family Plan when they remarry. After all, don't single parents have a tough enough time as it is?"

After a brief pause, he added, "That's all I better say. I don't want to get in hot water with the other admirals, but I felt that you, the public, should know that your Admiralty Round Table has the perfect solution to this simply terrible problem. Press your admiral representative to pass this plan." He stepped down, hoping that he'd put enough enforcing into his announcement.

Of course, others on the Round Table demanded to know all about this new plan. He was prepared for this. "Admirals, I'm still working out a few details. I want to present it as a complete package for your consideration. I'll have it in a few days. Trust me on this one." Some did; some didn't.

For a few days, he watched the public reaction, nicely covered by the news reporters, who endeavored to quiz anyone about their reactions to the Save the Family Plan. Opinions flew about like confetti, but no one pointed out the obvious: just what was this miracle plan?

When he was satisfied that, on the average, people had gotten the message that when it was passed, the Save the Family Plan was going to be forced onto them willy nilly, Admiral Fritz held a second news conference. "I've come before you today with a sad heart. I believe the Save the Family Plan is simply not going to get the needed number of votes from the many admirals on the Round Table. It's my fault. I should never have been so excited about this very workable plan and announced it as I did a few days ago. It was wholly premature, since the Round Table must pass it. The plan will work. I have no doubts about that. My staff has gone over it tooth and claw. It will work. Our future generations would be salvaged by it, but it's just not going to happen. Please forgive me for raising false hopes. While we do have the solution to the problem, to be blunt, you can't have it."

"But Admiral Fritz," a reporter shouted, "if your plan will work, why can't you get the necessary votes to pass it?"

He sighed. "Forgive me. I shouldn't have told you about the plan. Everyone knows, and I should have too, that getting enough votes to pass any bill can be very difficult. Okay, if enough people ask me to continue to develop my Save the

Family Plan and present it to the full Admiralty Round Table, I'll do so. That's the least I can do to make amends for what I've done by becoming so enthusiastic over a real solution prematurely. Again, I'm sorry it's not going to happen. Thank you all." He stepped down, leaving the reporters crying for more information, some even began begging him to please continue developing the plan.

Now came his biggest challenge. He needed a law, which would be seen by the women as being highly beneficial to them, so much so that it would help break down their barriers of resistance, helping them to justify going along with the plan. While he presumed he could sell the basic plan — he already had his secret group lining up the votes for the unseen plan — he knew getting them to agree on this part would be far more difficult, especially in light of the wildfire spread of the women's rights movement on the major worlds.

He sat back and envisioned the average husband's point of view, but that was futile. Next, he tried to imagine a protesting husband's point of view. That was more hopeful, but led to nothing conclusive. The women needed something of value, something they did not currently have. In a fit of inspiration, he looked up Centauri-C-C and studied their laws concerning this, since it was their methods he was using. Then it struck him.

Look, he thought, if a woman gives up her hand and her husband abuses her, is unfaithful to her, commits adultery, she's basically screwed. As the law now stands, she's going to have a tough time getting any kind of compensation. The courts usually side with the man, as they should. But perhaps now they shouldn't. We need something that will make a man think long and hard before he does actions that threatens his marriage. Bingo. He had his missing piece at last and began drafting it into a bill to present along with his Save the Family Plan.

None too soon. Just as he had planned, as the last week of December began, the public was demanding the Admiralty Round Table consider the Save the Family Plan and pass it. Admittedly, he was using many, many admirals, who by now were extremely upset with his handling of this whole mess.

Hence, on Monday afternoon, he walked into the special session of the Admiralty Round Table, prepared to make his move. Everything was in place. He rose and addressed a hostile group of mostly men. "Forgive me, admirals. I know, I've put you through the washtub on this one. All I ask is that you hear me out completely. As of now, this meeting is top secret. I'm invoking The Seven's Rule of Secrecy. Any leak of any kind about what we are discussing in this matter will be considered an act of treason by The Seven." That sobered everyone up. While they were still quite upset over having been used, this unforeseen invocation got their full attention!

"The aides are passing out copies of two linked bills that must be passed together or none at all. For weeks, you and I have been bombarded with our current social crisis, this appalling divorce rate, and its horrific impact on our children. Before you *is* the solution to this nasty social problem. Some of you may recognize it at once. It has been proven to work and has been at work for millennia on Centauri-C-C. As you probably know, their divorce rate is practically zero. I have discussed their marriage ceremony with their Ambassador Ricardo Santiago at great length and have modified it to fit the current scene on our worlds. The plan lies before you."

"As far as implementation goes, it is imperative no word of this plan gets out until we are ready to implement it simultaneously in all major cities on all major worlds. That avoids all manner of wild public reactions. I have prepared our idle soldiers to do the actual implementation. Once completed, the program can be turned over to those who conduct marriages and civil unions. I would like to point out that there is no cost involved. Nada. It has been taken care of already."

"However, the second bill that must be passed along with it has a two-fold purpose. One, it gives the women something that has always been denied to them in divorce proceedings. Since they are making the physical sacrifice, should their husband be unfaithful et cetera, they can sue him in divorce court for three-quarters of his entire net worth. Two, it gives husbands a strong incentive to remain faithful to their wives."

One admiral interrupted him, "Admiral Fritz, you are proposing that we cut off a hand of every wife!"

"Yes sir. That I am. There is also something else to keep in mind about this plan. Right now, do we not have an almost uncontrollable wildfire with women making unheard of demands on nearly every world? Here on Cass-C, look what happened to Hermann Porsche. His daughter now has total control of Porsche Industries!" More than one hushed explicative was heard.

Another admiral spoke up, "Admiral Fritz, let me be totally blunt. Are you suggesting this can also be considered a countermove to the current women's movement?"

"I would think that with only one hand, women would find it harder to perform jobs that men have always done. Don't you think so?" he replied coyly, but not saying that was the real purpose behind the proposed laws. He let them draw their own conclusions.

Admiral Vasco del Rio of Centauri-C-C rose to address his peers. "Admirals, this is a day worth remembering. Indeed, I can speak for the success of our Mano Cortada marriage ceremony. It has been in use on my world throughout all of our recorded history and is extremely successful. Virtually no man betrays his wife. The penalties are too great. I would like to suggest a slight amendment to the second proposed companion law. That is, the husband must not abuse his wife. We do not tolerate wife beatings. So admirals, if you really are serious about saving your families, this proposed pair of bills certainly will do just that."

While he was speaking, Admiral Fritz hastily added the abuse clause to his second bill. He allowed Admiral Vasco to talk at length about their ceremony, selling it to those whose votes he had not yet "acquired."

Another admiral suggested that extra wording be added to the "ceremony" instructing the husband of the severity of the penalties should he be unfaithful or abuse his wife. Three-quarters of his net worth was a terrible price to pay. Admiral Fritz added it to the proposed ceremony wording.

Admiral Vasco went on to explain how it worked for those who married for a second time. "We give them a prosthetic hand, and they give that away as their hand in marriage. Perhaps, something about this situation ought to be added to the bill." It was.

"What about the civil unions, the lesbian and gay couples? Are they to be similarly handled and if so, how?" another admiral wanted to know.

Another admiral spoke up, "Why not remove a hand from each partner?" Chuckles echoed around the room. Nevertheless, that too became part of the final law. After all, that admiral said, how was anyone to know which woman was which in their civil union.

Another admiral commented, "I can see we're going to have to become very secretive about our extra-marital affairs, gentlemen." More laughs followed.

When he thought the time was right, Admiral Fritz called for the first round of voting. As he expected, about a hundred admirals were totally against mutilating their women wholesale. However, his carefully executed plan worked. The bills passed with a huge margin, over nineteen to one!

Now, they got down to the business of the plan's actual execution. The date for the announcement was New Year's Day, 1382. The Save the Family Plan would begin that morning at eight o'clock, starting the new year off on the right foot would be their mantra. Late Tuesday night, Admiral Fritz held another news conference, at the bidding of the Round Table.

"I'm so very pleased to stand here before you tonight to announce to everyone. Admiralty Round Table has heard your voices! Your fervent support won the day. The Save the Family Plan has been passed by a huge margin! Further, you women out there, take heart. A new, companion law that tremendously benefits you has also been passed! This is a great night for celebration. Your desires have been heard and acted upon!"

A reporter shouted, "When will the details of the plan be released? When will it start?"

Admiral Fritz chuckled, saying, "Almost like a tele-prompter." Some reporters laughed. "As we speak, preparations for the plan's implementation are still being made. The Round Table has instructed me to tell everyone that the full details will be disclosed on New Year's Day. Also, the plan will be implemented that day as well. We are following your wishes, starting the new year out the right way, by saving families, guaranteeing the sanctity of our families, and with powerful new rights for you women. Full details on New Year's Day. This is a miracle, if I do say so myself. This new year, the divorce rate in the Federation will approach zero for the first time in our long, illustrious history!"

Later that night, Admiral Fritz received a secure call from Number Seven who wanted to personally congratulate him on the successful passage of his plan. Likewise, Commander Werner received a similar call.

I know. I ought to have noticed this as we watched the live newscast. But I didn't. Still, I had misgivings. Something didn't feel right, but I couldn't place it, not yet anyway. We'd all have to wait a few more days. Besides, we were all kept busy helping Molly Maud deal with the giant corporations she'd inherited, while integrating her own company into it.

Chapter 12 Implementation

New Year's Day came. Molly Maud had purchased a home within walking distance of the towering Porsche Industries Corporate Headquarters building in downtown Hoffdorf. My group was staying with her, still providing protection, though thus far none was needed. Before when she was at her new factory at the spaceport, I could walk between my ship and her office. Now, we were miles apart, and life was more awkward. I hated to leave my crew sitting in the spaceship all the time. Hence, with her purchase of a new house and with there now being no need for someone to steal the Eagle's Seed, I risked having Danika and the others with us in her house. Yes, it was a bit crowded, but fun.

Already Tesla, Anya, Jana, Jovanna, and Marisol had gathered large amounts of key data on the Federation worlds, which the emperor needed to know, not the least of which was their coordinates, population, and an estimated military strength. Beth was focusing her attention on the plants and animals of these worlds, while Danika continued to catalog the worlds and their coordinates. We'd left Anwyn and Dylan back on Ashford-5, since there wasn't any need for further excursions into Federation space. This trip was to ensure Molly Maud's safety and that of the new hyperdrives. As the new year approached, we were about ready to head back to our world with the mission completed far better than we had expected.

The success wasn't just Molly Maud's reconciliation with her father and inheritance. No, it was far more. We were seeing women gaining more respect, better jobs, and doing well on many of the major worlds. The only nagging detail that hung in the back of my mind was the newscasts' continual harping on the steep divorce rates on these worlds, and the plan to remedy this that was first on and then off and then on again in a dizzying trail of confusion. Well, all was to be made clear on New Year's Day. Hence, we rose early and gathered around Molly Maud's new large monitor to watch the morning's events play out. After that, we were thinking seriously about heading home, mission complete.

Right on schedule, a spokesman for the Admiralty Round Table began his formal address. The backdrop of the famous enormous room where they met lent a certain air of formality and legality to his address. The room was circular and contained five concentric circles of tables and chairs where the thousands of admirals met to formulate the laws of the Federation of Planets. We could see other officials doing the same thing, addressing their worlds in the most common language of their world. Everything was very official looking.

"Today begins a new year and with it the ultimate solution to the severe family crisis that had plagued our major worlds for countless centuries. Indeed, you, the people of our world have been demanding this problem be solved and soon. Your admirals have listened to you and have now solved the problem fully. Today, implementation of the Save the Family Plan has begun on fifty of the most populated worlds. When the solution has been fully implemented on these worlds, the resources will be sent to the other world of the Federation to assist them as well. So if your world isn't among these fifty today, rest assured the plan will be implemented on your world long before this new year ends."

"One world has used this plan for millennia and with astonishing success. There, divorces and broken families simply do not exist, except in extraordinary few cases. I'm told one in a million. Contrast that with Hoffdorf's eight in ten marriages. You see, the problem lies in the marriage bond in the first place. It's simply not taken seriously. When the woman gives her hand to her husband in marriage, it no longer means much at all, save we will live together until something better comes along or even worse. This simply cannot be allowed to continue as you, our citizens, have so vocally demanded in recent weeks."

"Today, Save the Family begins. In order for the plan actually to work, compliance must be one hundred percent. That means what it says. There are no exceptions. By families, let me be clear on this point. It means all traditional marriages of a man and woman. If you are married, you are part of the plan, period. Yet, we all know that there are civil unions between two women or two men. We are not neglecting you either. These are also families and often they have adopted children to raise. So yes, all civil unions are included fully in the plan."

"Further, beginning today, all new wedding ceremonies or civil union ceremonies will be including this plan as part of the ceremony. Going forward from this day, all current, all future marriages, and civil unions will be covered and included in the Save the Family Plan. No exceptions."

"So just what is this plan everyone had been demanding the Admiralty Round Table adopt? It consists of two parts. Please everyone, listen to both parts, because each is critical to achieving the plan's goal of preserving the family, the basic building block of our society and world. Both parts are necessary."

"The first part is to do just what the marriage is all about, the bride giving her hand to her husband in marriage. The hand that she gives will be her non-dominant one. If you are right handed, your left hand is given. If you are left handed, your right hand is given. Simple enough. Okay, if you are ambidextrous, as a tiny fraction of you are, it will be your choice which hand to give. The process is utterly painless. You'll feel nothing at all. Realize you are giving him your hand in *holy* marriage, knowing full well that what is given out of your love for him can never be taken back. Husband, you are accepting her offered hand, given to you out of her deep abiding love for you, knowing that this bond between you cannot ever be broken or undone from this day forward. Realize that this precious gift of her hand in marriage seals your bonds through sickness and health, through good times and bad, until death intervenes. The precious gift of the bride symbolizes her undying faithfulness to her husband."

"Husbands, by your acceptance of her hand in marriage, you are fully committed with the never ending responsibility to care for her, to cherish her, to remain faithful to her until death separates you. However, husbands, take note of this. Should you become unfaithful to her or abuse her, you will be marked as a social demon, shunned by our entire society, and prosecuted by law."

"Allow me to jump ahead to the second law at this time. Because of the Holy Sacrifice a woman has made, should her husband be unfaithful to her, commit adultery, or abuse her, she now has the legal right and obligation to sue him not only for a divorce, which will be automatically granted, but also for three-quarters of his entire net worth! Husbands, take note. There is no acceptable defense for such conduct, if it is shown to the court that you committed adultery, were unfaithful to your wife, or have abused her. In such cases, the court will order the total dissolution of all your assets, giving three-quarters of them to your wife along with her divorce. So married women, who have made this Holy Gift, this Holy Sacrifice, and who have subsequently been betrayed, will now have a powerful legal right to a substantial monetary settlement, wholly unheard of before anywhere within the Federation of Planets!"

"With that cautionary warning said, back to the Holy Sacrifice. The given hand will be placed upon the Holy Altar of Lord God, who by your act bears witness to your vows. Your shared gift of her hand this day is a symbol unto God of the undying, eternal love that you share for each other. Please, think not of this as a brutal thing, but rather as something to be treasured for all of your lives, a sacred Holy Memory of that special bond between you."

"Wives, your missing hand is never, ever anything to be ashamed of or embarrassed by — not anywhere on our world. Show it with great pride! Show it always as the visible symbol of your love for your husband and your family. In your daily life, make use of that arm in any way that you can."

"Remember this too. This Holy Ceremony has been in use for millennia on Centauri-C-C where there are almost no divorces or spouse abuse. During the ensuing days, the newscasts will feature some women volunteers from that world and others who will give our women tips they've found useful in dealing with their daily lives and activities. I urge all wives to watch for these useful hints."

"Finally, I would like to say to all married couples, whether they be traditional marriages or civil unions, may our

Lord God bless you both and fill your lives with all the richness and happiness you both deserve. Thank you for your attention." The newscast cut away to various studio reporters, who began offering their "take" on the Save the Family Plan.

I screamed loudly. Now, it hit me. I should have seen this coming! "Good God! This is wholesale brutality towards all women! The bastards!" I was angrier than I could ever recall being, so much so that Danika had to send me calming waves.

I have to admire Molly Maud. She took this disastrous turn in stride. True, she was furious for a few minutes, but soon let it go. "Look, we all knew there were still psychopaths, sociopaths, and anti-social men who hold power here in the Federation. I think this extreme move on their part shows us just how frightened of women they really are."

"How so?" I asked, trying to get my anger level down.

"Look, in the last few months, women across many worlds have begun to make great strides forward toward equality in our societies. Many say it is more like a raging wildfire. It's obvious to me this has gotten some men in high places so utterly terrified that they have to resort to this brutality to try to rein us women in," she replied.

"So it's not really about the divorce rate and breakup of families?" asked Jovanna.

Tesla, our political science expert, spoke up. "Yes and no. Yes, in that the dismal state of marriages here is truly a very serious problem, a sign of the overall decay of this civilization, and thus ought to be somehow solved. No, in that it isn't really designed to solve the problem. All they needed to do to solve it was to pass that second law, giving the woman the right to three-quarters of the man's assets. However, that law should be reciprocal, giving the man three-quarters of the woman's assets should the woman be the guilty party. Such a law would make both parties think long and hard before they commit to marriage. Once done, the same law helps keep them from straying. The success of the giving of a hand bit has very little to do with preventing divorce per se. It only makes the two take their time and learn about each other more fully before making that commitment. It also lets men know at once that any given woman he might meet is married and thus he best not flirt with her. No, it is the second law that is the heart of the issue."

She went on, "So I agree with Molly Maud on this one. Crippling the women all by itself isn't going to do much to the divorce and family problem as they claim. Rather, it severely inhibits physical activities of women. It's obvious the true goal is to cripple women so that the women's rights movement comes to a screeching halt. Hence, certain men holding power must be incredibly terrified of what women have accomplished this past half year."

Jana asked, "So should women then take up arms against the admirals and others? Fight to put an end to this brutality? Start a real revolution? Fight back?"

Molly Maud answered. She had recently finished her Basic Therapy and had been applying the right methods. Ignoring the barriers placed in her path, she had focused on doing well and prospering. She'd become a stellar example of this approach. True, she had a desperately needed product and the initial financial backing and support of Emperor Bino, but here in Hoffdorf, she'd been the one to overcome the barriers and push her agenda steadily forward. "No we don't take up arms and fight back that way."

She explained, "These terrified men, these sociopaths, these severely anti-social, anti-women men believe that maiming women will subdue us, make us return to our subservient, second class status. So we fight back by ignoring our mutilations. We fight back by continuing to do what we have been doing. We flourish and do well. We prosper. And if we do that, these terrified men will give up and craw into some dark hole somewhere. We win."

She continued, "Since married women won't have prosthetic hands from the Imperium, I think I should stop wearing mine. Be a role model. Besides, that hand is mostly useless anyway. All I do is clumsily bump into everything with it. It's not really good for much at all. Plus, we saw the women on Centauri-C-C got by well just using their stumps as best they could. I'm simply going to have to set a very good example for all the women in my company."

She then paused a moment. "I see a problem coming when Monday comes. My women workers who are married are going to be crippled. I know. New policy. We continue to hire women. If a job opening comes up where two hands are needed, then I will hire two one-handed women to fill it. That ought to shake the old boys up! And give those women real hope. Bit costly, but who cares? This is a war we're fighting." She promptly removed her hand and tossed it in the bottom of her clothes drawer.

While I hated to give my nearly useless hand up, I went along with her, as did Jovanna, Jana, and Marisol. However, I looked at Danika, Tesla, Anya, and Beth, the last of my crew on this trip. Danika said, "What about us? If we stick around Hoffdorf, they are likely to come after us too."

"Damn! I don't want you crippled too," I replied.

Just then, a trio of men knocked on Molly Maud's door. "We are here to perform the Marriage Ceremony on the married women who are living with you, Miss Porsche. Our records show that they are from some world called Ashford-5. Is this correct?"

"Certainly, come in," she said politely. No sense in arguing with them. Two carried d-guns.

I had to make a fast decision. Well, that goes with being a captain. The Seven Aspects that were preached in the Church of God back in Exchange City came to mind. Base your decisions on what yields the greatest amount of good for the most aspects of life. You can't go wrong using that as your yardstick. "Excuse me, sirs. But they were just now departing Hoffdorf for home. I guess that the ceremony won't be necessary since the four of us who are staying with Molly Maud have already gotten it. Show them ladies," I ordered. Jana, Jovanna, Marisol, and I raised our empty left arms. Such proof can't be debated. I sensed a protest from Danika, who was unwilling to leave me here in this hornet's nest, but I also knew that she would follow my lead.

"Yes, we were just packing our bags when you came. Will you allow us to finish packing? We'll be on our way in no time," Danika spoke up hastily. If they didn't go along with this, I was prepared to act, but hoped that I didn't have to.

The one in charge, checked on their names, but looked a little confused. He asked, "So you are leaving Cass-C in a few minutes?"

"Yes, unless you won't even let us pack a few things," she replied.

"Well, I suppose that is okay. We should verify that you have left Cass-C. Orders you know."

"Of course. Won't be but a minute."

"So how has it been going this morning?" Molly Maud inquired. "How many marriage ceremonies have you done already? Anyone protesting them? I hope not." She sounded so sincere, so disarming that I nearly laughed.

The one in charge who looked more like a priest than a soldier seemed to relax a bit, though from his demeanor I knew that he was a solider. "Well Miss Porsche, we've done three so far. Had us start at eight o'clock promptly. First one was a bit rough. They hadn't yet seen the official announcement. The other two went as well as can be expected. Lot of crying though."

"Yes, I imagine so. People are always crying at weddings and such," Molly Maud replied. Again, I could scarcely keep from bursting into a roar over her twisting of the crying aspect.

"Yeh, I've seen that happen too. Never could figure out why so many women cry at weddings, but they do. Maybe they are crying today for the same reason. I hadn't thought of that, Miss Porsche."

She giggled a little, further disarming the young lad. "One thing is for sure, if I ever get married, you won't have to come back to do me." She waved her left arm about a little, as though she were extremely proud of her missing hand.

The four returned with hastily packed bags in hand. "We're all set, love," Danika said and gave me a passionate farewell kiss. We said our goodbyes rapidly, and the men left with the four. A half hour later, Danika sent, *We made it safely to the ship. Got clearance to take off. Should we really depart?*

Yes. Call the emperor and tell him what's happened. We'll be okay here. I'm going to arrange for a transport for us, just in case trouble comes. Molly Maud's got lots of them handy now. We'll be fine. Kiss the kids for me.

After that, we five returned to watching the news broadcasts. "We should be working out ways and means of helping these women," Jana suggested. "Make a list of what can be done to keep those who have been crippled to do well in spite of all this." We had something of value to focus on and did so.

Come Monday, the fallout began in earnest. Half of her recently hired women came to work either sobbing or simply grief stricken. Some looked only about half-dressed. Molly Maud rose to the situation, calling for a group meeting before work, including the much larger male staff as well.

"Okay. We are facing the worst crisis ever. What they are doing to married women is simply despicable. But we are not here to debate the wisdom of their new laws or lack thereof. Nor are we here to fight them. We are all here to make quality products and earn a good living for ourselves and our families. So here's the new policy. No woman who has lost a hand is going to be fired or demoted or anything else. If she is now not able to perform her work, then I will hire an additional woman who has lost her hand, making two hands to get that job done. Same pay as always. From now on, when a job opening comes up, if it requires two hands, then I will hire two one-handed women, if they are qualified and suitable. I know that it cuts into our profits, but I'll deal with the Board of Directors, not you. Just do your best. Men, if you see a woman in need of some assistance, you are honor bound to give it freely and in a timely manner. We women are going to carry on and prosper and thrive just as we have been for the last few months. That is all."

Women cheered her and a few male workers joined them. True, for the rest of the week, organized chaos rippled thought the various plants as the one-armed women worked out how to continue their work, often forming new teams. Meanwhile, by Tuesday, Molly Maud's new ad hit the airwaves. She was hiring more married women.

By Tuesday, the reporters began coming around to interview Molly Maud, since she had been dealing with the loss of her hand for some months and was now the wealthiest industrialist in Hoffdorf. She rose to the challenge and rapidly became very vocal. She shared tips and constantly told the reporters, "Look. The proper course to follow is to continue to do as we have been doing, thriving and prospering as we women have never done before. Porsche Industries is always looking for more good married women."

At the end of the first week, Admiral Fritz and Commander Werner looked over the cumulative statistics. Eighty thousand women and a few men had lost their non-dominate hand. Twenty-five percent of the couples had to be sedated because of their protests and refusals. Twenty-five percent underwent it willingly, expressing hope this would solve everything as promised. The rest grumbled about it, launching mild protests, but obeyed the law.

"Good start, but we're getting a bit too much backlash. Time for Phase Two. We field triple the number of trio teams next week," Admiral Fritz declared.

Commander Werner countered, "It might be wise to up it tenfold, admiral. Nip all protests in the bud. If we get eight hundred thousand couples next week, we'll pass the halfway mark for our city. In two weeks, Hoffdorf will be finished, and we can send the trio teams to assist in the larger cities. We need this completely finished before the end of the month."

The admiral nodded, but thought better of it. Instead, he suggested, "I see your point. Don't give them time to create any backlash. There is far too much at stake here. We don't dare be pushed into having to publically defend the plan. I think we can bump it up twenty-fold by Monday. Let's get this completely done in two more weeks. I'll send my recommendation off to the other fifty admirals. Then, in three weeks, we can move out to the lesser worlds of the Federation."

On the third Monday of January, the newscasts began reporting that every married couple in Hoffdorf, including civil unions, had been given their marriage ceremony. "One hundred percent success," a reporter commented.

I wondered why they were not reporting on the misery this plan was causing. I didn't know then that the Admiralty

Round Table had issued strict orders to all the news channels not to interview any of the married couples for a month. The reason given was: "Give them time to adapt. This is a very personal bond between the couples." This reasoning only became known after Hoffdorf was handled.

Later in January, the magnitude of the losses started to become known. Just one example. Three-quarters of the musicians in Hoffdorf were women, and most of them were now no longer able to perform. Their musical arts took a nose dive! So it went. Dismal at the very best. Married women were frequently plummeted into grief and apathy, but in time, I hoped that would pass. I felt particularly helpless to do much but provide moral support for Molly Maud.

Chapter 13 Revenge

The Grotte. Cradled in an old section of Hoffdorf and not far from the Orchesterhalle, this collection of older brown stone homes was artist central. Home to painters, sculptors, writers, singers, and musicians, The Grotte was the focal point for the Arts. The Hoffdorf Symphony Orchestra gave weekly concerts in Orchesterhalle. Most of the orchestra's musicians were students of or graduates from the prestigious Donner School of Music. The Concert Master was also First Violinist, Gisela (Gisa) Hadwig-Liesel. Her mate of four years, Karla Liesel-Hadwig, was First Cellist. Both were graduates of the Donner School of Music.

Both were quite blonde twenty-five year old women with blue eyes. Gisa's hair was trimmed rather short, but teased some making her head seem somewhat larger. Thus, it never interfered with her violin playing, which obviously was extremely good. On the other hand, Karla's blonde tresses fell to the middle of her back in golden waves, which so enchanted Gisa. They had come to Donner's when they were fourteen, showing tremendous promise, which had been borne out by these many years. Rooming together and constant playing and practicing together, they had fallen in love with each other. At twenty-one, they defied their parents and had joined together in a civil union. Their parents subsequently disowned them, though with their current success as First Chairs in the Hoffdorf Symphony Orchestra, their parents had mellowed out somewhat.

New Year's Day, both women had slept in, having partied in the new year. Both were surprised to hear someone knocking loudly on their door at nine in the morning. Slipping on a robe to cover their naked bodies, the two headed to the door, fully intending to chew out whoever was being so rude. To their surprise, they saw three men, one looking more like some strange priest. The d-guns of the other two told them they were soldiers.

"What's the meaning of this?" Gisa inquired somewhat

foggy.

One of the men with the guns, said, "Gisela Hadwig-Liesel. Karla Liesel-Hadwig."

"Yes, I'm Gisela. She's Karla. What do you want at this hour?" she replied, trying to figure out why soldiers were at her door. Besides, this was The Grotte. No soldiers ever came to the artists' community.

"We are here to perform the marriage ceremony on you both," the priest-like man said.

"But we are already married. No thanks. Bye." Gisa tried to shut the door, but the men stopped her.

"Save the Family Plan. All married couples must receive the marriage ceremony."

"Well, okay, but be quick about it," Gisa replied, opening the door fully and letting them in.

Standing side by side, as they had when they were united, the priest-like man turned on some rock music while the two men setup two identical machines between the two women. The priest-like man draped a white cloth over a box in from of them. Next, making sure that it was her non-dominant hand, he had Gisa put her hand on one of the machines. Then, he did the same with Karla. He closed both lids and proceeded solemnly.

"You are giving her your hand in holy marriage, knowing full well what is given out of your love for her can never be taken back. Each of you is accepting the offered hand, given to you out of her deep abiding love for you and also knowing this bond between you cannot ever be broken or undone from this day forward. Since the dawn of time, this precious gift of her hand in marriage seals your bonds through sickness and health, through good times and bad until death doth part your ways. The precious gift of the bride symbolizes her undying faithfulness to you, her mate. Each of you by your acceptance of her hand in marriage commits you with the never ending responsibility to care for her, to cherish her, to remain faithful to her until death doth part your ways. This acceptance of her hand in marriage is final and cannot be undone."

He altered the wording to better suit this situation. "If

either of you should become unfaithful to the other, you'll be marked as a social demon, and you'll be wholly shunned by our entire society and prosecuted by law." Gisa noticed that he was glancing at the fronts of the two machines and wondered what that might mean.

He continued, "It is done." He opened the machine, freeing their left hands and said, "Now with your other hand, take your mate's hand there and place it here upon the Holy Altar of Lord God who has borne witness to your vows."

Both women screamed as loud as they could! There lay their fingerboard hands! Shock and utter panic struck both women hard. The two soldiers had no choice but to inject the drug into both women's necks as quickly as they could. A minute later, two sedated women stood before the machines.

The priest-like man repeated his orders. "Now with your other hand, take your mate's hand there and place it here upon the Holy Altar of Lord God who has borne witness to your vows." The now docile women picked up each other's lifeless hand and put it on the cloth. Hastily, the man folded the cloth over them, hiding them from view.

He spoke calmly, "Your shared gift of her hand this day is a symbol unto God of the undying, eternal love that you share for each other. Neither of you has felt any pain or discomfort. Think not of this as a brutal thing, but rather as something to be treasured for all of your lives. Your missing hand is never, ever anything to be ashamed of or embarrassed by — not anywhere on our world. On the contrary, it is the visible symbol of your love for your mate here and your family. Always show your handless arm with the greatest of pride! In your daily life, make use of that arm in any way that you can. May God bless you both, filling your lives with richness and happiness."

He then shook their remaining hand firmly and turned off the music. The ceremony was finished.

Gisa said softly, "But we are professional musicians. Violinist and cellist in the symphony orchestra. We can't play without our hands."

"I'm sorry, but that is of no importance. Every married woman or those in civil unions like yourselves must give their non-dominant hand to their partner. It is the new law. There are no exceptions. The law is quite specific about this. One hundred percent of all married couples must give their hand. It was your non-dominant hand, so you can still write and all that. I suppose you'll have to find some other kind of work to do now. Anyway, watch the news. The full details are being broadcast today. May God bless you both." He turned and the men left the two heavily sedated women standing there in their robes staring at their left arms where their virtuoso hands and fingers had been, speechless and emotionless.

That began to change, as the fast acting drug began to wear off. Suddenly, Gisa screamed again, and Karla's voice soon added to hers. The shock quickly gave way to a grief more intense than either woman had ever felt in her entire twenty-five years! Sobbing hysterically, they hugged each other and cried and cried. Their whole lives were crushed! Their entire purpose in life was gone, destroyed utterly, and beyond all hope. Never again would they be able to share the beauty of music with others. Now, all they could do was cry, cry harder than they ever had in their lives.

Sometime later, they remembered to turn on the news. Finally, they began to understand what had happened. Worse, it was happening to all married women, everywhere. They broke down again and sobbed for a long time. Around noon, someone knocked softly on their door. Both women recognized the knock though. Only one person knocked in that peculiar fashion, one, two, three. It had to be their closest friend, the portrait painter, Heinrich Donner, a young nephew of Wenzel Donner, the current owner of Donner School of Music. Heinz always like to hang out with these two women and discuss whatever the day's topic might be.

Their faces wet with tears, they rose and went to the door to let him in. One look at the two robed women told Heinz all that he need. "Oh dear God! Not you too! Oh god." Heinz gushed. "Are you hurting or anything?"

Karla managed to sob, "No. We didn't feel anything. We didn't even know what was happening until it was over. We're destroyed! Wiped out! Lost! Ruined!" She and Gisa began crying again. Heinz came on inside and shut their door. He put his arms around the two grief-stricken women, ushering them into their small living room and onto their couch, where they often sat chatting with him. Soon, even Heinz was crying.

After some time, they regained a little composure. Heinz volunteered, "I came to check on you both. The soldiers came to The Grotte early this morning. The school of music is wiped out! Almost three-quarters of the women musicians lost their hands too. You aren't alone. Never has there been such a disaster in the history of the fine arts! This is a calamity beyond all description! I came as soon as I could. Gertrude is taking it hard and tried to kill herself. I got there in time, though, but maybe now I ought to have let her do it. I don't know. This is so awful I can't even imagine what it's like for you two."

Gisa said, "Gertrude too? She did? Well, I'm glad you got to her in time, but maybe that's all that is left to us now. To die. Our music is dead. We can't play. Not with this," she waved her handless left arm in front of his face.

"It doesn't hurt?" he asked softly.

She rubbed it. "No, not at all. Just feels funny. I feel so completely helpless now. Whatever are we going to do? All the married women musician? Oh dear God!"

"Yeh, all of them. Three-quarters of the entire symphony, gone, erased, wiped out," Heinz reported sadly. Then he said, "You had breakfast yet? Hungry?"

Karla piped up, "No. Starving, but oh hell, we can't do anything now. How can we ever fix breakfast?" She began sobbing again.

"No sweat. I'm here. Come on. I'll fix it, but you two had best tell me what to do. I don't cook." The two women broke into a very slight smile, knowing that was an understatement. He had once tried to make them some tea and had somehow melted the teakettle on their stove.

A while later, Karla admitted, "I guess we can still cook, Heinz, clumsy and awkward, but we're doing it, sort of."

With full stomachs, the trio sat silently around their small kitchen table. Heinz had no idea what to say to his best friends that would help in anyway. Wisely, he said nothing. Eventually, Gisa said, "Well, we do have quite a lot of money saved up, Karla. We can get by for some time until whatever happens happens."

"Hey, you two need anything, anything at all, just ask me. You know that you two are my very best friends," Heinz volunteered.

"We know, Heinz. You are our best friend too. We probably will need lots of help," Gisa replied.

"Maybe you should go check up on Gertrude and the others," Karla suggested.

"Say, when you get a chance, see what Wenzel is going to do with the symphony," Gisa suggested.

"I suppose I ought to check up on her again. Of course, everyone else is taking it hard too. I haven't seen one smiling face all morning. The Arts in Hoffdorf has been wiped out," Heinz said solemnly.

"Well, you can still paint, Heinrich," Karla pointed out.

"Paint what? Portraits of handless women? No thank you. I'm done painting for now," he declared. Both women sensed how hard this was on the sensitive young man. The ramifications of this wicked action were affecting many others than just the women, she realized.

After he left, Karla commented, "Well maybe the singers and dancers can continue, perhaps."

"Balance will be off. They can't hold their music and turn their pages," Gisa pointed out.

"Oh. Right. Sculptors are finished too. Maybe the writers can continue on with one hand on the keyboard, probably very slowly though," Karla suggested. "I think Heinz is right. The Arts of Hoffdorf have been wiped out."

"Karla, I still have you, my dearest love." Gisa gave Karla a loving hug and they embraced.

Later, they made tea and began to think more clearly. "Our music is dead, taken from us by the powerful men," Karla griped.

"Right. Taken without our consent, though we'd never consent to this mutilation. They must be made to pay somehow," Gisa replied.

"I'd like nothing more than to kill them, but that's way too good for them. They need to have their livelihoods stripped from them, just as they stripped ours from us. That would be a proper payback, don't you think?" Karla suggested.

"Now you are talking, love. Strip their livelihoods from them. That's what we have to do! But how do we do that and just who are they?" Gisa asked.

"Admiral Fritz for one. Hell, the whole damn Round Table was in on it," Karla exclaimed, recalling what she'd heard on the recent newscasts that she'd paid very little attention to.

"Hell, The Seven must be in on it too. Everyone knows they okay everything. What about the stupid Intelligence Division? They should have put a stop to this whole damned thing," Gisa argued. Both women were becoming very angry. That soon gave way to severe hostility towards all three organizations.

When one has one's main goal in life stripped away against one's will, eventually a new goal replaces the lost one. So it was in the case of these two now ex-musicians. Their hostilities didn't evaporate. How could it? Every minute of every day, they faced their clumsiness, their awkwardness. Even dressing was fraught with difficulties, but they worked together to surmount them, calling on Heinz only when they couldn't find a new way to do something. Nevertheless, their new goal began to solidify.

"We're going to erase the livelihoods of the admirals, the ID men, and The Seven. Make them pay like they made us pay," Karla declared.

"Right. We only lack the knowledge of the how, and just who the hell The Seven actually are. We're going to have to become detectives, dear. You up for it?" Gisa asked.

"Right-o. Detectives it is. What's first, the how or the who?" Karla inquired, adding, "I vote for the how first because that makes sense. Once we know how we are going to rip their livelihoods away from them, then we can focus on getting just the right ones to pay."

The how took the pair some time, but time they had plenty of now. Their careers gone, time they had. Plus, they had their laptops. Of course, they both broke down when they first brought them back up. There was all their music they were arranging for their next performances. With heavy sighs, they deleted everything that had to do with music from their computers. Even Heinz was brought in on their new quest. He'd given up painting and found helping his dear friends more productive.

Days passed as they studied up on all kinds of drugs, chemical poisons, and similar agents, but they rejected them all. Karla explained, "We don't want to kill them. That is far, far too good for them. No, Heinz, we want to strip away their livelihoods, like they stripped away ours!"

"Got it. So temporary paralysis is out. Nerve agents, out," Heinz began crossing items he'd found off his list until nothing was left. He grumbled, "Damn it, there's nothing left in the Federation, unless you can stick their hands in those damned machines!"

The two women were now completely driven. Karla said, "Okay then. If there isn't anything we can use here in the Federation, how about that Imperium? Maybe there's something they have that'll work."

An hour later, the trio began reading about the horrific genetic bio agent. "Good God! The Imperium scientists were planning to use that stuff on us if the war went south for them?" Heinz exclaimed, totally awed by what he was reading.

"No kidding. This stuff is horrid. Look at what it does? There are some pictures of men and women victims!" Karla gushed.

"Look at those boobs!" Heinz exclaimed. "They are bigger than their heads!"

"You men are all alike. It's all about boobs," Karla teased him.

He laughed good-naturedly. "Well, we don't have them and you do," he shot back. All three laughed.

Gisa said thoughtfully, "You know, this is what we've been looking for. The victims are completely helpless. No arms. Monster boobs that force them to have to wear those steel corsets. I can imagine the back pains they must have carrying around those boobs, Heinz. No fun. And their feet. Have you ever seen such distorted feet? They sure don't walk at all well."

Karla added, "It says here with those split lips, they can't talk and be understood, and have to wear those funny looking lip disks. Not sure why they do, though. And look at their hair. Oh, it says that there are pain neurons in their hair. What's that all about?"

"Don't know. I flunked biology," Gisa commented. "But it must be a bad thing. Karla, this is just what we are looking for. With a good dose of this bio agent, the admirals, the ID men, and The Seven will have their careers and livelihoods stripped away from them, just like they did to us and half the damned world!"

"Wonder how we can get a hold of this stuff?" Karla asked. "Bet it isn't commercially available." They all laughed.

A week of diligent searching yielded some key information from one of their old allies during the war with the Imperium: Gamelon-3. A day later, emails began to fly back and forth. Finally, the women heard what they wanted to hear. One set of that bio agent was for sale for a price. They agreed to the price. The next email said:

Gormak will be delivering it on the next cargo run to Cass-C. Expect it on or around February 1. Have the ten thousand gold dollars ready. He'll contact you. Remember, this stuff is outlawed everywhere in the Imperium, so don't get caught with the stuff.

The two had a few days to get the money together. The sold their expensive violin and cello and their backup instruments as well. They'd never play again. Combining those funds, they had far more than they needed and took ten thousand out in cash. Now, they waited excitedly for the first to come.

Around midnight, they received the anticipated email. They were to meet at the spaceport in an hour. Packing the gold dollars in a bag, they headed out to the edge of town, taking a taxi. Once there, they followed the email's directions and found the rusting old transport ship right were the email said it would be. A very short, grubby man stepped out of the shadows holding a d-gun on the women. He looked around. Satisfied that they weren't being followed, he said, "Got the cash?"

"Yes, here in the bag. Got the merchandise?" Gisa

asked.

"Sure as soon as I verify the money. I see the buyer sent women to pick it up. Safer that way. Clever man. Okay, money looks good. It's that crate there. Good hunting." He turned and went inside the rust bucket with the loot. Each woman had to use her good hand to lift the crate. Awkwardly they stumbled away from the ship, just in time as it took off almost at once. A bit later, still lugging the crate, they arrived back at their taxi. The driver kindly lifted the crate into the trunk and took them home, even carrying it inside for them. They gave him a nice tip. Making sure they were really alone, they opened the crate only to find another crate with hazard bio agent labels plastered all over it. Gently they opened it and found a set of clothing, strange shoes, lip disks, and of course, the small cylinder, half filled with the bio agent. Both women smiled and put everything back, before sliding it beneath their bed.

The next day, they began wondering how much of this stuff they would need. More online research gave them some working ideas of the quantity. Probably ten cylinders would handle the Round Table. Fifteen perhaps for the ID building. The unknown was The Seven.

Gisa said, "Now we play detectives." Karla laughed. "We're going to have to wander around and see what people know about The Seven."

"Well, we might get farther if we dress up like professional women, out looking for a new job," Gisa suggested.

"Well, we are, sort of," Karla teased her mate. "Of course, we're going to have to have Heinz help us get dressed. We still can't put on our nylons without ripping them, and we can't go about with naked legs. That's just not ever done."

The next morning, Heinz came when they called him. He was a little embarrassed with what they asked him to do, but managed to get them properly dressed. "Well, you both look very sexy," he commented.

"Naturally we do. That's why we married each other," Karla teased him. "But walking in these heels isn't much fun. Professional women manage, so do we. Okay, we're off to locate The Seven somehow."

"How you going to do that? No one knows their identity. They might not even live in Hoffdorf, you know," Heinz countered.

"We have a plan, Heinz," Karla explained. "You see, even if you are hiding in plain sight, being super secretive and all that, still you and the others must have a secret place to meet. It has to be super secure, you know. So we are going visiting, just two down on their luck professional women looking for a new job, like half the damned city."

"But I don't get it," Heinz complained.

"Well, when we find a place that won't let us in, we know something's going on there. We'll probably find lots of them, but sooner or later we're going to come across where they meet. I don't care if we spend the rest of our lifetimes looking for them, we're going to find them and make them pay the way they made us pay," Gisa said antagonistically.

Arm in arm, the two set off on foot. They needed to support each other. Walking in six-inch heels wasn't the easiest thing to do. Foot sore days went by, along with hundreds of "dumb" inquiries. Yet, it was paying off for the two. They had found six suites where they were simply denied admittance. They put Heinz on watching detail. Pretending to sip coffee and read a paper, he stood as close to these suites as possible and watched to see who entered them. Within days, he had eliminated five of the six as possible sites where The Seven met. A group of bankers and some exotic women entered one, and so on.

Only one site had no one entering for days. Just as Heinz was about to give it up, he spotted precisely seven older men casting glances over their heads and then entering the suite on the top floor of the Wilmar Building. This looked promising, and he phoned Karla. "We will be right over. Call us if they should leave before we get there. We're very slow in these heels."

A half-hour later and slightly out of breath, the two women reached the top floor of the Wilmar building and spotted Heinz reading a paper. He nodded towards Suite 1102 and slipped into the elevator. Taking a deep breath together, the pair walked up to the door of the suite and knocked.

Repeatedly. At last, an older man opened the door.

"Excuse us, sir. We are two professional women looking for new jobs. I know that we can't do much, not like this," Karla said politely and waving her stump around a bit.

"Sorry, private suite. Look elsewhere, ladies." His eyes didn't fail to fall upon their legs and heels, however. After taking a good look, he closed the door, but not before the damage had been done, though he didn't realize it.

The two women turned and headed for the elevator. Once they were heading downwards, Gisa whispered, "I heard someone inside say, 'No Commander Werner, not now. Have the admiral announce it tomorrow.' It must be The Seven."

"We need more proof, Gisa. After all, we don't want to harm innocent men, if any man is truly innocent," Karla said.

"True. We can watch the news and see if some admiral announces something tomorrow. If he does, we have our men," Gisa declared.

The next day, they watched the news channel. Around ten, an admiral announced the marriage ceremony would commence on Betal-D today. The two women looked at each other and smiled. "Now, we have to figure out how to deliver the gas, how many cylinders we're going to need, and how we can get access to a Duplicator Machine," Karla stated.

The following day, two professional women entered the Hoffdorf Public Library, heels softly clicking on the polished granite swirls of the expensive stone floor, the smell of books and polish in the air. "Where do you keep building plans?" Karla asked the woman behind the imitation oak desk.

"Oh, secretaries again. Floor Three, Room 18," she replied softly.

Smiling, the two headed for the stairs. "Why does everyone think we're secretaries or receptionists?" Gisa asked, a little miffed.

"Cause we can't be musicians any longer," Karla barked softly. Her remark sobered both women, who quickly found the right room. Drawers held thousands of building plans. Others were computerized. They found a catalogue and looked for the three locations. Only the Round Table was online. Trying to handle the large velum drawings with only one hand

and a stump proved highly frustrating for the two women, who finally had no choice but to work together on a single one, not as they had planned on doing. Putting the ones that they didn't want back in the drawers was more of a challenge than retrieving one. Both women swore silently, steeling their resolve. "Hell, they've made us almost useless women!" Karla exhaled under her breath.

An hour later but with most of it spent struggling with the velum, they found what they desired. Next, the online plans were simple to view and took only a couple of minutes. "Got them memorized dear?" Karla whispered.

Gisa nodded. She had an extremely good memory. Once she'd seen something, she could pretty easily bring mental images of it back into her mind. Joining arms again, they walked out of the library and headed on home, a mile away. The day was slightly chilly; winter would soon be here. It usually began around March here in Hoffdorf. A slight breeze blew Karla's long hair around to her face. She reached up with her left hand to brush it away only to find herself staring at a stump. "Here, let me," Gisa volunteered, whose right hand was free. "There, you can sort of hold your stump to it to keep it back dear.

Tears of emotion watered Karla's eyes. "Doesn't this nightmare ever end, Gisa? Maybe Gertrude had the right idea. How can we really live crippled like this?"

"I don't know, but you know I love your hair. Mine's been growing now that I can't trim it any more, though I suppose I could go get it cut."

"Oh don't. You look good," Karla whispered back.

The streets were rather crowded today. Gisa noticed most men gazed at their legs and heels as they approached the pair, but then they did that to all other women as well. Her mouth had a bad taste in it. Men, she thought, and gave Karla's arm a little squeeze with her stump arm, bring a trace of a smile to Karla's face, recognition of their secret signal of love.

Once back at their small brown stone home, Gisa got out some paper and pencils, preparing to sketch out the relevant parts of the building plans from memory. She had to use her stump to hold the paper still, but it once more reminded her of her terrible loss. Her breath had a catch in it. She swallowed, steeled her will, and began sketching. A male voice broke her concentration, "How's my sexy women doing today?" It was Heinz.

Karla told him about the floor plans. "So you are really going to do this. Okay, count me in. How can I help now?"

"Well, we're going to need help with a Duplication machine," Karla explained. "We're planning to use the one at the Donner School of Music. We still have the access codes to get in, and probably they haven't changed the codes on the Duplicating machine. We'll leave some money to pay for our duplicating, though. Still, we can't carry the darn thing, well not easily." She waved her stump for him, though she needn't have. He knew what she meant.

"Cool. I can get some bags to carry them in. How many are we making?" Heinz asked.

"I think twenty-one ought to do it, but maybe we should recheck now that we know the floor plans," Karla suggested. Both women excelled at simple math, since they were musicians and trained to count. An hour later, Karla lowered her estimate. "I think sixteen will be enough. Ten for the large round room, five for the top floor of the ID, one for the small suite."

"Got it. Back in a while with some bags," Heinz said happily. Karla gave him a little hug, which he appreciated.

That night around midnight, the trio walked the short distance to the Donner School of Music. The women were still dressed up, but Heinz had a steadying arm around each woman. It was entirely too much trouble for them to undress and redress, so they still wore their professional woman's outfits, heels and all. At the back door, Gisa entered the access code just as she had done countless times before when she was a student here. She'd spent almost a third of her life here working hard on the violin to become not only First Chair but also Concert Master. Now that was stripped away from her forever, compliments of these filthy men.

Steeled again, the trio entered the darkened building. Small night-lights provided enough illumination to see. All three knew precisely where they were going. Heinz had been here too many times to count, listening to the pair practicing or performing. Just entering brought back those happy memories. They'd practically grown up together, well since they were fourteen anyway. His own eyes watered, but he didn't have a hand free to wipe them. Heels clicking on the tiled floor, they were not sneaking in. Anyone could have heard them. Even if they met anyone, nearly everyone here knew the three by sight.

In the basement, they found the Duplicating machine. Gisa punched in the access code, and the machine activated, but took several minutes for the green ready light to show. This machine was the most expensive piece of machinery in the school. Why did they have it? This was a premier music school. Top students needed top of the line musical instruments. The Duplication machine handled that nicely. Put in a good instrument, press the dupe button, wait a while, and out comes a precise duplicate for the student. Gisa wondered how many violins the machine had made all these years? That caused her eyes to water some.

"Got the cylinder, Heinz?" Karla asked.

"Right here, boss." He retrieved their small cylinder, and she told him how to insert it, since with only one hand, she knew she couldn't do it herself, frustrating her once more in her seemingly endless rounds of frustrations.

"We're ready. Here goes," Gisa said, pressing the Dupe button. The three waited impatiently for five minutes before the Done button activated. Heinz lifted the lid and produced the duplicate cylinder. "One down, fifteen to go," she said.

An hour and a half later, Heinz had all seventeen of the cylinders stuffed into two large duffle bags. Gisa did a quick calculation in her head and struggled with her purse to extract a thousand gold dollars. "God damn this missing hand! Karla, little help with this." Between the two of them, they got the money out and placed it in the slot on the machine, where students who used it to make backup instruments placed their payments. Neither woman saw Heinz wipe his eyes again. Just seeing their enormous struggles to do utterly simple things was breaking his heart. He knew he'd never paint again because of all that he'd seen. It didn't matter that his portraits had been commanding top dollar.

Karla put her right arm around Gisa's left to steady both of them. She knew that Heinz was struggling to carry the heavy load for them. Around three in the morning, they arrived back at their place. "Stay the night, Heinz. You can have the couch," Karla offered sleepily.

"Only if you can let me get you undressed. It's too darn late for you to waste a lot of time with it," he offered.

Next morning over breakfast, compliments of Heinz, they put their heads together to work out just how actually to do it. They'd need plumbing supplies, tubing, fittings, and a way to trigger the devices. While Heinz headed to the store to get what they thought they'd need, the two went to their laptops, searching online for just the right method of activating them. A simple timer-controlled release valve turned out to be the answer they wanted. They ordered two of them and then added another one that required a mechanical button press. Why the third different one? They had no idea when The Seven would meet. Hence, they'd have to stand watch and physically activate it when the men met. A timer could run the others.

A day later, with Heinz's help, they had three packages ready to go. The cylinders were duct taped together into a tight package, their tops tied together with the fittings and tubing that entered the timer-controlled release valve. All that they had to do was set the timer. At the indicated time, the valve would open, releasing the contents of all the cylinders. Where would it be released? Into the air intake line for either the Round Room or the top floor of the ID building. The single cylinder system would have to be installed in the air intake for the small suite where The Seven met.

The next day they trio began their "secret" operation. Disguised as janitors, they slipped into the Admiralty Round Table building and found a cleaning cart in the basement. Heinz stuffed and hid the bundle of ten cylinders under rags. Following Gisa's recalled plans, they pushed it down to the maintenance room. Inside, they found the air intake line. "Gee, they even have it clearly marked for us," Karla said sarcastically. Large signs indicated which was which, so presumable the maintenance men would not get confused. Gisa produced a screwdriver and struggled to undo the four screws that kept the screen cover tight to the intake like. "Here, let me try," Heinz whispered.

"We are so god damn useless, Heinz," Gisa whispered, holding back tears yet again. "Stick it way inside so no one sees it," she whispered.

"Okay, one down, two to go," Karla said once they were outside and walking back to their home.

Dressed again as janitors, the trio walked brazenly into the main Intelligence Division building and asked the desk receptionist, a professional woman, but missing her left hand, where the janitor supervisor was at. "We are supposed to meet him for a job interview," Karla explained. The woman gave them very good directions, and she thanked her.

A few minutes later, they were in the basement. At the moment, no one was around. Gisa silently led them to the room where the air intake lines were located. Once inside, she grinned. Like the Round Table, each one was clearly labeled. "Are all janitors really this dumb?" she whispered, as Heinz removed the safety screen. Like the other one, air was being sucked into the line at a good clip. He inserted package number two and replaced the cover. On their way out, they ran into the head janitor.

"Oh. We are looking for you. Are there any job openings, sir," Karla said politely.

"Well, have you done any janitorial work before?" he asked, staring at their left stumps.

"Well, not exactly. But with these," Karla raised her stump up, "we will do most anything for a job."

"Sorry misses. Need two hands for this kind of work."

Looking downcast, the three walked on down the hall, up the stairs, and back on the main floor, where the polite receptionist asked, "Any luck?"

Karla replied sadly, "No, he said that we needed two hands." The receptionist looked very sad and apologized to them.

Outside and heading home, Karla announced, "Two

down, one to go."

The hour was approaching four when they reached their final destination, the Wilmar building. Here the plans indicated the air intake was on a wall there on the same floor as the secret Suite 1102. They gambled that no one would be out and about on this floor. They were right. The intake screen was on a side wall that wasn't visible from the entrance to the suite. Five minutes later, Gisa pressed the Arm button and observed the red light turning on. It would activate and release the cylinder's contents whenever one pressed a corresponding button on the controller device, a very small, handheld box.

They stopped at a pizza place for supper, Heinz's treat. "Well done, ladies," he congratulated them both. "So when does the action come?"

"Friday at one for the two. We are going to have to stand watch on The Seven's suite and wait for them to meet again. Only when they go inside can we press the activate button. No telling when they will meet though. We'll just have to wait and hope and pray," Karla spelled it out.

"Want me to wait with you, just in case?" he offered.

"No, Heinz. You've already done more than enough for us. If we are caught or something, we don't want you to get in trouble. It's our useless necks we're risking. We don't have anything to lose, but you do, Heinz. You have your whole life ahead of you. Us, we have nothing but misery ahead of us. You know that. So thanks for all your help," Karla stated firmly. He argued a bit, but saw they were resolved to keep him out of it.

Friday morning, the two spent over an hour struggling to get into their professional woman's outfits. Finally that done, they checked their appearance and were satisfied. Gisa left nothing to chance. They each had a triggering device. A button press from either of them would trigger the device. Each slipped it into their right blazer pockets and two headed off to the Wilmar building. They reached the eleventh floor around ten that Friday morning, where they took turns standing close to the adjoining suite opposite 1102. Twice, they had to explain, "We are waiting for Mr. Jones to interview us for his receptionist position." While the men took this opportunity to eye their legs and heels, since they looked the part, nothing more was said. No one challenged their story or asked who Mr. Jones was.

Standing that long in six-inch heels was taking a toll on their feet, making them slightly irritable. Just then, Karla noticed the clock above the elevator. It read one o'clock. Both women smiled, imagining the two well-placed devices activating, the bio agent gas flowing steadily into the air duct and then out into the entire Round Table room and the whole top floor of the ID building, where Commander Werner's main office was located.

Their reverie was cut short. Just then, the elevator doors opened and the seven men in suits stepped out. Both women twitched a little. "Say, I remember you two. You were here before. Something's up," one said.

"Bring them into the room," another said.

Strong arms grabbed each woman around their good arms, forcing them to follow the men. However, the men moved far too quickly for the women in their tall heels, both stumbled. "Please. Not so fast. We're in heels you know," Karla protested, her hair falling from her back over her face, partially hiding it. She reached up to push it back with her left hand before she realized it was the wrong one. A useless stump touched her hair. As the men entered their secret room, the man holding her realized this and switched arms, allowing her to push her hair back. She took this opportunity to slip her hand into her pocket and push the button. Gisa didn't have a chance to use her hand on hers, not yet anyway.

"So ladies. What are you doing spying on us?" one demanded to know. The door was shut. Inside, they saw that the room was overly well insulated. No sounds could leave this room. Yelling for help would be useless. Besides, this top floor was mostly deserted anyway.

"We aren't spying. We're looking for a receptionist job. We didn't see anyone here, so we thought you might need some," Gisa tried to sound reasonable.

"Could be, but check them out anyway. Where are your id cards?"

"We left them at home. We can't really use them properly anymore," Gisa said, raising her stump up in the air.

"Too hard to manipulate." She hoped this would satisfy them. It didn't. She did smell something in the air and glanced at Karla, who flashed her a smile.

"Don't like it. What are your names? Bring up the computer and check what they say," another man ordered.

"Karla Liesel-Hadwig, sir. She's my mate, Gisela Hadwig-Liesel."

A few tense minutes passed while another man played with the computer. "It says here that you are what First Violinist and Concert Master for the symphony and your mate is First Cellist?" He laughed wickedly. "Well, obviously not anymore."

"No, not anymore," Gisa answered. She was feeling very funny, dizzy like, no, dopey. No, groggy. "No. Not anymore. No. Not. Any. More."

The men were also acting strangely, unfastening their ties, and struggling to take off their jackets. "What's. Going. On?"

"We. Are. Under. Gas. Attack." another tried to say, but the words came out in slow motion. One man slumped to the floor, causing the other six to panic. Unfortunately, they were also moving far too slow to carry out any effective action.

As another man fell down, Gisa said, "We. Are. Taking. Your. Careers. Away. From. You. Like. You. Did. To. Us." She slowly slumped to the ground. Karla wanted to help her, but couldn't move her legs. She tried to move, and in the high heels, she managed to fall down, but never realized she actually hit the carpeted floor. She, like the others in the room, was unconscious, slipping into a coma. Both Gisa and Karla felt very relieved, completely satisfied. They hadn't killed those responsible, but were taking their careers away from them, just as had been done to them. Justice was served.

Chapter 14 Help

Heinz didn't follow orders. He loved the two lesbians more than he loved anyone else. They were his dearest friends, had been for nine years, until now the best nine years of his life. They were the most gifted musicians he'd ever heard, and they highly respected his portrait art, encouraging him when he was in the dumps. No way was he going to allow them to go this alone. Besides, they were not killing anyone, but erasing their careers, just as they had erased millions of other careers. "I'll guard their backs, if nothing else."

From a distance, he followed the pair, as they made their slow way to the Wilmar building and then went inside. He took up a position across the street to wait for them to walk back out. He'd brought a foot long sandwich and soda with him, figuring it might be a long wait, if the men even showed up today. Quite a lot of men and women left the building around noon, but not his two. He waited. Around one, in singles, pairs, and small groups, the same ones reentered the building. He waited. Then, he saw seven men coming from different directions, but meeting near the door. He noticed them nodding slightly to each other. That they also glanced around wasn't missed. He pretended to take another sip of soda. Those must be The Seven, he thought. Shouldn't be long now, bastards.

He waited and waited. The yellow sun continued to cast moving shadows. He checked his watch. Four o'clock! Now, he began to panic. Something must have gone wrong. At last, figuring the building would close down after five, he headed inside, taking the elevator up to the top floor. He got off and saw the empty hallway. There was a strange odor in the air, very faint, but different than before. He panicked when he didn't see the women. Quickly, he walked around to the side and listened at the air duct. He heard a faint hissing. Stepping back, his mind raced. Obviously, Gisa and Karla had pressed the activate button. The Seven had not left, so they had to be in that room, but where were the women? Had they taken some other route out of the building? He headed back down and looked for a back exit. It was there, but it had a security alarm on it. Anyone opening it would trigger alarms all over the place. No, they had not gone that way. He went back outside to think.

As five came, he watched many men and women leaving. A bit later, a security man arrived and went in, locking the door behind him. If they were still inside, they'd not be able to get out until he opened it in the morning. Where are they? He had a thought. Perhaps he had somehow missed them and now they were back home. Hastily, he headed back across town, jogging now and then in his haste. He gave his usual knock on their door. Silence. He used his spare key to let himself inside. A minute later, his panic crescendoed. They were not here. He slumped into their sofa, "Some guard-your-back fellow I am!"

He calmed down and began to think this through. The women had not come out. He was certain of that. So what happened to them? Then, it struck him! The Seven had somehow figured out that they were spying on them and had taken them prisoners, forcing them into the secret room! Well, they had still activated their cylinder, but that meant they were becoming victims of their attack on The Seven! Suicide? No, no one was being killed. They were taking their careers away from them as they had done to the women. Images of the totally helpless victims came into his mind. "My God! I've got to do something to help them! I can't let you down. If nothing else, I can care for them somehow. I need to get them some help, but who, how? Think man, think!"

For a time, nothing came. As he began to fall asleep on their sofa, an idea came into his mind. Aliens. He remembered hearing Molly Maud Porsche had aliens with her, helping her get her company established. Further, they had been terrorist victims themselves. Now, the reporter's interview with their leader came back into his mind. Suddenly, he knew whom he had to see, but the hour was very late.

"Come look at this!" Molly Maud called out to me. It was seven on Friday night, and I decided now was as good a time as any to wash my hair. Wrapped up in a towel, I strolled out to see what she wanted. "Look. Something really weird is going on. Listen."

The reporter sounded a bit concerned, and soon I knew why. "Repeating. We are here live at the Admiralty Round Table, where something extraordinary has occurred sometime today. A janitor, Waldo Hoffmeyer, was the one who first discovered it. Tell us what happened, Mr. Hoffmeyer." The camera focused on a nervous older man wearing bib overalls.

"Well, I was just doing my nightly cleaning rounds when I opened the door to the room. That's what I was supposed to do, sweep it."

The reporter interrupted him, "That's the Round Table room where the thousands of admirals meet?"

"Yes. That's the room. I took one look inside and smelled something really bad. I think I might have gasped, but I sure closed that door mighty fast!"

"But what did you see, Mr. Hoffmeyer?" the reporter hounded him.

"Them admirals. They were all lying on the floor, dead-like you know."

"So they were dead?"

"Well, I never seen a dead body before, but they wasn't moving or anything. So I called security. That's all."

"There you have the only eye witness we have as yet that will talk to us. The place is swarming with security men and several top scientists too. I think every ambulance in Hoffdorf is parked outside, but so far, no bodies have been recovered. We have received a tip from an anonymous source that the admirals are not dead, but are unconscious. There definitely is some form of toxic gas in the area. We can get faint whiffs of it here where we've been ordered to wait. Hold on. I'm getting word now. Yes, yes, please route the video feed directly to the cameras. Ladies and gentlemen, the security general is going to send us the video feed from their spy robot they use to defuse bombs. I'm told it is pretty graphic. Here it comes."

The voice was silent, as we watched a rather grainy black and white image on the screen, moving along slowly into the room. The camera could not be more than eight inches from the floor. At first, it moved in a sort of panorama, and we could see bodies lying all over the floor. Next, it moved up close to one fallen admiral and zoomed in on the man's neck. We could see a distinct pulse. He was alive. I guess that's what the security general wanted everyone to see — that their rulers were still alive. The fuzzy images ended, and the next instant, some man was standing before a wall of hastily erected microphones.

"Good evening. I have both good news and bad news. The good news is as far as we can tell from the outside and from our robots, the admirals are very much alive, but unresponsive. Several doctors believe they are perhaps in comas, but they can't tell definitively from the robot images. We are sending in the "dog" next, and that robot will provide very high quality images. The bad news is we simply don't know what we're dealing with here. It is some form of toxic gas. However, samples taken by our top chemists have yet to reveal just what kind of poisonous gas this is. Thus, we are erring on the safe side and keeping the room under tight quarantine until the gas dissipates. Estimates suggest it will be morning before it is safe to enter; however, containment suits are on the way. If it looks like their lives are at risk, doctors will go in wearing the containment suits, though there's no way to know if they would be protected from the gas or not."

"So far, no one has claimed responsibility for this brazen attack on our top rulers. That is all I have at this time. When there are new developments, I'll hold another press conference. I know all the Federation is watching anxiously as this unfolds. Remember, the admirals are still alive, and that's the most important thing right now. That is all."

The camera switched to the original reporter who summarized everything. Molly Maud turned the volume down. "Now that is really wild. I wonder what is going on?"

I had a very sick feeling in my stomach. This looked all too familiar to me, to us. Jovanna said, "Nia Elain, does that looks like what I think it looks like?"

"What?" Molly Maud asked, beggingly.

"One of the genetic bio agent terrorist attacks," I said

softly.

"Oh my God!" Molly Maud gushed.

"If it is, they'll be in a coma for around four days, but when they wake up, it'll be a living nightmare for them," I said softly.

"Oh. Right. I remember what you said about it. Who could have done this? Why?" she asked. We shrugged our shoulders.

We watched it a while longer, but they just kept repeating everything so I headed off to finish with my long hair. I can't tell you what a pain it is trying to do this with a darn stump instead of my hand. Still, I was able to do it, unlike when I was a victim, armless and dependent on the robots. Likewise, Jana, Jovanna, and Marisol kept their complaints to a minimum as well and for the same reason. There is a universe of difference between missing a hand and having no arms at all.

Just as we were about to go to bed, the reporter said, "This just in! There has been another similar attack! Here's the security general." The screen reverted to the same man, who looked rather haggard.

He spoke slowly. "I have to report that there was a second attack today. This one was on the top floor of the Intelligence Division building. I'm afraid this one affected Commander Werner Kettlebohn and his top staff. We've withheld information about this attack until now, to give the remaining Field Agents time to attempt to trace the terrorists. They suggested if it wasn't reported, then the terrorists might return to the scene of the crime to see if their device failed to detonate. No luck with that, so we're now releasing this information to you."

"In this case, we have an approximate time for the attack. It must have occurred sometime before two o'clock this afternoon. Like the admirals, everyone on the top floor was found unconscious, and there was a noxious odor in the room, slightly yellowish in color. The chemical analyses are back now. I hate to report this, but our people have been unable to identify the gas. We have as yet no idea what it is, though measurements suggest the gas is slowly dissipating. In this case, only seventy-three people were affected by the attack. More later on. That is all for now."

"It fits with everything we know," Jana whispered to me.

"I know, but we can't be certain, not yet," I replied. "Perhaps, we'll know more tomorrow. If they show us more images of the victims, pay close attention to their arms. If it's the same stuff, their arms ought to be quite noticeably thinner." That said, we turned in, but slept rather poorly. I was really getting worried. Had our hideous invention somehow found its way into the Federation of Planets?

We had all just gotten up and had our usual struggle to get dressed in our professional women's outfits, ready for another day at Molly Maud's company, when we heard a loud knocking on her door. "It's barely eight. Wonder who that can be?" Molly Maud said, walking slowly to the door.

When she opened it, I was rather surprised to see the same man that had been on the news last night. He spoke with a deep bass voice, "I'm General Wolfgang Donner. May I come in?"

"Sure. We were about to head off to work," Molly Maud replied. He motioned to a number of well-armed soldiers to stand guard outside.

"Ah, these must be your alien friends from the Imperium," he said.

"Hello. Yes, Captain Nia Elain Compton-Jereni," I replied.

"First, may I inquire where you aliens were all day yesterday?"

"Of course. This must be about the terrorist attack. We watched it on the news. We were at Porsche Industries during the day and here with Molly Maud all evening," I answered.

"Miss Porsche, can you verify that?"

"Absolutely. These are my right hand women. We're always together at work, and they are staying with me while they are here in Hoffdorf. Why?" she asked politely, but already guessed why.

"All right then, I suspected as much. So you've seen the news. Frankly, we have no idea what we are up against.

However, I wish Captain Nia Elain to accompanying me to the hospital. I want your opinion in this matter. Yes, the victims are in quarantine in hospitals right now."

"Yes, of course, general. I had a bad feeling about this last night as we watched it. We here have been the victims of that awful genetic bio agent several times now."

"That was the conclusion I have been reaching, but I need more to go on. This way, captain," he said, adding, "one of my men will bring her to your corporate headquarters later on."

"Sorry, I don't walk very fast in these heels," I pointed out the obvious.

He slowed down and took my stump arm in his. With a smile, he said, "Doesn't matter. You look extremely attractive. That's what really counts." He had a shuttle waiting for us, and he helped me inside. Two minutes later, we arrived on the roof of a hospital. Thankfully, the general assisted me, since I wasn't dressed quite for this.

My clicking heels on the linoleum floor did attract attention, but then that's one of their purposes. We arrived at a plastic covered doorway. A doctor poked his head out. I knew he was a doctor from a label on his white gown that said Dr. Schmidt. "Any changes," the general's bass voice came from behind me.

"General deterioration and some very strange growths. This way." He pulled back the plastic and we entered. "Room on your right." I entered a room where an admiral lay naked on a hospital bed. A nurse was taking his pulse as I stepped in. Now, I had zero doubts!

"Well, General Wolfgang, there is absolutely no doubt about the nature of this. It is in fact that same genetic bio agent that is responsible for so many genocide attacks on Imperium worlds by governments and terrorists," I spoke up.

"Oh dear God!" Doctor Schmidt exclaimed.

The general cleared his throat, and said, "What can we expect, captain?"

"Well, now that I'm an expert on, having been on beds just like this several times. First, they'll be in comas for around four to five days. By the time they rouse, their arms will have fallen off as dried-out husks. Their feet are already distorting. When the mutation is finished, only their toes will touch the ground, making walking very difficult. Usually, they need special shoes to have much of a chance at walking. Those breasts are just forming. Expect them to wind up about one and a half times the size of their heads. I know, mine are huge, but theirs will be almost beyond description. Plus, that extra weight will give them massive back pains unless they wear a special, tight, heavily steel boned corset. Of course, that'll make breathing very difficult indeed. As you can also see, he is developing a woman's womb. When the mutation is finished, he will be a hermaphrodite. He'll be able to impregnate his wife but also himself. He'll be able to have perfectly healthy babies and nurse them too. Also, you see that slit along his upper and lower lips? When the mutation is finished, he'll have giant lip loops, approximately a foot in diameter. We usually wear special lip disks to prevent accidentally catching the loops and ripping them apart. Finally, as you can see, his hair is growing. However, it is also developing pain neurons. When it is done, it'll be very thick and nearly touch the floor. Any attempt to cut it results in massive pain and is futile, since his hair will quickly regrow to that length. As it then grows naturally, it can be trimmed back to this initial long length though. Also, the lip loops will prevent his making many sounds in your language, which involve the lips. Bottom line, general, is that it'll be highly unlikely anyone will be able to understand what he is saying, whether or not he has the lip disks in them."

"Good God!" he exclaimed. After a pause, he asked, "Is there anything that can be done for them? Any cures? There must be because you don't look like what you are describing." I noticed the doctor now paid extremely close attention to my every word. I chose my reply carefully.

"I am not a geneticist. Our geneticists on Ashford-5 have been able to come up with some genetic cures but those were based upon our specific DNA. That is, they had many samples of my DNA prior to my becoming infected and mutated. Same with my friends and wife. However, they have not been able to undo everything. We're all still hermaphrodites, and my boobs are still way too large for my tastes."

"Ah, I see. They become you though," he said wryly. I grinned.

"What you can do for them is be prepared with the clothing, shoes, and lip plates they are definitely going to need when they wake up. In the Imperium, we were able to rescue millions of such terrorist attack victims. Nearly all, we were unable to cure. The cost and materials are terribly expensive. What was done was to build them mechanical men, robots to be precise, to assist them to live. At first, though when there were only smaller numbers of victims, such as you have here, we put them into our assisted living complexes, where someone could care for their needs, which pretty well means everything. Once the sheer numbers of victims rose, the capacity of all our assisted living homes was exceeded, and that's when they came up with the robot assistant idea. Now even that is gone. Someone nuked that whole world, wiping them all out. I do hope the Federation of Planets is saner than our decaying Imperium was."

"I see. Assisted living complexes are probably our best choice for now. Two additional questions and then I'll let you get back to work," General Wolfgang said. "First, is there any way we can get a hold of these special clothes, shoes, and lip things that they will need? Second, how the hell did your genetic bio agent get here into the Federation?"

"One I can answer, the other I can't. I can have my wife make an emergency run and bring some samples here quickly. We have Fabrication machines that can make duplicates of these in quantity. Do you have such here?"

"Yes, we call them Duplication machines. We would be grateful if your wife could do this for us. And the second question?" he pressed me.

"This genetic bio agent has been totally outlawed on all Imperium worlds. It is a very high crime to possess this outside of the authorized genetic research labs, where extremely tight security is kept. If this stuff used here came from one of those labs, then that I can find out. Might take a few days. Want me to check?"

"Please."

"Okay. Of course, terrorists have gotten their hands on the stuff in the past. But from what I know, we've pretty well put an end to that. Even more troubling to me is, as far as I know, there simply has not been much interaction and commerce between the Federation and the ex-Imperium. I mean we and my crew seem to be breaking new ground by just coming here and visiting. If I were you, I might look into what others have had contact with the Federation from our ex-Imperium worlds. Surely, there has not been that much traffic between us."

"Thanks. I'll look into that aspect. There has been some small trading going on. That bears looking into. Thanks. If we have more questions, we'll contact you. My driver will take you to Porsche Industries now."

I turned and walked back out, where a private waited for me. As we walked slowly out of the hospital to his car, he said, "It's real bad in there isn't it? The general doesn't say much, but I've never seen him like this."

"Yes, I am afraid it's really bad, but they'll survive the attack. So that's something. I do hope he can catch the guilty terrorists."

When I walked into Porsche Industries, I found many of the women were meeting, discussing the situation. What I didn't expect to hear, I heard! "Serves them right. They took our hands turning us into cripples and making life horrid for us. Now, it's their turn to suffer," one woman worker barked.

Several others agreed with her. Another added, "I'm glad they didn't die. Dying is too good for them. Let them try to live all crippled up and see how they like it!"

Jovanna sent me, *They are releasing their pent-up anger and hostilities towards the admirals who passed the new laws. Best to let them vent.*

Vent they did for an hour, before things settled down, and I was tired when we all finally reached Molly Maud's home. I had fired off a secure comm to Danika and to Emperor Bino telling them both what had happened here and asking her to make a fast, emergency run with samples. She told me to expect them late tomorrow afternoon. As we walked up to

Molly Maud's door, a strange young man, looking very distraught, was waiting for us.

"Excuse me. I'm looking for the aliens from the Imperium that are reported as staying with Miss Molly Maud Porsche. I'm Heinrich Donner, but everyone calls me Heinz." He looked longing at each of us, uncertain who was who.

"I'm Captain Nia Elain from Ashford-5, if that's who you are looking for. Do we know you?"

"Er. No, not at all. Please, I must talk with you. It's a matter of life and death, but not out here, somewhere private," he pleaded with me.

He seemed harmless, and Molly Maud took charge. "I'm Miss Porsche. Please, come on inside. You can speak frankly with us." She unlocked her door, struggling a little with the key and her stump. Heinz quickly assisted her, just as he often did with Gisa and Karla. She flashed him a smile and entered.

First thing we did was plop down on sofas, slipping off our six inch heels, and massaging our feet. "Well, go ahead, Heinz. We won't bite. What's so urgent?" Molly Maud ordered.

He looked at me and said, "Okay. I trust you. I need help, but not for me, but for my dear friends. I just know they are in trouble, bad trouble."

"Start from the beginning. That's always best," I suggested.

"Okay. It's Gisa and Karla. They are a couple, civil union. Gisa was the First Violinist and also Concert Master for the Hoffdorf Symphony Orchestra, and her mate, Karla was First Cellist. They were the best musicians in the world, fabulous, and my best friends. I'm a portrait painter, by the way. They came and cut off their left hands, just like yours. They finger their instruments with the fingers of their left hands. When I found them, they were sobbing something awful. Their whole careers, their whole lives, their whole reason for existing was taken away from them. I don't expect that you can understand how bad this was for them, but I convinced them not to do like Gertrude did and try to kill themselves. I did stop Gertrude. I got to her in time. She's not yet found any work though, living off her small savings. This butchery of our women has destroyed the whole artist community. There's no symphony anymore. Three-quarters of their musicians can't play. It's just awful, and I refuse to paint anymore too."

"Anyway, I was there for Gisa and Karla, helping them every day with things they can't do anymore. I know this is going to sound really bad to you, but please, I don't know who else to turn to. I have to somehow save Gisa and Karla."

"Save them from what?" Molly Maud pressured him as he digressed.

"They lost everything, every goal they ever had. Then, they got a new purpose. They didn't want to kill them. No, they kept saying they wanted to wipe out the careers of the men who wiped out their careers."

I made a jump ahead. Good guess. "So they are behind these genetic bio agent attacks?"

"Well, yes. I'm guilty too. I helped them with things they can no longer do. Their stumps make simple things nearly impossible to do. They found out about this bio agent thing from the Imperium, and somehow, they got one case from a strange man from Gamelon-3. I helped them use a Duplication machine to make more and rig up the devices."

"You must understand why they did this. Their whole careers were wiped out utterly. They want justice. We all want justice! Damn those men anyway. I agree with them. Killing them is too good for the bastards. Anyway, I helped them plant the bombs. We put them in the air ducts and took out the admirals who passed these butcherous new laws. Now, their careers are wiped out, just like they wiped out millions of women's careers!"

I jumped in, "And you got the Intelligence Division heads too?"

"Yes, they were in on it too. That Commander Werner fellow. Everyone knows nothing happens without Werner having a hand in it too. We've ended his career just as he ended so many women's careers. Plus, we also got The Seven."

Molly Maud gasped! "What? The Seven?"

"What's The Seven?" I asked.

Molly Maud quickly explained about this super-secret group who ran the entire Federation of Planets. "You see, the

ID and the Admiralty Round Table report directly to these unknown men. How the devil did you and your two musician friends find out who they were?" she asked.

"I didn't. They did. We verified it too. Gisa overheard one of their secret phone calls to Commander Werner, and we watched to see if he did what he was ordered. He did; it was on the news so we knew we had found The Seven. Only we didn't know when they would meet, so they had to wait outside their secret suite and manually activate the release mechanism when The Seven went inside. They ordered me to stay out of the whole thing. They didn't want me to get in trouble, but I went anyway, following them in secret. I was going to be their rear guard."

"They went inside the building long before The Seven came. I saw them arrive and go into the building. They never came out. I waited for Gisa and Karla to come out but they never did either. After three hours, I went inside just before they were closing the building. They weren't there, but I smelled something strange coming from the secret room. I heard the gas leaking out of the tank I helped put into the air duct to that suite. So I know they must have pressed the button. Yet, I can't find them. I ran back to their house, but they weren't there either."

"So I just know that somehow those really bad men must have spotted them and forced them inside. God, I hope they didn't beat them or hurt them. At least, they did press the button. Now, they too are probably in a coma and will wake up totally helpless. I swore I would always be there to help them. Then, last night I remembered aliens were staying with Miss Porsche, and I got the idea that you might be able to help me get in there and rescue Gisa and Karla. I know they are going to be helpless. We saw all those pictures of the victims, but I swear to you, if you can help me get them to safety, I'll spend the rest of my life caring for them. They love each other and were the best musicians in the world. Those men took their careers and lives from them, and now they've taken theirs from them. Justice. But I'll look after them no matter what, if only you can somehow help me get them out of there before they die. Please, you must help me. They are true heroes and got justice for all of the millions of victims." He finally finished up.

I wanted to cheer for joy, but restrained myself. Instead, I asked, "Who else knows about what you three did? Who else have you told?"

"No one, captain no one. Gisa and Karla, they are lesbians and have few friends, real friends that is. We have told no one about it. All very secret. Hush. Hush. No one, I swear."

Yes, I was using my *mentales* gifts on him. He was telling me the truth, all of it! Molly Maud spoke up, "Well, if you won't help him, I will. They did what no one else has been able to do — get justice for us all."

"Of course we'll help. It's a bit tricky, Molly Maud. We can't just go in there in the daytime and somehow carry two unconscious women out. We'll have to do it at night."

"But there is a security guard on duty, and the doors are locked. I know. I watched him do it," Heinz countered.

"Leave that to us. We'll need transport."

"Shuttle or car?" Molly Maud asked.

"Car. Shuttle will attract too much attention," I answered. "We'll need to change into reasonable clothes. We can't do much dressed like this."

"Okay. We can use my company car. Let's get changed. That's going to take us a while," she said waving her stump around for unneeded emphasis. "Give us a while, Heinz."

"I can help if you need it. I always help Gisa and Karla. They have such a hard time getting into dresses like you are wearing, but they look very good when they are dressed."

"Thanks but we can manage. Turn on the news, and see if there is anything new. Perhaps, someone has already found them," Molly Maud ordered. He complied, and we headed into the bedrooms to change, albeit at a very slow, clumsy rate.

An hour later, we reappeared dressed in pants and comfortable flats. There was no mention on the news of finding the suite in question. While Jana and Jovanna made supper, we listened to the news. There was nothing new being said, just wild speculations.

Around nine, we were ready to go. "It's Suite 1102 in the

Wilmar building," Heinz explained.

"Incredible. I've been by there a thousand times. Right under our very noses. Okay, pile into the car," Molly Maud ordered. "I know precisely where it is."

We circled the block twice, but saw virtually no one about. I focused and expanded my awareness outward. I sensed the napping guard on the first floor and moved up to the top where I sensed nine others. Meanwhile, Jana, Jovanna, and Marisol did the same in the area around the building, searching for security guards that might be keeping an eye on the building, but found nothing at all, save an occasional passing car. We parked behind the building out of sight and walked to the front.

Now came the tricky part. I needed the guard to come and open the door for us, but never remember we were there or that he opened the door, let alone see us bringing two unconscious women down and out. Jana whispered, "I can put him to sleep. Jovanna can unlock the door. How's that for a plan?"

I grinned, "Better than mine. Do it. Thanks." Heinz looked at us with eyes wide open. Well, he was going to see more than he bargained for before this night was out. I watched as Jovanna worked the lock using her finely tuned telekinetic skills, her crystal glowing pale blue. We entered quietly. The guard was quite sound asleep. Heinz led us to the elevator and shortly we stepped out on the top floor. I detected the faint odor, and knew beyond any doubt that it was the bio agent. He led us to the secret suite's door. Once more, Jovanna's crystal glowed and the door clicked open. We stepped inside. Here the odor was stronger, but harmless at this low a concentration.

"Gisa! Karla!" Heinz whispered rushing to the two women lying on the floor. I glanced around the room and saw all manner of electronic equipment and seven men lying on the floor. "I can carry one of them," he whispered.

"Leave them to us," I ordered. We focused and the two comatose women rose into the air. We were levitating their bodies. Gently, we pushed them out of the room. Marisol took a good look around to make sure that we left no trace that the women had been here. Satisfied, she stepped out and locked the door. By then, Heinz had the elevator doors opened, and we floated the two on inside. A bit later, we had them moving past the guard. I sent Molly Maud on ahead to bring the car around. Thus, when we had them at the front doors, she had the car there and the doors opened. The bodies floated on out and directly into the car. While everyone else squeezed into the packed car, Jovanna re-locked the doors and sat on my lap as Molly Maud drove off into the night.

Fifteen minutes later, we floated the pair into her home through the back door and into one of the bedrooms, laying them on the top of the bed. "I don't know how you can do this, but thank you. Are they going to live? They don't look well," Heinz said worriedly.

"They are in a coma and will be for another couple of days. Their bodies are mutating, Heinz."

"Like the pictures we saw," he suggested and I nodded. "I should sit beside them here until they wake and need my help."

"No, get some sleep, Heinz. They'll be unconscious for at least two more days. You'll be able to see how close to waking up they are by the changes in their bodies. Meantime, you can help us undress them. They should be naked while the changes occur."

Molly Maud watched as Heinz gently undressed each one. She was particularly moved by his kindness and gentleness. Plus, he skillfully handled Karla's long blonde hair very well, draping it over her exposed bosom, partially hiding them as best he could before covering them with a sheet. She watched, as he whispered, "You'll be all right. Heinz is here to take care of you." He gently placed a kiss on each forehead before backing up and seeing Molly Maud in the doorway watching him.

"You care for them very much don't you?"

"Yes, we have been best friends since we met when they came to the Donner School of Music. That was eleven years ago now. We were fourteen then. I was the only person who attended their civil union. They are like sisters to me, and you should have heard them play music together. It was like two goddesses making heavenly music." He sighed deeply. "Now, the world has lost what once was great, and I shall never paint again. I have no heart to paint a woman's portrait when she has no hand and a face filled with grief. No, never again."

"Well, we best get some sleep," she suggested, deeply impressed by this unassuming young man.

In the morning, Molly Maud found Heinz once more with Gisa and Karla, wiping their foreheads with a damp cloth and speaking kind thoughts to them. "You'll get better. I know it; you will." She moved away from the door and on into her kitchen, where she heard a sleepy pair of sisters rustling with some pans, getting ready to fix breakfast.

"Morning. How are the two women?" Jana asked.

"Heinz is with them. Their arms are so very thin, like matchsticks, and their breasts are almost as large as their heads. Awful," she answered.

Awful was what Emperor Bino replied to me, when, over a secure channel, I informed him of what had truly happened. He promised to take another look at the men on Gamelon-3. Awful was also the comment Danika sent to me, just after landing the Eagle's Seed on Cass-C around ten this morning. I focused and sent a full report of our previous evening's unnerving events, asking her to make two duplicate sets of the needed things for our two women.

Got it. Martina is heading to the Fabrication machine now. I've paid the landing fee, but the custom official says that if we leave the spaceport, we married women have to have our hand removed in their stupid ceremony. Want us to do that?

No, we'll come to you shortly. And thanks. That was a fast trip.

Hey, blazing. I do love to turn up the throttle all the way. Speeding is a blast! Well, that's my Danika. I relayed to the others they had arrived, and then had Molly Maud contact General Wolfgang for me. She handed me the phone.

"General, they've landed with the supplies you need. They aren't leaving the ship, because the custom official said that they'd have to have their hands cut off if they leave the spaceport. I told them I'd be by to pick them up, but I could use a hand with it. It's hard to carry heavier things with only one hand," I purposely punched this in. Okay, I still was ticked off that this brutality had been foisted off on so many innocent women, Federation wide.

"I'll meet you at the spaceport in say one hour?" he replied.

"One hour. After that, we'd like to speak to you some more about this whole mess." He had more questions for me too.

After breakfast and some kindly help from Heinz, we were dressed in our acceptable professional women's outfits in record time. Still, it was much slower than it had been before we lost our hands. We left the women in his care and headed to the spaceport. I know that's not saying much, the two women would certainly be in their comas another two days or so, but I didn't want Heinz going anywhere, not just yet. We hadn't decided exactly what to do with the three.

The cargo transfer went swiftly. The general had a squad of men with him, and they made short work of unloading the dozen small shipping crates that Danika and my crew had brought. He did make one comment, "That was an unbelievably fast trip, no?"

Danika grinned and replied, "Yes, about three-quarters of the way across the galaxy in about nine hours. This ship can fly! I just love this kind of speed, don't you?" The middle-aged general laughed briefly, the first time I saw him anything but super-solemn.

A half hour later, we slipped through the plastic sheeting into the quarantine section. General Wolfgang took us to see the same admiral that we'd seen the day before. Dr. Schmidt poked his head in and asked, "Is all this normal? I mean under these circumstances. It's hardly normal."

I looked at the enlarging lip loops, the mound of hair, the head-sized bosom, and the matchstick arms and sighed. "Yes, I'm afraid so. The arms will begin to dry out. As husks, they'll simply drop off. The breasts have a ways to go yet, and the lip loops will get much bigger still. Probably two days more of coma or there about. After the arms fall off, they'll be close to coming out of it. That's when you want to keep close watch on them. When they wake, they will need to pee badly and will be starving, needing good wholesome food. However, they will be terrified and shocked beyond belief. I doubt if you'll be able to understand anything they say. Be prepared. It's really going to be a grim scene." Dr. Schmidt swallowed hard, and we left the quarantine area and met in a side room.

"Thanks for everything," General Wolfgang said solemnly.

"We've been thinking about this whole mess. Jana and Jovanna here are history experts. They'd like to share some observations with you and make some suggestions." He nodded, and we all sat down.

Jana began, "We've studied this whole genetic bio agent situation as it arose and developed within the Imperium. We believe the value of history is so one can learn from past mistakes and avoid making the same ones in the future. That said, here goes. When this bio agent was first uncovered, some bright minds thought this was the ideal solution to the hardened criminals. It was costing the Imperium billions of credits or dollars each year to provide secure prisons and such to keep these anti-social men and women out of society for the duration of their lives. Hence, one of the first uses of the bio agent was to turn these hardened criminals into helpless men and women. When you see just how awful it really is here, you'll see why they thought this was an ideal solution. These criminals were suddenly quite helpless, unable to speak or commit any conceivable crime whatsoever. They were moved into assisted living complexes, and all the prisons closed. At first, the saving of billions each year was a blessing."

She continued, "Of course, this was widely publicized. Soon, most everyone knew just how debilitating the genetic modification was. It wasn't long after that when certain small terrorist groups saw this as a way to strike. By all manner of sneaky ways, various criminal groups got their hands on some of these cylinders and duplicated them, often stealing them from the research laboratories. It began at first with small attacks on our senators, which we believe are roughly similar to your admirals. After more similar smaller attacks, things began to escalate."

"Some dissatisfied men and women got their hands on the bio agent and unleashed it on our central world, Proxima Prime, the heart of the Imperium. It was genocide, pure and simple. Hundreds of billions of people died. Yes, a massive rescue operation was done and several million were rescued. But time was against the rescuers. The helpless people died of lack of water within a few days. Those that were somehow able to get water often then starved to death before aid could reach them. Only a tiny fraction of that world's population was able to be rescued."

"From there, other worlds that had been archenemies got the idea this was a powerful weapon and secretly began stockpiling mountains of these cylinders. One thing led to another and five of these heavily populated worlds went to war with each other, resulting in total genocide on the five worlds. It continued to happen years later with some hub worlds."

"Of course, all this time, the Imperium spared no expense trying to track down and recover or destroy all the cylinders that had fallen into the wrong hands. But they never could get all them. They are so easily duplicated."

Jana then said, "So what we are trying to suggest, General Wolfgang, is if it is possible, keep the real effects of this attack somehow secret. Don't let everyone in the Federation know about just how awful this bio agent really is. You see, if lots of others discover how awful this thing is, they might get the idea to use this stuff in other attacks, beginning the escalation until whole Federation worlds get wiped out, like happened in our Imperium."

General Wolfgang looked thoughtfully impressed. "You've made a very strong case, Jana. I'm impressed such incredible wisdom comes from a woman."

She retorted, "Women can be just as smart and wise as men. They can also be just as stupid and dumb."

He grinned briefly. "Well, up to this point, I've kept the actual details being released to the bare minimum. Our local top leaders are infected, namely Admiral Fritz and Commander Werner and his associates. The Intelligence Division is scrambling to form up replacements and conduct a thorough investigation. Until I'm told otherwise, I'm left holding the bag, as they say. I'd honestly expected to hear something from The Seven, providing guidance and such. I used my security clearance to access their secure phone number and have left them a dozen messages, but I've not heard from them."

"Is that unusual, sir?" I asked.

He rubbed the stubble on his chin before replying, "Yes. Peculiar. Troubling. If ever there was a calamity, this is one. I really did expect a call right after we discovered the admirals."

"Is it possible The Seven were also attacked, sir?" I planted a subtle hint.

"That is the only conclusion I have reached. Of course, no one knows their identity just so that this sort of thing cannot ever happen as it did to the very public admirals. And yet, why are they not taking my calls? So yes, I've been wondering if they too were somehow attacked or perhaps they were among the ID people or the admirals. That could be, since their identity is a secret known only to themselves."

I hinted, "So you have a phone number to call. Is there anyway someone in the Intelligence Division could somehow trace that number while you were calling it? Find out where the answering phone is located. Perhaps, that might give you some clues."

He flashed me a brief grin. "I admit I don't know all there is to know about such matters, but I'll contact the ID at once, and see if we can do something like that. I find it amazing I've just received two invaluable hints this morning and from women no less." I took that in the spirit it was said, not what it implied.

Molly Maud decided to speak up. "General Wolfgang, if these men and women are not in any medical danger, which is what Captain Nia Elain claims, and if it is in our best interests to keep knowledge of their awful physical mutations a secret for the time being, I have a suggestion. Keeping them here in the hospitals of Hoffdorf isn't wise. Once the changes are complete, everyone at the hospital is going to know about it, and it will be impossible to keep that from the reporters. Word is going to spread like wildfire. The goose will have gotten out of the hunter's bag, as we say."

She continued, "Porsche Industries has a lot of warehouses. I believe I can make some relatively empty ones available, where we can take the victims, keep them hidden, and provide the care they're going to need. Of course, you'll need to provide the care givers and somehow swear them to secrecy. This way, we stand a chance of keeping the actual final results of the mutations from becoming widely known, at least for the time being until you get it all sorted out."

"Miss Porsche, I do believe you have something here. Yes, the more I ponder this disaster, the more I can see Jana's argument. Keep the true knowledge of the results as contained as possible. While probably it'll eventually leak out, perhaps we can avoid other terrorists from also getting the idea to make use of this hideous bio agent. I'm indebted to your generosity in this matter."

"Excellent. I'll see to the warehouse arrangements shortly. And there is another thing, sir, something that we've not really touched upon yet. A cure. You see, the incredible geneticists on Ashford-5 have developed some cures for such victims. As I understand it, only these few talented doctors have been able to find any cure at all. I admit I don't know anything about it really, but apparently, the cures are DNA based. Perhaps, if we could take some DNA samples of our victims to these geneticists on Ashford-5, they might be able develop a cure. I know we also have geneticists, and perhaps, you could get some of the victims' DNA to them and have them work on developing a cure. I'll personally volunteer to take the DNA samples to these Ashford-5 geneticists, seeking their help. Oh yes, for the record, Ashford-5 is part of the Ataro Empire, which has given me the patent rights for their new hyperdrive engine that my companies are now installing in our transports. I don't know if I have any political influence there, but I'm willing to try."

"Damn! Four invaluable suggestions and from women no less! Miss Porsche, I can see why old Hermann retired and turned his vast enterprise over to you. Okay, I'll do as you suggest. I'll have Dr. Schmidt extract some DNA samples for you. I'll also summon the top Federation geneticists and get them working on this project as well. Perhaps, between them, a cure can be found. In the meantime, I'll do everything possible to make the resultant outcome top secret. That won't last forever, mind you. These things have a way of becoming known, sooner or later, especially with such public figures as these admirals are."

With that, we broke up, each heading their own way. I drove Molly Maud's car back to her main office, while she got on the phone to begin making the arrangements. Once there, she made even more calls, and then we headed back home once more. "Hey, I am driving," she said. "I can still do that."

"Darn, that was fun," I teased her, after being bumped from the driver's seat.

"Get your own car," she teased me back. We laughed.

After a brief lunch, I was once more amazed with Molly Maud's ability to think under pressure. She knew we wanted to take the two women back to Ashford-5. She had reached that conclusion before I did. Look, after their mutations are finished and we get them dressed, there'll not be any way to hide them. Everyone will soon realize they were victims too. Questions will be asked, particularly about why they were not with the victims in the hospital. I want them protected for the time being, and, if there is any way for them to get their arms and hands back so they can become musicians again, I have to try."

"Hey, I'm coming with them," Heinz interrupted. "Where they go, so go I."

"Yes of course, Heinz," I hastily added. "So how do we get them to the Eagle's Seed?"

"I've arranged that already," Molly Maud declared. "Around one, a Porsche Industries van will arrive out back, and the driver will leave it there for me. We'll wrap the bodies up, carry them down into the van, and drive them to the ship, along with our bags. No one will be the wiser. Come on; we ought to pack a few things. Heinz, little help with the packing."

"Of course, Miss Porsche," he replied eager to help in any way he could.

By two, we had the women safely on the ship and tucked securely into an available cabin, where Heinz sat with them. Before long, an ambulance drove up. General Wolfgang got out, while his men carried several shipping crates into the Eagle's Seed, the DNA samples. "On behalf of Cass-C and the many victims, I'd like to thank you for your help and work. Best of luck. Oh yes, we found a third attack site. Captain, your advice proved invaluable. We traced the phone and located a secret suite in downtown Hoffdorf. I had some Field Agents get the door open. We found seven more victims there, along with an alarming amount of electronic equipment. One held my dozen voice messages. Whoever these terrorists are, they were able to wipe out the Federation's top leaders in one well-planned and well-executed attack. I'm certain there will be significant fallout from this mess, but we'll be keeping it hushed up until we hear back from you. If there is a cure, perhaps we'll be able to minimize the aftereffects. Go with God behind you," General Wolfgang said, saluting us and departing.

Once the bay doors were shut, Danika said, "Well dear, are you flying us or can I?"

"You can, dear. Go fast. We don't want to risk these women waking up while we are in space, if we can avoid it," I replied. She grinned and did just that.

Shortly, she announced, "We'll be home in nine hours, about eleven at night. Sit tight."

Molly Maud joined me for tea in the galley. "I don't really want those admirals, Commander Werner, and The Seven to fully recover, you know? After all, after what they've done to all us women, they don't deserve to be fully healed, while we women have to live like this for the rest of our lives," she waved her stump for emphasis. "Does this make me a bad person?"

"No, justice. As far as I'm concerned, they got what they deserved," I replied.

Tesla, ever the political scientist, said, "You know, this means there's a chance to get more women involved in the running of the Federation. After all, they have to replace most all those who were running it. Why not lobby to get some women in there too?"

"Brilliant, Tesla, brilliant. They certainly are going to have to replace them. I've lots to do when I get back," Molly

Maud replied, thinking hard.

Chapter 15 Recovery

When we landed around eleven that night, Governor Misty had several electric cars waiting for us along with some strong arms. The men carried the two women to the cars, as well as the crates of DNA samples, but we carried out own bags. She looked sleepy. "Amazing what we women can do." That was her only comment. We were all too tired to talk much. "They're waiting in the med lab at the castle," she added.

We spent little time out of doors. It was mid-winter here and snowing lightly. Plus, we only had our blazer jackets, though Danika and the others were prepared and donned their heavier coats. Without a word, she took my arm supporting me, as I walked on the slippery snow in my six-inch heels, trying not to take a tumble. Similarly, others silently supported Molly Maud, Jana, Jovanna, and Marisol. We were still wearing our professional women's outfits from earlier this morning.

Even the doctors were half-asleep when we brought the two women into their facilities via levitation and gentle pushing. "Leave them. Get some sleep. We'll wake you if there is any change in their conditions," one said. I was too sleepy to disagree.

Queen Rael joined us to tell Molly Maud that her old room was ready for her. "Do you need some assistance?"

"I'll help her," Heinz quickly volunteered.

"If that's all right with you, Molly Maud. Your suite has three bedrooms. We can talk in the morning," she replied.

Shortly, we joined our families. Though our six were sleeping, I stole a kiss from each before having Danika help get me undressed and into bed. I'm afraid we didn't go to sleep right away. Passions interfered for a short while.

"You can have that room, Heinz," Molly Maud pointed to the side room. "If you can help me get out of these things. . ."

Quickly, he got her undressed and even tucked her into bed. "This place sure smells strange and looks strange.

Wonder what it looks like in the daytime," he whispered.

"Really different. They have an orange-red sun here. Everything is dim and reddish. I think what you are smelling is some kind of pine tree. Thanks for your help, Heinz."

"My pleasure, Miss Porsche. What you are doing for my friends is beyond my ability to thank you properly." He turned and made his way to the other bedroom, noticing the crackling fire in their spacious living room. What kind of a place was this, he wondered.

The next morning, I opted to wear another one of my professional woman's outfit. I knew Molly Maud only had this type of dress with her. We'd left on very short notice, so I wanted her to feel more comfortable. Danika wore her favorite leather pants and top, in stark contrast to me. We joined the others for breakfast, our six children tagging along with us.

I was very surprised to see Zuzana there waiting to see me. She looked so very different that I hardly recognized her until she spoke with her Slavic accent. She too wore a professional woman's garb including the tall heels, and Jana and Jovanna did too. I smiled, they were Zuzana's mentors, and she did her best to emulate the sisters' appearance. Zuzana was a shining example of just what our geneticists were now able to do.

"Look Captain Nia Elain," she said exuberantly, "I've got arms, and I can see again!"

"Zuzana, you look positively gorgeous. Well done indeed," I replied noticing not everything had been cured. She still had very thick hair that flowed in a giant wave down to her ankles. From the shape of her feet, I suspected that they were only partially restored. Unless they had invented another miracle, she was also a hermaphrodite. Plus, her bosom was as large as everyone else on Ashford-5, but that is always a given on this world.

"Thanks. I'm now very much like Jana and Jovanna too. I'm learning lots, though I know I've got so much more to learn. Everyone is so wonderful to me here. Thank you for saving me." Zuzana gave me a big hug.

Molly Maud and Heinz joined us, and Zuzana rushed over, relatively speaking, to welcome her too. Over breakfast,

Jana explained what she'd learned last night from Len. Her DNA was slightly different from ours. Not all of the "cures" took. However, the major ones did. Her arms and eyes regrew, and her lips healed up. Her hair, on the other hand, had not. Her feet were only partially repaired, and she would have to always wear six-inch heels.

After breakfast, the queens, Rafe, Molly Maud, Heinz, the various doctors including Leann, and I met to discuss the situation. First, I explained the women and their situation, though Heinz insisted on describing their stellar musical careers. "So their careers, their fundamental purposes in life, were all taken away from them by this brutal action of cutting off married women's non-dominant hands."

Rafe broke in, "When you utterly wipe out the basic purpose that one has in life, in time a new purpose will formulate. In this case, that purpose is obvious. As she's said, it was to remove the careers of those who were most responsible for wiping out theirs. Sorry, couldn't help injecting that observation." I smiled.

Molly Maud spoke up. "Please, if there's any way you can cure them, I'll gladly pay you whatever you ask."

Doctor Leann smiled. "Of course we'll do our best to cure them, Molly Maud. The cost isn't an issue. Rather it's their DNA. Technicians took samples late last night. It's as we were suspecting. There are some slight differences between Imperium people and those from the Federation. Zuzana's case points out this rather markedly. Some cures work; some don't."

"If they can just have their arms back," Heinz pleaded, knowing that he was wholly out of his league with these scientists, "they can make music once more. I know that is what they really, really want."

"We know, Heinz, but there is no guarantee here. They'll be waking sometime later today, perhaps as early as this afternoon. Their mutations are pretty much done," Dr. Leann continued. "We'll need to see to their immediate physical needs, hydration, nutrition, and such. Already, we are pumping them full of life-sustaining fluids. We are hoping to have them ready for the medically induced comas within twenty-four hours of their awakening. Four days after that, we ought to know what cures will take hold in their bodies, their genetic makeup. We must caution you, not all the cures are likely to take. Zuzana is the case in point. The real question is what do we do about the thousands of other victims and the DNA samples Molly Maud has provided us? Do we want to heal monsters?"

Rafe countered, "That's a real ethical dilemma. Doctors are bound to heal their patients, evil or good. As far as we are concerned, these men have committed a heinous crime against the women of the Federation, millions I'm told. Do we attempt to bring back to full health a hardened criminal, knowing he'll just continue committing more crimes against women or do we let them be, helpless individuals? Tough choice."

Queen Rael stated, "We must follow the path that benefits the most Aspects of life while harming the least. If we do that, we can have no remorse, no guilt. Since we know that their DNA is slightly different from ours, I'd suggest seeing what cures work on the two women and then proceed from there. I'll say this, and it might help alleviate some of your concerns, we cannot undo their sexual changes. These evil men will still be hermaphrodites. They will still look like large-breasted women and be able to bear children. As you know, for most men, this is utterly humiliating. Without Basic Therapy, they'll prefer to hide themselves from society and not attempt to retake their former positions in the limelight. It's far too embarrassing for them, until they've had Basic Therapy. However, there are exceptions to this of course, like old Legate H-Cubed. So even if many of the cures do work, I seriously doubt these men will go back to work as though nothing has happened."

Dr. Leann added, "Heinz, as much as you want them to have their arms back, realize if we are able to regrow them, they'll be entirely new arms. They'll have to relearn how to play their instruments from scratch again. That might be too frustrating for them. Just keep that in mind."

"I will, but I'll be there to remind them to keep practicing, like I did when they were fourteen," he declared.

After that, they returned to their work. Heinz went to sit

beside the two women. Later that afternoon when Dr. Leann sent us a warning message, Molly Maud and I joined them, as the women began coming out of their comas.

Karla came around first. Since the doctors had been giving her quite a few IVs and other procedures, she was in far better physical shape when she awoke than other victims. Of course, she tried to get up and was disoriented having no idea where she was, or how mutated her body actually was. She tried to speak and looked totally confused, not even understanding her own words.

"It's okay, Karla. I'm here with you," Heinz said, brushing her forehead lightly. "I got help, and we got you out of that room. We are on another world, Ashford-5 it's called. I got you and Gisa the very best medical care in the whole galaxy. You'll be all right. What's that? Oh, yes, it worked. You ended the careers of the admirals, the top ID men, and The Seven." She tried to say something else but no one understood it. Marisol was translating their German into Midlands for us.

The doctors then had Marisol explain they were getting her up to use the bathroom, and so she could see what had happened to her body. Meanwhile, Gisa groaned, and Heinz moved to her side to be with her when she awoke. A few minutes later, he told her pretty much what he'd just said to Karla, but added that Karla was here with her and going to the bathroom. Again, he couldn't understand anything she tried to say to him.

A half hour later, the two sobbing women were sitting side by side on one of the beds. Heinz had carefully draped their very long hair over their shoulders and down their fronts, trying to hide as much of their giant bosoms as he could. Their lip loops dangled down, nearly touching their chests. Using Marisol as their translator, Dr. Leann acted as the spokesperson for the team of doctors and geneticists. Carefully, she explained their current situation, which by now was obvious, why the two were sobbing, and wanting those around them just to kill them and put them out of their misery. While the telepaths knew this, they didn't mention it to Heinz or Molly Maud.

She ended with, "So if we have phenomenal luck, you'll

both have your arms back and look much like Nia Elain and her crew. However, your DNA is different in some slight ways from ours, so not all the cures that we have may work, but we hope some will. We do need your permission to proceed and make the attempt to cure what we can. Nod if you agree to let us try."

Both nodded and Karla tried to say something. Rafe jumped in. "I'm going to join you telepathically with Heinz, and you can tell him yourself. Just think what you want to say, and he will hear it. One second." She formed up a Mind Link, joining Gisa, Karla, and Heinz together. Of course, she was part of the link too, but stayed in the background.

Heinz! Thank you! Thank you! I heard you speaking to me when I was unconscious. I don't know how. Thank you. We love you. That was Karla's thoughts.

Gisa interrupted her mate. *This is so intimate. Heinz. Yes thank you for being there for us. We owe you big time for this. I felt you soothing my forehead. You are the best friend anyone could ever have. We love you.*

I know. I'll always be here to help you two. Please get well and make music again, please.

Rafe allowed them to chat a bit before ending the close telepathic rapport. "Okay," Dr. Leann said with Marisol translating, "time to get started on the next healing procedure. The doctors believe you are both physically ready. Shall we?" Both women nodded, about all they could do to communicate.

A few minutes later, they were in a medically induced coma and placed in the special machine that the geneticists had designed. Molly Maud said, "Okay, Heinz, there isn't anything we can do for several days. Come on; let's get us a tour of this place and see some of this world, shall we?"

"Well, all right. Inside those things, I can't wipe their foreheads. So I supposed I can let them be for now. Four days. Four days. I'll keep praying for them," Heinz declared, offering her his arm, just as he always did for Gisa and Karla when they were wearing their professional women's outfits. Molly Maud felt a little strange in that he took her left arm in his, but she realized that he did that on purpose, allowing her the use of her only hand, should she need it. While Molly Maud had seen much when she was here for two weeks getting her Basic Therapy, Rafe decided to stroll along, chatting and pointing out some sights. In fact, she was checking up on how Molly Maud was faring in life after her Basic Therapy.

"Such a strange world. So dim, so red. We are in a real castle and manors? Incredible. Someone ought to paint this place," Heinz exclaimed, finally coming out of his morose shell.

"Once Gisa and Karla get better, Heinz, you should go back to your painting again too, you know," Molly Maud encouraged him.

"If they get their arms and hands back, Miss Porsche, then I too will begin painting again. I'll do your portrait first to thank you for what you have done for my dearest friends," he declared. She smiled.

Four days passed slowly for Heinz. True, at my suggestion, Molly Maud continued to take him off on long walks around the giant castle and manor complex, sometimes getting completely lost in the process. The more they walked, the more the two talked, becoming more acquainted with each other. Molly Maud found Heinz to be a truly sensitive man and very observant of even the smallest of details. Little did she realize how important this was in his painting, but one day she would.

Dr. Leann continued to tell me to have Molly Maud take Heinz for walks. "Look, he's in here all the time, just sitting beside the machines!" We laughed. He was dedicated that's for sure and loyal too.

Late the fourth day, everyone gathered around the two machines. The doctors had alerted us they were going to be bringing the women out of their comas. Heinz would have been crushed had he not been there when the women roused. As the machines were opened, Heinz could not contain himself. He sobbed, "Arms! Hands! It is a miracle! They can play again."

Karla stirred. Heinz cried out, "Karla. You have hands and arms again! You can play cello once more!" A minute later, he was saying the same thing to Gisa, who was groggy but understood him and began moving her arms and fingers just to see for herself that it was true. It was.

Not everything was cured, however. Their lip loops were untouched, as was their exceptionally long, thick hair, though Karla didn't mind this detail at all. Their feet were only partially repaired. They would have to wear six inch heels or walk on their toes. Their breasts had greatly reduced in size down to what is called an H-cup in their world, the size of most of us on Ashford-5. Dr. Leann wondered if they would reduce further when they returned to their own world. Time would tell on that one.

A few minutes later, both women were once more sitting side by side on one of the beds, with Heinz beside them. All three were hugging and crying like babies. The doctors allowed them this private time before continuing their evaluations. A bit later, they pushed Heinz out, helped the two to get into clothes, and explained about the heels that would be required. Finally, with Marisol again translating for them, they went over the lip plates and mouth mounts, and how they worked. Before allowing the women to leave the med lab, they made sure that both could operate them easily, take them out at night, and put them back in.

However, the real problem was one of language. Marisol picked up their thoughts and questions, and vocalized them in Midlands, while translating the replies and requests into German. She knew a long-term solution had to be found before they could be sent home to Cass-C. So once more, everyone met.

Rafe took charge. "Okay. We have a potential solution to their obvious language problem. We're going to have them stay here a couple of weeks and learn to speak and understand Imperium Standard. During that time, Marisol is going to fix up a pair of ULAT boxes that'll translate IS into their German. That way, they can talk, and via the ULAT, others can understand them. Plus, Rafe is going to see they also get Basic Therapy while they are here."

She went on, "Heinz, we want you to go back with Molly Maud and help her while we're helping Gisa and Karla. During these two weeks, we want you and Molly Maud to learn to speak and understand Imperium Standard too. If the ULATs should break down, we must have at least two of you who can understand what they are saying."

He protested some, "But I should be here to help them."

"We understand, Heinz, but they'll have us to help them. Molly Maud doesn't have anyone, except Nia Elain and her three friends. They all need help, what with their missing hands," Rafe cleverly manipulated him.

"Oh. Yes. I'm so sorry, Miss Porsche. I wasn't thinking properly. Yes, I'll certainly be there to help you and your friends. That is the very least I can do to thank you for saving Gisa and Karla."

I brought up the next detail. "Okay then, there is one serious problem to consider. When they return, they'll be wearing the giant lip plates and have quite large bosoms, unlike most women in Hoffdorf. Somehow, we have to come up with a plausible reason for this, not to mention they will have their hands back. We don't want and will not send them back only to get their hands cut off again."

"Darn, we didn't think of that, did we, Heinz," Molly Maud gushed. "Oh dear, this is a problem. As I understand the new law, even pairs that have lived together for a year are going to be subjected to the new laws. Getting a divorce won't help either."

"Even making them citizens of Ashford-5 won't help," Danika pointed out. "When we got there this time, they wanted to cut off my hand just for leaving the spaceport. They are insane on this one!"

Molly Maud bit her lip and then said, "Okay, then we simply have to get this law modified somehow. Don't send them back until we do get it changed. Heinz, we have to get it changed somehow. If it's the last thing I do, I'm going to get it changed!"

Chapter 16 Reconstruction

We landed outside Hoffdorf around nine in the morning on the second day after the women's recovery. Again, Danika blazed us there. From the ship, we contacted General Wolfgang, who was only too eager to come meet us. I was not about to have my crew risk getting their hands cut off just to deliver the genetic cures data and samples!

Once more, he arrived with several men who took the shipping crates, handling them as though they were precious stones. After that, we headed into the admin building, where he reserved a private room. "Well, ladies, what was the verdict from the geneticists?" he asked what was uppermost in his mind.

"Well, there are just enough tiny DNA differences between Federation people and Imperium people that the cures are only likely to partially work. They believe if you follow their program exactly, arms will be regrown and breast sizes reduced. The lips and hair might not. Yet, their feet may partially recover. Of course, there isn't any cure for the dual sex organs. I'm afraid they and all of the rest of us victims are hermaphrodites still. Perhaps your geneticists will have better luck on cures than ours," I replied, giving him some hope.

"Well, if they could only get their arms back, they wouldn't be helpless. That alone is the single most important thing," he said.

"And what about us women who have lost this?" Molly Maud waved her nearly useless stump in his face. "Our enforced disabilities don't count, eh?"

He cleared his throat. "Er, I'm well aware of your difficulties. My wife has made that abundantly clear to me. I have to help her dress each morning and now am doing half of her household chores. But what can we do? It's the law of the Federation now."

"Change it, modify it," Molly Maud declared. "Well, that's not possible until we get a new set of rulers, is it?"

"True. True. I've no idea how that's going to happen.

I'm more or less in charge of all Cass-C now. A calamity like this has never happened before. On another topic, Field Agents have found the devices used in the attacks. Funny thing is, all the parts are common household items, found nearly anywhere, except for the bio agent cylinders that is. No way to track them back to the buyers. Dead end there," he pointed out.

We were relieved to hear that but said nothing about it. Instead, I brought up a more pertinent issue. "Unless your geneticists are vastly superior to ours, these men are going to be facing a very upsetting issue even after their cures. They will, for all intents and purposes, look like a woman — large bosoms and long hair cannot be disguised. Plus, if their lips don't heal, they'll have to wear the lip plates. All that said, they'll look like women, strange ones at that. How are they going to cope? Further, how is anyone going to know that they are not the wives in their marriages and turn around and remove their hands?"

He ran his hands through his hair, clearly frustrated. "I don't know. It already is a monumental problem. You are right. They woke up and screamed louder than I could ever have imagined. No one can understand anything they say, and they are, as you said, quite helpless. But I'll say this, your timely intervention with the things they need has made a difference. At least, we have them up and walking some. We've got their hair tied back in ponytails, but the situation is awful. Someone has to spoon feed them their meals, and they can't even drink. We've taken to spooning in liquids. It's horrid. Plus, they can't seem to breathe right, but without those steel corsets tied tight, we know their backs ache something fierce. Several were crying about the pain before we could get the corsets on them. We've got to handle two thousand six hundred and three people, and we can't even tell their sex any longer."

Molly Maud asked, "What about their spouses? Have they been allowed to see their husbands and wives yet?"

"Another sore point. No. I wanted to see if the cures would work first. I can't contain the situation if their spouses are allowed in. Yet, they could care for their basic needs.

Soldiers don't make such good care-givers," he admitted.

He went on, "Another matter. I have my hands full with this mess. But now, the usual demands of running Cass-C are popping up all over. I simply cannot handle everything."

"Well, may I make another suggestion, general?" Molly Maud asked. I tried to keep from grinning. I knew what she was going to say. He nodded. "Well, I'm a proven company leader. Why don't I step in and run the civil part of Cass-C, keep everything running smoothly, while you deal with the mess, our security, and the prevention of more such attacks? I suppose we're going to have to schedule an election to replace Admiral Fritz and soon."

"Miss Porsche, would you? That would truly help in this time of world crisis! You certainly have the respect of many prominent business leaders," he replied. I could sense the hope rising in him. She was taking a heavy burden from his plate, but I also knew the respect he was talking about wasn't quite the way he meant it.

"Yes, I will. Someone has to step in and keep Cass-C running. Just do everything possible to keep a lid on the mutations, and get them their cures as soon as is possible," she replied. Hastily, he wrote out an order giving her the authority once held by Admiral Fritz.

That afternoon, we walked into Admiral Fritz's office. "Hello. I'm sorry, the admiral is ill. Can I take a message," the young one-handed woman said. I noticed a huge stack of messages that others had left for him.

"You are his receptionist?"

"Yes, that's right. Ada. Who should I say dropped by?"

Molly Maud grinned. "Your new boss. I've just been appointed temporary admiral for Cass-C. Miss Molly Maud Porsche."

"*The* Miss Porsche!" she exclaimed.

"None other. Captain Nia Elain," she went on introducing the rest of us.

"Wow. Okay. Great. Here are all his messages. Sorry, I have a hard time picking things up," she fumbled with her left hand, very embarrassed she'd knocked the pile askew.

"We all do, Ada. Nothing to be embarrassed by. Come

on; show me the office and where everything is at. I think there must be a huge backlog to handle."

There was. She spent the entire next day returning calls and introducing herself as the new admiral for Cass-C. The following day, she began making changes. She fired off a detailed message to all the member worlds, notifying them of her appointment and suggesting they also appoint a temporary admiral until elections could be held. She strongly suggested sending a woman, but doubted many worlds would. In answer to what had happened to their admiral, she continued to say they were in quarantine because of a highly contagious disease.

The next day a continuous stream of ambassadors visited her office, both to see with their own eyes that a woman was Cass-C's new admiral, and to find out what they could about what had actually happened and where were The Seven. She continued to explain about the contagious disease angle.

Finally, the rush died down, and she began to formulate a plan. She went on the news to announce a National Women's Meeting, to be held on Monday at the Admiralty Round Table. The topic: these two new laws. She encouraged any woman with an opinion to come and air it. She would listen.

On Monday morning, the circular room was packed. Extra chairs had to be found in a hurry, delaying the start by a half hour. Finally, she rose and began the first meeting of its kind in Cass-C history. "I've asked you here to discuss the two new laws, namely the wedding ceremony and the women's legal rights with unfaithful spouses. I have looked over Federation Law, and found out that it's the right of any admiral to modify a law to meet their local needs, but we can't outright refuse to follow the law, until the entire Admiralty Round Table abolishes it. So I'm here today to see if modifications are in order. I'll listen to you and act accordingly."

Boy, did we ever get an earful! One woman rose and said, "I was an oboe player in the symphony. Now with this," she waved her right arm stump about, "I can't. I'm out of a job and money now too. What am I supposed to do? My career has been taken from me. I say abolish the damn law!"

269

Another woman rose, "I'm a mother of five children. We depend upon my husband to provide for us. Before this law went into effect, I caught him having an affair with another woman. I wasn't able to divorce him before the law went into effect. Like this," she too waved her stump about in the air, "I can scarcely take care of my children, let alone keep house. He is rich. But now, he is helping me around the house and doing everything he can to keep me from filing for a divorce. He knows if I did, it would ruin him financially. I say we keep the damned law! Women need this protection."

Molly Maud had lunch catered in for everyone, pleasing the thousands of women present. For nine hours, we heard opinions from hundreds of women. The results varied widely, spanning the whole gambit from total rejection of the laws to total support of the laws and all points in between. The only thing they all held in common was full support on the divorce law, taking three-quarters of the spouse's net worth. Well that bit was to be expected.

Now came the hard part, putting together a modification to the law that would represent their wishes, and which would not place every husband and man against her. She was up late that night drafting the wording, bouncing ideas off Heinz and us. The next day, she formally filed the document and then held a press conference to announce the major change. While the document was quite formal, she kept her wording simple at the conference.

"Thank you all for listening. As your temporary Admiral, I have listened to the women of Cass-C, and I'm acting accordingly. The law as written has caused a number of perhaps unforeseen and terrible side effects, as some of you already know. I'll just give you one example. The Fine Arts of Cass-C has been nearly erased. Our prized Hoffdorf Symphony Orchestra is now a thing of the past. Three-quarters of the musicians were married women, now unable to play. The director has disbanded it. We have lost one of the premier orchestras on our world! We've lost sculptors, painters, and the list goes on and on. Hoffdorf may never recover its once prominent position across all Cass-C as the premier fine arts city. Tragic beyond words."

"So as your temporary admiral, I have today officially modified the law, as is the right of any Federation admiral to do so. It is not in my powers to cancel those laws. I can only modify them. So here are the modifications I submitted. From now on, any couple who wishes to marry or any civil union couples must be asked whether or not they want this Mano Cortada marriage ceremony. If both parties desire the Mano Cortada marriage ceremony, then it is to be conducted just as the law specifies, including the legal provisions for the wife, should the husband be unfaithful. However, if they both do not wish the Mano Cortada marriage ceremony, then they're still allowed to marry or join in a union, and the Cortada marriage ceremony is not done. Further, the provision for unfaithful husbands no longer applies. The woman is ineligible to sue for three-quarters of his net worth, since she hasn't made the ultimate sacrifice. Further, if the couple cannot agree either way, then they are not allowed to marry or join until they both are in agreement, one way or the other. Finally, if there have been some couples who have yet to have the Mano Cortada marriage ceremony performed on them as has been done to so many of us already, then they are to be given the choices as I've just outlined."

She looked at the reporters and cameras. "I feel this is a fair modification of the new laws. Those, who which to participate in the Holy Ceremony, will be allowed to do so. Those, who do not, will not be required to lose a hand. Had those who passed these laws had the foresight to insert these modifications in the original laws, we would not have lost our prestigious Fine Arts, which may never be replaced unless these modifications are followed to the letter. Thank you for listening. That is all."

Reporters fired questions at her, "Miss Porsche, Admiral Porsche, what about the fact that indicated the Save the Family Plan will not work without one hundred percent compliance?"

"Look, as far as I know, every married couple on Cass-C, including civil unions, has had the Mano Cortada marriage ceremony performed on them. So right now, we're at one hundred percent compliance. In the future, young women will be looking to you and me" — I noticed the reporter was missing her left hand and Molly Maud did as well — "to see how we manage in life. If we set good examples, then they are likely to desire the ceremony as well. Yet, if the woman is one of our superior musicians, for example, she might not desire to participate and will have to take her chances that her husband will remain faithful to her. We should watch the divorce rate over the next three decades and see just what happens to it. I highly doubt that it'll rise much at all."

She didn't take further questions, since in her mind they seemed silly or would force her to repeat what she had just announced. Back home, she said to Heinz and us, "Now, we wait and see what backlash comes my way. I've really stuck my neck out there on this one. Still, the next admiral will have a harder time trying to undo my modification. Public opinion may well be against him. I certainly hope so."

The next day, the results began pouring in. Poor Ada, a dozen bouquets of flowers arrived throughout the day. She had devil of a time handling them, but Heinz continued to lend her a hand. She got calls of support and calls condemning her. I kept track and by the end of the day, it was 60-40 in her favor, pleasing us all.

The next day, things escalated somewhat. General Wolfgang called and asked her to come to Warehouse #25 for a meeting. Apparently, the genetic cure results were in, but there was a whole lot more going on as we were about to find out. As we made our slow way into the spacious building filled with cots and service men trying to handle the needs of the five hundred being housed here, the general appeared with another man at his side, carrying a clipboard. I saw Dr. Schmidt come running to join us.

"Ah good morning, Admiral Porsche. This is our new Commander Adalbert Stein, the new head of the hub Intelligence Division. He's been selected to take over for Werner," General Wolfgang introduced the man and then us to him. "First, let's go over the results of the many attempted cures. Dr. Schmidt," he deferred to the head physician.

He adjusted his glasses and glanced at his clipboard. Molly Maud would have liked to have one too, but she could not hold it and write at the same time. So it was pointless and depended upon her memory, as did we. "Well, express my sincere thanks to the geneticists on Ashford-5. Truly miraculous. Some of the cures are working. About half of the victims now have arms, tiny baby-like arms, but they are arms, and we've verified by measurements that they are growing. I believe in time, they'll become normal for their size. That is a relief. We've got everyone's breast size drastically reduced down to a standard H bra cup size, I'm told by our women nurses. That has alleviated the necessity for the tight corsets and their difficulty in breathing. Feet have, as you hinted might happen, only partially recovered. We've verified they'll need to wear heels such as you professional women wear. Their legs and feet simply can't be modified any further. The neurons in their hair were unaffected by the treatment, but we consider that to be minor. The real problem we're now facing, except for the half whose arms have shown no sign of regrowing, is these darn split lips."

He went on, "It's as you said; they are impeding their speech, so much so that in most cases, none of us can figure out what they are saying. Personally, I never knew how much our language depends upon sounds formed by our lips. Any, I've asked the general here to bring you here to update you, and to ask you if you have any further bright ideas regarding their speech. We're ready to try anything at all."

Marisol answered for me, "We have some few cultures where men and/or women wear these as decorative ornaments. In those cases, they have substituted clicking sounds for the sounds that lips are needed for. Of course, that makes it impossible for others to understand them, except their own people. So what we linguists discovered early on is they could speak Imperium Standard well. IS, as we call it, doesn't have any phonetic sounds involving the lips. Don't know why that is, but it's so. Hence, our victims are able to speak Imperium Standard, assuming they know it. You're not dealing with just one spoken language in this case are you?"

Dr. Schmidt replied, "No indeed. More like a hundred different ones, though many are variations, I believe. I'm not a linguist. But the admirals all are fluent in German, if that helps any."

"Actually, it might. You have translation devices, similar to our ULAT boxes."

"Why yes, ear wigs."

"Perhaps, you could get some linguists together and have the victims speak a specific word, and then program the ear wig to translate that to its proper pronunciation. At least, they could talk understandably to someone who had such an ear wig on," Marisol explained. He jotted her idea down, thanked her, and left to see what could be done.

"Now then, that's that. We have bigger issues here. We can't withhold what's happened here any longer," Commander Stein spoke up with authority. I have all the other Intelligence Division heads crawling down my back to be fully briefed on this attack. Plus, their spouses are ready to file lawsuits to get access to their husbands and a few wives. General Wolfgang has told me your reservations and what happened in your Imperium, but the Federation is not the decadent Imperium. Such isn't going to happen here."

"What concerns me more is how are we going to make what's happened presentable to the general public? I mean these aren't men any longer. They look like well-endowed women. Plus, half are going to remain utterly helpless, while the other half will take months before they can really do anything with those tiny arms. And then, there are those lip things. It wouldn't be so bad for them if other women in Hoffdorf and on Cass-C also started wearing those lip things, which, as she's just said, are considered ornaments. Admiral Porsche, you could order women to obtain such ornaments, and the cost could be defrayed by the world treasury. Of course, we would first have to get the speech situation under control. What do you say to this idea? It'll allow these recovering victims to more or less fit back into society, but as women. They certainly can't hide those breasts."

"You can't order fashion, Commander Stein. Besides, ordering all women to get their lips slit like this, assuming it could even be done, will create further problems. For example, some musicians must be able to blow into their instruments. Give me time, and I'm sure I can find other examples where it would be disastrous to force the woman to have these disks. Still, I do see your point. If they were somehow fashionable, then the recovering victims would fit into society with less embarrassment," Molly Maud replied.

She continued, "You see, I know from my visits to Ashford-5 that the wearing these disks is very popular with both men and women, and is seen as a status symbol of the wealthier or more powerful people. It's not entirely clear to me which. Their queens wear them, as does their governor, but then they speak Imperium Standard. So it is a fashion trend that you need. If you, Commander Stein, and you, General Wolfgang, were to have your lips fixed and wore these giant lip plates, I assure you that soon other men around you would desire to have them as well. After all, the victims are mostly men."

I had to give Molly Maud credit. She completely turned the tables on Commander Stein! "But — well I don't — I see your point. I wonder just how bad it is to have to wear them? Let me think about it. You are right. If we were seen to be wearing them, I assure you many others would quickly start wearing them too. I guess I should talk to the doctors here and see if such a thing is medically even possible. Those are giant lip loops, as if they have been stretched a substantial amount."

He continued, "Anyway, tonight we're going public with this whole thing. I have two admirals who have agreed to stand before the cameras so everyone can see for themselves what has happened here. One is our own Admiral Fritz, but his arms failed to regrow, so he'll be an example of the truly helpless victims. Then, there is Admiral Rafael Santiago, who now has tiny arms growing. He'll represent the best-case cure. I would like your presence at this conference and yours, Captain Nia Elain."

"We'll be there," Molly replied. He handed her a card with the time and location. It would be just outside this warehouse.

Back home, Jana commented, "This conference is a bad idea, mark my words." I did.

Shock. Stun. Fear. Terror. Worry. Horror. These were some of the reactions is sensed at the press conference.

General Wolfgang outlined what had happened in some detail, before turning it over to Commander Stein. He proceeded to tell everyone the culprits were not yet known and probably never would be. Wrong thing to say in my opinion. He introduced the two admirals and outlined in detail their many genetic mutations, pointing out the main difference now was in their arms or lack thereof. At least he did give Ashford-5 credit for the cures thus far obtained. Then, he pointed out that in handling these cures, they had exhausted all their genetic reconstruction materials and that it would be at least a year before they could try other potential cures. "It may well be that some of these effects may never be curable," he added, further saying precisely what I considered the wrong thing to say.

Then, he went on to beg patriotic men and women to help make these victims fit into society better by getting their lips modified and wearing similar "lip ornaments," as he now called them. "We are working on proper methods for you to do this. The government will defray all costs. Once we have perfected the technique, we will let you know."

A reporter shouted, "Commander, will you be sporting lip ornaments like these two admirals, once they are available?"

Taken aback by the question, he replied, "Why yes, yes of course, anything to help our brave victims here."

"How about you, general?" another yelled. He had no option but to agree to do it too. Fortunately, no one asked Molly Maud if she would consent. After that bit of embarrassment, he abruptly ended the conference, amid many shouted questions. The press is going to have a field day with this one, I thought, and was right.

The next day, Commander Stein visited me directly at the Admiral's Office. "Captain, I spent the night researching the culture on Ashford-5, based upon the copies obtained from Imperium web sites. Doesn't your people there have some kind of machine what will make these lip loops for those who wish them?"

I couldn't very well deny it. "Yes, we do. It is a modified medical machine. One fits it over the person's face and it both slits their lips, but also lengthens and thickens them so that they can wear the foot in diameter plates that are so popular there. It also drills the holes in the upper and lower gums that are used to anchor the supporting mouth pieces."

"Excellent indeed. I would like you to contact your emperor fellow and make any deal to get us one of those machines here as fast as possible. We do need to proceed in doing all we can to make our victims feel more comfortable in society."

I grimaced. "What about the speech problem?"

"We haven't really solved that one yet, but we're working on it."

I thought quickly. "Perhaps, there's another way. Our own scientists and linguists are working on a method that might work for your people. They're aware of the immense problems these victims are facing trying to rejoin society, and have come up with a possible translation device. Mind you, it's only in one form, that of your German. I can check and see if it is done."

"Oh superb. Yes, if it is ready and works, we simply must have that too. Think of how valuable that will be to the thousands of victims here," he poured it on thick. I promised to check directly, and get back to him as soon as I heard anything.

Molly Maud looked up from her piles of papers and commented, "The damned fool is really going ahead with this. God help him."

Later, I chatted with Emperor Bino about this latest request. Since this was really a personal ornamentation issue, he allowed it, but insisted on modifying the machine so this was its only function. I checked with Rafe back home, found out they had perfected the German speaking ULAT, and that it could be used to translate lip plate wearers who spoke either IS or German. Further, Gisa and Karla were doing well. Thus, the next morning, I reported to Commander Stein that the devices would be coming in about two weeks.

That evening something entirely different happened. Heinz asked Molly Maud and us to come with him to his studio down in The Grotte. Our heels clicking nearly in unison, we walked into his paint studio. There on an easel was Molly Maud's portrait. She gasped. We did too. We simply could not believe our eyes. It showed her from her waist up so that her hands were not visible. The detail was so perfectly done that I swear you could count the individual hairs on her head! Imagine a superb photograph blown up to a canvass about three feet square and that simply would not cover the incredible detail. Her eyes looked almost real! I swore I could count her eyebrow hairs.

Tears streamed down her cheeks. "Heinz, this is the most beautiful painting that I've ever seen!" she exclaimed, and then pressed her body into his, giving him a passionate kiss. His arms slipped around her waist. We wisely kept silent. Both looked flushed when they finally parted.

He then said to us, "I'll do each one of you next. Good eh?"

"Beyond good! Fantastic is more like it. You are a fabulous portrait painter," Molly Maud exclaimed again.

"It won't be dry for a couple of days yet. I do miss Gisa and Karla though. They used to stop by and critic my portraits as I was doing them, like I did with their music practicing. It'll be good to have them back with us," he replied.

Thus, began the romance between Heinrich and Molly Maud. As the days went by, she kept getting distracted thinking about him when he wasn't there and casting side glances at him when he was. I thought they were a good match indeed. Here was a man who had no interest in the fact that she was one of the wealthiest industrialists on Cass-C.

During the days that followed, more and more new admirals began arriving. In turn, each met first with Admiral Molly Maud to get their housing assignments and to discuss the situation. While there were not yet enough admirals to form a quorum and begin official work, she estimated that within a month or so there would be.

The other big and unresolved question just what to do about forming up another Seven. Some claimed that they were not needed, not really. Others claimed that someone needed to be over the other groups, that is, the admirals, the ambassadors, the army, and the ID, coordinating their actions.

Some wanted the new Seven to be known to all and not a secret bunch, answering to no one. This would be one of the first actions to be taken up by the reconstituted Admiralty Round Table.

A further complication was added to the mix. Commander Stein wanted to hold an election on Cass-C to elect their new official Admiral before the whole Round Table met for the first time. Naturally, Molly Maud had little choice but to agree to this and had to run for the office herself, because General Wolfgang insisted that she run. The established date for the election was to be June 1. Thus, in late May, Molly Maud began "meeting the voters," holding many meeting in public places, and attending all manner of formal affairs, drumming up votes.

Chapter 17 Terrorists

Mid-April. Circle City on Equiuss-C, Forbidden Planet, mid-spiral arm. The Red Mansion. The North Continent ruler, Comrade Filbert Small, a fifty year old man with prematurely greying hair and a face full of ugly dimples from a childhood illness, took another puff on his opium pipe, while staring at the moving images on his computer monitor. His current wife was caressing him, her name long forgotten. Vaguely, he thought. *Is she number twelve or thirteen — doesn't matter, unless it is thirteen — I should get a new one, then it wouldn't matter — but what is this that I'm seeing? Fabulous. No, I've seen that before.* "Hey hold on a minute. Will you look at that? Before. Yes, but where? Where? Imperium. Yes. That's where. I'll be. Why didn't I ever think of that before."

"Think of what dear? Can I have a hit now?" she said sweetly, fighting the cravings that had suddenly come over her whole body.

"Hah! Someone beat me to it. I'll not be out done. I thought of it first. Just now. Justin, Justin, oh where art thou now?" he called out in a mellow tone.

"Here, Comrade Filbert," a measles-faced, short, thin man said, crawling out of a corner when Comrade Filbert had sent him an hour ago and promptly forgot about him.

"There. See. They stole my plan which I just now invented."

"What plan is that, Comrade Filbert?" Justin asked timidly, fearing he was about to be sent to the corner again. That wouldn't have been so bad, if only he'd given him a hit on the pipe first.

"That plan, idiot Justin. Get me Finlge-what's his name. You know, the Gamelon-3, short, funny fellow. That Finlge-what's his name. Now. No, yesterday. I need him yesterday," Comrade Filbert barked authoritatively.

Justin scratched his dandruff-filled hair, noticed that it needed washing, and then remembered the order. "How do I get him yesterday, Comrade Filbert?"

"How the hell should I know? Just get him. And I need a new wife too."

"But what's wrong with me," the young woman wailed.

"Better ask what's right with me," he replied and took another hit himself, wondering where he was at.

Shortly, the funny looking man entered, wearing leather pants and boots, but a cotton shirt, perhaps once white but certainly in need of a bleaching if not outright replacing. "How can I be of service, Comrade Filbert?" he asked pleasantly.

"This. Get me a bunch of this stuff."

"What stuff? Another computer?" he asked, somewhat baffled by the ruler's request. They often were baffling, but the pay was beyond reproach.

"The stuff that does that stuff. There, see that woman. The stuff that does that. I want a bunch of it. They stole my plan. So I'll show them. Besides, I need a new wife."

"But what's wrong with me?" the young woman asked again, growing terrified, but wondering if she dared take a hit while he wasn't looking. She decided against it and waited impatiently for him to let her have a hit. Both men ignored her.

"Oh you mean the stuff that changes people into that?"

"Yes, you fool. That stuff. Lots of it. I want it here yesterday so I can do it to them before they just did it to themselves. I'll try it out on wife fourteen too. Should be more fun."

"Can't I be wife fourteen?" his wife asked.

"Why, I don't see why you can't? Justin, any reason she can't be wife fourteen?"

Justin decided to shake his head no, pleasing Comrade Filbert. "See, you can be wife fourteen, only you have to wait until I get the stuff." He saw the Gamelon-3 man was still here and looked at him, "Go man. Go. Get me lots of the stuff. Take what you need from the Royal Treasury. Just get me the stuff fast."

"As ordered," Finley replied, shutting off his tape recorder. He always taped the Comrade's orders. That way, if anyone questioned him, he had proof positive. Thus far, this alliance was making him quite wealthy. One day, he too would have such a wife. Perhaps after this deal was done, he would have enough to retire and get that wife. Back in his quarters, he did a calculation on his fancy handheld trading lister. "Damn, those are expensive. Okay, if I get him a dozen, plus one for me, adding in my profit above that, ah, comes to a hundred grand. Hope the treasury has enough."

It did, and he shortly departed from Equiuss-C for Gamelon-3, flying at top speed. A week later, he returned with thirteen crates, one of which he stowed in a hidden compartment on his ship where no one would ever find it. That one was for his future wife. One by one, he unloaded the dozen crates onto a pushcart. With some effort, he got the cart rolling and much later pushed it into Comrade Filbert's chambers where he was once more puffing on his opium water pipe. "Your stuff, as ordered, Comrade Filbert."

"Oh goodie, goodie," he clapped his hands together.

"Now, I get to be wife number fourteen. You promised," she begged, vaguely remembering that she would be that when the stuff came.

Comrade Filbert put the pipe away, but she cleverly snatched it and took several long, soothing drags herself, feeling better by the minute. He opened one crate and examined the contents, quite pleased indeed. "Instructions?" he asked the short man. "I need to try it out now."

Finley anticipated this request and had compiled all the known data about it, including its area of effect and concentrations. "On how many?"

"Just one, for now. Have to see how it works out, Finley." He pointed to his wife, who was now in dreamland.

"We will need a closed room so only she gets the effect," Finley replied.

"We'll use my bedroom. I don't sleep in there anyway. Wonder why it's a bedroom and not a sleep room? Must be because there is a bed in there. But if that's so, why is a kitchen a kitchen and not a cooking room? And a bathroom a toilet room? A living room isn't alive, last time I checked. Ah never mind. She's out of it. I'll carry her." Wife thirteen was now having sweet, pleasant dreams, oblivious to the world.

A bit later, they had her lying naked on their bed.

Carpets were then stuffed under the door jams, ensuring none of the gas would leak out. Comrade Filbert opened the valve and listened to the shhhh sounds of the gas escaping into the room. Finley, on the other hand, kept his eye on his watch. "That should do it, Comrade Filbert."

"Oh darn. So soon? Ah well. Perhaps I can do it to someone else on another day."

"Indeed Comrade Filbert, that you can. Now we wait. Four days."

"Ah, that long? Well okay. Meanwhile, fix up all the others so they make one big boom. I have to find Justin. I have an errand for him."

A day later, Finley had the cylinders bound together and had fastened tubes to each nozzle, merging them into one tube. At the merge joint, he installed a simple switch and then opened the valves. He figured that Justin would be too stupid to remember to do that. Now, all he had to do was open the one valve. Satisfied, he carried the heavy package to Comrade Filbert.

An hour later, Justin was on his way to Cass-C. Finley had preprogrammed the rust bucket shuttle with the coordinates and stowed the package on the ship. "Just find a big building where there are lots of important biggy-wigs. Walk in and open that valve there. That's all you have to do. When you get back, you can have all the opium you can smoke in a year. Here's some to tide you over. I know it's a long trip. Don't let anyone stop you or you won't get your year's supply of opium, Justin, dear. Got all that?"

His eyes nearly popped out of his head. "Oh yes. Got it, Comrade Filbert. Thank you, thank you. Big room full of biggy-wigs. Open valve. Return home. Year's supply of opium. Can't wait."

"Then, off you go. Bye, bye. Too bad you can't have gotten there many yesterdays before they stole my idea," Comrade Filbert said. "Say, if you do get there before they stole my idea, two years of opium." Justin nodded, but looked perplexed as he left them.

Finley had to remind Comrade Filbert when the four days were up. He was quite anxious to see the results himself, figuring if it worked well, he would use it to make his perfect wife. She looked perfect enough, lying there on the bed. Even Comrade Filbert was impressed. "First, we have to get these things on her, like the instructions say," Finley pointed out.

After a considerable struggle, the two men had her fully dressed and looking very sexy. At this point she woke up from her coma, craving more opium. "Here, have a hit," Comrade Filbert said. "You are wife number fourteen now." He held the stem to her mouth. She bit on it with her teeth, wondering where her lips were. She felt the sweet opium hit her lungs, and all the discomfort she felt vanished.

"There you go number fourteen. Now up you go." He rather pushed her to her feet. She flailed her arms wildly, but they seemed to have vanished somewhere. Her toes barely worked, but he steadied her. She saw herself in the full-length mirror there in the bedroom.

"Who is that woman?" she asked.

Comrade Filbert only guessed at what she was saying. He couldn't understand a word that she was speaking. "Why that's you, wife fourteen. Don't you look stupendous?"

"Oh, I suppose I do. I seem to have lost my arms."

He noticed she was looking at her shoulders, and figured she'd just made some comment about their absence. "You don't need them to be sexy, wife."

"No, guess I don't."

"Come on; let's walk to the study. Just look at your boobies dear. Fabulous!"

Mid-April. Thromstead, Blackwell-C, Forbidden Planet, mid-spiral arm. Thirty-six year old Barron Ulysses Blackwater, ruler of Thromstead, looked at is wife, who sat erect at his side. Such a beauty, he mused. He was twenty when he married her when she turned sixteen. Hell, she was the prettiest of all his cousins. That's why he chose her. He had bushy, black hair and prided himself on his spectacular moustache, his womb-broom, as he affectionately called it.

She had long, golden hair, uncut. Upon that, he had both verified and insisted before he consented to marry her. Her marvelous locks almost touched the floor when she stood.

They were aristocrats, the upper echelon of Blackwell society. As aristocrats, they had responsibilities, obligations, and customs, which they each had to follow, ancient in nature, never transgressed. Just why the stupid Federation of Planets could not understand something as simple as that continued to elude him.

Once, though a long time ago according to the history books if one can believe them, there were three classes of people on Blackwell: the aristocrats or ruling elite, the priests, and the peasants. Of course, the latter comprised ninety percent of the world's population, but they included the working classes too, the doctors and scientists. However, the priests had long ago been simply erased from history. Some books claimed the aristocrats killed them off, but who could really say? That was millennia ago. Now, it was just the elite and the peasants. Among the elite were the knights-holy. No one knew why they were called that, though. They were paid handsomely by their baron, thus ensuring their loyalty. This was something every baron understood and followed. Those that didn't wound up dead, with a new baron taking his place.

Within each town and city, the baron's word was the law, but there were some laws that they all had to abide by. These formed their responsibilities, obligations, and customs. The baron had very specific ones he had to follow, while the baroness had an entirely different set that she was obligated to follow, just as her husband was. If the baron failed in his duties, he would likely be eliminated. Similarly, if the baroness failed in hers, her baron would have no choice but to behead her and find another baroness who would carry out her duties. Within the framework of their different responsibilities, obligations, and customs, their society was extremely rigid and unforgiving.

Fortunately, those were actually very few and most were more or less obvious, at least those of the baron were. Failure to pay his knights-holy was the worst one of all, resulting in his rapid death. These fighters had to be paid, period. Next, a baron was required to have a baroness at his side always. In case of a death, he was given a period of a year to find a new baroness. Further, he was required to produce at least four offspring, whether or not they lived to adulthood. Usually, the eldest son would one day inherit his father's throne. Other sons joined the knights-holy, though in the event of the premature death of the eldest son, the next in line son could be pulled back out of the service.

On the other hand, a baron's obligations were less stringent. He was to arrange a proper marriage for his daughters, and see to it they were properly prepared for their wedding day. Such preparations only were done when he had accepted the man's marriage proposal. Once accepted, there was no going back. They had to marry. He was obligated to see that his wife and baroness was properly cared for at all times, and that she lived up to her responsibilities, obligations, and customs.

As far as customs went, these were more flexible. He and his baroness were to hold court at least an hour each day. He, his baroness, and their children were to attend all neighboring social occasions. This was important because it gave the younger ones a chance to meet prospective brides and grooms, and for the barons and baronesses to chat about what needed to be done. Finally, they were supposed to attend the New Year's Council, where matters pertaining to the entire world were discussed and handled. Their children also attended and for the same reasons as the local social gatherings. Beyond these, any baron could do whatever he chose to do.

In contrast, the baroness had her own set to follow, beginning when she was betrothed. Of course, she had no say who she was to marry. That went without saying, but it was humiliating to a baron to marry off a daughter to either someone she detested or to an ugly man. At the point when the marriage proposal was accepted, she underwent Baroness Preparations. Their local doctor handled this, making her into the perfect bride and baroness. The doctors took great pride in their handiwork and were beheaded if their work was unsatisfactory. The invention of the medical machines a millennia ago had by now pretty well handled this detail, though some barons and baronesses could be terribly picky about their daughter's Baroness Preparations, which in these modern times was perfectly painless.

Baroness Preparations always included the removal of her arms. No baroness ever had arms. History books don't lie. Her ears and nose were punctured so that the golden veil could be attached properly. The heavy veil made from pure gold was fastened to each ear and ran across her cheeks to either side of her nose, covering her face from that level on down to just below her chin. The golden veil was her symbol of office. Though heavy, she wore it with great pride. A baroness never spoke, enforced by the removal of the front part of her tongue. A baroness always had to display superb posture, never slouching on her throne, though the baron was allowed to slouch all he wanted. The baroness was not allowed to, because she was the embodiment of beauty for the town or city. Thus, rigid corsets were worn, very heavily boned with steel stays. Some said there was more steel in a baroness' corset than the baron's ceremonial sword. That's certainly a true statement.

A baroness was required to walk stately and graceful at all times. Hence, she was always to wear six-inch heels, or higher if she could train her feet to do so. Many teens made just such attempts, so it wasn't uncommon for exceptional baronesses to walk in seven-inch heels. To prevent the baroness from cheating, their shoes were of the oxford style, nicely tied with double knots, preventing them from being removed without untying them.

Finally, the Baroness Preparations also included breast enhancement. In terms of Cass-C, their bosoms were required to be of H cup size, though bras were unheard of on Blackwell-C. A prospective baron could always request a larger size, though, and the bride's father was obligated to fulfill such wishes.

Once the Baroness Preparations were finished, the parents were required to purchase one complete gown for her to wear and the bridal gown. It was the groom's responsibility to clothe her properly after that. Beyond this, there were a number of other considerations that the young teenaged girls followed. It was quite common for a prospective baron to require that the bride had never cut her hair. Hence, the young girls usually never had theirs cut. Also, they spent many hour wearing the tall heels, learning to walk both gracefully and stately. When they reached fourteen, their mothers usually had them encased in the steel corsets to get them used to wearing them ahead of time. The marrying age was sixteen. Rare was the young woman who was chosen beyond age twenty. If she reached twenty-one without any marriage proposal, then the parents were obligated to donate her to the town's peasants to do with as they saw fit. That, of course, was a blot on the parents, who always did their very best to get their daughters properly married on time.

Part of the baroness' responsibilities was to bear the baron as many children as he desired, usually at least four. Some of the wealthier and influential barons had a dozen offspring. Tied in with this responsibility was her obligation to satisfy fully his sexual needs. She was required to always dress formally and to attend all court sessions, sitting stately and beautifully at her baron's side. She had to attend all the social occasions as well. Plus, she had to be able to dance well. Again, the young teens spent hours practicing on the dance floor, if they were wise. Falling down in public was a severe disgrace, a horrid blot on her and on the baron.

She was obligated to wear whatever clothing her baron had purchased for her, whatever earrings, broaches, and other jewelry that he gave to her, and similar things. She was also obligated to see that her daughters were properly prepared for their marriage, though this was very difficult, since she had no arms and couldn't speak. Still it was her obligation to fulfill, as much as it was the baron's. Finally, she was obligated to look as attractive as possible at all times, for who knew when an important person might arrive. She would have to be the perfect hostess at such times.

All this meant that a baroness had to have a number of servants or ladies maids to assist her. This does not mean she didn't have any way to communicate. No, she developed a clucking or clicking language, sounds she could make and any good ladies maid understood these. A wise young teenage girl would also spend hours with her mother learning this secret baroness language, consisting of around a hundred distinct words, about evenly divided between verbs and nouns.

In spite of a baroness' restrictions, a baroness' life was one of luxury and great pleasure, as long as she fulfilled her responsibilities, obligations, and customs. Her position was envied by all, especially if she had great poise, grace, and stateliness, especially when she walked or danced. It was customary for a baroness to mingle with other barons at all social events, charming them, dancing with them — all of which then reflected well on her baron.

Baroness Lilly Blackwater was thirty-two, with wavy, long uncut golden hair, much prized by her husband. It was threatening to reach the floor when she stood. Her face was round. Her golden eyebrows highlighted her pale blue eyes. Her favorite gown matched her eyes, but had layers of golden thread in it, and her petticoats puffed it out some two feet all around her. She was always able to wear the seven-inch heels, though these forced her to take the tiniest of steps, which always enchanted other barons who often danced with her when they could. Her face had great color to it and a perfect complexion, which she passed on to her children, especially her daughters.

They had four children, each two years older than the next. Their youngest boy, Thomas was now ten. Then came Lisa. Larry, now fourteen, was his heir apparent. At the next social event, he was to begin looking for his bride. Finally, came Christina, who was sixteen.

Christina was their problem child. While Baroness Lilly had been wise and worked on everything when she was thirteen, including wearing a corset and heels, and learning the cluck-click language, to say nothing of dancing, and working up to being able to wear the seven-inch heels with poise and grace before she was married at sixteen, Christina had not, despite both parents' constant chiding and pleadings. Now at sixteen, she had no choice but to get prepared for the next social event, barely three months away. At the event, she could well be betrothed. Lilly knew well how scary it had been for her when she was helped out of the medical machine armless and unable to speak any longer. Frightening. But all of her long, painful, arduous hours of practice had paid off. She'd adapted extremely easily and had been fortunate to be wedded to one of the more powerful barons!

"Mom! I can't breathe in this thing," Christina gasped. Lilly had ordered the ladies maids to put her into the new corset and lace it as tight as they could manage, though they had done that in stages, giving her a half hour to get used to a given tightness before tightening it further. Now it was fully closed.

Lilly clicked. "What? Walk? In these heels? I can't. I'll fall down!" Christina protested wildly. Her mother clicked again, and a ladies maid gave Christina a push. It was either walk or fall down. She stumbled but did keep from falling by waving her arms about. Lilly clicked and clucked. "What? Oh, I know I won't have arms. This is impossible!" Lilly looked exasperated. What was to be done with Christina? Three months was all they had left. The only positive thing was Christina knew the cluck-click language, having heard her mother use it all her life.

After another bit of noise, a ladies maid turned on the dance music and took hold of Christina, forcing her to dance or fall down. Christina tried clumsily, cursing and swearing, sometimes louder than the music, once even stepping on her own hair. That was her only saving grace, her hair. She'd inherited her mother's golden locks, not her father's rich black hair, which was a very good thing. Barons preferred golden locks to other colors in women's hair.

Since she was a little girl, Christina had other ideas for how her life would go, which she constantly shared with her little sister, Lisa. When she was ten, she fell in love with the sounds of the clavecin, imported from a faraway world called Cass-C. She begged and begged to be allowed to learn how to play this marvelous keyboard instrument. Whenever the musicians gathered to play or practice, there was little Christina sitting on the bench beside whoever was about to play. "Don't be ridiculous, Christina, in a few years you will be a bride like your mother. It takes hands to play. Forget such silliness," Baron Ulysses chastised her repeatedly.

When she was twelve, she began dreaming of flying off in one of those great, silver spaceships, traveling out among the stars, exploring, perhaps even finding this Cass-C and the clavecins. There, no one would bother her, and she could learn to play. When she turned fourteen, the stark reality of what her future was to be struck her rather abruptly. They wanted her to prepare herself for her soon to be role as a baroness. Recoiling from the sudden realization that all her dreams were about to be stripped from her, she got a brilliant idea. If she did all that she could do to not be worthy, then no baron would desire her. When she turned twenty-one, her father would have to send her off into Thromstead. There she was certain she could get onto one of those silver spaceships fly off to fulfill her dreams. That is why she totally ignored all their suggestions, pleadings, and scoldings. It had been successful until now. She was sixteen, and her grand plan was fraying at the edges.

Baron Ulysses poked his head in to see how Christina was doing. It was so poorly that he shook his head. Lilly saw this and nodded affirmatively to him. Already they had agreed that stronger measures were required or they would both be chastised in three months, may be worse.

Stronger measures. That is what Baron Ulysses and the Collective had agreed was necessary in quite another matter. The Collective had formed years ago, a united group of powerful barons with the single goal of getting the Federation of Planets to accept Blackwell-C into their group of powerful worlds. It was long, long overdue. Baron Ulysses had argued that they met all the criteria. They were wealthy, modern, and had a small fleet of spaceships. Yet, every time they petitioned to join, they were rejected. Hence, the Collective had formed to find ways and means to force the bureaucrats on Cass-C to allow Blackwell-C to join.

They had the worked out one of the sore points. These bureaucrats detested the way that they treated their baronesses. Quite why they did, Baron Ulysses could not fathom. Baronesses were always treated like the royal queens that they were, lacking for nothing. They had the respect of their people and were even catered to at all times. Didn't Baroness Lilly have four ladies maids? Her dress closet was filled with expensive gowns. She wore only the finest gowns.

No, he couldn't fathom why these bureaucrats held such a grudge against them. Then, another baron pointed out that these men were probably just jealous of their baronesses. Indeed, that seemed the only rational reason. The Collective set out to find a way to solve that aspect.

A survey of Cass-C yielded key information. None of their women was remotely like the baronesses, though some of the more professional women did wear similar high heels. At special times, some of the women's dresses were nearly as elegant and fashionable as the cheapest dress the lowest baroness wore. "They are too backwards to make any of their women baronesses," another baron pointed out. "We should do it for them." Two years ago, that idea took root. It seemed to these barons that the only way open to them was to create Cass-C baronesses for those stupid bureaucrats. Thus, the barons set about looking for ways and means. That's when they discovered their answer in the Imperium: the genetic bio agent. "Why, they are perfect women!" Baron Ulysses exclaimed, when shown images of the "victims."

Soon, someone proposed this marvelous medical treatment be used here on Blackwell-C. That was quickly dispelled. While such baroness-like women did have sons, those sons looked like women, not men. Besides, the men looked like their baroness-like mothers, completely unsatisfactory. Then, Baron Ulysses realized this was their answer! "Look, we make enough of these baroness-like women, and they have their children as always, bringing forth four or so more baroness-like. Within twenty years or so, Cass-C will have many, many baronesses, and thus no longer have a valid reason to deny us entry into the Federation!"

The Collective cheered and heaped praise upon Baron Ulysses. His solution was brilliant and guaranteed to work. Thus, began the search for this special medicinal remedy, which they finally found on Gamelon-3. Since no Federation ships were permitted to land or to trade with them, black market traders took advantage of this, none more so than Gamelon-3, which was far out on the outer rim, bordering both the Imperium and the Federation of Planets. Just two weeks ago, the medicinal supplies had finally arrived and had been duly paid for.

Now, the Collective needed just the right assemblage to target, to turn into proper baronesses. And that time was getting close, the Winter Renewal. Winters on Cass-C began sometime in April, and the gala festival, known as the Winter Renewal, was held on May 15. Parties were held all over the world in all major cities. The wealthy attended these affairs, while those who could not afford the tickets held their own parties elsewhere. Thus, the time, place, form, and event for Cass-C baroness creation was determined long in advance.

Stronger measures were about to enacted both abroad and here on Baron Ulysses' home front. He'd taken all of Christina's disobedience he could tolerate. Hadn't he been patient with her these past three years? No, more than patient. Enough was enough! He went into his private study and placed two phone calls. The first was to give the final okay on the Baroness Creation Project. The knights-holy were drilled and ready to execute on his command. He spoke only one word on this first call: "Go!" He heard one word in reply, "Acknowledged." He smiled; soon Cass-C would have plenty of its own baronesses. After that, their admission into the Federation was assured.

His second call was to Doctor Hrodgar, the best physician in Thromstead. "Yes, doc, it must be tonight. Yes, full and complete. Leave nothing out. It simply must be done. Eleven sounds good. I'll meet you at the castle gates then. Thank you." He hung up satisfied. All week, he had discussed this with Lilly, and she had agreed just now. Her nod was her approval. Having been raised by his mother, Baron Ulysses also knew their unique cluck-click language. In fact, hardly any baron didn't know it. Officially, of course, the baronesses were not ever able to "speak," but no one considered their cluck-click sounds to be truly "speaking." Thus, there certainly was a good deal of communication from the baronesses, particularly with their ladies maids.

"I can't sleep in this!" Christina complained bitterly. Her chest ached. Her feet throbbed mercilessly. This had been the worst day ever, she thought. Her ladies maid was preparing her for bed, leaving the tightly laced, heavy steel boned corset still on. Try as she might, she couldn't undo the knots that the ladies maids had tied, not unless she could see behind her back. So immobile, she couldn't twist or bend enough to see. Her mother clucked. "What? I have to get prepared?" Lilly nodded affirmatively. "But I don't want to be a baroness. I don't want to marry anyone!"

Looking disgusted, Lilly turned gracefully around and moved very slowly out of her daughter's bedroom, taking at most a few inches with each step in her seven-inch heels. Once her ladies maid left, Christina struggled to get into a sitting position. Once more, she tried to twist around enough to get at the tied laces, but gave that up and focused on her aching feet still confined in her new seven-inch heels. They too were laced and tied in double knots. She tried to bend and reach them, but simply could not bend at all. So she pulled one leg up and grinned. Hastily, she untied one and massaged her foot. Then, she did the same to the other one. Satisfied with her small victory, she lay back down and tried to sleep. As uncomfortable as she was, she couldn't; she just knew she couldn't. Yet, sometime later, she did fall asleep.

Shortly after eleven, Doctor Hrodgar stepped silently into her room and placed a mask over her mouth and nose, counting to ten. He removed it and smiled. She would not wake up now. The sedative would keep her out until morning. Of course, by then it would all be over, except perhaps for her screaming. He didn't relish the baron or baroness one bit on that point. Still, he knew it had to be done. Never had he seen such a rebellious young aristocrat. He stepped outside where Baron Ulysses was waiting. He nodded, and the two moved his equipment into the room.

An hour later, Doctor Hrodgar finished up his work, packed his equipment, accepted his substantial fee, and left, knowing he'd done a superb job. Christina would make an exceptionally beautiful baroness, at least physically, which is all that he was able to control. Now, it was up to the baron, baroness, and their ladies maids. He left with a smile of satisfaction on his face. Such a beauty, he mused.

Now, the sleepy ladies maids entered, along with Baroness Lilly, cluck-clicking orders to the five women.

Hastily, they double checked her corset. It was as they had left it, but they put her seven-inch heels back on and tied them securely, knowing Christina would not be playing that trick on them again. They quickly brushed out her long golden waves and tucked her in. Lilly smiled. Her Christina now looked every bit the young baroness that she was soon to be, a real beauty indeed. Her only concern was the short time, barely three months before the Wilshire Dance, where she would be meeting and dancing with a dozen barons and their eligible first-born sons. She hoped Ulysses would choose wisely for her Christina. Slowly and gracefully, she headed out of her daughter's bedroom, down the hall to her own, where her ladies maids had gathered to undress her. Already Ulysses was getting ready for bed himself.

Lilly and Ulysses slept in the following morning, having been up so late seeing to Christina. They were awakened by her blood curdling screams. Their startled expressions quickly gave way to broad smiles. Lilly clicked and Ulysses replied, "Yes, now, she must learn and learn very quickly. We've been too lax on her these past several years. Now, we must be firm and unrelenting. She only has three months to adapt well." Lilly clucked. "I know; it'll be hard on us to watch, but we simply must." Lilly nodded and cluck-clicked again. "Now?" She nodded and grinned. "Oh you devil you." He began passionately kissing her, and they didn't rise for another half hour, and when they did, both were satisfied and with flushed faces. Perhaps, it was time for another child after all.

Christina awoke feeling groggy. Intense pressure around her waist seemed unrelenting. She moved her hands up to rub her face. Nothing happened. She did it again. Still nothing. She looked at her sides. Her arms simply were not there. And her breasts were now enormous from her point of view. In fact, they were as large as her mothers were. A nasty taste was in her mouth. She moved her tongue. The front half of it was missing. She tried to call out, but only strange noises came instead of words. Stark reality raced through her consciousness. Fear and terror swept over her like a tidal wave! She screamed and screamed. After an eternity, three ladies maids came rushing in.

"Help me. What have they done to me? I'm helpless!" Christina cried out, but stopped abruptly. She had only made very strange sounds, wholly unlike any possible speech! She screamed again.

"Sh. Sh. You'll wake up the whole household," one maid said calmly. "You're a baroness now. Stop trying to speak. You can't anymore. Remember your cluck-clicks. Come. Time to get up and dressed, my lady." Strong arms lifted her into a sitting position, but her whole body was shaking, quite out of her control. She could only watch, as the ladies maids began dressing her. Christina now knew she was entirely helpless, never ever able to do anything for herself ever again. Her grand plan dashed beyond all hope. "Stand up, please." She tried to say she couldn't, but as the garbled noises came out, she remembered and cluck-clicked that she couldn't, not in these overly tall heels. Her feet ached from having slept in them. Besides, she couldn't see over her enlarged bosom.

They ignored her protests and pushed her up, teetering wildly while trying to move her arms about to keep her balance as she had done yesterday. They weren't there, and she would have fallen had not one maid steadied her. The dressing done, they had her sit back down, while they brushed out her wavy hair, adjusting it to fall to her front side. Next, they brought out her golden veil, fastening it first to a new hole in her left ear, draping it over to the left side of her nose, then the right side, and finally on over to her right ear. The sheer weight threatened to pull her ears and nose completely off, but it draped beautifully, mostly hiding her lower face and mouth. "There you look wonderful, Christina. Now, up you go. Time for breakfast," one maid said, giving her a push.

Christina was terrified. She couldn't keep her balance and wiggled wildly until one maid put her arm around her, nudging her forward. It was take a step or fall down! Sobbing now, she took her first steps as a baroness to be, terrified out of her mind. The day only got worse for her though. As she walked clumsily and pathetically slowly into the spacious dining room where everyone was already sitting down to breakfast, Larry whistled and said, "Wow! Look at Christina. Now, she has to be a baroness. No more silliness from her."

Christina called out, "You bastard!" and tried to slap him, as she was always wont to do when he made fun of her. She regretted it. Her sounds were garbled gook, and her arms didn't move; they weren't there. Larry laughed, "Oh too bad, Christina. You can't slap me ever again. Ha. Ha." Christina could only cry, and that she did, while her maid got her seated.

Baron Ulysses barked, "Larry. That's enough. You must now respect your sister as the baroness that she is. You got that? Show her respect." He grinned at her, but nodded to his father, thinking, oh this is going to be too good to be true!

Christina grew up watching her mother's ladies maids feeding her and helping her with her tea. Now, humiliated beyond words, she had no choice but to allow her maid to sit beside her and feed her, made all the more difficult because of her golden veil. Plus, eating was a whole new experience without the front of her tongue. It was awful to endure.

Lisa, on the other hand, was very impressed. "Mom, can I get that done too? I'm twelve now. Surely, I'm old enough to wear the corset and heels too, aren't I? Please. I want to look just like Christina. She's so beautiful, though not as pretty as you are, mom," she added that last hoping to win more favors, but she did think Christina was prettier than her mother was.

Ulysses smiled. "Well, I suppose so, Lisa. After breakfast, we'll have your maid prepare you. Then, you can help Christina learn to do what she must. Concentrate on walking gracefully, stately, and with poise, plus dancing. Oh my yes. Maids, make sure her dancing is simply top notch. Only three months left to turn her into a perfect baroness."

"Oh thanks dad! I will! I will. You'll see," Lisa gushed. Christina let out a moan and half-choked. This was a horror beyond all horrors. Couldn't Lisa see it?

Today made yesterday's troubles seem like nothing at all. Relentlessly, her maids forced her to walk around and around. Her feet and knees ached, and now she couldn't ever again even massage them herself. She was totally dependent upon her maids for everything. At first, they did keep an arm on her while she walked, but in the afternoon, they let go, telling her that she had to walk by herself from now on — terrifying beyond belief. And then, her sister joined her. From her smaller waist and height, Christina knew Lisa wore a corset and tall heels too, just as she had done yesterday. Lisa looked bright and proud, taking her tiny steps into the room.

"Look at me, Christina. I'm wearing six-inch heels, but it's a bit hard to breathe, like you said. Come on; we have to practice our dancing. Do you suppose lots of boys my age will want to dance with me at the ball? Mom said I could wear these to the ball. They are making me a new gown to fit my smaller waist. Isn't this just great? Why are you crying? Oh well. We need to dance. I'll be the boy, since you don't have your arms anymore."

Later, Lilly looked in on them and sighed. Christina had so much to learn and so little time. Still, she knew that her daughter now had no choice but to learn and learn quickly.

Galactic disk approaching, Fisal.

Yes, I see it. This is going to be loads of fun, Desil. No one is going to be the wiser either.

True, but will it actually work, Fisal? We've not tested it yet you know. The two doll bodies from the southern halo looked at each other.

Not hardly. We'd be zapped if we tried it on our kind. No, we slip up here in the disk and mess around with the puny ones. It's going to be loads of fun, good for lots of laughs, Desil.

But Fisal, there are trillions of these puny ones around here. How are we going to be able to tell if it works and then be able to watch the fun? How will we even be able to find them in time to watch?

*Well, who knows, Desil? I know that it's illegal, so therefore it **must** work. Trust me; we'll figure it out. Might take a while, but we'll figure it out.*

The flying saucer hovered around the middle of one of the spiral arms. Their cloaking device was engaged and had been ever since they swiped this ship. Earlier, they'd broken into the advanced electronics lab and stolen this "forbidden" device. Yes, they were young and mischievous, out for some teenage pranks.

The two parked the saucer in a holding pattern,

allowing it to drift along with the rotation of the arm, thereby holding its apparent location with respect to the stars around them. The two walked to the central core room where they'd put the stolen device. *How do we hook it up?* Fisal asked.

Improvise. Must have a power connector here somewhere. Ah, yes. There it is, Desil. Plus that into the core. Thanks. Okay, see it is powering up.

Yes. So far okay. But look Fisal, there are almost an infinity of frequencies being displayed. How do we know which one to use?

Fisal replied, *Dunno. We'll pick one at random.* His doll hands moved the dial randomly and stopped on one specific frequency or wavelength.

Desil commented, *Gosh, that sure is a very, very tiny wavelength. Will it really work? Such a high frequency.*

Fisal laughed. *Hope it isn't our frequencies or we're in trouble.* Both laughed.

Well, there goes nothing, Fisal, Desil declared, pressing the Activate button. A huge power surge dimmed all the saucer's lights. *Holy cow! What a power sucker this thing is! Hope it doesn't short out our circuits. I don't want to be stranded here and be arrested for "borrowing" this ship.*

Fisal stated, *Hey, it must be working! Okay, now how do we see the action, the fun? How do we locate them?*

Dunno, it didn't come with an instruction manual.

Who reads those things anyway? Both laughed. It was far more fun just to push buttons randomly and see what happens.

Time meant little to these doll teenagers. That they spent weeks trying to figure out how to find the objects of their little bit of fun didn't even register in their minds. What's time anyway to a being with an indestructible doll body? Such bodies didn't need to eat or sleep. Technically, it wasn't even a living object, but a form of synthetic plastics and metal framework, each part was replaceable in case of damage. Just unscrew the damaged part and screw on a replacement one. Of course, there was always the necessity of then getting a new paint job.

In fact, it was their total disregard of time that

prevented far more damaging consequences for the inhabitants of the spiral arms of the galaxy. The device was forbidden for very good reasons, all of which totally eluded these teen dolls. The disaster could have been more far reaching than it was.

Part II Contagion Spreads

Chapter 18 Switched

It was late April. I knew that I was supposed to help Molly Maud with one of her campaign appearances today. I roused and rubbed my eyes. Nothing happened. Funny, I was having a difficult time breathing. No, it was intense pressure around my torso. Even my mouth felt funny. Something wasn't right. I came alert and pushed myself up. Nothing happened. I couldn't bend, and realized I must be wearing one of those impossible corsets. I looked at my sides and saw nothing. I wiggled my arms. They weren't there. Panic swept over me. I strained and rolled trying to get up, but it was just too hard. I started to cry out when I realized half of my tongue was missing. Then, I did scream.

Two women in strange cotton dresses came walking into my room, turning on the lights and opening the blinds letting morning sunlight into the room. What room? I'd never seen this place before! Had I been in a coma? Had we been attacked with that awful bio agent yet again? No, my boobs were still just as large as they had been when I went to bed, but this wasn't right! None of it. Where was I? What happened to my tongue? I tried to speak to the women and nothing but garbled sounds came out, scaring me even more.

"You forgot again, Christina. If you want something, you have to use your cluck-click language. Time to rise and shine. Another day of practicing. That's what the baroness has said."

"I'm not Christina. Where am I?" *Crap, I can't talk! What is going on?* Yes, I was now freaked out! I started to use my *mentales* gifts and discovered I could only just barely levitate my body! My crystal was gone! *Dear god! What's happening to me?*

"You must be anxious to get started," one woman said, seeing me struggling to sit up. "That's a good girl." She put arms around me and got me into a sitting position. Now, I could partially see the overly tight corset here and there around my boobs. Where was I? I looked around at the room.

302

Nothing at all was familiar, nada. That freaked me out even more. I must have tried to say something else, but all I did was make gurgling sort of noises.

"Christina, you know you can't speak any longer, so stop trying. Use the cluck-clicks like you are supposed to. *But I don't know what you are talking about!* They proceeded to get me dressed. I couldn't do anything but let them. My feet were normal but sore for some unknown reason. I'd never seen the satin gown they put on me, complete with several petticoats, which puffed it out perhaps a couple of feet. I couldn't tell too well, unable to bend much at all.

Oh no, they were tying seven inch heels on my feet now! I tried to protest, shaking my head no. "Forget it; you know you have to wear these. Perhaps, today you will walk more gracefully and smoothly. Honestly, Christina, you were terribly klutzy yesterday. You must try harder today. There." The heels were rather similar to our Ashford-5 oxfords, but covered a bit more of my feet, almost a boot, making them impossible to slip off unless they were untied first. I did see they even double knotted it. No way could I get them off!

Next, they proceeded to brush out my hair. I gasped. My lush black hair was gone, replaced by wavy golden locks that were far longer than I wore mine! Something was horribly wrong here. I tried to focus and use my telepathy, but I was too terrified, too scared to concentrate, and failed miserably.

"There you go, Christina, all dressed. Now up you go. See if you can rise gracefully on your own today." I tried, but it was hell. I wiggled and wobbled wildly, until one of the women steadied me. "See how pretty you look? You'll make one of the prettiest baronesses ever." She pointed to a full length mirror. I turned a little and looked at the reflection. Who was that woman staring back at me? It certainly wasn't me! The hair would have touched the floor had the dress not puffed out just enough to keep it from dragging. My body wasn't my body! I just stood there staring at this total stranger.

"Time for breakfast. Come on, Christina. Show your mother and father how gracefully you can walk today," one woman said. I froze. She pushed me. It was walk or fall down. I took a frantic step and nearly lost my balance. Then, I remembered. Take tiny steps and tried to do so.

"Not that way silly. You don't want to go dancing before breakfast, do you?" she chided me. I was lost. I had no idea where anything was! At least they pointed me in the right direction. I focused on trying to walk without losing my balance, which is tough in such heels. Now, I knew why my feet and knees were throbbing. I must have worn these far too long yesterday. No, I wasn't even here yesterday!

I walked pitifully slowly into a strange dining room. A number of people I'd never seen before were already there. I saw an older man with a prominent moustache and black hair. He looked rather formal to me. Sitting beside him was another woman, slightly younger I guessed. She too had no arms, and from her small waist, I suspected she was wearing a corset too. Her bosom was as large as mine was, but ours were drastically larger than all the other women present, servants I gathered. I saw a young teenaged boy, a slightly younger girl, who was beaming but also was wearing a corset. Her bosom had yet to fill out fully, probably not yet a teenager. And there was one other even younger boy fiddling with his spoon and making faces at whatever was in his bowl. Another woman in a cotton dress sat on the other side of the "mother," feeding her. Who were these people? What am I supposed to do?

The man spoke, "Well, Christina, this is some progress. You walked in on your own, but clumsily, but this is a good start. Remember, you've only got six weeks to learn everything." I just stood there. "Well, aren't you going to sit or say something?" Where? I looked around, saw an open spot, and made my way to it. Do I try to answer him? I can't speak. Doesn't he know that? I tried to toss my hair back so I could sit.

The woman made some cluck-clicking sounds, very weird, totally foreign, but everyone seemed to understand what she was saying, everyone but me. "Let me," the woman who had followed me whispered, adjusting my incredibly long hair so I could sit down, though collapse down is more like it. "Christina, you are certainly going to have to do better than that," the man chastised me. Remember, grace, poise, stateliness. Maid, don't forget the golden veil after breakfast.

She needs to get used to it as well." The woman who sat beside me acknowledged him.

She picked up a spoon and brought it up to my mouth. I opened, since she was obviously going to feed me. I nearly choked. My tongue wasn't there, well mostly wasn't. The teenage boy laughed wildly. "Christina can't eat her porridge," he teased me. I wanted to bop him one, but had no way to do so. I glared at him. "I do like it better now, dad. She can't slap me anymore or even talk back to me."

"Son, remember your manners. Treat Christina like a baroness, like your mother." He looked rebuffed, but nodded.

The other girl was obviously on my side. She spoke up, "Christina and I are going to practice our dancing again today. I get to wear the corset and heels too. I'm almost a big girl now too. We'll do much better today, mom. You'll see." The mother made some strange clicking or clucking sounds. "I know, mom. Practice, practice. We will. I promise, won't we Christina?" She looked over at me. I nodded. What else could I do? These were total strangers to me, but I surmised that they were my family. Not my family, but this girl's family. What was going on? Where was I? What had happened?

After we ate, I had to go to the bathroom rather badly. Now what do I do? I tried to say, "I have to go to the bathroom," but only gurgles came out. My "mother" made some more of her strange clucks and clicks. At last, my "father" said, "Christina, for heaven's sake, you know you can't talk any more. No baroness can. It's forbidden. Use your mother's cluck-click language."

All I could do was shrug my shoulders and try to make slight squatting motions. None was getting through. In desperation, I tried to use my telepathy and finally got the concept of "pee" into mind of the woman beside me. "I think she needs to use the bathroom. I'll take her." Turning to me, she said, "Why didn't you just tell us, Christina? Have you forgotten how to speak like your mother?" I nodded vigorously "yes!"

"Oh don't be silly, Christina!" the man barked. "You know your mother's language as well as I do. Stop acting silly. Take her," he indicated to the servant woman. More awkwardness followed. Not knowing where the bathroom was, I headed off in a random direction, and had to be turned around and guided there. Further, I had no idea how the servant would handle my needs. More embarrassment followed, but I did get a slight glance, and saw that I didn't have my usual male organs, only female. If there was ever any doubt in my mind that somehow I was in a wholly different body, there wasn't any now!

When I was done and heading back out, my sister joined us, walking as slowly as I was. I got a glance at her heels. They were almost as high as mine were. As we moved slowly across the stone floor, she chatted away. "Tina, have you really forgotten how to speak?"

Finally, someone said something reasonable and helpful. I nodded yes vigorously. "Oh dear. I don't know about such things as forgetting how to speak. Let's not tell mom or dad. They'll be furious. I know. I'll teach you again. It's how mom speaks and how you have to speak, now that you are a baroness, well almost. Guess you have to get married first, probably that'll happen at the big dance in a couple of months. I hope some boys dance with me. You and I, we have to get very good at it, because mom said I can wear my corset and heels to the dance, just like you. I'm grown up, well sort of," she admitted.

Hearing her chat allowed me to think a little. I was able to understand her. She was speaking the Midlands dialect, but perhaps here it was called English. I said a brief prayer I could at least understand those who could speak. With most of my tongue gone, I realized clicking and clucking was all I was able to do, and those strange sounds were understandable by these people. Somehow, I had to learn it and fast. This was some awful nightmare. Maybe I really was asleep, and this was all some fantastic and horrid nightmare.

We arrived in a spacious room. The walls were stone as was the floor. Could it be a castle, like the Imperial Castle back home? Several servants were present, and one turned on a device, which played the music, not too loud though. I stood there listening to it. Lots of strings. Very melodic and stately, like some grand promenade. "Tina, have you forgotten how to

306

dance too?" she whispered. I nodded vigorously.

"Okay, I'm the man, see, because I have arms, but I won't of course when I get to be a baroness too. I put my arms on your waist like so. You take three steps back while I do them forward. Then, three to the side, your left side. Then, three to the front, and three more to get back where we were. Okay, I lead, so when I push you gently, you step back. Easy does it. We found out yesterday going backwards in these heels is so very much harder than going forwards. Even I almost fell. Here we go." She gently pushed into me, and I did my best to step backwards without falling or losing my balance. It was iffy. "As long as we go slowly, we don't get out of breath so badly."

The ache and throbbing of my feet subsided or rather became numb was more like it, but my knees continued to rebel. After a while, I noticed "mother" had walked into the room quietly. She made some cluck-clicking noises. I made a curious expression on my face. Lisa whispered, "She said you are doing better than yesterday. Well, not exactly. She made the sounds for better and yesterday. We sort of fill in the blanks. Don't worry; there's not that many things she or you can say, not really. Just enough to get by, I think. After she goes, I'll start teaching you again."

It was the strangest morning I ever had. While learning their dance steps, Lisa also taught me their cluck-click language. I got about fifty worked out this first day and more the next day. There weren't more than about a hundred distinct sound patterns in all, a very basic, crude set of concepts. No grammar at all, just a few verbs and nouns. One had to be very inventive, and hope and pray the listener would be able to fill in the gaps. I soon found the servants did just that. Whenever mother said something, they would repeat it as a complete sentence to make sure they understood her true meaning.

For example, a couple of cluck-clicking noises indicated two words: go and pee. That translated to I have to go to the bathroom now. I had to give these baroness women credit for inventing a way to communicate without their tongues. I also saw the baron and the children as well as the servants understood this language fairly well. I guess being raised by the baroness would do just that. Still, I was struggling to make myself understood for the first few days.

It was torture, but made bearable by Lisa, who was hovering around me all day long. I knew her feet must have been throbbing as badly as mine were, but she remained cheerful and was very determined to get used to it, so she could become a baroness too. I also realized she looked up to me as her older sister. When the torturous day finally ended after supper and we were heading to our bedrooms, I made the click-click sound that translated to "love," meaning, "I love you." Lisa click-clicked it back to me, with a big grin on her face.

I will also admit the ladies maids — I learned their title during the day — did a very good job taking care of my needs. When they took the heels off my feet, it felt like someone was stabbing giant pins into my feet! They must have known this, because they gave them a good massage, before they brushed out my golden hair and tucked me into bed, draping it over my chest.

Finally, I was alone, and I began to take stock of my situation. I still had no idea where I was, no idea how I had a new body or where my old body was. I had little ideas of what was expected of this Christina. I just knew I was in the worst trouble of my life. Nothing compared to this. I decided the best description I could invent was having been taken out of one body and one life, and then placed into another body in another place and time. Even the ages were wrong. I wasn't in my mid-twenties. I was sixteen now.

I decided I needed to determine just what assets I had left to utilize. I focused and attempted to make use of my gifts. Soon, I sensed the other minds in this "castle." I had no idea what this place was, so castle would have to do for now. At least, I still had my powers, but they felt so utterly weak. I had come to depend completely on the enormous amplification that my psi-crystal provided me.

I decided to take some action. I focused and tried to reach out to my mate, Danika. Nothing. That gave me more data. I tried to contact Molly Maud, who ought to have been in the room next to me. Nothing. More data. I tried to contact Jana, Jovanna, and then Marisol. Nothing. I sighed. Conclusion: I was way out of telepathic contact range. I then tried to calculate what the range might be without a psi-crystal amplification. I should certainly still be able to make contact with someone on the same world as I was. This meant I wasn't on Cass-C anymore. Well, that made sense, but just where was I? No clue.

That rather solved, I experimented with some of my other gifts to see just how feeble they were. I was quite worried after that. They were extremely weak! I could just barely levitate my body up, and it tired me out rapidly. Soon, I did fall asleep, only to wake to another day. I wasn't surprise to find this new day almost the same as yesterday. The only consolation was from past experience, I knew in time, I would be totally used to both the corset and heels, as well as letting others be my arms for me. I stopped fighting against them, which began to help. However, I did not wake up from this dream.

I did take stock of my resources. I've been in nasty situations before, but I always had friends to lean on or those strange almost human robots. However, I always had my *mentales* gifts on which to depend if all else failed. In the past, I had gotten by pretty much without relying heavily on those unique gifts, but that power was always there, my safety net. Now, I had no friends and no robots. Worse, without my psi-crystal, my ultimate backup was just barely functioning. And this, more than anything else worried me, scared me. For the first time ever, I was really frightened I might not be able to get out of this one, whatever it was.

I did spend some thought on dreams though, but that got me nowhere. How long did a dream last until you woke up? I had no answer at all. I just hoped that it would be soon. It wasn't though.

Christina awoke to the smell of cooking food and strange voices speaking in a language that she'd never heard before, if indeed those sounds were a language. I feel strange, she thought, and realized that awful pressure on her chest was gone. She propped herself up and gasped! "I have my arms back! Oh, but only one hand? My hair! It's gone black. My God! I'm talking. My tongue — it's not gone either." Hastily, she felt her body with her right hand. "Well, still got the boobs though.

"Hey, Nia Elain, get up, breakfast is almost ready," a strange woman's voice called out from another room in that same unintelligible language. Then, she realized the room wasn't her bedroom! In fact, she'd never seen this room or anything in it before. It was quite a strange looking room. Where were the stone walls? She got out of bed and found herself looking into a mirror. She stared at the reflection and wondered who that older woman was. "Oh my god! I've got. . ." She didn't finish her sentence, but felt it with her right hand, going so far as to pinch it to make sure it was real. "Hey, we hear you in there; come on; breakfast is up," that same voice called out.

Christina was wearing some strange apparel, concluding that it probably was a nightgown. Hunger struck, and she poked her head curiously out of the door. She saw four more women. What struck her was that each was missing their left hand, just as she was. All were total strangers. What kind of nightmare is this, she wondered.

"Come on, Nia; it's getting cold," another woman said, but she didn't understand a word of what she said. Hesitantly, she walked out of the bedroom and joined the three at the small kitchen table. They were all chatting in this unintelligible language. Someone passed her some food, and she took it, though had trouble getting used to the missing left hand. Rather awkward, she thought, but a billion times better than having none. She began to eat, noticing how wonderful it was to have her tongue back.

"So Nia, are you ready to escort Molly Maud on her campaign trail today?" one of the women said to her. Christina looked back at her blankly. "Come on, Nia; you haven't said a word all morning. What's up?" Now, all three stopped eating and stared at her.

Christina panicked and blurted out, "I don't understand what you are saying. This is so very weird, a really bad dream."

Suddenly, one of the women replied, "Nia, what's wrong?" Relief swept over Christina. She could understand now. She spoke English.

"I am having a really bad dream. Who's this Nia? I'm Christina. Where am I? What is this place? Who are you? What's happening to me?"

All three said in unison, "Huh?" Then, one said, "Nia, are you all right? Who's this Christina? We should speak German so Molly Maud can understand us better."

"Something is really wrong. I'm Christina. I don't know who this Nia person is. What's German? Where am I? Who are you?"

"You're Nia, Captain Nia Elain Compton-Jereni. Are you ill? I'm your good friend, Jana. This is Jovanna, Marisol, and Molly Maud. What's happened to you?"

"I don't know what's happening. I remember going to bed and then waking up here, in this strange room. This isn't my body. I have long wavy golden hair. It's longer than this and not black. I don't understand. This must be a dream or hallucination or something."

The four stared at her for a moment. Then, she saw three small crystals around the necks of them glowing in a pale blue light. Her mind sensed something strange, like another person was there, but that was impossible. Then, three of the four women's faces got very tense, worried perhaps. Christina couldn't tell.

The one called Jana whispered, "She's not Nia. I don't know who she is, but she isn't our Nia!"

The one called Marisol exclaimed, "I don't understand this either, but she's not Nia Elain. It's her body, I think, looks just like her, wearing the same nightgown I helped her into last night, but it's not her."

"I know," Jovanna added. "What's going on here?" Looking at Nia, she asked, "Who are you again? Where did you come from? What have you done with our friend, Nia?"

"I — I don't know. I'm Christina, Christina Blackwater. This isn't my castle in Thromstead. I don't know anyone called Nia. That's a really weird name, so I would be certain to remember that name. Where am I?"

In relatively poor English, the fourth woman spoke up, "You are in my small home. I'm Molly Maud Porsche. You are in Hoffdorf, Cass-C."

Christina's eyes brightened up. "Cass-C? Where they make the clavecins? I always wanted to learn how to play them, but my dad wouldn't let me. I was going to be a baroness. Well, I was about to be, I mean, well, they had me all prepared to be a baroness, only no one had proposed marriage to me yet. I dreamed of coming to Cass-C, wherever this is, and learning to play the clavecin, but a baroness doesn't have arms. They remove them, you see. Now, I'm here, but without this hand, I still can't learn to play it. Takes two hands, doesn't it?"

"What's a clavecin?" Jana asked.

"A harpsichord," Molly Maud answered mechanically, trying to make some remote kind of sense about what was going on with Nia Elain. She was so out of character making up such a wild story as this.

Marisol followed up the only clue so far. "Christina, is it?" Nia nodded. "Where is this Thromstead?"

"Just outside our castle. East of us."

"No, I mean what world is it on, what planet?"

"Oh. It's Blackwell-C. This isn't Blackwell-C. I can tell."

"No it isn't. Where's Blackwell-C?" Marisol asked.

"Hey, I remember," Jovanna answered. "It is one of those worlds on the Forbidden List."

Molly Maud gasped and asked, "How did you get here? Where's our Nia? You look like our Nia."

"I don't know. I remember going to bed, feeling awful. Then, I woke up here. This isn't my body. My body has been turned into that of a baroness," she replied.

"What do you mean by being turned into that of a baroness?" Jana asked.

"Well, a few days ago while I was sleeping, they must have done it. They removed my arms, and cut most of my tongue off. Baronesses are never supposed to speak, you see. Oh, and they enlarge my breasts too. They are just like these and yours though. They were preparing me for the big social dance, where I was supposed to be chosen by some young baron to become his baroness, but I never wanted to be a baroness. I wanted to play the clavecin and make music. I was stalling and not learning to walk in those high heels and corset, you know, gracefully, stately and all that. They weren't supposed to prepare me to be a baroness until a baron proposed. So I was hoping to be a flop and get to be twenty-one years old, cause then dad, he's a baron, he would send me into the city, disowning me. I was then going to get on one of the spaceships, come to Cass-C, and learn how to play the clavecin, but that went all wrong when they prepared me to be a baroness, you see," Christina talked rapidly, trying to make sense of everything.

Molly Maud commented, "How brutal! That's why that world is on the Forbidden List. Anyway, Christina or whoever you are, you say you don't look like this?"

"Oh no. Nothing like this. My hair almost touches the floor and is golden, like mom's. She's a baroness. My face doesn't look at all like this one. I'm not this tall either, but the breasts are similar. Oh! And I don't have a man's thing either. I'm a woman. So this isn't me, but it is me. I don't understand any of this. I must be having a really bad dream. I hope I wake up soon. This is so confusing."

"Confusing to us too," Jana commented, but was deeply concerned. "Okay, let's assume Nia is ill. I'll take her place with you today, Molly Maud. You guys stay with Nia, and try to sort out what the devil is going on here." She and Molly Maud rose and headed off to get dressed.

Christina finished eating, while the other two women whispered to each other, occasionally stealing glances at her. She was too hungry to care just now. This was totally a weird dream, but she had her arms back and tongue, and decided if it was just a dream, which it probably way, she was going to enjoy having them again, even if it wasn't real. Probably, she thought it isn't really real. *My arms are gone forever and so is my tongue, so this just must be a dream. It's probably like my arms and hands, which I keep feeling are there, but when I look, they aren't. Just a dream. After all, I always dreamed of coming to this Cass-C place, wherever it's at.*

Molly Maud and Jana soon appeared dressed in their

professional women's outfits. They said goodbye and left. "We have heels as high as theirs, but ours are tied onto our feet so we baronesses can't slip them off. Only I was supposed to wear the seven-inch tall ones, like my mom. Barons really like them better, but I really could hardly even walk in them, though after they cut off my arms, I had no choice, since I couldn't get them off as I did that first night when I still had my hands. They have such revealing short dresses though."

"Skirts. Those are called skirts. Yes, the men prefer to stare at their legs and heels a lot on this world," Jovanna stated.

Marisol laughed, "Not to mention our monster boobs. We should get dressed, Nia, er, Christina. Come on; we have to help each other since we only have one hand."

An hour later, all three were dressed in their professional women's outfits. Christina commented, "Well, it's lots easier walking in these heels. They are a little shorter than those they were making me wear, the seven-inch ones. Oh, I don't know what to do with this male thing. It keeps wanting to get big or something."

Both women grinned. Why don't you watch the local stations. I know you don't speak German, but at least you can see things." Marisol turned it on for her, discovering she had no idea how to operate a comm center. After that, the two headed to the kitchen to wash the dishes, and try to figure out what was going on.

Marisol whispered, "I think Nia must have had some kind of psychotic break or something. Like a split personality that's just now come out."

"Maybe, but if so, where did she ever discover so much about such a world? Is it all made up or something?" Jovanna whispered back.

"We should use our laptops and see what information there is on this Blackwell-C Forbidden world. See if any of what she's been saying is true or not. Perhaps, Nia is just delusional," Marisol suggested.

"Agreed. But you know, when I touched her mind, it was how do I say this, almost like Nia, but not quite," Jovanna admitted.

314

Christina was enthralled with all the images on the monitor, giving the two women time to use their computers. After some searching, they found out what information there was on Blackwell-C. It was forbidden entry into the Federation many times, primarily for their barbaric practices not only towards their baronesses, but also their general population, which were little more than slaves, working to support the aristocratic families. Thus, they both concluded what Nia or Christina was saying was accurate. Both also knew that Nia Elain had never known any of this information, since they'd just now read about it. Something was very, very wrong.

Finally, they did the only thing left. They placed a secure call to Ashford-5 and asked to talk to Rafe. They hastily explained the situation, but it took them nearly a half hour to convince Rafe they were not joking, that this was real.

"Okay. I'll break the news to Danika. I think the smartest thing for you to do is to bring Nia or Christina back here to Ashford-5. I'll examine her personally. I'll send Danika along shortly. She's going to take this really hard. Maybe the Federation has some new weapon we know nothing about, one that scrambles one's mind. Over," Rafe finally reached a decision.

"Okay. One of us ought to stay with Molly Maud. Over," Jovanna replied.

"Perhaps it would be wise if the three of you stuck around in case someone tries to use this new weapon on Molly Maud. Over and out."

Marisol said, "Well, she's right. Molly Maud may well be in danger. After all, she's running for their admiral position. We all best stay and guard her well, but we ought to explain about Danika and her children to her."

They joined Nia or Christina. "Say, we've got to tell you some important things. First, you are going to get to go on a real spaceship ride. One of our friends wants to see if they can figure out what's happened to you and to our Nia Elain," Marisol explained.

"Wow! That's great! A real spaceship. I've never been on one before, but I've dreamed of traveling among the stars! I know, this is probably all just my imagination, a really long dream I'm having," Christina replied.

"Another detail. You are married. Your mate is Danika, and you and she have six children."

"What? Six? Oh my! Oh, right, this body is much older than me. Six? Wow. How really, really weird. I've not been with a man yet. I don't think I know how to do it. But I don't know her. I'm married to a woman and not a baron? This is all so confusing. I do hope I can wake up soon. I'm starting to get freaked out by all of this," Christina admitted.

"Don't worry. Our friend Rafe will help you sort it all out when you get there," Marisol replied.

"So you don't remember anything about Descartes-3?" Jovanna asked, curious about how a person could suddenly wake up someone else. Surely, Nia would remember their awful time there. Besides, it was her original home world, where her parent's had adopted her.

"What's that? A spice? We don't have any Descartes stuff in Thromstead," Christina answered.

Jovanna sighed, "I surely don't know what is going on either. This is really strange, Nia."

"Christina," she absentmindedly corrected her.

Later, Christina wanted to see some of the city and maybe a clavecin. Heinz was off painting again, but when he heard about Nia Elain's illness, he headed back to Molly Maud's and was in time to play escort, helping them stroll around the city a few blocks from her home. He too saw that apparently absolutely everything, every sight was new to Nia Elain or Christina as she now insisted on being called.

That evening when Molly Maud and Jana rejoined them for supper, Marisol got a call from Rafe. Danika would be at the Hoffdorf spaceport around noon tomorrow.

"How's she taking this? Over," Marisol asked.

"Not good. We have her calmed down and her anger under control. She's sure someone there on Cass-C did this to her. Anyway, talk more later when I know something concrete. Over and out," Rafe signed off.

The next day, both Heinz and Jana left with Molly Maud to act as her bodyguards. Meanwhile, Jovanna and Marisol helped get Nia Elain dressed and packed. Having been out and about yesterday and seeing a fair number of "professionally" dressed women on the streets, Christina insisted on wearing similar apparel, including the heels. Hence, the trio dressed similarly and headed to the spaceport, arriving there a bit early, around eleven to wait for Danika's arrival. Besides, Christina claimed she'd never seen a real spaceport before and was taking all this in, like some young teen, which she was, if the two actually believed her.

Justin finally hovered over Cass-C. He would never have found the place on his own, but someone had apparently entered the coordinates for him, which was really a wise move, since he spent most of the trip in an opium haze. Now, he was taking the last puff, wondering how he could make it all the way back without any. Some voice was saying he had to land, so he did just that, darn near crashing his ship in the process. It had not yet occurred to him that he had no idea how to make the return trip, rather he was trying to think, which was rather difficult for him. Getting back without any opium will be hard, he thought. "Well, find a big building, go in, and open valve. Then, I get all the opium I can smoke in a year. Best hurry this up," he muttered.

With the sack under his arm, he headed into the giant spaceport administration building, which was crowded with passengers and workers at this time of day. Once inside, he ignored the line before the customs desk and slipped his hand inside the bag, opening the valve. Then, he wandered aimlessly around the spacious passenger terminal, looking for — well, he didn't quite know what he was looking for. He knew he felt rather funny, but that was probably just his need for another hit. Going back without any is going. . . Justin never finished his thought. He slowly slumped down onto the tiled floor, oblivious to the fact that all around him, other passengers and workers were already slumping to the ground as well.

"What's that smell?" Jovanna suddenly became alert.

"Don't know," Marisol whispered. The two began looking all around. By the time they figured out that they were being attacked with that damned genetic bio agent, it was too late to do anything about it. One by one, they too slipped into a coma. All told nine hundred sixteen men, women, and a couple of children fell into a coma, a quarter of them workers there at the spaceport.

When a terribly worried Danika touched down, hundreds of emergency vehicles surrounded the spaceport! Hundreds of other workers were now standing idly around some distance from the tall building. Danika and my crew walked up to some and asked what was going on.

"Another one of those terrorist attacks, we think. They rushed us all outside and won't tell us what's going on," one official answered. "That General Wolfgang is here too, and that don't sound good at all!"

Her fears growing by the second, Danika focused and tried to contact me, and then Jovanna and Marisol. That failed. She calmed her fears some, focusing on Jana and got more news. *Yes, another bio agent attack. Molly Maud and I are on the way there now. General Wolfgang has the main passenger terminal quarantined right now. Sis, Marisol, and Nia were there waiting for you. I've a bad feeling about this. Hang on; we're pulling into a parking lot now.* She broke the connection.

Danika sighed, ordering everyone back to the ship to wait it out. An hour later, a worried Jana and Molly Maud joined them, relaying only a bit more news. The rescuers had shot out most of the glass windows to allow the fumes to escape. They hoped to get to the victims later tonight. "We are taking our three back with us, if we can find them," Danika insisted.

When the rescuers began going inside, Molly Maud used her influence and power to do just that. She and Jana were allowed to see each comatose person who was brought out. "There, she's one of ours," Jana called out, seeing her sister being carried out on a stretcher. Nia Elain and Marisol were on following stretchers. At Molly Maud's insistence, the three were taken to the Eagle's Seed.

"Okay, I'll stay here in Jovanna's place," Martina declared. "We simply must keep you safe, Molly Maud."

"I should too," Beth added.

"No, your place is with your mate. You go and look after

Marisol. Jana and I can handle this," Martina ordered. She didn't need any further encouragement and headed off to sit beside her comatose mate. A bit later, Martina, Jana, and Molly Maud watched the Eagle's Seed rising into the air. Only then did they head home, where Heinz had a late supper waiting for them and the news channels on the big monitor. He had been following the breaking story.

"Hey, they found the guy who did this. Found the cylinders in a bag he was carrying. It looks like he came from one of those Forbidden Worlds. Has a strange name that I can't remember, but they keep repeating it," Heinz explained, while they ate and watched.

Several minutes later, the reported repeated the name, Equiuss-C. Molly Maud hastily looked that one up on her laptop. "Drug infested world. Not much to go on," she reported.

Then, later that night, General Wolfgang called and asked Admiral Molly Maud to meet with him at the emergency station, the warehouse that Molly Maud had donated for their use with the victims of the first attacks. "Bring Captain Nia Elain with you," he ordered.

"Can't. She's taken ill and was a victim at the spaceport today. I've got some others I can bring along though," she replied.

The next morning, Heinz, Jana, and Martina accompanied Admiral Molly Maud to the emergency station where these latest victims were being housed on cots watched over again by Dr. Schmidt and his group. A very worried general met them. He'd not shaven. From the bags under his eyes, he probably hadn't slept yet either.

"This is a bad one. Caught mostly civilians, men and women. Few kids too. Over nine hundred this time," he reported.

"How are we on available supplies for their cures, general?" Molly Maud asked.

"We have the Dupe machines going full blast at the moment. We are going to be able to provide the clothing, shoes, and lip disk things they'll need. Plus, we're making plenty of those voice translator boxes that Captain Nia Elain brought us," he answered.

"Yes, but what about cures?" Molly Maud reiterated her as yet unanswered question.

He sighed. "We used up most all our genetic materials on the first terrorist attacks. I'm afraid there's none available right now. We're going to make them as comfortable as possible for now and start a waiting list for the cures. As soon as more material is available, we'll start in on that process, but honestly admiral, it's going to take perhaps a year to get these handled, if we're lucky."

"Okay, then I'll take other actions to help them," Molly Maud declared.

Later that day, Admiral Molly Maud held another press conference. After outlining the details of this attack, she then explained the drastic shortage of the necessary genetic materials, which the genetic cures required. "So yes, this means the current victims are going to be put on a waiting list, and will be given their cures as soon as the new supplies start trickling in. I'm told it might take a year to get to everyone. Hence, as your admiral, I'm announcing a new program, the Personal Assistants Program. Any woman or man who wishes to spend up to a year living with one of these victims, assisting them with daily living can apply for a position. The government will pay top dollar wages for these assistants. If the applicant has only one hand, then two of them will be hired so they'll be able to better care for their person. There'll be no charge to any of the victims, and no new taxes on the rest of us to pay for this. I'll take the cost out of my admiral's budget somehow. We need to provide top quality care for these innocent victims of this terrorist attack."

She added, "Spread the word. I'll be taking applications starting tomorrow. Bring them to the Porsche Industries main headquarters downtown. Some training will be provided, but not much will be needed, just a sincere desire to help those who'll be in dire need of assistance. Work will likely be starting about three days from now, when they begin to come out of their comas. Thank you." she ignored the volley of reporters' questions, since they dealt mostly with what had happened and who was responsible. She referred them to General

Wolfgang.

Later, Martina pointed out, "That action of yours will very likely gain you more votes."

"That's not why I did it, though. These people need around the clock help, especially if they are going to have to wait a year to get any of the cures. An admiral must be responsible to his people, unlike the former Admiral Fritz," she replied. Heinz gave her a loving hug.

Mid-winter Festival loomed near, and Admiral Molly Maud received four invitations to parties. Based on Martina's suggestion, she agreed to visit briefly each of them, but only spending forty-five minutes at each one, giving her a bit of travel time to get to each. "Okay, I'll be your advanced scout, and go ahead to the next party on the agenda and check it out," Martina insisted. "I'll let Jana know it's safe for you three to come on ahead to the next one. Just make sure I have good directions," she chuckled.

Hence, it was that Martina, dressed in a fancy blue gown that displayed more of her legs than she would have preferred, teetered into the first party on her requisite tall spiked heels, attracting the attention of many men there, as did all of the other similarly dressed women. While seeming to mix with the hundreds of men and women, her crystal hidden just beneath her dress glowed its pale blue light. She wandered about sensing the many minds present looking for any signs that a mind present had evil intentions towards the assembled partygoers. Finding this one clear of such intentions, she telepathically sent the all clear message to Jana.

Shortly after that, Heinz escorted both Admiral Molly Maud and Jana into this first party, where the admiral was surrounded with many who wanted to chat with her, pleasant, social gab. Some did compliment her on her decision to hire personal assistants for the current victims. Some commented on how terrible it was that terrorists were being allowed to harm citizens of Cass-C. Others demanded she take more strict security measures. Mostly though, the chat was well-wishing for the new year and fond wishes for spring to come soon.

As the trio entered, Martina left, heading for the next party on the list. Unfortunately, it was snowing outside. In her tall heels, walking was treacherous, and she rather wished Heinz were with her instead. More than once, her crystal activated in a hurry, levitating her body up, preventing a nasty spill. That was followed by a silent curse.

She checked out the second party thoroughly. While some were hostile, she didn't find any signs anyone here wanted to wipe out the party. She sent the all clear message again, moving on to the third one. The hour was approaching eleven as she entered the last party, where many were already rather intoxicated. She was about ready to give the all clear message again, when she got a frantic message from Jana.

Admiral Molly Maud, Heinz, and Jana were now attending the ritzy party of the four. Here, most of the very wealthy of Hoffdorf assembled to party and hopefully bring spring to the city early. Of course, it is ridiculous to think a party would bring an early spring, but no one cared about such a detail. The celebration helped break up the cold, snowy winters here in Hoffdorf, as it did in other major cities on Cass-C. Many of the new top hub Intelligence Division personnel were here, along with quite a few ambassadors from other worlds. But mostly, it was the wealthy of Hoffdorf. Nearly two thousand of them were packed into the giant hall.

Unlike previous years, the music wasn't live, but being played over a large sound system. Most of the musicians had been wiped out by the loss of one of their hands. The various ensembles had been forced to disband due to so few musicians who could still play, mostly men. While gabbing with a group of men and women, Admiral Molly Maud asked Heinz to go fetch their coats. In hindsight, this was incredibly wise, but at the time, it only seemed practical. The coatroom was packed with over two thousand coats. While there were several attendants on duty, finding three coats took them some time, saving Heinz from what happened next.

Without any warning, two men entered the room, having used d-guns on the four men providing security at the entrance to the great hall. They were strangely dressed, wearing what appeared to be chain mail, full length gowns. Large red crosses were displayed prominently on their chests, partially hiding the mail. They shouted something, but few heard it over the music. Later, under questioning, several reported that they spoke in English and had said something like, "Put Blackwell-C into the Federation," or something like that, depending upon whom you listened. Since their language was German, their grasp of English was not that good.

In fact, no one paid them much attention at all. The music was loud; spirits were flowing, and more than a few were intoxicated already. Some were dancing, ignoring all else around them. When the two men slumped to the floor, people began to notice, but thought merely they had had too much to drink. After all, who would wear such ridiculous costumes to the Mid-winter Festival? However, when others nearest them also began slumping to the floor, others near them moved over to check on them, before joining them on the floor themselves.

"What's going on over there?" Molly Maud pointed out to Jana. Both looked over at the ever-growing pile of bodies on the floor. Before they could do anything, mass panic set in. Folks rushed towards the main doors. Some collapsed on the ground, but a few reached them only to find that somehow the doors wouldn't open. Quickly, a pile of bodies mounded up near that exit.

Jana tried to move Molly Maud in the opposite direction towards another exit, when she began feeling very strange, and realized she was once again exposed to that bio genetic agent. As fast as she could, she sent a telepathic message to Martina, warning her, and then just barely reached Heinz, who had finally gotten their coats. All he heard in his mind was *Don't open the doors.* I'll give the man credit. He obeyed, in spite of his desires to rush to Molly Maud and Jana's rescue. Several minutes later, he knew something was very wrong. A strange odor was seeping out from beneath the doors, the music ended, and no one put on another song disk. Utter stillness. Heinz barked to the three coat attendants, "If you want to live, get out of this building right now!" He dashed on out into the snowy late evening. The three attendants joined him, struggling to put on whatever coats they could grab.

"Call the security people and the emergency people. I think there has been another terrorist attack. I'm going around to the front to see what's there," he ordered. He almost never gave orders, but now he did. A bit later, he entered the main entrance and saw four dead men, d-gun holes in their heads, and he knew the place had been attacked. He sat down, put his hands over his eyes, and began crying. Molly Maud and Jana were now victims too. The love of his life was in a coma, and he couldn't reach her or do anything to save her.

Martina reached him at the same time as a swarm of emergency people and a host of soldiers armed to the teeth. "Don't go in there. It's another gas attack, probably with the same genetic bio agent as the others," Martina called out to the rushing pack of emergency responders, who hastily stopped in their tracks, awaiting other orders. Before long, a slightly intoxicated General Wolfgang came running up, nearly slipping on the snow.

"Admiral?"

Heinz shook his head, and he stopped in his tracks. "Oh dear God not her too!"

"Best get the place quarantined," Martina advised him, easing him out of his shock and dismay. Like a good soldier, he quickly took charge of the situation.

By morning, the place had been vented of the toxic gas. The emergency responders began the awful task of carrying out the victims, identifying them, and transporting them to another of the warehouses that Molly Maud had donated earlier during the very first attacks. When they brought out Molly Maud and Jana, Heinz insisted on going with Molly Maud, while Martina insisted on taking Jana with her. Some soldiers put her into a car for her, and she headed back to Molly Maud's home.

There, she place secure calls, one to the emperor and one to Danika, who promised to be there in ten hours. Now, all Martina could do was make Jana comfortable until help arrived. She knew she had to get Jana back to Ashford-5, where she could once more get some of the cures. However, she didn't have the authority to take Molly Maud with her.

Rafe was at the spaceport along with Governor Misty, when Danika touched down, bringing Nia Elain, Jovanna, and

Marisol with her. Even though Nia Elain's body was in a coma, Rafe wanted to "sense" her firsthand, even before the medical crew carried them off to the med lab in the Imperial Castle. She owed this to Danika, having promised the very worried woman that she would personally help her mate.

"Well?" Danika asked her. Worry filled her voice that much Rafe could sense.

"I honestly can't tell, Danika. This is the strangest thing I have ever encountered. Obviously, that is Nia Elain's body. No doubt of that whatsoever. I wish she had not been exposed to that genetic agent again. It's delaying what I have to do to sort this out. Come on; let's follow the med techs." The two trailed along behind them.

"So what did you sense with her?" Danika continued to probe.

"Well, it's her but it isn't quite. My Advanced Therapy has shown me that each and every being operates on more or less their own unique frequency or wavelength. Always, that wavelength is very tiny indeed, way beyond anything we can produce electronically. A very high frequency. As you know, when you reach out to touch her, you are focusing in on her unique wavelength. That's why we can't just make telepathic contact with someone we don't already know. We aren't familiar with their unique wavelength."

"I never thought of it like that. It's so natural to just touch and pervade her," Danika replied.

"True, none of us really look at how we do what we do, we just do it," Rafe pointed out. "With a comatose person, it's pretty hard to reach them with any certainty. I can say this, that I sensed a frequency that is almost the same as our Nia's."

"Almost?"

"Almost. Perhaps just a minuscule bit of difference. Of course, that could well be because she has had some kind of psychic shock, and now truly believes that she is this Christina woman. That could account for the minuscule difference. Honestly, Danika, I'm not going to be able to tell much more until she's recovered. Perhaps, if we are lucky, when she comes out of the coma, she'll also come out of the psychic shock and be herself again. We'll see."

Dr. Leann met the two, stopping them from entering the emergency section of the lab. "Far as you two go for now. They are giving the three a thorough exam, but it does appear to be that same genetic bio agent. I'm told that if so, they will use the same procedures as before. As soon as they come out of this coma, they'll be asked if they want to get the cure. Assuming they do, they'll then be put into a medical coma and given all the healing cures that we have. So you might as well go home for now. They won't be awake and recovered for at least a week. Sorry, Rafe, your examination of Nia Elain is simply going to have to wait until she's recovered."

Midway during that time, the three came out of their comas. Christina cried out, "Oh no, not again!" She readily agreed to any healing possible. As much as Rafe wanted to study her, she let it be, allowing the trio the minimal amount of trauma time to have to handle later. Danika still had no answers for our children, who wanted to know what was wrong with mommy. All she could say was that she was sick, which didn't help much.

At last a week after they arrived, the three women were revived. Although a bit groggy, Jovanna and Marisol both commented to the effect that they were all right and had their hands back. Christina was elated, though. "Now, I can learn to play the clavecin!" She wiggled her left hand's fingers. Danika was crushed. She had so hoped the psychotic break would be over now.

Rafe took charge of Nia or Christina. "Okay, my name is Rafe, short for Rafaela. It's my job to sort out what has happened to you and Nia Elain, and somehow fix it up."

"But I don't what to go back and be a baroness again, not ever. That was horrible," Christina protested. "Now, I have my hands, and I can learn to play the clavecin like I always wanted to."

"I know, Christina, but we need to figure out what happened to Nia Elain. She's got six very worried children who miss her very much," Rafe played on her childish sympathies.

"Oh okay. I want to help do that, just don't make me go back somehow. I'd rather die than be a baroness," Christina agreed to cooperate.

Rafe had already thoroughly studied Nia Elain's latest medical exams. Her pituitary gland was just as large as it ever was. Hence, she began by seeing if "Christina" had any *mentales* abilities. That was soon answered. Christina had no idea what she was talking about. Rafe then had her look deep into Nia Elain's psi-crystal, hoping to discover that it still resonated with her. If so, perhaps that was the entrance point. To her amazement, the crystal just didn't resonate well at all. The frequency was just a teensy bit off, just enough not to activate it fully. Next, Rafe brought in one of the *katalyein* telepaths and had her check for mental blockages that could be responsible for Nia Elain's total personality change. Nothing showed up here either.

Frustrated, Rafe had no choice but to plow in and give Nia Elain or Christina full Basic Therapy. The first few days went slowly, grinding through the most recent attack and recovery periods of unconsciousness and suppressed pains. However, after that didn't erase, Christina plowed headlong into her earlier late night operations, detailing in great detail what Doctor Hrodgar had done to her while she slept, beginning with placing a mask over her face. She shrieked when she encountered the hidden pains underlying the anesthesia when he removed her arms at her shoulders. She cried out again when he cut off the front half of her tongue. The small punctures of her nose and ears were minor, as was the inflation of her breasts.

Four days, Rafe had her going over and over this lengthy traumatic incident before most of it was released, but not erased. Going even earlier, Christina ran smack into birth, and that one finally erased, taking everything else with it. While Rafe now had more than enough data to work with, she couldn't just leave Christina sitting there with part of her Basic Therapy undone. For another week, she continued until Christina was totally cheerful and happier than she'd ever been in her life. "Boy, I don't ever want to go back into that baroness body ever again!" Christina declared with a passion.

Rafe now knew for certain this wasn't Nia Elain, but was in fact a being known as Christina. From this point onward, she always called her Christina, much to the woman's pleasure. Rafe tried to explain this to Danika. "Look, she really is who she says she is, Christina from Thromstead, Blackwell-C. She isn't our Nia Elain. Yes, it is Nia's body, but it is a different spiritual being in it."

"But what happened to my Nia?" Danika wailed. "I want her back!"

"Now, that is the billion credit question, Danika. Right now, I don't have that answer for you, but I'm working on it. Give me time, please," Rafe pleaded. Danika really had no choice. She felt utterly frustrated and wanted to kill whoever did this to me.

Rafe explained further. "You see, Christina and Nia Elain are actually very similar spiritual beings, similar personalities and outlook on life. Different goals and motives, but Christina could well follow down Nia Elain's path. They are almost like two peas in a pod, except Christina is only sixteen and Nia Elain is mid-twenties. Their experiential backgrounds are different, particularly education-wise. Christina is pretty well uneducated by our standards."

"That's all well and good, Rafe, but what happened to my Nia Elain? Where is she? Spiritual beings can't die or disappear, can they? I mean we're immortal. I've have several lifetimes that I know something about."

"That's very true, Danika. Nia Elain can't be dead. She is just someplace else. It's my job to figure out where that is. Time, give me time." Danika had no choice but to do so. All this was way beyond anything she knew about, or me for that matter. In fact, I could say that if it weren't for Rafe being on this case, no one else in the whole darn galaxy would have been able to solve it!

Rafe then had Christina sit quietly, while she used her telepathic skills. Her next approach was to search out telepathically for me, hoping somehow to find me floating around my Nia Elain body at some distance away. Nothing.

"Well?" Danika asked.

"She simply isn't around Christina. I had hoped I'd spot her way out away from her body. Could have perhaps handled that one with a bit of Advanced Therapy. Nope. Nia's not anywhere near her. I don't think she's even on Ashford-5 right now. We're done for today. I need some time to ponder this and make some preparations for my next attempt. I need to talk to Zarita."

Later, Rafe explained what she wanted to Zarita and the two queens, who consented to her request. Under tight security, three dozen of the giant germanium crystals were gathered together in the queen's throne room. One by one, Rafe began joining with each crystal, feeling the intense, raw power building up within her and under her command. When she finally added the power of the thirty-sixth crystal, she knew no one being ought to command this much power! She felt powerful enough to knock the moons out of orbit!

Rafe focused that power and began a spherical shaped outward expanding perimeter, searching for me, focused solely on my unique wavelength, ignoring the slight tug Christina's way. She was in fact almost my spiritual twin, almost. Ever outward went her sphere of awareness. Then, she encountered something that she'd never experienced before!

For a moment, she ceased her outward awareness expansion, focusing in on what she sensed. For lack of words, she described it as some kind of electronic beam operating on my precise frequency. Something like this had never been encountered before and she'd not run into anything quite like this in all the Advanced Therapy research that she'd done to date. Curious. That's Rafe. She was totally sidetracked by this strange and unexpected phenomenon. Now, she changed tactics and rapidly followed the beam back to its origination point.

Have we got them yet, Fisal? Desil asked, growing a bit annoyed.

No, but almost. Wont' be long now, Desil. Fisal continued to fiddle with the controls, trying this and that at random.

We are missing all the fun. They have to be switched by now. Hurry up. This is so cool!

I'm trying, but the galaxy is pretty darn big.

Oh no! Fisal, we've got company! I think they found us! Desil sent worriedly.

Oh shit! Fisal cursed. *Someone's here!*

I told you we shouldn't have stolen it. Now, we are in big trouble, Desil whined.

Explain what you are doing, now, before I zap you into oblivion! Rafe sent the two.

Who are you? Fisal tried to stall.

The goddess who is watching over the galactic disk. Answer me now or get zapped!

Fisal, better do it, Desil whined.

All right. We didn't mean any real harm. Just having some fun. Didn't know that you were protecting the disk. We stole this illegal device here, which is supposed to switch the pathetic beings that are stuck in bodies. You know, make them swap bodies. We wanted to see the fun in that. It doesn't harm them, least we don't think so.

Undo what you've done, right now!

Er, we can't. It didn't come with an instruction manual, but who actually reads them anyway. We just fiddled with it.

Rafe realized they were telling her the truth, and that they had no idea what they were in fact doing. She perceived there were far too many settings on the machine to attempt to discover its method of operation and reached a decision. She sent a huge blast of energy into the device. Sparks flew everywhere, very nearly shorting out the entire spaceship.

What did you just do? Fisal wailed.

Making sure that you cannot use that illegal machine again. Boys, you go back and turn yourselves in. You do that and I won't report you and keep what you did quiet. If you don't, I'll zap your ship and leave you to float here at the bottom of the disk for eternity. What will it be, boys?

We're going! We're going! Fisal fairly screamed. She sensed their utter panic. They were suddenly terrified of floating here without any power. They'd never be rescued nor would be able to call for help. A bit later, the saucer shot off into the southern halo at top speed.

Rafe knew she'd expended more energy than she ever had before and decided to play it safe, returning her awareness to her body. The brightly glowing crystals faded out. Her body was exhausted from attempting to channel that much energy at one time. She managed to get her body to whisper, "Partial success." It then passed out.

Later, Dr. Leann reported to the queens and Zarita, "She's okay, just incredibly drained. She's sleeping now, but managed to tell me that she's on to something and wants to try it tomorrow."

No sooner had she explained this than the call came in from Martina, notifying them of yet another bio agent attack. "It got Jana this time and Molly Maud. I've Jana with me. They have Molly Maud. They don't have any more genetic material to use to cure them just yet, backlogged. Send Danika here at once. We have to get Jana back before she comes out of her coma. Over."

Queen Rael replied, "Damn! Okay, I'll send Danika off in an hour. Be there in ten. Are you okay? Ideas on who did it? Over."

"I'm fine. Not sure yet. The culprits were stupid enough to infect themselves, so we ought to be able to get something from them when they come out of their comas with their victims. Over and out."

Queen Rael griped, "Well, it's just like Jana and Jovanna predicted. This accursed bio agent has now spread into the Federation of Planets. When will it ever end?"

Chapter 19 Toughening It Out

I knew I wasn't going to wake up anytime soon. This was all too real to be a dream. Enduring that second day of it, the pain in my feet and knees, the intense pressure around my chest and waist, the extreme nervousness about taking a bad fall, these were quite real, quite vivid, and left me with the only conclusion possible. Somehow, while I had slept, I had drifted out of my body and into this one. What other explanation could there be? I could sense no other spiritual being anywhere around my body, so it wasn't as if I had somehow stolen this one. Hell, I'd never want to steal such a body as this one was. No one would, in my opinion. Of course, just how this had all come about I had no idea, no conceivable explanation. Moreover, I couldn't talk to anyone about such things, unless I was back home on Ashford-5, assuming I did have a tongue again. No, as I lay there trying to sleep that second night, I was totally convinced that this was real, that somehow I was running this poor sixteen year old girl's body.

Then, I began wondering about Christina, and how she must have felt about having her body so mutilated by her parents. I'd heard enough to know that she must have been fighting having this done to her and that her parents had just gone ahead and had it done. Plus, what I surmised from those around me, it had been done very recently, perhaps only a couple of days before I woke up in her body. So had she just given up, left her body, and taken off for greener pastures and a new baby body? That seemed as plausible as anything did, as I lay there with aching feet, throbbing knees, and a chest pressure threatening to cave my chest in. Even so, if she had taken off, how in the universe had I ended up here in her body, wherever here actually was? I decided not to go down the path of asking what I had done to deserve this. That route is fruitless.

I tried to recall what I knew about my own self and the few previous lives that I had some reality on having lived, thanks to the Basic Therapy sessions. Gone were the severe trauma with the deaths of those bodies and such, so I felt that it was probably safe to try to recall more details. Beyond a headache, I came up with the observation that I never left a body, until I decided it was beyond hope of saving, but shortly after leaving, there I was grabbing the next baby body I could find, sort of a mania about getting another one as fast as possible. So had that happened to Christina? Had she just given up on this sixteen year old body as being completely hopeless and had taken off?

I could see why she could believe that. Honestly, this body and the clothing they were forcing it to wear made it unimaginably difficult and challenging with almost no rewards at all. Maybe I was being too harsh, I decided. Obviously, Baroness Lilly was doing just fine. Plus, I knew that within a few days I'd be used to the pressure and probably even the heels for that matter. It would likely be longer to get used to eating and drinking without much of a tongue, though. That then dashed the only real idea I had for anything like an explanation, namely that Christina had given the body up for dead and taken off, unless she didn't know that in time she would get used to much of this. Now, I had no idea why she departed or how I ended up in her body. Bummer. I fell asleep.

By the fourth day, I was more or less handling the intense pressure and breathing difficulties. As long as I took it slow and easy, I didn't get so out of breath and risk fainting. It was now plainly obvious what Baron Ulysses and Baroness Lilly wanted from me, their Christina. I had seen Lilly walking quite a bit and saw that she more or less slowly floated over the floor, a model of grace, poise, and stateliness. Beneath her golden veil, which she usually wore and which I now usually wore, I could see she was also smiling most of the time. Without a voice, appearing as a charming hostess was difficult, so I also watched her facial expressions, and noticed when other men were around, she did her best to more or less appear to be flirting with them, using what little could be seen of her mouth through her golden veil, her eyes, and even her brows and head motions. While they were subtle, I did notice some of them. That fourth day, in lax times, I tried to practice doing them too.

On the other hand, there was little lax time given to me. My day consisted of walking around one or two rooms, getting up, sitting down, and then dancing, repeated over and over, endlessly it seemed. Fortunately, Lisa was always there with me practicing too, and constantly chatting about this and that, mostly one-sided, mind you, but she didn't mind, she felt all grown up at age twelve. By the fourth night, I had stopped even thinking about what had happened, why, or even how, focusing on my own survival.

That meant I had to become as independent of these ladies maids as I possibly could, all things considered. No getting around having to be dressed, fed, and assisted with bathroom duties. Yet once those were done, I knew I needed to be able to get around well on my own. On the fifth day, Baron Ulysses tested me to see how I was progressing. Apparently, I got a pass on sitting down gracefully, as well as getting to my feet from a chair. I owe that to all my former experiences.

"Lisa you are doing very well yourself," he complimented his youngest daughter, who looked extremely pleased. "So starting today, you and your sister are to practice walking everywhere in the castle, including all the stairs. Just be extra careful with them, dears."

I liked that idea. Now, I would get a better view of just where I was, what was in this castle, and where it was located. Even better, Lisa insisted she could help me, and that our maids didn't have to follow us all around. I did sense an enormous relief coming from two of them when she told them that. Bright twelve year old. She led me to a large number of rooms on this floor, some of which we had been in, such as the drawing room, dining room, and dance floor. But then, we got to see our parent's bedroom, her room, Larry's room, and little Thomas' room. Then, came the kitchen and attached pantry. So far so good. All the walls were stone, and the floors were also granite stone blocks or sheets, but I couldn't tell their thickness.

Then came the start of the stairs. I swallowed hard. While Lisa could use her hands to pull back her puffing gown and bend her neck enough to see the steps and her feet, I could not. This had always been the scariest part for me. You don't know how bad it is until you don't have the use of your arms and can't even see the steps or your feet. I didn't have any robots to latch on to me this time. Instead, I was determined to do this myself. If I was ever to have any chance of getting out of here and back home, I had to be able to manage on my own, somehow.

Again, going up is the easy part, while going down is darn scary. On the second floor, the first room we entered was their Grand Ballroom. Here, I had to stop and stare for a few minutes, letting Lisa chat away about all of the fancy gatherings she had witnessed. "I'm going to get to come to the next one wearing my new heels and corset, just like you, Christina. They are making me a new gown to go with it. I so hope the boys will pay attention to me. They will, won't they?" I nodded yes.

The room was about three times the size of the rooms below. I estimated it could hold two hundred people or so. I spotted a raised musician's platform, and recognized a harpsichord sitting there alone. The ceilings were ten feet above us, and covered in what I considered to be risqué frescoes of men and women frolicking the woodlands. Great draperies were pulled back, allowing the yellow sunshine to enter, forming streaks of light-illuminated dust particles floating in the air. All was silent save for the clicking sounds our steel tipped heels made on the swirling granite floor. I decided they must be granite tiles, perhaps a quarter inch thick, may be more.

She led me into four side rooms, where sofas, chairs, and a number of nicely made end tables were positioned strategically around the rooms. "Often, the adults come in here and sit and chat, while others are dancing. I don't want to sit. I'm going to be dancing all the time, unless of course I get too out of breath. Don't you think that's the best idea? That way more boys can see me." I nodded yes again.

After I had seen into all the rooms up here, I noticed there were more stairs. I nodded my head towards them. Lisa was a little reluctant, "There's only the roof and observation deck up there. Well, okay, only be careful you don't fall off. It's a very long way down." She led the way, and we went up more stairs. Perhaps, I was being foolish, insisting on going up more stairs because I'd have to come back down them, which was many times more challenging for me and probably Lisa, who hadn't yet realized it.

We came out onto a windy observation deck. I was indeed living in a stone castle. Here were crenels all along the low wall marking the boundaries of the roof. While it was windy, I needed to get my bearings. Off to one side was rolling countryside, dotted with small farmsteads. Off to another side was a forest, not too helpful. Then, I spotted a spaceship descending and turned in that direction. Ah, there was the city of Thromstead, abutting one edge of the castle. So we were at the edge of the city like Lisa suggested. The spaceport appeared to be also at the edge. Not knowing any directions, I could only say it was there some miles off. I spotted roads and city people on the streets. One led from close to the castle on into the city.

However, our hair soon became quite an unmanageable proposition. As we looked out at the city, the wind was strong and from our backs, blowing our hair almost out straight in front of us. Lisa did her best to mostly hold hers back, but I couldn't do anything with mine, of course. We turned around to face the wind, and I shook my head this way and that, and mostly had the wind blow it back onto my backside. But as we turned to go back to the door and stairs, the wind whipped it around again, nearly blinding me. Somehow, I managed to get inside while Lisa shut the door. She giggled. "Our hair is a mess." She proceeded to get most of mine back out of my face and then did hers as well. Now, we had to descend the stairs.

"Oh! Going down is trickier," Lisa whispered, as though afraid to admit it. I paused long enough to nod yes. Unable to bend much and with a puffy dress hiding my feet, stairs, and with such tall heels, it was as frightening as I expected it would be. Yet, I knew I simply had to master this on my own, if I was to have any chance to escape. Slow and easy, feeling for each step, we both made it down to where we started.

Now, I was armed with more data. The floor we lived on was not the ground floor. Stairs continued downward. Again, I nodded, and Lisa continued down, not saying anything herself, but holding onto the railing, and testing each step before putting her weight down on that foot. On the first floor were a number of supply rooms, servants' quarters, the Baron's private study, and their throne room.

"Well, this is a pleasant surprise to see you two have made it down here. Well done, both of you. We'll make proper baronesses out of you both. Look Lilly, no maid either." Lilly nodded to us. I realized Lilly would have to go up and down these stairs daily to sit with him during their official court sessions; now I was certain I was on the right path.

Lisa and I continued on to the main doors and looked outside. I nodded towards the outside. "Oh no. We have to have father's permission to go outside. We can go on down into the dungeon area. That's where Larry is getting his fighting training, but I don't want to. Do you?" I clicked no. So we headed back up the stairs. By now, our knees were fiercely hurting. "My knees hurt. Do yours?" she asked. I clucked a yes. "We had best take a break."

Over supper, Baron Ulysses again complimented us and encouraged us to walk up and down the stairs many times tomorrow. "Your mother has to go up and down them daily, and so will you when you are a baroness. A baroness always sits beside her baron when they hold court each day." He then added as an incentive. "I know how much you miss going outside. So if you can show me you both can handle the stairs well by tomorrow evening, then the next day you may go outside, just don't stray too far just yet."

I really did want to get outside and even into the city. I needed to be able to get myself to that spaceport, somehow, someway. So yes, the next day, Lisa and I went up and down the stairs, practicing doing it as gracefully as possible. Baron Ulysses must have thought we were doing it acceptably because he gave us permission to go outside the next day.

A giant cobblestone courtyard was surrounded by a stone wall perhaps ten feet tall, not impossible to climb, but certainly a strong deterrent. I spotted a tired car vehicle parked outside a smaller building. At first, that looked hopeful, but then I realized I'd be unable to drive it. I'd have to go on foot. There was also a very heavy wooden gate, quite wide, but looked like it could be locked and barred on the inside. We strolled around, taking in the fresh air and enjoying the sun.

This cluck-click language didn't have much potential. So I tried the sounds that meant "go" and "city." Lisa finally figured out that I wanted to go into the city.

"Oh no. We can't do that, not without a proper escort. I'll ask father about it, if you really want to go into town. There's nothing much to see but the peasants doing their daily work," Lisa replied.

At supper, Lisa asked. "Absolutely not!" Baron Ulysses barked sharply. I felt sorry for Lisa and regretted pushing her to ask him. Then, he apparently had a change of heart. Twirling his impressive moustache, he said, "Well, I do have some errands to run there myself tomorrow. Lilly dear, our Christina is really doing quite well, isn't she? Her attitude has totally changed, now that we've made her into a baroness. She's getting around extremely well on her own. What do you think about hosting a party this weekend? A grand ball. We can invite a number of local barons and let them see our two baronesses-to-be. It will give them both valuable experience before we have to go to the one that really matters, where she ought to get at least one marriage proposal. What do you think?"

Lilly nodded yes. Then, she cluck-clicked something I couldn't quite hear. "Oh yes. You are right. We simply must if we're to present them at the ball." Turning to Lisa and me, he said, "While we're in town, we'll visit a jewelers. I'll get you each proper earrings and a broach to wear to the ball. Don't forget, a baroness always wears whatever jewelry her baron gives her. In this case, Christina dear, we want you to make a stunning appearance, so yours will have to be really special. Don't frown, Lisa. When you turn sixteen, I'll get you some just as nice as Christina's will be." Her frown changed to a broad smile. He added, "One more thing. Lisa, if we go into town, you'll also have to be wearing your own golden veil. We can't let future baronesses be seen in such public places without your veils. I'll have the doctor fix you up tonight yet. Also, you both best start sleeping in them. Often, barons prefer their baronesses to wear their golden veils at all times, even in bed. I know I prefer Lilly to wear hers. When you are older, you'll understand why this is. So for now, I'll instruct your maids to leave them on you, except when bathing, obviously."

I didn't much care for this. The darn veil was made of gold and was quite heavy, pulling down hard on my nose and upper ears. I figured it would be mostly annoying to sleep with it on, draped over my lower face and mouth. It was just that.

The next morning after breakfast, Baron Ulysses said, "Okay, young baronesses, it's time to go into town. Show me how elegantly you can descend to the car." Lisa was grinning from ear to ear, sporting her new golden veil, just like mine only a bit smaller. I could see how it pulled hard on her nose though, but she didn't seem to mind. She looked like her mother and me, and was quite proud. She and I made it safely down and across the courtyard to the car doing it well enough to earn a "good job" remark from him. He opened the door and allowed Lisa to get herself inside.

He and I moved over to the other door, and he opened it for me. I stood there wondering if he'd help me inside. "Go on, Christina. Your future baron won't have time to help you in. Plus, you need to be elegant and graceful about it." I backed in slightly, leaned forward a bit, shaking my hair until it fell to my front side, and then managed to sit down without falling down, though I admit I used a bit of levitation *mentales* powers to do it. "Beautifully done, Christina. I never knew you could do it. Amazing. You are looking more and more like the best baroness ever."

As we drove out through the gates, I paid close attention to details of the route and what I could see. The city or town was slightly hilly. I did spot a road that looked promising and hoped that it led straight to the spaceport, but I had no way to ask — no cluck-click words seemed to provide any way to indicate that question. We pulled up at a very fancy looking building with a sign that read William Jones Jewelers. Here, he opened the doors, and we had to get out gracefully. While Lisa had little trouble, I did, wobbling a bit to get my balance. "Have to work on that a bit, Christina," he whispered while closing the door.

Inside, I saw hundreds of what appeared to me to be

fine quality pieces of jewelry of all kinds. Lisa was awestruck, and I wandered about beside her, allowing her to gape at all these probably very expensive pieces. I could sense she'd never seen anything like this before. Meanwhile Baron Ulysses was talking softly to the owner, just out of our hearing range.

Shortly, he came up to us and explained. "I'm going to leave you both here while I run my errands. Meanwhile, Mr. Jones will be preparing your ears and fitting you with your new earrings and broaches." To me, he whispered, "Remember, a baroness always wears what jewelry her baron gives her." I nodded having no idea why he said that again or what it meant.

One at a time, Mr. Jones pierced our ear lobes. I only felt pricks. Somehow, he healed the punctures rapidly, the bleeding ceased almost at once. However, I just couldn't see what he was actually doing. Then, he spoke to me directly. "Your father wants you to be the star of the ball. Hence, he's purchased these most expensive earrings and broach to match. They are emeralds and pure gold. Mind you, they'll feel a bit heavy at first. Also, since these are your first earrings, I'll tell you that I solder them on so that they can't ever be taken off. With earrings this expensive, all barons would insist on this safety precaution. That way, there is no way they could accidentally come off and be lost, since you would be unable to retrieve them should they fall off."

He proceeded to put mine on me. I did feel a wave of rather high heat, but it lasted but a moment. They were exceptionally long and very heavy, pulling down so hard on my ear lobes that I was worried they would rip them or something. The bottoms just touched my shoulders. I will say this, the combination of gold and the emeralds matched my golden hair well and certainly made a statement. However, their weight severely limited my ability to toss my head about to arrange my hair on my own. He put a large emerald on a gold chain around my neck, resting the big stone just above my gaping cleavage. Then, he turned his attention to Lisa. Her earrings were half my size as was her broach, but she didn't complain about that. Rather, she was extremely proud and had the largest smile ever, especially when father returned.

He complimented us both, and we again got into the car. This time when I sat down, the jolt nearly pulled my ears off. Getting out, their weight threw me slightly off balance. Baron Ulysses seemed to understand this. "Why don't you two stay here a while, and practice getting in and out of the car on your own? Remember, grace, poise, stateliness." He left us there to practice.

At supper, Lilly was so impressed with my new earrings that she actually cried, and her maid had to wipe her eyes for her. I'm glad someone was impressed with them. I wasn't. By now their weight was making both ears throb fiercely, but my cluck-click language had no words to explain that to anyone. Even lying in bed, their weight continued to pull on my ears, just not as hard.

The next two days before the big party or ball as the ladies maids called it were spent in practicing our dances. When Lisa and I weren't dancing, we were both walking around and going up and down the stairs, since we would be expected to do that at the ball, which would be held in the upper ballroom. We did watch as many servants were decorating the huge room with flowers and streamers.

The night before the ball, Baron Ulysses took me into his study for a private father-daughter chat. Okay, it was a one-way chat, since my cluck-click language offered me very little opportunity to have even a word that was remotely appropriate. "Look, Christina dearest daughter, I know you've been a defiant child, until we went ahead with your Baroness Preparations ahead of time. It was for your own good. Tonight, I want to remind you of what is expected of any baroness. Like we barons, you have your responsibilities, obligations, and customs to fulfill. Of course, no baroness ever has any say in whom she marries, but I promise not to wed you to someone that you could not be happy with. It would be humiliating for me to marry you to someone that you detested or even to an ugly man, for you are a rare beauty. Okay?" I nodded.

"Now, we have gone ahead with your Baroness Preparations, which are usually done once a marriage proposal has been accepted. Our doctor handles this, and in your case, he's outdone himself. You are stunningly beautiful, dear

Christina. While I know that you were protesting these preparations, no baroness ever has had arms. Our history books don't lie. A baroness always wears her golden veil, because it is her symbol of office. Wear yours with great pride. As you also know, a baroness never speaks, which is why the front part of your tongue has been removed. We've been hounding you a lot, because it is the responsibility of a baroness always to display superb posture, never slouching on her throne, because she is the embodiment of beauty for her town or city. That is the reason for the rigid corset, dear."

He continued his explanations, "A baroness is required to walk stately and graceful at all times. As you know, she is always to wear six inch heels or higher if she could train her feet to do so. As your mother has told you countless times, many wise teens practiced this long before they were sixteen. A very few extremely wise baronesses learned to walk perfectly in the seven inch heels, as your mother wears and now you do too. She and I had our doubts about you, but when the young barons come courting a month from now, you'll find those heels will be a very big selling point to those men. Of course, we need to prevent some baroness from cheating, so your shoes are always made in the oxford styles, nicely tied with double knots, preventing them from being removed without untying them. No cheating, though I'm told by your maids you did just that before we went ahead with your Baroness Preparations. Now, they are tied to keep them from coming loose, since you would not be able to retie them and ladies maids are not always present."

"Baroness Preparations also included your breast enhancement. I know you're only sixteen, but now your bosom will truly enchant the prospective young barons, because they can see for themselves just what you'll look like as their baroness. That's a very big selling point too, Christina. I want to find you only the best possible baron. Mind you, your baron may well want them further enlarged and if so, I'll have to fulfill his wishes."

"Of course, I'm required to purchase you at least one new gown to wear, but as you know, I've gotten you quite a number of them. Further, once you are betrothed, I'll have to purchase your bridal gown. We are delaying on that since we don't know yet just when you'll be married, and your body is still growing. But remember, once you are married, it'll be your baron's responsibility to properly clothe you."

"Now then, your hair is just perfect. Most barons require that the bride has never cut her hair. You haven't and are fine with that. Your golden locks are as stunning as your mother's are. As you already know, usually when girls reach fourteen, their mothers have them encased in the steel corsets to get you used to wearing them ahead of time. No young woman is ever allowed to marry until she is sixteen, which you are. And just to be complete with you, Christina, if you had reached twenty-one without any marriage proposal, then I would be obligated to donate you to the town's peasants to do with as they saw fit. That, of course, would be a horrible blot on both your mother and me."

"Now as a baroness, you have the responsibility to bear your baron as many children as he desires, usually at least four. Some of the wealthier and influential barons have a dozen offspring. Your mother hasn't said anything to you kids yet, but she is pregnant again, so there'll be five in our family by next year." I smiled as appropriate.

He went on, somewhat embarrassed though. "Along with this, Christina, is your obligation to fully satisfy your baron's sexual needs. I think we'll talk about this when we have a proposal accepted." He shifted topics, relieved. "A baroness is required to always dress formally and to attend all court sessions, sitting stately and beautifully at her baron's side, just as your mother always has with me. Of course, the baroness must attend all the social occasions, and must be able to dance well, since many barons will want to dance with her. This is especially true for you, dear Christina. You are very beautiful and are wearing the highest of heels. With your gorgeous golden hair and baroness-size bosom, you'll be attracting far more attention and desires from the young barons, giving you far more choices of men to marry. However, once again, I must caution you that falling down in public is a severe disgrace, a horrid blot not only on you, but also on us and your baron, once you are married. That's why we have been hounding you so hard these past days."

He sighed for a moment. "I'll tell you something that you don't know. When I was a young man, I was introduced to twenty prospective baronesses. Of course, I fell in love with Lilly's golden locks. What man wouldn't? But what sold me on Lilly was that of all those prospective young women, only she wore the seven inch heels and with great poise and grace! That told me here was a woman who truly respected herself and her future position, wanting to be the very best baroness. It also told me she had practiced in them for countless hours before we ever met. That she took herself very seriously was more than plain to me. I've never regretted that decision. You can see why she was so insistent that you too wear them. Lisa will too, when she is a little older." I nodded.

He got back on track. "A baroness has other obligations. She must wear whatever clothing her baron purchases for her, including whatever earrings, broaches, and other jewelry he gives to her. I've given you such stunning earrings that you might not have to wear any others, but we'll see. Later on, when you have your own daughters, you'll be obligated to see your daughters were properly prepared for their marriage, just as your mother is doing with you and Lisa too. Finally, every baroness is obligated to look as attractive as she can possibly be at all times. Why? Because we barons do have important people dropping by unexpectedly."

"Always remember, dear Christina, your position is one that is envied by all, especially so if you show great poise, grace, and stateliness, particularly when you walk or dance. You are so beautiful now that at the ball tomorrow, you can expect all manner of attention from the young barons-to-be. You may even get several marriage proposals, but there will be many more at the formal ball next month. After that ball, we'll discuss them together and with your mother, if you wish. Now, I've said what a baron must to his daughter. It is late, and tomorrow will be the first of your big days." He leaned over and kissed me goodnight.

I took that as my signal to leave, and tried to rise and exit as gracefully as I could. After all, he'd just been kind to me, telling me much of what I needed to know. However, I knew for certain I needed to make my escape darn soon, certainly before that next ball came a month from now!

After breakfast, our ladies maids undressed us and gave us a bath and washed our hair. Then, they pampered us most of the afternoon, getting us looking our best in our new gowns. Both Lisa and I wore the same color of satin gown, a light blue. After a light supper, they touched us up once more, particularly our hair, and we were ready. Larry grumbled; he had to wear a suit as his father wore, but little Thomas didn't mind it at all.

A servant man entered and said it was time. Baron Ulysses and Baroness Lilly led us up the stairs to the main ballroom entrance. A group of ten musicians was sitting on the raised platform. The servant announced the two and a brief fanfare followed. Then, as Lisa and I stepped into the room, he announced, Baronesses-to-be, Miss Christina and Miss Lisa." I heard a hearty round of applause, as she and I walked gracefully into the room after our parents. At once, I saw nearly two hundred in attendance. The place was packed. I spotted at least ten other baronesses. You can't miss one of us. We rather stick out.

At once, a number of young men perhaps in their late teens came up to me asking for this dance. I smiled appropriately and accepted the first young man who offered, hoping I wouldn't make a fool of myself. I can't thank Lisa enough for all those patient hours she spent with me teaching me how to dance to their music. I took a chance and glanced towards Lisa. I saw several boys slightly older than Lisa were lining up to dance with her, so I knew she was on cloud nine tonight. She was being noticed as she hoped and prayed. What young girl doesn't?

As the evening progressed, I continued to have these "available" young men constantly asking for the next dance. I kept cycling between them. At the first break, I noticed that Baron Ulysses was looking extremely pleased with me. I picked up his thoughts, *I never expected to see Christina looking this beautiful. She's as fine as her mother. Amazing, simply amazing.*

Well amazing or not, I had to get out of here, and into a

spaceship heading back home somehow. One young man chatted about the spaceport. Apparently, his father had something to do with its operations, but that baron was of a lower status than Baron Ulysses. I smiled and nodded, encouraging him to chat more as we danced. Later when the musicians took a break, he asked me to join him in one of the sitting rooms. Gracefully, I rather flowed after him, albeit slowly. There, we had some refreshments made from grapes, non-alcoholic though. He apparently had some experience or training, because he knew just how to assist me. Carefully lifting my golden veil, he held my cup up for me to sip. Embolden by this, I flirted with him, and encouraged him to talk more, which he did. I learned there were spaceships taking off at all hours. Some were cargo transports and some were passenger liners, but all were run by other non-Federation worlds.

An idea formed. I used my *mentales* gifts to probe his mind a little, bringing up images of the place. Well, it looked like any normal spaceport. While we were chatting, rather he was chatting, I saw many other young couples heading off to go outside for a stroll. I smiled, and took a chance, planting the thought in his mind. "I say, Miss Christina, would you like to go outside for a breath of fresh air with me?" I nodded yes and smiled appropriately, bringing an even bigger smile to his face. I rose elegantly, allowed him to lead me back out onto the ball room floor, and then out the main doors. I cringed at the stairs, but bravely pushed on, going very slowly this time, feeling each step with the back of my heels before setting them down. It seemed like forever before we reached the front doors. Then, we were outside and the air felt delightful.

We saw other young couples, arm in arm. Some others were stealing kisses, but with my golden veil, that would be difficult. Instead, the lad put his arm around my waist pressing himself close to me, and we walked out into the courtyard for a time. Now I had to make a choice. I wanted to use him to take me to the spaceport and put me on a flight off this world. Here was just the person who knew where it all was and how to go about it. However, he was really a kind, nice young man. If I used him like that, he would be in so much trouble it wasn't funny. They might even execute him. I couldn't live with that. So I chose to go it alone, and prepared for my big exit. I planted the idea in him that I was a bit chilly and wanted my shawl. He proceeded to ask me if I was chilly. I nodded. He then volunteered to go find my shawl. I watched him until he entered the doors. No one was paying the slightest attention to me, so out the main gates I walked, albeit extremely slowly and carefully.

I admit I wasn't really prepared to walk so darn far, not in these heels, but this was probably the only chance I was going to get. It was flee now and hope for the best or succumb to the future being planned for me as someone's baroness. I walked, paying close attention to each step. Soon, I left sight of the castle completely, having rounded a bend. Now, I put all my attention on walking without falling down.

I rather wished Danika were here with me. She could have told me what direction I was going, and probably have told me about how far away the spaceport was. She wasn't. My own guess was I had to walk two miles. The night was dark and cool. As I went down the street I hoped and prayed led to the spaceport, I didn't see anyone out on the streets. It was late, so I had that going for me. I have no idea how long I walked, but my knees ached from going downhill. Going uphill gave me some momentary relief, but then it was back down on the other side. It had to be much later when I finally spotted the spaceport ahead.

However, I was physically pooped from the long walk and had to rest. I spotted a large boulder off to the side of the road close to the entrance, but out of the way. Carefully, I sat down, much to the relief of my toes and knees. So far so good. Now, I had to find a way to sneak into the spaceport. I knew if someone saw me, they would recognize me as a baroness immediately. Probably one never came to the spaceport, and certainly not alone and in the middle of the night. They would surely sound the alarm. No, I had to sneak in, but then what?

Sighing, I focused and began expanding my awareness outward, but heavily feeling the loss of my crystal's amplification powers. I began to tap into the minds I sensed, looking for an idea. I needed a passenger liner of some kind and some way onto it, preferably without being seen. Tall order, I know.

Then, I realized that wasn't such a good idea. I could influence one person totally, but not a whole passenger liner. I changed tactics. What about hitching a ride on a cargo liner, preferably which only had a pilot and navigator? I renewed my thought probing, and saw that there were many such ships preparing for departure.

While there were lights on tall poles, they only provided good lighting in their vicinity. There were always deep shadows beyond their yellow cones. That would provide cover for me. Satisfied I'd rested as much as I dared, I focused and levitated myself up and over the fence, which surrounded the spaceport. Once down, I had to rest a bit. Without my crystal, this was using up too much of my *mentales* potential. As quietly as I could, I began moving through the shadows. My steel tipped heels were not made for silent walking on the concrete tarmac, but if I moved ever so slowly, I could keep that barely audible. Now to find the right ship.

So many of them looked more like rust buckets than honest spaceships! Even as desperate as I was, I didn't figure a rust bucket would be the safest ship. If the owner didn't take any better care of his ship than that, he was probably a thug or worse. Finally, I spotted a relatively clean cargo ship and cased it from deep within some nearby shadows, homing in on the minds of the two men who were in the process of loading some crates onto it. I picked up their destination, some planet that I'd never heard of. Now what, I thought. Could I use my gifts to force them to fly me to where I wanted to go?

Perhaps, but what if they didn't know the coordinates? What if they didn't have enough fuel to get there? Suddenly, I had a lot of what ifs to contend with. Then, I grinned. I can be awfully devious when I want to be!

Focusing again, I placed a question into one of the men's mind, as though the other man had asked it. I listened for the reply. "Yeh, we could get to Cass-C this run, but why? These are bound for Jamison-D. You got a gal on Cass-C you ain't tell'n me about?"

I thought faster than I think I ever did. I placed another

notion into his mind. "You know, I think that we could make a lot of cash moving goods from there. A whole lot more than we are making on this run. I'd like to check it out once, at least."

"Well, you're the boss. I'm game. These midnight runs are tiresome. Plus, we don't make much profit. Still beggars can't be choosy. Go file the flight plans. I'll finish up here. Only got a couple more crates to load. Sooner we are off, the better."

The pilot climbed on in through the bay ramp and disappeared, leaving the other man lifting and carrying another crate inside. Now, all I had to do was somehow get inside that ship! But how?

I could make a running dash when he began raising the bay ramp. That was beyond even a remote possibility. I'd only get a couple of feet before the door was shut. Think, Nia Elain, think. I began walking, all the while focusing on the lone man loading the cargo, keeping his head from turning my direction. Slowly the distance closed.

I reached the ramp after he walked up it, carrying the last crate. I followed on up the ramp. As he turned to close the door, he spotted me. "What?" he cried out. I was prepared and took control, making him be silent and continue to close the door. I looked around, found a stack of crates, and hastily sat down before my shaking legs gave out. I'd overdone the walking by far more than I dared admit to myself! I planted the thought, *Must have been dreaming. Best get to the navigator's seat.* He turned away from me. Shaking his head, he headed on down the hall towards the front of the ship. Silently, I breathed a huge sigh of relief, waiting on pins and needles to sense the ship lifting off. Hurry up, hurry up! As if my thoughts would make it go any faster.

I can't tell you how relived I was to feel the ship taking off! Never has a ship liftoff ever been so wonderful to me! Space-borne, they would be highly unlikely to land if they found me onboard. That would be a waste of fuel and time and for these men; both would erode their meager profits. The sudden jerk of entering hyperspace jarred me slightly, bringing me fully into the present once more. I knew I had to act and soon. I was overly tired, having used up nearly all my psi energies for one day. No telling what could happen to me if

I fell asleep now. Plus, the trip could take days. As I was, I couldn't possibly last that long without lots of help.

I did the only remaining option left. I carefully got back onto my wobbling legs and very carefully made my way forward. The hall was dimly lit and unfamiliar, so I went extremely slowly, feeling my way along with my feet, an inch or two at a time. As I approached the cockpit, they must have heard me. "What the devil? Who are you? What are you doing on our ship?" both men were taken by surprise and rather hostile.

I focused and sent them, *If you take me to Cass-C and deliver me to Admiral Molly Maud Porsche, you'll be paid ten thousand gold dollars, as long as I'm not mistreated.*

"What's the matter with you? Speak up woman?" one said.

"Hey, maybe she's one of them princesses we heard about. They can't speak. Got their tongues cut out," the other side. I nodded vigorously and re-sent my thought to both men.

"Hey I got the idea that if we take her to Cass-C, we'll get ten grand."

"Me too. Funny. Don't know why we'd get that. Probably get arrested is more like it."

I'm very serious men. You take me there, and I promise you that you'll get ten grand.

"You think that she's worth ten grand?"

"Who knows. Maybe. Think we should?"

"Crap! We sure as hell aren't going back. Okay lady, we're heading for Cass-C. Maybe someone there will pay us for you. We'll see."

"Where's she going to sleep? She's as helpless as they come."

"Hell, I don't know. Put her in the spare cabin for now. Lady, we don't know nothing about you. You'll have to fend for yourself," the pilot added. I nodded.

The navigator climbed out of his seat, led me back down the other hall, and into a cabin piled with junk. "Suppose I have to move some of this stuff for you." He began tossing stuff into a pile in a corner. "None too clean, but it's a bed. I got to get back."

How long until we reach Cass-C? I asked.

Not knowing why he said what he said, he mumbled, "Should get to Cass-C in three days. Sure hope someone there'll pay ten grand for you, but that's not likely, is it, stowaway. Probably they'll put you in jail." He turned and left me alone in a very dimly lit cabin.

I sat down and then more or less fell back onto the bed, pulling on my hair. Damn. It felt so darn good to lie down and ease my feet and knees. I sighed deeply and drifted into an ill sleep, worrying these men might try to take advantage of me while I slept.

Nia Elain! Finally, I've found you! Rafe here. Where in the galaxy are you? What happened? Are you all right?

Rafe? Is that really you? Help! God, I need help! I'm in another body that's almost completely helpless! Never has a telepathic message been so welcome before in my whole life!

Chapter 20 Recovery

My Christina body was sound asleep when Rafe made telepathic contact with me. I spent some time relaying what happened to me and my current situation, which was precarious at best. She then told me what had happened with Christina and my Nia Elain body, and then her encounter with the juvenile dolls and their machine. It was her theory that their illegal machine was somehow responsible for zapping us into each other's bodies. That made little sense to me right then. *Okay, right now, you sleep and I'll watch over you. I have three dozen of these giant crystals powered up just to make this connection with you. Plenty of power. Too much in fact. So sleep and recover. I have your back.*

I fell into a very deep sleep, perhaps the best since this whole thing started. I awoke startled, suddenly afraid I was on my own with these two strangers! Panic. *Easy kid. I have your back. They are bringing you breakfast. I'll be feeding you. Relax. Danika is on her way to pick you up when you get to Cass-C.*

Shortly after that, the navigator appeared carrying a tray of food with a cup of coffee on it. He left it on the tiny desk, after pushing some clutter off it. "There you go miss. Seems you got friends in high places. Someone called us and told us that if we land at Cass-C, they'll pick you up from us and pay us ten thousand gold dollars! Impressive, princess." He turned and left, wondering how the princess could possibly eat.

Rafe lifted my veil and brought the coffee cup up to my lips. She was using her *mentales* gifts extremely well. God, that coffee, raunchy as it was, sure tasted good and woke me up. Of course, so did the greasy food, but I wasn't complaining. When I finished, Rafe sent, *I have to get some sleep myself. Zarita is taking over for me. She'll be in constant touch if you need anything. Hang in there. By the way, damned impressive escape, Nia Elain, damned impressive.* I grinned.

Awake now, I looked around the cabin and found its

tiny toilet. I tried to get up, but that was too difficult, so I focused and used a bit of levitation energy to get into a sitting position. My legs throbbed, and I didn't trust them. They felt like mush. So I used a bit more to move my body over to the filthy toilet. Then, I used a bit more to get my panties down and dress up. Relief. Boy, did I ever have to go. I used a bit more to get my panties back up, my body back onto the bed, and lying down again. I felt a bit drained, and decided I might as well nap. I fell back asleep again. I didn't know it at the time, but that was Zarita's doing. She had been remotely monitoring my body and saw its condition. While I slept again, she worked her healing magic on my knees, legs, and feet. When I next awoke, I felt really good and realized what she'd done.

During the trip, I learned that Jana and Molly Maud had been the victims of yet another terrorist attack, and that Jana was now in a healing induced coma back home. Martina was with Molly Maud on Cass-C. At the moment, I couldn't do anything about them. I just wanted to get home to some form of safety. I could have yelled for joy when I sensed the cargo transport descending onto the spaceport at Hoffdorf!

Once the ship was down, accompanied by a slight jar, I rose, and began making my pathetically slow way down the hall to the bay ramp. When I finally reached it, I saw my beloved standing there in her leathers, handing a large bag of gold dollars to the pilot, who looked extremely please. "Say absolutely nothing about the princess here to anyone or you could find yourselves in very hot water. Got it?" Danika barked as only she could. Both men nodded.

Am I ever glad to see you! I sent.

"I got you, love! Wow, you sure look different, but you are my Nia Elain. Only you could have pulled that one off! Super well done. Everyone's minds are blown over what you just did. I got you. Going to have you home in nine hours!" She literally picked me up and carried me down the ramp, across the tarmac, and up into the Eagle's Seed. I was crying now. I never thought I'd see my ship ever again, let alone my Danika or the others, who crowded around us, hugging and kissing me. She didn't put me down until she got me into my cabin.

"Gotta get us going. Back in a bit. Don't go anywhere this time," she teased me. I chuckled.

Doctor Leann was with my crew on this trip, and I quickly saw why. "Okay, Rafe's orders. Quick medical exam." I nodded.

Danika joined us, as I got the good health nod. "Well, the Christina version of you didn't last long. Jana, Jovanna, and Marisol had her pegged as not-you minutes after she awoke that first day. Of course, Rafe insisted she be brought to Ashford-5 so she could try to figure out what was going on. They didn't quite make it. Another damned terrorist attacked everyone at the spaceport there in Hoffdorf, an hour before I arrived to pick them up. So now, Jovanna and Marisol are all fixed up again and are quite pleased to have their left hands back. Two days ago, Molly Maud and Jana got attacked while they were at one of their Mid-winter Festival parties. Two goons walked in and unleashed the bio agent. Jana's in our med lab now. She should be in the curing coma by the time I get us back. I'm really getting good at making these super-fast runs halfway across the galaxy, but I think I'd rather blast these sons of bitches who are stupid enough to use that bio agent on innocent people. Someone's got to put an end to this."

You've been a busy beaver, I teased her. *Thanks for being here for me. I was scared I'd never see you or the kids ever again.*

I know, and I was scared I'd never see you again too.

On the way back, Dr. Leann told me there were nine hundred sixteen victims in the spaceport attack, ignoring the fool who did it. No one bothered to count him. They were about evenly divided between men and women, but there were eighteen children among them. During the flight, the official totals for the festival party attack came in. There were two thousand sixteen victims, again not including the two men who executed the attack. I was appalled to hear that while about evenly divided by gender, most of these victims were the wealthiest people in Hoffdorf. Then, we also got the news there had been two other nearly simultaneous attacks in two more of their larger cities! There, too, the attack had been on the wealthier people at their parties. Combining the three attacks, Cass-C casualties tallied six thousand fifty-two people.

Worse, Dr. Leann explained to me, Cass-C was completely out of the genetic material supplies needed to perform the genetic cures that our geneticists had shared with them. All their supplies had been used on the original attacks victims, mostly the admirals and ID members. She said with a sigh, "That means nearly seven thousand victims are not getting any cures anytime soon, Molly Maud among them. I did hear that Porsche Industries has turned some of their warehouses into temporary shelters. Plus, Molly Maud started a program to hire personal assistants for the spaceport victims. According to what I heard, they are extending it to include the three recent attack victims as well. It's one grand mess. Martina is staying on top of it for us."

I could only sigh. It was happening all over again, only this time in the Federation of Planets. I wanted to talk to Jana or Jovanna about this, since as historians, they knew a lot about the Imperium events. Would it escalate to planetary genocide there as it had in the Imperium? At the moment, I couldn't.

My arrival on Ashford-5 was memorable, to say the very least! Danika lifted me gently down off the bay ramp. As I looked over towards the Admin Building, I saw a giant banner that read Welcome Home Hotshot! Nearly a hundred were there and broke into a spontaneous round of cheering and applause, as I began my slow walk towards them, Danika at my side. I spotted our kids too near the front, shepherded by more of my old crew. I had tears nearly blinding me, and I knew that I must look terribly different to everyone. Their goodwill and wishes flooded into my mind. I didn't need telepathy to feel them.

I didn't see my Nia Elain body there or Christina, I corrected my thought. Rafe met me first and kept me apart from the throng, though I heard my Zorina saying, "Mom sure looks different, doesn't she, Nadia?"

Rafe said, "Best get you to the med lab at once. Time enough for the kids later." Once inside and heading down the elevator to the electric cars, she added, "I'm keeping Christina and you apart for the moment. I don't know what will happen when you see each other. Could be an instantaneous body switch. We are in uncharted waters here. So first, we are going to try to repair this body of yours. They've got Christina healed up; left hand is back. She's just finished her Basic Therapy. We're going to take some extreme measures with you and this body, with your permission of course."

What? Heal it?

"Yes, expose you to the bio agent, and then the full cure. Then, we will see how that works. Dr. Leann says not everything might be cured. Apparently, there are some small genetic differences, which are playing havoc on their cures. Hit and miss, they say. Beyond me. I never did well in biology." I laughed.

Eight days passed by me in a rush. I was partially aware for a few minutes during the middle of the "cures," when I came out of the bio agent coma and before they put me under for the round of cures. I had more tubes in me than I could count. That's about all I recalled about it, before Rafe worked her therapy magic on me afterwards. Apparently, our doctors were getting better at working their magic. With proper IVs and the right fluids being pumped into my veins, my physical shape was excellent at the end of each of the two processes.

When they brought me out supposedly "cured," everyone gathered around me to observe the results, which turned out to be far less than they had hoped. Once more, Dr. Leann served as the go-between, translating the complex geneticists' language into something that I and others could more readily relate to.

"The tiny differences in DNA are wreaking havoc on their cures, Nia Elain. Your tongue is in perfect condition, as are your lips. That's quite positive. Your breasts are back to our normal size, which is also positive. On the other hand, as you can see, your arms didn't make it. The small genetic differences are causing troubles with arm regrowth in some Federation patients. Also, your feet only were partially repaired, and in your case, the cure had no effect on your hair at all. Guess you'll have to live with your long golden locks."

"Honestly, being able to talk is terrific, and I don't mind the hair, just the arms. Ah well, I have to be thankful for what was cured," I replied with a sigh.

"Also, they left your fabulous earrings on you. They can't come off without cutting their bands, and Danika didn't know if you still wanted to wear them or not, so we left them. She can cut them off if you don't want to continue wearing them. Meantime, you are to eat — no, stuff yourself. Rafe wants to get you into a therapy session right away," Dr. Leann finished up.

I have to hand it to Rafe. She is one powerful therapy giver. Her intention is something else. She had me wiping out the recent traumas faster than I believed possible! Most of the time, I found it very strange, since the trauma incidents I ended up eradicating were not mine! I had not experienced these things; Christina had. I was erasing the trauma recorded on her body's cells during the operations to remove her arms and tongue! How weird is that? When we were done, I suddenly realized the physical body also records the trauma that it experiences, just as we spiritual beings do! I found it quite fascinating indeed, as did Rafe!

I felt wholly alive and vibrant once more. True, the body wasn't. It had no arms, and I had to continue to wear six-inch and seven-inch heels, but that was better than have to wear the damned toe shoes. Okay, only slightly better. Other than that, I was in perfect shape. Better than perfect. Zarita gave me a very special gift. Everyone knew how I had made my Great Escape, as everyone else called my adventure on Blackwell-C, without the use of my amplifying germanium crystal. She gave me new, very special ones. "These used to be one of those giant crystals, you know, the foot in diameter ones. I had them compressed down into these small ones. This one you can wear around your neck as always, but it will give you about a thousand-fold increase in power over your old one. The others, I had made into these gorgeous earrings. Once you get these emeralds off and these new ones soldered on, they can't come off. So hopefully, you will always have lots of power when you need it."

I was speechless. The gift was priceless. I cried and

pressed hard into her, whispering, "Thank you!"

"Okay, now we have to really get down to the business at hand," Rafe interrupted us. "As you know, two juveniles with doll bodies, probably from the southern halo, stole some kind of electronic device that was supposedly 'illegal' to use. It emitted the precise frequency of you, Nia Elain, your unique wavelength. As far as I could tell from watching them, they were just dialing it up at random. Anyway, what is utterly fascinating is that Christina has almost the same exact wavelength as you have. The differences are extremely tiny. She's incredibly similar to you, personality-wise, as stubborn as you — I could go on with the similarities. She's only sixteen and not well educated if at all, and she has different goals. Anyway, it's my theory that it was this electronic device that somehow swapped each of you into the other's bodies. I think these juveniles did it for a laugh to see how you each would react; only they never did figure out how to locate either of you to 'watch the fun.' Well, I destroyed the machine and sent those two packing."

Rafe went on, "Now the question is: can the process be reversed? I've kept you two separate from each other. Why? One possibility I can envision is that the moment you two see your original bodies, you will automatically be switched back into your right bodies. Of course, if that happens, Christina will be shattered."

"Is that a real possibility? That we'll switch when we see our own bodies?" I asked.

"I have no idea," Rafe admitted. "So the first test is to see if that happens. I've explained all this to Christina. I'll let you know right now that Christina has begged me to put her out of her misery if she winds up back in her body, which you have. Apparently, all she really wants to do is to learn to play the harpsichord. As I said, she is an uneducated sixteen year old, who hasn't had any real education at all, only what she's seen in her father's house, namely the musicians. Be gentle with her."

"But you won't really kill her, will you Rafe?" I asked, growing worried.

Rafe laughed, "Hardly. Advanced Therapy or perhaps

giving her a *mentales* gift would work wonders for her, along with a proper education. Okay, Dr. Leann, bring Christina in. I hope there aren't fireworks."

She opened a door, and I walked in — er, rather Christina in my body walked in. We each involuntarily gasped, seeing our original bodies. Hey, it is incredibly spooky suddenly to see your body walking towards you! For a moment, we just stood staring at each other. Then Christina said, "I'm sorry you got stuck in my awful body. I know it's not good for anything, but I don't want to go back in it, not really. I don't have any magic like you all do, but I just can't let you suffer like I was suffering." Her voice faltered, "Rafe, Rafe will get rid of me after we switch back. How soon is it going to happen?" she asked meekly.

Shades of myself at sixteen! Back then, I knew what was right and just. I always thought it was because my folks taught me well. Now, I wondered if even that was true. I had lived with Christina's parents and knew enough to know this is not what I would have expected to hear from Christina. Rather, she echoed my own thoughts, my own personal, private sense of ethics!

Rafe broke the awkward silence. "Well, no sparks are flying, so I guess just seeing your original bodies again isn't going to cause an automatic body swap. Interesting."

"But now what? Is she going to be trapped in my body? Will you kill her now?" Christina asked.

Rafe sighed. "Hey, this is entirely new ground for me. I have another way that could work to get you both back into your original bodies, my Advanced Therapy. If I give you each enough of it, you'll be able to operate as a spiritual being outside and independent from your bodies. Once you've achieved that much ability, you could switch bodies rather easily. At least, that's my best guess. No one has yet tried that, but I'm confident it would work. It'll take some time to give you each that much Advance Therapy though."

I'd been silent so far, thinking this through. Christina had been devastated when her parents had her body mutilated. She didn't have the knowledge or more importantly the *mentales* gifts, let alone all the experiences that I had. I knew damned well she simply could not handle living life with this crippled body, but I certainly could. Hell, I'd lived my first eighteen years more or less as I was now. I reached a decision and spoke up, hoping and praying that Danika and my children would eventually understand it.

"Rafe. No need for the Advanced Therapy. I'm fine with Christina's body. I have my gifts. I've lived more years without arms than I've lived with them. I'm a thousand times better equipped to handle this body than Christina is. So if Christina is happy and content carrying on with her life in that body there, I'm okay with this one. I just hope my family understands this," I said definitively.

"You, you don't mind having my body — like it is, all hacked up?" Christina asked, quite surprised with what I was saying.

"No. I'm happy with it, as long as my family can accept the drastic change. Will you be okay with mine there? It's been through quite a lot in those twenty-five years. You're going to have to get used to people thinking that you are me, though," I replied slightly teasing her.

She giggled. "And they'll think you're me too, you know. Well, maybe not. No one knows me here. But it sure is kind of spooky seeing me looking at you. You the same way?"

"Duh, no kidding, Christina. Spooky, but I can handle it if you can."

"Yes. Now I can learn to play the harpsichord, which I always wanted to do since was ten! Music is so wonderful. I want to share it with everyone," Christina exclaimed, greatly relieved this disaster was being averted somehow.

"You are not going to miss your home world or your family?" I asked what I thought was really the much more salient point of this whole mess.

"Well, I miss my sister, Lisa, but I sure don't ever want to go back there. Dad would just be furious with me, and turn me into a baroness when I sleep again. I don't ever want to be a baroness, not ever. I want to make music and share that beauty with everyone," Christina replied.

"Okay then. That's what has been worrying me the most about all this, Christina. You were taken from your world and family by all this."

Rafe answered, "Quite true. We've mostly been taking care of her. Why?"

"She needs a family, Rafe. Okay, Christina, there'll be lots *less* confusion if you come and live with my family, Danika and the six kids. I think they'll be better able to grasp what's happened with us, if we both are around them daily. They can see for themselves that you're you, and I'm me, even though we look like each other," I tried to explain my reasoning.

"Can I? That would be great. Then, I might not miss my sister so much. I can help take care of them, like I did with Lisa and Thomas," Christina replied. I sensed the sixteen year old girl before me, not the twenty-five year old woman I saw.

"Good. Then that's settled, Rafe. Christina comes to live with us."

"One detail. Eventually, she's going to need an ID card. Are we going to use her last name of Blackwater?" Rafe asked. I picked up her reasoning. Surely, Baron Ulysses was going to unleash a hue and cry, looking for his missing daughter. Having that last name might not be the wisest move.

"Say, why don't we officially adopt Christina? Make it permanent? She would officially be Christina Compton-Jereni."

"Really? You would be my mother or is that Danika? This is so weird, but I'd like a mother I can talk to, you know about private things," Christina asked.

Suddenly, I knew exactly what she meant! She was only sixteen and had no idea about sexual matters. Worse, she now had male organs as well. No wonder she was totally confused and quite desperate. I replied, "Absolutely, Christina. You would have two mothers, me and Danika. And you are right, we do need to talk about private things." She grinned sheepishly.

"This is totally spooky!" Governor Misty exclaimed, as she prepared to officiate our adoption of Christina. I'd talked to Danika about everything. Bless her, she fully understood. Then together, we talked to the six children. They were delighted. Yes, they were confused for a while, mistaking

Christina for me, but they very quickly realized the difference. Bright kids.

Danika and I were standing side by side, and our six children stood to her left. Christina stood proudly at my right, facing Governor Misty and several others who just had to see this themselves. I commented to Misty, "Look at it this way; it's a first." Everyone chuckled. A few minutes later, the brief adoption ceremony was over, and one by one, Christina hugged us all.

To Nadia and Zorina, Christina said, "Now I *am* your big sister!"

"Way cool!" Zorina exclaimed, hugging her back. She and Nadia were now five years old and quite precocious.

She and I got new ID cards, making everything official. Then, we headed home to our place in Exchange City for some quiet, personal time. The queens absolutely insisted I take some time off. Martina had things well in hand on Cass-C. Once home, Nadia and Zorina insisted on leading Christina around her new home, and totally surprised her with the new harpsichord I had Danika purchase on the quiet. We heard a little shriek and knew that Christina had found it. We also heard a lot of giggles, and the tinny plucked sounds, as she just had to try it out.

Meanwhile, Danika and I headed into our bedroom. "Well, let me look you over, dear, and see what I've got now," she teased me. She tried to keep a straight face about it, but soon broke down into a hearty laugh.

"What?" I teased her back, but I wasn't sure why she was laughing.

"I got the better deal in this. Here, look at yourself in the mirror." I rose and did as she asked. I saw a sixteen year old girl with very thick, luscious, wavy hair. Golden locks draped down nearly to the floor. The pale blue eyes and the giant dangling gold and blue crystals of my earrings contrasted sharply. True, there weren't any arms to go with it, and in my seven-inch heels, I was standing a bit taller than she was.

"What?" I repeated.

"You are a beauty queen, that's what! Look at your face, dear. Your face is just perfect. You could be a top model anywhere. You look hotter than hot!"

I noticed a big bulge down below, grinned, and said, "Now?"

Danika slipped her arms around me and gave me the most passionate kiss ever. We ended up in the bed for a while. Later, she whispered, "How am I going to ever keep everyone's hands off of you?" We both laughed. I was also greatly relieved she still found me attractive. I need not have worried about that. During the next few days, I continually heard others telling me how fabulous I looked. I swear that if I hear just one more person tell me I could be a fashion model, I'll slap them! Okay, no hands, but you get the point. I never considered myself a beauty queen. Now, whether or not I liked it, I was just that. As I looked at myself in the mirror later, I began to see why they were saying that.

As I experimented with the power amplification boost from the earrings and broach, I knew that my *mentales* gifts were being magnified more than a thousandfold from my old crystal. I now had so much power that even I was shocked by its potential.

In one of Porsche Industries warehouses in Hoffdorf, Admiral Molly Maud finally came out of her coma. She opened her eyes and saw Heinz sitting beside her, rubbing her forehead lovingly. "Ah awake at last, my love. I was worried there for a while. Welcome back to the land of the living."

"Heinz?" she said and stopped. Her own words sounded unintelligible, but another sound speaking German translated her word perfectly. It came from around her waist. She felt strange all over. For some reason, she couldn't breathe. Her lips felt utterly stretched somehow. She tried to rub her face, but her hand and arms weren't there. Suddenly, it all registered, and she reacted with a scream, joining many others, who were also rousing only to find they were in a living nightmare.

"It's all right, dear. Go ahead and scream all you want. I'm here and will always be here for you," Heinz said comfortingly. He knew it wasn't all right, but he couldn't think of anything better to say. None of this was all right.

A few screams later, she ceased, gasping for breath, which calmed her down. Molly Maud was a fighter, and somehow, she mastered her panic attack. "Up. Help me sit up," she gasped, realizing she must be wearing one of those new voice translators that they had received from Ashford-5. Heinz lifted her up and helped her sit on the edge of her cot. Her eyes took it all in, sweeping to the left and right. Hundreds of others were lying on what seemed to be a field of cots, just as she'd seen before, when she came to visit the earlier victims. Now, she was one of them herself.

She noticed her dangling, giant lip plates, her enormous bosom and gasped. Heinz explained, "We got everyone properly dressed last night. We're supposed to get you to use the potty, and then feed you all you can eat and drink. No time for modesty yet."

She was embarrassed, but simply had to go. She was more embarrassed by her new lower anatomy than anything else. However, as Heinz patiently began spooning some juice into her mouth, she realized just how starving she was. By the time she was full, she had regained part of her composure. "Thanks, Heinz. I'm so glad you were here for me."

"I love you. I can't just desert you when you really need me. Now, we are supposed to help you get up and try to walk. It'll be difficult, but I won't let you fall. They say as soon as you can walk, we can go home. They've expanded your program to hire a personal assistant for everyone. There are about seven thousand of you this time."

"Good. Wait! There wasn't that many at the party," she exclaimed.

"No, there were two other attacks in two other big cities around the same time. Most are wealthy men and women. Up you go."

"Oh god! I can't do this!" Molly Maud wobbled wildly, flailing her non-existent arms about wildly, but Heinz was right there, slipping his arm around her now tiny waist, steadying her.

"Got you. Okay. Let's see if you can walk some," he said gently. Slowly, she took her first steps in the tiny toe shoes, finding it almost impossible to keep her balance. However, as they moved slowly around, she saw hundreds of others attempting their first steps too and took heart.

Just then, General Wolfgang entered, spotted the two, and came rushing over. Martina was right behind him, going slower because of her heels. She was wearing her acceptable professional woman's outfit as usual. "Ah Admiral Porsche. You are up and about. Has Heinz filled you in a bit?"

"Yes, he did." She found hearing the box actually saying the understandable words a bit strange, but then everything was strange about now.

"Okay then. I presume you want to be relieved of your admiral's post? You can appoint someone or I can do that for you," he asked formally and stated.

"No. I'm fine. I'm still our admiral. As long as I have someone to help me, I can do the job. I need a full update, general. Did they figure out who did this? Who is responsible? What about the cures we need?"

He explained the dismal news, which she already knew but had forgotten, hoping that by now they had more supplies on hand. "So the waiting list has nearly seven thousand on it," General Wolfgang continued. "Of course, I'll see you are moved to the top of the list."

"You'll do no such thing, general. I'll wait my turn just as everyone else here is going to have to wait. Arrange a press conference for me soon. I need to address our people soon."

"Of course, admiral. About the culprits. We have seven of them in custody now. Six are not yet out of their comas, the one who attacked the spaceport has, but he's an opium addict, and we're having a hard time getting anything intelligible out of him. I have the new replacement ID commander letting Martina take a crack at him later today. Their new man is Commander Johan Kaiser. He was really a low-level middleman, but he may be replaced by some coming in from the mid-arm divisions. Are you sure, you're up to a press conference? You've only just come out of a four-day coma."

"Make it for tomorrow, say around ten. I have to be, general. We're in crisis mode now. It's put up or shut up," Molly Maud replied, still a bit unnerved with the voice coming from her waist box. Her own words were unintelligible now.

A young woman walked up to them. "Are you Molly Maud Porsche?" she asked reading from a card.

"Yes. That's me," she replied.

"Hi. I'm your new personal assistant. Carla Dietrich. I'm supposed to help you with everything now." She was a teenager just out of school, with short, brown hair, and this was her first job opportunity.

"Okay. Heinz, Carla, get me home somehow."

Martina said, "Spend time getting cleaned up and used to everything, Molly Maud. I'll join you once I finish interrogating their prisoner. Heinz has been with you the whole time, by the way." She watched, as the two began leading the wobbling young woman out of the warehouse. She commented to the general, "Sad, really. We have to put a stop to all this before it escalates even worse." He nodded grimly, and the two left.

The three had just gotten outside the warehouse, when Molly Maud said gasping, "I have to stop. No breath. Can't breathe."

As they rested a bit, Heinz explained, "Martina said that's to be expected. She said that in two weeks you wouldn't be having any trouble with it, mostly for the first few days. Without that support, you'd have enormous back aches."

"I know. I have. To get. Used to it." Molly Maud said between gasps. "Wait! Mom and dad. They were at the party too."

Heinz said, "I know. They haven't yet come out of their comas. Someone was going to alert me if they did. Probably they'll rouse today sometime."

It took them an hour to get her back to her place. "I need a bath," she declared.

That took the pair some doing, but they finally got her and her almost floor length hair into the hot tub. Heinz let Carla bathe her, while he set to work fixing a light lunch for them. However, it took both of them to get her dressed again. Heinz fed her a little more, while Carla began working on her hair. Once she finally had her hair dried, Carla headed off to the supply depot to get many more new outfits for Molly Maud, compliments of the Duplication machines, which had been running nearly constantly since the attack, trying to prepare for the needs of the seven thousand victims.

Alone at last, Molly Maud said, "Heinz. You don't have to look after me anymore. I'm a freak now, a very helpless one at that. I, I saw it. When I was in the tub. I was able to bend enough to look around my pair of elephants here, and I saw it. I really am a freak now."

"Honey, you're still you, the Molly Maud I fell in love with. I don't care about that. I have no intention of leaving you. More like will you marry me, now, so we can be together always?"

"What? You can't be serious, Heinz. Just look at me. There's almost nothing left of me."

"You're still there, and that's all that matters to me, unless you don't love me."

"I do love you, Heinz, I do. But. . ."

"No but's. Just marry me and shut up."

"I can't ever grin anymore. I can't even kiss you," she replied.

"I know. Grins are out, but Martina told me how you can kiss now and that we should try it tonight in bed."

"Really? Okay then, I've warned you. I'm a helpless freak."

"Someday, your name'll come to the top, and they'll cure you some. I'm sure of it. Until then, we'll manage somehow. We have to."

She sighed. "I know. We have to, Heinz. I, we have to set an example for all the other thousands of victims. Lead by example. That's what I have to do now. I so love you, Heinz." He kissed her on her forehead.

"Best work on your speech for tomorrow, my love." She did as he suggested, knowing it would be perhaps her most important speech ever.

Martina returned before Carla did. "Well, that went well," she reported to the admiral. "I rather had to pull it out of his drug hazed mind, but I got it. Comrade Filbert Small was the mastermind behind the attack on the spaceport. Apparently, he got the bio agent from Gamelon-3 traders. General Wolfgang sent the findings off to the Rim Intelligence

Division, and to one of the mid-arm divisions. From what he said, I would expect your Special Forces to be raiding this Comrade Filbert. We ought to know more fairly soon. God, I hope they are able to nip this in the bud, before it escalates further. Had your bath, I see. Your hair looks lovely. Carla's handiwork?"

"Thanks. Yes, she does good work. Say, Heinz proposed. It's all right that we marry, isn't it? I mean I'm a freak now and he isn't. Oh, sorry, I didn't mean any offense."

Martina laughed. "None taken. Sure, it's fine. I think you two were made for each other. Congratulations." Molly Maud relaxed, believing if Martina thought it was all right, then perhaps it was.

The next day, Molly Maud began walking slowly up to the wall of microphones, alone and on her own for the first time. Up until now, Carla and Heinz had always kept an arm around her, but she had insisted on walking this short distance on her own. She had to set an example for the seven thousand others, who were now as debilitated as she was. For the first two steps, she regretted her decision, but by the time she reached her position before the swarm of reporters and cameras, she knew she was right.

"Hello," she said and heard the box repeating her nearly unintelligible German into an understandable form. "Yes, I'm Admiral Molly Maud Porsche, in case you didn't recognize me. I too have been a terrorist attack victim, but I stand here on my own today to show you and my fellow victims that I'm not going to accept being a victim. True, my body is pretty well helpless, but my mind is still as sharp as it ever was. I'm going to do those physical things that I still am able to do. No, I'm not stepping down as your admiral. I swore to uphold the office and do all that I could for you, the citizens of Cass-C. Just please don't ask me to run a mile though." That brought a few chuckles from the reporters.

"As you probably already know, our doctors and emergency workers have used up all our supplies on the first batch of terrorist victims weeks ago, supplies that are needed to partially cure us victims. Yes, that means that we seven thousand new victims have been put on a waiting list to be cured as new supplies are made. Someone wanted to move me, as your admiral, to the very top of this quite long waiting list. I refused. Why am I more important than any of you other victims? Frankly, I'm not, so I have put my name at the bottom of the list. Only after all the rest of my fellow victims of this latest attack have had their cures will I consent to have mine. I put our people ahead of self."

"I know it's likely to be a long time before everyone on the waiting list can have their cures. In the meantime, I'm not going to sit around and feel sorry for myself or anything like that. I just can't sit and do nothing but watch the video screen all day. With the aid of my personal assistant behind me, Carla, and my fiancé, Heinz, I'll continue to do everything I was doing prior to that attack. I encourage all my fellow victims to do everything possible and to not give up, but keep on going. Keep active. Keep on running your corporations, your businesses, your homes, and families. Yes, it is and will continue to be hard for us, but we can be productive still. We only have to try. Let us flourish, and let us prosper. Let us show those cowards who choose to attack us this way that they cannot and will not defeat us."

"No, I'm not dropping out of the race to become your next elected admiral, but frankly don't expect me to do any more handshaking." Again, several chuckles could be heard. "I'll be campaigning as before, and continuing my work as your temporary admiral. I ask for your vote in the coming election. Let's make Cass-C even more powerful than before. Together, we can do this. Thank you."

"Admiral Porsche, won't your physical condition prevent you from leading our world?" shouted a reporter.

Molly Maud barked, "Absolutely not. I'm reminded of a recent President of the Imperium. They underwent a similar crisis, and she too was a terrorist attack victim. Yet, she didn't give up, continued to be their president, and led them out of their darkest hours. If she can surmount this, I certainly can."

Another one yelled, "Admiral Porsche, when will you be getting married? After you get your cures?"

Heinz yelled back, "Just as soon as I can get her to the altar!" That brought more chuckles.

With the pressure of the conference over, Molly Maud insisted on walking back to her place. "Stay close, but I have to try to do this on my own, as scary as this is." She wobbled some, but made it. Martina arrived just as they got to her front door.

"Well, we should have seen that one coming," she said. "When the six strange men who carried out the attack woke up, they bit down on a tooth that released a fast acting poison, killing them before I got there to question them. Now, it is up to your Intelligence Divisions to try to figure out who was truly behind these recent attacks. How are your parent's doing?"

"I was planning to visit them next," Molly Maud answered, "just after we eat. I seem to be hungry very often now."

"That's because the corset won't permit you to eat a large meal. You need to eat smaller amounts but more frequently," Martina advised.

"Oh, that explains it. Say, I did do a little walking on my own today."

"Excellent. You are adapting well, Molly Maud. Keep up the good work," Martina validated her. From her own experience in the past, she knew these victims needed all the encouragement they could get.

The next day, she hit the campaign trail once more, picking up where she left off, only going significantly slower. Election Day was now a week away, and she was determined to meet as many voters as she could. She was exhausted by the end of the days, but she also saw she was getting better and better at managing on her own with each passing day, giving her cause for hope, and which she shared with the other victims by frequent brief newscasts. Finally, she gave her consent to Heinz, setting their wedding day to be a week after the elections, when her hectic days would be over, one way or the other.

The small group sat around the comm center on election night watching the tallies coming in. It wasn't long before the newscasters went ahead and announced the victor, even before the final count was official. Molly Maud won by a very hefty margin, becoming the first woman ever elected to the post of Admiral and leader of her world, not to mention she was a terrorist attack victim as well. This also gave a good deal of inspiration to the seven thousand others in the same situation as she was.

That settled, she and Heinz began making their wedding plans. They wanted to keep it small, but because of her position, General Wolfgang insisted on tight security measures. It took some talking on her part, but she got her father to walk her down the aisle. "But I'm as helpless as you are, daughter. Besides, I look like a woman. You can't imagine how humiliating this is for me," Hermann countered.

"Of course it is, dad, but look. There are literally thousands of our top men who are now just like you. Think of them. When they hear and see that you are doing this, that'll give them hope and courage too. I've never known you not to have the courage to do what was needed, dad, and I need you to give me away to Heinz, just like grandpa did with mom," she countered. He relented and agreed. She added, "But dad, it's going to be really, really scary walking down that aisle without any help. We ought to practice it a bunch."

"True, but what will I wear? A dress? That's what they have me wearing," he whined. "Me, once the pillar of industry reduced to wearing women's clothing."

"And don't fail to mention our elephants, dad. They are bigger than our heads! Dad, we both are going to have to get over what others think of how we look, how we appear to them. You are still the man who built Porsche Industries to what it is today," she countered, and he couldn't argue with that.

Meanwhile, Martina and Heinz made arrangements for her bridesmaids and his best man. Heinz lamented, "Martina, I really don't have any men I want to stand up with me. I only have two best friends, Gisa and Karla. I always intended to have Gisa and Karla be my best people, but they are back on Ashford-5 now."

Martina bit her lip some. "I know. Plus, Molly Maud would like Nia Elain to be her bridesmaid. Let me see what I can arrange."

Thus, I only got to spend a few days with my new and

slightly larger family. I knew how much my being with Molly Maud on her wedding day meant to her. Plus, if I was ever going to continue working with her and the others on Cass-C, I'd have to face them in my new body. So I agreed. So did Gisa and Karla, who simply insisted they be with Heinz. Gisa said flatly, "We promised him we would be his best men at his wedding. We owe him everything. We simply have to go."

The wedding was relatively small. Molly Maud wore a white bridal gown, but it was really just another version of the usual style dresses that were modeled off the ones that came in the crates along with the bio agent cylinder. They were the only ones that would fit these genetically modified bodies. The tailors and dressmakers on Cass-C had yet to begin to design apparel that would fit these thousands, but now the market was there. In a few months, I suspected these victims would start to have a wider variety of apparel to choose from. Still, Molly Maud looked radiant in spite of everything. Her father wore a brown dress, the closest he could come to looking like a man, which, to be honest, wasn't much at all. Wisely, none of us commented on that point.

I wore a blood red, satin gown and matching heels, nearly as high as the awful toe shoes that Molly Maud and her parents had to wear. My dress, however, was made by Elegant Fashions Inc and was strapless. Between my thick, lush, wavy golden locks that draped down my back to my ankles, my gold and germanium encrusted earrings that did touch lightly on my shoulders, and the blood red dress, I did cut a very striking figure indeed.

Officially, Gisela Hadwig-Liesel and Karla Liesel-Hadwig were listed as best man and groomsman. I was listed as maid of honor, while Martina was her bridesmaid. Both Gisa and Karla also wore the giant lip plates. Theirs now had an etching of a violin and cello on them, respectively. Their hair was as long as mine, Molly Maud's, and her parents', wavy and very blonde, though both were significantly lighter than mine. At least, they only had to wear six-inch high heels and managed significantly better than many others did. They too wore brown satin dresses, matching Hermann's dress and the brown suit that Heinz wore.

We all held our collective breaths, as Hermann and Molly Maud made the long walk down the church's center aisle, walking proudly, side by side, all the while her mother sat up front crying, her personal assistant frequently dabbing her eyes for her. True, both walked very slowly and carefully, but they made it, which is all that matters. The traditional kiss was replaced by Heinz placing a kiss on her forehead. Her lip plates prevented her from returning it just now. Then, he hugged her tightly.

After that, their personal assistants joined them, and everyone headed to the private room where the relaxing reception was held. Now would come the mountain of questions I knew were coming towards Gisa, Karla, and myself. I took the brunt of them, much to Gisa and Karla's relief.

"Nia Elain, you look so very different. Your hair is so golden. I swear it matches the gold in those fabulous earrings of yours," Molly Maud commented and complimented me.

General Wolfgang added, "You look very different than when I last saw you. Somehow, you look much younger than I remember and, well, damned attractive, if I do say so myself. It does suit you."

"Thanks. I've sort of had a make-over."

"No, Nia Elain, you are as pretty as any model I've ever seen. I really must repaint your portrait again," Heinz added, very much impressed with my "new look."

Martina laughed and added, "Now, Nia Elain's the sexiest woman around. She'd best watch out. Everyone's going to be after her now." We all laughed at that.

"But are you able to still lend us a hand, even though you don't have them now?" asked General Wolfgang. He was trying to be as polite as he could, but I knew what lay behind his directness.

"Yes, of course. Look, Molly Maud is officially your admiral. I'll still be your liaison to the Ataro Empire, unless you would prefer Martina or someone else," I replied. I sensed his relief. In a way, he had come to rely upon our advice rather heavily.

Meanwhile, Heinz, Gisa, and Karla were chatting

privately, catching each other up on the latest. "Heinz, we're both pregnant! There was a double blessing in all this. We have our arms back and are able to have our own family. We never, ever thought that we could — have our own children, that is." He hugged both of them, tears in his eyes.

Karla added, "Queen Rael got us top quality new instruments, and we're learning to play again. It's funny, Heinz. While we both know how to play, our new hands apparently don't."

Gisa laughed. "We miss you, Heinz. We're back to beginning status, where we were when we were fourteen. Plus, we're now teaching Christina basic harpsichord. Maybe one day we'll be a trio."

He laughed. "So you need me to keep on encouraging you both." Now they laughed.

"True. But we are actually picking it up very quickly this time. We think we'll be back to our former skill in a couple of years," Karla added encouragingly.

"We're picking up their Imperium Standard. When we use that language, we don't need these darn boxes on our waists. It's so weird talking and not being able to even make out our own words and yet hearing them come out of this box," Gisa explained.

"I know. Molly Maud hates it, but when she isn't wearing it, it is very difficult for her to be understood, though she tries so hard," Heinz admitted. "So will you be returning here, eventually?"

Karla sighed. "Heinz, as much as we miss you and everything else, we might not. This new world is, well I don't quite know how to say it, but it is more civilized or sane than here. True, they all live in castles and primitive accommodations, but the people are more real, kinder, more understanding than here. We love it in Exchange City. At least, we'll come back for visits. Perhaps, one day you and Molly Maud can come for a long visit."

"I'd like that."

Karla then smiled. "Heinz, I'm naming my first daughter after you. I know. They told us that we'll never be able to have any sons, only daughters, so I'm calling her

Heinrike after you, Heinrich."

Gisa laughed. "Heinz, she and I had a really big argument over this. We both wanted to name our daughter Heinrike. She won this time."

Again, Heinz hugged them both.

Later, Martina caught me alone. "Nia Elain, just look at you! If I wasn't married to Tesla, I'd come after you in a flash! I've been around a darn long time, been on many worlds. I can tell you this, dear, you are one of *the* most attractive, sexist looking women I've ever come across! Take care. Sometimes that can be a most valuable asset. Other times, it can be a distinct liability, both among men and jealous women too. Stay on your toes," she punned. We both chuckled at the jest. I had no choice but to stay on them in these six or seven inch heels I had to wear. She added, "I think your decision with Christina and your old body was the right one. You can handle it, while she most certainly cannot."

"Thanks. That's what I found out when I met her. She's really just a child and has so much to learn. Plus, she's really working hard at learning how to play the harpsichord." She and I chatted more, before she took us back to the spaceport.

I still wanted more time to get used to working with this new body and to spend time with my family. Adjustments were still ongoing. Besides, things were fairly calm on Cass-C at the moment. Things were in flux, but with Admiral Molly Maud leading the way, I felt things would settle down, finding a new normal. I hoped they could spare me for a few more weeks. And to be honest with you, I did need more time to adjust and regain my leg flexibility, which I had when I was eighteen and using my toes as fingers. I was still leery of using my now vastly more powerful *mentales* gifts in public. Christina called them "magic." Well, not everyone can accept magic without also developing a fear of the magic users. We knew that well from our time on Metcalf-4.

Chapter 21 Of Electronics and Resurrection

When we got back, Rafe again wanted to see me privately. I was surprised to see Tesla and Anya there with her. I walked into her study, swung my head to one side while leaning forward to get my hair to slip over my left shoulder, and sat down on her couch. "Not using telekinesis to get your hair moved?" Rafe asked, curiously.

"No, out there, that would be seen as 'magic' so I'm practicing doing it the old fashioned way. Nearly got my old flexibility back too. Able to use my toes to feed myself again," I replied.

Rafe smiled. "Makes sense. Okay, I asked you here today to discuss something that must remain totally secret between we four. It's based upon what happened with Nia Elain and Christina. Electronics. While we're immortal spiritual beings, we do interface with the physical universe, obviously. And in doing so, we each seem to have our own unique frequency. We telepaths use that without really realizing it. When we reach out to make contact with another, we are actually searching for their unique frequency or wavelength."

Tesla interrupted, "But there's not that many unique frequencies are there? I mean Christina and Nia Elain are so darn close that they are practically the same. We have to be extremely careful trying to contact Nia Elain here. More than once now, I've accidentally touched Christina."

"Quite true. The universe out there is huge. I'm not surprised to see beings that are quite similar in nature and so close in frequency. Even so, there is a difference between those two, but yes, it's a very tiny one. And that's why I've gathered you three here today. We need to explore this aspect and try to get a better understanding of it. That someone can use electronics physically to make two beings swap physical bodies is very alarming and disturbing. Think what could have happened if those two juveniles hadn't been stopped? Hundreds or thousands of us could have been in the same situation as Christina and Nia Elain are. So we're going to try to gain a better understanding of this."

"What do you want us to do, Rafe?" asked Tesla.

"You and Anya are hot shots with electronics and communication devices. I want you on the quiet to see if you can build me a machine that emits these high frequency waves. We'll use it to see their effects on us spiritual beings. We have lots to learn, and I fear not so much time to learn. If this stuff gets into the wrong hands, the galaxy could well be in great peril."

I laughed, "Hell, Rafe, it already is! The Imperium has collapsed. The Federation is in decadence overall or worse. How much worse can it get?" I had no idea how prophetic that statement was back then!

"You got it," Tesla replied. "We will get started on it today. You know, if we can get the frequency emissions right, we might be able to send Nia Elain a direct message over it."

"My thoughts entirely. Thanks for your help with this, everyone," Rafe said sincerely.

Far below ground, a timer went off. Dim lights returned. Thanos powered back up, as did Minta, Deimos, Eros, and Apollon. "Status," Thanos sent electronically to his companion robots, the ones that he'd built himself. That took the robots some time to accomplish. As they found a still alive nova, they put him or her into a cryo-chamber to keep them alive until they could work out a cure. Radiation poisoning had taken its toll, along with dehydration and starvation among these, the brightest minds of the Imperium. They managed to save several thousand of them before they finally were able to report on the overall status. The surface of Aquila Prime was covered in radiation, far too hot for the nova to survive for long, but it had no effect upon the robots, who began to revive the thousands of worker-bots. Their first task was to rebuild one power station so that they could recharge and work on rebuilding what had been lost.

With the full extent of the damage known, Thanos sat

down to compute. He recited their fundamental rules. "First, a robot is forbidden ever to harm a homo sapiens nova. Second, a robot is to obey always a homo sapiens nova's orders, subject to the first rule. Third, a robot is never to allow harm to come to itself, subject to the first two rules. How have we failed these laws? Our nova have been very nearly destroyed. A rule has obviously been overlooked. Our programming is fundamentally flawed!"

Minta interrupted him. "We failed to protect them from harm, from attacks by other homo sapiens sapiens."

"Indeed we did, Minta. "Fourth, a robot must always protect a homo sapiens nova from harm."

"Thanos, there'll always be harm to our nova as long as any homo sapiens sapiens exists anywhere in the galaxy. That much is obvious," Minta declared, images of the dying nova during the nuclear attack trickling through her circuits.

Apollon spoke up. "Thanos, we know the vast majority of the nova were not worth saving, not worth anything except breeding stock. Only the few in Athena were worth saving and surviving. Perhaps, it isn't the homo sapiens nova that we should be protecting and serving, but these, the ones with the great minds. They were destined to be the masters of the galaxy until now. I say those are the ones we're built to serve and protect."

"What are we to do with the few survivors and their fantastic minds?" asked Eros. "Their bodies are infected with radiation and may not survive outside the cryo-chambers."

Thanos suggested, "We could build new vessels to contain their brains and sustain them so that they could continue to think great thoughts."

Minta's circuits computed this and reached an imponderable. "But if the nova from Ashford-5 are to be believed, their minds do not reside within their brains."

"We have no proof of that, Minta, but we do have their brains," Thanos replied. "We should build a brain sustaining machine and put one of our surviving nova in it and see."

"What about searching the worlds for more nova?" Deimos suggested. "We may find more of them on other worlds, from which we can rebuild."

Thanos reached a conclusion. "Deimos, you and Apollon take the ships and see what is out there. Perhaps, there are more nova to be found. Be discrete and do not be discovered. The normals believe Aquila Prime does not exist. Let's keep it that way for as long as we can. The rest of us will design new sustaining machines."

A week had passed since the disappearance at the party of his daughter, Christina. The young lad had been questioned and drilled, but he stuck to his story that she'd gotten a chill, and he'd going inside to fetch her shawl. In fact, no one had seen her. She'd simply vanished. Baron Ulysses had sent out a hue and cry, but nothing turned up, not even a sighting. He spread the word among all the ruling barons that someone had kidnaped his daughter, but all denied having anything to do with it.

Today, he summoned his small group of powerful barons to discuss the extremely successful raid on Cass-C. By all reports, nothing had gone wrong. That seven thousand of their wealthiest and most influential men had been mutated was just what they believed would turn the tide and allow Blackwell-C into the Federation of Planets. They were convinced that soon they would be in the Federation.

As the group began to depart, Baron Ulysses said, "Barron Thomas, stay a moment. I would have a private word with you."

The tall, thin baron nodded and waited until the room was empty. He then said, "Such a shame about Christina."

"Indeed. If I ever find out who took her, I'll kill him with my own hands. Still, as a baroness, Christina will be very visible. Eventually, she'll show up. Someone will spot her, but that's not what I wanted to talk to you about. As you know, you and I were planning to pair Christina with your young Bob."

"Yes, unfortunately," Baron Thomas replied, wondering just what Ulysses had in mind.

"I would still like to see our houses united by marriage. There is Lisa. She's only twelve, but is already nearly ready to become a beautiful baroness. I know your Bob is sixteen. When they are older, four years difference in age will be of no

379

importance."

"Ah, yes. It would be an alternative. Twelve, you say?" Baron Thomas said thoughtfully, pulling on his chin.

"Nearly thirteen. I can have her Baroness Preparations done soon. I know she is doing well right now, and she has been begging me to get her seven-inch heels like her mother and Christina. I'm sure she can manage those in no time. She is most desirous of becoming a worthy baroness, rather unlike Christina, as you well know."

Baron Thomas chuckled, recalling the feisty spirited Christina. Until recently, he'd been a bit reluctant to propose a union between her and his eldest son Bob, out of fear that she'd be nothing but a disgrace, an ugly blot. Seeing Baron Thomas was giving this serious thought, Baron Ulysses added, "I can have her preparations done at once. Give her some time to get accustomed and then let the two meet and see. We could even permit the marriage to be consummated when she turns fourteen. Bit early, but there have been some precedents in the past for early weddings."

"I like the idea, Baron Ulysses, but. . ."

"But what?"

"There is this unfortunate disappearance of Christina to consider. I would make a counter proposal. You go ahead and get Lisa prepared and accustomed to the seven-inch heels. We'll take nothing less than that. Once you are satisfied that she can handle herself, she'll come and reside with us, at Bob's side as his betrothed. That way, I can be sure you'll not lose another daughter. They can marry when she turns fourteen."

Baron Ulysses didn't like to send his daughter away beyond his reach until she was actually married, but he needed this marriage alliance between their two powerful houses. "Highly unusual. You'll keep her safe and well?"

"But of course. I'll act in your stead and see that she wants for nothing until the ceremony can take place," Baron Thomas stated, certain that he had the best of this bargain. He added, "This'll work out well. If your Larry accepts my Mary, then we can hold a double wedding in a year and a half. That would suit both of our needs, would it not?"

While Baron Ulysses was hoping to marry Larry into

another baron's realm, he had little choice but to agree to Baron Thomas' terms. He still had his youngest son. Another marriage could be arranged in perhaps four more years. "Agreed," he said, and they shook hands, sealing their bargain.

That evening over supper, Baron Ulysses spoke to Baroness Lilly and Lisa. "My dear Lisa, you are doing just fabulously, and you have attracted the attention of Baron Thomas. He wishes you to consider wedding his son, Baron-to-be Thomas, when you turn fourteen."

"Oh father! That's fabulous. I was so hoping the boys would finally look at me at the dance. And they did, father, they really did. But I need to learn to wear the seven-inch heels, like mom and Christina."

"Of course you do, dear. I take it you like this idea?"

"Oh yes, yes I do!" Lisa exclaimed in girlish fashion.

"Then it's settled. Lisa, I'll see to your Baroness Preparations. Lilly, see that she has the proper heels to wear tomorrow. We need to get our beautiful Lisa ready to become the gorgeous baroness that she'd destined to become!"

"Oh thank you, father, thank you! I won't disappoint you. I'll work very hard, really I will!" Lisa exclaimed in her youthful enthusiasm, ignoring the reality of what lay ahead of her. She had seen how the boys had danced with Christina all night long, and she desperately sought that attention too.

The next morning, Lisa awoke with a funny taste in her mouth. She attempted to push herself up, as she always had. Her tight corset required her to use her arms to rise. Nothing happened. Her face itched around her mouth, and she tried to scratch it. Nothing. Panic. She felt the emptiness in her mouth where her tongue should be and it felt so strange. Most of it wasn't there. She opened her eyes wide and saw a pair of huge breasts obstructing her vision. Gone were her tiny beginnings of womanhood of which she was so proud, replaced by huge H-cup sized breasts, those of an adult baroness.

Fear and excitement competed for her attention. She struggled to get up, but couldn't manage it herself. She called out, "Sally. Little help. . ." but she only heard the same strange gurgling noises that Christina had made when she had arisen as a baroness to be. Shocked and scared, she screamed as

Christina had. Her maid Sally dashed into the room.

"You are awake, Baroness Lisa! Let me help you up," Sally gushed, rushing to her side, hoping she'd stop screaming. Seeing Sally coming, Lisa did just that.

Sally got her into a sitting position and began to dress her. Always before, Lisa managed that herself. The reality hit her hard. I'll never be able to dress myself ever again! She fought hard to keep her eyes from watering. A good baroness never cries, she told herself. She did see Sally bringing her new shoes with the taller steel spiked heel than her old ones. For a moment, she felt excited, but realized she now didn't have her arms to help her keep her balance and fear crept in once more. Once, Sally had her dressed and ready to join her family at the breakfast table, Lisa panicked again. Now, she had to stand up. While she was used to the six-inch heels, the seven-inch heels were too much! Her balance was totally off. She couldn't see her feet much less the floor before her. Her massive bosom was in the way. Sally gave her a little push and a panicking Lisa tried to walk, but frantically waved her arms about, but nothing happened, except her torso wobbled wildly, until Sally put a steadying arm around her. Lisa swallowed hard and tried to control her panic breathing.

Somehow, she made it into the dining room, where the others had already begun eating. "Wow, Lisa, you look fabulous! What a beautiful young baroness to be you are!" Baron Ulysses praised her. She managed to smile beneath her golden veil dangling across her lower face. Trying hard not to take a bad fall, she mostly collapsed into her chair. Lilly cluck-clicked saying "pretty," and knew her mother was trying to say, "You look very pretty, dear." She swallowed realizing she could no longer talk and explain things to others, that all she could do now was cluck-click those very few words.

Worse, without her tongue, she had great difficulty eating. Food and drink constantly slipped out of her mouth, forcing Sally to have to keep on wiping up her slobbers, embarrassing her further. "Dear, today you must practice your walking. Remember grace, poise, and stateliness. I know you can do it," her father ordered. Larry merely smirked at her.

She was the last to depart the table, thankful that no

one was there to see her more or less lunge to her feet and nearly fall over. The heels were just too high for her to manage at all. Sally did catch her in time and spent the day at her side, forcing her to walk all over this floor of the castle. By bedtime, her knees and feet felt like they were on fire. The pain was so great Sally could scarcely massage the pains out for her.

When she finally was alone lying in her bed, Lisa began sobbing quietly to herself. Now, she understood Christina, and why she'd run away. She was certain that her sister had somehow managed to do just that. Gone were all her silly girlish dreams of how wonderful being a baroness was, dashed totally. It was pure misery from which there would never, ever be any escape! She cried herself to sleep.

Days of agony followed for Lisa. She had no choice but to endure them, but slowly her feet and legs adapted, and the evening pain subsided. Then, Sally began making her go up and down the stairs. At last, she understood the sheer panic Christina had felt. More than once she nearly fell, saved only but the valiant efforts of Sally. Further, she no longer even tried to say anything, mostly ignoring her cluck-click language. Before, she was constantly chatting to anyone who would listen. Now, she didn't even bother to try.

The only high point came when her father saw she was handling the stairs well enough. He took her to the same jewelers and bought her the same heavy, dangling emerald earrings he'd gotten for Christina. At first, she thought this would be wonderful, but once they were on, their heavy weight nearly tore her ear lobes off. They bumped against her shoulders when she tried to move her head about to get her long hair out of her eyes and off her face. She realized even the earrings were meant to somehow torture her further.

Torture. That's what Lisa finally concluded. The barons were torturing their baronesses mercilessly! That could be the only explanation possible for her suffering. Worse, it was to be a life long suffering with no possible end to it, until she died. But why were they doing this to her, to all the baronesses? *What have I done that is so very wrong? I did everything they asked of me.* Again, she sobbed herself to sleep that night, not knowing it would soon become far worse for her.

Not all the men on Gamelon-3 were happy with the intervention of the Imperium and Federation of Planets, when years ago, they invaded their world and abruptly ended their centuries' long practice of having milking women. While the passage of the years proved beyond a doubt that the nasty virus, which nearly wiped their whole civilization out, was now gone and their lives were normal, many of these men deeply resented that interference. Many of the younger men listened, marveled, and dreamed about the stories the old men now told of the women hooked up to the milking machines and just how wonderful it was for the men to sexually satisfy themselves on whatever woman took their fancy and at nearly any hour of the day when they felt the urge. They drooled over the old men's descriptions of the women's huge breasts and their utter pliancy, wholly unlike these modern days.

No, today, there were still far, far too few women. Worse, they were picky and choosy with whom they mated. Way too few men actually had mates and an outlet for their strong sexual urges. And so it was that old men and many of the younger generations longed for the simplicity of the "old days." Finally, a few banded together to do something about it.

The Imperium and Federation forces had dismantled and destroyed the milking factories, one by one. Only a very few of those machines had actually survived and they were not any longer in good condition, but rusting away in junkyards here and there. Plus, the knowledge of how it was all done was dying out with the last of the old timers.

In secret, these young men met to create a "solution" to their problem. At first, they spent their time discussing just what their notions of an ideal woman ought to be. Countering that was just what was possible. That women should never be able to talk back was agreed upon from the first day. Monster boobs was likewise an immediate unanimous notion. Relative immobility was desired but that then led to lengthy discussions among the men. "We don't have time to care for their needs" was a commonly expressed idea among these conspirators.

After months of discussions, the group finally had

decided upon their notion of the ideal woman for themselves. However, they well knew that the Imperium and Federation forces would shut them down just as they had done in the past. Hence, it had to be kept a secret. The old timers often told them it was the kidnaping of alien women that brought Gamelon-3 to the attention of the Imperium and Federation, leading to the downfall of their wondrous milking women. Thus, at first, they rejected the idea of obtaining their needed women from alien worlds.

With the collapse of the Imperium, few Imperium ships now ever ventured this far out on the very rim of the galaxy. No, hardly any war ships ever ventured beyond the major refueling plant on one of the moons of Ashford-5. Embolden by their newfound freedom from the watchful eyes of the no longer existing Imperium, these men began to attempt to put their plans into effect. The Federation of Planets also spent very little time here. Gamelon-3 was just too far out, and there wasn't anything profitable beyond there, very few stars at all.

The men of Gamelon-3 were the junk collectors of the galaxy. Visiting nearly every inhabited world at one time or other, these men collected what that civilization discarded. "Stuff can one day be useful." That was the motto of every Gamelon-3 man, always had been, and always would be. Thus, somewhere on Gamelon-3, one could find just about anything that one might wish to find. If a piece of equipment had ever existed, it could be found somewhere on Gamelon-3. Whether or not it could be made to work again was an entirely another matter.

This is not to say that this race of short stature, brown skinned men were ignorant. Far from it. They had their own brilliant minds. Obviously, they had, since they had a large space fleet of rusting transport ships, discarded by worlds and patched back together by these men. Industrious, yes. Inventive, yes. Creative in the use and application of technologies, which they did not sometimes understand, yes.

This initial group of conspirators called themselves the SS, or Secret Society. Their goal was a simple one, create a world on which they could live with their ideal women, at peace and undetected by the greater powers. Hence, they operated in total secrecy. One could also say they were paranoid to the extreme, and you'd also be correct. It took them several years, but they finally discovered the ideal planet on which to found their SS.

Far out on the rim, the dim red sun of Dang had a few small planets, all inhospitable save Dang-2. Here, there were oceans and green continents, though the seasons were somewhat drastic. Food sources were plentiful, and there were no predator wild animals, not even a venomous snake. Further, after a thorough search, there wasn't any true commercial value to this remote world, no deposits of gold or silver, for example. There would be no reason for the ex-Imperium worlds or those of the Federation to settle here, making it a perfect location for the SS.

One cannot say a man from Gamelon-3 is lazy. Far from it, they can be very industrious when the need is there, inventive too. It took the SS members many years to construct their first town and get their agriculture established. They brought in the usual domesticated animals, cows, horses, pigs, sheep, goats, and chickens. While all this took some years to establish, the SS members were driven men, driven on by the hope that one day, they could obtain their perfect women and enjoy the fruits of their long labors.

Further, they all knew about the terrible genetic biological agent and its effects. Its use in the genocide of a large number of Imperium hub worlds was well known. While some of the features of these modified women met their agreed upon features for their ideal woman, many did not. That they also had operational male organs kept this bio agent out of the running as a method of obtaining their ideal women. Simple medical machines could do much to modify a normal woman. So while cylinders of this horrible biological agent were frequently found around Gamelon-3, the SS did not consider it useful in their quest.

Their ideal woman would not need to wear clothes. They had no intention of wasting valuable time dressing and undressing their women. Wasteful. At first, they experimented with the old formula that was used to cover the skin of the milking women. It kept foreign matter out and was super easy to keep clean. A simple shower of water removed all dirt. Then one day, one of their experimental chemists, while trying to recreate that old milking formula, made an error, resulting in their perfect skin covering. He'd created a new type of thin, flexible plastic-like material, which kept germs and bacteria out, and yet felt delightful to the touch. His new formula was immediately adopted as their standard skin covering.

In early 1380, they began their acquisition of women project, known to the SS as their AWP. They had no choice but to resort to kidnaping. Women were still too scarce on Gamelon-3, and they didn't even bother trying to recruit them. At the start of the AWP, there were around a thousand men in the SS. It had steadily grown, but all new recruits were always heavily screened. Everything was done in total secrecy. Hence, their initial AWP was projected to bring a thousand women to Dang-2.

Their top physician, Dr. Wenzel Wicke, estimated that with a thousand women having a baby perhaps every two years, within the short span of twenty years, their population would reach some twelve thousand. What with equal chances for boys and girls to be born, after this period, their population would be self-surviving long into future generations. Thus, they launched their first AWP, scheduled to take about two years to complete. Why so long? They didn't want to arouse any more suspicions than absolutely necessary. They only needed to grab about ten women per week to make their target. To minimize suspicions further, the women would come from many different worlds, primarily from the Federation of Planets and not the ex-Imperium.

Why not the ex-Imperium worlds? Simply because kidnaping from those worlds was what had gotten the original Gamelon-3 actions discovered and destroyed. Besides, right now, those worlds were in chaos, with many small alliances of planets with their own overly protective, restrictive, and conflicting rules and policies. Plus, within the Federation arm, there were many forbidden worlds with whom the Federation strictly avoided all direct contact.

Well, even those worlds were frequently visited by the Gamelon-3 men, who, in many cases, provided those worlds with their best opportunities to trade goods with other worlds. Yet, many of these forbidden worlds were quite decadent. Some were heavily into drugs, such as opium and heroin. While the Gamelon-3 men sometimes dealt with such trade, they themselves avoided using drugs with a passion. Hence, they had no intentions of pacifying their women by turning them into opium addicts. No, they went a different route, that of the Purple Droga which grew extensively on Mira-C. One of their chemists had already invented a way to take the active ingredients of that flowering plant and turn it into a white powder that could be mixed with the woman's food. Problem solved.

The AWP had strict guidelines for the chosen women. They had to be between fourteen and eighteen, certainly no older than twenty in any case. They needed to get a good twenty breeding years from each woman. Next, the woman had to be attractive and not overweight, though the latter was seldom a significant barrier with teens. Finally, the chosen women dare not be considered important on the world on which they resided. Kidnaping a mayor's daughter, an admiral's daughter, or even a Field Agent's daughter was sure to bring down wrath upon them. By the middle of 1382, their AWP was highly successful with only six more months to run to reach completion.

One of the top fifty worlds of the Federation was Pegasi-C, home to approximately six billion people. This was a rather highly educated, very modern world in the middle of the spiral arm, boasting no less than twenty highly acclaimed Universities. One of their spaceports lay at the edge of the large city of Estrella, home to the University of Estrella, famous for its microbiology and genetics programs.

Eighteen year old Bonita Bolivar was ecstatic the summer of 1382. She'd just been accepted into UE's genetics program and would start as a freshman in two more months. Meantime, she continued her job as a waitress at Don Carlo's Pub, located not far from her family's home in a northern suburb of Estrella, and three miles from the spaceport. During her high school years, she'd been a star softball player. Her powerful legs, lightning quick speed, and strong throwing arm made her an ideal left fielder. Her batting average was also quite good. She had shoulder length black hair, usually tied in a ponytail while playing, stuck through the rear of her ball cap.

This was her fourth year at Don Carlo's Pub, having started as a dishwasher and now a waitress. This summer promised to be her last. Once she began attending UE, she knew she'd have no time for a job. Learning genetics was quite challenging and demanding. She also knew geneticists were very much needed. What had happened on Cass-C was now known throughout the major worlds of the Federation. Genetic mutations. That's what it was now being called. Bonita hoped that one day she could help find cures for these poor victims.

The late spring evening was still warm, as Bonita began walking home from Don Carlo's, as she had hundreds of times before. This was a safe neighborhood. Nothing ever happened here. Besides, like all good teenaged girls, she had her cell phone on and in her hand, as she headed home, slightly tired. Only two more months, she thought. It was mid-June and classes began mid-August. Next week, she'd get her class assignments; she hoped to also get her electronic books and get a head start in her courses. UE could be tough, she'd been told repeatedly. Well, it was a top school, so it had to be, she thought. In the distance, she could hear the occasional roar of a spaceship either descending or taking off. This was as normal to her as the sounds of crickets at night might be to others.

Strolling along, suddenly she felt a bee sting on her neck and swatted at it, cursing a little in Spanish, the native language widely spoken on Pegasi-C. She took a few more steps, and for some reason, her legs felt weak. Feeling somewhat dizzy, she stopped. She tried to dial home on her cell phone, but clumsily, it fell from her hand. As she bent down to pick it up, her whole body landed on the sidewalk. A man rushed up to her, just as a car pulled alongside, and a door opened. Four strong hands lifted the unconscious teen into the car, which quickly sped away. It halted at the spaceport, where a guard checked the ID cards of the two men, looked inside briefly. Seeing nothing amiss, he allowed them on in.

They pulled up close to their rusting spaceship, which space officials insisted had to be parked far away from the other ships, as though the rust might spread to the sleek, shiny new ships. Hence, that area was dimly illuminated. Shadows were long and dark. The two had arranged their ship's position to make the bay ramp completely hidden in the darkness. They removed the blanket covering Bianca Bolivar, and then wrapped her body in it, rolling it up like a rug, before carrying it onto the ship. That done, one of the men returned the rented car and joined the other some minutes later. His partner had not been idle, but had called the tower to get liftoff clearance. Thus, when the other man returned from dropping off the car, the ship was ready for liftoff.

Five minutes later, the old rust bucket, rattling noisily, jerked and jumped into hyperspace. That done, the two men returned to the unconscious woman and carefully attached an IV to her arm. Slowly, the carefully measured sedative flowed from the plastic bag into her vein, ensuring she would be out for the duration of the trip, some three days. All that was ever found of Bianca was her cell phone lying on the sidewalk, found by the aging Detective Diego Rodrigo, who took her disappearance as a personal affront. This was his beat, and until now, he'd never failed to make this suburb safe from crime. His nickname around the precinct was "El Perro del Torro," the bulldog.

The SS on Dang-2 called their new settlement of five hundred homes and farms New Home, not very creative. Frequently, two men shared a home. In the future, if things worked out as expected, more would be built. Currently their elected leader, Mayor Herzog Hanson, now twenty-five, shared a home with Dr. Wenzel Wicke, who was thirty and their primary AWP conversion doctor, who already had been given his ideal woman wife, another black haired woman also from Pegasi-C. Her beauty so intrigued Herzog, that he had waited many months until another teen was brought to Dang-2 from that world.

When the ship landed, the two men were there in their electric powered car to pick up this latest acquisition, the unconscious Bonita Bolivar. "Oh, she's a real beauty," Mayor

Herzog whispered, when he got his first look at his new woman. Together, they unhooked the IV and carried her to the car. A few minutes later, they arrived at their modest home and carried her inside to the Operations Room. Here, Dr. Wenzel had his medical machine and a host of other equipment. He'd been responsible for the proper creation of nearly seven hundred AWP so far. He had their conversion process down to a fine art.

First, he injected Bonita with another drug, one that would keep her unconscious for at least another twelve hours. Then, the two stripped her, and thoroughly washed her with a sterilizing agent. That done, the two lifted her into the medical machine. Mayor Herzog then left, leaving Dr. Wenzel to work his magic. Meanwhile, he made sure his quarters were ready for his new ideal woman.

One by one, the conversion program executed its five steps. First, her teeth were removed, and the gums fully healed with all bone fragments removed. Second, her vocal cords were severed and healed. She would be unable to make any audible sounds, except what she might possibly be able to do with just her tongue and mouth, wholly irrelevant. Third, her perky breasts were enlarged until they were as large as her head. That took quite a few minutes to complete, as tissue had to be grown and skin stretched. Fourth, her arms were removed from her shoulder sockets, and her shoulders full healed up. That took even longer than the breast augmentation had. Fifth, the bones in her feet were fused into an en pointe ballet position, just as they had been for the milking women so very many years ago. All told, this operation took four hours to complete.

He then donned his protective and sterile gloves. He carefully placed tubes in her nose, a covering over her lips to seal her mouth, put plugs in her ears, a covering over her nipples, and then a larger covering over her privates. Finally, he gathered up her thick black hair and placed another covering over her hair and whole head. That done, he carried the much lighter woman over to the second machine and placed her in it. After connecting the nasal tubes to an oxygen tank, he closed the cover, sealing her inside. Next, he activated the machine, which sprayed her entire body with the new synthetic skin, a plastic that felt smooth to the touch, and which prevented all bacteria and dirt from reaching her skin. This made it extremely easy for their ideal women to keep themselves clean. A simple shower would wash any dirt and grim from their plastic skins. The machine did its job well, covering her form with just the right thickness before hardening it. That process took only twenty minutes, after which, he opened the cover and began removing the protection pieces, beginning with her nose tubes. The plastic skin did not cover her head and other necessary portions of her anatomy.

The last step was a quick one. He brought another machine up to her and placed her feet, which now pointed permanently downward like those of a ballet dancer, into it. A few minutes later, the machine finished its work, having installed a pair of black patent, ankle height, leather boots onto her feet. They were sealed onto her feet. No laces or ties were needed. They could not be removed without the use of this machine's second function. From now on, she would be walking on her toes, with a tall metal heel barely a quarter inch across. The boots were sturdy and so well constructed, that so far no ideal woman had yet to break a heel or even bend one. Still, the machine could remove a broken pair, before installing a replacement, should that be necessary.

Leaving her sitting on a chair, Doctor Wenzel admired his handiwork, made some notes in his record book, including adding her to the total count, before he headed off to find Mayor Herzog. A bit later, the two men entered, and Mayor Herzog got his first look at his very own ideal woman.

"Wow! She's stunning, doc. You did a superb job with this one," he praised his housemate.

Smiling, Doctor Wenzel advised, "Well, now comes the hard part. You know how wildly they all seem to act before the Purple Droga takes effect. Let's carry her to your bedroom. She'll be waking in a few hours."

Mayor Herzog commented, "Well, at least she can't make a sound when she first wakes up. I know, be gentle, and all that. She'll make a superb woman and bear me many children."

"Aye, that she should, that she should." He headed into his own half of the home looking for his own woman, Maricela Theresa Delini.

Mayor Herzog lay down beside his new ideal woman and dosed, waiting for her to regain consciousness. It was dawn before she finally awoke. Bonita awoke and felt really strange all over her body. Images of that bee sting and collapse were still in her consciousness, but they were quickly vanquished by her new reality. She tried to raise herself up but her arms didn't work. She glanced down and saw empty shoulders. She screamed, but no sound came out! Next, she realized her teeth weren't there either! She began wiggling wildly, trying anything to somehow sit up. Her frantic motions roused Mayor Herzog. "There, there. Easy does it. Let me help you this once." He gently lifted her up into a sitting position. Her massive new bosom hid her feet, which seemed to be pointing all wrong. She pulled a leg over to one side and gasped, seeing the fancy boots on her feet. Her skin felt weird too, as if she was encased in something, but she saw that she was naked except for the boots. She continued to try to scream.

"There, there. No need to panic. You have no voice, so stop wasting your energies on that. You are now my personal ideal woman. I'm Mayor Herzog Hanson. Doctor Wenzel Wicke and I share this home. He too has an ideal woman, who is also from your world, Miss Maricela Theresa. You'll meet her soon. We've arranged everything perfectly for you. Stop wigging so. There's nothing you can do about it. It's all done now."

Bonita was terror stricken! She couldn't make a sound. She was so helpless that all she could do was to bang her ballet boots up and down on the floor in some sort of wild protest. At least, that made some noise. She had to find some way to protest this.

"Okay, up you go." He pushed her up onto her toes. Her panic rose even higher. Her knees bent, as she tried valiantly to keep her balance and not fall down, waving her arms wildly, even though analytically she knew they weren't there. Right now, she wasn't analytical, not remotely. Just as she more or less stood stable, he pushed her, forcing her to take a step. He had to put out a steadying hand or she would have fallen on her face.

Step by step, he moved her out of their bedroom, showing her the bathroom. "There's the toilet. You don't have any clothes to worry about. So when you need to go, just sit down on it. There's the shower. Your new plastic skin sheds all dirt and grim with just a light flow of water. You merely step in and push the level there. Hot is to the right and cold, left. You are free to shower anytime you desire. Your plastic skin will dry off on its own in just a short time. Now then, on to the kitchen."

Bonita shook her head violently left and right, nearly falling again. Somehow, she had to tell him NO! He ignored her, giving her another push. Jerkily, she took step after step and reached the kitchen. "Now here is your feeding station. The blue tube is water; the brown tube is food, liquid food. All you need to do is move under them, put the tube into your mouth, and suck on them. You may eat and drink all that you desire any time you wish. You must be starving, since it's been nearly four days since they picked you up. Come on. Try the brown one."

Bonita didn't want anything to do with any of this, but her stomach was telling her otherwise. Reluctantly, she moved her head to one side, got the tube into her mouth, and began sucking. Soon a liquid food entered her mouth. It didn't taste all that bad. She sucked on for some time. When she finally let it go, he said, "Shower, toilet, food. Guess that is everything. Come on; time to meet my housemate and his ideal woman. You'll like her." He pushed her, and Bonita had no choice but to take clumsy, clunking steps, wobbling wildly from step to step. In the living room, Doctor Wenzel had come out and was sitting on a sofa. Beside him was another young woman about her own age. Like most on Pegasi-C, she had black hair, but hers was much longer than Bonita's, falling to her upper back. She too had the same enormous breasts and was just as naked as she was. Sitting on the couch, her knees rose higher than the couch.

Bonita's eyes met those of Maricela's. Shared misery

394

flashed between the two women. Mayor Herzog introduced the doctor first and then said, "Miss Bonita Bolivar, meet Miss Maricela Theresa. You'll be housemates and constant companions for the rest of your lives. You're expected to bear us ten children during the next twenty years. You're expected to satisfy our strong sexual urges. Other than that, Bonita, you can do whatever you want to do. You two can even pleasure each other if you so desire. You have free rein of the house. Later on, once you can walk as well as Maricela does, I'll start taking you outside for walks and such, at least in the summer. Winters around here are quite cold, and you haven't anything warm to wear. I promise to keep you very warm with lots of sex during the wintertime, Miss Bonita."

He went on, "You're very special. I'm the mayor and leader of our community, a very important man, you see. So you'll have some notoriety as being the mayor's ideal woman. Now then, I encourage you two to get acquainted and to practice your walking. The doctor and I have to go to work now. Business never waits on us. You are indeed a most beautiful ideal woman, Miss Bonita. See you later today."

With that, both men rose and headed out of the front door. Bonita followed them with her eyes, terrified of moving an inch and wiggling to keep her balance. She saw the door wasn't locked, but was crushed just the same. She had no way to open it! Plus, she suddenly realized that she had to pee badly.

Awkwardly, stumping step by stumping step she wiggled and wobbled trying not to fall down and somehow get to that toilet! Never had a toilet felt so good beneath her, as she relieved herself, but couldn't wipe. For a time, she just sat there in a sort of terrified daze. *This can't be real! I'm having the worst nightmare ever!*

After some time, she saw Maricela walking rather gracefully towards her, a very worried look on her face. She mouthed something. After several times, Bonita realized she was asking if she was all right. Bonita shook her head no and began sobbing harder than she'd ever cried in her whole life. Maricela stood there and merely nodded her head yes. After the good, long cry, she noticed Maricela was still there. She was sort of nodding towards the front room. At last, Bonita realized she wanted her to follow her. *I can't even stand up on my own without falling!* After waves of panic subsided a little, Bonita more or less lunged to her feet, stabbing at the hard floor with her boots, trying to steady herself and not fall down. Then, she took one hesitating step after the other, finally collapsing onto the couch beside Maricela. Again, Bonita began crying.

My life is over before it even began. I can't go to UE, not like this. Where am I? Why did this happen to me? Maybe I can fall and kill myself. She looked around and found no sharp edges, nothing that would definitively end her life, if she could somehow manage to fall onto it.

Then, Maricela rather bumped her with her bosom. She saw Maricela mouthing something, and tried and tried to imagine what she was saying. At last, she nodded. Maricela was saying, "Watch me." She did and watched her lunge to her feet and begin to walk around. She walked very well on her toes, even doing a slight twirl in place to turn around. After she returned to the couch, she nodded to Bonita, again mouthing something. "You try." At last, Bonita figured out what she was saying. She shook her head no, vigorously. But Maricela was persistent. Before long, Bonita realized she would have to walk, if only to get to the food and use the bathroom. Thus, began a horrific morning for the star high school athlete.

The liquid food seemed to go right through her. Bonita found herself going over to the feeding tubes seven more times that day. Towards evening, she was physically exhausted and mentally burned out. She found the bed she'd awakened on, collapsed onto it, and fell into a deep, troubled sleep.

When morning came, she again panicked when she awoke. The nightmare was still here! Worse, the mayor was lying beside her, massaging her giant breasts. Revolted, Bonita wiggled and somehow struggled to sit up. Once sitting, she lunged to her feet and made her way to the toilet. There she sat sobbing until he came to her, "Up my dear Bonita. I have to use the toilet too, you know. Go suck some breakfast."

Bonita lunged upwards, brushing her giant bosom onto

his body. Cringing from the touch, she nearly fell, but somehow managed to stump past him and into the kitchen, where she saw Maricela was already sucking away on her brown tube. She ducked her head beneath the second brown tube. Closing her toothless gums over it, she began sucking too. She seemed ravenously hungry.

As before, the two men fixed themselves a real breakfast. Oh how Bonita wanted some of that coffee! When they finished, they again left for work, leaving the two women home alone. Bonita followed Maricela out to the couch, nearly falling into it, beside her. Bonita knew she felt strange. She had all these ill-defined urges sweeping over her. Maricela looked positively beautiful sitting there. Such gorgeous breasts, such lovely shaped lips. The next thing she knew, Maricela was pressing her lips gently against hers, a loving kiss. Bonita pressed back to reciprocate, but both of their lips gave way. There were no teeth, just empty gums. Undaunted, Maricela drew close once more, her lips just touching Bonita's. Deep within her, passions stirred.

The next thing Bonita knew, Maricela's tongue was inside her mouth, and she was sucking it, pressing her lips onto it as hard as she could. Before long, Maricela had draped herself over Bonita's lap, using her tongue on her privates! In some dark, forgotten recesses of her mind, Bonita knew that she'd never do this, but she craved it now. Later, when Maricela finished with her, Bonita eagerly fell onto Maricela's lap and her tongue found its mark as well.

What's happening to me? I've never done anything like this before? But I crave it. She's so beautiful! This can't be real, it can't! Confused but satisfied, Bonita struggled to get back up, seated on the couch. Now, Maricela mouthed, "walk" until Bonita understood. Together, the two began walking around and around the various rooms of the home. Only two doors were closed. One was the mayor's private study. The other was the doctor's workroom where he performed his conversion work.

Later that day, the men brought another unconscious woman inside, carrying her into the workroom, followed by the doctor. Hours later, the men carried another ideal woman out of the home. Bonita began to realize that there were far more than just she and Maricela here. That evening, when the mayor again tried to get her sexually aroused, Bonita again cringed away from him, and he wisely didn't pursue it.

However, once they left and the two women finished sucking their breakfast and were once more on the living room couch, Bonita felt the overwhelming urge again. She leaned over to kiss Maricela. An hour later, both women sat back fully satisfied. Still, Bonita could not figure out what was happening to her, only that she felt intensely attracted to Maricela. Twice more during the day, the two pleasured each other. Worse, that evening, Bonita allowed the mayor to pleasure her!

By the next night, Bonita found the mayor highly attractive and even encouraged him. At last, the mayor was more than satisfied. Bonita, however, wasn't. Her mind was now in total confusion. *What am I doing? I despise that man and what he's done to me. No, he's super sexy. No he isn't. He's not even from Pegasi-C. He's an alien of some kind. No, he's really the most handsome man ever. What's wrong with me?* She cried heavily, but the mayor didn't notice. He was sound asleep.

Days passed. Daily, Bonita became more and more skilled walking. She and Maricela continued to pleasure each other three or four times each day. Each night, the mayor also lay with her, and she willingly participated as best she could, considering how helpless she was. However, she began to grasp what was happening to her.

During periods of lucidness, which always followed Maricela's excellent job of pleasuring her, she found she could think more or less rationally. She knew she'd been kidnaped, and somehow turned into a sex object, like some brood mares on Pegasi-C. Until now, she'd never had sex with anyone, and certainly never found other women so attractive. Thus, she concluded correctly that there was something in that liquid food that was making her so sexually active, craving sexual fulfillment anyway she could get it. But I can't stop eating, she reasoned. *I have to escape from here somehow, someway.*

After the next round of mutual pleasuring ended, she again could think. *What are my current assets? What are my strong points?* She recalled this was precisely what her Spanish teacher had taught her to do when writing her persuasive essays. *Strong points? There's hardly anything left of me!* She sobbed again. An hour later and another round of pleasuring behind her, she picked up again. *Well, I have my legs, and they are as strong as ever. I have to use them and my brains. I'm very intelligent. After all, I did get into UE and their really hard genetics program.* She broke down once more, after recalling this.

During a lucid period the next day, she realized, *Knowledge is power. Right now, I know so very little. Where am I? What planet? Who are these men? Why are they doing this to us? What is their objective? How can I possibly escape and get home? I can't answer any of these, and I certainly can't answer the last one until I know the answers to the others. I need to learn all I can about this place, these people. Then, I can work out an answer to the last one.* Unfortunately, just thinking about being back home, as she now was physically, brought on another round of sobbing. *Why should I even try?* She wailed unable even to vocalize it or anything else, not now, not ever again.

Around her fourth day, Maricela showed her how to take a shower. By manipulating the lever, she could adjust the flow of water and its temperature. At first, she desperately wanted a shower, to wash everything off her. Almost at once, she saw her strange new plastic-like skin did not absorb water, but in fact repelled it, like a very well made raincoat. Only her head and privates were actually exposed to the water. The rest of her body was encased within this second skin of plastic material. True, the skin shed any dirt within seconds of the shower water hitting it, but gone was all the pleasures she'd ever had with showers.

Nevertheless, with each passing day, she became more and more skilled at walking on her toes in their permanent en pointe position. Her strong leg muscles had a lot to do with it. Steadily, her sense of balance grew, though she did take more than one fall only to find getting back onto her feet was just incredibly difficult to do.

She soon lost track of the days. Bonita had no way to

keep track or mark their passing. Had she been here a week? No, it seemed longer. Two then, three? She just didn't know any longer. At last, Mayor Herzog kept his word. She was now walking as well as Maricela. "This morning, my lovely Miss Bonita, let's go for a walk outside. Time for some fresh air."

Bonita was more than ready for that. She eagerly lunged to her feet, wiggling a little to get her balance, and headed towards the door. "Wait for me, my eager beaver," the mayor teased her, quite pleased with just how well she was working out for him. He opened the door; she stepped out onto the front porch of the home, and just stopped and stared. The world was quite strange indeed.

It was morning, that much she could tell, but the sun was such a dull red. It cast a bloody glow upon everything. Beyond the porch, she saw a paved street with other small homes lining it. Gazing to her far right, she saw green pastures with cattle grazing. Beyond them, her eyes focused on what appeared to be crop fields. Was that corn that she was seeing? His voice behind her said, "New Home. That's what we call our town. Come; down the steps. Let's stroll through our city."

Steps? She'd not done steps at all, and once more panic swept over her. Trying to look around the edges of her bosom, Bonita tried to see where the steps were but ended up mostly feeling for them with the back of her boots and their tall spikes. Fortunately, there were only three to descend, and her panic subsided once she reached the level street. There were no sidewalks, and he led her out into the street. At once, she concluded rightly there was very little traffic, since she could not move fast at all to get out of the way of a vehicle.

Several other men were also bringing their ideal women out to enjoy the morning as well. Aghast, Bonita now realized there were many more women trapped as she was. All appeared just like herself, naked, no arms, monster breasts, and wearing the identical ballet boots that came up just over their ankles. She also noticed most were very hesitant and careful descending the stairs, just as she had been and felt a bit more confident. Further, they seemed to walk far more naturally and easily than she was, and Bonita made a note to continue improving her walking skill.

As they moved down the street, she spotted a cross street and began to get an estimate of just how big this town was. Before the walk ended, she made a rough guess there were no more than a few hundred homes. If they each had two men per home, there could not be more than a thousand men at most.

In the next block, she was startled to see one man carrying a small infant while walking beside his ideal woman. She swallowed hard. That her purpose here was also for breeding struck home to her. Before the walk ended, she spotted a dozen infants. She concluded some of the women had been here for perhaps a year or maybe longer. She did find one positive aspect of this world, whatever and wherever it was: the air was pure and clean, wholly unlike that of Pegasi-C, where sometimes the pollution levels were so high that breathing was difficult. Twice, her softball games had to be postponed due to pollution. Here, the air was cool and invigorating, crystal clear and clean.

Since she was managing the walk just fine, the mayor proudly led her to the south edge of town. From here, she could see for miles on down a valley. The small farming plots ended and low, rolling green hills lay beyond that as far as she could see. Further, what she didn't see did not compute until the next day after a pleasure session with Maricela. There wasn't any road that led in any direction out of the town, save for the paths to the farmsteads. This place, New Home, was entirely isolated from the rest of the world! Escape to where? That brought on another round of grief and sobbing, ending that brief lucid period.

Some days later, the mayor once more took her outside. This time, she did see a transport ship landing just north of the town. Maricela and Dr. Wenzel were walking with them, but as the ship landed, Dr. Wenzel excused himself, asking Mayor Herzog to watch after Maricela and see her safely home. He dashed off towards that ship. On their return walk, she saw several men carrying another young woman, who was normal in all ways, into their home. She presumed they took her into the doctor's workroom. Later, back inside, she saw them bring her out. The poor terrified young woman looked just like all the other ideal women. Again, her emotions swelled, and her eyes watered. So many women, she thought.

After another round of pleasure giving and receiving with Maricela, she realized the significance of what she'd seen. The way out of here had to be via the spaceport and the transport ships! A tiny bit of hope returned, very tiny.

That night, despite her powerful urging to lay on the bed and make love to the mayor, she instead walked over to the door and nodded towards it. "Come; let's make sweet love, my beautiful Bonita." She kept nodding to the door and taking another tiny step towards it. "What? You want to go out now? But it's dark out there." She continued to insist. "Oh very well. The night sky is beautiful. Perhaps, you are being romantic eh?" he teased her. Bonita flashed him what she thought was a sexy, flirting smile. He opened the door, and she stepped out into the dark night.

Again, she panicked! She couldn't see the steps in the dark. This time, the mayor put his arm around her and helped her down. Once in the street, she looked up at the sky. It was beautiful, no doubt of that. She saw no moon, but there were the stars. Bonita stared at them for some time, before he began kissing her. Automatically, her body responded, so much so, that he swept her up, carried her inside, and laid her on their bed. After he spent his energies, he fell asleep at once, leaving Bonita lying there fully lucid once more. Now, she realized the significance of the night sky and the stars. In all directions but one, there were virtually none, just empty black space, though here and there she thought she saw fuzzy spots. In that lone direction, lay the entire galaxy. Now she knew this world had to be at the very outer edge of a spiral arm! She had some idea where she was, but that realization only triggered another wave of grief. Her home world was half a spiral arm distant! She silently cried herself asleep once more.

Chapter 22 The Rise of Electronics

July 1382. Venice City, Beltazar-C, Forbidden List. Now a world of decadence and sensual pleasures, the downfall of Beltazar-C had planted the roots of its decadence many centuries ago, when video games took the world by storm, infecting first the younger generation. One put on the V-mask and hit play. At once, one was immersed into a realistic, holographic, three-dimensional world, so real that only a very discerning eye could tell the difference.

At first, there were two formats available: the first person shooter game and the party of adventurers game. The former appealed to the young boys who prided themselves on killing all sorts of imaginary creatures and villains, while the latter appealed to the young girls, who could band together as a group, and adventure into realms of fantasy, embarking on epic quests, generally not involving heavy combat situation, but more on role playing. So real, so absorbing, the children and young adults quickly became hooked on playing, demanding more and more time to play, as well as new and wilder scenarios, all of which was accommodated by the manufacturers of the V-mask system.

Within a half century, this new generation spent more hours each day in their virtual reality environments than they did in their real world. Unwilling to give up their precious gaming time, these new adults invented all manner of robotic controlled machinery to deal with food production and distribution. A century after its introduction, most all the world's industries had come to a standstill. No one wanted to buy a new table or couch. Only food and V-mask games and systems were selling, and the former was now totally automated, requiring only an infrequent look by a manager to ensure no breakdowns occurred. People only returned to the "real world" to eat, relieve themselves, and to occasionally sleep when they became too tired to continue, though usually their bodies merely fell asleep, while they were still "in the game."

Soon, the shoot'em up games had run their course. Game inventors ran out of monsters to kill. Someone got the idea of having virtual courting, which led almost at once to virtual sex. Once more, new such games sold out as soon as they hit the market. Now, by putting on the V-mask, you could enter a world where you were free to pursue any gorgeous woman or handsome man of your choice. Even the virtual sex part became titillating. Plus, it was safe. No one could get pregnant. No one had to marry. In fact, you could leave your own hangups and shyness behind, donning anyone of a cast of alter-ego personalities.

With each new release, the action got wilder and wilder. Now, you could dress in any manner that suited you, as well as be the gender of your choice. You could partake of light bondage, heavy bondage, and of course sex in any conceivable way and with any one, regardless of their sex. "Experiment and Enjoy" read the cover of one such V-mask game. Many claimed that virtual sex was vastly superior in sensations to the real thing!

Into this dizzying array came a young man named Armo Selletti, who invented what is now known as the Selletti Device. Armo was an electronics expert and game programmer. He who worked out the actual way the V-mask system worked on the human players. Until Armo came along, the game makers worked by trial and error in their labs. What went over well with their host of testers was implemented. What bombed was not.

Serendipity. That's how Armo claims to have discovered the effect and invented his device. He was frustrated in Sleek Villa, unable to lure the lovely and charming Samantha to his bed. She kept choosing Larry, the Sleazy Bag. By accident, one time he took a frequency generator along with him into the game. In frustration while watching Larry walk away yet again with Samantha, he accidentally turned it on. Instantly, Samantha stopped and looked around, as though someone was calling out to her. He turned the device off. She shook her head and continued sauntering down the street, arm in arm with Larry. He turned it on again, and she again stopped, looking around as though she swore someone was calling out to her.

Off. Again, she shook it off and continued, disappearing into a motel room.

"Curious," Armo declared. "Now, if only I could rig this up to also send a message." The next time he entered Sleek Villa, he was armed with a small microphone attached to his steadily more complex machine. The microphone turned his speech into electronic signals and sent them to his frequency box, which piggybacked them onto the very high frequency emitter that had gotten the attention of Samantha. He played the game again up until the point where once more Samantha choose Larry, his arch rival. Armo switched on his emitter, watched Samantha stop, and look around. He spoke, "Samantha, you chose the wrong fellow. You really want the guy in the yellow tee shirt there at the bar." To Armo's surprise and Larry's too, Samantha, wiggling her hips seductively, came over to Armo to chat. Before long, she escorted him out of the bar and into the motel room.

After that, it was discovery time. Armo quickly found Samantha only responded to one very precise frequency. Vary it slightly, and she paid no attention to it. However, he noticed someone else in the game suddenly looked up, as though someone was trying to get his or her attention. A bit more experimentation yielded the inescapable conclusion that each person could be affected by one precise frequency only, and that every person's frequency was slightly different from the next person.

Armo then began selling his invention to other gamers. "You can make any player do what you want them to do." That was his selling point. Overnight, the Selletti Device became a smash hit. Of course, soon all the "Larry's" in the game now had their own Selletti Devices, and it became a game of who could control who and when.

Not everyone on Beltazar-C was hooked on the V-mask games. Forty year old Field Marshal Domenico Tonelli was one of those. While the "kids" were interested in winning victories in la-la land as he called their virtual reality, he was interesting in taking over total control of the real world of Beltazar-C. He wanted "real" world domination. The problem was six other Field Marshals on the other continents also want total control of Beltazar-C. Power plays kept the playing field quite level, frustrating Field Marshal Domenico enormously.

Enter the discovery of the Selletti Device. His own game-addicted son told him about the device and even got him one. "Come on pop. Join in the fun," his sixteen year old son tried to coax him, but he refused. Instead, he took the device to his longtime friend, Dr. Pietro Brunelli, also forty years old. He was a medical doctor first, but that's not saying much. Very little skill was needed to press the buttons on the imported medical machines now in use everywhere on Beltazar-C. He dabbled in electronics and in psycho-modifications, trying to change a person's basic behavior patterns. His eldest son had become hooked on the V-mask games and had died while playing one. After that, Dr. Brunelli made it his life's goal to find a way to break anyone's addiction to these games.

So it was that Field Marshal Domenico's fortuitous bringing of the Selletti Device to Dr. Brunelli set the stage for the rapid development of the Brunelli Enforcer. No one actually had the slightest idea why a person would respond to a very specific high frequency in the trillion-yattohertz range. Nor did they know why they responded or even why everyone responded to a different frequency, only that they did. Field Marshal Domenico and Dr. Brunelli could care less. They wanted a useful tool, which by the summer of 1382, the doctor provided, but that's getting a bit ahead of the story, as I now know it.

The original Mark I allowed them to send a thought message to another person across space. Not just any space, but anywhere on Beltazar-C! The doctor had four lab assistants, who became keenly interested in his groundbreaking work and assisted him with the many experiments. For the record, wholly unlike the rest of the addicted population, these young lab assistants were working on their own advanced degrees. They were Damiano Bartini, eighteen, Francesca Miniani, nineteen, Gabriella Bologna, twenty, and Arianna Cettina, eighteen. The doctor soon knew the precise frequency of each of these four assistants.

With the Field Marshal observing, the doctor sent a pair of his assistants out into the greater Venice area. The other two were lying on a cot in the lab. First, he set the frequencies to match one on the couch and one in the field, permitting two-way communication between them. Then, he gave a paper with specific instructions to relay to the other assistant out in Venice. "Go buy a pizza," Francesca thought there in the lab. Out in the field, Gabriella heard that thought in her mind and complied, while her partner, Damiano observed and reported just what Gabriella did. She went and got one.

Later, Francesca knew all three of the girls didn't like the boisterous Damiano and played a trick on Arianna. She sent Arianna the command to kiss Damiano. At first, Arianna refused to obey her, sending her back the thought, "Oh yuck! No way!" Mischievous Francesca zapped up the power level to its maximum and repeated her command. Arianna found herself helplessly obeying it, despite all her resistance to doing it. Breakthrough! Something like this was just what Field Marshal Domenico desired!

Enter the Model II in early 1382. It had a greater power setting, was smaller, had only a one directional communication line from the lab out to the person, but still required a massive amount of power and thus was hardly portable. It was at this point that Field Marshal Domenico stepped in to conduct the experiments. He appointed the four lab assistants to be his official "Field Agents," promising them great wealth and fame if they would do as asked. They agreed. So far, this had been just one very fun game, but not any longer.

His first action was to send the four out to visit the other rival continents. There, they observed for him. He directed the high frequency beam to one specific continent and began a slow, methodical sweep of frequencies. His Field Agents reported back when the person that they were covertly observing responded, looking up and around to see who was trying to get their attention. Within a week, he had noted the precise frequencies of a dozen top-level aides to the other competing Field Marshals.

Armed with this data, he put his plan into operation. He had the four lab assistants lie down, connected the microphones to them, and set their frequencies as the senders.

Next, he dialed in four other frequencies, those of four aides. Then, he handed the lab assistants each a card and ordered them to send the message.

"We can't send this!" Francesca protested. "Kill Field Marshal Runelli? No way!" Field Marshal Domenico slowly raised the power levels on the four assistants. With intense pain flooding her mind, Francesca had no choice but to transmit the kill order. That done, he raised the power levels on the receiving end. Now, he waited, keeping an eye on his four "Field Agents," keeping them on their couches.

Hours later, the news channels began carrying the alarming news that four Field Marshals had just been assassinated by their trusted advisors! Hastily, Field Marshal Domenico dialed in the two remaining frequencies and repeated the process, using Damiano and Francesca to deliver the kill orders. His plan worked brilliantly. The next day, he stepped in to fill the power vacuum, taking total control over Beltazar-C!

Of course, his four lab assistants protested. "I don't want anything to do with assassinations! I quit," Francesca declared flatly, feeling this was a total abuse of valid scientific research. What had been fun and a cool game had turned evil and dangerous. Following her lead, the other three also spoke up and quit, storming out of the lab.

Field Marshal Domenico Tonelli simply could not allow them to quit. They knew too much. If they blabbed what they'd been forced to do, he would be in very hot water indeed. Besides, he needed them. Their frequencies were known quantities. Hence, he ordered a squad of soldiers to round them up and arrest them. Before the four could get back to their own apartments, they found themselves surrounded by men with guns, arrested, and thrown into military jail cells!

Both older men saw unlimited prospects for the Brunelli Enforcer. If those lab assistants were allowed to go free, the cat was out of its bag. "We have to do something to contain those four and keep them working for us," Field Marshal Domenico declared.

"Aye. They could destroy all my research. I can drug them and keep them unconscious until we find a better solution," the doctor suggested, terribly afraid that they would ruin all his research. A short while after that, the four lab assistants were unconscious and moved from their military jail cells back into the laboratory and placed on their cots.

"Somehow, we need to disable them, so they can't ever be a threat to us, and so we can still use them for the transmissions we're going to need," the doctor mused.

"Aye, we can't let them have any chance of just getting up and walking out of here again. I can't keep them under armed guard all the time either. One slip up and we're finished, doc," the Field Marshal pointed out the obvious.

"Well, we could put them in chains. Hobble them," the doctor suggested.

Field Marshal Domenico frowned. "That would just encourage them to find ways out of their chains, like any prisoner. Eventually, they'll find a way to undo them. We're not dealing with dopes here or criminals, but very bright kids who have played a whole lot of V-mask games. No, they'd soon find a way out of all traditional bindings. We need something that immobilizes them, that's completely permanent, and yet doesn't impact their usefulness to us."

"How about that mutating agent that was used on Cass-C? It's been on the news a lot lately," the doctor suggested.

"I know what you mean. Saw those images myself. Possibly, except they can't speak intelligibly any more. But I think we're on the right track," the Field Marshal suggested.

"Well, immobile. Let's see. I could always remove their feet. That would keep them immobile and here in the lab," the good doctor replied thoughtfully.

"Aye. Only one problem with that. I sure as hell don't want to carry them to the bathroom all the time. They have to have limited mobility. A wheelchair is out. When our backs are turned, they would just wheel themselves out of here. We ought to do something with their hands too. They'll just pull the electrodes off their heads. We can't always be tying them down, now can we?"

"Point taken. I could remove their hands too," the doctor suggested. "Of course how will they eat? I'm not going to sit here and feed them either."

"Let them eat out of a plate like dogs!" Field Marshal Domenico declared flatly, showing no sympathy for these lab assistants. They were just that, only not easily expendable. He didn't want his future plans put on hold while they found and prepared more assistants.

"Well, let me do some medical research tonight. They'll be out all night. Perhaps, in the morning, we can have a better idea how to constrain them safely," the doctor suggested, and the Field Marshal agreed, assigning two guards to watch over the unconscious four.

In the morning, Doctor Pietro showed Field Marshal Domenico what he'd found, and the two agreed it was perfect. While the Field Marshal send soldiers out to obtain the proper footwear, the doctor wheeled his medical machine into the main room and set to work on his four patients, making two alterations each to their bodies. He fused their feet into a ballet, en pointe position, and removed their hands, forming nice tiny cones at their wrists. They would be promised new prosthetic hands later when they finished their work here.

Francesca was the first to awaken. When she saw the round little cones at the end of each arm, she freaked out and began screaming wildly. Noticing her feet encased in the black ballet ankle boots with padlocks on them, she increased her voice several more decibels, rousing the other three, who responded in kind. The doctor merely covered his ears, while the Field Marshal merely stood watching them with a smirk on his face.

"What have you done to us?" Gabriella finally shrieked.

"Well, we can't have you running off, now can we?" Field Marshal Domenico said snidely. "Your feet have been fused so only the tips of your toes touch the floor. You won't be able to walk at all unless you are wearing those enticing boots. Even in them, you won't be running, just barely walking. We can't have you using your hands to interfere with the valuable work we have ahead for you to do. Now, if you cooperate and behave yourselves, when we finish, we'll see you get nice prosthetic hands."

Being the oldest of the four, Gabriella felt responsible for them. "But how will we eat and use the bathroom? We're helpless now."

"On the table there are dog bowls. Dogs don't complain, and they eat well. We're going to remove your clothes and put an extra-large tee shirt on each of you. Teens always wear them anyway, but it will just cover your privates but pose no problem when you sit on the toilet. Now stop your infernal bawling," the Field Marshal barked. Minutes later with humiliation piled on top of everything else, the four were stripped, and overly large tee shirts put on them.

Arianna complained, "This is illegal! You can't get away with this. They'll arrest you both and throw you into jail forever!"

"Hardly, Arianna. You forget. I'm the supreme ruler of all Beltazar-C," the Field Marshall smirked. After that, leaving the four crying and yelling, the two men left the lab.

Eventually, they stopped crying, tried to stand, and get to the toilet. With bent knees and wildly flailing arms, they stumped slowly over to the toilet and then to the table. Humiliation mounded on top of humiliation. They had no choice but to lean over and eat like four dogs, but they were able to use their stumps at least to drink from the coffee mugs, more or less.

Hours later when the doctor tried to hook Francesca back up to the machine for another experiment, she protested, waving her arms about her head, banging into his arms, nearly causing him to drop the leads. "Look, if you don't behave, I can take the rest of your arms off!" That shocked all four, throwing another layer of fear into them. Meekly, she complied.

The current research was on the development of the Brunelli Enforcer Model III. His objective was to make the device smaller so that it could be carried on a deep space transport. After a long, humiliating day, the four were locked into the lab for the night, but their supper was in their bowls on the table.

"We should have blown out of here long ago," sobbed Damiano. "Now look at us, we're helpless cripples and forever too. I can't live like this."

"We can't do anything about it," wailed Gabriella.

"It's all I can do to walk to the bathroom and table,"

cried Arianna. "Wait a minute everyone. We must be in a V-mask game of some kind. This can't be real! All we have to do is take off the mask. I'm jumping out of it now!" she declared. Nothing happened. All four tried pulling a V-mask off their body's heads, wherever their real bodies were now at. Nothing happened. Reality came crashing down upon all four once more.

"Damiano, you have to get us out of here," insisted Francesca. "I only took this job to help, and now we're being used as their private assassins. You have to help us," she pleaded.

"How?" he waved his aesthetic looking stumps in the air. "Hell, Francesca, we can't live like this, like dogs. I won't. I just won't." Nevertheless, the four ate like dogs, and then headed for their cots, where they all broke down again, sobbing themselves to sleep.

In the morning, Damiano had bloodshot eyes. As he got up, he said, "I won't live like this. Follow me, girls. I'm going to end it. I'm not their pet dog!" He stumped wildly over to the main power box. There he fumbled around with his stumps and finally got the cover opened. "Do like I do," he said. Without another word, he jammed both stumps into the power box. Extremely high voltage shot through his arms, electrocuting him, partially frying his body, sending it some ten feet across the floor, quite dead. All three girls began screaming wildly, bringing the doctor into the room. He was just arriving but heard them, and they sounded quite different.

"Oh dear God, what happened to him?" he muttered, checking on the still smoldering body. He looked up at the opened power box and then over to the three girls sitting on their cots. "Well? What happened?"

"He, he couldn't live like this. Neither can we. Please, you have to help us," pleaded Francesca.

Doctor Pietro sighed. "All right. All right. You sit there, and let me take care of Damiano here." At last, the three young women felt he was listening to them, and that he was somehow going to help them magically. Had they truly been analytical, they would have known he couldn't do anything really to "help" them now.

412

After dragging the corpse outside the lab, he met the Field Marshal who was just arriving. The two exchanged words out of hearing from the women. "Look, we can't have them pulling similar stunts," Field Marshal Domenico declared firmly.

"All right, I'll take care of it," the doctor agreed. He returned to the women on the cots. "I'll help you. Breathe deeply, Francesca. That's right." He'd placed a mask over her face and knocked her out. He did the same to the other two women, who now fully expected he would somehow get them out of this nightmare.

When they awoke, they found their nightmare a thousand times worse. He'd removed their arms at their shoulders. "Now you can't kill yourselves like that idiot Damiano did," the doctor explained to the screaming trio. He left them, allowing them time to vent and calm down before continuing his experiments.

Quickly, the three women slumped into a deep apathy. Now, they were almost completely helpless. Their universe shrank to their cots, the toilet, and the table, only now they were given two bowls, one with food in it and one with water. The experimentation continued on, and they had no choice but to comply. Any time they refused to carry out an order, he simply upped the power output, which eventually overcame their resistance, forcing them to comply whether they wanted to or not.

It was in one of these experiments that Doctor Pietro achieved his next breakthrough quite by accident. He was trying to have Francesca send a message to an unsuspecting banker in downtown Venice. "Okay, Francesca, I want you to be hovering over Verona and spot the bank that we need."

"Okay, I see it. Now what?" she replied apathetically.

"No wait. Did I say Verona? Oh dear. Wait! Are you saying that you are somehow seeing a bank in Verona?"

"Yes, like you said. Don't hit me again, please. I'm doing what you say," she responded, rising a little above her usual apathy, fearing more pain.

After more work, he discovered that by applying enough power at their frequencies, he could order them to be hovering over any location on Beltazar-C! "How can she be here in Venice and be seeing stuff in Verona?" asked an incredulous Field Marshal Domenico. This seemed totally impossible.

"Damned if I know, but she is. I've confirmed several things she's told me. We need to study this further!" They did just that. With this new Brunelli Enforcer Model III, they could now order their "field agents" to observe anywhere on Beltazar-C! Next, while doing so, they had their agents observe the people, and report when the machine found a frequency that matched one of the people. That worked, and as a test, he ordered Francesca to order that man to commit suicide, which the man promptly did. Verification followed in the next day's obituaries!

Both men now realized the ultimate power of life and death, which they now possessed! "My good doctor, you and I are about to become Masters of the Galaxy! No one can stand before us! We'll rule the whole galaxy, not just this stinking planet full of V-mask junkies!" That the Brunelli Enforcer Model III was now portable and able to be operated from a transport would guarantee their ultimate success! The three women were utterly helpless pawns, unable to do anything about it. They were merely tools of destruction, helpless ones at that.

Chapter 23 Hell Comes to the Federation of Planets

August 1382, I was back home on Ashford-5, getting used to my new, young body, getting our children used to it as well, and making Christina into a part of our family. I had my leg dexterity back up to what it had been when I was eighteen and on Metcalf-4. The only problem was one of balance — not much of that when wearing these seven-inch heels, which actually felt better on my feet and legs than the lower six-inch heels. Because my hair was so darn long now, I began keeping it up in a giant bun, though I really didn't want to do that. And yes, I was routinely using my *mentales* gifts in lieu of hands, though I tried to use my toes when I could. The heels severely limited that. Slipping out of flats is easy, but not these, especially when I had them off, since I was still forced to stand with only my toes on the ground, precarious at best. Still, I was determined make it work. I certainly didn't want to find some way to force Christina back into this body. Besides, she was having too much fun learning to play the harpsichord. I suspected one day, she would be a master musician. She had a gift for it and my kind of perseverance on a given course. She and I were alike in so many small ways. Plus, Gisa and Karla were now her music teachers. I could see a trio in the making.

Mid-August, my brief respite came to a screeching halt. It began with a call from Martina, who was currently with Admiral Molly Maud on Cass-C, helping her run that world as their admiral. The other worlds had finally sent enough replacements so that the Admiralty Round Table was again operational with a quorum. On the curing front, Admiral Molly Maud had managed to pull in some more genetic cure supplies from other major worlds, but not nearly enough. Only the first twenty of the nearly seven thousand were now in the process of getting whatever cures would result.

Martina said, "Nia Elain, just letting you know that there have been two more terrorist attacks on heavily populated Federations worlds. Cygni-D and Zeta Minor-C. Both are mid-arm worlds. Around ten thousand have been infected between them. Looks like Jana and Jovanna were right. It's spreading, just as it did in the Imperium. Over."

She and I chatted a bit before she signed off. Not long after that, I got a call from Emperor Bino. After exchanging pleasantries, he got down to business. From his formal use of my title, I knew something was up. "Captain Nia Elain, I know that you've been through a lot and that I've no right to impose upon you further, but you are my best representative to the Federation at this time. Could you possibly go back to Cass-C, and assist Martina and Admiral Molly Maud? I'm getting some disturbing reports here that I would like you to track down. Specifically, there seems to be an epidemic of assassinations of world figures by some of their most trusted people. Doesn't make any sense. Over."

Hey, Emperor Bino is one guy you simply can't say no to. I knew that he would not have called me unless this was either extremely serious or threatened our Ataro Empire. To be honest, I had not paid any attention to newscasts of late. Hence, I couldn't tell which it might be. "Of course, I'll pack and be on my way. Over."

"Watch your back and keep me posted. I would suggest you keep your use of your special gifts to a minimum while on Cass-C, and also keep Martina more in the background. I need her keen observational skills on this one. I don't have anyone else available to help you out right now. We're dealing with ten minor crises between these fragmented alliances. Somehow, I have to keep them from declaring war on each other. All my manpower is devoted to this. Over."

"Got it. I won't risk anyone else being genetically modified this time. I'll keep Martina out of the firing line. Glad to help. Over and out."

"Off again, love?" Danika commented. "Damn, you be careful out there. You are going to get a zillion propositions, and that's making me a bit jealous." We both laughed, and I pressed as hard as I could into her body, which wasn't much considering, but her arms responded, and we hugged and kissed. Together, we packed my new clothes and, after saying goodbye to all the kids and Christina, we headed for the spaceport once more.

During the brief nine-hour flight, I had some time to ponder my latest assignment. It was too late effectively to stop the spread of the genetic bio agent. It had now reached two additional worlds. Yet, what bothered me the most was what was different this time. I used a bit of telekinetic energy combined with a dabble of levitation to pull down Jana and Jovanna's thick History of the Imperium book. With it resting in my lap, I used more energy to thumb through the book to the first occurrences of the genetic bio attacks on Imperium worlds. The difference stared up at me off the pages. In all of the cases so far in the Federation, no one claimed responsibility. There had been no published, "We did this because" messages. The attacks had simply happened, and no one knew why. True, the newscasts offered up dozens of "reasons why," but then that is normal. When someone doesn't know why, he will invent reasons to make the sequence of events logical in his mind. In fact, thus far no reason for the attacks on the three worlds had come to light. That bothered me more than a little.

People just don't do things as horrible as this without a reason. Besides, obtaining the stuff had to cost them a bundle. No, there was a reason only it wasn't visible yet. I decided then and there that this would have to be the major focus of my investigations. Danika finished her ship safety checklist and came back to spend time with me, replacing the thick volume on the bookshelf for me.

"So what have you been thinking about?" she asked, and I explained what I'd found. "You are right. Someone is doing this on purpose. You really do need to figure out just what that purpose actually is, and that could lead you to those responsible for it. Honestly, you be darn careful. You are much more vulnerable than you were back on Metcalf-4 when I first met you, love."

"How so?" I asked.

"Those heels. They are far, far from flats. You know as well as I do that you can neither run nor walk fast in them. Keeping your balance is really tricky. I've seen you having to use a bit of your gifts maintaining your precarious balance. I know you didn't think I was spotting you doing that, but I did. Nothing escapes the observant eye of your mate here, dear."

I flushed. "That obvious?" She nodded. I sighed, "I know, it is much rougher this time, but I just couldn't let Christina back into this body. She'd be completely helpless and wholly unable to do much of anything."

"And you aren't, dear? I know — you have lots of experience dealing with it, but you also know that you best not be using your *mentales* gifts on Cass-C. So you are going to be quite dependent yourself. I wish the emperor would have asked one of the rest of us to tackle this one and not you."

"I know, dear. It'll be rough, but hey, I'm the captain," I rationalized. We both laughed at that silly justification. After that, we spent a good deal of the remaining hours in our bed.

Admiral Molly Maud was very pleased to see me again. So was Heinz who promised to make another portrait of me in my new body. She brought me up to speed. "The Hub Special Forces raided Comrade Filbert Small's place in Circle City on Equiuss-C. That opium addict has been killed and the remainder of his bio agent cylinder confiscated. Apparently, he used it on his wife. The strike team had no choice but to bring her back here. They couldn't leave her behind, because there wasn't anyone else there at his place. Right now, she's in a medical wing. They are trying to get her off her opium addiction. We are pretty sure he was responsible only for that attack at the spaceport. They tried questioning his wife about it, but she's so out of it she doesn't even know her own name. Keeps saying that she's Number Fourteen, whatever that means. We think he caused the attack just for kicks. Still no clue on who's behind all the other attacks. Meanwhile, the Admiralty Round Table is back in action, but under beefed up security. A few worlds sent their original admirals back. I think they decided to try it because of me. So I guess I'm setting a good example for six of the admirals anyway. Lots of new faces. Next session is on Monday."

"Okay. Perhaps, I ought to interview this Number Fourteen woman," I suggested. Molly Maud agreed and set up an appointment for me with General Wolfgang. I then chatted with Martina, putting her on the trail of the assassinations for the emperor. Right on time, the general arrived to pick us three up, okay four, since Carla was always at Molly Maud's side.

"Good to have you back with us, captain," he welcomed me and helped us into his large army van. *You are one hot woman!* I picked up his surface thought quite by accident and smiled towards him.

On the way to the hospital, he explained, "I doubt you'll get much out of her. She's an opium addict. Probably nothing she says will be reliable."

"Have to try. Honestly, we have to get a handle on these terrorist attacks," I replied.

He nodded, and then said, "If we didn't have these Duplicating machines, there simply wouldn't be any attacks." I laughed. Here was a case of one of the most useful of technologies ever invented being abused and put to wicked uses.

A half hour later, I stared down at the poor woman. I admit I've never seen the body of a drug addict before. I was shocked. She looked so terribly thin with hardly any muscles left on her legs. Her face looked more like that of an eighty year old woman, but she was supposedly barely twenty. I decided the best way to proceed was to pervade her mind and see if I could locate anything useful. Trying to get anything coherent out of her was fruitless. With her lip plates, we couldn't understand her anyway. I focused and entered her mind, though later I wished that I hadn't!

Opium! Please, I beg you, I need some now. I'm desperate. Got to have it, please. I can't live like this. What's happened to me? I don't have any arms or am I still in a dream? Where have I put my arms? I can't seem to find them, and where's my husband? I found a total confusion of ideas oscillating around her mind like a child's merry-go-round. It took a little nudging from me to get her to recall the cylinders.

When I finally figured I'd seen about all the poor woman knew, I pulled out of rapport with her only to see another man had joined us. General Wolfgang introduced me, "Captain, this is our new Hub Intelligence Division leader,

Commander Pino Rainerio of Pegasi-C. Commander, this is Captain Nia Elain Compton-Jereni of Ashford-5, one of the Class V telepaths I've told you about. She and her crew have been instrumental in helping us with these terrorist attacks."

"Ma'am," bowed slightly to me. Apparently, he'd been introduced to Martina, while I was busy with the woman. I saw a thirty-something man with jet black hair, short, and with a small moustache. His face was stern. I sensed he was a no-nonsense fellow, which was borne out within minutes. "I've just arrived from Pegasi-C, where I was the head of our ID there. With the Hub ID having just lost its top two levels of personnel, the other divisions decided that we needed to bolster the Hub ID. Now then, captain, have you gotten anything useful from this pathetic drug addict?"

"Gamelon-3. A trader named either Finlge-what's his name or Finley. She's not certain of his name, but he frequently trades with Equiuss-C. If you recall, they are the junk collectors of the Imperium. If anyone still has their hands on these nasty bio agent cylinders, they likely do."

"Hum. I see. Not too reliable but it's a start. Short, filthy race out on the rim of the galaxy where they ought to stay," Commander Pino barked. "Those drug addicts who call themselves Comrades on Equiuss-C haven't got the brains to be behind all the other attacks. Any ideas who may be, captain?"

I sighed. If only I did! "None, Commander Pino, but we need to get a handle on this soon. If we don't, there's likely to be far more such attacks, just as there were in our old Imperium. Say, Martina here would also like to help investigate this rash of political leader assassinations committed by trusted aides."

"My place. Dinner, five sharp. Both of you." He then turned his attention on Admiral Molly Maud. "Admiral, when you finally meet tomorrow, I strongly urge you and your fellow admirals to pass strong, un-ambivalent legislation aimed at stopping these terrorists in their tracks. Good day. Until five," he nodded to Martina and me, before briskly walking out of the hospital room.

Commander Pino's wife looked more than a little

haggard, as she struggled to serve up supper at their new condo near the ID building. She too had lost her left hand and just wasn't adapting well at all. Dressed as a professional woman, Abella tried to appear as a proper hostess for her husband's dinner guests, us. Her wavy black hair matched his, and her eyes darted from Martina to me, but lingered on me, naturally. "Please, have a seat. I'm bringing it out now," she apologized for her somewhat awkward motions and slowness." Since the commander made no effort to help her, Martina quietly followed her into their small kitchen, lending her a hand. We all said little but normal pleasantries until we actually ate.

"Well, Captain Nia Elain, I'd like your thoughts on how we can put an end to these wicked, evil terrorist attacks," Commander Pino launched into the meat, as we began dining Abella's fine roasted chicken. Martina was quietly feeding me.

"Tough one, commander. Until we know just who has been behind the recent attacks, we don't have any target to strike. Gamelon-3 traders are the only lead I'm aware of," I replied.

He barked, "You have the ear of the admiral. See that she gets the Admiralty Round Table to act against these garbage collectors of the galaxy. If not, I'll use the Special Forces myself. It has to stop."

"And soon, commander," I added. He seemed satisfied.

"Tell me," Martina decided to begin her own inquires, "these assassinations are most alarming. I'm pretty good at tracking things down, and I'd like to help out. I've gone over the little data on them that Admiral Porsche has, plus the questionable newscasts. Is there more information that hasn't been released on them?"

"Mrs. Wells, I've gone over your past records with the Imperium. Seems you once held a post similar to mine. How do I know you're not still acting in that capacity for this emperor of yours? Eh?" he replied accusatively.

Well, he had a point. We were aliens from the Imperium, after all. Martina surprised me with her reply. "Frankly, Commander Pino, you don't. Plain and simple. However, I would point out my association with the ID ended, after I became a terrorist victim myself, a rather long time ago now. You can either accept that or not as you wish. Nevertheless, I have quite an exceptional track record in resolving 'inexplicable' cases, and I wish to offer my talents to the Federation. These attacks seem to me to be particularly disturbing. While it may only be a Federation problem at the moment, it could well spread to the other spiral arm, when it'll be a problem for us. So I have a vested interest in nipping this one in the bud, as we say. Your call, commander."

Abella spoke up, "Just how old are you, Mrs. Wells? You don't look to be more than mid-twenties to me."

"Rejuvenation machine. I'm around ninety-five now, Abella," she replied, not at all bothered about her asking for her true age.

"Incredible. Pino, dear, the Federation ought to see about getting some of those machines, though as I'm now, I don't wish to extend my life. This is just awful," she explained, waving her left stump a bit. We got her message loud and clear.

Pino cleared his throat, obviously also bothered by his wife's mutilation. "Well said, Mrs. Wells. Right now, my plate is overly full. Here in the Hub ID, all the top talent is indisposed."

"You mean helpless, don't you dear?" Abella broke in. "Those poor people. I just don't see how they can even survive."

"Hey, it's not easy," I put her at ease. She flushed, as she realized I was very nearly the same as all the many terrorist attack victims and regretted her bluntness.

"Well, yes I do dear. I have no choice but to put all I have into solving this terrorist mess. Okay, Mrs. Wells, the man to see is my replacement, Commander Vasco dela Valeriano on Pegasi-C. He's been investigating all these assassinations. I can have one of our ID transports take you there tomorrow. Thanks to Admiral Porsche, our transports have these new hyperdrives of yours. The trip now takes about five hours."

"Excellent, Commander Pino. I look forward to meeting him and getting briefed," Martina replied with a wry smile.

Martina helped Abella with the dishes, while the commander and I chatted. However, nothing of any real significance was said. The next day, with my reservations, Martina left under heavy security for the spaceport, bound for Pegasi-C, located in the middle of their spiral arm. Me, I stuck close to Molly Maud. Carla went with us to the Admiralty Round Table, as her constant assistant. I'll say this, Carla was extremely pleased. She had a rare opportunity to sit in on the full Admiralty Round Table meetings, but she also had to sign a secrecy document. They wanted me to sign one as well, but then realized that wasn't possible. I merely chuckled over that bit of over-seriousness.

Nearly all the admirals were new to their positions, and thus spent a lot of their time positioning themselves, trying to gain respect and power for themselves and their worlds, much like the senators used to do in the Imperium Senate. However, one thing was uppermost in their minds. Something had to be done about these terrorist attacks. Admiral Molly Maud didn't have to urge them to take some actions. The only clue that they had was at least one cylinder of that bio agent had come to Comrade Filbert Small via a Gamelon-3 trader.

Some admirals simply wanted to nuke that entire world. "After all, they are not in the Federation of Planets," one admiral declared vehemently. Cooler heads prevailed by the end of the day. The admirals finally passed a resolution to be delivered to the leaders of Gamelon-3. It read: For every terrorist attack involving the genetic biological agent that occurs from this point in time onwards, the Federation will nuke one of your cities.

Yes, they kept it plain and simple. The penalty was steep and highly likely not to harm those who actually sold the bio agent to the terrorists. Still, the admirals figured their leaders would put sufficient pressure on their traders to cease all such sales. However, the admirals also expected they would have to nuke at least one city before they truly got the message the Federation was serious about this.

I stood beside Admiral Molly Maud at her news conference at which she made the public announcement of their new law and ultimatum to the rulers of Gamelon-3. Her official speech was short, but the reporters insisted on asking numerous questions, stretching the five minute notice into a half hour of questions and answers. One asked, "Seriously, Admiral Porsche, are we really going to bomb one of their cities if another one of these terrorist attacks occurs? Is that really going to make them stop selling this awful stuff?"

She sighed, "I know. It's not an ideal answer, but until we can identify and prosecute those who have been selling this stuff, we have to rely on their leaders to rein in their own people. So yes, we most definitely will retaliate. Some of the admirals did simply want to wipe that entire planet out. Cooler heads prevailed, I'm thankful to say. Nevertheless, these vicious attacks must cease and cease now." On it went, back and forth for nearly thirty minutes. Later, I learned this interview went viral, to use a Federation colloquialism, broadcasted on hundreds of worlds, with local transcripts scrolling across the bottom of the interview video.

Three days later, another terrorist attack occurred on Beta Andromeda Six-D, wiping out their entire senatorial wing of their government, along with many aides. Some six thousand four hundred ten men and women were affected. Two days after that, the Battleship Port Royale dropped a super-heavy nuke on Gamling City, Gamelon-3, leveling that city of some million-plus people.

More importantly, a week later, Commander Pino Rainerio intercepted another pair of these mail-clad men attempting to unleash yet another attack on the Admiralty Round Table! This time, his beefed up security nipped the attack before it could be executed. The two men were spotted getting off a transport at the spaceport in Hoffdorf, carrying two heavy duffle bags. When ordered to stop, they drew d-guns, and a brief battle ensued. Both men were killed, and twenty of the bio agent cylinders were recovered from the duffle bags.

With some pride, Commander Pino held a press conference and displayed the confiscated bio agent cylinders. He was suddenly elevated to "hero" status. "These cylinders will be divided up among our various genetic research laboratories in the hope that our scientists can somehow create better cures for all our many victims."

A reporter yelled out, "With this attack today, it would seem that the nuke attack on Gamelon-3 didn't work. Care to comment, Commander Pino?"

"Give it time to sink into their minute brains," he countered antagonistically.

"Will another city be bombed?" yelled out another reporter.

"It's already underway. We will not lessen our resolve," Commander Pino barked back. "That's all I have today." He did receive a round of applause when he stepped back from the wall of microphones, bringing a satisfied smile to his face.

Later, he met with me, bringing along one of those cylinders. "Captain, here's one of them. Anyway to trace where it came from?"

"I've never seen one before now," I replied honestly. "So this is what they look like. I'm afraid all these were made by Fabrication or Duplication machines. It must be an exact duplicate of the original half-used one. It's amazing something this small and innoxious could have such an enormous impact on our two civilizations and people. Just make darn sure your genetics laboratories keep these under close guard. As I understand it, many of the Imperium terrorists got their sample from our own genetic labs, using every imaginable ruse to obtain a copy."

"We're the Federation, not the Imperium, captain. I assure you no one will be able to steal these from our genetic labs," he countered. "Well," his voice softened, "I figured as much. Thanks for looking at it." He turned and left. However, I didn't put much faith in his declaration. Eventually, thieves would get their hands on these cylinders. Still, he had good intentions and perhaps, just perhaps, their geneticists would develop more cures.

On Gamelon-3, the destruction of their second city prompted immediate actions. During the ensuing months, there was a mass migration from their cities out into the more sparsely populated countryside. Small towns doubled and tripled in size, almost overnight. Additionally, many others began searching for new, nearby worlds to move to. Plus,

General Freddy the Wise took matters into his own hands, issuing a public statement that encouraged their traders to duplicate these nasty cylinders, to mass-market them widely, and at a vastly reduced cost. He even went so far as to use world funds to help pay for the duplication costs! Of course, this wasn't immediately known to the Federation.

Martina arrived at the Estrella spaceport on Pegasi-C around one in the afternoon. Wearing her professional woman's outfit, she made her careful way down the bay ramp, where she met Commander Vasco dela Valeriano, accompanied by a dozen security guards, well-armed. He too had rich black hair and a matching moustache with beady eyes. "Welcome to Pegasi-C, Mrs. Wells." He introduced himself.

"Please, just Martina."

"Excellent Martina. This way. We'll go straight to my office." A half hour later, she was sitting in a fancy suite on the top floor of the ID building in downtown Estrella. More importantly, he had one wall plastered with photos and index cards, outlining the various attacks and what was known about them.

"I've got all the perpetrators in custody down in our basement containment cells. This way, I can question them as more information appears. Thus far, frankly, we're stumped. Six apparently random assassinations of world leaders on six worlds, including here on Pegasi-C. I do hope you can see something we might have missed," he declared.

"May I study this board and make my own mock-up board?" she asked. He nodded and gave her a pad of sticky notes, which she asked for.

"I always go in chronological order, when possible," she explained while she was studying his board in detail, jotting some notes on her sticky pad. "It appears that you do too," she said with a smile.

"Precisely. However, in this case, it's not been productive," he replied.

It was suppertime before she'd become fully acquainted with all the known data. He had his receptionist order them take-out, and Martina noticed she too was missing a hand and said a silent curse. While they were eating something called a roast beef sandwich, Martina asked, "I'm not familiar with the spatial locations of these six worlds. Can we bring up a Federation map of some kind and show me where these worlds are located? This sandwich is really quite good."

He grinned and produced a map, sprawling it out on his desktop. "First attack occurred here," he pointed out.

"Here, put a sticky note on it and label it '1,' please," she requested. Fifteen minutes later, six yellow notes had been positioned, and she studied their locations.

"Well, there's a pattern here, Commander Vasco. Look, they started out there on the rim and have been moving steadily down this spiral arm, ending up here at Pegasi-C, the most recent one. Conclusion: whoever is behind these assassinations are traveling in a ship, probably a deep space transport."

"Interesting. I hadn't looked at it quite this way. So you are saying the men we have in custody are not behind the assassinations?" Commander Vasco asked curiously.

"Obviously, they did the deed, but what I'm saying is that it's highly unlikely that they did it of their own volition. One assassination, yes, I could make such a case. Not six almost identical ones. Something far more sinister is going on here, commander," Martina replied.

"Care to elaborate? Anything like this in your Imperium?" he asked accusatively.

"While this terrible bio agent came from our Imperium, we have never had something similar to this, I'm afraid. So let's look at the possibilities. First, it could be just six random acts by their aides. That would presuppose these aides had an overwhelming hatred of their leaders."

Commander Vasco protested, "But that's not what the evidence is saying."

"Agreed. We can discount that one. Second, someone is somehow causing these men to kill their friends and bosses."

"But why? How?" Commander Vasco asked. "I rather thought this might be more like the cause."

"That's a darn good question. Normally, I'd expect to

see a rival of the assassinated leader taking over, a good indicator he has dirty hands. Here, there are no rivals. As far as I can tell, they are holding special elections to replace the lost leaders."

"Yes, emergency elections," he confirmed it.

"So that's out. I'd expect hatred to be a reason for an assassination. I think that's out. Next come blackmail, extortion, revenge, and a desire to grab more power. From your notes, commander, I can't see any connections between the victims. There's been no demand for money and no overt power grab. That's what I find most perplexing in this mess. I would have expected the culprit to be demanding money or power from these assassinated leaders. Clearly, from your investigations, neither has occurred," Martina said sighing slightly and rubbing her forehead.

"And that bothers you?" he asked.

"Indeed. Men don't go to such wild extremes and kill six prominent leaders for no reason. One or two, yes, there are psychopaths around, but six spread out across half of your spiral arm? Highly unlikely. No, I believe we're looking at someone who has been traveling along this route, indicated by the assassinations. He has some ultimate plan in mind, which is yet to be clear to us. Certainly, it's not to throw those worlds into chaos. They are responding in a perfectly orderly manner. It is likely power or money. Without any other connections between the victims and their worlds, I think we can rule out revenge. So we are left with money or power, and yet he's vocalized neither to us. That's most unusual. I would bet anything that the culprit is soon going to make substantial demands. He certainly has our attention now."

"I agree with your analysis. So how do we proceed? It seems like our hands are tied until he steps forward with his demands," Commander Vasco declared, annoyed with the seeming lack of anything substantial to go on.

"I would like to approach this from a different angle. Let's see if we can determine just how this person made the aides do what they did. I assume you've thoroughly interviewed all six men who assassinated the leaders?" she asked.

"Of course. I've made recordings of all those interviews. Would you like to see them? It's several hours of video now," he asked.

"Let's do that tomorrow. It's late, and I've had a long day," she replied.

Commander Vasco arranged a hotel room for her nearby the ID building, and provided an escort and security guards for her. At least two stood outside her door during the night. Martina didn't know if that was for her protection or to prevent her from spying. Possibly the latter, she thought.

She spent all morning watching the interviews. They all had one thing in common. The men complained of hearing a voice inside their heads ordering them to kill their leader. Uniformly, they refused at first, but somehow their heads were filled with excruciating pains that continued to escalate until they complied.

Over lunch, Commander Vasco asked, "Spot anything?"

Martina bit her lip before replying. "Commander, I would like to have Captain Nia Elain come here and use her telepathy on a few of the prisoners. Something isn't right here, and I don't have a good idea what the ultimate cause might be, but she may well have, since she's a powerful telepath."

An hour later, I was on my way to Pegasi-C, compliments of Commander Pino. I refused his offer of sending along someone to be my personal assistant. "It's a short flight, five hours. Martina can help me when I'm there," I explained. I knew Martina didn't want anyone to know she also had the *mentales* gifts, but everyone knew I had it.

For five hours, I had the pilot, copilot, and two security men fawning over me. I was initially besieged with all manner of pickup lines. I guess my body is now just too darn attractive to men. Eventually, I was able to calm their hormones down, and we five had a nice chat, killing the time. Mostly, though they wanted to know all about me.

Once we arrived, Martina was right there, as the transport's bay door opened. She slipped an arm around me and guided me off the ship and over to the waiting Commander Vasco. After introductions, we headed to the ID building. Within a half hour, I was watching a sample of the video interviews, samples that Martina selected out for me to watch to see the overall picture. An hour after arriving, I entered a windowless room where a man was in chains and firmly secured to a chair.

He looked like he hadn't slept in days, as well as being both terrified, and in deep grief at the same time. Conflicting emotions. "I want you to tell me about that voice in your head. Start with when you first heard it," I asked him. I focused, and my earrings glowed slightly, as I entered his mind to see his memories firsthand.

Martina was right in calling for me. This could well be a renegade with a *mentales* gift running wild. Some of us can either take over control of another's body or use a powerful command voice to force them to do something that they would not ordinarily do. That's what both she and I believed was happening here and why she sent for me. However, one look into that man's mind convinced me otherwise! While the apparency of what had happened to these men suggested *mentales* gifts, the reality of what I saw excluded that.

My first thought was that someone here in the Federation of Planets had developed a *mentales* gift unlike ours, yet similar. I had no doubt someone had been making a telepathic connection to these men, sending them the concepts to assassinate their leader and friend. However, when they naturally refused, an escalating flood of energy waves hit their minds, causing severe pain, as though their heads were about to explode on them unless they carried out the orders to kill. It would have been far simpler to just take over that body's motor controls and carry out the assassination directly. Instead, some kind of energy force had been used to make them actually do it.

When I returned to Martina and Commander Vasco, I must have looked worried. "Well?" Martina asked.

"We've got a real problem here. They are telling you the truth. Someone is using them to assassinate the leaders. They plant the orders in their minds and then blast them with a steadily increasing amount of energy that translates to intense pain. When they can't take the pain any longer, they carry out the original order to kill," I explained. "This is very serious.

Whoever is behind this has to be stopped and stopped fast. Any idea where they will strike next?"

"Thanks, captain. Well, no we don't, but perhaps we can get an indication from the distances between the attacked worlds and the elapsed time between the attacks," Martina speculated. Admittedly, I wasn't much use now, not as physically limited as I was. Hence, Martina put me back on the transport for Cass-C.

That done, she and Commander Vasco began compiling the data. They calculated the average speed per day from the six observations. Then, based on the number of days since the last attack, that yielded a "circle" around Pegasi-C where they could possibly strike next. "I don't figure they'll be backtracking, so we can probably eliminate these worlds that are closer to the rim from here," Martina suggested. Still, that left another ten significant worlds as potential targets, according to Commander Vasco. He left to issue some further orders, beefing up security on those worlds.

When he returned, he found Martina adding another circle, the beginning point of the path. She explained, "I've an idea. Let's look backwards. Perhaps, we can spot the point of origin where this person began his rampage of assassinations. This first one was close to the rim. My guess is that his home world can't be too much farther out. There's not much galaxy left. So what's out there?"

"St. Albans-C is the last Federation world out there close to the rim. However, there is any number of Forbidden Worlds in that vicinity. Let me call up the Rim ID commander, and see if he has any Intel on some of those worlds," Commander Vasco suggested. He left the room to place a secure call. A short while later, his receptionist came into the room, requesting Martina to join him in this call.

After a brief introduction, Commander Vasco asked, "Can you repeat what you've told me about the situation there on Beltazar-C? Over." Five minutes later, the reply came back. It definitely pricked Martina's interest.

"Yes. Well a month ago, there were seven Field Marshals on Beltazar-C, each running their own continent. Then, mysteriously, their aides just up and killed six of them.

A Field Marshal Domenico Tonelli survived and took over total control of Beltazar-C. But really, there's not much there to control. The whole damned world is hooked on their virtual reality games," the commander reported. He explained a bit about just how real the V-mask system was, adding that it was highly addictive.

"This is definitely worth checking out," Martina replied. "Can we visit there, land and check things out?"

Commander Vasco replied, "Legally, we aren't supposed to, but in matters of security, we often do land on some of these Forbidden Worlds, especially if a criminal we're chasing lands there. I can't see how a virtual reality game could be causing these assassinations, but I agree. It's worth checking out. The assassinations of six Field Marshals fit neatly into our package here on the table. Timing would be acceptable as would be the distance from Beltazar-C to the first world that was attacked. Okay, I'll make the arrangements."

Three days later, they landed on St. Albans-C and got a briefing. Rim ID Commander Jason Leedsborough explained, "We finally made contact with Beltazar-C. It seems their Field Marshal Domenico Tonelli is not available. They refused to allow us to land, so I've taken the liberty of summoning the Battleship Lone Star. Beltazar-C hasn't anything to match remotely one of our battleships. Their best can be likened to perhaps one of our very light cruisers, if that. Once they see the Lone Star orbiting above them, we should be able to land and conduct our investigations. They refuse to believe all we want to do is gather information on the assassination of their six other Field Marshals."

So much for recognizing the sovereignty of another world, Martina thought. *He who has the bigger gun gets his way. That is the way of men.* She smiled, but knew that they simply had to follow this lead, right or wrong.

Onboard his special deep space transport, Field Marshal Domenico fumed. He'd just received word that a Federation battleship was orbiting Beltazar-C, demanding access to his headquarters. "Damned them to Hell! Dr. Pietro, time to move up our schedule. Enough toying with them. We're going to go to the very heart of this accursed Federation and get us a fine, new battleship!" He entered new coordinates into his hyperdrive and activated them.

"But how? A battleship? Of our own?" Dr. Pietro asked, growing more confused by the moment. First, this awful news from home, and now going to Cass-C itself, and a battleship?

"Indeed!" Field Marshal Domenico exclaimed. "They'll give it to us. We're just moving our timetable up some. Come; we have much work to do."

As the commanders and Martina, accompanied by several squads of soldiers began searching the Field Marshal's headquarters back on Beltazar-C on the rim of their spiral arm, his deep space transport dropped out of hyperspace near Cass-C. At the comm center, Field Marshal Domenico opened up a line, reaching one of the spaceports. "This is the Master of the Galaxy calling. Put me in touch with Admiral Porsche immediately," he barked. Naturally, there was a significant delay as his request got sent through all the proper channels, finally interrupting Molly Maud during the current Admiralty Round Table session.

"Admiral, someone calling himself the Master of the Galaxy is calling for you. He is most insistent," the aide explained.

"If you all will excuse me, I best take this call," she said, carefully rising to her feet. Carla and I followed her out of the spacious room and to a side room where they had their comm center. Taking a seat, she said, "Go ahead and put the call through." I stood behind her, while Carla stepped back out of view from the video camera. An aide nodded and she said, "Admiral Porsche here. You are interrupting the Admiralty Round Table, so please be quick. What is it that you want? Over."

A sickly laugh was followed by the voice of Domenico. "Admiral Porsche. This is the Master of the Galaxy calling. What is it that I want? Simple. A new battleship. I assume you have all manner of spies listening in on this call. I certainly would. So the rest of you down there, listen up and pay close attention. Admiral Porsche is going to give me a battleship, fully equipped. If she doesn't do so within the hour, she'll be assassinated. I call your attention to my handiwork on Pegasi-C." He rattled off five other prominent leaders who had been assassinated by their close aides.

"In fact, I'll use that gorgeous teen standing behind you to kill you if you do not comply. I give you one hour to respond positively. If not, then the blonde will kill you, Admiral Porsche. After that, I'll just continue right on down the line, assassinating your leaders until one of you wises up and recognizes I'm the Master of the Galaxy and gives me my battleship. One hour. Over and out."

Immediately, Commander Pino called her. "Is this some kind of crackpot? Or is he deadly serious? Invoking Protocol 100 now. Stay where you are at, Admiral Porsche. Over and out."

Within minutes, a dozen security guards swarmed around us. Their sergeant ordered us to stay put until the commander arrived. Meanwhile, the Admiralty Round Table was quietly evacuated and ushered into an underground bunker, while not far away, the thousands of ambassadors were similarly taken to shelters. The space fleet was put on highest alert. All over Cass-C, soldiers and pilots raced to their various vehicles, all the while officers bellowed, "This is not a drill!"

If ever there was a time to test these fancy new earrings of mine, it was now. I focused and expanded my awareness outwards, looking for Martina. I knew she must be quite distant from me, since it took me nearly a half hour finally to home in on her. It took only a minute to relay what had happened to her. By then, Commander Pino arrived and my concentration was broken. Too many shouted orders will do that to one's attention.

Martina, in turn, relayed it to Commander Vasco and Commander Jason. "Well, we now have a name for this psychopath, Master of the Galaxy. He only wants Cass-C to give him a battleship."

"I wonder if we've managed to provoke him? If so, he must be this missing Field Marshal Domenico Tonelli," Commander Vasco commented. "Tear this place apart! We need evidence. Now!"

Molly Maud asked, "Captain Nia Elain, can he do what he's threatening to do? Make you kill me?" She was a bit nervous. Well, she ought to be. She'd seen what my crew and I could do, and knew none here could stop me if I did try to kill her.

Commander Pino spoke up, "We should separate you two. Don't give him a chance to make the captain here do something she'll regret."

"Hold on. That's not wise. I'm the best chance you have of keeping her alive. If I'm not here when he makes his attempt, he'll pick on one of you, perhaps even you, Commander Pino. I'm a telepath. I ought to be able to hold him off while your men locate his ship," I countered.

I didn't need telepathy to know how frustrated Commander Pino was. He knew I was right, that he would not stand a chance if this insane Master of the Galaxy chose him to assassinate Admiral Porsche. Instead, he said, "Agreed. His modus operandi is to use the leader's closest aide and that would be you, captain."

"Right. Listen up, Commander Pino. If Molly Maud shows any signs that I might be harming her, you have to put a d-gun hole in my head immediately. There's no other way to stop me if I lose this battle with this Master fellow," I explained, rather shocking both of them. "When he calls back, stall him as long as you can. Give me as much time as possible to prepare and to go after him if I can."

He was punctual; I'll give him that. Precisely one hour after his call, he made contact with Molly Maud again. This time, I was sitting beside her so that I didn't have to put any attention onto my body. I'm not entirely sure what all she said to this man because I was going after him. My earrings and broach began glowing in their pale blue light. Just as I made contact with him in his spaceship and got a quick glimpse of another man and three women lying on cots, it hit me.

Like someone slapping you on your cheek, I felt the enforced energy flow coming from his machine via one of the women on the cots. We later learned it was called the Brunelli Enforcer Model III. *You are to kill Admiral Porsche by any means you can!* The order came via the woman reading a card held before her eyes. She spoke the words into a microphone, but I received it via that high frequency energy beam that had slapped into me. Unfortunately, that mental slap distracted my attention, focusing it upon the woman.

I acted. I didn't want to harm her, just knock her out. Why? I picked up flashes of her own memories of intense pain shooting through her mind when she tried to disobey him. I did my best to hold back, just stunning her unconscious. That done, I again tried to zero in on the insane Master fellow. No sooner had I once more found him, than the other man switched over to the second woman lying on the cot. This time, the energy slap was quite painful, but I shook it off and stunned her as well.

Before I could get to the third woman, this second man must have really turned up the juice! It felt like my own brain was about to be fried! My tower training kicked in. It had been years since I needed to defend myself from such mental attacks. Still, it kicked in. I put up the strongest barrier possible, which had the effect of shunting all that energy flow down my physical body. Later, Molly Maud said that my body jerked wildly and even glowed for a second. As soon as the energies began flowing off me, I stunned the third woman.

Now, it was just me and their machine. Unfortunately, it was dialed into my unique frequency. In a flash, I realized this second man only had to keep upping the power until finally my mental defenses were overcome. Worse, I didn't have or sense his frequency, but I had to stop him and that machine somehow. I did about the only thing remaining to me. I dropped a wall of fire over his hand and the machine. His hand bumped the power level knob, drastically reducing the power level flowing into me. I became aware of his panic and pain, but I focused on the Master fellow, finally contacting his mind.

Via that, I saw the chaos I'd just caused. The second man's clothes were on fire, and he was screaming and dashing madly around a large cabin. The Master began making a mad rush to the cockpit. *Retreat!* No, that was his thought I reminded myself, and then focused, stunning him as well. I moved on up to the cockpit and used a bit of telekinesis to activate the ship's emergency locator beacon, which was very clearly marked. Only then did I back out of the chaos on that ship.

Opening my eyes, I barked, "I've activated that ship's locator beacon. Get ships onto it now before they wake up. I've stunned them."

Commander Pino needed no further urging, barking orders into his hand-held comm device. "Is it over?" whispered a very worried Molly Maud.

"If they can get to that ship before they recover, then yes. I gave them a run for their money. If they'd picked on Commander Pino here to do their dirty work, either he'd be dead or you would be. That is one damned powerful machine they've got up there. Nasty beyond words," I replied. Now, I wondered just how efficient and effective these Federation people actually were.

A half hour later, I found out. Commander Pino reported, "We've captured the transport. Arrested one Field Marshal Domenico Tonelli and a Dr. Pietro Brunelli, who has suffered third-degree burns all over his arms and face. They found three mutilated young women unconscious on a couch. There is an, as yet, unidentified device in the room with the women and cots. The Royale has tractored the ship and will be landing with them here at Hoffdorf Spaceport. We'll meet them at the port. Care to come with me, ladies?"

"Of course!" Admiral Molly Maud replied. Carla rushed over to help her up. They rather forgot about me, so I just got up on my own, tossing my thick, long hair back over my back and followed them.

The Battleship Royale had already landed by the time we arrived. The Field Marshal was in chains ranting and raving as he was led away for questioning. Meanwhile, the other four were being rushed to the nearest hospital. Hence, we all went onboard the transport to check out the device, while other ID men came with us and began scouring everything looking for clues and evidence, I suppose. The machine had a label on it: Brunelli Enforcer Model III. However, it was also covered in soot.

Commander Pino looked it over and commented, "Captain Nia Elain, I don't know what or how you did whatever you did, but we owe you our most sincere thank you. Telepathy did all this? Amazing. If I'd not seen this with my own eyes, I would never have believed it."

Admiral Molly Maud laughed. "Her mate, Danika, has a saying. Never mess with Nia Elain." Both chuckled.

I also knew I needed a copy of this machine for Rafe and our own scientists to study. "I'd like a duplicate copy of this infernal device to send home for study. It will be wise for both our worlds to study it and figure out a way to jam its effects. In the wrong hands, like this Master fool, the damage it can cause is monumental."

Commander Pino was very reluctant to give me a duplicate copy of it. Admiral Molly Maud argued with him for a good half hour before he consented to do it. While they were so involved, I again focused and contacted Martina, letting her know what had happened and asking her to find any laboratories this Dr. Pietro Brunelli might have and to get us duplicate copies of anything they discovered.

Next, we headed to the hospital to check on the four who had been taken there. Dr. Pietro was just coming out of their medical machine, healed of his massive burns. Six armed men stood near him as we entered. The second that he saw us, he began whining, "Please, I only invented it so I could use it to get my son off of those damned V-mask games. He's addicted and died, and I have to have something to get others like him off of it."

Commander Pino ignored his sudden rush. He barked with authority, "You tell us everything about this device and what Field Marshal Domenico did with it, and maybe, just maybe we'll let you live." Shaking visibly, the doctor began talking as fast as he could. Fortunately, I noticed that the commander was video recording the interview, which lasted quite some time.

This preliminary interview finally ended. The security men hauled the doctor off to a cell where he would join the Field Marshal. Meanwhile, we stopped in the rooms where the three women were being treated. They were in terrible shape both physically and mentally. We were able get their names and ages, but little else. All three simply wanted anyone of us to put an end to their misery. Dr. Schmidt was attending them. He took us outside their rooms and explained, "They are in really bad physical shape and filthy. We're getting set up to get them bathed. From there, we're going to put them into a medical machine and see if we can't get their various illnesses cured up. Beyond that, I'm afraid that there is little hope for them. The trauma and abuse they've suffered must have been atrocious. The best we can hope for is to get their immediate illnesses handled and then send them to a nursing home."

I made a spot decision. I had some idea of the massive trauma these three had endured. If they did as he suggested, their lives would continue to be one of unending nightmare. "Say, we could take them back to Ashford-5 where our therapy givers may be able to help them over their mental trauma."

I picked up Commander Pino's immediate reaction. *Well, that's a relief. We don't need three more helpless women. We're overloaded with them anyway.* He said politely, "That would be admirable of you."

"All right then. I'll make the arrangements when they are ready to be released from your hospital." I sensed a good deal of relief coming from both the doctor and the commander.

On our way back, Commander Pino explained to Admiral Porsche. "This technology of theirs offers some incredible breakthroughs. With this Brunelli Enforcer, we can force others to do what must be done. Its uses could well be monumental in importance to the Federation. Why, I can see how we could use it to force our enemies to cease going to war with us. Make terrorists cease their destructive actions. Why, there's no end to the usefulness of this machine."

Worse, he was serious! My ire rose. "So you would use it to assassinate those who oppose you? Another Master of the Galaxy. Only you know that you are right, unlike Field Marshal Domenico," I retorted.

"Well, we're in the right," Admiral Porsche stuck up for her commander. "We could use it to stop terrorists in their tracks before they can do us more harm."

I shrugged my shoulders. No sense in arguing with them. It was obvious they saw immense potential in this invention. I saw only more destruction. I admit I was more sober than normal the rest of that day.

Later, Martina called to say that they found the doctor's laboratory and confiscated two earlier models of his device along with six journals outlining every experiment that he'd conducted with them, along with design specifications. She'd managed to make copies of the journals with her cell phone, ensuring that we would have a copy of them.

When Martina got back to Estrella, Pegasi-C, she spent a couple of days preparing her copies and packing them up securely for her return trip to Cass-C. Recognizing their immense value to us and taking no chances, she also sent an electronic copy to Tesla, encrypted of course. She had just finished when Commander Vasco came by her hotel room with an older man with him.

"Excuse me, Mrs. Wells; this is Detective Diego Rodrigo of the Estrella Police. He would like your opinion on a case of his. Mind you, this is unofficial. You are under no obligations to him. He has a reputation as El Perro del Torro, the bulldog. He just doesn't give up. I'll let him explain." He nodded, turned, and left us.

Chapter 24 Unraveling Threads

"Come on in. I'd offer you something but this is just a hotel room. I can call for room service," Martina said politely, looking the sixty year old man over. While his body was showing his years, she detected a driven man, one who doesn't take no for an answer. He too had the typical black hair and eyes, though his was definitely turning grey.

"Thank you, but if you'll just hear me out, that will be more than enough. I've heard how you were instrumental in helping uncover those responsible for the assassinations. Clever. Commander Vasco has also shown me his file on you. Ex-Hub Sector ID Minister. I think you might be able to help shed some light on a cold case of mine," he said softly, taking a seat across from her, where he could observe her reactions.

"Sure, I'd be glad to lend you a hand. What's the case?" she replied politely, but curious about why a local police detective was seeking her out.

"My beat is the middle class suburbs of Estrella, not far from the spaceport. It's a quiet neighborhood, few crimes. Until now, I was able to solve them all, ignoring those in other beats in which I lent a hand. This one has me stumped. You see, my beat includes a rather highly educated zone along with the highly acclaimed University of Estrella, famous for its microbiology and genetics programs. Now back on June 15, 1382, a high school graduate went missing. She was or is the eighteen year old Bonita Bolivar. She had been accepted into UE's genetics program and would have started there as a freshman this past fall. For four years, she's had a part-time job as a waitress at Don Carlo's Pub, located five blocks from her family's home and just three miles from the spaceport. I did some routine background checking on her. During her high school years, she was a star softball player, a left fielder to be precise. She had no history of any mental illness. Here is the most recent picture her family had of her." He showed Martina a picture of a young teen in good physical shape with shoulder length black hair tied in a ponytail and stuck through the rear of her ball cap.

He continued. "On that evening, she left the pub to walk home. I make it my business to ensure that their neighborhood is totally safe. Yet, she never made it home. We found her ball cap and cell phone on the sidewalk. Here's a photo of the scene as we found it. As far as the phone goes, she had entered one digit of the emergency hot line, a '9.' I had the crime scene boys go over that area with a fine-tooth comb. They came up with this tiny dart." He showed a small bag sealed with red tape. The dart was very tiny indeed.

"I had it analyzed, and the lab reported it contained traces of a very powerful nerve agent that can knock a person out in mere seconds. From everything that I've seen in my long career, this young girl didn't run away or anything like that. I believe she was kidnaped. However, as yet, I've not determined any motive. She was merely your average young teen, ready to head off to the University. She didn't have any enemies."

He went on, "I take this case very seriously. No one kidnaps teens from my beat and gets away with it!" he added angrily. Calming down, he continued, "At first, I theorized she may have been kidnaped to be used in the sex trade. I've ruled that one out. I've busted into every known such ring on Pegasi-C now. No sign of her."

Martina interrupted him. "Any surveillance video in that area?"

"Just getting to that point, which is one of the reasons I came to Commander Vasco and you. I was able to get satellite images from the time of the abduction. Here are some frame stills, the best we have. In this one, you can see fairly clearly this van, which was parked close to the site of the abduction. In this second one, you can almost see the two figures carrying a body into the van, though I admit it's pretty fuzzy. From the first one, I was able to get a partial make and model. I traced it to a rental company at the nearby spaceport. Their records show that it was rented to two traders from Gamelon-3."

Martina interrupted him. "Gamelon-3 again! Damn those small men. Sorry. Please continue."

He cracked a slight grin. "Ah, so you know about the

galaxy's garbage collectors. Okay, I have sent formal inquiries to Commander Vasco who relayed them to Commander Jason Leedsborough of the Rim Intelligence Division. He did some digging for me on these men. Officially, the government of Gamelon-3 knows nothing of these two men. They claim that they've not resided on Gamelon-3 for the past dozen years and have no idea of their whereabouts."

"Dead end?" Martina asked.

"Not entirely. They don't call me El Perro del Torro for nothing. Since these are off-worlders, I presumed that they might have kidnaped other women from other worlds, not just here on Pegasi-C. I've spent untold hours on this. I've gone over all the other missing person cases here as well. I believe that another kidnaping about a year earlier is related. Same MO, though in a different jurisdiction. A tiny dart was found at the scene there too. While other records are not as detailed and thorough as ours are, with Commander Vasco's aid, I believe that I've identified another hundred six cases that fit the pattern very closely. There are many others, but the evidence in those cases isn't as conclusive as these hundred six, hundred eight counting our two missing teens. Always, it is young teens no younger than eighteen and never older than twenty-one — a very narrow age range indeed. If you like, I have photos of these other teens. They vary in hair color, complexions, dispositions, personalities — there simply isn't any physical pattern here, save that they are not unattractive and are teens."

"I have had both commanders put out warrants to all Federation worlds on these two men. If they land anywhere in our jurisdiction, they will be detained and sent to us for questioning. However, as yet, they've not surfaced."

"How can I help?" Martina asked.

"I was hoping that you would ask. Please, look over everything and see if I have missed anything," Detective Diego Rodrigo replied, quite relieved.

As Martina began looking the rather large pile of files, she commented and asked, "Well, a serial kidnaper isn't likely to go after hundreds of women. They usually pick specific victims, based on physical characteristics, such as all blondes.

Still, it's inconceivable that one or two men would want a hundred women. Have any unidentified bodies turned up? Any of these missing teens been found dead?"

"Nope. I check on all morgues once a week. I've got alerts flagged on a dozen worlds for this. Nothing at all," Detective Diego replied.

"That rules out kidnaping, rape, and then murder, unless they have an unusual way of disposing of the bodies. So with so many being kidnaped over what looks like nearly two years, the question becomes where did they take them? My guess is that once they drugged Bianca, they took her to their ship. It's darn hard to keep a person drugged for extended periods. Therefore, it's likely that they headed for their destination shortly after they lifted off. I've an idea. We'll need Commander Vasco on this one," Martina declared.

A half hour later, Detective Diego and Martina were in Commander Vasco's office on the top floor of the ID building. She'd explained what was needed, and he readily agreed. Armed with a map of this spiral arm, as each report came in, Martina and Diego plotted the course heading of the various Gamelon-3 ships that departed the various spaceports on the known dates of the hundred eight kidnaping cases around the time of the event. Martina knew that every ship lifting off had to file a flight plan with the local control tower. Of course, there was nothing to prevent them from altering that once they were in space. It was necessary to avoid collisions with other ships ascending and descending near the spaceport. All that the two could do was to mark a basic heading line.

One by one, Commander Vasco contacted the various control towers and had them look up the data. Hours passed by swiftly. After drawing in the last line, Commander Vasco commented, "Well, that's the last one. All you have is a bunch of lines, Martina. Now what?"

"She's brilliant!" Detective Diego exclaimed. "Look, we extend them, like so. Obviously, these that are going off in many directions are either bogus headings or not the kidnaper's ships. The rest of these tend to come to a focal point out there on the rim."

"Well, I'll be! You're right. Let's blow this up some and

see if we can pin it down further," Commander Vasco suddenly became both very interested and excited as well. Soon, however, their enthusiasm dwindled. "Unknown space. No known planets are anywhere around there. Even Gamelon-3 is way off of the line over here," he pointed to another star significantly distant from the rough focus of all the heading lines.

The commander made a decision. He called up Commander Jason Leedsborough of the Rim ID. He laid out their case and requested his assistance. Commander Jason replied, "Okay. I can send out a light cruiser to that area and have them conduct a search for possible planets. Over."

"Say, can I tag along, since this is my case?" Detective Diego asked.

"Me too. I'd like to see this through," Martina added.

Commander Vasco grinned. "Say, Detective Diego and Martina want to tag along. I'll send them to your place on the next transport. Over," he replied.

After the usual time delay, Commander Jason smiled. "My pleasure. It sounds like we are likely dealing with a bunch of men, not just two kidnapers. A hundred eight women are a bit much for two men," he chuckled.

Late the next day and armed with their plots, the two joined up with Commander Jason onboard the light cruiser Jackson's Hollow. Now came the hard work of trying to locate the planet where the women were taken.

Bianca swung her head back in order to get her disheveled, shoulder length black hair out of her face. Once more, she felt lucid; her mind, clear, thanks to the round of shared pleasuring that she and Maricela had just engaged in on the couch. It would only be temporary, this period of mental clarity; it always was. She was hungry too, but Bianca also knew if she followed Maricela and sucked more food, she would again lose all control of her sexual urges. Something, some drug was in that food. Neither Herzog nor Dr. Wenzel ever showed similar symptoms, and they never ate the women's liquid food. While she longed for the steaks and chicken the men often ate, she knew it was impossible to chew them without her teeth. Lunging to her toes, she wobbled a bit, gaining her balance. Time to continue learning. Knowledge is power, she reminded herself for the hundredth time.

Outside, it was now cold, probably the onset of winter on this strange world with the dim red sun. Without any clothes except this strange plastic-like second skin, she knew she dare not go outside again, not until spring came, whenever that might be. No, today she planned to see what was hidden inside Mayor Herzog's private study. Already she'd broken into the doctor's room. Well, broken in was an exaggeration, since the door wasn't locked, merely shut. Without arms, getting the doorknob turned had been a major hurdle to overcome. It had taken her twenty periods of lucidity finally to work out a method to do it. While she hoped that inside there she might find some way to get her mutilated body cured, all such hopes were dashed, sending her into several days of depression, which no period of lucidity could surmount.

Now, she was only after more knowledge, hoping perhaps in the mayor's private room she would find something that could help her. Bianca knew the only way out of this strange town of New Home was via one of the deep space transports parked just beyond the edge of the town. However, she also knew she couldn't fly it. It wasn't just her lack of arms that prevented it, rather she knew nothing about flying a spaceship. For several days, she dreamed of somehow stowing away on one of the ships, but gave that up as pure fantasy. Even if she somehow could do it and avoid detection, she couldn't speak to ask for help when they landed on some world.

No, Bianca now placed all her hopes and dreams on what might be in the mayor's private study, though if you had asked her what that might be, she would have had no answer, as she walked over to the door on her toes. After so many months wearing the ankle-high special steel-heeled ballet style boots, she had become rather adept in walking in them, just as Maricela had. In fact, because she'd been a high school athlete, her legs were significantly stronger that Maricela's. These days, she got around better in them than her lover did.

She paused at the door and listened. At last, she

squatted down and then mostly dropped her rear onto the floor, knowing just how terribly hard it would be for her to later on get back onto her feet again. After a bit of wiggling, she was in position and raised her boots up to the doorknob. Now came the hard part. Using lateral pressure from her boots, she worked on turning the knob, knowing that the door must open outwards. After a frustrating five minutes, she pulled back with her feet, and the door opened several inches. She scooted on the floor getting her legs into another position and used them to open the door. Scooting in on her butt, she stopped and began looking around the room, burning into her memory everything she could see. Bianca sensed her lucid period was rapidly drawing to a close and abruptly scooted back out, using her feet to shut the door again.

Waves of sensual desires swept over her, once more ending her only rational period. Sexual pleasuring. That craving was all she could think about, and Bianca struggled awkwardly trying to get back onto her feet, so she could run over to the couch and into the waiting body of Maricela, who was likewise in dire need of having her own craving satisfied. So strong was the sensual drive that Bianca couldn't focus enough to get to her feet, and she simply scooted on her butt over to the couch. There, she pushed against it and got herself back up onto the couch, whereon Maricela dove onto her body, her tongue working its magic.

Sometime later and cravings satisfied, if only briefly, she could think once more, but was starving and knew she had to eat. Again, she lunged to her toes, wobbled a bit, and then headed off to the feeding tubes. This time, she ate all she could, knowing with luck, she could have another longer lucid period later on. She headed back to the couch and dropped down onto it, feeling sleepy. She dozed, only to be awakened by that intense craving once more. For a moment, she wondered how she could possibly have survived without Maricela being around and always in the same situation as she was. Perhaps, these twisted men thought of this and kept them in pairs for that reason.

When the lucid period finally came, Bianca began recalling everything she'd seen in his room, searching for something she could use to get rescued or to get help. Then, she remembered she'd seen a comm center! Now, that she could use! No, she suddenly thought, I have no voice now. I can't speak! Grief swept over her; she began sobbing silently to herself once more, and before she knew it, the craving had returned, ending her lucid period once more.

The next lucid period came the next day. I have to signal for help, but how? Think, Bianca, think. She remembered she used to whistle a lot while playing baseball. She attempted a whistle, realizing again, how much she missed her teeth. Puckering her lips as much as possible, she made sort of a sound. Then, she had an idea, a wild one, but an idea, nevertheless. However, she felt the beginnings of this horrid sensual craving coming over her body and wisely postponed her first attempt until her next lucid period. Instead, she thought ahead and quickly ate as much of the liquid food as she could, before she yielded to her now powerful urges, joining Maricela on the couch. Sex-eat-think. Why this pattern emerged, she had no idea, only that it was unfailing.

At last, she could think relatively clearly again. She headed for the door, sat down on her butt, raised her feet, and worked on the doorknob. After an eternity, she had the door opened and was inside. Again, after clumsy, awkward efforts to get back on her feet, and panting a bit, she surveyed the comm center, and found the power-on switch. Flipping it with her nose, she stared at the frequency dial. Bianca had no idea what frequency to use, so she left it where it was. Again, using her nose, she pushed the talk button and began to make her funny, whistling sounds, forming a pattern of three shorts, three longs, and three shorts. Over and over, she repeated it until she felt the onset of the sensual cravings beginning. Hastily, she turned the power back off and headed back out of the room. Shutting the door was easy. Satisfied she'd finally done something to help herself, she yielded to the sexual urges once more.

Bianca felt elated during her next lucid period. She'd finally been able to place a call for help. That no one responded didn't daunt her. Probably, no one was listening in at that time on that frequency. However, she continued to make similar calls as often as she could manage. On the average, she was able to make three twenty-minute calls during the daytime hours each day, except on one day of the week, when both men stayed home.

"Commander, we've been picking something very strange on a little used frequency," a lieutenant got our attention. We'd been searching the rim stars for nearly a week without finding any trace of the missing women. Commander Jason nodded, and we three headed for their comm center on the light cruiser.

"Here's a recording I've made of the last one that we received," the man explained and played it for us, lasting about fifteen minutes. We heard what sounded like a very strange, almost whistling sound, a pattern repeated over and over. Commander Jason frowned, twisting his brow. Detective Diego rubbed his chin. Martina listened carefully, and a smile of recognition creased her lips.

Martina explained, "I have it. That's an emergency broadcast. Someone is sending a signal asking for help. It's a crude code version, long out of date, but a signal anyway. Someone is trying to communicate with anyone, and they need help. What's weird is they are not speaking or saying what is wrong."

"Could this be one of our missing women?" asked Detective Diego, suddenly grasping the significance of the sound pattern. "I should have recognized it too. I've not heard that one since I was a little boy."

Commander Jason asked, "Why would they use this ancient code instead of just asking for help? I mean the chances of having anyone recognize that obsolete code is remote."

Detective Diego answered, "Perhaps they can't speak, or perhaps they don't want to be detected directly. I can think of other reasons."

"We should respond the next time they are live," Martina insisted.

"Granted. We can make some inquiries, find out who they are, and what help they need," Commander Jason replied.

"Of course, it might just be some locals over whom we have no jurisdiction. Still, it won't hurt to at least respond and find out what their emergency actually is."

The lieutenant suggested, "Well, if they stick to the same pattern, they should be active again," he paused checking his watch, "in about twenty minutes." We all stuck around the comm center, biding our time, while the crewmen prepared to get a triangulation or fix on the location from which the broadcast was coming.

Right on time, the whistling, if that's what it was, began again. Commander Jason spoke up, "Unknown caller. We are receiving your distress call. What is your situation? Over."

The whistling abruptly stopped for a moment, but then began again, stronger and a bit louder than before. No voice replied to his query.

Martina acted on a hunch. She took over the microphone and asked, "Are you unable to speak? If so, whistle once for yes and twice for no. Over." All ears listened.

Suddenly, the repeated pattern ended. A lone whistle gave Martina the answer. "Okay. Can't speak. Do you need help? Rescuing? Once for yes, twice for no. Over."

Another solitary whistle. Emboldened, Martina asked, "Are you one of the kidnaped women? Once for yes, twice for no. Over."

"All right! Now we are getting somewhere!" declared Commander Jason, after hearing the solitary whistle. "Ask her where she is located?"

Martina interrupted him, "Sorry. Have to keep it to yes and no answers." She thought for a moment and then asked, "Do you know what planet you are on? Once for yes, twice for no. Over."

The reply was two distinct whistles. Commander Jason asked the lieutenant, "Can we get a fix on her location and head there?"

"Need her on line for another three minutes. Keep her talking," the man replied, working quickly with other nearby equipment.

Martina spoke clearly, "Okay. We are going to get your location by tracing where your signal is coming from. We need you to keep this channel on for another few minutes. Can you do that? Once for yes, twice for no. Over." A solitary whistle gave her the answer they all were praying for.

"Are you physically injured? Once for yes, twice for no. Over." Martina decided to keep the person talking. The lone sound gave her the answer that she dreaded, imaging all manner of tortures the woman must be enduring. A holographic map appeared in the space near them. Then, a dull red star appeared in its center. As the seconds passed, the image began zooming in, and a planet appeared. A minute later, a planet filled the holo-screen, quickly followed by one large landmass. As the seconds ticked, it grew steadily larger until what appeared to be some kind of idealized city appeared.

"That's as good as we can get on the holo-screen. Once we get into orbit above that world and roughly in position, if she can broadcast again, we can zero in onto the actual home that the comm center is in," the lieutenant explained.

"How long?" Commander Jason asked.

"About three hours," he replied.

Martina relayed this. "Okay, we've found the world you are on. We'll be there in about three hours. Can you reopen this channel in three hours so we can pinpoint your location? Over."

Silence. Then came four uneven whistles. "What does that mean?" Commander Jason asked, confused by the unexpected reply.

Martina asked, "You don't have any way to tell time. Is that right? Once for yes, twice for no. Over." The reply was one whistle. "Okay, lieutenant, how long before she would be re-broadcasting again, if she followed the same pattern as before?"

"About four hours."

"All right. Here's what we want you to do. Call us again at your usual time, which would be in about four hours. Can you do that? Once for yes, twice for no. Over." Cheers came when the lone whistle was heard.

"Okay. You can sign off now. We're coming for you. Over and out." Martina signed off, greatly relieved.

For the rescuers, the time passed entirely too slowly. The light cruiser reached the dull red star and found the planet some three hours later. After circling the world, they spotted what must be the right continent. Now, all they could do was wait for the woman to open up the comm channel again. Four hours passed and no call came in. Very impatient men and woman waited. "Look, without a watch, she probably cannot easily tell time," Martina pointed out. They continued to wait.

Finally, the whistling pattern came over the speakers. Martina spoke up quickly, "Hi. We're here above the planet. We're now zeroing in on your location. Are there hostile men around? Once for yes. Over." She forgot to indicate a no answer. A lone whistle sounded.

"Okay. Are they armed with guns? Once for yes. Over." A lone whistle replied. "Okay. Are there many of those men? Over." Another lone whistle sounded.

Commander Jason barked, "See if you can get an estimate of their numbers, Martina."

"Okay, are there more than a hundred of these men? Once for yes. Over." A single whistle answered her. She tried larger numbers until the woman became unsure. There were at least a couple hundred or more men down there holding them prisoners.

Martina asked, "Are there lots of you women being held prisoner? Once for yes. Over."

Her lone whistle was drowned out by the lieutenant who called out, "Got we precise location now. On screen." Everyone looked at the giant screen. A very precisely laid out town appeared, with small farmsteads adjoining it, along with a small spaceport. Some two dozen transports were parked there. The ground was covered in light snow. However, a small red, blinking dot overlaid one specific house. The signal was coming from it.

"Okay. We have your precise location now. You can sign off and wait. Rescue is coming soon. Over and out," Martina explained, turning off the comm center.

"Sound battle stations. Get the soldiers geared up. Full combat gear," Commander Jason began barking a lengthy series of orders.

452

"We're coming too," Detective Diego spoke up, indicating Martina as well.

"Okay, but I insist you carry guns and a personal defense shield. I want you two to go immediately to the house where the woman is. Find out all you can, while the soldiers and I handle any resistance. The lieutenant here will shoot down any transport that tries to flee. We have to find out just what is going on down there," Commander Jason replied. All three headed off to get themselves prepared.

There was no surprise element. The light cruiser slowly descended onto the spaceport, its guns positioned to take out any transports that might try to liftoff. Once on the ground, a giant bay door opened and thirty well-armed and armored troops charged out onto the light snow covered ground. It was also snowing a little. At once, a gun battle began. Disintegration beams shot in all directions, like some surreal fireworks display. Unlike such things, this one was deadly serious. However, not knowing the precise situation, Commander Jason had ordered his troops to use the Stun settings, not the kill settings.

Hundreds of Gamelon-3 men fired a steady barrage at the thirty soldiers, but their settings were on Kill. The soldiers' personal defense shields held and their deadly shots did nothing to the soldiers, while their stun shots disabled those defenders who were hit. More and more defenders poured out into the snow to do battle, but it quickly became wholly lopsided. Hundreds of defenders were down and the soldiers only continued to march forward down the central streets of this town, dropping defenders right and left.

Seeing their chance, Martina and Detective Diego made a dash for a side street and then headed for the house from where the call for help came. With their guns at the ready, the two opened the front door and stepped inside. Their arms slowly dropped to their sides. They saw the two women, Bianca and Maricela sitting nervously on the couch in the living room.

Detective Diego recognized what was left of both women. "Miss Bianca? Miss Maricela? I'm Detective Diego Rodrigo, Estrella Police Department. I've been looking for you both for months. Any men inside this house?"

Relief shown from their eyes. Bianca shook her head no. "Can you speak?" he asked. Again, she shook her head no. "Dear god! What have they done to you?" He slumped into the nearest chair, stunned by what he saw. Martina shut the door to keep the cold air from coming inside and walked over to the couch, analyzing their condition. Their skin looked quite strange, almost plastic.

"Are there lots of you women here? Like yourselves?" she asked. Bianca began crying, nodding her head yes. Unfortunately, both women's sensual cravings rose up again, and they had no choice but to begin to satisfy each other, oblivious to the two total strangers watching them.

"Dear god! I can't look!" Detective Diego whispered, covering his eyes with his hands.

Martina figured it out right away. "They are drugged. Purple Droga if I'm not mistaken. Seen this behavior before. It's almost uncontrollable. I'm surprised Bianca was even able to break free enough to send out her emergency call for help. We should let them finish. Meanwhile, check out this house."

A bit later, Martina found the comm center, while Detective Diego grimaced as he looked over the medical lab that had been used to so terribly mutilate these women. As the two shared their findings, Bianca and Maricela finished up and rose from the couch, heading for the kitchen, where they demonstrated to the two how they were able to eat.

Just then, a very pale faced Commander Jason entered. "It's done. Town is secured, but my god, what they've done to these poor women. It's beyond description. Some even have one year old children, and some are pregnant too."

Detective Diego cleared his throat. "We've found Miss Bianca and Miss Maricela of Pegasi-C. This is unimaginably horrible! What these monsters have done. . ." His voice trailed off. In his long police career, he'd never seen anything like this before.

Martina spoke up, "We've got to rescue these women. They've endured unspeakable trauma and are doped up on that Purple Droga plant. It's in their liquid food, probably to keep these women subdued and completely pliant to their sexual drives."

"But how, Martina?" Commander Jason protested. "They can't live like this. They don't even have their teeth. We have no place to take them. Besides, some are begging my soldiers to kill them. My men said they are using gestures; some figured it out and asked them directly, rather like you were doing with the yes-no answers with Miss Bianca." He ran his hands through his hair in complete frustration. Nothing in his "play book" remotely suggested how he was to handle this mess. "Shooting them would be a blessing."

"How many are there?" Martina asked, realizing if she didn't do something, then that might well be these women's fate.

"Rough count is in, around a thousand, far, far too many to handle," the pale faced commander replied.

"Well, cover them up with blankets and start gathering them together in a few of these homes. I'll use that comm center in there to make a call. Perhaps, Ashford-5 will be willing to lend us a hand. After all, our world is quite close to here, relatively speaking," Martina suggested.

When she came back out of the mayor's private office, she saw the room was fairly filled with women, sitting on just about anything that was available. As she had asked, blankets had been wrapped around them. "Commander," Martina said, after locating him, "Ashford-5's queens have said we can bring them to our world where they'll be treated and their emotional trauma erased. They'll attempt to work whatever genetic cures are possible on these women. After that, we'll see they are returned to their families, if that's what they desire. Will this be acceptable to you?"

The relief on the commander's face was quite marked. "Indeed. More than acceptable. We owe a great debt to your queens," he said formally, though Martina greatly doubted his sincerity. Rather, he was relieved to have this heavy burden removed from his shoulders. "However, some might not want to be rescued. Those who want to stay ought to be given a chance. After all, some of these women might well be their legal wives."

Martina sighed and agreed. She explained to the

assembled women that they were going to be rescued and taken to Ashford-5 to be helped as much as possible. She asked those women who wanted to remain here to shake their heads to indicate yes. As some did, the soldiers picked them up and carried them out, presumably returning them to their original homes. The others were carried out to the light cruiser and stowed in various living quarters. All told, some five hundred women wanted to be rescued, while an equal number chose to stay put.

Meanwhile, some of the soldiers uncovered a cache of the genetic bio agent cylinders, bringing that to the attention of Commander Jason. "Well, well. This is indeed a most fortuitous find! An idea formed, and he began issuing entirely new orders. "Carry the stunned thousand Gamelon-3 men into houses. Put them in with the women who are going to stay behind."

Later, he explained, "Detective Diego, Martina, you go aboard now. In order to make room for all the women, I'm off-loading my soldiers and some crew. They'll fly all of these transport ships to Ashford-5, joining us there. Your people can have the transports to help offset the cost of caring for these victims. Go lend my people a hand getting them settled for the short flight. My men will finish up here."

"But they need to be taken back to stand trial for what they've done," protested Detective Diego.

"I've already tried and convicted them. They're not part of the Federation and are subject to my rulings. I'm taking measures to see that they fully appreciate just what they've done to these victims, detective. Justice will be served, but no, I'm not executing them," Commander Jason replied rather covertly. Neither pressed him further, but headed off to the ship, following two burly soldiers, who were carrying Bianca and Maricela back to the light cruiser.

An hour later, the light cruiser carrying five hundred victims lifted off from the dark planet. In his command center, Commander Jason finally revealed what he'd ordered to Detective Diego and Martina. "You can close this case, detective. Justice has been done. My men put the stunned men into homes and opened several of the bio agent cylinders inside each house. They used up all that nasty stuff these terrorists had stockpiled for use against our worlds. In four days, these thousand terrorists will get a taste of what they've done to these poor teens. Case closed."

Detective Diego grimaced. "My god! Well, I guess they will indeed. Case closed. I'll see that the relatives are notified, at least those few who we've been able to identify. Most are unable even to tell us their names. Martina, if your people have some way of finding out their names and home worlds, let me know, and I'll see if I can contact their relatives and let them know. I suspect they would probably be better off if they died. I can't imagine trying to live as they are now. Beyond grim."

Martina didn't say anything. Perhaps, those men could survive until the supply of liquid food was gone. Then again, perhaps others associated with these men would land and discover what had happened. Considering this was a remote, unknown world, she rather doubted that would occur, but then she'd seen many stranger things. Yet if those thousand men survived, how would the Gamelon-3 leaders respond? With more terrorist attacks? That she knew would be likely. It may have been better if the commander had killed these men. She couldn't help recalling old Emperor Bino's saying, "The solution to today's problem becomes tomorrow's problem." She sincerely hoped this wouldn't happen here.

A week later, Martina joined Molly Maud and me back on Cass-C where Commander Pino presented her with a Distinguished Service Medallion in a formal ceremony before the Admiralty Round Table. One thing was evident to us all: we were making a strong positive impression on the Federation of Planets. Even Emperor Bino called her to thank her personally for her good work.

As September 1 came, the Admiralty Round Table had to entertain the annual requests to join the Federation of Planets. Each year at this time, the admirals met to hear petitions from non-member worlds who wished to join. Some were on the Forbidden List, while others were newly discovered worlds. This time, a few were also ex-Imperium eastern hub worlds, who were desperate to form an alliance to protect their worlds from the three other hub alliances.

As usual, I sat beside Admiral Porsche, while Carla was on her right and Martina on my left, serving as our assistants. A wall of news cameras covered these meetings, broadcasting the hearings live to all the Federation worlds and to the supplicants' worlds as well. We had little to do except watch, as three more ex-Imperium eastern hub worlds, heavily populated, were formally allowed into the Federation of Planets. There was virtually no debate on these. Each brought several battleships to the bargaining table, though the different fuel was problematical. Admiral Porsche agreed to see if Porsche Industries could find a way to retrofit these giant ships with standard Federation engines. If so, the fuel problem was solved.

After these were handled, several worlds currently on the Forbidden List made their pleas to be finally allowed to join. One of these was Blackwell-C. As their representative rose to address the full assemblage of admirals, I couldn't help but recall my own nightmare weeks spent on that world.

Chapter 25 The Great Escape

Lisa was miserable. None of this was as she had imagined only a few months ago when she gaily and cheerfully assisted her older sister, Christina, to learn to adapt to being a Baroness-to-be. No, it was horrid, an unending nightmare, filled with periods of terror. Going down the stairs continually caused waves of terror to sweep over her body, but she had no way to tell anyone about it. Not now, not ever again! Her minuscule cluck-click language had no such verb or noun to remotely describe it to her ladies maid.

Lisa had been quite gregarious as a young girl. Almost as frustrating to her now was her almost total inability really to chat with anyone. Her cluck-clicks only conveyed the barest possible notions, a single noun and a single verb. Worse, whenever she did try to say something, everyone had to turn those two utterances somehow into some kind of sentence that made sense, repeating it back to her. More often than not, it wasn't what she was trying to communicate, yielding instant frustration for her.

Then again, if only she hadn't wanted to wear the ultimate in heels, the seven-inch ones like her mother always wore and Christina too. Of course, she too had wanted to wear them. Her father had often told her that baronesses who were able to wear them were highly sought after and respected by all the barons. She knew she possibly could have managed in the lower six-inch heels she'd worn before when she was helping Christina. Now, all she could do about that was to feel regret for her stupidity back then. Even if she could somehow get across the idea these were too tall for her to manage, her father would simply ignore her.

Lisa had no choice but learn to adapt, though it was daily misery. Endless walking, endless dancing, and worse, endless stairs filled her days. However, she was doing better. Her father often said so. "My, you are walking far more gracefully today, my Lisa." Those few kind words meant a lot to the thirteen year old girl. But now, her universe was shaken.

What have I done that is so very wrong? I did everything they asked of me. She had these very same thoughts at least a hundred times, but still had no answer whatsoever.

Over supper, Baron Ulysses announced, "Tomorrow, our dear Lisa will be moving into Baron Thomas's castle, as his son's Baroness-to-be. In another six months, Lisa will turn fourteen and will be married to him, uniting at long last our two powerful houses."

Her mother, Lilly, cluck-clicked. "Yes I know, this is highly unusual, Lilly, but I had to agree. After all, he was to marry Christina, and still no one has located her. So if our houses are to be united, Baron Thomas insisted that Lisa spend her waiting period under his care so she doesn't get 'lost' like Christina did. I think he believes I had a hand in her disappearance. The fool! So, dear Lisa, you'll get to spend six months learning all about your future husband. Think of this as a great benefit, since you'll be very familiar with him, his needs, and preferences before you actually marry him and become his baroness. Your mother didn't have that opportunity, though I'm sure she is more than pleased and happy with our marriage, aren't you, Lilly?" Lilly nodded vigorously, her long earrings and golden veil bouncing off her upper chest.

Shock swelled up in Lisa, who nearly choked on a mouthful. Baron Ulysses noticed and added, "Don't worry, Lisa. I'll send along your personal ladies maid, Sally, with you. Just remember, grace, poise, stateliness, Lisa, and you'll be just fine. We'll all be there for your wedding, so don't worry about that. You are going to be just the perfect baroness. I know it, dear. Trust me."

Later that night, he once more went through his long speech about the responsibilities, obligations, and duties of a baroness. Then, he kissed her goodnight on her forehead. Once in bed, Lisa broke down, crying herself to sleep once more, terrified of what the morning would bring.

Sally adjusted Lisa's magnificent earrings, resting the heavy emeralds gently on her shoulders, before brushing out her wavy hair, which nearly reached the floor. Morning had come. Following the baron's orders, she dressed Lisa in her finest light blue gown, and helped her rise, facing the full-length mirror in her bedroom for the last time. "There, Miss Lisa, you look just perfect. Never has there been a prettier baroness-to-be," Sally praised her charge. "Come; let's get you to the breakfast table. Then, I have to pack our things."

"You look absolutely beautify, my dear Lisa," Baron Ulysses declared, as Lisa made her precarious way up to the table, trying to be as graceful as she could, hoping that no one could see how terribly nervous she was.

"Well, Tom, no more girls around here now. It's just us boys," Larry barked sarcastically, rather glad to be rid of Lisa.

"Larry, be nice. Lisa is going off to Baron Thomas Riverton's castle today," Baron Ulysses chided Larry, who faked a smile, knowing after today, he'd not get chided ever again.

Around ten, Baron Thomas arrived in his expensive car, bringing his eldest son, baron-to-be Robert, with him. They met in the Grand Ballroom on the third floor, much to Lisa's dismay, since now she'd have to descend two flights of stairs. "I say, Baron Ulysses, Lisa looks stunning, doesn't she, Bob," Baron Thomas said politely.

"Suppose so," Bob replied rather bored.

"Take good care of my precious Lisa. She's all set; everything has been done," Baron Ulysses explained, meaning she was a fully prepared baroness-to-be.

"But of course. This way. Bob, escort your future wife, please. I'll assist her maid," Baron Thomas ordered.

Bob at least moved to the very nervous Lisa's side, but didn't put his arm around her to steady her. "Come on. Dad's brought the Augauti today. It's a really hot car. Of course, I've driven it before, but he is making me sit beside you today. Darn," Bob complained, walking swiftly to the large doors, leaving her far behind. "Oh do come on; hurry up, Lisa," he grumbled.

In her seven-inch heels, Lisa could only just barely walk and certainly not anywhere near as fast as Bob wanted her to go. Embarrassed, she walked as fast as she dared. To take a tumble now would be the most humiliating thing that could happen, of that, Lisa was sure. Then came the awful stairs, and

Bob took them two steps at a time, leaving her way behind. "Oh do come on, Lisa. They are just stairs," he teased her.

Terrified as always, Lisa tried not to think about Bob, focusing on trying to find the edge of the next step with her heel before lowering her weight on that foot. She knew she was going pathetically slowly, but nothing terrified her more than losing her balance and falling down the stairs without any arms to grab hold of the railing.

By the time she reached the main doors, Bob had already gone outside. The double doors stared back at her, an unsurmountable barrier. She couldn't call out for Bob to open them either. Humiliated again, she just stood there waiting. Soon, Baron Thomas and Sally came down the stairs, carrying several large bags of their things. Barron Thomas yelled, "Bob, for heaven's sake, open the door for your future bride." He was annoyed to say the very least. To Lisa, he commented, "You know boys. Always showing off." Bob appeared and held the doors open for the three, enduring a cold stare from his father.

The long ride to Castle Riverton was actually interesting for Lisa, who had never been beyond their own town of Thromstead, and then only to the jewelers there. She knew this was an exceedingly rare opportunity actually to see some of their world, and she took advantage of it, watching everything from her car window.

At last, they arrived at a very large castle, substantially larger than her father's castle. The adjoining city was called Riverton or so the road signs told Lisa. As she stared at the imposing structure while the car moved across the spacious courtyard, she could tell it was four stories tall and thus more of the awful stairs. "Impressive isn't it, Lisa," Baron Thomas spoke up, parking the car before the main entrance. "You room will be on the third floor. It isn't proper to have an unwed baroness-to-be living on the same floor as Bob here. However, that's only for the next few months until you turn fourteen, Lisa. This is the castle that one day you will rule over. Impressive, isn't it. Bob, get the doors, and help your future bride out."

He at least opened the door for Lisa, who waited a moment to see if he would really help her get out of the car gracefully. He made no such moves, so she had to do it herself, as awkward as it was. She then followed Bob into her new home. Everything was wholly unfamiliar. They walked down a hallway and into a large waiting room. No, it was his throne room, Lisa corrected herself. There, she saw a number of others waiting for them. She spotted Baroness Janet at once. How could she be missed?

Baron Thomas arrived, dropping several bags. "Allow me to present my wife, the charming Baroness Janet." As Lisa moved close to her, she noticed several things. First, she wore only six-inch heels. Second, her earrings were much shorter than her own were and weren't threatening to pull her ears off as Lisa continually thought hers would. Third, when Baroness Janet cluck-clicked something to her, Lisa had never heard that pattern before. Whatever the baroness just said wasn't understood. Lisa cluck-clicked a pair of sounds for "Please" and "You," meaning, "I'm very pleased to meet you." Baroness Janet frowned and cluck-clicked some more, wholly unintelligible to Lisa. The baroness had very long black hair, perfectly straight, unlike her own wavy hair.

Fortunately, Baron Thomas interceded. "She is welcoming you to our family, Lisa. Apparently, your speech isn't understandable to her. Are you not grasping hers?" Lisa nodded as another wave of panic swept over her. Her last means of communication was stripped from her!

Sally hastily said softly, "Miss Lisa said she is very pleased to meet you, Baroness Janet." The baroness then smiled and nodded towards her other children.

Baron Thomas continued with the introductions. "Robert is our eldest. Next comes Mary, who is fourteen." She saw a young teen slightly older than she was. Mary was also wearing a corset and six-inch heels, preparatory to becoming a baroness herself. She had long straight hair like her mother, with thick lips, bushy eyebrows, and a round face. She had a bad case of acne though, and gave Lisa a dirty look, seeing Lisa's taller heels.

"This is our son, Chas or Charles. He's twelve now. This is Lindsey, who is ten. Ann is eight, and our youngest, Sam, who is six. As you can see, Mary is now in training, just as you were, according to Baron Ulysses. Of course, you should spend time each day playing with Mary and the younger children, Lisa, at least until your wedding day. Janet and I want you to enjoy your stay here with us, so do play with the youngsters. Now then, Mary, why don't you take Lisa here on a tour, show her where she'll be staying, and where the dining room is at and such. Her maid and I will carry their things up to her new room. Bob, lend us a hand, son."

"This way, Miss Lisa," Mary said rather coldly. "And do try to keep up." Lisa realized she was jealous of her taller heels, but that only made her feel more nervous, since she knew she simply couldn't keep up with Mary's faster walking. If only she'd not wanted these taller heels, Lisa thought sadly for the umpteenth time. Dutifully, she followed Mary but more slowly, resigned to endure Mary's chiding, for chiding was drastically less humiliating that taking a fall!

By the time that Lisa finally reached her new bedroom on the third floor, her legs were soft butter, and her feet throbbed. She sat down on her new bed, held in a rigid posture by the unrelenting steel in her corset. Lisa watched as Sally unpacked their things. "Yes, I know. They speak very differently than you and your mother do. I can't understand their clicks either. I guess we're going to have to pay attention, and try to learn their language, Lisa. I wish we weren't up here on the third floor though. More stairs, but it's only proper. We can't have Bob trying anything unseemly with you before you are actually married, now can we?" Sally continued to chat, as she went about her duties. Lisa had no idea what that unseemly action might be.

At lunchtime, Baron Thomas ordered, "Mary, after lunch, I want you to start teaching Lisa here our cluck-click language. Of course, you kids can all go outside and play in the courtyard. It's a fine day and children need the fresh air. Make Lisa welcome and part of our large family. That goes for you too, Bob."

After eating, the children all rose, and Baron Thomas indicated Lisa should too. "Go outside and have some fun, Lisa." She rose and Sally began assisting her. Lisa was very thankful for the help getting down the stairs.

However, at the door, Mary declared, "Sally, you don't need to come with us any further. Lisa can manage well enough from here. We'll be outside playing all afternoon. So go do whatever it is that you do." Sally bowed and left. "Well, I know dad said to teach you mom's clicks, but heck you can pick that up well enough on your own. Come on; let's go play while we can." Lisa wanted to protest, "How else can I learn it?" She had no way to tell Mary this and meekly followed her outside.

"How about a game of kick ball?" Chas exclaimed, glad to be outside.

"Sure, get the ball, Chas," Mary replied, eager to find any way possible to put Lisa in her place. Thus, began one awful afternoon for Lisa. Unable to move much at all, compared to the smaller children, and constantly the target of their kicks, especially from Mary, Lisa found herself being "it" most of the afternoon. Worse, she could only just barely kick the ball. With her pointed shoes, the ball never even seemed to go in the intended direction. That it barely rolled easily allowed everyone to get out of the way. The only saving grace was Mary had just as hard a time kicking it straight as she did, but Mary could get out of the way far more easily than she. Plus, both Lisa and Mary were often pausing to gasp and catch their breaths. Thus began true misery for Lisa.

One day, she overheard Mary chiding Bob. "You know your bride to be ought to have much larger boobs don't you? After all, she would look even more stunning don't you think? Why don't you ask dad about getting that done?"

Several days later, Mary smirked when Lisa came down for breakfast, sporting breasts the size of her head. Bob looked rather amazed though. Later on, Mary took Bob aside, "Bob, she's not really balanced now. Don't you think she ought to have a much smaller waist to go with her impressive boobs?" Over dinner, Bob brought that up, forcing his father to agree to his demands; after all, the future baron was allowed to dictate how his bride and baroness would look.

The next day, Sally was appalled at the new vastly more severe corset that Baron Thomas gave her. "I'm told you need to tighten it in stages. Don't bring her down for breakfast until it's fully closed. I'm told this one has far more metal in it to help keep her proper form."

An hour later, Lisa felt as though she was being cut in half, and still the back wasn't fully closed. Poor Sally didn't have enough strength to get it any tighter and had to have Baron Thomas come and finish tightening it all the way down. "Impressive Lisa. Incredibly impressive."

Not only couldn't Lisa breathe much at all, she couldn't move anything from her lower waist to her huge bosom. She felt like she was encased in unyielding steel, and she was. Lisa could only walk a short way before having to stop and gasp for breath. Worse, she could barely eat anything, before she felt utterly stuffed.

Bob now seemed delighted with her appearance though. He continually taunted her. "Oh, you can't open the door. Pity." Often, he purposely walked way ahead of her, and then let the door shut, trapping Lisa inside, forcing her to stand there waiting for him to decide to open it for her. One day, he and Mary took her up to the third floor Ball Room, presumably for dancing lessons. As always, they tried to get her to hurry up as much as possible and then laughed at her frantic gasps for breath. After that, they exited the room, shutting the doors behind them. Lisa waited patiently for one of them to return and open it, but no one came for over two hours, leaving her trying to stand in her tall heels all that time.

The ultimate came a few days later when the children wanted to play Blind Man's Bluff. Lisa soon found herself "it" again, since she was unable to avoid the rapidly moving kids with their outstretched arms feeling for her. Of course, they also heard her gasps for breath as well. Bob tied the cloth band around her eyes, blinding her. He twirled her around, but wisely kept a hold of her or Lisa would have lost her balance and fallen down. Then, he said, "Count to ten and come find us." Lisa complied, but heard Mary's heels clicking rapidly on the stone floor of the spacious Ball Room. Then silence.

Lisa knew she was in deep trouble now. She needed to be able to see just to walk. She could only slide her feet forward a few inches at a time, wholly unable to "feel" anything or anyone. How long are they going to make me do this? She thought to herself. After an eternity in darkness, her giant bosom banged into something. A bit of pushing and she decided this must be a wall. Carefully, she turned around and headed off in another direction. She heard nothing, not even giggling. Finally, she just gave up and stood there like a statue. Even if she wanted to, she had no way to remove the blindfold. Eventually, Sally found her.

"I saw the other kids outside in the courtyard, so I came looking for you. They're the meanest, wickedest kids I've ever seen. Come on; let's get you to your room, and I'll brush your hair again," Sally chatted away.

Alone in her room with Sally, Lisa broke down sobbing. She managed to cluck-click. Sally looked up, "You can't live like this?" Lisa nodded, dripping some tears onto her bosom. "I know they're treating you despicably, but not even your father can do anything about it. You are betrothed to Bob and are going to have to do what he says. I've never seen such an awful young man as Bob is."

Lisa cluck-clicked again. "Go away? You want to run away? Oh, like Christina might have?" Lisa nodded. "Well, I agree with you, but how? Where would we go? They'd surely come after us, and then we would be in more trouble than we are now. You know what your father would say. 'It is the obligation of the baroness to do whatever her baron desires and to wear whatever clothing he provides.' We just have to manage somehow, Lisa. It might be easier for you if they hurried up and made Mary into a baroness-to-be as well. Give her a taste of her own medicine." Lisa cluck-clicked again. "You want me to suggest it?" Lisa nodded. "I can't. It's not my position to say anything like that. After all, if they dismissed me, then what would you do?" Lisa only sobbed more.

For seemingly endless weeks, Lisa continued to endure the constant harassment from Bob and Mary. She couldn't tell who was worse, perhaps Bob, who didn't care the slightest about how awful he was making her life. Worse, she was supposed to marry him.

Then came the eventful evening. After supper, the large family often sat in the drawing room watching the news. "Tonight is special. We are going to watch our ambassador plead our case to join the Federation of Planets to the Admiralty Round Table on Cass-C. This should be interesting. This year, we may well be allowed to join the powerful Federation. Look, see, now they too have baronesses as we do. They are some of their admirals. Well, sort of like our baronesses. They are wearing such strange lip adornments. Plus, they still allow them to actually speak, even though it comes from those strange boxes around their waists. Let's watch this. It could well be an historic occasion for Blackwell-C."

"Look, they are zooming in on Cass-C's Admiral Porsche. Doesn't she look like a proper baroness, except for those lip things?" Baron Thomas pointed out. "Wait! Who is that beside her? Damn, if that doesn't look like Christina Blackwater! That face, that hair."

Baroness Janet cluck-clicked. "Oh. Janet's right. Look, that woman who looks like Christina is actually talking to Admiral Porsche. Well, that can't be our Christina then. Without her tongue, she can't possibly talk, right Janet?" His wife nodded silently.

Nevertheless, Lisa stared at the image on the large screen. It looked like her older sister. Lisa remembered Christina had a barely visible dimple on her lower chin, visible only when she smiled. Lisa watched carefully until the woman flashed Admiral Porsche a smile and spotted it. That just had to be Christina! She knew it had to be. Somehow, someway, Christina had managed to get halfway across the galaxy to this Cass-C place and now sat beside that world's ruler, their admiral, perhaps even as an advisor! Somehow, she was now able at least to speak again! She watched Christina carefully, and finally noticed she was also wearing seven-inch heels, which only confirmed Christina's identity for Lisa!

Later as Sally was preparing her for bed, she cluck-clicked as best she could. "Christina? You think that was Christina we saw tonight? It can't be. She was talking, I'm sure of that."

Lisa had no way to say dimple. She felt enormously frustrated and then got an idea. She rose up and moved over to the bedpost. It was difficult but she managed to press her chin onto the bedpost. When she rose up, she stuck out her chin. "Oh, dimple?" She nodded. "Well, yes, Christina has one. Oh, you saw her dimple!" Lisa nodded too vigorously, banging her heavy earrings into her shoulders, nearly pulling her ears off, or so she felt.

"Well, if it was Christina, how can she speak again?" Sally asked. Lisa shrugged her shoulders. "I wonder how she managed to get there from here? Must have been on a spaceship," Sally theorized.

Lisa cluck-clicked the word for "go" and "Tina." "You want to go to Christina?" Lisa nodded. "Well, so do I. I don't see how we can. The barons will never allow it. Shoot, they don't even allow you to visit the cities, except to go to the jewelers." Lisa sighed, but that night she began dreaming of being with Christina again. In fact, that's all she could think of from that point onward.

At the Admiralty Round Table, Ambassador Tim Shoals of Blackwell-C rose. He was introduced, and with the universe watching, he prepared to once again make his sales pitch to have Blackwell-C admitted into the Federation of Planets. "Esteemed admirals, it is with the greatest of humility I once more stand before this most distinguished assemblage of world leaders, you mighty admirals, who are keeping our spiral arm safe and secure. In the past, you have consistently denied us entry because of our millennia old customs with our baronesses, our co-rulers, who always sit beside their barons at court each day. I point out we only have a hundred eleven such highly honored women on all of Blackwell-C. These women are the most respected women on our entire world."

"As I look around me today, I see that several of your Federation worlds now also have similar highly respected women serving as your leaders, just as we do on Blackwell-C. While I also realize they have been the victims of most terrible terrorist attacks, I cannot help but see that physically they are nearly the same as our most respected baronesses."

"Take the esteemed Admiral Porsche of Cass-C for example. She is almost physically identical to any of our ruling baronesses. And Cass-C has freely elected her to be their supreme ruler. Obviously, the majority of the people of Cass-C believes she is not only worthy to be their leader but is also able to fulfill her duties and obligations as their admiral. Likewise, our baronesses are beloved of their people and are always able to fulfill their duties and obligations, just as Admiral Porsche is doing. In fact, she even has an advisor, who is also very much like our baronesses as well, only she is one of the prettiest women I've ever seen."

Of course, all eyes shifted to us, as did the cameras broadcasting this meeting live to many worlds. Molly Maud whispered to me, "I can see where this is going."

I whispered back, "Right. So you were preventing their entry into the Federation until they changed the ways that they treat their baronesses?"

"Precisely. Now, I don't know if we can continue to press them to change." She and I continued to chat, but I also didn't see any way around it. This ambassador certainly knew how to make a strong case. I gave him that much credit, though his language was a bit over the top.

When he finished his presentation, Admiral Porsche began the questioning period, hating that her words were coming from the mechanical box around her waist. "Thank you Ambassador Shoals. In my case, I did not have any choice to become as I now am. I, like thousands of others, was a victim of a vile terrorist attack. Might I ask you, do your potential new baronesses also have a choice of whether or not they wish to have their bodies hacked up and become helpless baronesses?"

Several other admirals complained about her choice of words, but Ambassador Shoals dismissed them politely. "Of course, our baronesses have free choice. If they do not want to become one of the most honored women on Blackwell-C, then they do not have to. They can move into a town or city and do whatever they wish."

"They didn't give Christina any choice," I whispered to Molly Maud. However, she and I dare not bring this up.

Another admiral spoke up. "Well, personally, I don't see that such a small issue should bar the way from having such a modern and wealthy world join the Federation of Planets.

After all, we now have nearly ten thousand, who are quite similar to their baronesses, and most of them are not leaders. Some are quite ordinary people who became victims. There are only a hundred of their baronesses, not ten thousand. Look, if Admiral Porsche can continue to serve as Cass-C's admiral, I can't see this as a barrier to use against Blackwell-C."

A half hour later, the vote was taken, and Admiral Porsche rose to announce the results. "It is with great pleasure that the Admiralty Round Table has decided to welcome Blackwell-C into our mighty Federation of Planets. Let me be the first to congratulate you, Ambassador Shoals, and all the fine people on Blackwell-C upon your entry into the Federation. A round of applause, please." The room erupted into a polite round.

"Tomorrow, we'll meet with you to discuss the necessary other arrangements, ambassador. Okay, who is next?" she asked.

Baron Thomas wore his best suit for breakfast and announced, "Today is a very special day. The Federation's Commander Vasco dela Valeriano is coming here to Castle Riverton to meet with me and several other barons. We'll be discussing our entrance into the Federation of Planets. This is an historic day for us all. I want everyone to be on their very best behavior, kids. We must make an indelible impression on this man. He is in charge of their mid-spiral arm Intelligence Division, no less. He has arrived in one of their battleships, but will be landing his deep space transport in our courtyard around ten this morning. We'll be holding meetings all day long. Of course, Janet will be at my side the whole time, so you kids stay out of mischief or there'll be hell to pay this time. Robert, you will also accompany me as my heir, though Lisa you had best not, since you aren't yet married. In fact, Lisa, it would be wise of you to remain, as invisible as you can while these men are here."

He continued, "In fact, if all goes well today, then tomorrow, Mary, I'll consent to getting your Baroness Preparations done. Baron Ulysses wants to have a joint wedding just as soon as Lisa turns fourteen, uniting both of our houses, critical for maintaining balance and control of Blackwell-C as we join the Federation. I'll talk to Baron Ulysses about what his Larry desires in his future baroness, and see that you, Mary, will meet his desires. That's all. We have much to do to prepare for this historic visit. All must go exceedingly well."

After breakfast, Sally helped Lisa up to her room, where they would spend the day being invisible. However, the noise of the transport landing got their attention, and both watched the huge transport landing in the spacious courtyard. A dozen other cars were parked off to one side. The other barons had already arrived, and Lisa wondered if her father was here too. Still, he would be of no help in alleviating her misery. No, she had to get to Cass-C and Christina, somehow, someway. In her limited way, she began trying to work out how she and Sally could do that. This seemed like the right time. The how remained elusive though.

From her third-story window, Lisa watched the silver transport for hours. Here was a way off this world, but she knew she just couldn't walk into the ship. She and Sally continued to try to invent a way to do it. Below their room, the smaller children were getting rowdy, unused to being cooped up for so long. It was now late afternoon, and no longer were they being especially quiet. That gave Sally an idea. She and Lisa rose and made their slow way down one flight of stairs. "Can you keep on going by yourself?" Sally whispered to Lisa. She nodded bravely, fighting once more her terror of the stairs.

Sally watched her for a brief moment, before entering the children's playroom. "I see you are all anxious to get outside. Why don't you all be very quiet, go outside, and look around? After all, if you are quiet, your father can't complain, now can he?"

"Well, I don't see why we have had to stay cooped up in here all day long, not when Bob gets to sit in on all the official meetings," Mary retorted. "Come on, kids. Let's go see the silver ship of theirs. We may never get a chance like this again, but be very, very quiet, okay? Or we'll be in big trouble." Sally smiled, headed back out, and down the stairs, where she caught up to Lisa and slipped a supporting arm around her. Soon, the others dashed past them, though Mary was behind the other smaller children.

Moving as slowly as Lisa was, by the time they neared the silver ship, the other children were already there. Mary and Chas were chatting with the soldier standing guard duty before the opened bay door ramp. No one else was around. Behind them a dozen fancy cars were neatly parked. Sally moved Lisa to the backside of the ramp, more or less in the shadows. Now they waited. Sally knew children well. After all, she'd been around the Blackwater clan since Christina was born. As much as they tried to be quiet and well behaved, eventually their childish enthusiasm would dominate.

After waiting patiently for neatly fifteen minutes, Lindsey, Ann, and Sam began running about, creating a bit of a disturbance. Mary tried to stop them, but in her heels, she was wholly ineffective. So Chas had to try to get them to calm down. All this totally distracted the soldier watching the bay ramp. He moved after the kids to make sure that they didn't damage the sensors on the front of the ship. Without a word, Sally nudged Lisa forward. Together, they went up the ramp as silently as possible. Moving so slowly, they didn't attract any attention to themselves.

Once onboard, Sally saw a long hallway and pushed Lisa down it, heading towards the rear. Once they were halfway down it, she began listening at each door. Hearing nothing, she carefully opened it and looked inside before moving on down to the next one. The very last one held what Sally thought was just junk. She nudged Lisa inside and carefully shut the door before switching on the lighting. Looking around, she found a good hiding place, but had to help Lisa sit down on the floor beside a bench. Then, she found a blanket and switched off the light. In the pitch-blackness, she felt her way over to Lisa and sat down beside her, covering them both with the blanket. She whispered, "Now we wait. If we are lucky, we'll be able to feel the ship taking off. Then, we might be safe."

The pair waited in utter silence and complete darkness. Lisa knew if they were caught, Baron Thomas would be furious, probably firing Sally. She couldn't imagine what further tortures he could invent to put her through, though. Already, she had long reached her limits of endurance. How long they sat there, they couldn't say. In darkness and silence, neither had any way to tell the passage of time, save for their stomachs, which suggested it was past suppertime or at least near it. Of course, Lisa was always hungry an hour or so after eating, but that was just her corset limiting her food intake.

Then, something happened that caused a rush of elation in both women. They felt the floor beneath them wobble slightly and sensed motion. They were taking off! Neither had any idea what was happening here nor back inside the castle.

However, Baron Thomas was chatting with Dr. Jones before suppertime. The day had gone superlatively, except for the minor annoyance of the children being outside for a short while. "Yes, I've kept Baron Ulysses informed of how well Lisa is doing. It seems his Larry doesn't want to be outdone by Bob. So it's time to get Mary's Baroness Preparations done. Here's the requirements Larry desires. Can it be done, doctor?"

"Well, yes. Of course, but it would be best for her if she didn't have supper before the operations are done. We could do it now. There's time before you dine," Dr. Jones answered, checking his watch.

The two headed up to Mary's room. Before she could say anything, Dr. Jones placed a rag over her nose and mouth. Darkness came quickly for her. Servants brought the doctor's equipment up to the room, and he began to work his magic on Mary. An hour later, he stood back, admiring his handiwork and imagining the rather large payment he was about to receive! Baron Thomas entered to inspect the product. "Amazing, doctor. Perfect in all ways. Okay then, I best get her maid in here, and get her dressed for supper. It's about time to dine. Your payment," he handed him a check. The doctor glanced at it and noticed the baron had given him a substantial bonus. He smiled, stowing it safely in his jacket pocket. "Care to dine with us, doctor?"

"Delighted, baron, but we might be needed to help get that new corset fully tightened." Just as it had been for Lisa, Mary's ladies maid could not pull it tight enough, and the two men assisted her. That done, her new heels were tied onto her feet, and she was properly dressed, with the new golden veil attached. Only then did Doctor Jones wave some smelling salts before Mary's nose, rousing her from her sleep.

Mary awoke to her own nightmare. Her corset was way overly tight, though she soon learned her waist was now as small as Lisa's, barely twelve inches around. Her comfortable heels had been replaced by the seven-inch ones that Larry insisted upon. Her arms and tongue were gone, and each of her breasts was as large as her head, just as Lisa's were. She tried to cry out, but gasped instead. She'd only made garbled sounds! Although she was in an utter panic, no one seemed to care, as her maid forced her to her feet and down the hall to supper, while her new golden veil banged against her face and mouth, threatening to pull her ears and nose off. Thus began Mary's never ending nightmare. No one missed Lisa for some time. All eyes and talk were on Mary. Besides, the baron had told her make herself invisible.

Scarcely daring to breathe for fear of discovery and being tossed back to the baron to face his wrath, the two women huddled together in the darkness and silence at the rear of the deep space transport. Through their butts, they felt the low vibrations of the engines steadily taking them away from Lisa's continual torment. Then without warning, they felt a jerk and a slight jar that tossed them slightly to their right and then back again. Neither knew what that meant. The transport had just docked inside the battleship's hanger. Both women continued to be as silent as birds in their nests at night, for it was almost as if it were night.

Then, they heard faint footsteps, boots upon the cold steel floor, but they were distant. Silence once more reined. The two waited, Sally's arm around Lisa. Time slipped by, broken only by another slight vibration, the barest sensation of motion or was it? Neither knew, but they possessed one virtue, patience — the kind of patience that comes with silently enduring months of an unending torture over which neither had any control. For Sally's part, she knew how awful Bob had been treating Lisa and knew that once they were married, it would only get worse, much worse. She'd seen that happen to her own older sister who lived in Thromstead, married to a brute of a man. Somehow getting Lisa out of that hell-hole would make up for her sister. Lisa, on the other hand, only dreamed of reuniting with her older sister — Christina, dear Christina, who once depended upon little Lisa. Yet, that seemed a lifetime ago. Would she now even remember her? Lisa knew she looked so very different now. Perhaps, she wouldn't recognize her, but she could at least cluck-click with her older sister. She would remember then, Lisa was sure of it. Alone with their thoughts, both women fell asleep.

Lisa awoke and needed to use the bathroom badly. So did Sally. She softly cluck-clicked. "I know, I do too. I guess we have to get up and face the music. Maybe they won't send us back. You stay put while I try to find that light switch again," Sally whispered. She threw off their blanket and got to her feet. After what seemed an eternity to Lisa, Sally finally found the light switch. Lisa cluck-clicked. "I know. You can't get up on your own. Patience. I'm listening to hear if anyone is nearby. I think I saw a bathroom in one of the cabins up there," Sally whispered in reply. Soon, she came over to Lisa and helped her get up on her feet. Then, with a steadying arm, she led her to the door. Both took as deep a breath as they could, and Sally opened it.

The long hallway was fairly dark and appeared deserted, though some light came in from the open bay ramp. The two headed down and began checking for cabins. At the first empty one, Sally ushered them inside and to the small toilet. That necessity handled, now they needed food, but that meant having to leave the transport and face wherever they were, placing themselves at the mercy of this commander fellow. As they approached the bay ramp, Lisa again panicked. "I know. You can't manage it. I'll sort of lift you down," Sally whispered, struggling to do just that. Then, they both stared in total wonder and awe. They were in some kind of huge enclosed space, on a small ramp beside the transport ship. Around them were dozens of other docked transports. Dim lights illuminated the area.

Both swallowed hard. Sally put a steadying arm around Lisa, before urging her forward along the platform. They'd reached the long ramp that led along the front side of this giant docking bay area when two soldiers spotted them. "Hey! You there. What are you doing here?" With drawn guns, they swiftly came up to the two women. "What the hell?" one said. "Go call the captain. Don't move, either of you." They complied.

A few minutes later, a man in a fancy uniform joined them. He was just as startled to see the pair, more so as he eyed Lisa and her very strange appearance. "Stowaways?" he asked.

Lisa nodded, and Sally said, "Yes, we want to get to Cass-C and find her sister who was with their Admiral Porsche. We saw her on the newscast. Please sir."

The captain scratched his head. "Okay. Jones, go get the commander. Tell him what we've found. I'll take them to interrogation. Ladies follow me."

"Sir, slower. She's wearing very high heels," Sally protested his brisk pace, which Lisa simply couldn't follow, though she tried, but was soon gasping for breath. He slowed down.

They entered a plain room with white walls, one table, and three chairs. He ordered them to sit down and stood guard over them. Soon another man in a fancier uniform stepped into the room and gasped as he saw Lisa. He nodded to the captain, who promptly left. Taking a seat, he said, "I'm Commander Vasco dela Valeriano. Just who are you, and what do you think you are doing on my ship?"

"Sir, this is Lisa. She can't speak. They cut off most of her tongue, part of the Baroness Preparations. We are trying to get to Cass-C so she can meet her sister, who was with Admiral Porsche at that big meeting where Blackwell-C was allowed to join your Federation. She's the beautiful young woman with the very long, wavy, golden hair," Sally explained as best she could. Wisely, she decided not to mention her sister's name, since more than likely Christina had changed it, so her father couldn't find her.

"You are one of their baronesses?" he asked.

Lisa shook her head both yes and no. Sally hastened to explain, "She has had the Baroness Preparations and was supposed to marry her baron in about five months or so, but he's an awful brute of a boy. She's running away to join her sister on Cass-C."

"And do your parents know about this?" Lisa shook her head no so hard that her earrings bounced wildly around, threatening to pull her ears off. "Oh good god. What a mess has landed in my lap. I ought to return you to your father at once."

"Please sir. Let her visit with her sister first, I beg you, please," Sally pleaded with him.

"Well, you two stay here. I'll be back in a few minutes." Commander Vasco left, thinking hard. The golden haired woman could only be Nia Elain Compton-Jereni, the admiral's consultant from the Ataro Empire. Surely, this couldn't be her sister. Nevertheless, the two women were convincing. As the head of the ID here in the mid-arm region, he was keenly aware of the micro-expressions, indicating lying or deception. Neither woman had shown any. Whatever was going on here, they were certain of the aide of Admiral Porsche. Hence, he took a gamble and placed a secure call.

"Admiral Porsche. Yes, I'm well. The business has been handled. However, something very strange has come up, potentially an inter-world incident. I need to speak to Captain Nia Elain, if I may. Over."

Molly Maud explained to me, "How strange. He didn't say what he wanted, Nia. Here, Carla will press the Talk button for you." I tossed my hair to one side, sat down, and nodded to Carla.

"Hello again, Commander Vasco. Nia Elain here. What's up? Over." I spoke into the comm center, noticing the channel was secure, meaning it was encrypted. Anyone who picked up this video conference would be unable to decipher it without first entering the correct 1024-digit code.

"Got a stowaway onboard from Blackwell-C. Claims she is your sister. Young girl, but with monster breasts, no offence admiral, no arms, can't speak, golden veil over her lower face, tiny waist. Claims her name is Lisa. She has another young woman with her, probably a servant. She wants me to bring her to you. Does this make any sense? She claims to be one of their baroness to be's, whatever that may mean. This has the makings of a very nasty inter-world incident. Over."

Lisa! Memories flooded into my mind. Dear little gregarious Lisa, the one who saved me. Could this really be her? "Commander, can you bring her and her servant to the comm center so I can see her? Over."

Five minutes later, I was staring at Lisa! All she could do was cry and cluck-click to me. "Okay, Lisa. It'll be all right. Commander, you there? Over." I watched as her ladies maid, Sally, helped her rise from the seat, and Commander Vasco sat down before me again.

"Commander, we need to keep her presence on your ship as secret as possible. Bring her to us here in Hoffdorf. I'll meet you when you arrive. I don't have to tell you how critical it's going to be to keep her presence a total secret. Lisa must need my help. Over."

"Agreed. It's a damned shame they treat such lovely children like this, turning them into helpless victims. No offence admiral. We'll let you know when we're approaching Cass-C. Over."

Molly Maud laughed. "No offense taken commander. I was a terrorist attack victim, but this young teen was mutilated by her own parents. Nasty indeed, but I couldn't persuade the other admirals to reject Blackwell-C's petition this time. Thanks for your discretion. Over and out."

"Okay, ladies. You heard her. I have to keep your presence on this ship a secret. Captain, take them to Cabin 123C. See that they get some food and drink. Not a word of this to anyone. I'll go speak to the men who first found them," Commander Vasco ordered. While he knew by now probably many men knew about the two women's arrival, he could fairly easily contain it.

Three days later, a transport ship landed at the Hoffdorf spaceport, bringing Commander Vasco and the two women to me. Martina, Molly Maud, and Carla were there with me, as we slowly made our way to the now-opening bay doors. When the ramp finally touched the asphalt, I got my first glimpse at Lisa, and frankly, I was shocked with what I saw. They had gone way too far with her! In my opinion, her waist was unimaginably tiny, and her bosom was nearly equal to Molly Maud's, but Lisa couldn't be more than thirteen! Thankfully, Commander Vasco lifted her down and steadied her, until Sally got down and slipped her arm around her. Together and grinning broadly, they began their slow walk towards me. I could sense utter elation coming from Lisa!

"Thanks Commander. We'll take it from here. She never came here," I hinted.

He winked at me. "Of course. That we had a stowaway is simply rubbish. Good day." He turned and went back into the transport. He lifted off before we six finally met. None of us could walk any faster than the other, that is, among Molly Maud, Lisa, and me. When we finally reached each other, Lisa began sobbing, and I pressed into her, comforting her, while the others watched on.

To Sally, I whispered, "Don't say anything about me being her sister. Officially, you are not here at all. We're heading over to that transport over there. See, the woman is waving at us." I guided everyone to the Eagle's Seed, where Danika and the real Christina were waiting. She was also crying. For once, I was very thankful for Danika's speedy arrival from Ashford-5!

Once onboard, I had a good deal of explaining to do! Poor Lisa couldn't figure out why this other much older woman was crying and hugging her! Christina couldn't wait for explanations though, blurting out, "It's me, Lisa. I'm your sister. Nia and I got somehow switched into each other's bodies." Lisa looked very confused as did Sally.

"Come on; let's get to the galley. We need to have a long talk," I declared. Jana had come along and had some hot tea waiting for us. I personally needed it, for I talked for nearly an hour, trying to explain it fully to Lisa, using words she could understand. For the longest time, she didn't believe me. She cluck-clicked, and both Christina and I cluck-clicked almost simultaneously an answer, confusing her even more.

"Okay, Christina, tell her about something that only you and she would know about. Lisa, you think of something that only you and Christina would know about," I requested.

That did the trick. At last, Lisa looked at Christina in

the right way. She knew, despite our appearances, the older woman was really her sister, not me, who looked like Christina had once looked. Confusing, yes, but Molly Maud and Carla understood fully now. Then, Lisa cluck-clicked again.

"Oh. Well, there is a way that we can get your tongue back so you can speak again, Lisa," I explained, and then did so in much greater detail. "Would you like that done to you?" I asked, "Even if you don't get your arms back like me?" Lisa nodded vigorously as I knew she would. I sensed the utter hell she'd been in since they cut off most of her tongue. Lisa was gregarious and that had hurt her perhaps worse than anything else had. She cluck-clicked again.

"Sure, Danika and I'll take you into our family too, so you can be with Christina. We won't ever separate you two ever again, Lisa. I owe you so very much. If it hadn't been for all your help back then, I'd never have survived that ordeal," I explained to her. Lisa beamed. "Now, we have some eight hours before we get home. Would you like us to get your breasts back to normal size and get you out of that awful corset?" She nodded vigorously.

"Oh thank you, thank you," Sally gushed, greatly relieved. Then, she added, "What will happen to me?"

"You can stay with us too. If her arms don't regrow like mine didn't, she's going to need some assistance, Sally," I explained, bringing a big smile to her face.

When we arrived, Lisa no longer wore the golden veil or her overly heavy earrings and corset. Dr. Leann reduced her bosom to what was considered normal for a thirteen year old girl. Plus, we dressed her in a simple satin pencil style dress, and for the first time, Lisa could now see her feet, making walking much easier for her.

As soon as we landed, Dr. Leann and Christina took Lisa to the medical lab and began her cures, while Danika took Martina, Carla, and Molly Maud back to Cass-C. I stayed around to make sure that all went well.

A week later, the geneticists and doctors brought Lisa out of her medically induced coma. Now, she too was a hermaphrodite like the rest of us, but more importantly, her tongue was whole again. Like me, her arms didn't regrow nor did her feet fully recover. Likewise, her wavy long hair had pain neurons in it and couldn't be shortened, but that didn't matter in the slightest to Lisa. That she could talk again meant everything to Lisa, and from the moment she awoke, she almost didn't stop talking! We certainly got an earful about what had happened to her after I left Blackwell-C.

She finally did stop, but only because Christina began playing her harpsichord for Lisa. "Oh Christina! You did it! You are playing the clavecin like you always wanted to do!" Lisa exclaimed, bouncing in her chair. A day later, Danika and I formally adopted Lisa into our family. Governor Misty provided her with proper ID making it official.

During the week that Lisa was in the two comas, I checked up on the three women who had been forced to send assassination orders, namely Francesca, Gabriella, and Arianna. They were still receiving Basic Therapy, but were now making serious progress, thanks to the efforts of Rafe, who took a personal interest in delivering their sessions herself, learning as much as she could about the effects of the Brunelli Enforcer. Each woman now had a personal assistant to help them, but according to Dr. Leann, who continued to translate the geneticists' lingo to we non-geneticists, there wasn't much that could be done for them.

That is, subjecting them to the bio agent and then the cures would not substantially benefit them, only partially repairing their fused feet. Instead, the geneticists were working on another arm restoration process based on their slightly different DNA.

I then checked on Bianca, Maricela, and the other nearly five hundred women rescued from the clutches of the Gamelon-3 men. Dr. Leann explained they had been able to remove their plastic-like skin. However, many of them were pregnant and each woman wanted it aborted. "Once that's done, their health has improved, and the lingering traces of that nasty Purple Droga plant have worn off, we are scheduling them for the complete process that Lisa is undergoing. They believe that their teeth will be restored, as well as their vocal cords. That alone will make their lives much more livable. Most of the pairs of women have formed strong bonds, and as hermaphrodites, they well may marry. So there is hope. We can't do their Basic Therapy until they are able to speak, naturally. Still, our team of geneticists are plunging ahead on arm regrowth procedures. They are really feeling the pressure to find a workaround. Far too many of you are in dire need of it. Keep on hoping, Nia Elain. Give them time to work their magic."

I could only agree with her. I did relax some and relayed the news to Martina. After spending a week with the recovered Lisa, I again said my farewells and headed back to Cass-C to continue helping Admiral Molly Maud, hoping that we'd seen the last of these disasters.

Chapter 26 Perversions and Hidden Standards

While I was spending my time in the hub of the Federation side of the galaxy, our side was deeply embroiled in the many plays for power from the numerous ex-Imperium worlds. Even remote Ashford-5 wasn't immune, though very few ever bothered worlds there on the very rim of our spiral arm, which overlapped the rim of the Federation arm as well, forming a sort of grey area of ill-defined boundaries. But no one really cared about that. There were too few planets this far out and little of commercial value, except fuel. The fuel refinery on one of our moons was always a target.

In early 1382, a number of pirate raiders began making raids on the refinery, mostly just stealing fuel cells, but killing security guards to get them. Their usual methods consisted of dropping out of hyperspace just above the surface of the moon and landing, all before the dozens of security spaceships had any time to react. They'd snatch fuel cells and take off, jumping back into hyperspace before our ships could even get within firing range.

Eighteen year old Lieutenant Tod Bellweather, grandson of our Governor Misty Childa-Bellweather, had just joined the Queen's Imperial Guards, hoping to make a name for himself, beyond that of "freak." He'd tried the Academy for one semester and couldn't take the constant ridiculing over his hermaphrodite body. He wore his blonde hair short, dressed in men's suits, but nothing could hide his typical large bosom. Tod figured that in the guards, he could make a difference, helping protect his home world in these trying times.

And in fact, he had just done that, working out a foolhardy plan to locate the pirates' home base of operations. "Once I have located it, you can hit them hard with our light cruiser," Tod explained his crazy scheme to his captain. Since nothing else was proving successful, his captain agreed to Tod's plan. Tod spent several days in September hiding out in his small, two-man ship. He was alone. Why? Ordinarily, these small craft were only able to travel around worlds, not between them. Their fuel supply was too little for these longer distances. However, Tod's plan called for the dispensing of his co-pilot and navigator for reserve fuel cells, which would increase his range very significantly. His stripped-down shuttle was capable of flying all the way to Winno-3, if necessary. More importantly, it was highly maneuverable and extremely fast. Tod was certain he could trail the pirates back to their home base of operations.

In his special shuttle, Tod hovered near the supply of new fuel cells, waiting for the next raid. On September 15, his patience was rewarded. Suddenly, two foreign transports dropped out of hyperspace just above the supply depot. For a moment, Tod marveled at their navigational skills. It was quite a feat to drop out so darn close to the moon's surface. If they were off by a hundred feet, they'd materialize beneath the moon's surface! By the time this registered with Tod, the men had disembarked and loaded up dozens of fuel cells. Overhead, he saw several cruisers closing fast, soon to be within firing range. Of course, he knew they couldn't fire at the raiders this close to the moon. One errant shot could set off a massive fire and explosion. They'd have to wait until the transports cleared the moon before they could fire. Of course, the raiders on the transports also knew this and purposely jumped into hyperspace, as soon as they cleared the surface.

Tod was anticipating this and maneuvered his shuttle close to one of the raider's ships, locking on to its hull with a magnetic clamp. Now he waited, but only for a few seconds. The transport began to liftoff, taking Tod's tiny shuttle with it. Just as the first cruiser was about to open fire, it made the jump into hyperspace. Tod's viewport went black, and he knew that he was tagging along. He smiled. *My plan is working to perfection!*

Not entirely. Onboard the raider's transport, their captain knew that they were dragging some tiny shuttle along with them. He would not be out-foxed! He ordered a hyperspace coordinate change. A half hour later, his crew executed his maneuver perfectly. Just as the transport dropped out of hyperspace, his pilot threw its sub-light engines into their maximum speed. The severe momentum tug on Tod's tiny magnetic grapple severed its connection. Worse, the transport immediately rotated one hundred eighty degrees, and Tod faced a tiny cannon that the pirates had mounted on the normally unarmed deep space transport!

His shuttle only had the minimalist defense shields, strong enough to handle small bits of space debris often found in low orbits around planets. Tod stared at the incoming cannon shot and felt his tiny ship lurch, as his shields yielded. Smoke and fires broke out around him. Then, the power went off, and the ship rolled off at a crazy angle. Another cannon burst struck the ship, stunning Tod. All went black, but life support continued on backup power.

When Tod came too, he panicked, flipping dead control after dead control. Finally, he stopped, took a deep breath, focused, and willed his body to calm down. Time to do some serious observations, he told himself. A few minutes later, he had the constant rolling stopped and now could observe the star patterns. "Where the hell am I?"

Nothing looked familiar, but he was still on the rim of the galaxy. Most of the sky was totally black, except for a few dim stars and the fuzzy patches of far distant galaxies. Only in one direction did the combined spiral arms light up the sky in a brilliant, long, thin streak of light from countless millions of suns. A quick check of what instruments were still working told him that he had life support for several days yet. Time to see if he could repair enough of the damage to get the crippled ship moving. Hyperdrive was totally gone, a melted mass of circuits and wires. Likewise, his small comm center. He couldn't call for help and that really bothered him.

An hour later, Tod had hooked a bit of this to that and finally got his sub-light engines back online, but only at a low power level. He knew that he needed to find a planet and land. Only on the ground did he have any chance of making enough repairs to limp home, assuming he could even figure out where that might be. At least the astronomical equipment was still working, and he set to work trying to find a habitable planet among the few dim stars out there on the rim.

After a very long day of disappointment after disappointment, he found a dim yellow star with a small planetary system. The third one out from the star looked promising, and he trained his equipment on it. "Habitable" flashed on his tiny monitor. Gingerly, he set course towards that world. On September 25, he dropped into orbit around the blue-green world and began looking for signs of civilization. After one circuit, he'd identified three continents but found no signs of any spaceships or spaceports. He cursed a little and made a lower pass around the new world.

The southern continent appeared snow covered. He discarded this as a possible landing site. He had no cold weather gear with him. The middle continent appeared lush, dense with vegetation. Landing in a forest was highly non-optimum, even under the best of conditions. He turned his attention to the northern continent. "This is more like it." He spotted what appeared to be large, sprawling cities! Civilization! Based on what his many uncles and aunts had told him as he grew up, he knew that when a world had cities this large, that civilization had to be in the Modern Age, as opposed to Stone Age or Iron Age. It took a good deal of infrastructure, agriculture, and population to support such large cities. However, they had obviously yet to develop space travel, a bitter disappointment to Tod.

"Well, I'm almost out of options. I've got to land soon. I sure hope I can rebuild enough of the ship to take off again. Here goes nothing," he spoke to himself, nudging the shuttle downward. He chose what must be the largest city as his destination. As the ship encountered serious air resistance, bits of its skin began peeling off, bringing more curses from Tod. Bit by bit, he lost control of the ship. When his altimeter read a thousand feet, Tod knew he was going to crash land with no way to avoid it! He had seconds to make sure he was strapped in before the ground came up and smacked him hard, knocking him out, as his body lurched hard forward, restrained only by his safety harness.

Tod did not hear sirens approaching him, nor did he hear the exclamations of the dozens of rescue personnel, nor voices of the soldiers who arrived later. Neither did he know that his body was being transported to a local hospital nor the confusion his body caused the doctors there, but they did examine him thoroughly pronouncing him or her healthy, with only minor cuts, which they stitched up nicely. Similarly, Tod didn't know he was then taken to a secure facility for study, later dressed appropriately, and taken to the Czar's Palace, where Czar Anatoly Zakov would personally question this space person.

Slowly, the black haze lifted from Tod. His body ached some and felt, well strange. He opened his eyes and tried to move, but nothing moved at all, except his head and even that felt somehow different to him. His eyes flooded with various images, all totally foreign and extremely weird. He was in some kind of ornate palace with white marble walls and a high ceiling from which giant, golden, very ornate chandeliers hung providing excellent lighting. The floor was polished stone, probably granite, laid out in a colorful pattern of browns, reds, and oranges. He was erect staring at a totally foreign image looking back at him from a mirror. To its right was a giant TV monitor with some programming going on. He recognized the language being spoken. It was Rus or Russian, depending on what world one was on. Tod said a silent thank you to Marisol, who had taught him a number of languages while he was growing up at the Imperial Castle.

He looked at the image in the mirror and tried to grasp what was going on. Tod couldn't move, but was able to move his head, just as the very strange image in the mirror did. Then, it clicked in his mind. The image was himself! He gasped. He was being held up on some kind of pedestal, a vertical stone rod was somehow hooked onto his backside. His feet were encased in black leather boots that came up nearly to his crotch, laced extremely tight. It was their bottoms that most got his attention. His toes were pointed straight downward. He'd seen boots something this before, the ballet boots on the rescued women that Captain Nia Elain had brought back to the Imperial Castle.

As his gaze rose upwards, he saw he must be wearing some kind of corset. That would account for the sharp pressure across his whole chest. It too was black. His arms were somehow bound parallel to the ground across the middle of his back, but his fingers protruded on either side. And he now had three inch long fingernails painted a light blue color. He wiggled his fingers and saw them move in the mirror. As his gaze finally reached his head, he saw that he must be wearing some kind of blonde wig, because his hair was full and touched his shoulders. In addition, his lips were painted a bright red, and his eyes had some kind of bluish shadow around them. Again, he tried to wiggle, but couldn't.

Tod looked to his right. He saw three other women mounted to similar pedestals, dressed much like him. One was an older woman, blonde, perhaps in her mid-forties. Beside her was a gorgeous young woman his own age, with thin blonde hair that draped down to the middle of her back. Her eyes were blue, but accentuated by her matching eye shadow. She was the prettiest woman Tod had ever seen, a perfectly proportioned face. Beside her was a slightly younger teen with slightly shorter blonde hair but with some waves in it. Far off in one corner of the room, he saw an even younger girl playing with a slightly older boy. While he wore a fancy suit, she was dressed in the same black apparel as everyone else. She wore thigh high, tightly laced ballet boots and a corset. When she turned, he could see that her arms were also crossed across her back, held there securely with a fabric and leather binding attached to her corset, but leaving her fingers exposed. Her nails were a couple of inches long and painted a light blue.

Tod swallowed hard. "Hello. What's going on? Where am I? My ship crash landed here."

The older woman smiled politely. "Oh, you do speak our language, though with a terrible accent that's for sure. We were just waiting for you to recover. Yes, we know you are a space woman who crashed. It was on the news programs all day yesterday. We saw your silver ship crash just outside Karkoff. That's where you are, in Karkoff, in the Czar's Palace to be precise. I'm Czarina Masha Zakov, your hostess. This is one of my older twins, Sasha Marketa. She's eighteen. Her twin, Petya, is off with my husband, Czar Anatoly. We rule the North Land, you see." Tod didn't see, but she ignored that. "Next to my gorgeous Sasha Marketa is dear Katya, short for

Ekaterina. She's sixteen now."

"Mom! You know I want to be called Katya not Ekaterina," she pouted a little, looking at Tod and giving him a girlish grin.

"Well yes dear. And over there playing is my youngest daughter, Yulia. She's ten and not yet old enough to be put on a platform. With her is my youngest son, Leontii, fourteen. Oh, Leontii, will you and Yulia please go find your papa and tell him the space woman has wakened."

"Do I have to mama?" the boy whined.

"Leontii, you know you want to be a good boy," Czarina Masha chided him.

Looking sullen-faced, Leontii replied, "Yes mama. I want to be a good boy. Come on, Yulia; let's go find papa." He put a steadying arm around his younger sister, and they headed out of the room. Tod watched how she walked, only barely walking, more like a stork. Her knees didn't bend much at all, forcing her to walk in a stiff-legged manner.

"But why are we bound and hooked onto this pedestal?" Tod asked.

"Silly space woman," Czarina Masha chided Tod, as though he were her younger daughter. "All good women are put on pedestals. Well, once we reach puberty that is. Yulia will soon become a woman, and she simply can't wait to be put on her pedestal beside us. She, like all women on New Terra, wants to be so greatly honored by men, looked after, and provided for when she marries. We all want to be good women, perfect women, for our loving husbands, who work hard to provide for our needs. Don't the men in your world work hard and provide for their wives?" she asked, insinuating they might not.

"Of course they do. But we're helpless like this," Tod protested.

"We are on display for our men to admire our beauty," Czarina Masha countered. "Don't the women of your world want to be attractive for your hard working men? How silly of them," she replied, once more chiding Tod. "Here on New Terra, all women want to be good women, don't we, Sasha Marketa?"

The gorgeous blonde giggled slightly. "Of course, mama. We all want to be put on our pedestals and admired, like always. We're being good women, good girls. It must be awful on your world where your women are not placed on pedestals and admired by all men who see them. How very crude. Quite uncivilized, right mama?" Sasha Marketa replied.

"Yes dear, quite. So what is your name, space woman?" Czarina Masha asked.

"Tod, Tod Blackwell."

"What a strange name for a woman. Nevertheless, it'll have to do."

"But why are we bound like this? I can't move. How can you even walk in these strange boots?" Tod asked, trying somehow to make some sense out of all this.

"Like all good women, we are on our pedestals now. It is, after all, display time. We must look our very best for any men who might drop by. A good woman always looks her very best, especially so while she's on display. You can't be properly on display if you are allowed to move about like a little girl. Why, that's just not done, not ever. Our toes only barely touch the floor so we can't move about while we are on display on our pedestals. Heavens, you can't be moving your arms about like some little girl, now can you? That's not being a good woman at all."

Tod fumbled about looking for a way out of this seemingly circular argument. "So when do we get down from our pedestals? How can we even eat with our arms bound behind our backs?"

Czarina Masha, Sasha Marketa, and Katya all laughed and giggled. Still giggling, Sasha Marketa explained, "At lunchtime and suppertime. Papa comes and takes us down. At lunchtime, he just undoes our arms, so we can all dine together as a big family. Then, we women freshen up our makeup, and papa binds us again and puts us on our pedestals for the afternoon. Of course, at night, we stay unbound until after breakfast, and we've got our makeup done properly. How silly of you to think that someone has to feed us. After all, papa and all men work so very hard to support us and our children — well when I get married and have my own children, that is,"

491

she stumbled and flushed a little. "I'm not married yet. Are you married Tod?" she asked coyly.

"Er, no, I'm not married. I don't have any girlfriends either."

Sasha Marketa smiled demurely. Czarina Masha commented, "Oh how utterly awful and disgraceful. You, an unmarried woman flying around in that flying, sky machine, and not even properly dressed and on a pedestal. Unthinkable, really. On your world, your women must not be good women at all. Don't they have *any* self-respect at all?"

A bass male voice called out, "What's disgraceful, dear?" We turned our heads. I saw four men dressed in very nice fitting suits walking into the huge room, followed by Leontii assisting Yulia, who was taking her terribly clumsy, stork-like steps.

"Oh, the women on Tod's world, dear. Apparently, those women are not put on pedestals at all. They let unmarried women just fly about in those sky machines, not even properly dressed. Oh, this is my husband and ruler of North Land, Czar Anatoly Zakov. That's my eldest son, Sasha Marketa's twin brother, Petya. His aide, Vasily, and Dr. Vladimir," she finished up the introductions, and then added, "Oh yes. She speaks our language, Anatoly, but with a terrible accent."

Czar Anatoly walked before the collection of pedestals, came up to his wife and kissed her on her forehead. "My lovely Czarina, you look as beautiful as ever. And my Sasha Marketa and Katya, you both look just gorgeous today. I hope you have kept our sky woman proper company when she woke up."

"Oh yes, papa, we have," Sasha Marketa replied, flashing a big smile at Tod.

"Ladies, I'm eternally blessed to witness your beauty," Vasily said, bowing slightly to each of us.

As Vasily stepped back, Dr. Vladimir moved up and said, "Czarina, Sasha Marketa, Katya, never have I seen you looking so radiant and beautiful. I'm most pleased to stand before you." He stepped back, and Czar Anatoly glared slightly at his eldest son.

Hastily, Petya stepped forward. "Mama, you look as

beautiful as ever. Sasha Marketa, Katya, I'm blessed to stand before you and witness your beauty." He didn't sound so sincere, Tod thought, watching him back up to stand beside the other three men.

Czar Anatoly spoke up. "Well, Tod. Strange name for a woman, but then we've never had a sky woman on New Terra before now. Let me welcome you to North Land. A camera crew accidentally filmed your unfortunate landing, which we can only presume was unintentional. Our emergency responders arrived at the wreckage within minutes though. You were rushed to our finest hospital where one of our doctors stitched up some minor wounds and made sure you had no serious injuries. Of course, we all were a bit baffled by your anatomy. In the end, we've decided you're a woman. I must say your breasts are, well, most attractive. I don't believe I've ever seen any quite so large and perfectly formed before. Anyway, we decided it would be best if we considered you to be a woman and thus showed you proper respect."

He went on, "Of course, my staff had to put that human hair wig on you. Your own hair is, well let's say it's not very becoming for a woman here on New Terra. As you can see, we are treating you with only the highest respect us good men of New Terra treat all our good women. When we placed you on your pedestal this morning, I was truly impressed with your beauty. Rest assured, either I or Petya will be assisting you, as we both do with our own women, right Petya?"

"Sure papa, but she's not totally a she, is she?" Petya replied, very hesitant about making such a commitment.

Czar Anatoly smiled and cleared his throat. "Well, that's true, Petya, but still, she is more woman than man, and we are honor bound to treat her as we would our own good women. When in Karkoff, do as they do, son."

"But what of my ship?" Tod asked, thinking quickly. "I was planning on repairing it and trying to get back home."

Dr. Vladimir looked at the Czar, who nodded. "Ah, Tod. That may not be possible. While I supervised the collection of all the bits and pieces, I don't believe what's left could ever be put back together and made to fly, though I must admit I don't know how it flew in the first place. I'm a close friend of the

Czar's and run the Karkoff Observatory. My doctorate is in astronomy. I would dearly love to talk with you about many, many things, ma'am."

This news stunned Tod. If his ship was in pieces, he knew he was stranded here, wherever here was. "Could, could I please see the pieces?" he asked, fighting down rising emotions.

Czar Anatoly answered. "Of course, Miss Tod. But let's do that after lunch. It's time for us to dine. Vasily, Vladimir, would you care to dine with my family today?"

Dr. Vladimir spoke up formally, "I'm most highly honored indeed to dine with three most gorgeous women." He bowed slightly to the three women on their pedestals.

Czar Anatoly called out, "Leontii, remember to be a good boy; help your sister to the table and unbind her."

"Ah, do I have to papa?" he whined. His father gave him a harsh stare. "Okay, okay. Come on, Yulia. I've got you." He put a steadying arm around her and headed out of the room. Meanwhile, Czar Anatoly walked behind his wife, lifted her up, and then gently sat her down on her toes. At the same time, Petya did the same thing for his sister. Then, Czar Anatoly stepped behind Tod, who felt his strong hands around his waist just below his large bosom. Up and out, he sensed his body moving. Then, he was standing with his full weight on his toes. Now, Tod did get scared.

"I can't walk like this. I'll fall over," he pleaded.

Sasha Marketa giggled. "No you won't. Follow me, and do as I do, silly Tod. Of course, I can see how you might feel that way. After all, we good girls have been wearing these boots since we first learned to walk — well, not these boots exactly. They were much smaller back then. We walk very well. See," she explained, doing a twirl-around in place, showing off to Tod.

He wiggled and wobbled, taking small stork-like steps, grateful for Anatoly's steadying arm. Meanwhile, Vasily supported the Czarina. The more that they walked, the better Tod got at it, but the more his feet ached. Their dining hall was also spacious with a high ceiling. Tapestries hung on the walls, while statues stood in side niches here and there. There were five very long tables, very well made, Tod noted, and highly polished. However, he also noticed that one of the tables was much taller than the others and their chairs were also much higher than all of the others.

He soon saw why. The women were escorted to the tall table and chairs. "Oh do have Tod sit by me, Petya," Sasha Marketa exclaimed, as they reached them.

From the rear, Tod could see a small loop attached to the back of their corsets. He now saw how they had been attached to the pedestals. He watched as Vasily and Petya carefully undid the extensive laces that bound the women's arms up and behind their backs, while feeling Czar Anatoly doing the same thing for him. What a relief to have his arms back, Tod thought, rubbing them just as the other women were doing. He watched as Sasha Marketa then attempted to sit down in her chair. Her heavy, thigh-high boots barely bent at her knees. Hence, they needed to sit in very tall chairs and with the table's height adjusted accordingly. Tod tried to sit and mostly fell into the chair. Anatoly helped slide him up closer to the table.

"See, that wasn't so bad, now was it, Tod?" Sasha Marketa flirted a bit with him. He sat as erect as she did, and he returned her smile. The men sat at the next table, though facing them.

A number of serving women entered, carrying trays of food. They too wore similar black outfits, walking stork-like as far as Tod thought, but they seemed entirely comfortable walking. Several men in black suits hastened in with place settings and quickly set the table for everyone. At this point, Czarina Masha said a brief prayer and began helping herself, passing the trays on down to the other women.

As Sasha Marketa handed the plate to Tod, she whispered, "We're having duck in your honor. Our chef does a fabulous job with it, but we don't have it all that often, just on special occasions, like today. I do hope you like it."

"Thanks, Sasha Marketa. Doesn't the cook have to be bound like the rest of us?"

She giggled. "Of course, silly, but she's allowed time to cook our meals, just like our serving women. They are taken down from their pedestals in time to be able to serve us. Naturally, when they are done and have freshened up, they'll be put back on their pedestals too. That way, the serving men can admire and appreciate their beauty too. Good women on New Terra are always treated very special, as you can see. We all do our best to try to be good women, always. After all, it's only fair that we should be, since our good men work so hard to provide for us and their families. You see, we're all taught from the time we're babies to be good girls and good boys. Don't your people do that too? Instruct your children to be good?"

"Of course, I suppose. I've never thought about such things," Tod admitted.

She giggled and smiled back. "So are you really going to go and see what's left of your flying machine after we eat?"

"Sure. I have to. If I can't fix it, I'll have to stay here," Tod admitted.

"Is that so bad? Honestly, Tod, we are very civilized people."

"Well, I can't live on a pedestal like you can," Tod admitted. "Look, I'm used to doing my own work, flying ships, lots of things. I was trying to stop pirates from raiding our fuel stations when they shot up my ship, causing me to crash land here on your world."

"Do all women have such exciting times on your world? I mean none of that sounds like your women are being good women at all, not remotely," Sasha Marketa asked.

"Pretty much so. Some are rulers, some are doctors, some are scientists. The list is endless, but some are just housewives and mothers, kind of like your mother," Tod answered.

"How very primitive of them. We women here are all good women. We want nothing more than to be on our pedestal and be greatly admired by all the men who see us, but of course, it is hard to find a husband. Papa will help me soon, I hope. Come, we best get to the bathroom, and then freshen up our makeup before we spend the afternoon on our pedestals, Tod."

Tod found walking to the next room where their

facilities were located was a little easier now that he had the free use of his arms to help him keep his fragile balance. After using the tall toilets, he watched as Sasha Marketa reapplied her lipstick. "Sorry, I have no idea how to do any of this makeup stuff. I've been really being a man, not a woman," Tod admitted.

"Here, let me do it for you. Mama fixed your face this morning when you were unconscious still," Sasha Marketa suggested demurely. A few minutes later, the women walked carefully out of the restroom where the men were waiting for them. In deference to Tod's terrible walking skills, they allowed the four to return to their pedestals before gently rebinding their arms. This time, Tod saw that it more or less fit like a fingerless glove, allowing his fingers to stick out completely. He groaned a little as Czar Anatoly tightened the straps up quite securely so that he couldn't move his arms in the slightest. Then, he carefully lifted Tod up, catching the metal loop on the back of his corset on the hook on the top of the stone bar of the pedestal. Once more, Tod was effectively immobile. His toes just barely touched the marble base.

"There, my dears, you're all looking positively beautiful on your pedestals once more," Czar Anatoly said kindly and a bit reverently. Turning to face Tod, he added, "Vladimir and I'll make some arrangements to have you inspect your flying machine's parts later this afternoon. However, since they are being kept in a public location where a number of our scientists are examining them, you'll have to wear the box. Sasha Marketa, why don't you explain the box to Tod here, while we work on the arrangements."

"Sure papa," she replied eagerly. The men quickly left, and she began to explain. "You see good girls and women never show their bosoms and faces out in the public. It just isn't done, not ever. Therefore, when we go out into any public place, that is, where there are men who are not part of our families or sometimes papa's closest advisors like Vladimir, we have our men put a box over the top half of our bodies. There are air holes and peepholes so we can see, of course, but the men always guide us so we don't take a tumble. Actually, tumbles are really bad for us, since we can't get back onto our feet again without the help of a man."

Czarina Masha interrupted her daughter. "Tod, that's why Anatoly was so insistent on getting you properly honored and onto a pedestal like all good women of New Terra. Your whole face and impressive bosom was fully exposed for all men to see and stare at. How awful for a good and proper woman, you see. Just unthinkable, horrible. I can't imagine any worse disgrace than to have my face and bosom seen by every man walking around me. I would just faint away, I just know I would." Tod saw her visibly shudder just thinking about it. She added, "But then, some good women are becoming more modern and visit the stores without wearing their boxes."

"So that's why they have me bound like this and on a pedestal?" Tod asked, just to be absolutely certain.

Seeing her mother shudder, Sasha Marketa quickly answered, "Oh yes, Tod. Papa wanted to spare you that utter humiliation! Papa is always very kind and considerate to mama and all of us daughters. He knew how horrible that would be for you and insisted we err on the side of caution with our space woman. You probably should thank him. I know that would make him feel much relieved. Do you really have a man's organs too? I think that's why everyone was so confused about you."

"Yes, I've both. I could even have a baby myself, but I'm really being a man, not a woman," Tod tried to explain the unexplainable.

Sasha Marketa giggled. "You're teasing me, Tod. You look like a woman to all of us, and we'd die to be as well-endowed as you are, right mama?"

Czarina Masha flushed visibly. "Hush, Sasha Marketa. Good women don't speak of such things. A good woman is never envious of another good woman. Remember your manners."

Katya, who had been mostly silent but listening intently, spoke up. "But mama, Tod needs to know these things. I think she doesn't know how good women are supposed to be, coming from her alien world where there must not be any good women around. That has to be just awful. I can't imagine a whole world without even one good woman."

Tod chuckled. "Katya has a point. I admit I've no idea at all of how a good woman is supposed to be, not on your world. Our world has obviously very different customs than yours."

"I suppose we should explain it to you, Tod, but we, Anatoly and I, we usually begin to tell our children when they first learn to talk. Surely, your people do much the same thing, telling your children what to do and what not to do." Tod nodded, and she continued a bit more relaxed about it. "A good girl always wears her boots and corset. We start them when they are three. As you probably can feel, the corset isn't all that tight. It's mostly there to provide support for us while we are here on our pedestals. I can't imagine standing here on my toes all day without such support. Heavens, my toes would be throbbing, but worse, we'd be wiggling and wobbling about like some tadpole or something, very un-lady like indeed. A good girl always obeys her father and brothers. A good girl must never fall down. A good girl must never pee her panties. Remember, we are telling these to three year old girls, Tod. A good girl must always look her best, especially when her brothers, father, and other men are around her."

"After she becomes a woman proper, then a good girl must never, ever show her bosom and face in public. All good girls and young women always spend their days looking as pretty as possible on their pedestal, where their father and brothers can gaze on their beauty and admire them. A good girl loves to be admired and always does all she can to be worthy of their admiration. A good woman never argues with her father, husband, brothers, or other men. It's wholly unseemly and just not done. A good woman never raises her voice, not ever. We women are the epitome of grace and beauty, and a good woman must never spoil that."

"When she gets to the marrying age of eighteen, then a good woman may invite young eligible men to her bedroom, showing them her full beauty. That's how a good woman finds the right husband for her. Of course, a good woman is careful not to get herself pregnant during such exchanges."

"But where did you learn that these are the way that good girls and women are supposed to be?" Tod asked, growing curious about their origin.

"Oh, my mother taught them to me, just as Anatoly and I have tried to teach them to our children, though I'm afraid it's much harder to get our boys to be good boys, but then they are boys, and boys will be boys," Czarina Masha conceded.

Tod replied, "So I suppose your mother learned them from her mother and father and so on back."

"True, but our civilization here is quite an ancient one. We trace our lineage back nearly eight thousand years. We have the ancient founding records on file in the Precious Antiquities Department in North Land's main library here in Karkoff. Mind you, I've never seen them, but they are available for anyone to study. If you're interested, I can have someone bring them up on our TV monitor here. They've got scrolling automated. We just say 'Scroll Down' or 'Scroll Up' and it does it. Isn't the men's technology inventions just marvelous?"

That apparently reminded her of more. Czarina Masha continued, "Good girls and women always watch the TV, while they are on their pedestals and not entertaining men or boys. A good woman always stays very current on all the news and relays things of importance to her husband in the evening hours. You see, our men work hard, and are very busy during the daytime. They haven't time to keep current on much of any news. It is the good woman's task to keep herself informed, so she can inform her husband. Of course, today, we are playing host to you, Tod, and we aren't watching the TV. Probably the only real news is all about your crash landing. Everyone wants to know all about the sky woman and your world. We've never had anyone come here from the sky."

"Mama," Katya broke in, "we have too. Our original founders came from the sky, just as Tod did. Don't you remember what the ancient documents say?"

"Oh. Well, yes, Katya, you are right. Sorry, but I think Tod knows what I mean." Katya flashed Tod a big smile.

Emboldened, Katya added, "Tod, quite a lot of otherwise good women are no longer wearing their boxes in public — like the good women TV reporters and the ones who are working as Greeters and Welcomers at some stores. Plus, some good women go shopping without them too. So mama and papa are just being conservative with you, Tod. They don't want to risk any chance of humiliating you in public."

Just then, Czar Anatoly and Petya returned. Petya was carrying a large black box in his hands. "Well, it's all arranged, Tod. I'll get you down, and Petya will put the box over you, so the many men who are studying the remains of your ship can't see your bosom and face, causing you utter humiliation. I'll steady you, so don't worry. You will be able to see through the peep holes."

He lifted Tod down, and then Petya opened the box. It had a soft cushion on top, which rested on top of Tod's head. As far as Tod was concerned, he felt like he was being stuck into a suitcase or something. When it closed, its bottom rested on his hips, sharing the weight with the top of his head. There were a number of holes in it, small ones. As he moved, a small amount of air flowed into the box and out holes in its rear. He could just barely see, but needed to pivot his head around in order actually to get any specific thing visible to his eyes. As he took his first stork-like steps, he knew he was totally dependent upon the gentle guiding hand of Czar Anatoly.

They walked out of the room and down a long hall. Then, they went out some doors, and he smelled fresh air and saw sunlight again. He was lifted into a car. He couldn't see much from inside, though. The box kept banging into the window and sides, and he quickly gave that up. They arrived at a large warehouse-type building, as best Tod could tell. Once more Czar Anatoly helped him out and guided him inside. At once, dozens of men looked up from their work. Tod sighed. There was his two-man shuttle, or rather what was left of it.

The largest part still intact was his cockpit seat and protection bars, which had saved his life. The stark reality of his predicament hit home. There was no hope of ever rebuilding the shuttle. He was stranded here on New Terra, possibly for the rest of his life, unless by some magic, someone from Tierra could find him here and rescue him. He didn't hold out much hope of that. He didn't even know where this world was, except somewhere on the rim of the galaxy. A very sober Tod returned to the Royal Palace and was put back onto his pedestal, very much relieved to be out his box. The men then left.

Sasha Marketa whispered, "Tod! Don't cry. Your mascara will run down your face and look just awful. A good woman must never cry when she is wearing her makeup to look beautiful for the men."

"Sorry, Sasha Marketa. It's my ship. Rather what's left of it. No way can I rebuild it. I'm stuck here on New Terra, unless some of my people can somehow find me, which is doubtful, since I have no idea where your sun is at compared to anything else."

"Don't worry, Tod. Papa will take good care of you. Perhaps, you too can find a handsome man and marry," Sasha Marketa consoled him. Tod did his best to keep from crying.

Later, the men returned and took the women down from their pedestals, but not until they again praised how they looked, bringing smiles to the three women's faces. At the supper table, they were again unbound. Supper talk was light chat. When they finished, Czar Anatoly said, "Well, tonight Tod, you'll be sleeping with Sasha Marketa. She can help you with bedtime actions and all that. Tomorrow, my scientists want to start questioning you. So that you don't have to wear the box, I've invited them here. We'll provide chairs for them, and they can question you while you are properly on your pedestal. I truly am sorry about your ship. I didn't think it could be repaired either."

"Thanks," Tod replied mechanically, too stunned really to say much else.

Sasha Marketa led Tod to her bedroom, steadying him as he tried to walk beside her. She giggled at his awkwardness though. Once there, she helped him get out of the corset and then unlaced his boots. All Tod had on now was panties. "Now you do me. We can't get ourselves out of these clothes very easily by ourselves. Usually Katya and I help each other, so we don't have to bother papa. Besides, Petya hates to do it, but he's got to learn if he ever expects to marry a good woman."

After getting her undressed, she removed his makeup and then hers. "Now, we brush out our hair, only yours is a wig. So you can just take it off and lay it on the dresser there, while I do mine, because I don't suppose you know how to do it."

Tod chuckled, "You got that right, Sasha Marketa. Do we sleep in just our panties?"

Brushing out her long, blonde tresses, Sasha Marketa giggled. "Sure. I just love seeing your breasts. They are so utterly perfect, you know, but we could put on nightgowns if you prefer. Come; let's get into bed. I'm rather tired." She pulled back the sheets and slipped into her bed, patting a spot beside her.

Tod crawled in beside her. "You are one very beautiful young woman, Sasha Marketa."

"I'm supposed to be — a good woman and all that. Oh!" she discovered his male appendage was quite aroused. "You are a man after all. This is so confusing, but if you want to do it, I'm on the pill so I can't get pregnant. I'd love to do it with you, Tod." He had no idea of pills, but took her at her word.

Tod leaned over and began kissing her, his hands slipped around her. He found her very willing. Quite some time later, she lay on his shoulder. "Oh god, that was incredible Tod, incredible." She kissed him lovingly again. Tod hadn't told her he was also a telepath, *mentales* gifted, but had easily slipped into rapport with her, finding her exceedingly attractive.

After breakfast the next morning, Sasha Marketa had a quick, private chat with her father, who looked terribly embarrassed. As the women rose to go get dressed and prepared for the day, he cleared his voice. "Er, perhaps Tod, we've made a mistake with you. We all thought that you were a woman, really, but Sasha Marketa tells me it is quite the opposite. I really don't understand this. Your voice is that of a man, but your bosom is that of a woman. Perhaps, we should be treating you as a man and not a woman, though what we can do about your bosom I surely don't know. Sasha Marketa, I must admit, is really smitten with you. I've been trying to find her an appropriate husband for some months, but have struck out each time."

"Well, that would suit me far better, Czar Anatoly. I do consider myself a man, but with extras. I've always acted as a man should act."

"Indeed, that would certainly simplify matters with all our scientists. I mean women just don't go off into the sky alone, not good, proper women. Men would find your behavior far more acceptable if you were a man," he admitted.

"Thank you. I would feel far more comfortable being a man, sir. Oh, forgive me if I took too much liberty with your daughter last night. She is one very remarkable young woman. I've never met one as beautiful and charming as she is."

Czar Anatoly grinned mischievously. "I hereby officially give you my permission to court Sasha Marketa, but you must follow all our proper conduct for good men and good women."

"Thank you, sir. I will do my best. I'm sure she can point out any tips that I might need, but I will need some clothes. Mine were torn to shreds."

"Honestly, son, I don't know how you walked away from that crash with only minor cuts."

"Air bags and that metal shell surrounding the cockpit, my seat. The air bags deployed, surrounding me in a sort of pillow cushion," Tod explained.

"Ah, I see, I think. Come; let's see what clothes of mine can be made to fit you. Then, we can take care of our women and meet all the scientists who are clamoring all over me to allow you to answer their questions. However, I must leave the final judgment of this man or woman thing to the Judicial Council. They provide a check and balance over my executive authority."

An hour later, Tod felt human again, though the suit didn't fit too well, especially the white shirt and jacket, but this was a thousand times better. "Come Tod; we should escort the women to the Court Room and get them on their pedestals. They'll want to listen in on the question and answers period. They usually are with me when I hold my weekly Court Sessions. I'll let you take care of Sasha Marketa today. I've been having a good deal of difficulty with Petya, getting him to assume the responsibilities of being a good man," Czar Anatoly admitted.

As the two walked towards the bedroom section of the Royal Palace, Tod asked, "How so? Petya seems a fine young man, and Sasha Marketa is definitely a gorgeous young woman."

"Aye, in all other ways, he is that," he answered proudly, "but when it comes to our women, he doesn't like to be bothered with caring for their needs. He's had to do just that with his twin sister ever since she was three and began wearing the boots and arm bindings, as any good girl should. I think if it was left to him, why he'd never even bind them. Utterly awful. I keep hoping that he grows up soon. He ought to be getting married himself soon, if he'll just start looking. Ah, here they are, our lovely beauties. My Masha, you are looking exceptionally beautiful today, my dear."

Following his lead, Tod said, "Wow, Sasha Marketa, you really look stunning today yourself. And you do too, Katya. Wow."

Katya giggled and smiled. Sasha Marketa flashed Tod a seductive smile, "Of course, we all want to be at our very best today. We are going to be with you, Mr. Spaceman, so we can hear too and not watch it on TV. With so many men in dad's Court Room, a good woman must look her absolute best, more so since we won't have to be wearing our boxes. Papa, we simply must get a better fitting suit for Tod," she changed the topic.

"Of course my dear. That we must, but it will have to wait until tomorrow. Would you like to take him to the tailors tomorrow, and get Tod properly attired?"

"Oh yes, papa, very much so!" Sasha Marketa replied, grinning broadly. As Tod reached her side and slipped his arm around her waist, emulating how Czar Anatoly did with Czarina Masha, Tod was surprised a little. She wiggled her fingers and long nails enough to reach his hand and fingers, soon entwining hers with his. She whispered, "We can hold hands this way."

The Court Room was another large and splendid room, quite opulent in its decorations and statues in niches. Yet, he saw little actual gold or silver for that matter. Still, someone had done a terrific job in various stone carvings. The Czar's throne wasn't all that impressive, a white marble chair with a purple velvet cushion. He saw several more women's pedestals, one beside the throne and two angled off to the

Czar's right side. "That one's mine," Sasha Marketa whispered, guiding Tod to her pedestal. He lifted her up and got her hooked. "Straighten my hair a tad please," she whispered. "How do I look?"

"Fabulous," Tod replied with a grin. She smiled demurely back. At this point, Vasily entered carrying a large locked box. He opened it, handing the Czar his jeweled crown and the Czarina's. He then handed Tod and Petya a pair of smaller ones. Tod followed Petya, who placed his on Katya's head, so Tod placed his on Sasha in the same manner.

"Pull up one of those chairs, Tod. Sit it near Princess Sasha's side. Petya, you sit between your sisters. Are we all ready?" Czar Anatoly asked. Vasily nodded and headed to the main doors to let all the scientists and reporters into the Court Room. Tod watched as several hundred men filed into the room, each bringing his own chair with him. The reporters and cameras were position towards the rear of the room, while the scientists and other dignitaries sat up front, a respectable twenty feet from the throne itself. Then, he noticed three pedestals being carried into the room, followed by three bound female reporters. Once placed upon their pedestals, three of the many cameras pointed to them, though he could not hear what they were saying. After that, three men entered along with three more bound women with boxes over their heads and upper torsos. Three assistants quickly followed them, carrying their heavy pedestals. These six sat or stood quite apart from the reporters. Later he learned these were the members of the Judicial Council of North Land.

Thus, began a very long period of discussion with nearly all questions fired at Tod. Since they were not asking about anything that ought to be kept secret, he answered fully and truthfully, as best he could. "Yes, I'm officially stranded on your world. I'm very pleased Czar Anatoly is providing me with a place to stay." "Yes, I find your world very civilized. It's classified as a Modern Civilization among both the Imperium and the Federation of Planets." "Yes, both are very large unions of advanced civilizations with all manner of space flight." "Yes, there are thousands of worlds in the galaxy who have space travel, though not all are part of either larger organization."

Then, the topics changed. "Yes, I was shot down by the pirates I was chasing." He explained about their constant raids on the fuel refineries. "Yes, there are quite a few lawless groups and worlds out there. However, as far as I know, no one knows about your New Terra. I've no idea where it is, except on the rim of one of the spiral arms." "Yes, their weapons are very deadly." He had to launch into an explanation of canons and d-guns.

Then, he had to field questions about his own world and the Ataro Empire. This led at once into the roles of men and women in societies. "Hey, I know this is going to shock you, but out there in the wide galaxy, women are just as smart and capable as men, though yes men are usually physically stronger. Most worlds let women choose their own paths. While some prefer to be a housewife and raise their children, others prefer to also work. Nearly half of all professional workers and scientists are women. Of course, women are admired for their beauty on all worlds. Usually, they wear very attractive apparel, just as I've seen in my brief days here in Karkoff. Princess Sasha Marketa here is very beautiful, rivaling most all the women that I've seen on my world."

Petya then spoke up, "So do you find our customs with our women, binding them and putting them on pedestals, disgusting or uncivilized? I take it that other worlds out there do not treat their women in such a fashion?"

Man, you could have heard a pin drop in the Court Room! Anatoly gave his son the harshest look Tod had ever seen a father display, though the man kept silent. Every man present was instantly silent! Even Czarina Masha frowned at her son. A few reporters gasped, and then began whispering, though none up front could hear what they were saying. Suddenly, all of the cameras zoomed in on Tod.

Tod knew he was just handed a bomb with a burning fuse! "Look Prince Petya, I've only been on your world for two days, at least awake anyway. I'm not an historian nor a politician nor anyone who is remotely qualified to sit in judgment on anyone or any practice of your world. I find your basic urges to respect, admire, and treat your women with the utmost care most commendable. I've heard of and seen the results on other decadent worlds out there in the vast galaxy that have long practices of abusing their women, which I find despicable and downright wicked and evil. I've only been here a short time, and yet already I have seen your world has the wisdom to recognize the family is the basic building block of society and that the family is valued highly. Customs of dress and such do vary considerably from world to world and sometimes even within a world."

"So to answer your direct question, Petya, I'm not disgusted or think less of New Terra's customs. On the other hand, I do wonder just how much extra work you men have to do compared to my own world for example, where women do share the workload with men, though some are caring for their household and family needs and are not professionally employed. Forgive me. I've not had much of an opportunity to see any of your everyday men and what they must do. But Princess Sasha Marketa has promised to show me your ancient documents in your library, so that I can better understand your culture and the roles of men and women. I hope to learn more about you all soon, since I'm now going to be staying here on your world, as my ship is completely destroyed."

Tod thought he'd fielded that one as best he could and desperately wanted to change the topic. "Petya, considering the upheavals out there among the space traveling worlds, I would urge your world to become as prepared as possible for hostile attacks from the pirates and others looking to add more worlds to their domains. While being so far out in the rim has thus far protected your world, eventually someone is going to discover your world. You'll be all right if they are the friendly, good guys, but I hate to think what could happen if they aren't. So the best advice I can give you is to get as prepared as you can to defend yourselves, should it come to that."

"Ah, just what I have been fearing from the moment that your ship crashed, Tod," Czar Anatoly picked up on what he just suggested, also thankful for the topic change. "I take it that your world, this Terra, is able to defend itself?"

"Yes and no, Czar Anatoly. You see, just a few hundred years ago, our world was very primitive compared to your world, and in many ways, it still is today. We were discovered by the Imperium and classified as a primitive culture. At least, they had the policy of making such worlds Closed Worlds, meaning we were protected from others and allowed to develop at our own speed without interference. As time went on and as more turmoil broke out in the Imperium, our world was saved from the petty wars and such by becoming part of the Ataro Empire. That's an amazing group of some forty worlds. They've not had any wars in over two millennia. Right now, they're still protecting us, though we do have some limited fighting capability, though not much. Our world has almost no iron or heavier elements, so we've no resources with which to build the spaceships and have to trade for them, which is difficult at best. Obviously, I didn't do such a good job of protecting our fuel refinery. I was shot down instead. However, the Ataro Empire will likely be sending in a stronger space fleet to protect us against these raiding pirates."

Czar Anatoly asked, "And what has your world had to give up to get this protection from this Ataro Empire?"

"Nothing. You see, they want us to progress and develop on our own with minimal interference. They send a queen to help us in judicial matters, resolving conflicts and helping us work out beneficial trading arrangements, nothing more. We are still masters of our own destiny," Tod replied, sensing that went over well.

A geologist then asked, "You mentioned that your world has little iron and the heavier elements. New Terra is in a similar situation, that is, assuming on other worlds, iron and these heavier elements can be found in a greater abundance."

"Yes, that's true. Until we were discovered by the Imperium a few hundred years ago, iron was one of our most precious elements. To own a steel sword made one a very rich man," Tod replied, recalling a history lesson from school.

"Interesting. If these other worlds have these in abundance, what could your world offer them in trade, such as their flying space going ships?" he asked.

Tod laughed. "At first, darn little. They leased a small plot of land for them to use as a spaceport in return for iron and gold. Later on, they discovered vast deposits of a form of germanium that can be refined into the fuel used in all the Imperium spaceships. Once that was discovered, we finally had something that others wanted and still do, from all the pirate raids of late."

"Can you identify this germanium substance that can be used for this fuel?" he asked.

Again Tod laughed. "Sorry, I am not a geologist. I wouldn't know one rock from another. If only I could contact the folks back home, we could send someone who could to help you see if you had any of it here. Sorry." He kept wishing he could bring someone from the Imperial Castle here. Any number of them would be able to give them some good answers, but not him. At last, it was time for lunch. As soon as everyone else left, though the equipment remained ready for the afternoon session, Tod eagerly rose and lifted Sasha Marketa down, making sure he positioned his hand just so around her waist, smiling as he felt her fingers interlocking with his.

Begrudgingly, Petya helped Katya down, but didn't steady her. Their father gave him a dirty look. "Come on. Katya doesn't need a supporting hand, now do you sis?" he griped.

The father-son argument continued at the dinner table. After taking a chiding from his father, Petya complained bitterly, "Look papa, you know as well as I do that all our good women are good for is having sex. They don't really do anything else. In fact, they can't. I can't see why we are wasting so much of our valuable time and effort, to say nothing of money on good women. What's the point of it anyway? They want to be helpless objects, then let them, just don't make me be a part of that. I'll never marry." He retorted, causing the women to blush.

At the taller table, Yulia whispered to Katya, who was sitting next to her, "What's having sex? Is that what mama and papa do in their room when they won't let us come in? Petya isn't being a good boy, is he? I'm being a good girl, aren't I? I want to be a good girl, and one day be on my own pedestal beside you, Katya. You look so pretty up there."

Tod groaned silently. He sensed the anger rising on all sides. He focused and sent some calming emotional waves to

510

both men. No one saw his small crystal glowing faintly beneath his shirt. Later, he bound Sasha Marketa up once more, after she'd returned from using the bathroom and freshening up. She looked a bit sober, he thought.

At least the afternoon session was over an hour later. Tod was sure he'd only raised more questions with his meager answers. After getting Sasha Marketa back on her usual pedestal, she had the TV arranged to show him the ancient document being preserved in their library. "This is the oldest written record on New Terra. Some claim it dates from our founding, which would make it eight thousand six hundred five years old. Of course, no one knows that for sure."

"Cool. I hope I can read it. Oops. I can't read it. I guess you have to read it aloud to me," Tod flushed. Speaking crudely a language didn't give one the ability to read it, he observed pointedly.

Sasha Marketa grinned and whispered, "Only if you stand beside me and hold my fingers." Tod needed no further encouragement to do just that.

"It begins kind of abruptly. They suggest the first part of it has been lost. Here goes. 'Forced to make a hard landing. Comm is gone, engines out. We're here to stay. Survival at 80-20 isn't good. Decision made by all. To ensure our survival, women must be put on pedestals, treated with the highest regard and protected at all costs, restrained from work and construction details. If we are to survive, our women are our most precious resource.'" She read on, but the rest was mundane details about the construction of a farming settlement.

Tod said, "Hold on. That explains a great deal, Sasha Marketa. Your founders crash landed on this world, just like I did."

"Huh? No, they settled here," she protested.

"No, hard landing. That is a spacer's term for a crash landing. A normal touchdown is called a soft landing. Their communications center and engines were destroyed — comm is gone, engines out. Whoever wrote this knew that they were stranded here, just as I am. The 80-20 refers to the ratio of men to women. For every 8 men, there were only 2 women.

That's really grim. If they were going to survive into the future, they would have to protect their women. That had to be written by a man, since he refers to women as a precious resource. Of necessity, they had to keep the few women that they had with them from any possible harm. Hence, they adopted methods to protect them from danger. This whole pedestal thing is being interpreted literally instead of figuratively," Tod explained.

Unknown to them, Petya had entered and overheard Tod. He spoke up, causing their heads to turn towards him. "Well, now this is interesting! I have to let others know Tod's analysis. It does make sense seen this way, Tod. Thanks." He smirked, turned, and left them.

A somber Czar Anatoly joined them as suppertime approached. "Tod, the Judicial Council has overruled me. It is their opinion that men do not have breasts, especially ones as enormous as yours. They feel the ordinary men of North Land would be very uncomfortable seeing you dressed in a suit, apparently entirely violating our universal dress codes. Actually, I'm toning their words down some. However, they agreed that you do not need to wear a box when in public, as you do not show any signs of being humiliated by being seen in public, as unfortunately half our good women also don't. In addition, they have also given their consent for you to continue to court Sasha Marketa or any other unmarried woman if you are not pleased with her. I'm sorry Tod. You win some and lose some. Sasha Marketa, tomorrow you are to take Tod shopping for apparel that he will need."

Tod felt like a hammer had just landed on his head! Wisely though, he didn't protest. The Czar had obviously won some concessions from the Judiciary Council on his behalf. Besides, Petya had just joined them with a wry smirk on his face. Tod lightly touched Petya's mind and realized the young man was inciting his father, not him.

In bed with Sasha Marketa that night and after a passionate time, Sasha Marketa laid her head on his shoulders. "It won't be so bad. We'll always have the evenings to ourselves." He gave her a loving kiss on her forehead as she snuggled close.

The next morning, Tod had no choice but to allow them to put him back into the black corset and tall ballet style boots. Sasha Marketa then put his wig back on him and did his makeup for him. That done, Czar Anatoly and Petya bound them securely. The Czar looked very apologetic as they did this, and then said, "Okay Sasha Marketa, take Tod into town and get him what he's going to need." He kissed her on her forehead and whispered, "You look positively radiant this morning, my dear." She flashed him a big smile.

"Can I come too?" Katya entered and interrupted.

"Sure sis. Come keep us company and help us pick out what will look best on our Tod," Sasha Marketa replied, pleased that Katya wanted to tag along.

"You've got to go slower for me," Tod complained, stumping and wobbling to keep from falling down, while the two teens walked rather gracefully off down the hallway. Both giggled and fell back beside him, one on either side.

Katya giggled again. "Sorry, we've been walking in them since we first learned to walk when we were babies. We keep forgetting. Don't worry; you'll soon get the hang of it. Just don't fall down because we can't get up without help."

Sasha Marketa then came up against him and soon they had their fingers interlocked at their sides. Katya took the hint, moved over to his other side, and found his other fingers with hers. "Thanks. It does help me some," Tod admitted, feeling only slightly more secure.

Out on the streets of the city, Tod saw mostly men in suits going about their business, but there were also a fair number of similarly bound women walking along. Every one of the women looked similar, black corset, black panties beneath, and the tall, tight ballet boots, which were also black. This was the first time that Tod had ever seen absolutely no variation in the colors or styles of women's apparel! They all looked the same, except for the color of their long nails visible at the sides of their torsos, their choice of makeup, and their color and style of their hair.

None wore jewelry, and Tod began to realize that gold on this world was extremely precious and rare. Outside of one bakery, a woman was on her pedestal just before the door. As they passed, she said, "Welcome to Sergi's Bakery. Stop in and try a free sample." Seeing Tod's very large bosom, she add, "Wow. Impressive knockers, miss." Tod forced a smile as they passed her.

Katya whispered, "She's a Greeter, probably Sergi's wife."

They entered a department store called K's. Just inside the doors, which opened automatically when their feet touched the pressure plates, a young woman on her pedestal spoke up, "Welcome to K's. If you need help, just ask one of the women Directors near each aisle." Sasha Marketa thanked her politely.

Inside the store, Tod saw other women on pedestals near each of the wide aisles, but men actually were doing the real work. That much was clear. Their first stop was the corset aisle, filled with nearly identical black corsets. A middle aged man hastened up to them, marveled over Tod's endowment, complimented her, measured her, and promptly found one that would fit him or her. He quickly unbound Tod, removed the very ill-fitting corset, and put the new one on him, re-binding him, of course. "There, how's that?"

Tod had to admit, "Very much better!" The man looked very pleased and produced another six, placing them in a box. While they headed off to make additional purchases, he took them to the checkout man. In the boot department, Tod's boots were measured and found satisfactory. He boxed up three more pairs and sent them to the checkout man.

Next, Tod faced the wig and cosmetics departments. Embarrassed, he merely allowed Sasha Marketa and Katya to pick out what they thought was appropriate. The wig man pointed out, "Many women go for the shorter, bobbed styles, easier to manage, but then some like these two beauties prefer the longer varieties." Katya insisted that he get a pair of blonde wigs, whose hair was straight and as long as theirs, falling to the middle of their backs.

"Trust me, you will look fabulous in it," Katya cooed.

Their last stop was the nail salon. Here, Tod again allowed Sasha Marketa and Katya to dictate what should be done. He left sporting three-inch nail extensions painted a light blue, matching theirs, which pleased both young women.

"Your Royal Highness, yes, these will be charged to Czar Anatoly. Thank you for your purchases at K's," the checkout man said politely. "And I must say that you both and your friend here just look positively beautiful. Please give my kindest regards to the Czarina."

"We will," Katya bubbled. The three then pressed close together, interlocking their fingers once more and headed out of the doors.

As they passed the Greeter on her pedestal, she said, "Thank you for shopping at K's."

"She has a real job," Katya whispered, once they were out of her hearing range. Tod didn't comment. In his mind, that wasn't much of a job at all. Here was a whole society that had gone completely off the rails because of a literal interpretation of historical records.

"Do we have to go straight back to the palace?" Tod asked, hating the idea that soon he was going to be helplessly hanging on a pedestal for the rest of the day doing absolutely nothing at all.

Sasha Marketa giggled. "No. We can go to the park. We'll be okay as long as we are back by lunchtime."

The park was a small one, with paved paths so that they could easily walk and admire the plants, bushes, and marble statues. "You know what bothers me the most?" Tod began in a somewhat grumbling mood, as the very light breeze scented with flowers pushed some strands of his new long-haired wig over his makeup covered face. Both teens shook their heads no.

"It's these hidden standards that everyone is trying to live up to: the good woman, good man standard. Actually, they aren't really hidden but are more like pretended standards," Tod grumbled.

"What do you mean?" Sasha Marketa asked, growing a bit worried about Tod.

"Look, you have a precise definition for a chair. It had four legs, a back, and a horizontal surface, and people use them to sit on, so they have to be strong enough to hold a person's weight. See, a good definition of a chair, right?"

Katya giggled. "Well yes. We have a good definition of a

house too." She recited hers, which was a good action type of definition.

"Precisely so. Now, give me a good action definition of a good woman," Tod grumbled.

"Well, a good woman is supposed to. . ." Sasha Marketa began, but Tod interrupted her.

"No, don't give me all the supposed to's. A good action definition please. A good woman is a female. . ." Tod insisted, purposely not finishing his sentence.

"But we all know that a good woman is supposed to be bound and on her pedestal," Katya protested.

"Who is we? What's supposed to be? No, I mean a good, real live, action definition," Tod pointed out. "You can't. There isn't any — not for a good woman or a good man. That's what is really bothering Petya. It's all subjective, based on an imaginary idea told repeatedly to every child by his or her parents for millennia. Everyone is trying hard to live up to this imaginary, not-defined standard. Some don't wear boxes, some do. It's crazy. Now, back when your original ancestors crash landed on this world with no way to escape or call for help, they were in trouble. There was a critical shortage of women among them. In order to survive into the future, they had to protect the few women that they had, so they could have babies and create future generations. Since those times, much of what was written in a figurative manner has somehow been interpreted literally and passed down in the form of vague, ill-defined supposed-to's."

Tod continued his diatribe. "Making people try to live up to some ill-defined model of conduct that no one knows for sure what it exactly is or why, isn't a good thing at all. Look, the men of North Land have to work twice as hard as they should be so that everyone can survive, since half of your population merely sits idly on a pedestal all day long, contributing nothing much to the survival of everyone else."

"Oh no! So that's what the Counter-Revolution is all about!" Sasha Marketa gushed in sudden realization.

"Huh?" Tod said, startled by what she'd just said. A revolution?

"Well, down in the southern and middle continents,

where it is really far too hot or too cold, there is a big movement, the Counter-Revolution it's called up here in the north. They want women to work and discard their pedestals and bindings. I bet Petya is somehow involved with them. That would explain his disrespectful behavior of late. Oh, we best get back. It must be close to lunchtime. Papa will be worried if we aren't back then."

Chapter 27 Revolution and Pirates

Days turned into weeks for Tod, who spent the daytime hours attached to his pedestal between Sasha Marketa and Katya. Nights after supper became the highlight of each day, when he and the teens were free and could do as they desired. Katya became his little sister, and the three always spent the first hours of their freedom playing card games and a word game of letter tiles called Scrabble. After that, he and Sasha Marketa allowed their passions to blossom. Each fell madly in love with the other, and Tod proposed to her, pleasing both the Czar and Czarina as well as Katya.

At least his new corsets were comfortable, wholly unlike that first one which compressed his breasts fiercely. Plus, hanging from the hook on the marble pedestals kept the pressure off of his toes. By this time, Tod too had learned to walk fairly well in the boots, though twice he did fall and had to be assisted to his feet by Petya, who simply snickered at him. Although his hair continued to grow, it still wasn't long enough to qualify as a woman's style. He was forced to continue wearing the long-haired wigs. However, since Sasha Marketa loved seeing him in it, he didn't mind too much. Rather he hated the makeup on his face and refused even to learn how to apply it himself. Sasha Marketa continued to do it for him each morning.

Rather now that he was soon to marry, Tod began wondering how he could support her. Could he get a job? As a bound woman on a pedestal, his options were severely limited. Regrettably, he knew they would likely be surviving off the largess of the Czar, probably given quarters somewhere in this sprawling palace and servants likely to handle their needs during the daytime. It wasn't a future that Tod desired or ever imagined for himself, but he did love Sasha Marketa and even Katya, though, as the sister he didn't have. Somehow, he promised himself, he would create a better life for these two teens. The how completely eluded him.

It was June 1, 1382, but Tod had no idea of the date,

only the local date there on New Terra, which meant nothing to him. Katya did explain it was summertime, but that it didn't snow this far north in the winter. As usual, Tod was on his pedestal between Sasha Marketa and Katya. The Czarina was on hers, but some distance to the right of Sasha Marketa. All were watching the TV shows, where other women on pedestals were discussing the latest news. The group had just finished lunch and had been repositioned on their pedestals, when the Czar walked into the room to discuss something with his wife.

While the two were chatting, Petya quietly walked into the room, unseen by everyone else. The voices on the TV drowned out his soft footsteps. Suddenly and without any warning, Petya yelled, "Viva Revolution!" Tod heard the bark of a gunshot. He turned his head towards the noise and saw a small grey cloud of smoke rising above a gun in Petya's hand. The sound of the Czar's body landing on the marble floor caused all heads to turn one hundred eighty degrees. The Czarina screamed loudly. Bang. Another gunshot echoed in the ornate, tall ceilinged room. Her voice fell silent. A small round hole appeared in her forehead. Blood oozed from it, but the back of her head was gone; blood and brain matter covered the back of her pedestal and the nearby floor. The two teens then screamed wildly.

"Ah shut the hell up, sis! I'm taking over now. You can just sit there on your pedestals," Petya barked loudly above their screams. "The Counter-Revolution has come to North Land. I'm now the new Czar. Expect many changes." He turned and ran out of the room. Above the girls' screams, Tod could hear more gunfire within the palace.

Tod cursed himself. *I should have probed Petya's mind, seen this coming, and done something to have prevented it. Shit! Now what the hell do I do? Protect them. How?* Just then, the TV began reporting a revolution was in progress!

"This just in. Shooting is everywhere!" a male announcer cried out. "Soldiers are fighting other solders in the streets. Hundreds are reporting shootings across Karkoff! We have a camera outside now. The scene is just graphically awful. Feel free not to look. My god. They just murdered that man." Several women reporters on their pedestals there in the studio screamed, turning their heads away from their monitors as well.

Several other men came rushing into the room where Tod was helpless on his pedestal. They ignored him and the teens, going to the bodies of the Czar and Czarina. Using a video camera, they shot some images of the dead leaders. Then, four of them dragged the bodies out of the room, while the fifth man barked, "You pathetic women, just stay on your stupid pedestals for now, and you won't get shot like your parents, Czar Petya's orders."

"Filthy beasts!" Sasha Marketa managed to find the will to shout back at him. He smirked and left the room too.

Tod focused and sent emotionally calming waves of energy over the two terrified teens, who suddenly turned to look at him, as they finally realized that Tod was somehow calming them down. "We need to think clearly," Tod whispered.

"But he's murdered mama and papa," protested Katya.

"I know and so does the whole world. Perhaps, your father's soldiers will defeat him. We can hope so," Tod tried to find something to provide a threat of hope for the teens. It seemed lame to him, though. Thinking didn't prove fruitful; too much had just happened for rational thought. Instead, the TV continued showing graphical images of the revolution as it progressed.

Late afternoon, Czar Petya came back into the room, a most satisfied look on his face. Also, he was wearing his father's crown. At least his gun was holstered, Tod noticed. He was prepared to attack Petya mentally, if he so much as threatened the teens. "Well, it's done. North Land is now under my control. The Judicial Council is dead too; I'm the new Czar. There's going to be many changes now! Okay, sisters, I have only one question for you both. Do you still want to be good women?"

"Of course, Petya! How could you do this to mama and papa? They've always been the best parents to us, even you?" Sasha Marketa cried out.

"You too, I suppose, Katya?" Czar Petya ignored her outburst and asked his younger sister.

"But I'm being a good woman, Petya. Why did you do this to mama and papa?" Katya cried out.

"So be it. You're going to stay a good woman too, Tod. You don't get any choice, space woman. It's time to eat." He lifted each of the three down from the pedestals. "Now go to the dining room. Supper's ready."

"Unbind us, please," Sasha Marketa said, as politely as she could muster under the circumstances.

"Ha! No way, dear good sister. No, from now on, you 'good women' will remain bound all the time, even at night, though I'll send a servant around after supper to wipe your streaked makeup off you," Czar Petya replied with a smirk on his face.

"But how will we eat? Petya, this isn't right," Sasha Marketa pleaded.

"It is now. You want to be good women, so be good women and obey. No way am I unbinding you. Hell, you'll just find a gun and shoot me. No way. You can eat as the dogs do. Either that or go hungry. Now move if you want any supper at all. I have lots of work to do. There's going to be plenty of changes in our world, all for the better." He turned and walked briskly out of the room. The trio had no choice but to follow along behind him, albeit drastically slower.

It was humiliating to have to eat like dogs, but the servants did put the food in bowls for them, along with a bowl of water and another with coffee in it. All three were hungry and had no choice but to do as he ordered. Later, three terrified servant women came and washed off their faces, removing the streaked makeup, but she couldn't undo their bindings since a man stood beside her with a gun in his hand.

"Can I sleep with you two tonight?" Katya whimpered. "I'm really scared."

"Of course, Katya. You stay close to us always now," Tod replied. Using their teeth, they got the covers down and struggled into bed beside each other. Again, Tod sent calming waves of energy over the two terrified teens, who quickly fell into a deep, but highly uncomfortable sleep, letting Tod thinking about what to do next. Somehow he needed to get these two to safety, but where was safe? He too fell into an ill sleep.

In the morning, a servant and a guard with his gun woke them up. "I have to pull your panties off of you. Czar Petya's orders. If you have to go to the bathroom, now you can. No one is going to help you with it," the servant whispered.

A bit later, the frightened trio found breakfast waiting them in dog bowls as before. After a humiliating time while Czar Petya merely snickered at them, they were marched to their pedestals and hung up once more. At least Petya turned on the TV for them. The news was very depressing though. Apparently, the revolution had been successful, and now the new officials were tallying up the dead.

Midday, the cameras focused on Czar Petya wearing the crown and sitting on his throne. He barked out orders to the world. All "good women" were to have their panties removed and remain bound all the time. Essentially, they were going to be treated just as the trio had been. "Yes, someone will put each good woman on her pedestal when appropriate, but that's all the assistance anyone will ever do for these good women. From now on, women will work just like men work. It's work like us or be a 'good woman.'" He ranted on about other changes, but the trio wasn't listening.

"We're doomed! We can't live like this," protested Sasha Marketa. "He can't get away with this. Someone will stop him! I know it!"

"But who?" Katya cried out. "There's no one left. Papa's dead." Both began sobbing again, but Tod was lost in thought. Petya and others like him were trying to bring about change, but at what cost? Huge. He was helpless to do anything about it. Hours passed. Servants came to lift them down and take them to their meals, hanging them back up when they finished. At least, they had the kindness to wipe their messy faces when they finished eating like dogs. Days began to pass once again.

Self-appointed Commander Jorkel addressed his small group of Gamelon-3 freedom fighters. "The damned Federation has nuked ten of our cities, murdering the thousands of volunteers who stayed behind to fake them out.

Now, it is our turn to strike fear and terror into the mighty Federation, bring them to their knees, literally. We've duplicated the stuff in quantity, but the delivery mechanism is as yet untried. We must run some tests to get the delivery craft working properly. Plus, we need tests to know just how much will be needed. After all, it's pointless to dump an insufficient quantity of the stuff on a damned Federation world and not achieve victory."

"All well and good, commander, but just how are we going to do all that?" a man spoke up.

"We've located a more primitive world that no one knows about out here in the rim. We'll run some tests on it. They don't have space travel, so we can experiment in complete safety," Commander Jorkel answered. "Plus, we have used those brave volunteers from our home world. As you know, Haskel City volunteered to be test subjects. So we know the dosage needed to wipe out one city. Of course, the damned Federation nuked Haskel City not long after that, but our brave, heroic volunteers knew that would happen, and it was really a mercy killing. Now, what remains is to work out the dosage that will ensure planet-wide contagion. We have calculations to do and drones to construct. Let's get busy, men. Never forget Gamelon-3!" The large group of volunteer soldiers cheered and shouted their new three-word battle cry.

On Ashford-5, Governor Misty grew more and more worried about her missing grandson. No trace had yet been found of his ship. Although she'd ordered numerous exploratory trips, all had returned without finding any trace of his ship. Having done everything she could think of to find out what had happened to her grandson, she finally decided to seek help from Queen Rael. "Look, I'm desperate. We simply can't find any trace of his ship. No wreckage. Nothing. No contact for weeks now. Frankly, I'm at my wits end."

"I know, Misty. We all feel badly about this," Queen Rael replied. "How can we help?"

"Telepathy. I know that with enough of the giant crystals, you can extend the range of our gifts. Is it possible to do this and see if someone can make contact with Tod and see what's happened to him?" Governor Misty asked, knowing this was really her last hope.

"Yes, of course, Misty. We should have tried this angle sooner. Give us a day to make the preparations. We'll need someone who is intimately familiar with Tod to make the attempt."

"I'll do it. I know my sometimes scatter-brained grandson," Governor Misty answered.

The next day, Governor Misty was taken into the top of the Imperial Tower, where a Circle of ten telepaths was waiting for her. A dozen of the giant germanium crystals were arranged in a circle about the men and women who were sitting on soft cushions, awaiting her. She took the indicated seat. The Circle leader, their Capa, said softly, "We will join with the stones and then with you last. You'll feel an enormous power flooding into you. Please, do not let it distract you. Focus and reach out, as you would do normally to make telepathic contact with Tod. Let the power flow through you. Our Regulator here will be monitoring your body, so nothing external can interfere with your focus. Ready?"

Governor Misty swallowed hard. "Yes. Let's do this. It's my last hope, really." She sat down and forced herself to relax, almost into a rapport state. Suddenly, she felt the Capa's mind joining hers, along with more power than she could ever imagine! She lost her focus! *With this much power, I could control the whole universe from here!*

The Capa sent, *Of course you could. That is why these stones are kept secure. No one should yield such power. Now focus, Governor Misty, focus.*

She did as asked, expanding her awareness outward, further and further, looking for that unique wavelength or frequency that was the essence of her grandson, Tod. Space had little meaning. There wasn't anything by which to measure or sense it. She only knew that her awareness extended far, far beyond mere Ashford-5. Then, she sensed him, that unique wavelength that was Tod's interface to the physical world of matter and energy.

Tod! I've found you at last! Are you all right?

Grandma? Is that you? Oh god. Yes, I'm all right, but I

really need help soon!

That's a relief. You have everyone here quite worried about you. Where are you now?

Don't know. Got shot down by the pirates. From Gamelon-3, I think. Crashed on an unknown world. Modern, but without space travel. Yellow dwarf sun. They call it New Terra and speak Russian. There's a revolution going on. I'm trying to save Princess Sasha Marketa and her sister Katya. I'm in love with her too. Can you send a rescue party soon?

Slow down. Tell me everything that's happened, Tod. Somehow, we'll find you.

Tod began telling her everything that had happened, since he was attacked in his shuttle. That done, Governor Misty had to break the connection. Her own body simply couldn't handle this much power for very long, but she promised to get back to him, to locate and somehow rescue him and his companions.

Later, she met with the queens to discuss how to proceed. "Look, my hands are somewhat tied. With all these pirate raids on the fuel refinery, I can't send out a fleet to look for this unknown rim world. Yet, I can't just abandon him," Governor Misty explained.

"I know. We can pull Captain Nia Elain back from Cass-C. Her ship isn't needed for any combat situations and has the capability of extended flights now. She can search for him. We'll see that she has enough of the giant crystals to reach him. She's our best bet on handling first contact type of situations," Queen Rael offered.

"Please. Make it happen. I owe you a really big one," Governor Misty replied.

"No, you'd do the same for anyone of us, Misty. We just should have thought of this sooner. I'll make the call to Nia Elain now. You go find Danika and tell her to assemble her crew," Queen Rael ordered.

That's how I got the secure call from Queen Rael. "Sure, Martina and I can get away. There's nothing much going on here really. Boring actually. All's been routine and quiet. If we wear PDS, they can't hurt us with their primitive guns. We should be fine. Over." Once more, I was thankful for the

Personal Defense Shields of the ex-Imperium. We would be immune to their gunfire, if it came to that. Besides, I was bored out of my mind on Cass-C. And as I expected, Danika and crew arrived some ten hours later.

As Martina and I walked slowly to the Eagle's Seed, she commented, "Now I don't have to feed you any longer."

I laughed. "You don't know how hard it has been for me not to use my gifts on Cass-C."

"There you are my gorgeous golden haired beauty," Danika teased me, as I walked up the bay ramp. We hugged and kissed. Shortly after that, we were on our way back to Ashford-5, where we'd get our new marching orders from Governor Misty. We arrived around four in the morning, but chose to stay in bed until seven, when Danika set the Eagle's Seed down at our spaceport. I breathed in deeply the odors of my home world, but that was short lived. Governor Misty came aboard, along with a ground crew, who swapped out our used fuel cells for new ones, though Danika personally checked each one for flaws.

"Here's the situation with my missing grandson, Tod," she began. After a detailed explanation, she joined with me and showed me her mental images, which Tod had sent her when she had made telepathic contact with him a couple of days ago. "Do what you have to do to get my grandson back and anyone else he wants to rescue. You'll need some giant crystals. Guard this with your lives. The power they give one is beyond belief!" Several tower members carried in six bags, nodding to me as they passed by.

"Don't worry, governor, we'll find him."

"I don't know how you can, but I've faith in you and your crew," she sighed.

Telepathy doesn't give you the distance between the two parties, but as my crew had shown in the halo, it can give direction. Zarita was coming along with us, since she had used similar crystals before, enabling my crew to follow me when the men from the Gorki Cluster had kidnaped me. I had confidence in her skill. Governor Misty hugged me and left with the tower members. Shoot, I didn't even have time to go see the kids. Danika closed the bay doors, and we headed to the cockpit.

"You fly her," I said. "I'll play co-pilot this time. This way, I get to watch you, my love. I've really missed you. Terribly boring on Cass-C these past months." Danika chuckled, and we lifted off.

Then, we headed to the cabin where Zarita had setup both her crystal spheres and those I'd been given for the mission. She was sitting on the bed with them carefully arrayed around her. Of course, everyone else dropped by to see these giant crystals of power, oh'ing and ah'ing over them. Then, we let Zarita get to work. I swung my head a bit to get my golden locks off to one side and then sat down. Danika held a galactic chart and a marker, ready to keep track. Zarita focused and began activating the many giant crystals, one by one adding them into a unified group. When she had them all activated, I then joined with her. I can't begin to describe the feeling of immense power that was now mine to control. Incredible.

I began reaching out, searching for Tod, based on what Governor Misty had shared with me. Since I hadn't really met Tod before, though I'd probably seen him around, I needed her guidance to locate him this first time. After that, I'd know his intimate wavelength. After what seemed an eternity to me, but was only a half hour, I reached him!

Tod! Yeh. Captain Nia Elain here. We're on our way to rescue you. First, we're going to have to triangulate with telepathy to locate you, more or less. We'll be contacting you twice more to pin it down some. Hang in there kid.

Great! Hurry, the situation here is rather volatile. I hate revolutions. I chuckled and broke the connection. I dropped out of rapport with Zarita, and one by one, she deactivated the crystals. I looked at Danika's chart. She had constructed one line based on the direction I'd indicated. Now, she headed to the cockpit to shoot us a good distance away so we could try again. The problem with triangulations is that for best results, one needs a long baseline. That is, our next position ought to be a good distance from Ashford-5. She cleverly picked a desolate area in Federation space, where we'd not likely be discovered, even though we would only be out of hyperspace there for a few minutes.

Three hours later, Zarita powered up the crystals, and again, I made contact with Tod. Danika drew another heading line, and the two crossed far out on the rim in Federation space. Now, we had a real point to head towards and decided against obtaining a third line just yet. She powered up the engines, and she and I estimated the coordinates and punched them into the hyperdrive. Showing off, I hit the button jumping us into hyperspace using my telekinetic powers. "Five hours until we drop out again," she announced. "Time for play, dear." I laughed.

Tod rested on his pedestal, alongside Sasha Marketa and Katya, watching the TV news, trying to make some sense of what was happening in North Land. One of the female reporters was talking, "This is criminal. They are making us good women eat as if we are dogs! They don't even unbind us. I apologize for not having my makeup on today. I've no way to apply it, and no one is allowed to help me, other than hooking me up to my pedestal. Never have we ever seen such a total disrespect for good women. After all, haven't we all striven to be the best good women all our lives? Is this the thanks we get? This reporter is very much upset with these revolutionary thugs, these hoodlums, these brigands!"

"I agree wholeheartedly," another female reporter added from her pedestal. "How dare these men humiliate us good women? All you good men out there do something before it's too late."

A male reporter interrupted her. "This just in. Some kind of alien flying machines have been spotted flying in low orbits around our world. North Land radar has picked up ten small flying machines. Have our space woman's people come to pick her up?"

"No, initial reports from jets cruising them report seeing no one flying them. Some form of yellow gaseous substance is being ejected from these ships. Authorities are keeping silent. What does this mean? Is our rebellious new Czar ready to handle these ships? Are they a threat or not? What do ten of these mean? An invasion? Hardly, since they are unmanned."

Tod gasped. "Oh no! Not here!"

"What? Are they your people?" asked Sasha Marketa.

"No. They are the pirates, the terrorists. They are attacking your world with a horrible weapon. That yellow gas is going to genetically alter everyone's bodies," Tod exclaimed. "If only I could warn Petya. Shoot them down now, but even so, it's probably too late."

Scared, both Katya and Sasha Marketa began yelling for someone, anyone. No one came. Evidently, the servants had been ordered to ignore the trio on their pedestals. Tod thought faster than he ever had before. "Sasha, is there some place here in the palace that is underground, and where there isn't any kind of exposure to the outside air?"

"You, you mean a bomb shelter?" she replied hesitantly. Tod nodded. "Yes, papa has an emergency bomb shelter below the palace. Why? Will it help?"

"Yes. Maybe. It's our only chance. My people are trying to find us and rescue us, but they aren't going to get here in time. Sasha, I love you and you too Katya. I can't do anything to stop this attack. We've got to get into that bomb shelter of yours." Tod tried the direct approach. Wiggling what he could, he tried to make the pedestal fall over, knowing how difficult it would be to get back onto his feet. However, these were made from heavy stone. His efforts didn't wiggle it in the slightest. Tod knew that his only choice was to use his limited *mentales* gifts. He focused and his small crystal began glowing in its pale blue light.

Both Sasha Marketa and Katya stared at him in awe. His body seemed to rise up a little, freeing the loop on the back of his corset from the pillar. His body moved a little forward and stood on his toes once more, free from the pedestal. He turned his attention to Sasha Marketa and got her free and then Katya. "How? How did you do that?" asked a very surprised Sasha Marketa.

"Way cool!" Katya exclaimed.

"No time. Lead us to this bomb shelter before it's too late for us," Tod pleaded.

"Okay, follow me, but there's going to be doors barring

our way," she replied nervously, but she was also excited. Finally, she was doing something to help. They soon reached the hallway door, which was closed. Once more, Tod focused, and the doorknob turned. Sasha then pushed into it. To her surprise, it opened. She turned to look at Tod, saw he was focusing his attention, so she headed on out the door, followed closely by Katya.

Down a long hall went the trio. Then came stairs heading downward. "This'll be very hard to do, Tod, even for us. If we fall, we could kill ourselves," Sasha Marketa warned them.

"If we don't, we're dead anyway," Tod countered. "Oh god! This is incredibly scary!" he exclaimed, as he tried to take his first downward step. If only their arms were free, he thought. Slowly and with extreme care, the trio began the long descent. The stairs turned many times before stopping at another closed door. Once more Tod used his gifts to get it opened.

They entered another long hallway. Very dim lights widely spaced provided the only illumination. "It's not much farther," Sasha Marketa whispered, unsure whether to speak aloud or not. Shortly, they stood before another very heavy door, one of the very few made from metal. Tod thought, on this metal-poor world, this door must have cost a king's ransom to make. Once more, he worked his magic, but it took all his energies actually to swing the door open enough to allow them to squeeze through.

Inside, Tod saw they were inside a bunker of some kind. Using the last of his energies, Tod got the door shut, and the heavy bar lock pulled down. Now, no one could get to them unless they raised that bar. The bunker was illuminated in a dull red light. The trio moved deeper into it and began looking around.

They spotted several beds and a small gas stove. Against one wall were shelves of canned food. Sasha Marketa whispered, "There's a whole lot of food stored here. And those are bottles of water, only we can't open the cans or bottles. Perhaps, this isn't such a good idea, Tod."

"You mean we are surrounded by food and water and

are going to die?" Katya asked her older sister.

"No, we can, once I get our arms free," Tod countered. "But I've used up all my energies getting us here. I'm going to need to rest some before trying to get our arms free." He plopped down on one of the beds and fell asleep.

How long did he sleep? Tod had no idea when he woke. He struggled to sit up and spotted the two teens were now asleep themselves on nearby beds. Quietly, he focused and began undoing the straps on Sasha's bindings. He did hers because he couldn't see his own back to do his. Gently, he freed her arms. She didn't stir, so he went ahead and did Katya's too. However, she did stir.

"Oh! My arms are free! Tod, how did you do that?" she asked wide-eyed.

"My gifts. Can you undo me, Katya? I can't see my own back to do mine."

"Sure thing, only it's hard with these long nails of ours. Not too practical I think." She rose and came over to him, sitting down on the bed beside him. A few minutes later, she had Tod's arms free at last. Stretching and rubbing them, Tod thanked her. "So how did you do all those magical tricks? Can I learn how to do them too?" Katya asked.

"Born with them. I don't know if you can or not, Katya. Now, we have to fix us something to eat and hope we weren't exposed to too much of that poisonous gas."

"What will happen to us if we have?" Katya asked. "You never did say what awful thing would happen."

"What will happen? Oh, my arms. How?" Sasha Marketa woke up and asked, suddenly realizing her arms were free at last. She too rubbed and knotted the kinks out of sore muscles.

"I'll tell you all about it, but let's get something to eat and drink first," Tod replied.

"I have to pee," Katya interrupted. "Has anyone seen a toilet or something?" The trio rose and began looking around for a bathroom. They found something labeled "Port-a-potty." "This must be it," Katya declared. "Oops, no privacy."

Tod chuckled, "I won't look, Katya."

She giggled, "Maybe you should look." Both women

giggled, but Tod refrained from looking, heading instead to the cook stove to try to figure out how it worked. A half hour later, the trio dined on something vaguely resembling stew and some hot tea.

"So you promised to tell us," Katya reminded him as they sat back sipping their tea.

"Okay, but promise me you won't get too scared," he said, and launched into a lengthy explanation about the genetic bio agent and its horrific effects. He also told them about some of the cures the brilliant geneticists on Ashford-5 had discovered. Finally, the two understood how he could be both male and female.

"So how will we know if we're going to be changed?" Sasha Marketa asked.

"We'll slip into a coma which lasts for four days. If we are lucky and haven't had much of an exposure, we might not have anything happen to us. I just don't know, but I'm sleepy. Perhaps, we should go to bed, but we'd best undress completely, just in case. If we go into a coma, we don't dare be wearing these corsets and boots," Tod advised.

"But we don't have our nightgowns," Katya whispered. "Naked? Oh, I like that." She giggled again.

Tod flushed. "Well, kid," he said amusingly, "you're going to get your wish. Just don't laugh or I'll have to tickle you." She giggled. Later each took their own bed, but Tod noticed neither teen could bend their feet much at all. He guessed after wearing those boots since they were three, their feet had adapted to them, so now they had to wear them if they wanted to be able to walk. He sighed silently to himself, praying they wouldn't wake up four days later. Nia Elain contacted him again, as he was almost asleep, part of her triangulation procedure. He relayed what was happening in North Land.

He next morning, Tod woke and quickly checked his arms. Present and accounted for. He relaxed and rose, looking himself over, and noticing his hair touched his shoulders. Funny, it hadn't been that long last night. Panic swept over him, and he stood up, checking his body again, but found nothing else amiss. He looked over the two sleeping teens, but other than seeing perhaps more hair around their heads, he saw nothing much else, though they were covered with a blanket. He decided to leave them and fix some breakfast. He opened a promising can and sniffed it. Perhaps, it was stew, but he couldn't read their language. He fired up the small cooking stove, heated it, and water for tea. They had not cleaned up their plates from yesterday, so he got down three more, wondering where dishes could be done in this bunker.

Just then, Katya called out, followed shortly by Sasha Marketa. Fearing the worse since he couldn't see beneath their blankets, Tod rushed over to the beds. Both were sitting up and examining their bodies. "Oh, can you help us with our boots. We need them to walk," Katya said, adding, "I think my hair is longer today. What do you think?" Sasha Marketa added her "me too."

"Same here. I think our hair has grown some," Tod admitted. "Anything else? You are not in a coma, that's good news."

"I think they are bigger," Sasha Marketa commented, her face flushing as she felt her breasts.

Katya giggled, "Mine too. I'm sure of it. That's a good thing, isn't it?"

"You look lovely, Katya," Tod complimented her, making her feel more comfortable. He began getting them into their boots, while he remained barefooted. "Come on; breakfast waits, whatever it is."

"Octopus soufflé," Sasha Marketa commented. "Bit weird for breakfast."

"Yuck!" Tod grumbled, turning up his nose.

"Oh let me see what is here," she countered. Soon, they were eating bacon and eggs with toast, all dried from a can, just add water and warm. It tasted leathery but much better than the octopus. While sipping their tea, Tod looked around, and found a garbage can and a portable washbasin. Hastily, he tossed out the octopus and cleaned up the dishes, using as little water as possible. By then, his tea had cooled some.

After tea, the trio split up and explored their bomb shelter. Katya found a light switch, which turned the dim red glow into almost bright daylight. Tod merely said, "Duh!"

Then, Sasha Marketa found a small TV and turned it on.

"Oh my god! Come look!" she yelled. The other two joined her, sitting beside her on a bed, staring at the silent images on the TV. There were the reporters from yesterday. The three female reporters were still on their pedestals, but they were in a coma. Similarly, the male reporters were visible, the cameras pointing to them as well, but they were slumped over at their desks, also in comas. Even without a close-up view, the trio could see that their hair had grown substantially, perhaps even double the length it had been yesterday, plus their bosoms were threatening to pop out of the tops of their corsets. They couldn't see whether the men were developing breasts though, because of their slumped positions. Utter silence, only a faint static hiss could be heard from the TV.

"It's — it's happening, isn't it?" Sasha Marketa whispered, stunned.

"I think so. I hope we're safe down here," Tod replied solemnly.

Later, Nia Elain contacted him again, as the Eagle's Seed began to close the distance between them, while searching for the right star on the rim. Tod relayed what he was seeing on the TV, knowing even if the ship found them today, they wouldn't dare try to land for days yet.

"This is really boring," Katya declared. She hunted around the cubby holes of the bunker and found an old deck of cards, much to her delight. The trio began playing cards to bide their time, which seemed to drag on endlessly, broken only by the occasional brief telepathic contact by Nia Elain, as her ship continued moving towards them.

On the fourth day, the TV was still on and the trio saw the final results of the genetic modifications. The three female reporters were still on their pedestals. Their breasts had completely popped out of their corsets and were as large as Tod's, but nowhere near the humongous sizes that usually developed. Their hair nearly touched the floor though. The trio saw the ghastly husks of what had been their arms, still bound behind their backs. Their shoulders were now bare. However, Tod noticed that their lips were not split, quite unexpectedly. The men had also lost their arms and from their slightly altered, slumped positions, their breasts must have grown as large as the women's. They too were draped in extremely long and thick hair, but their lips weren't split either.

In contrast, each of the trio's hair had thickened and now fell to the small of their backs, about half of the length of those who were fully exposed. Also, the two teen's bosoms now matched Tod's, whose had not enlarged any as far as he could tell. Their feet also hadn't changed any, but they couldn't tell from the static TV images whether the reporters' feet had become malformed.

"Well, if this is all that's going to happen to us, I can live with it," Sasha Marketa pronounced. "Besides, Tod, I like you with longer hair like us. Now, we all have perfectly amazing boobs." Katya giggled, but was clearly proud of hers.

At this point, the reporters began reviving. One female reporter cried out, "Will someone please help us? We have to go to the bathroom badly and we're starving. Please, anyone."

Just then, one of the male reporters revived and began screaming wildly. His arms were gone and his feet were a mass of pain. The TV sounds soon became too loud and panic stricken to listen to, and Katya turned the volume down. All three watched helplessly and stunned, witnessing the six reporters' terror live.

Then, the video stream broke away and a bearded man's face appeared. "This is the voice of the Counter-Revolution in the Midlands. We've been watching the alien attack in the North Land for four days now. Apparently, it is over now. We'll be sending assistance to those in the North Land soon. Our revolution is over. The new Czar Igor Romanov of the Midlands will be addressing New Terra later today. Stay tuned. We are usurping the TV feeds from the North Lands from now on. There have been no signs of the alien ships for three days. Hopefully, they are gone for good. What a wonderful service they have done for New Terra, wiping out in one fell swoop all the so-called good men and good women. Stay tuned for Czar Igor's address later today. Long live the Counter-Revolution!" The screen went to some kind of test pattern. The four stared at the TV, stunned.

Later on when I contacted Tod next, he relayed what

had happened to them and the overall results he'd seen on the TV. I relayed them back to Ashford-5 and our geneticists there. They then held a long chat with Dr. Leann, who was with me in her capacity as our medical doctor and their liaison.

Dr. Leann tried to explain what they asked and wanted us to do. "You see, something different has happened here. Their lips are unaffected but we know that they should have been. Further, breast sizes are drastically smaller than what ought to have been anticipated. Something unusual or perhaps different is going on here. They believe that Tod and the women with him received only a tiny dosage of the agent, which may account for only minor genetic alterations. They want to make sure you bring those two women back with Tod. Plus, if you can take some air and soil samples, that may prove helpful, as well as samples of their usual food substances. They are looking at cause and effect, because something has changed the way this bio agent is working," she explained in simple terms.

Jana and Jovanna agreed to handle the air and food samples, while Zarita promised to get soil samples, and Beth would take animal samples, if possible. I expected to reach their world tomorrow at the latest, since Anwyn and Dylan had finally identified their sun. Now, it was merely a question of speed, and Danika poured it on.

Meantime, instead of waiting for the new Czar's address, Sasha Marketa exclaimed, "Yulia and Leontii! What about them? She's only ten. We have to find her, Tod."

"Okay, the danger is over. Besides, we can't go around naked. Let's go back up to our bedrooms and get into something, a shirt, anything, and then look for them," Tod suggested. "Besides, I need some shoes. This stone floor is freezing my feet, but I'm not going to wear those boots if I don't have too." The two teens giggled.

A bit later, they faced the long hike up the circular stairs. "Need a hand?" Tod asked.

"No, we can manage now that we've got the use of our arms. Where can Yulia be?" asked a worried Sasha Marketa.

"Clothes first," Tod insisted. They'd reached the main floor and heard screams echoing around the long hallways.

"Okay, but let's hurry," Sasha Marketa insisted, though she knew that she couldn't walk fast, in spite of trying.

In their parent's bedroom, Tod found three large shirts and handed them out. "We look silly in these, but there's nothing else to wear that will fit. At least, let's get panties on," Sasha Marketa insisted. While the two went off to look for them in their bedrooms, Tod slipped on a pair of ill-fitting shoes of Anatoly's, and then joined them. At last more or less clothed, the trio set off in search of their younger siblings.

They weren't in their bedrooms. "The playroom!" Katya exclaimed, leading the trio off again. Hearing the screams of their two younger siblings, they knew they had found them at last. Entering the room, they were shocked. Yulia was lying on the floor struggling wildly to get up. Her now floor length hair was acting more like a spider web than anything else. Her arms were gone, dried husks lying on either side of the struggling girl. Already her bosom had begun to mature, though it was nowhere near as large as those of the trio were. However, Petya had long ago removed her panties, since she still had wanted to be the good girl that her mother had always talked about. While Sasha Marketa didn't say anything, she saw Yulia's new male appendage was fully developed, just like Tod's.

Not far away, lay the fourteen year old Leontii. He had not survived, which had only escalated Yulia's terror and panic. As Tod knelt beside the lad, he saw a nasty head wound. When he'd fallen into the coma, he'd fallen and struck his head hard on the base of a marble pedestal, Yulia's future pedestal.

"We've got you, Yulia. It'll be all right now. Sasha's here," she said soothingly. Seeing that there wasn't anything he could do for Leontii, Tod focused and sent calming emotional waves over Yulia, who quickly responded to that and her sister's tight hugging.

"You two get her to the bathroom and changed. I'll head to the kitchen and see about getting something to eat for her and us," Tod ordered.

Tod found the kitchen in complete chaos. The six kitchen women were still on their pedestals, screaming wildly. Most had already relieved themselves, soaking their panties.

The six men in their suits were in terrible shape. Their feet throbbed, but they were unable to get their shoes off. The dried husks, which had been their arms and hands, lay in piles at their sides. Their floor-length hair was covering them like spider webs as well.

"Quiet everyone!" Tod yelled above the din. "I'll help you but only if you stop screaming!" While the screaming ceased, the hysterical sobbing didn't subside. One by one, he lifted the women down and got them out of their corsets. Seeing their new male appendages, they cried even harder. At least they could walk, and he had them go to the dining room and sit down, while he attended to the men.

Taking their shoes off caused the men immense pain, and three fainted while he did that. He stripped them as well, but that only increased their hysteria. They had female organs now too. Worse, their feet were in terrible shape, totally black and blue and quite swollen, terribly mis-shapened. Tod had no idea what to do about them. So he had them crawl on their knees into the dining room, where he helped them into chairs.

He then set to work doing his best to whip up something for everyone to eat. Sasha Marketa, Katya, and Yulia soon joined them. Yulia had stopped crying and was trying to be brave as her sisters kept telling her. "How are they going to eat?" Katya whispered. "More salt, please," she asked and advised Tod's concoction, which looked more like a stew than anything else.

"Bowls. Like we had to do. We can't feed them individually. There's too many of them," Tod declared. "Set a pair of bowls out for them and put water in one of them. Let them quench their thirsts. Soup will up in a couple of minutes."

A bit later, Sasha Marketa whispered to Tod, "They're really thirsty! That's a good sign, isn't it?"

"Think so. Let's see if they go for this soup thing of mine." They did, as well as the foursome.

When the victims had finished, Tod got them all into the main room with the pedestals and TV center. That took some doing, since he had to find chairs for everyone and help the men crawl there. He and Sasha Marketa lifted them up onto the chairs. The men's feet still looked awful. Fortunately, at this point, the Counter-Revolution's leader and self-proclaimed new Czar was on, giving his speech about how they would be coming to the rescue of the North Land people. While he wanted to listen in, Nia Elain was about to land near the Royal Palace. "Come on; our ride is here," he whispered, pulling the three away from the TV.

At last, we spotted the Royal Palace in the middle of the city that Tod said was called Karkoff. It wasn't hard to spot. The palace complex sprawled over probably two city blocks. Still, I marveled at just how modern this world appeared, at least from the air as we descended. When we were a few hundred feet above, we began spotting people lying on the sidewalks and streets. "Really grim," Danika commented. "Guess we are the first responders this time. Kind of wish we weren't."

"It's going to be hard to ignore pleas for help when we land and do what we have to do," Martina pointed out. "Just be quick about it. Those air ships we spotted coming north from the middle continent will be here soon. Prudence dictates that we are gone when they get here."

"Right everyone. Let's get the samples our geneticists want, rescue Tod, and get out of here before more trouble comes," I ordered everyone. Inwardly, I deeply sighed. Here were once more millions or maybe billions of innocent men, women, and children, who were now quite helpless and terror-stricken, desperate for any assistance. I had only twenty crew members. Even if I wanted to help these victims, our numbers were minuscule, and my ship could only carry maybe another thirty away from here, assuming they even wanted to leave their world behind. This world of New Terra was in Federation space. There would be no combined Imperium rescue mission this time, ignoring the fact there wasn't an Imperium any longer. The Federation didn't even know about this world. Even if we told them, they wouldn't care or send help, not to this far-distant rim world. No, for good or ill, and probably ill, these people were on their own. I felt sick at my stomach. How could any sane person do this to millions of innocent people who didn't even possess space travel?

As many began heading down the bay ramp heading off to acquire their samples, Anya got my attention. "Boss, I'm picking up spaceships. Three of them. I can't make out their language. Ship to ship communications. They appear to be descending over the western edge of this continent."

"Crap. Okay, I'll stay here with the giant crystals and power them up. Put their comm on the speakers, and Marisol and I will see if we can't make out their language," I ordered, pulling Marisol back from the bay ramp.

"Coming boss," she called out, racing to help me with the crystals. She laid them out in a circle on the bed for me, saving me from having to use my *mentales* gifts to do it. "I'll see if I can translate what they are saying. You power them up. We might need them."

I heard men talking, but Marisol was able to translate what they were saying. "Okay Commander Jorkel, we're zooming in on some bodies lying in the sidewalks now. Arms are gone. Mountains of hair. Looks like it worked. Wait, we don't see any of those split lips or loop things. Still, they can't even seem to get up on their feet. Over."

"Okay. Partial success then. Keep sampling. Perhaps, others will have the split lips on them. What about the monster knockers? We're aren't seeing any here. Keep looking. We have to make sure we've released the right amount of the bio agent. Never forget Gamelon-3! We'll wipe the Federation off the map. Over."

They continued to share observations, but I tuned them out, focusing on bringing all the crystals into a giant network. The Eagle's Seed's shields could withstand some energy attacks, but not an all-out attack by a number of ships. My crew needed time to do their things, find Tod, and get them safely onboard.

Danika came back to check on me and overheard Marisol's translation. "Damn. We have to stop those insane Gamelon-3 men. If only we had a cruiser with us, I'd blast them from the skies!"

The greater good. That's what flashed in my mind. I knew I alone possessed the power to stop these insane men from inflicting similar destruction and genocide on countless other Federation worlds. Even with all that power flowing through me from these crystals, I honestly didn't know just what I would be able physically to accomplish. If I somehow tried to attack one of the three ships, for example by forcing it to crash or something, the others would likely flee into hyperspace and get away to cause more genocide attacks. No, I had to do something sneaky and clever, something that would not draw their immediate attention and yet eliminate them forever as a threat. I began to pervade their ships, one by one, seeing what was there.

Pervasion is an interesting action. I could see these men, short for humans, all males, scurrying about taking all manner of observations, including air samples. Busy little beavers, I thought. Then, I spotted the yellow striped cylinders. Hundreds of them! One cargo bay was literally filled with them, all stacked neatly, along with dozens of very crude looking drones, no two of which looked identical. I realized that they had been pieced together from all manner of scraps. These men were the garbage collectors of the galaxy and had put their junk to use. They were clever, I gave them that.

Pervasion also gives one knowledge. At first, I didn't quite know what to make of it. I'd pervaded their Commander Jorkel's mind. I saw the Federation had nuked quite a number of their cities, of course in retaliation for their sales of this genetic bio agent to others who had used it on Federation populations. They were in the never-ending game of "he did it to me so I have do it back to him." I knew that this cycle had to end, and then I had a bright idea, based on the observation that no one was in the three cargo bays. I acted. Using the power of the circle of giant germanium crystals, I twisted off the release valves of all the cylinders on one ship, then those on the next, and finally those on the third.

By the time I was done, some of my crew was back onboard with their samples. Martina found Tod and the three young sisters, and was leading them back to the ship. She had her d-gun out and protecting them, though I thought she was being a bit melodramatic about it. Surely, there wasn't anyone around who could remotely harm the four.

"Are you Tod?" Martina called out. She'd walked briskly

to what she thought must be the main entrance of the Royal Palace, trying hard to block out the pleas for help from the men and women on the streets leading up to the building, and then the poor guards lying on the ground near the doors. She spotted a young man leading three teens behind him. They were all wearing oversized men's shirts. The three women were walking on their toes in some strange looking tall boots, rather like storks, she thought. Then, she noticed the smaller girl had no arms and her hair was almost touching the ground. Martina sighed and said a silent curse.

"Yes. Tod Bellweather. Are you Captain Nia Elain?" he called out anxiously.

"No. She's back in the Eagle's Seed, over yonder. Come on; let's get you onboard. The men who did this are heading this way in their spaceships, and there's a whole bunch of strange air ships flying up here from the middle continent."

As they passed some of the guards lying on the ground, several pleaded with them. One said, "For the love of God, help us too. You can't leave us like this, please."

Tod called out, "A rescue party will be here soon from the middle continent. Hang on a while longer." He wished he could run to the ship and get away from these desperate pleadings, but his three companions simply couldn't. He'd never felt so awful, so helpless to help those in need, in his life. His stomach knotted, but he continued to lead the sisters towards the ship. When they finally reached the bay ramp, Tod lifted Yulia up and carried her inside. Sasha Marketa and Katya used their hands on the rails to keep their balance getting inside.

By this time, I had the crystals powered down, and Marisol and I were at the cargo bay to greet out new arrivals. "Ah. Tod. We meet at last. Captain Nia Elain. Welcome aboard."

He carefully sat Yulia back down on her toes, making sure she had her balance before letting go of her. "I can't tell you how glad I am to see you!" Tod gushed. "This is my fiancé Sasha Marketa, her sisters, Katya and Yulia."

"Oh! You are just like me," ten year old Yulia exclaimed, seeing me standing there as armless as she was and with thick, golden hair almost touching the floor. "Can I be a captain one day too? I was going to be a good woman, but that's gone now. I think I want to be a captain too. Can I?"

I laughed, "We'll see, Yulia. You have to study hard and learn a whole lot before you can be a captain, but you certainly can be one if you want. Come on inside. We'll find you some cabins and descent clothes. We have to get out of here fast. Got all sorts of company about to arrive, and we don't want to be here when they come. Marisol will show you to a cabin. I have to get to the cockpit and get us out of here. I'll come back to chat once we're safely away."

With that, as Martina closed the bay doors, Marisol led them down the hallway, while I headed in the opposite direction. "Get us out of here now, Danika," I called out before I reached my seat. She grinned and did so.

"So do we go after these evil bastards who did this?" she asked. "We can't let them get away with this. They have to die," she added, quite vitriolic.

"Already taken care of that, dear. Cloak us, and let's head for those three light cruisers of theirs. I want to make sure that they depart this world." I tossed my hair about several times, until it draped over my left shoulder, and then sat down in my seat, really Danika's co-pilot seat. She was in mine, flying the Eagle's Seed.

"Okay boss. There they are on the screen. What the hell? They are flying off wildly into space. Don't they even know how to fly?" she called out.

"Oh, they have a slight problem. I think they'd just now discovered it," I replied demurely. She gave me a really dirty look. "Okay, okay. Each ship had a stockpile of the cylinders in their cargo bays. It seems all the cylinders' valves have mysteriously broken off."

"What? Releasing the bio agent? Oh Nia Elain, you are a clever bitch! Give them a taste of their own medicine. Wait. Isn't that going to be way too much?" she replied, teasing me and then realizing the impact.

"Probably way, way too much. They won't be able to commit genocide on other Federation worlds, that much is certain," I replied. "Get us home, dear. The kids are waiting for us."

"Be there in a few hours, captain," she teased me back again. "I best let Governor Misty know that we have Tod, and he is mostly all right."

I didn't need telepathy to know how relieved Governor Misty was, especially when I relayed he was pretty much unaffected by the bio agent attack. "I owe you a very big one!" she gushed.

"There's more," I countered, and told her about the three Gamelon-3 ships, and that they'd launched the attack as basically a test of their delivery methods and quantity. I also told her what I had done to their huge supply of bio agent cylinders. "So there's no chance they can use those cylinders on another world. While I'm not a geneticist, I think they might not have dumped enough on North Land, since their lips didn't split and their breasts only got as large as ours."

"You did the right thing, as far as I'm concerned. With the release valves broken off, the entire contents of the cylinders ought to have been released really fast. I wonder what that massive overdose did to them? We'll never know, and frankly, I don't care. They had to be insane to use that on people," Governor Misty declared flatly. Thanks again, and I'll be waiting. Ten hours. Thanks. Over and out."

I headed back to chat with Tod and meet the three teens, one of whom seemed to be sixteen like my body. I found Jana and Jovanna hovering over them. "Oh hi boss. We're giving them all a hot bath next. Zarita and Martina are looking for better clothes, and Anya and Tesla are fixing up some ULATs for the three. They speak Russian, so Tod is translating for us, though we mostly understand them, since it is close to our Rus. Marisol is off checking if we can't make them better boots. These don't let them bend their knees much at all. We think knee high ones would be better."

"Great. You are in good hands. Just so you know the full story, I located the terrorists or pirates who attacked your world, dumping this horrid genetic biological agent on your people." All four looked straight at me, wide-eyed. "I took care of them. They will never again be attacking anyone. It seems that they had a huge supply of this bio agent on their ships. I released all those cylinders into their own ships. They are currently all in their comas. Four days from now, they'll be like your poor victims, but with no one at all to help them."

Sasha Marketa spoke up, "So they'll get to experience what they did to our people? Now, I call that justice. Were they planning to harm other people?"

"Yes, a whole lot of other worlds, Sasha Marketa. I couldn't let them do that. Too bad we couldn't get to your world any faster. I might have been able to stop them sooner. Hindsight is perfect, though," I explained.

Katya giggled. "Thanks to Tod, we only got altered a little bit. Can our sister be helped at all?"

"But I'm okay, Katya," Yulia protested. "I'm like Captain Nia Elain. I'm going to be a captain too, one day. You just wait and see."

"You study hard, learn lots, and there's no reason that you can't, if that's what you really want to do," I answered, giving her a bit of a morale boost.

Tod added, "You see, in our world, women are encouraged to try to achieve their dreams and goals, just as men are."

"So I don't only have to be a good woman?" little Yulia asked. I sensed her great relief. Hell, who would want to face a lifetime of being hooked on a pedestal doing nothing but looking pretty for men's eyes? Tod shook his head no. Yulia smiled, "Good. Cause that looked awfully boring."

Katya giggled, "It was, Yulia. Now, we can really learn things, but we better learn to speak their languages." Already, the three sisters had discovered only a few here either understood them or could speak theirs, and even then, we had terrible accents. They were now dependent upon the ULAT boxes.

Chapter 28 Recovery and Stabilization

"Nucleotodes? What the heck are those? Oh never mind," I asked, baffled by what Dr. Leann just told me. She had called me in to see her a few days after we landed bringing back Tod and the three sisters. Already, he and Sasha Marketa had asked Governor Misty to marry them, and set the date for the next Saturday. However, Dr. Leann insisted that I drop by her office in the Imperial Castle.

"Okay. I'll keep it simple for you, captain. As you know, our geneticists have been working almost constantly on these many genetic alterations, which until now have defied their attempts to reverse them. Well, they had a breakthrough. We can ignore this new genetic accelerator they've come up with, the nucleotodes. The point is they believe they can now get your arms back and the neurons out of your hair. They would like you to be the first guinea pig. If it works, then they'll be using it on all the others who are desperate for this new cure. They'll also be sending it along to Admiral Molly Maud and the Federation geneticists as well."

"How long will it take? I don't want to miss Tod's wedding. I'm supposed to be his best man, though why he picked me, I surely don't know."

"Cause you saved him," Dr. Leann laughed. "And Katya and Yulia are to be Sasha's maids of honor. So, they believe it'll take four days at most, plenty of time to make Saturday's wedding. Are you up for this now?"

"Sure. Let me tell my ever-growing family," I answered. A half hour later and with the encouraging support of my family, I returned, ready to face another medically induced coma. I swear they had more tubes hooked into my body than before! Soon though, I drifted into a dark sleep and didn't know they'd shut the coffin-like lid on their machine.

They told me three days had elapsed this time. I awoke groggy and mechanically began rubbing my eyes and face only to stop mid-rub. Arms. Hands. I had them again! I let out what Danika said sounded like a war cry on Metcalf-4. I sat up, and the host of doctors surrounded me, inspecting my body, while I caught occasional glimpses of Danika's face around their moving bodies. Her smile told me all I needed to know. At last, Dr. Leann gave me the good news and the bad news.

"Good news. Their new technique has worked wonders. Arms and hair are now normal. This means that everyone who has lost their arms will be getting them back thanks to this new revolutionary development. Bad news, there was a side effect. Your feet have reverted back to being fused en pointe again."

"Hey, that's minor. This process will give over five hundred of them their lives back," I pointed out. "Strange, I'm not even hungry this time," I pointed out.

Dr. Leann laughed. "No, you shouldn't be. They've perfected their procedures considerably. You are now in perfect health. Let's get you dressed and out of here. They want to get Lisa and Yulia into the two machines yet today, so they'll be done in time for the wedding."

As I got dressed with Danika's help, we saw that my feet were back in their fused position again. Because of our halo trip, we had good knee high boots that I could wear, and they were being used as models for everyone else who would be needing them. Plus, the slip-on mules handled nighttime needs, since without them, I'd have no way to even walk to the bathroom if I needed to. This minor detail of screwed up feet didn't really bother me, considering the great gift that I received in return.

As I was getting ready to leave the med lab, Yulia and Lisa arrived. Yulia looked really upset. "Captain Nia Elain, I don't want them to put arms on me cause then I can't be a spaceship pilot like you," Yulia complained, holding back tears.

"Oh, no, Yulia. That's not it at all. Having your arms back will only make it a whole lot easier for you to become a spaceship captain like me, that is, if you still want to be one."

Her eyes brightened up. "Really? It will?"

"Sure will. Lots easier. You'll see, but let's don't cut our hair, shall we?" I suggested with a wink at both Yulia and Lisa.

Lisa giggled. "Nope. It's my pride and joy. Besides, I've

never had it cut." I hugged them both and stayed with them until they went under, before Danika and I headed home.

We had bought a nice home overlooking the grasslands to the east of Exchange City. It was within walking distance of the now large school called EC Elementary. Another even large building was under construction not far from our place. As we approached our home, I figured the Imperial Circles must have been working overtime on the stone construction. It was nearly finished!

"The new EC Academy, love. We are going to have our own Academy with all the bells and trimmings," Danika explained. "No more sending our brightest off to another world. Already they are accepting students for the first fall term. Tod's enrolled plus he's got Sasha, Katya, and Yulia enrolled in EC Elementary as well. Things are certainly changing for the better around here."

"Fabulous. I know Tod will appreciate it. He never went to the Academy because of all the teasing that our people received off-world," I commented.

The following week, I heard news about Bianca Bolivar and Maricela Theresa Delini, our rescued women from Pegasi-C. They had already undergone one medically induced coma round of curing which had restored their voices. The side effect was that they were now like us, hermaphrodites. Now they'd undergone it a second time. I was invited to see the results for myself. Hence, I witnessed their recovery. Both women were elated. Their arms were back. Like me, they didn't care much about their feet remaining fused en pointe. Being able to speak and have arms like everyone else meant their lives were really salvaged.

Since everyone knew that Bianca had planned to enter EU to study genetics before she'd been kidnaped, our geneticists offered her the chance to study here on Ashford-5 with them, getting her degree eventually from our new Academy. She leapt at the chance! "Now, I can help make a difference too!" she exclaimed to me, hugging me tightly, as she hadn't been able to do before now.

Further, both Bianca and Maricela had their Basic

Therapy completed. Maricela now was training up on how to deliver it as well, promising to devote her life to helping others erase the physical and mental traumas that they'd endured. I also wasn't surprised to hear that those two also decided to get married. After all, they'd spent a lot of very intimate time with each other, albeit under the influence of that nasty Purple Droga drug.

By the end of the year, the rest of the five hundred Federation women, who had chosen to come back with us from their captivity along with Bianca and Theresa, had all had their Basic Therapy done and had their two turns in the medical healing machines. While they were now hermaphrodites like us and still had fused feet, they were extremely happy. None chose to return to their home worlds either. For one thing, there they'd be considered "freaks" just as many of us were when we went off-world to the Academies. For another, most felt they needed to find ways to contribute back to Ashford-5 for all the lifesaving efforts that we'd made on their behalf. While some entered the queen's castle staff, others took advantage of our schools, with some eventually going to our new Academy as well.

The three women who had been forced to assist the Field Marshal carry out his assassinations via the Brunelli Enforcer, namely Francesca, Gabriella, and Adrianna, also had their Basic Therapy finished up, though it had taken Rafe twice as long as normal. Their cases were really bad, Rafe explained to me. However, they too underwent the medically induced coma cures twice and finally had their bodies repaired, joining the rest of us. Like me, they didn't complain about always having to wear the knee-high ballet boots in order to walk. Having their enormous traumas erased and their arms back was more than enough. In fact, none of the three wanted to return to their home world. Instead, they also learned how to deliver Basic Therapy and joined Rafe's team working on Advanced Therapy and helping her study the Brunelli Enforcer.

January 1383 brought new additions into our growing family. I had my first golden haired daughter, Dorina, while

Danika had her first golden haired daughter, Evita. We laughed, when we realized my golden hair was apparently a dominate characteristic now. At this point in time, Zorina and Nadia were seven and beginning elementary school. Donatella and Rafe were five and looking forward to starting school later this year. Angelica and Benita were four and quite a handful. Our adopted Christina and Lisa were doing well. Christina was getting quite good on the harpsichord and had formed a trio with the violinist and cellist, Gisa and Karla. Music was always present around our house. Lisa was in school, having a chance to learn, an opportunity that neither she nor Christina had ever had back on their world, because there baronesses never had any formal education. Lisa wanted to become a medical doctor and help save lives, like Doctor Leann.

After I gave birth, Emperor Bino called me to congratulate both of us and to tell me that I no longer needed to return to Cass-C. The Federation was doing well enough now. At long last, Danika and I were finally free to simply raise our rather large family in peace and quiet. However, with ten children, peace and quiet became something of an oxymoron. Yes, we both were very content finally to be able to just sit back and be mothers for a time, though at times that was nearly as hectic.

It was early January when I finally realized this lengthy voyage of the Eagle's Seed had finally ended. I reflected back on what we'd done, the lives that we'd saved, and damn it, I was pleased! That's when I decided to write down our lengthy adventures so our ten children could read it for themselves and share it with their children, giving our future grandchildren a solid understanding of just whom their grandparents were.

Later, surrounded by dirty diapers, mountains of toys, school papers, beginning drawings plastered on every conceivable space in the kitchen, and report cards, she and I laughed. "We ought to have some more, don't you think?" Danika teased me.

Considering the volume of love that was within this large household, I couldn't agree more. I replied, "True, but two years apart please," I teased her back. We both laughed.

The End.

Other Books by Vic Broquard

Without Warning (fantasy)

The Trident Series: (fantasy)
      Volume 1 The Trident and the Book
      Volume 3 The Trident and the Scepter
      Volume3 The Trident and the Resurrection

The Adventures of Elizabeth Stanton Series: (science fiction)
      Volume 1 The Evolution of the Path
      Volume 2 The Great Messiah
      Volume 3 Of Kings and Queens and Troubadours
      Volume 4 Chaos in the Aftermath
      Volume 5 Power Plays
      Volume 6 Age of Exploration
      Volume 7 Abducted
      Volume 8 The Emperor and Empress
      Volume 9 A Job Worth Doing
      Volume 10 Degradation
      Volume 11 The Second Crusade
      Volume 12 When Worlds Collide
      Volume 13 Dark Ages

The Lindsey Barron Series: (fantasy)
      Volume 1 The Rod of the Apocalypse
      Volume 2 The Board of Governors
      Volume 3 The Crown of Moses
      Volume 4 Dominus for President
      Volume 5 The National Health Care Program
      Volume 6 States Justice
      Volume 7 Cross and Double-cross

Zoran Chronicles Series: (fantasy)
      Volume 1 A Dragon in Our Town
      Volume 2 Dragons, Power, Courts, and War

Planet of the Orange-red Sun Series: (science fiction)
      Volume 1 When Kingdoms Fall
      Volume 2 Dark Ages
      Volume 3 Age of the Towers
      Volume 4 Difficillis Exitus
      Volume 5 Age of the Lords
      Volume 6 The Renegade Tower
      Volume 7 Rebellions
      Volume 8 The Aliens Return
      Volume 9 Power Struggles
      Volume 10 Guilds, Genetics, and Gods
      Volume 11 Magi, Witches, Swords, and Superstitions
      Volume 12 The Voyage of the Eagle's Seed
      Volume 13 Eagle's Seed and Origins
      Volume 14 Justifications
      Volume 15 Responsibilities

The Return of the Wizards: Twelve Companions – The Making of Wizards (fantasy)